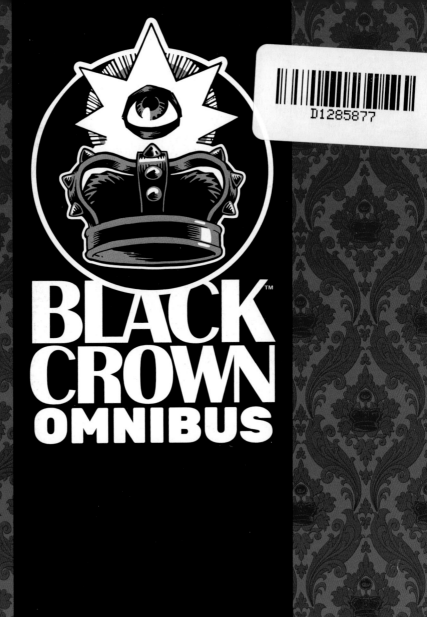

BLACK CROWN OMNIBUS

A YEAR IN REVIEW

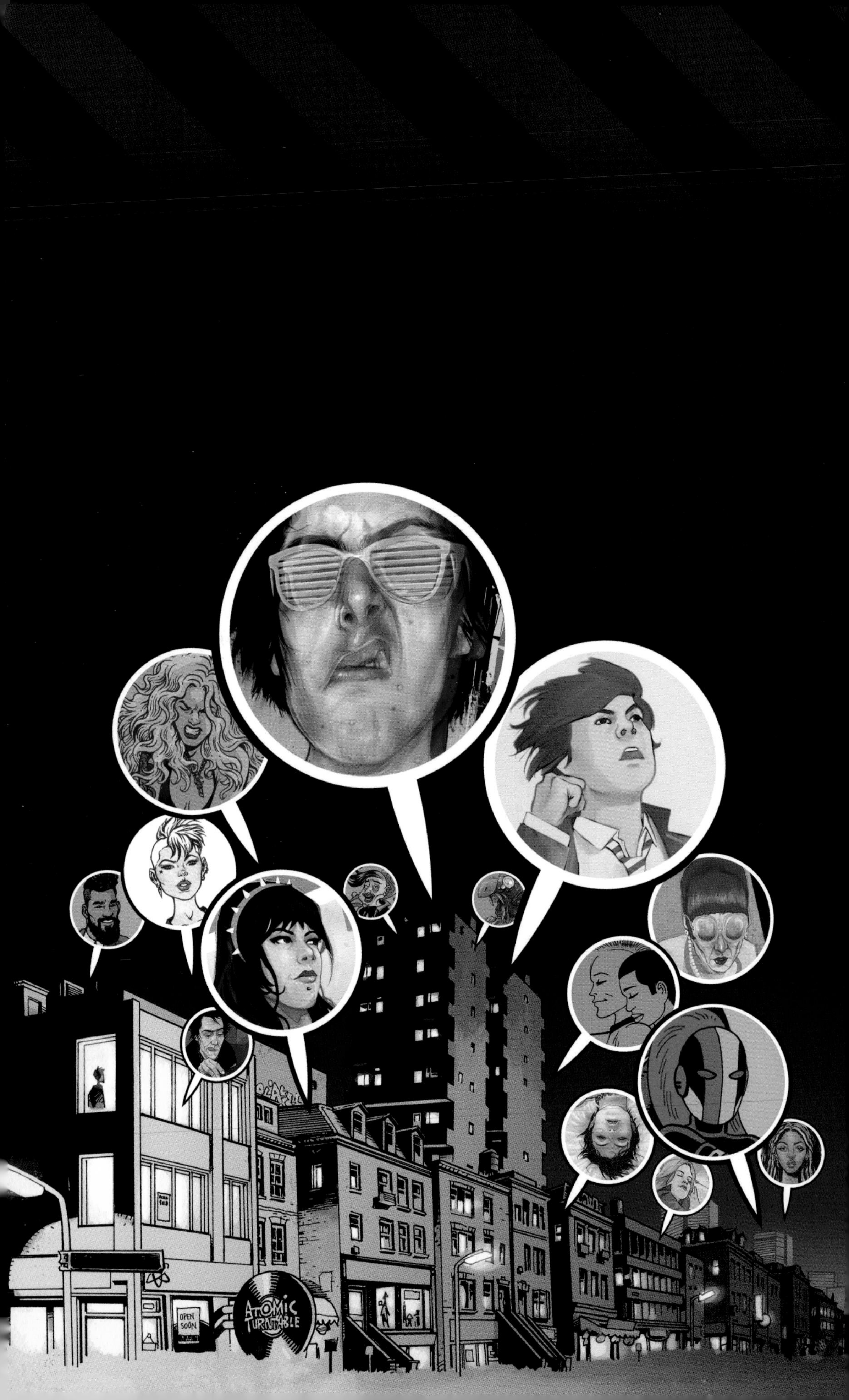
ATOMIC TURNTABLE
OPEN SOON

BLACK CROWN™ OMNIBUS

the compendium of comics & culture

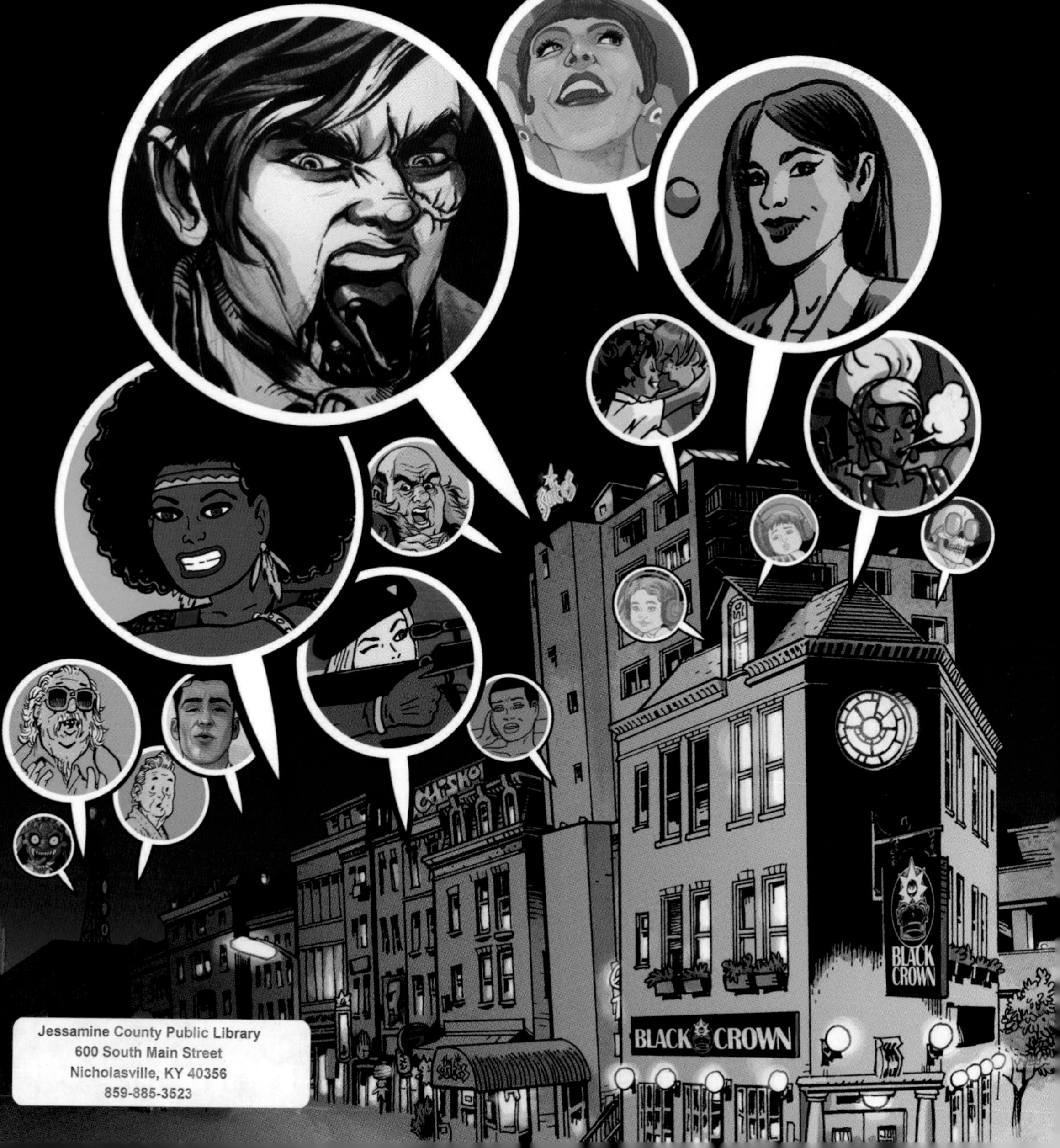
BLACK CROWN
BLACK CROWN

CONTENTS

For international rights, contact licensing@idwpublishing.com

ISBN: 978-1-68405-364-3

21 20 19 18   1 2 3 4

Greg Goldstein, President & Publisher • John Barber, Editor-in-Chief • Robbie Robbins, EVP/Sr. Art Director • Cara Morrison, Chief Financial Officer • Matthew Ruzicka, Chief Accounting Officer • Anita Frazier, SVP of Sales and Marketing • David Hedgecock, Associate Publisher • Jerry Bennington, VP of New Product Development • Lorelei Bunjes, VP of Digital Services • Justin Eisinger, Editorial Director, Graphic Novels and Collections • Eric Moss, Sr. Director, Licensing & Business Development
Ted Adams, IDW Founder

Facebook: facebook.com/idwpublishing • Twitter: @idwpublishing • YouTube: youtube.com/idwpublishing
Tumblr: tumblr.idwpublishing.com • Instagram: instagram.com/idwpublishing

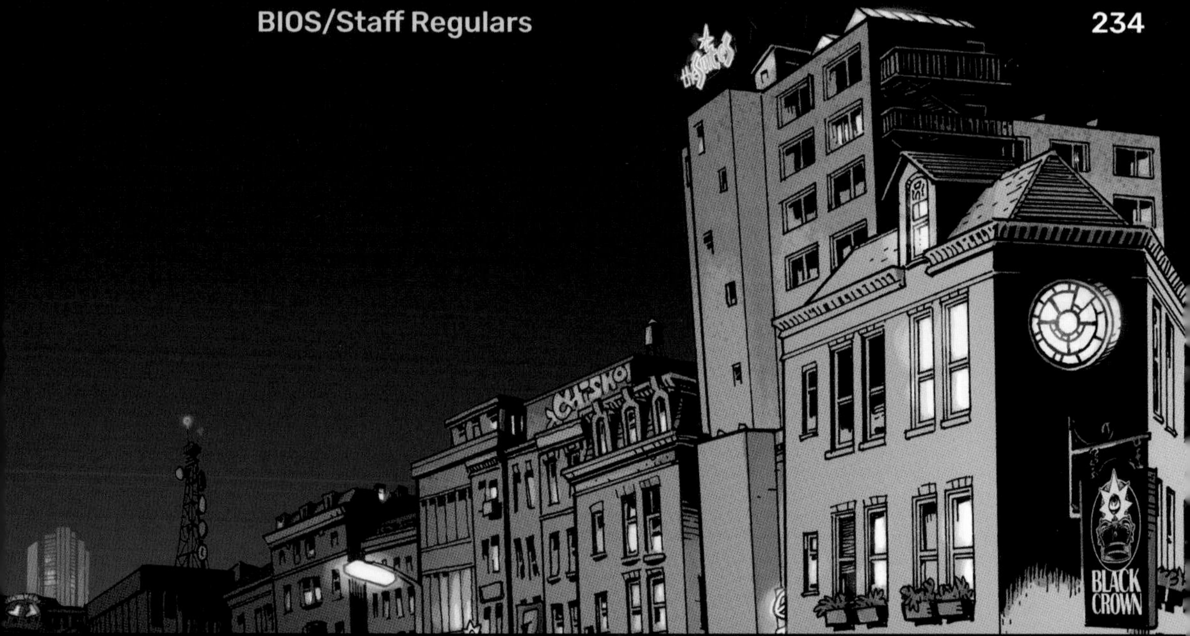
BLACK CROWN

BLACK CROWN HQ
Shelly Bond, Editor • **Chase Marotz,** Associate Editor • **Aditya Bidikar,** Letterer
Arlene Lo, Proofreader • **Philip Bond,** logo, publication design and general dogsbody
Greg Goldstein, President & Publisher

BLACK CROWN is a fully functioning curation operation based in Los Angeles by way of IDW Publishing. Accept No Substitutes!

The Convivial Times

blackcrown.pub

BLACK CROWN: THE RULING CLASS

Note: Loyal purveyors of pop fiction, my regularly scheduled column has been pushed aside for "breaking news" in the comic book arena. An e-mail with top secret curation information has come to our attention. Read at your own risk. — Eve Stranger, Social Correspondent, The Convivial Times

Dear Favorite Freelancer,

I hope in the near/now/far future I can count you in for IDW's BLACK CROWN. The imprimatur is two-fold: First and foremost, it's a line of comic books and graphic novels for readers who take on double dares without flinching. Second: The Black Crown Pub is a public house that anchors a mysterious street full of storefronts that correlate to each comic book series. While creators maintain a separate, singular vision within their comics, they also have the opportunity to own a chunk of real estate for their characters to interact as much (or as little) as they want to in this shared landscape. Imagine NYC's St. Mark's Place in the '90s or the high street you traveled to

through snow and circumstance on a boundless quest for that new 12" import or signed hardcover; the haven that welcomed freaks and inbetweeners with lots of eclectic reading material, cool garb and no franchises!

On her way to an important curation excavation, Bond neither confirms nor denies the leak.

Michael Allred can't commit to a project right now, but I gave him first dibs on the record shop. (Natch!) He's calling it The Atomic Turntable. And I want to give you carte blanche on another property. So what'll it be? We have an exclusive nightclub called The Violet Opaque, a '70s retro diner/

candy shop called Butterscotch and Soda, The National Dry Cleaners, Little Bear Sewing Machine, Vacuum & Raygun Repair, and Canonball Comics. We have a punk, rockabilly, new wave and glam clothing store called Electric Trash, Cauldron Coffee, and Winnie's Hot Wheels Roller Rink. We have a Post Office, Love's Letter's Lost. We could really use a barbershop that offers tattoos and piercings and an oxygen bar, but I'm definitely open to other ideas. Ultimately, we're making comics with swagger and soundtracks that are warped and weird with a bit of black humor to help us survive the way we live now.

I can't wait to open shop and roll out the black & white checkerboard carpet. But for now, let's keep this top secret imprint strategy just between us!

Best,

Shelly

Shelly Bond
BLACK CROWN HQ
Los Angeles
blackcrown.pub

Excerpt from BLACK CROWN PREVIEW, San Diego Comic Con, July 2017

BLACK CROWN
A discerning comic book selection of art & alchemy, opulence & madness.

Face it. Nobody likes an **OPENING ACT**

You've paid full price, so why bother with the tribute band when you can hang out with the headliners?

I'll keep it light.

What you're about to experience is a pop culture assault of sound + vision.

The Preamble is located to your left.

The idea behind BLACK CROWN was to go back to my indie roots and create comics I wanted to read again. Pair up people from disparate parts of the universe and let them loose on the page (vicious editor dog riding shotgun with refreshments notwithstanding). BLACK CROWN has always been a tremendous collaborative effort — we may *think* we're the be-all/end-all of the artform but we couldn't do it if someone wasn't willing to lock limbs and jump into the trenches with us. As a curation operation, we've managed to go beyond our audacious expectations with help from some amazing velvet curtain-pullers backstage.

Thanks to early adopters Chris Ryall, IDW Founder Ted Adams and President/Publisher Greg Goldstein of IDW for letting us break ground — and the rest of the IDW team for kicking off their kitten heels and getting down in the mud with us. Thanks to comics veterans who came to relive the good old times with their favorite editor (or who owed me favors), and the newer creatives who had no idea what they were getting into. I can assure you the young punks are now exhibiting better hair but they're fucking exhausted. [See my trusty collection of red pens.] And major thanks to my secret weapon, BLACK CROWN's general dogsbody (his term not mine), publication designer, favorite artist and favorite human, Philip Bond, as we go forth and continue to incite this neo comics revolution.

Viva comics!

Shelly

Shelly Bond
Editor/Curator

28 September 2018
Los Angeles
blackcrown.pub
@blackcrownhq
Built to Last
#therulingclass

GOD SAVE THE QUEEN

FROM THEORY TO REVOLUTION
a year in review

APRIL 2016
Due to org. chart restructuring Bond is restructured out from DC Comics. Sets out to enjoy first summer off since 1979.

Chris Ryall, (then) the CCO of IDW Publishing, emails to see if a working relationship with IDW can be cultivated.

MAY-AUGUST
Bond spends days & nights in the public library with the other bums, reading comic books and novels, writing, and crafting secret comic book imprint.

SEPTEMBER
Bond sends Ryall the imprint proposal for BLACK CROWN. Interviews with Greg Goldstein, Ted Adams and Chris Ryall at IDW's San Diego headquarters. Proposal includes a shared landscape/street component where creators and characters can commingle & corrupt, utilizing Bond's extensive Rolodex which brings hardcore veterans & punk neophytes together to inspire each other on the page.

Philip Bond designs the logo, nails it on his first attempt.

OCTOBER
Bond receives job offer and agrees to work remotely from Los Angeles starting in early 2018.

NOVEMBER
After the U.S. Presidential election, Bond asks IDW if she can Kickstart FEMME MAGNIFIQUE, a title from the imprint strategy. This anthology salutes women in pop, politics, art and science and promotes equality and empowerment. The timing for this project could not be more pressing.

NORMAL PEOPLE ON HOLIDAY

BLACK CROWN

BLACK CROWN

BLACK CROWN

BLACK CROWN

ACK°

2016
APRIL

SEPTEMBER OCTOBER   NOVEMBER

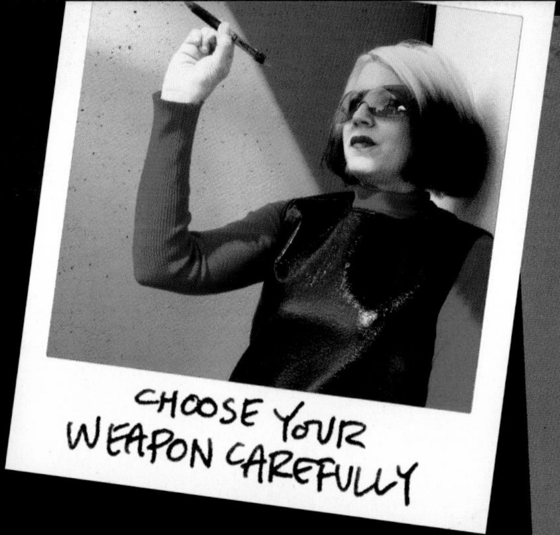
CHOOSE YOUR
WEAPON CAREFULLY

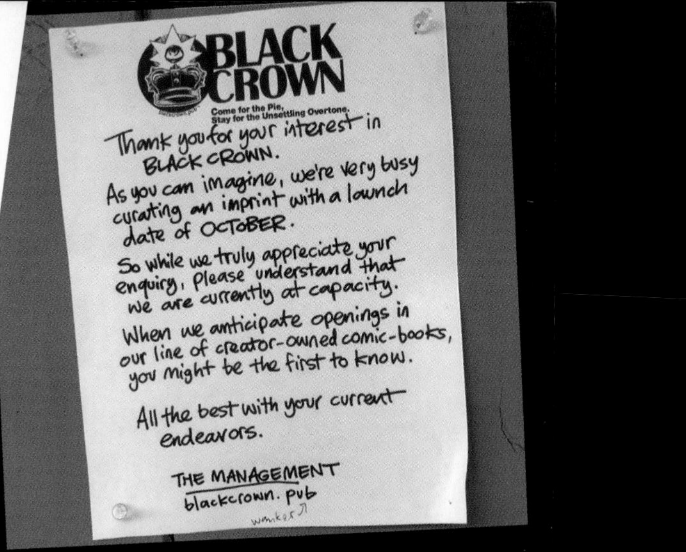
BLACK CROWN
Come for the Pie, Stay for the Unsettling Overtone.
Thank you for your interest in BLACK CROWN.
As you can imagine, we're very busy curating an imprint with a launch date of OCTOBER.
So while we truly appreciate your enquiry, please understand that we are currently at capacity.
When we anticipate openings in our line of creator-owned comic-books, you might be the first to know.
All the best with your current endeavors.
THE MANAGEMENT
blackcrown.pub

FEBRUARY 2017

With the help of co-curators Brian and Kristy Miller of Hi-Fi Colour Design, the FEMME MAGNIFIQUE Kickstarter launches on Valentine's Day and is fully funded in a matter of days.

Hands shook, papers signed, and the stars aligned, BLACK CROWN becomes real with steadfast support from Chris Ryall, Ted Adams and Greg Goldstein of IDW Publishing.

MARCH

IDW announces the new BLACK CROWN imprint at Emerald City Comic Con in Seattle. KID LOBOTOMY by comics legend Peter Milligan and artist Tess Fowler leads the pack.

APRIL

Launch books KID LOBOTOMY, ASSASSINISTAS and BLACK CROWN QUARTERLY are in motion. Bond and Fowler attend Wondercon in Anaheim to discuss the inner machinations of KID LOBOTOMY to a host of excited fans.

Blackcrown.pub happy hour is christened and convivial times would occur every Friday at 4:00 PST/midnight UTC. The goal: to provide glimpses of BLACK CROWN HQ behind-the-scenes and promote titles and the creative coterie.

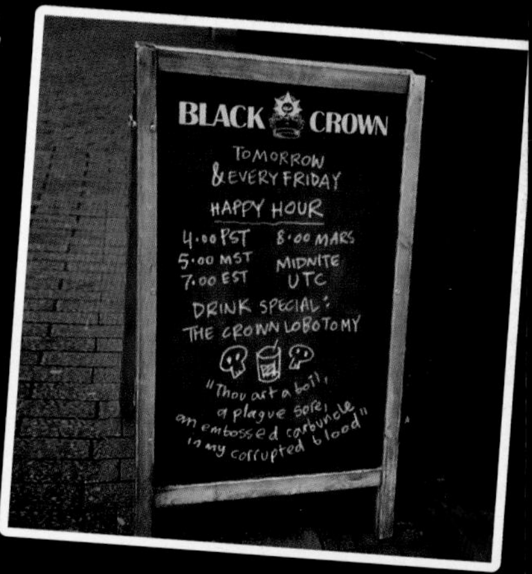
BLACK CROWN
TOMORROW & EVERY FRIDAY
HAPPY HOUR
4:00 PST 8:00 MARS
5:00 MST MIDNITE
7:00 EST UTC
DRINK SPECIAL: THE CROWN LOBOTOMY
"Thou art a boil, a plague sore, an embossed carbuncle in my corrupted blood"

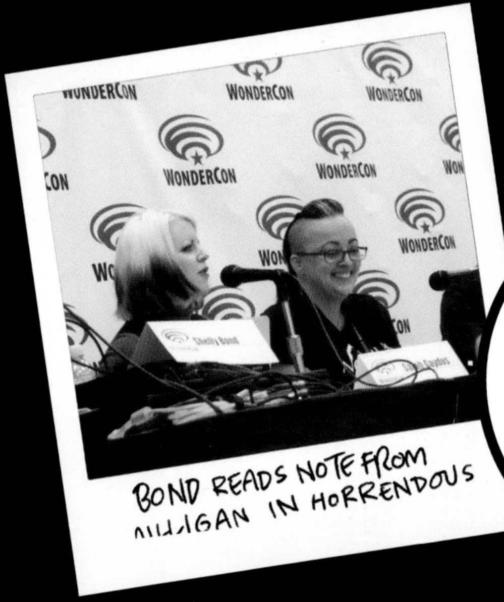
WONDERCON
BOND READS NOTE FROM
MILLIGAN IN HORRENDOUS

"It's a haunted hotel on crack."
— Tess Fowler on KID LOBOTOMY

2017
FEBRUARY
APRIL

FROM THEORY TO REVOLUTION

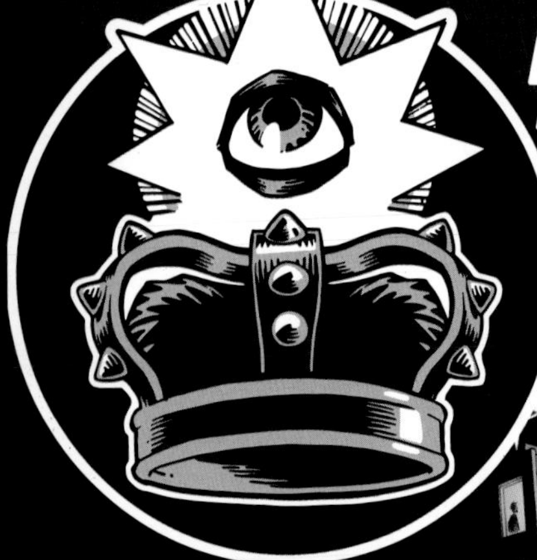

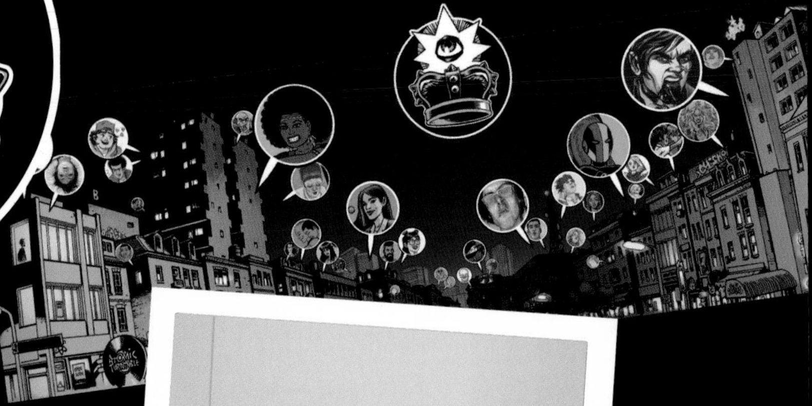

JULY
SAN DIEGO COMIC CON

BLACK CROWN has a huge presence with an extensive street display stretching across one side of the IDW booth. The ASSASSINISTAS team of rising star writer Tini Howard and Eisner Hall of Famer Gilbert Hernandez sign, sketch and break bread, and then announce their series at the BLACK CROWN panel.

A primer of the imprint philosophy and launch titles is handed out at the booth along with logo pins and a two-sided poster featuring KID LOBOTOMY and ASSASSINISTAS.

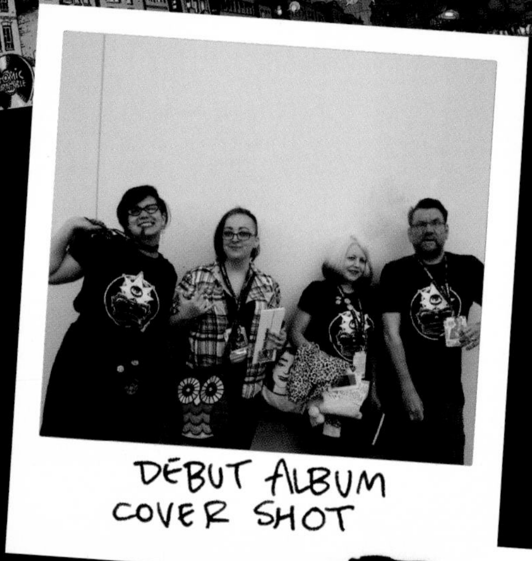
DEBUT ALBUM
COVER SHOT

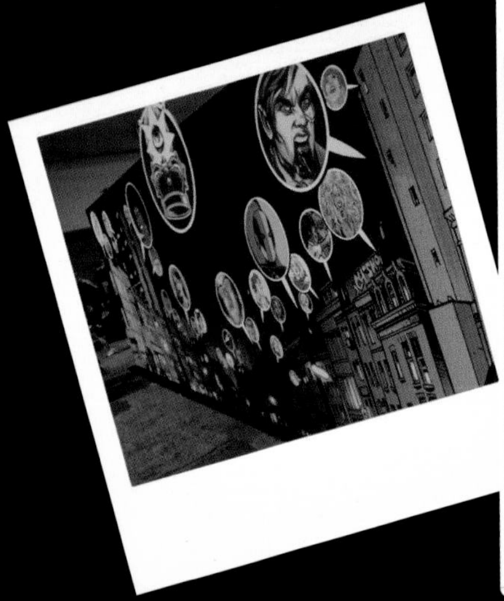

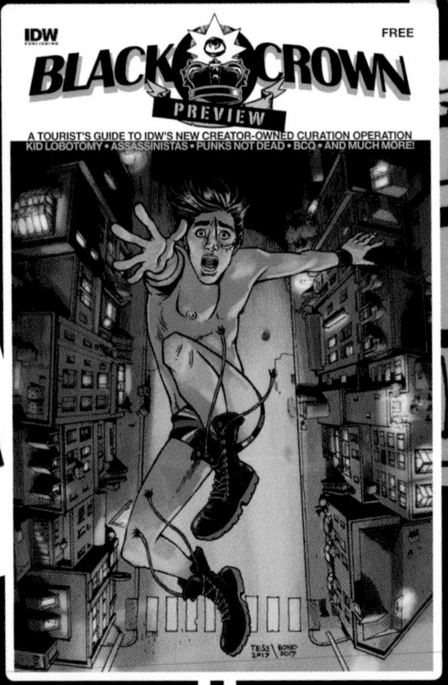
IDW
FREE
BLACK CROWN
PREVIEW
A TOURIST'S GUIDE TO IDW'S NEW CREATOR-OWNED CURATION OPERATION
KID LOBOTOMY • ASSASSINISTAS • PUNKS NOT DEAD • BCQ • AND MUCH MORE!

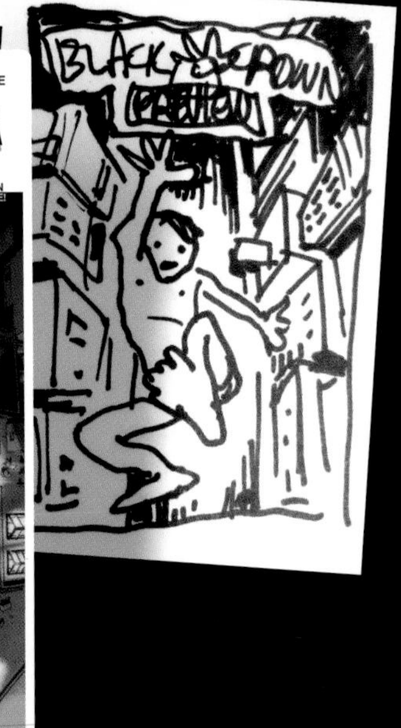

2017
JULY

AUGUST

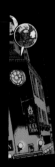

THE COMICS + CHAOS TOUR STARTS HERE! THIS IS ENGLAND 9/21/17

4 KIDS WALK INTO A HOTEL BAR IN LEEDS

SEPTEMBER

In under seven busy months, FEMME MAGNIFIQUE, the 208-page Kickstarter hardcover, is printed and dispatched to its backers.

Bond kicks off on the "Comics + Chaos Tour" in the U.K. at the Thought Bubble convention in Leeds and finally gets to meet and entertain the CUD band, AKA writers Carl Puttnam and William Potter. The BLACK CROWN: Comics + Chaos panel includes Rob Davis, the Black Crown Pub proprietor and writer/artist of Tales from the Black Crown Pub, the lead story in the BLACK CROWN QUARTERLY.

Also in attendance: House letterer Aditya Bidikar, Jamie Coe and the creative team of PUNKS NOT DEAD, writer David Barnett and artist Martin Simmonds.

Post Leeds, comic book shops in London (Orbital, Forbidden Planet, Gosh and Mega City) receive cold calls from Bond with swag in tow to garner excitement and procure advice for the new imprint.

BC REGULAR PUNTERS LEAH MOORE & ADITYA BIDIKAR

FEMME MAGNIFIQUE

A comic book anthology salute to

50

magnificent women who take names, crack ceilings and change the game in pop, politics, art & science

LEEDS · LONDON · NEW YORK · DURHAM

"KICK OFF YOUR CUBAN HEELS, COME FLY WITH ME." ♫ LEEDS/THOUGHT BUBBLE 9/23/17

SEPTEMBER

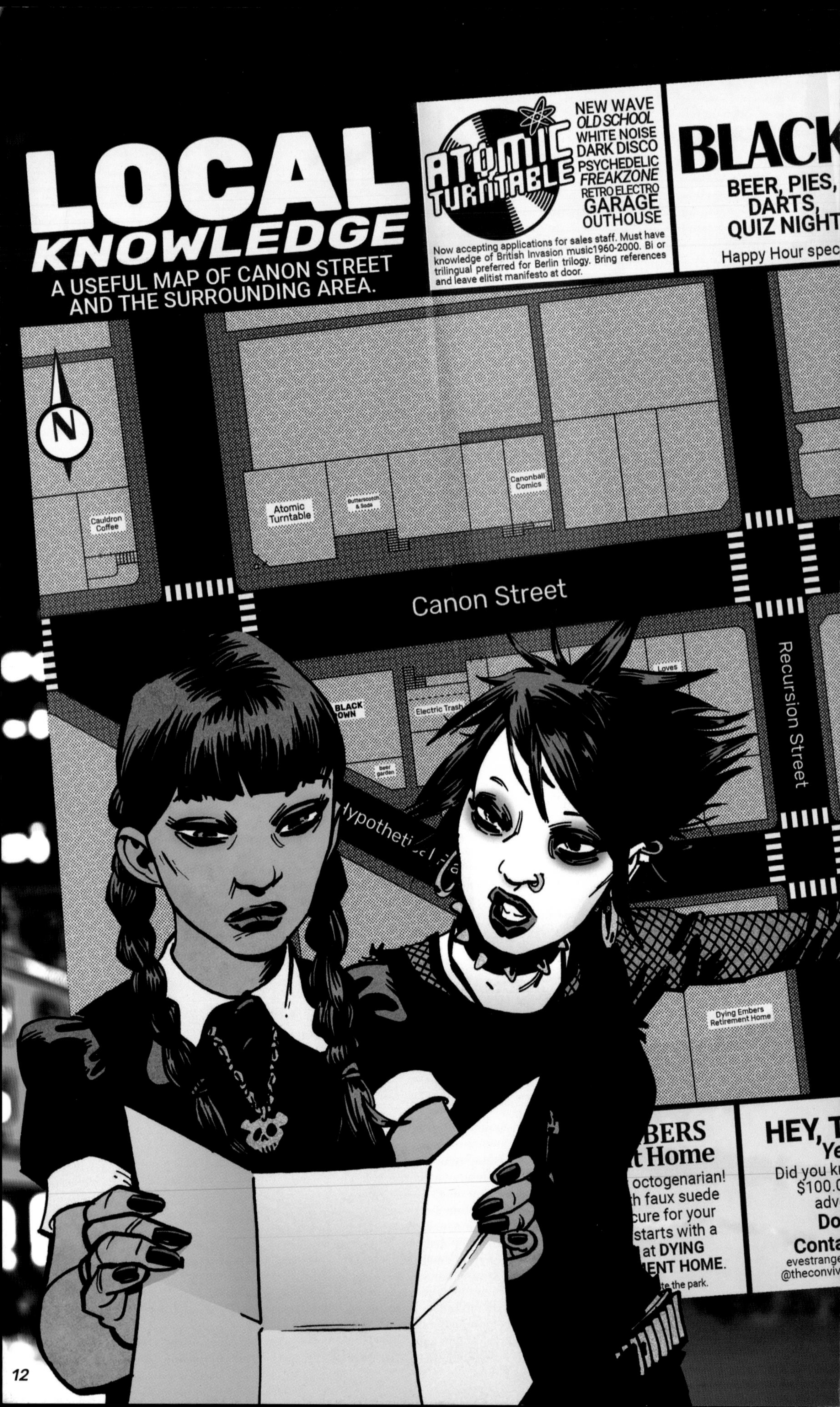
LOCAL KNOWLEDGE
A USEFUL MAP OF CANON STREET AND THE SURROUNDING AREA.
ATOMIC TURNTABLE
NEW WAVE
OLD SCHOOL
WHITE NOISE
DARK DISCO
PSYCHEDELIC
FREAKZONE
RETRO ELECTRO
GARAGE
OUTHOUSE
Now accepting applications for sales staff. Must have knowledge of British Invasion music1960-2000. Bi or trilingual preferred for Berlin trilogy. Bring references and leave elitist manifesto at door.
BLACK
BEER, PIES, DARTS, QUIZ NIGHT
Happy Hour spec
N
Cauldron Coffee
Atomic Turntable
Butterscotch & Soda
Canonball Comics
Canon Street
Recursion Street
Loves
Electric Trash
beer garden
Dying Embers Retirement Home
BERS
t Home
octogenarian!
h faux suede
cure for your
starts with a
at DYING
ENT HOME.
te the park.
HEY, T
Ye
Did you k
$100.
adv
Do
Conta
evestrange
@theconviv

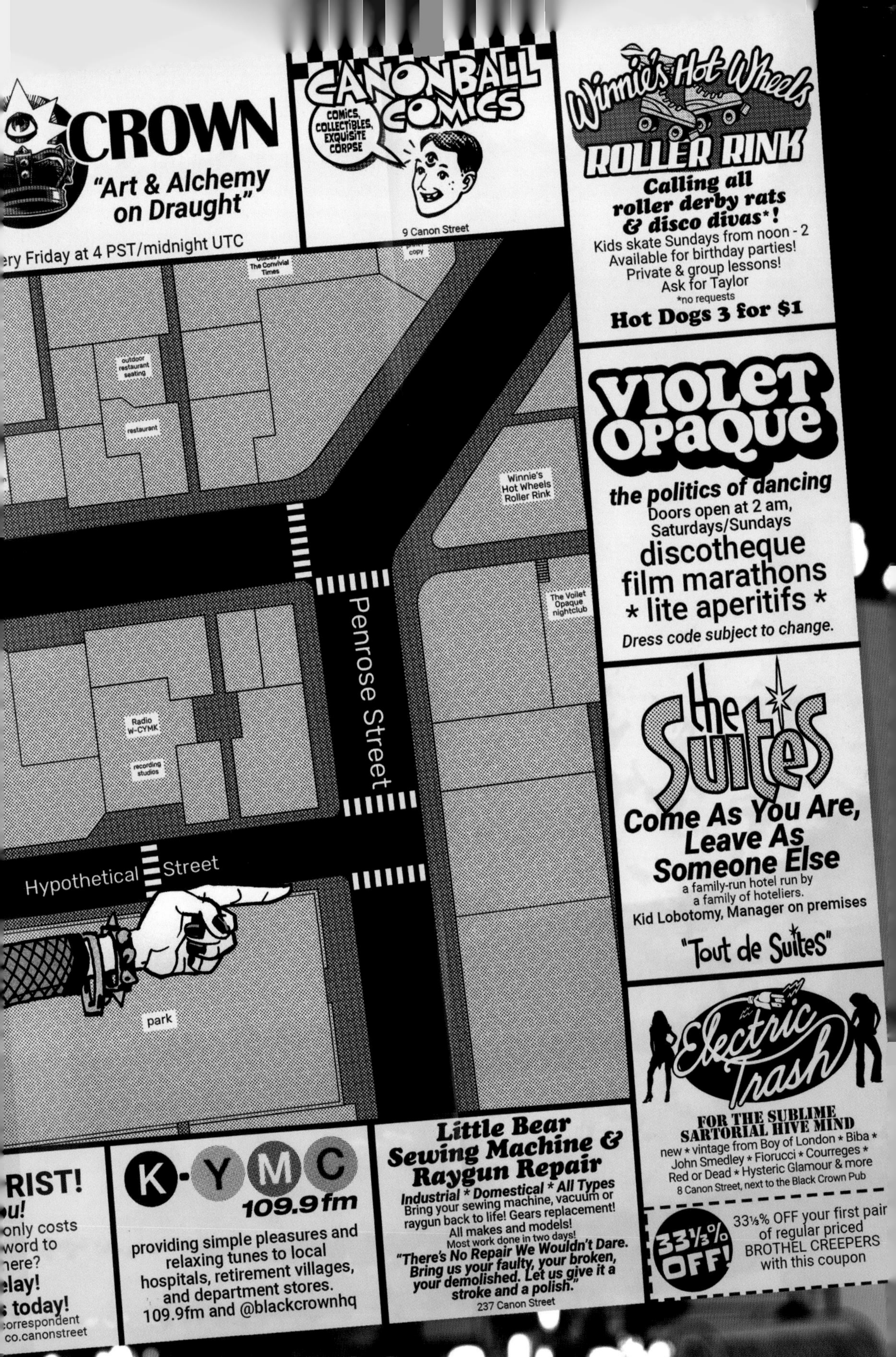

CROWN
"Art & Alchemy on Draught"
ery Friday at 4 PST/midnight UTC
CANONBALL COMICS
COMICS, COLLECTIBLES, EXQUISITE CORPSE
9 Canon Street
Winnie's Hot Wheels
ROLLER RINK
Calling all roller derby rats & disco divas*!
Kids skate Sundays from noon - 2
Available for birthday parties!
Private & group lessons!
Ask for Taylor
*no requests
Hot Dogs 3 for $1
The Convivial Times
copy
outdoor restaurant seating
restaurant
Winnie's Hot Wheels Roller Rink
The Voilet Opaque nightclub
Radio W-CYMK
recording studios
Penrose Street
Hypothetical Street
park
VIOLET OPAQUE
the politics of dancing
Doors open at 2 am, Saturdays/Sundays
discotheque
film marathons
* lite aperitifs *
Dress code subject to change.
the Suites
Come As You Are, Leave As Someone Else
a family-run hotel run by a family of hoteliers.
Kid Lobotomy, Manager on premises
"Tout de Suites"
Electric Trash
FOR THE SUBLIME SARTORIAL HIVE MIND
new * vintage from Boy of London * Biba * John Smedley * Fiorucci * Courreges * Red or Dead * Hysteric Glamour & more
8 Canon Street, next to the Black Crown Pub
33⅓% OFF!
33⅓% OFF your first pair of regular priced BROTHEL CREEPERS with this coupon
RIST!
u!
only costs
word to
here?
elay!
s today!
correspondent
co.canonstreet
K-YMC
109.9 fm
providing simple pleasures and relaxing tunes to local hospitals, retirement villages, and department stores.
109.9fm and @blackcrownhq
Little Bear Sewing Machine & Raygun Repair
Industrial * Domestical * All Types
Bring your sewing machine, vacuum or raygun back to life! Gears replacement!
All makes and models!
Most work done in two days!
"There's No Repair We Wouldn't Dare. Bring us your faulty, your broken, your demolished. Let us give it a stroke and a polish."
237 Canon Street

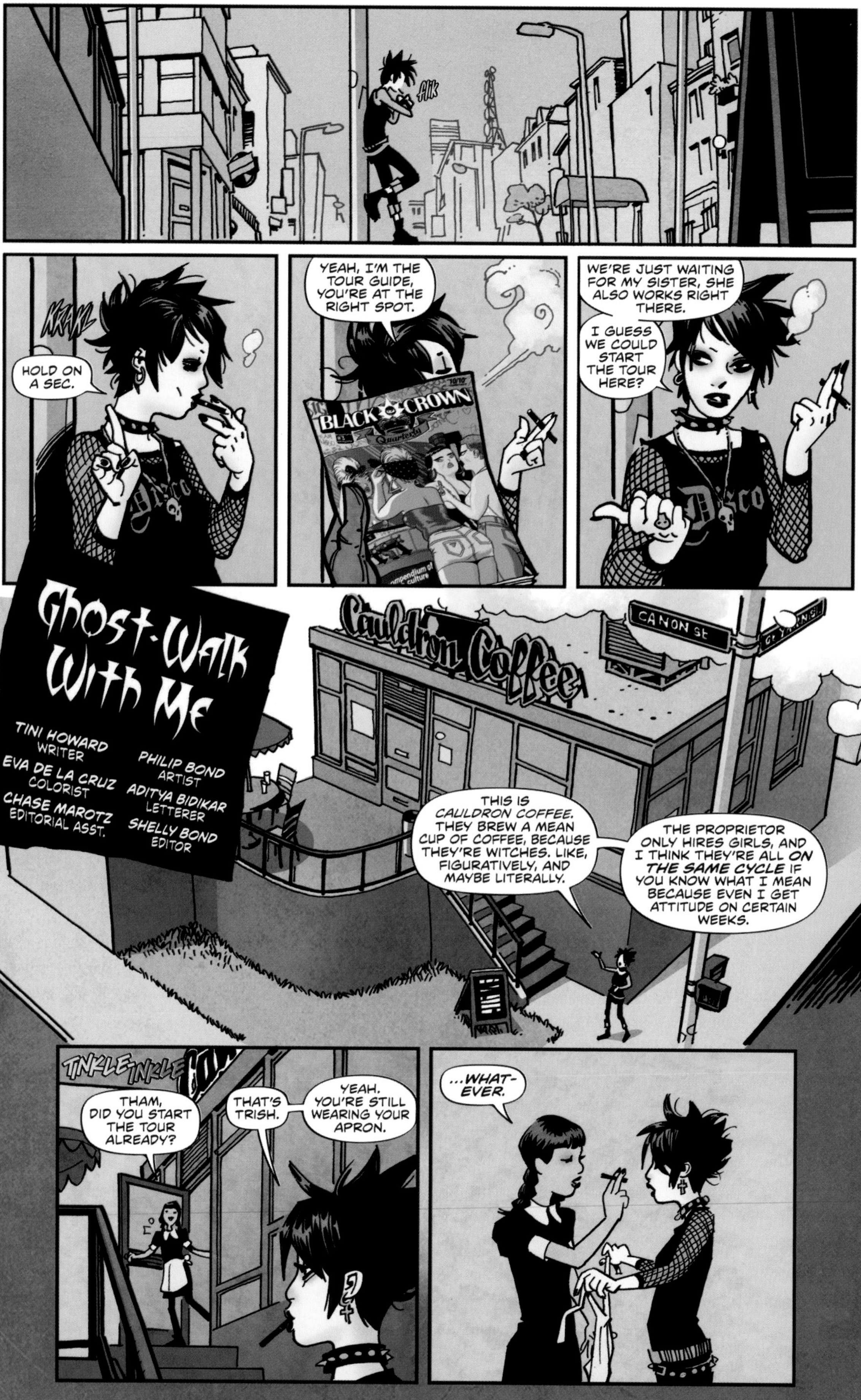
FLIK
KKAKL
HOLD ON A SEC.
YEAH, I'M THE TOUR GUIDE, YOU'RE AT THE RIGHT SPOT.
BLACK CROWN
Quarterly
WE'RE JUST WAITING FOR MY SISTER, SHE ALSO WORKS RIGHT THERE.
I GUESS WE COULD START THE TOUR HERE?
Ghost-Walk With Me
TINI HOWARD WRITER
PHILIP BOND ARTIST
EVA DE LA CRUZ COLORIST
ADITYA BIDIKAR LETTERER
CHASE MAROTZ EDITORIAL ASST.
SHELLY BOND EDITOR
Cauldron Coffee
CANON st
THIS IS CAULDRON COFFEE. THEY BREW A MEAN CUP OF COFFEE, BECAUSE THEY'RE WITCHES. LIKE, FIGURATIVELY, AND MAYBE LITERALLY.
THE PROPRIETOR ONLY HIRES GIRLS, AND I THINK THEY'RE ALL ON THE SAME CYCLE IF YOU KNOW WHAT I MEAN BECAUSE EVEN I GET ATTITUDE ON CERTAIN WEEKS.
TINKLE INKLE
THAM, DID YOU START THE TOUR ALREADY?
THAT'S TRISH.
YEAH. YOU'RE STILL WEARING YOUR APRON.
...WHAT-EVER.

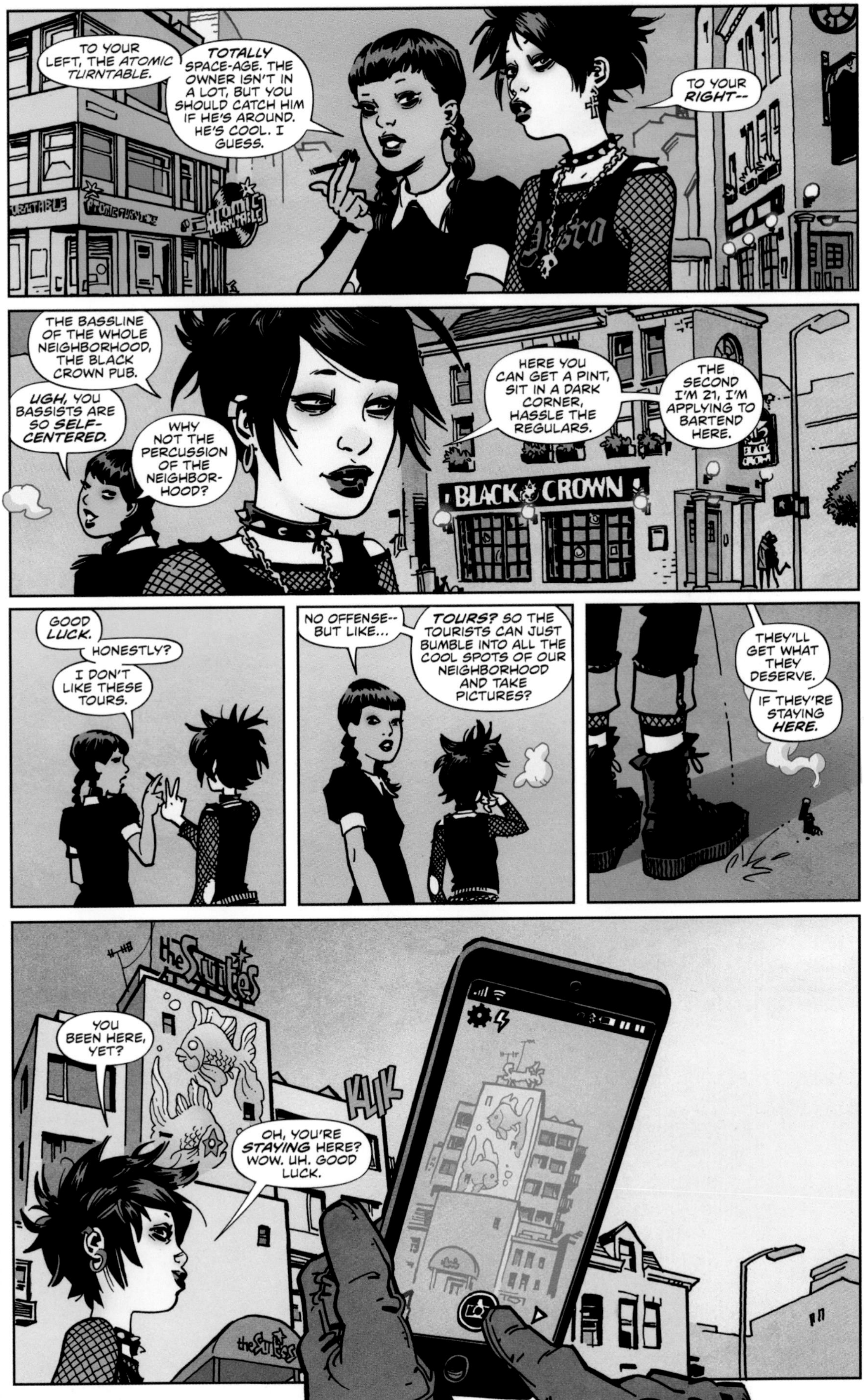

TO YOUR LEFT, THE *ATOMIC TURNTABLE*.
TOTALLY SPACE-AGE. THE OWNER ISN'T IN A LOT, BUT YOU SHOULD CATCH HIM IF HE'S AROUND. HE'S COOL. I GUESS.
TO YOUR *RIGHT*--
ATOMIC TURNTABLE
THE BASSLINE OF THE WHOLE NEIGHBORHOOD, THE BLACK CROWN PUB.
UGH, YOU BASSISTS ARE SO *SELF-CENTERED*.
WHY NOT THE PERCUSSION OF THE NEIGHBOR-HOOD?
HERE YOU CAN GET A PINT, SIT IN A DARK CORNER, HASSLE THE REGULARS.
THE SECOND I'M 21, I'M APPLYING TO BARTEND HERE.
BLACK CROWN
GOOD *LUCK*.
HONESTLY?
I DON'T LIKE THESE TOURS.
NO OFFENSE-- BUT LIKE...
TOURS? SO THE TOURISTS CAN JUST BUMBLE INTO ALL THE COOL SPOTS OF OUR NEIGHBORHOOD AND TAKE PICTURES?
THEY'LL GET WHAT THEY DESERVE.
IF THEY'RE STAYING *HERE*.
the Suites
YOU BEEN HERE, YET?
OH, YOU'RE *STAYING* HERE? WOW. UH. GOOD LUCK.

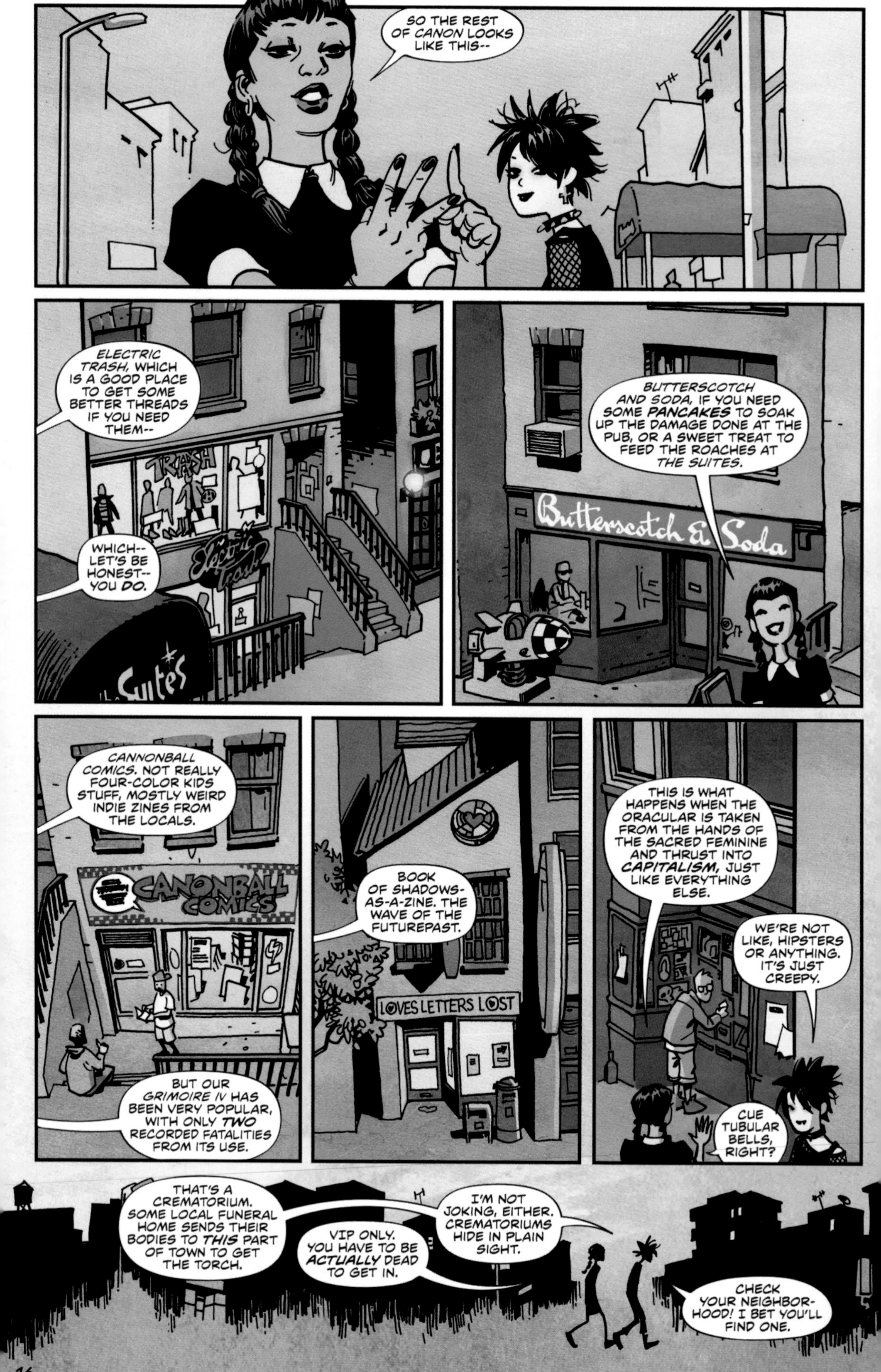
SO THE REST OF CANON LOOKS LIKE THIS--
ELECTRIC TRASH, WHICH IS A GOOD PLACE TO GET SOME BETTER THREADS IF YOU NEED THEM--
WHICH-- LET'S BE HONEST-- YOU DO.
SUITES
BUTTERSCOTCH AND SODA, IF YOU NEED SOME PANCAKES TO SOAK UP THE DAMAGE DONE AT THE PUB, OR A SWEET TREAT TO FEED THE ROACHES AT THE SUITES.
Butterscotch & Soda
CANNONBALL COMICS. NOT REALLY FOUR-COLOR KIDS STUFF, MOSTLY WEIRD INDIE ZINES FROM THE LOCALS.
CANONBALL COMICS
BUT OUR GRIMOIRE IV HAS BEEN VERY POPULAR, WITH ONLY TWO RECORDED FATALITIES FROM ITS USE.
BOOK OF SHADOWS-AS-A-ZINE. THE WAVE OF THE FUTUREPAST.
LOVES LETTERS LOST
THIS IS WHAT HAPPENS WHEN THE ORACULAR IS TAKEN FROM THE HANDS OF THE SACRED FEMININE AND THRUST INTO CAPITALISM, JUST LIKE EVERYTHING ELSE.
WE'RE NOT LIKE, HIPSTERS OR ANYTHING. IT'S JUST CREEPY.
CUE TUBULAR BELLS, RIGHT?
THAT'S A CREMATORIUM. SOME LOCAL FUNERAL HOME SENDS THEIR BODIES TO THIS PART OF TOWN TO GET THE TORCH.
I'M NOT JOKING, EITHER. CREMATORIUMS HIDE IN PLAIN SIGHT.
VIP ONLY. YOU HAVE TO BE ACTUALLY DEAD TO GET IN.
CHECK YOUR NEIGHBOR-HOOD! I BET YOU'LL FIND ONE.

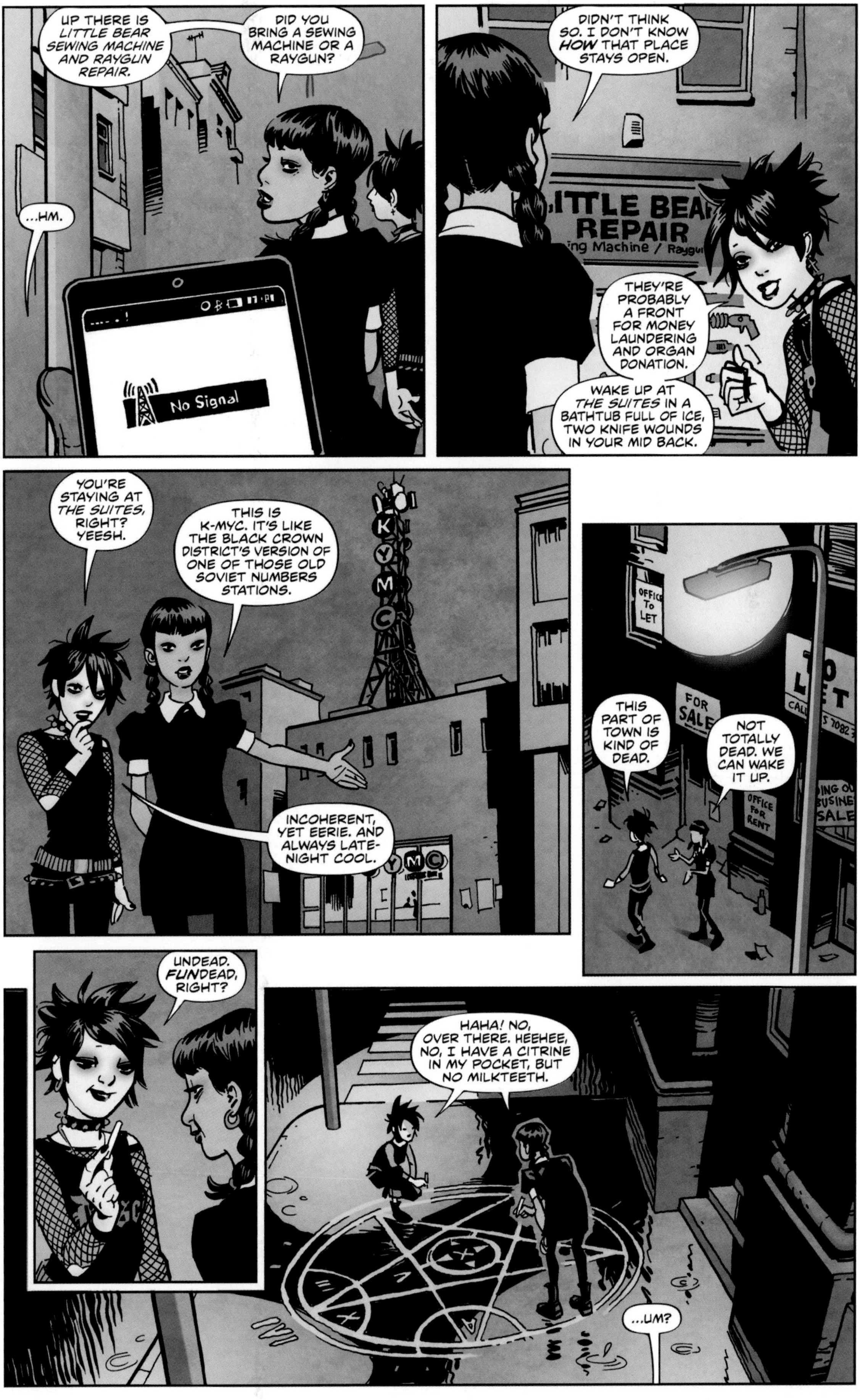
UP THERE IS LITTLE BEAR SEWING MACHINE AND RAYGUN REPAIR.
DID YOU BRING A SEWING MACHINE OR A RAYGUN?
...HM.
No Signal
DIDN'T THINK SO. I DON'T KNOW HOW THAT PLACE STAYS OPEN.
LITTLE BEA
REPAIR
ing Machine / Raygu
THEY'RE PROBABLY A FRONT FOR MONEY LAUNDERING AND ORGAN DONATION.
WAKE UP AT THE SUITES IN A BATHTUB FULL OF ICE, TWO KNIFE WOUNDS IN YOUR MID BACK.
YOU'RE STAYING AT THE SUITES, RIGHT? YEESH.
THIS IS K-MYC. IT'S LIKE THE BLACK CROWN DISTRICT'S VERSION OF ONE OF THOSE OLD SOVIET NUMBERS STATIONS.
KYMC
INCOHERENT, YET EERIE. AND ALWAYS LATE-NIGHT COOL.
OFFICE TO LET
TO LET
FOR SALE
THIS PART OF TOWN IS KIND OF DEAD.
NOT TOTALLY DEAD. WE CAN WAKE IT UP.
OFFICE FOR RENT
UNDEAD. FUNDEAD, RIGHT?
HAHA! NO, OVER THERE. HEEHEE, NO, I HAVE A CITRINE IN MY POCKET, BUT NO MILKTEETH.
...UM?

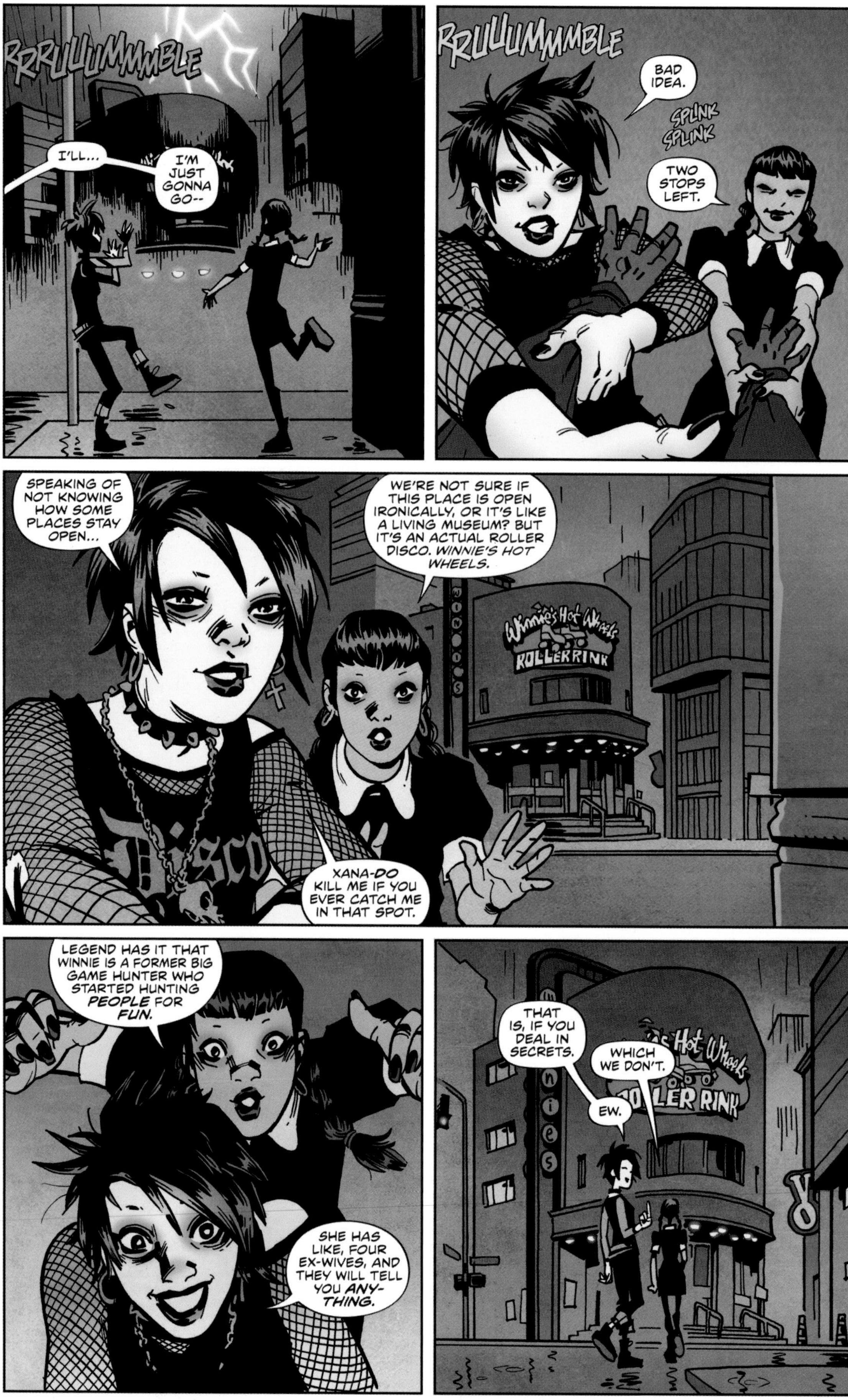
RRRUUUMMMBLE
I'LL...
I'M JUST GONNA GO--
RRUUUMMMBLE
BAD IDEA.
SPLINK SPLINK
TWO STOPS LEFT.
SPEAKING OF NOT KNOWING HOW SOME PLACES STAY OPEN...
WE'RE NOT SURE IF THIS PLACE IS OPEN IRONICALLY, OR IT'S LIKE A LIVING MUSEUM? BUT IT'S AN ACTUAL ROLLER DISCO. WINNIE'S HOT WHEELS.
Winnie's Hot Wheels
ROLLER RINK
DISCO
XANA-DO KILL ME IF YOU EVER CATCH ME IN THAT SPOT.
LEGEND HAS IT THAT WINNIE IS A FORMER BIG GAME HUNTER WHO STARTED HUNTING PEOPLE FOR FUN.
SHE HAS LIKE, FOUR EX-WIVES, AND THEY WILL TELL YOU ANY-THING.
THAT IS, IF YOU DEAL IN SECRETS.
WHICH WE DON'T.
EW.
ROLLER RINK

LASTLY, THIS IS THE VIOLET OPAQUE, WHERE OUR TOUR COMES TO AN END.

A *VERY* EXCLUSIVE NIGHTCLUB, FOR THE ELITE WHO KNOW BETTER THAN TO PATRONIZE MOST OF THESE OTHER PLACES.

OH, SORRY. YOU'RE NOT ON THE LIST.

BUT IT'S *RAINING*, AND--

OH.

IS IT?

KLICK

WAIT.

"DIDN'T YOU TWO MAKE IT RAIN?"

MERCI BEAUCOUP FOR JOINING US ON THIS INAUGURAL TOUR OF THE BLACK CROWN NEIGHBORHOOD! THE TOUR RUNS RAIN OR SHINE, AND AS SUCH, WE ARE NOT RESPONSIBLE FOR ACTS OF ANY GOD, SUMMONED PERSONALLY OR OTHERWISE. PLEASE BE SURE TO TAKE YOUR TOUR BROCHURE TO LITTLE BEAR REPAIR FOR 5% OFF YOUR NEXT RAYGUN SERVICE! --THE MGMT.

THE VIOLET OPAQUE

ALL NITE DANCING

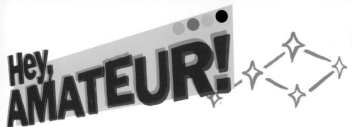

Hey, AMATEUR!

How to Spot A Galaxy!

by Emmeline Pidgen

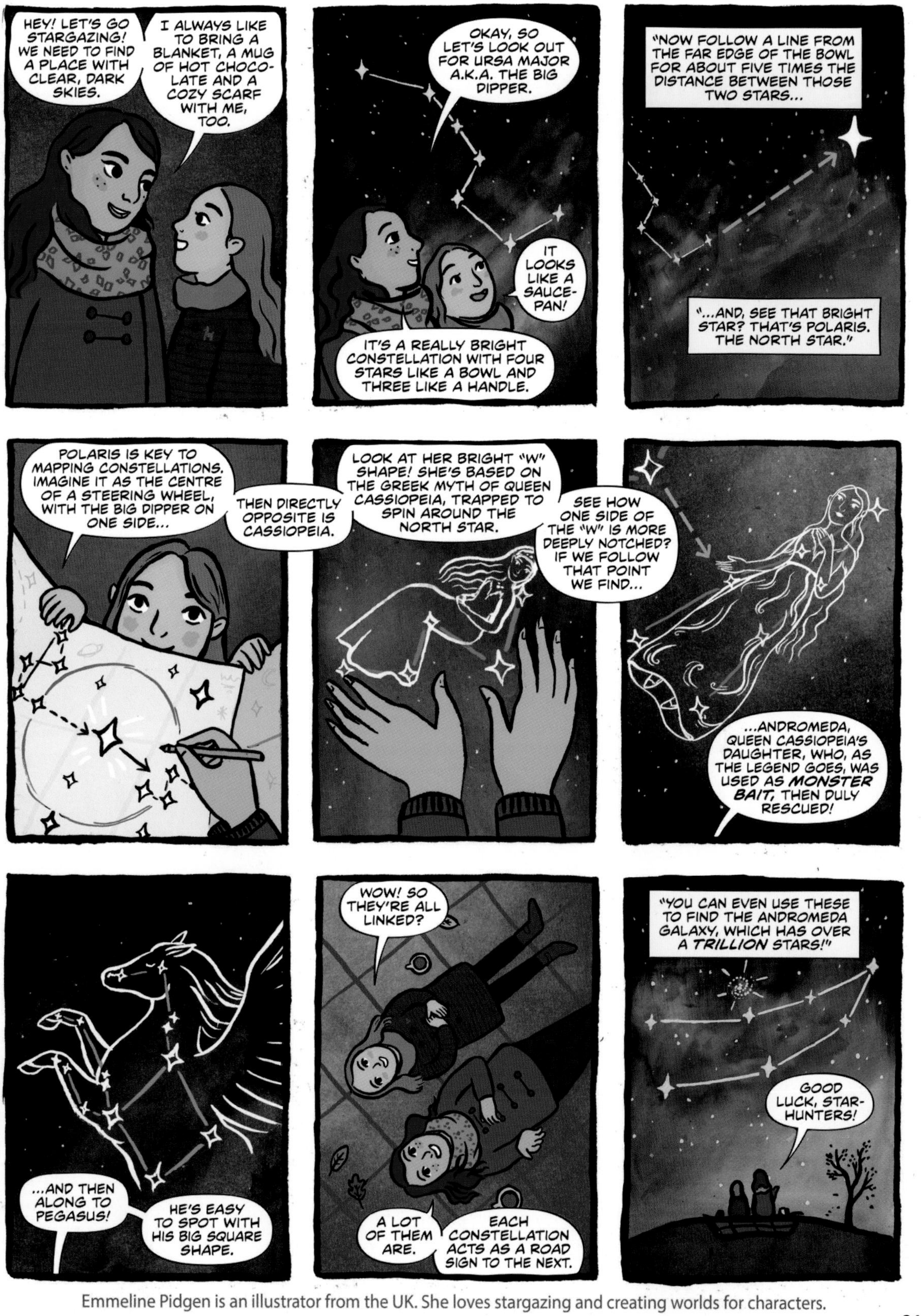

HEY! LET'S GO STARGAZING! WE NEED TO FIND A PLACE WITH CLEAR, DARK SKIES.
I ALWAYS LIKE TO BRING A BLANKET, A MUG OF HOT CHOCOLATE AND A COZY SCARF WITH ME, TOO.
OKAY, SO LET'S LOOK OUT FOR URSA MAJOR A.K.A. THE BIG DIPPER.
IT LOOKS LIKE A SAUCEPAN!
IT'S A REALLY BRIGHT CONSTELLATION WITH FOUR STARS LIKE A BOWL AND THREE LIKE A HANDLE.
"NOW FOLLOW A LINE FROM THE FAR EDGE OF THE BOWL FOR ABOUT FIVE TIMES THE DISTANCE BETWEEN THOSE TWO STARS...
"...AND, SEE THAT BRIGHT STAR? THAT'S POLARIS. THE NORTH STAR."
POLARIS IS KEY TO MAPPING CONSTELLATIONS. IMAGINE IT AS THE CENTRE OF A STEERING WHEEL, WITH THE BIG DIPPER ON ONE SIDE...
THEN DIRECTLY OPPOSITE IS CASSIOPEIA.
LOOK AT HER BRIGHT "W" SHAPE! SHE'S BASED ON THE GREEK MYTH OF QUEEN CASSIOPEIA, TRAPPED TO SPIN AROUND THE NORTH STAR.
SEE HOW ONE SIDE OF THE "W" IS MORE DEEPLY NOTCHED? IF WE FOLLOW THAT POINT WE FIND...
...ANDROMEDA, QUEEN CASSIOPEIA'S DAUGHTER, WHO, AS THE LEGEND GOES, WAS USED AS ***MONSTER BAIT,*** THEN DULY RESCUED!
...AND THEN ALONG TO PEGASUS!
HE'S EASY TO SPOT WITH HIS BIG SQUARE SHAPE.
WOW! SO THEY'RE ALL LINKED?
A LOT OF THEM ARE.
EACH CONSTELLATION ACTS AS A ROAD SIGN TO THE NEXT.
"YOU CAN EVEN USE THESE TO FIND THE ANDROMEDA GALAXY, WHICH HAS OVER A ***TRILLION*** STARS!"
GOOD LUCK, STAR-HUNTERS!

Emmeline Pidgen is an illustrator from the UK. She loves stargazing and creating worlds for characters.

BETTER LIVING THROUGH CANON: STREET DYNAMICS FOR EARLY ADOPTERS

People in comics are throwing around the word "curator" a lot. Blame me: I started a trend — and unless you really know your shit, it's as ambiguous as the term "editor." So in an effort to make the distinction between glorified paper pusher and Master Control, we need to start with urban planning. To paraphrase by definition it's *"...the design and regulation of the uses of space that focus on the physical form, economic functions, and social impacts of the urban environment and on the location of different activities within it."*

The Brief: To create an unprecedented environment wherein characters (the story kind and the creative types who enable them) commingle, corrupt and — this is important -- correlate to individual comic book series under the BLACK CROWN imprimatur.

For example, the good things in life revolve around food and drink (cue personal soundrack). Therefore, THE BLACK CROWN PUB makes an obvious anchor. Located at the cross street between Canon and Great Yarn, you're just as likely to catch an impromptu CUD gig (see The BCQ) as you are to share a frothy pint with the ghost of Sid from PUNKS NOT DEAD. (Don't ask, you always pay for it...)

Speaking of PND, its specific link to Canon Street involves "Electric Trash," a retro/vintage boutique where Julie Ferguson, Fergie's mom, worked in 198?. This may or may not be where Julie and Fergie's absent father corrupted, commingled and consummated. It's definitely not a sartorial destination for Dorothy Culpepper, MI-5's fearless leader of The Department of Extra-Usual Affairs. This brash, champagne-swilling old mod bird breaks into a rash just thinking about anything other than her own original couture. She wouldn't be caught dead or alive here.

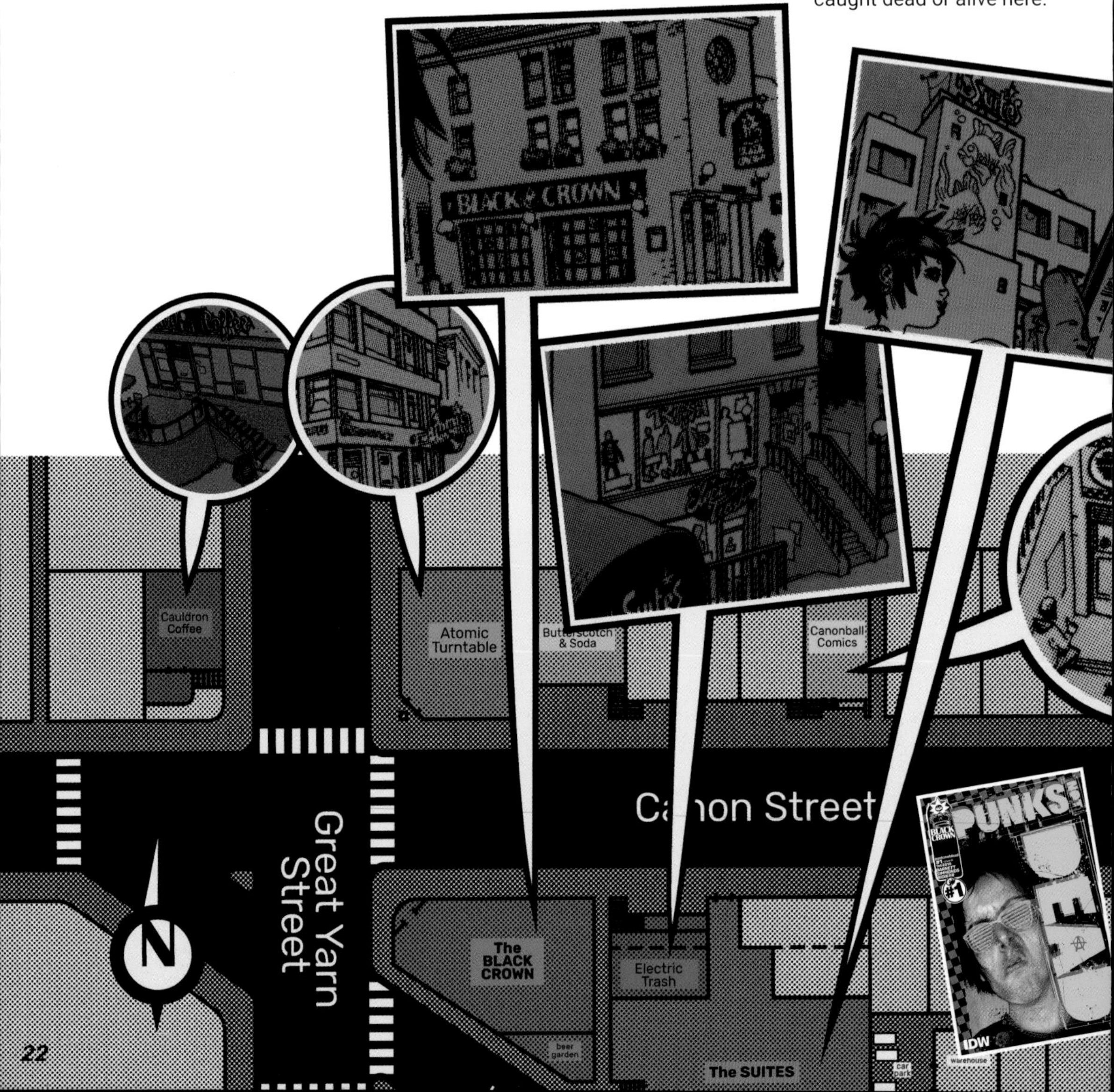

BLACK & CROWN
Cauldron Coffee
Atomic Turntable
Butterscotch & Soda
Canonball Comics
Canon Street
Great Yarn Street
The BLACK CROWN
Electric Trash
beer garden
The SUITES
car park
warehouse
PUNKS!
IDW

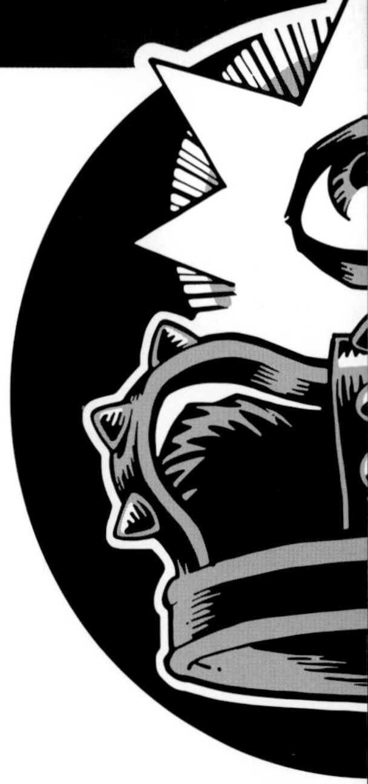

"Because urban planning draws upon engineering, architectural, and social and political concerns, it is variously a technical profession, an endeavour involving political will and public participation, and an academic discipline."

"The Suites" hotel is a sanctuary for Kid of KID LOBOTOMY fame, the youngest descendant of a dysfunctional family of hoteliers. A former rockstar/current manager (or madman), Kid has an unhealthy appetite for existential fiction, shapeshifting chambermaids, and performing lobotomies with his own special raygun. But he means well. Absurdist comedy in times of great societal and political upheaval? Check in: anytime. Check out: the twelvth of never.

Our ASSASSINISTAS knew the secret knock to get into Winnie's Roller Rink back in the day when duffel bags held skates with glittery laces and silver bullets for AK-47s. Although the trio has evolved, these badass bounty hunters still mean business when it comes to eradicating the world of CEOs who demoralize women, abetting sexual discrimination, injustice and inequality at all costs. Cracking skulls in your honor and proud supporters of #metoo.

"Urban planning concerns itself with both the development of open land and the revitalization of existing parts of the city, thereby involving goal setting, data collection and analysis, forecasting, design, strategic thinking, and public consultation."

No small feat, the communal landscape at large is clearly a labor of love. Immerse yourself accordingly. Additional real estate is under construction so check out our weekly happy hour updates every Friday at 4:00 PST/midnite UTC at blackcrown.pub. Beware naysayers and barefoot rockstars wielding harps and rayguns with equal vigor...unless you like that sort of thing.

BLACK CROWN: How it's done.

Shelly

Shelly Bond
Editor/Curator/
Urban Planner
BLACK CROWN
#therulingclass
blackcrown.pub
May 2018

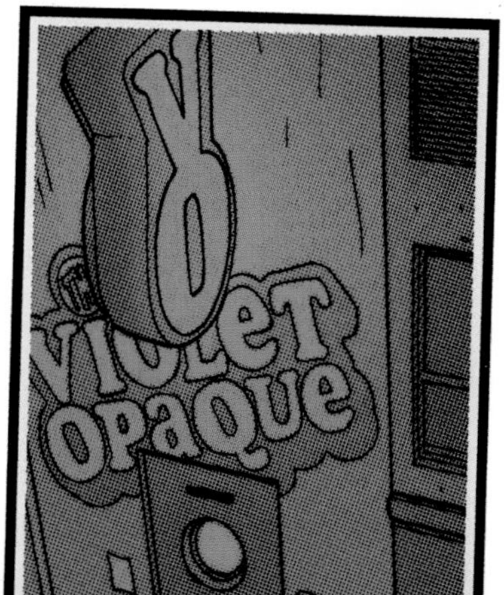
VIOLET OPAQUE

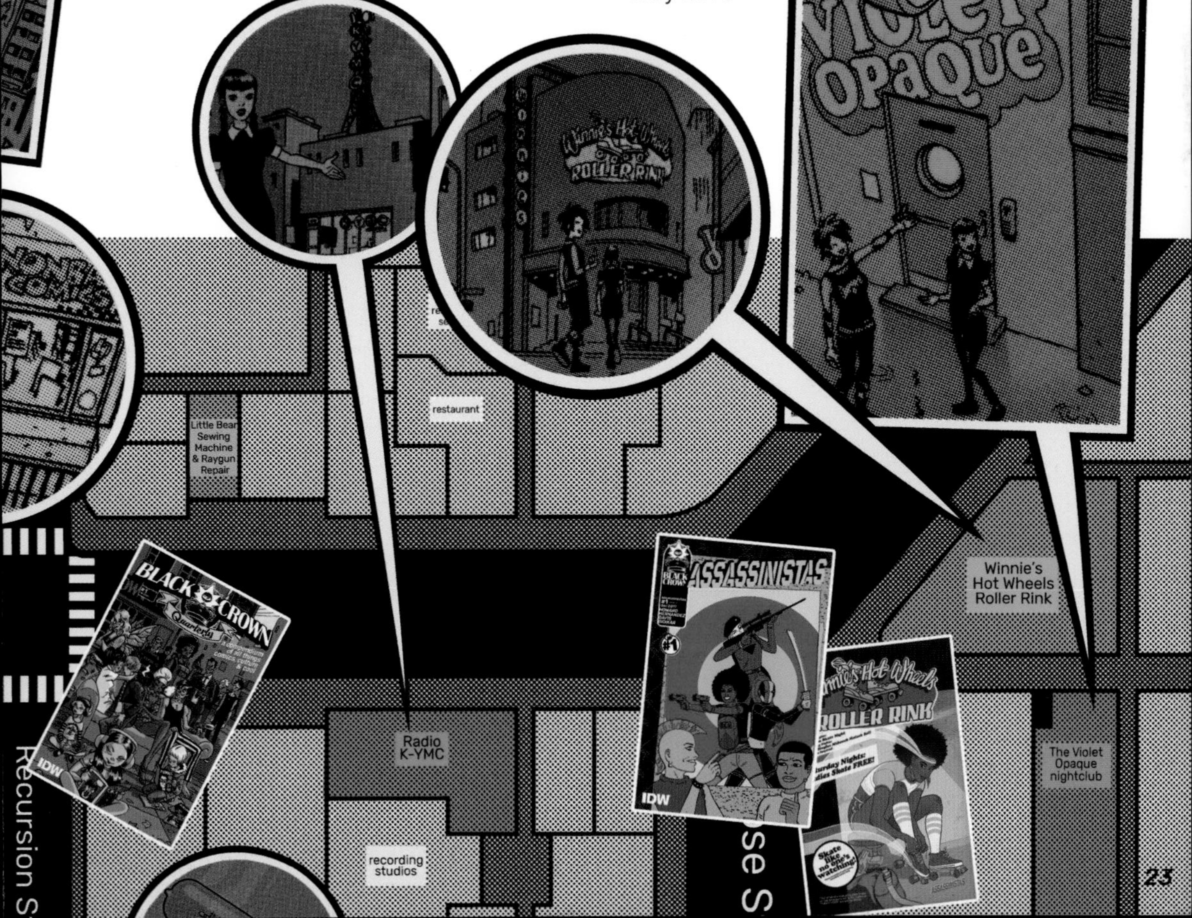
Little Bear Sewing Machine & Raygun Repair
restaurant
Radio K-YMC
recording studios
Winnie's Hot Wheels Roller Rink
The Violet Opaque nightclub
BLACK CROWN
ASSASSINISTAS
IDW
Winnie's Hot Wheels
ROLLER RINK

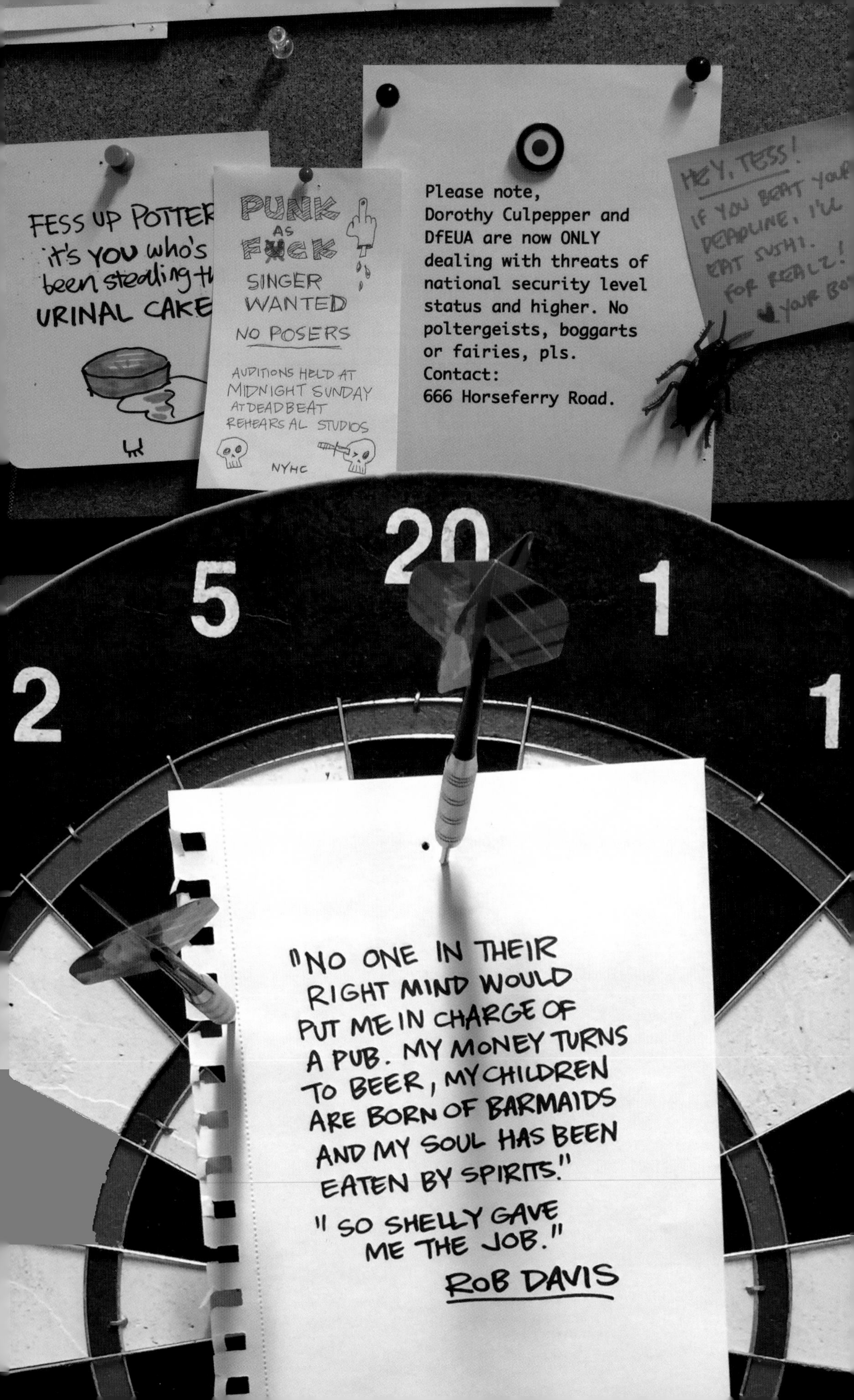
FESS UP POTTER
it's YOU who's
been stealing th
URINAL CAKE
PUNK AS F✗CK
SINGER WANTED
NO POSERS
AUDITIONS HELD AT MIDNIGHT SUNDAY AT DEADBEAT REHEARSAL STUDIOS
NYHC
Please note,
Dorothy Culpepper and
DfEUA are now ONLY
dealing with threats of
national security level
status and higher. No
poltergeists, boggarts
or fairies, pls.
Contact:
666 Horseferry Road.
HEY, TESS!
IF YOU BEAT YOUR
DEADLINE, I'LL
EAT SUSHI.
FOR REALZ!
♥ YOUR BO
"NO ONE IN THEIR RIGHT MIND WOULD PUT ME IN CHARGE OF A PUB. MY MONEY TURNS TO BEER, MY CHILDREN ARE BORN OF BARMAIDS AND MY SOUL HAS BEEN EATEN BY SPIRITS."
"SO SHELLY GAVE ME THE JOB."
ROB DAVIS

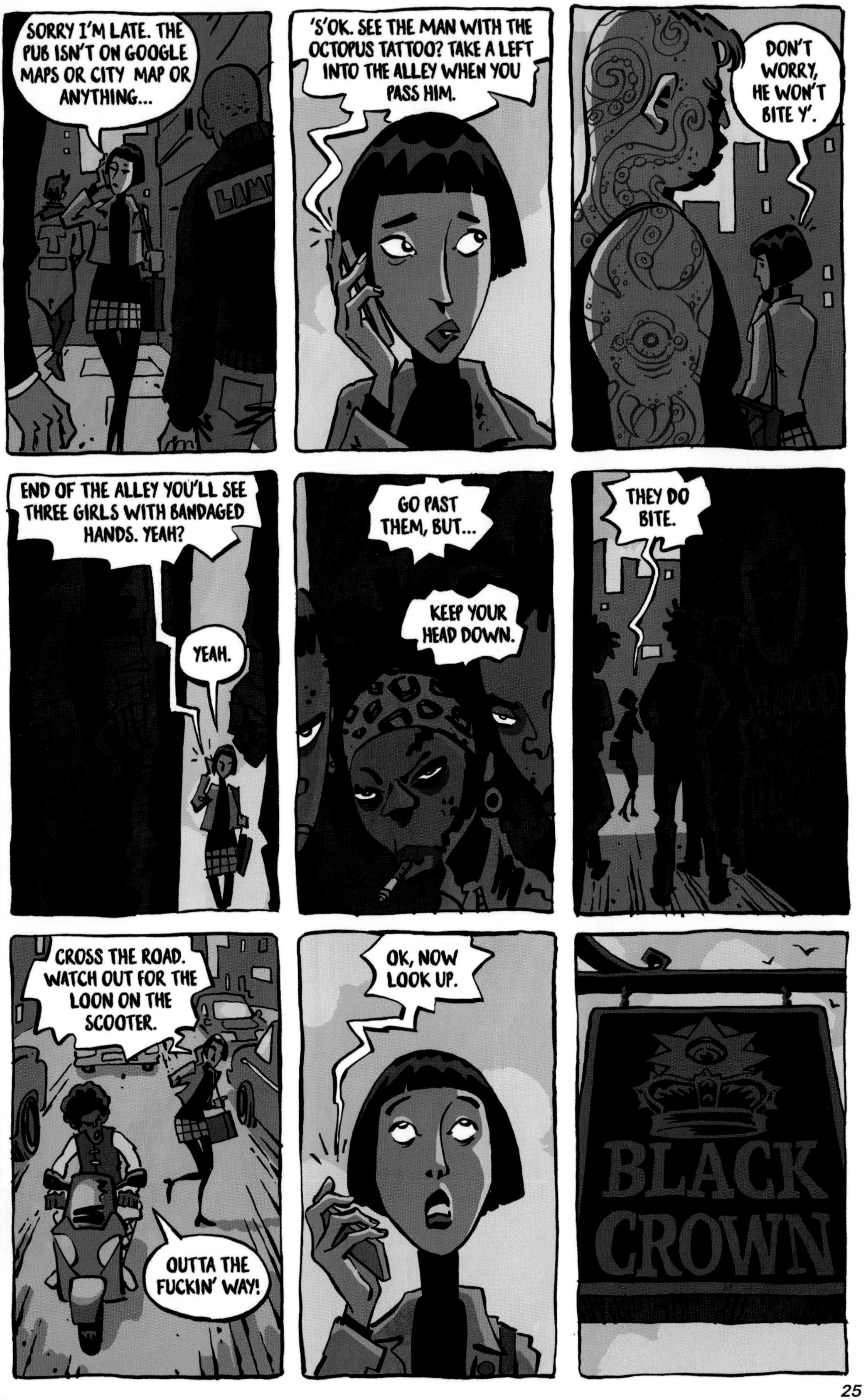
SORRY I'M LATE. THE PUB ISN'T ON GOOGLE MAPS OR CITY MAP OR ANYTHING...
'S'OK. SEE THE MAN WITH THE OCTOPUS TATTOO? TAKE A LEFT INTO THE ALLEY WHEN YOU PASS HIM.
DON'T WORRY, HE WON'T BITE Y'.
END OF THE ALLEY YOU'LL SEE THREE GIRLS WITH BANDAGED HANDS. YEAH?
YEAH.
GO PAST THEM, BUT...
KEEP YOUR HEAD DOWN.
THEY DO BITE.
CROSS THE ROAD. WATCH OUT FOR THE LOON ON THE SCOOTER.
OUTTA THE FUCKIN' WAY!
OK, NOW LOOK UP.
BLACK CROWN

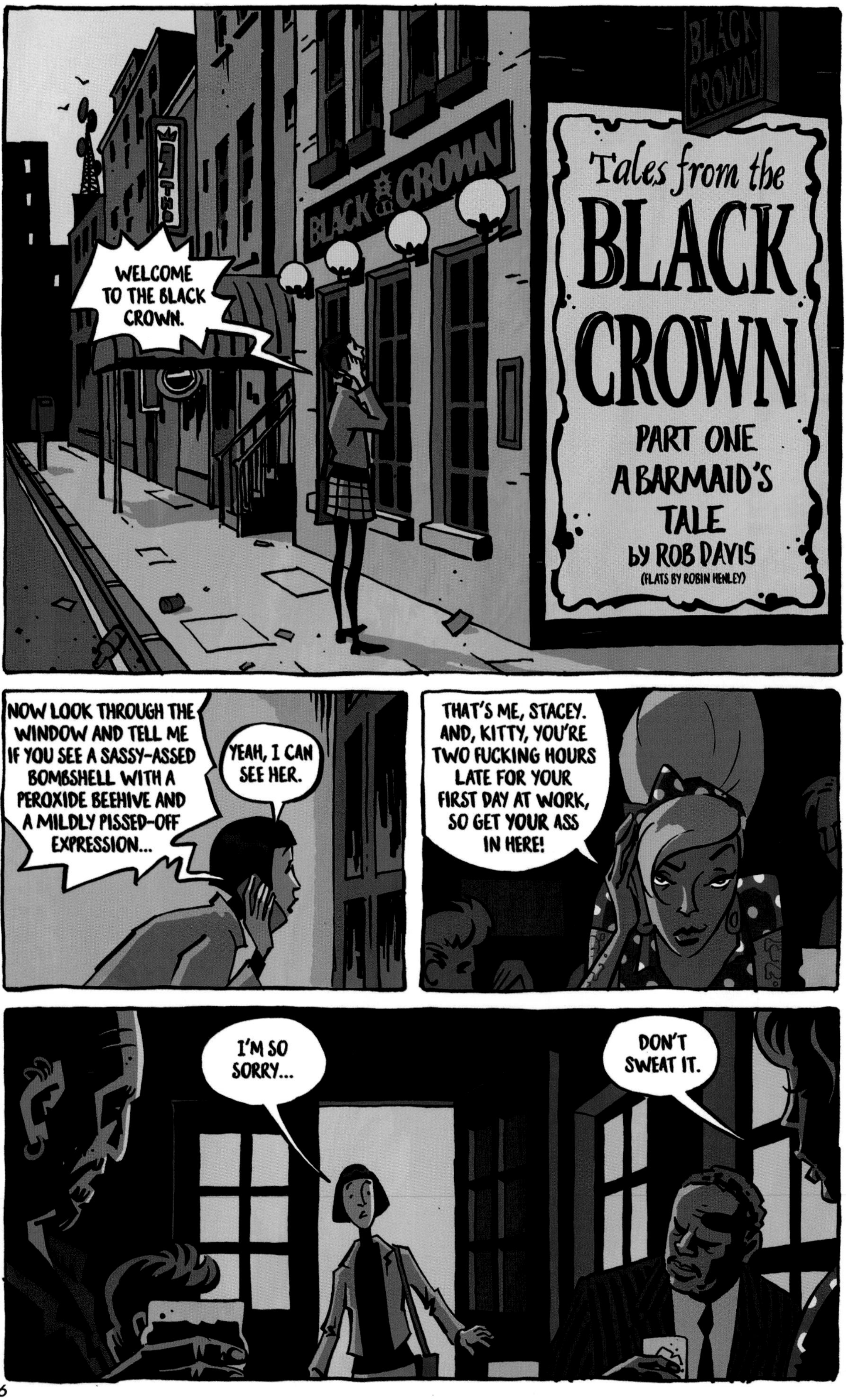
WELCOME TO THE BLACK CROWN.
BLACK CROWN
Tales from the BLACK CROWN
PART ONE
A BARMAID'S TALE
by ROB DAVIS
(FLATS BY ROBIN HENLEY)
NOW LOOK THROUGH THE WINDOW AND TELL ME IF YOU SEE A SASSY-ASSED BOMBSHELL WITH A PEROXIDE BEEHIVE AND A MILDLY PISSED-OFF EXPRESSION...
YEAH, I CAN SEE HER.
THAT'S ME, STACEY. AND, KITTY, YOU'RE TWO FUCKING HOURS LATE FOR YOUR FIRST DAY AT WORK, SO GET YOUR ASS IN HERE!
I'M SO SORRY...
DON'T SWEAT IT.

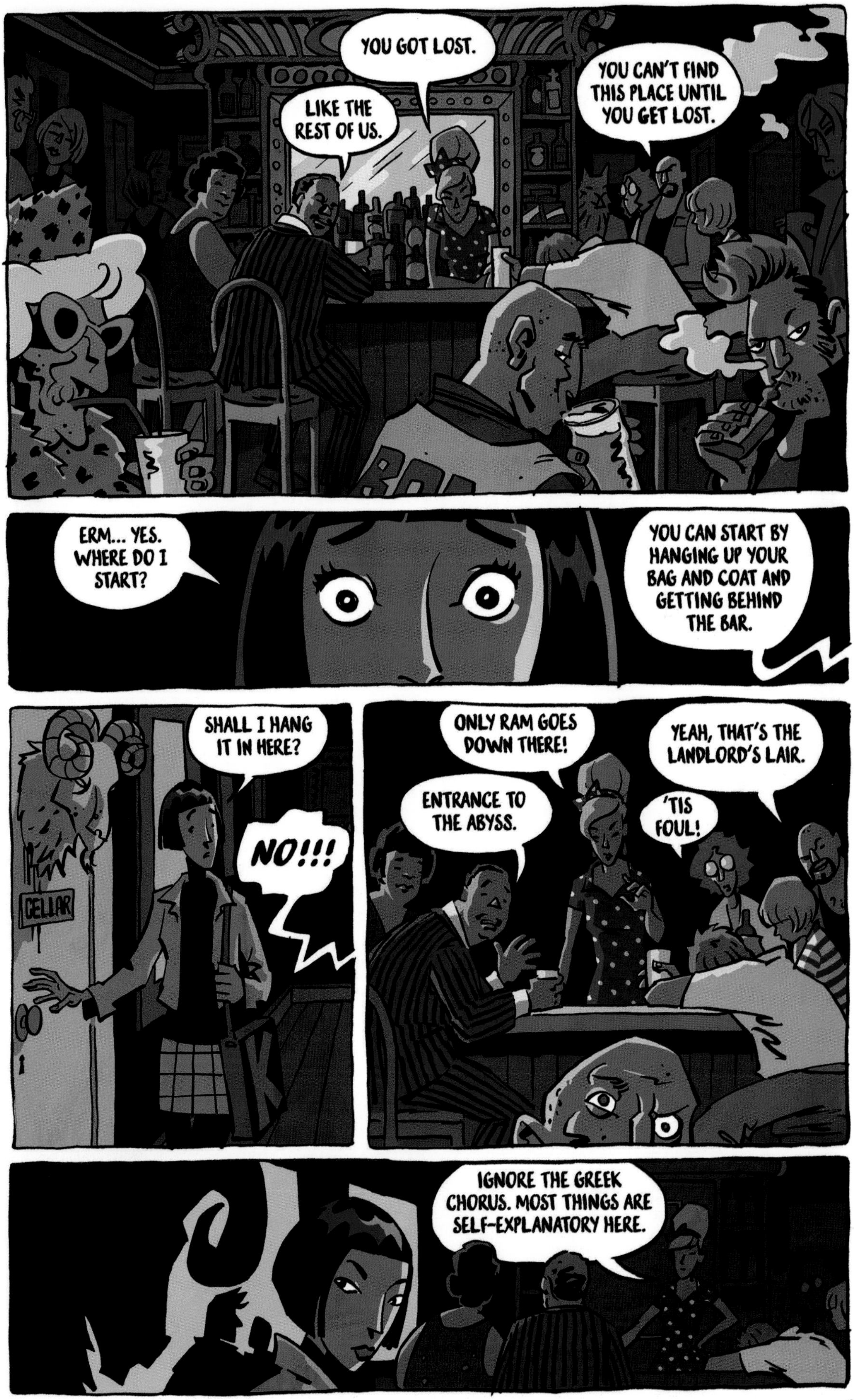

LIKE THE REST OF US.
YOU GOT LOST.
YOU CAN'T FIND THIS PLACE UNTIL YOU GET LOST.
ERM... YES. WHERE DO I START?
YOU CAN START BY HANGING UP YOUR BAG AND COAT AND GETTING BEHIND THE BAR.
SHALL I HANG IT IN HERE?
CELLAR
NO!!!
ONLY RAM GOES DOWN THERE!
ENTRANCE TO THE ABYSS.
YEAH, THAT'S THE LANDLORD'S LAIR.
'TIS FOUL!
IGNORE THE GREEK CHORUS. MOST THINGS ARE SELF-EXPLANATORY HERE.

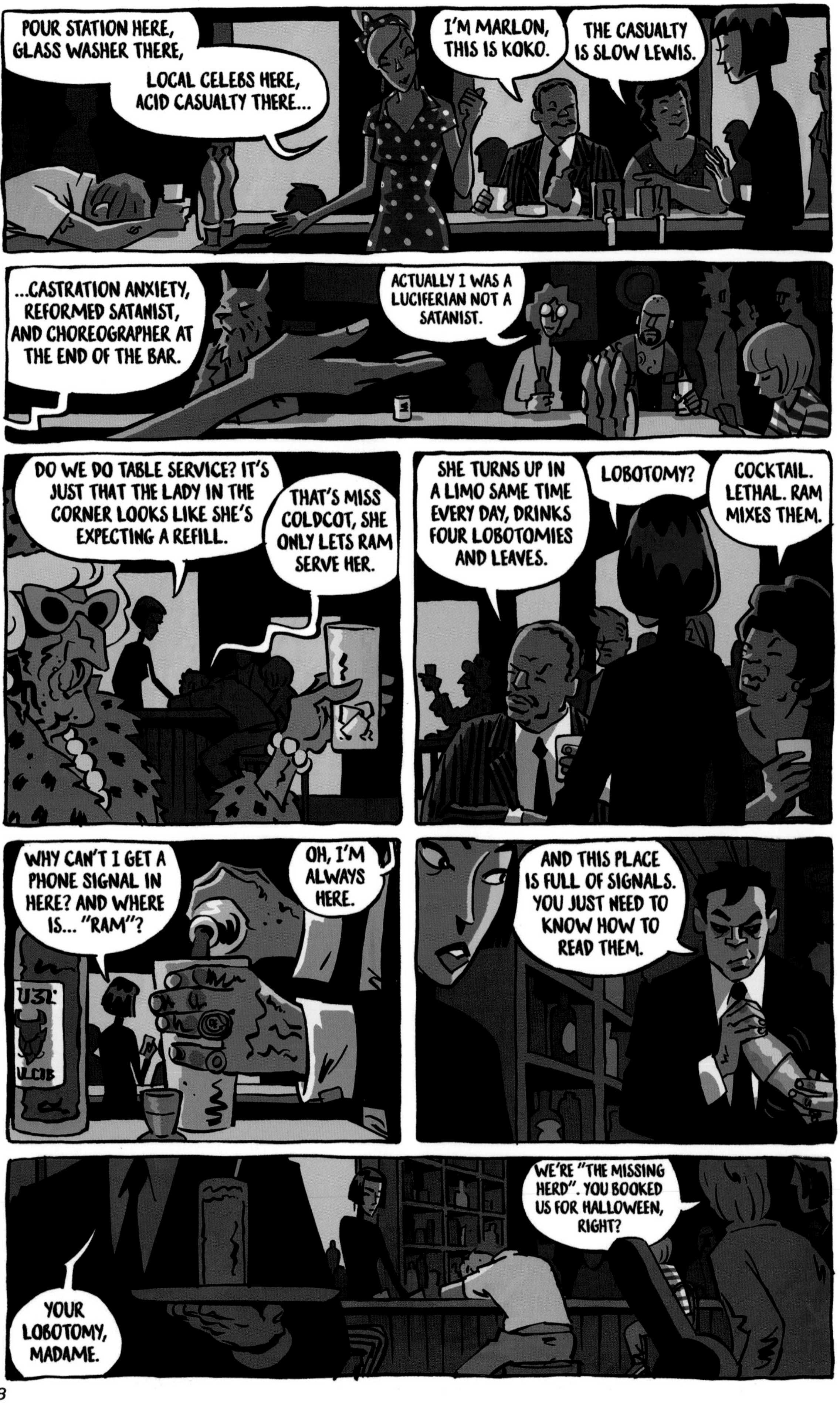
POUR STATION HERE, GLASS WASHER THERE,
LOCAL CELEBS HERE, ACID CASUALTY THERE...
I'M MARLON, THIS IS KOKO.
THE CASUALTY IS SLOW LEWIS.
...CASTRATION ANXIETY, REFORMED SATANIST, AND CHOREOGRAPHER AT THE END OF THE BAR.
ACTUALLY I WAS A LUCIFERIAN NOT A SATANIST.
DO WE DO TABLE SERVICE? IT'S JUST THAT THE LADY IN THE CORNER LOOKS LIKE SHE'S EXPECTING A REFILL.
THAT'S MISS COLDCOT, SHE ONLY LETS RAM SERVE HER.
SHE TURNS UP IN A LIMO SAME TIME EVERY DAY, DRINKS FOUR LOBOTOMIES AND LEAVES.
LOBOTOMY?
COCKTAIL. LETHAL. RAM MIXES THEM.
WHY CAN'T I GET A PHONE SIGNAL IN HERE? AND WHERE IS... "RAM"?
OH, I'M ALWAYS HERE.
AND THIS PLACE IS FULL OF SIGNALS. YOU JUST NEED TO KNOW HOW TO READ THEM.
YOUR LOBOTOMY, MADAME.
WE'RE "THE MISSING HERD". YOU BOOKED US FOR HALLOWEEN, RIGHT?

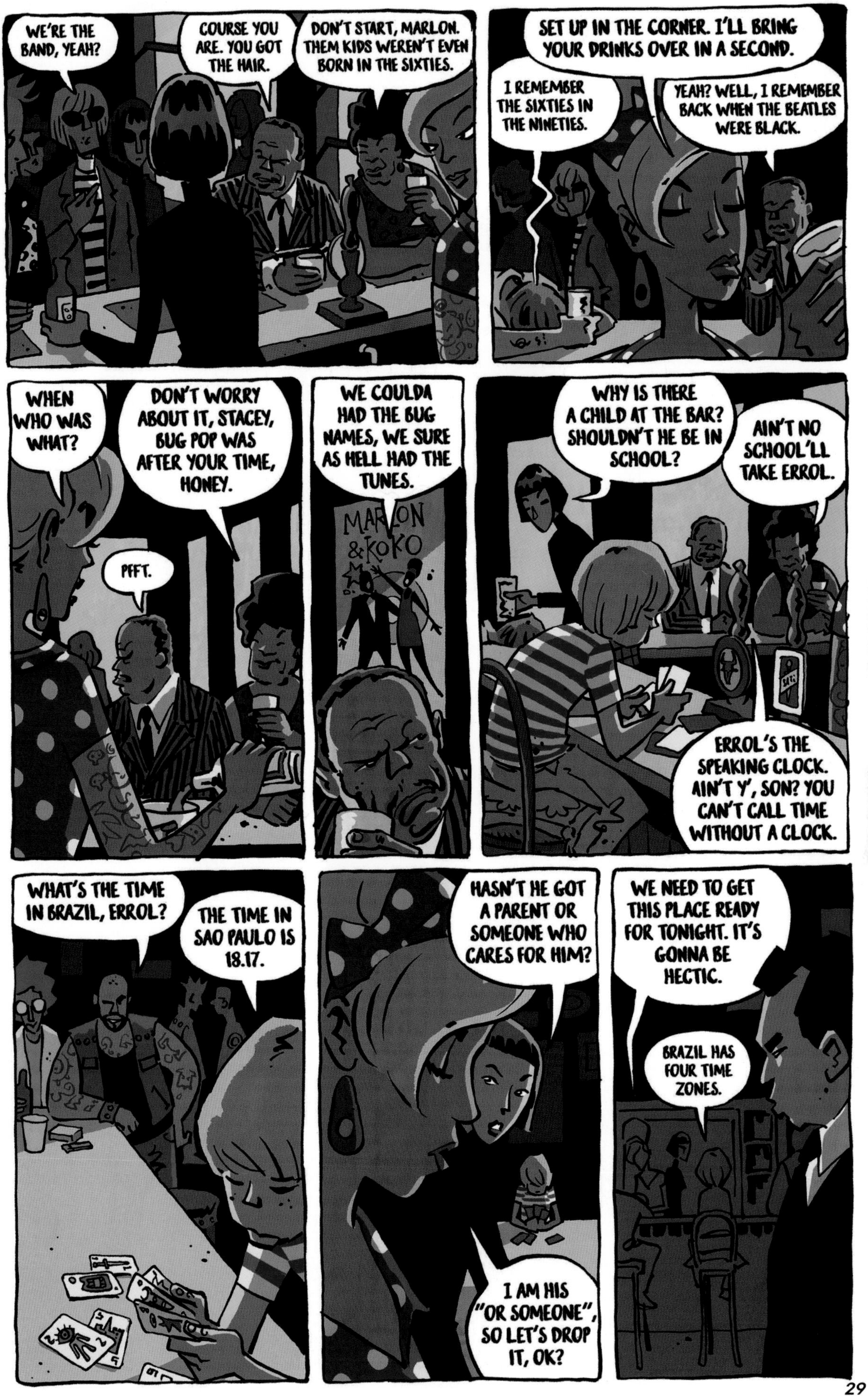
WE'RE THE BAND, YEAH?
COURSE YOU ARE. YOU GOT THE HAIR.
DON'T START, MARLON. THEM KIDS WEREN'T EVEN BORN IN THE SIXTIES.
SET UP IN THE CORNER. I'LL BRING YOUR DRINKS OVER IN A SECOND.
I REMEMBER THE SIXTIES IN THE NINETIES.
YEAH? WELL, I REMEMBER BACK WHEN THE BEATLES WERE BLACK.
WHEN WHO WAS WHAT?
DON'T WORRY ABOUT IT, STACEY, BUG POP WAS AFTER YOUR TIME, HONEY.
PFFT.
WE COULDA HAD THE BUG NAMES, WE SURE AS HELL HAD THE TUNES.
MARLON &KOKO
WHY IS THERE A CHILD AT THE BAR? SHOULDN'T HE BE IN SCHOOL?
AIN'T NO SCHOOL'LL TAKE ERROL.
ERROL'S THE SPEAKING CLOCK. AIN'T Y', SON? YOU CAN'T CALL TIME WITHOUT A CLOCK.
WHAT'S THE TIME IN BRAZIL, ERROL?
THE TIME IN SAO PAULO IS 18.17.
HASN'T HE GOT A PARENT OR SOMEONE WHO CARES FOR HIM?
I AM HIS "OR SOMEONE", SO LET'S DROP IT, OK?
WE NEED TO GET THIS PLACE READY FOR TONIGHT. IT'S GONNA BE HECTIC.
BRAZIL HAS FOUR TIME ZONES.

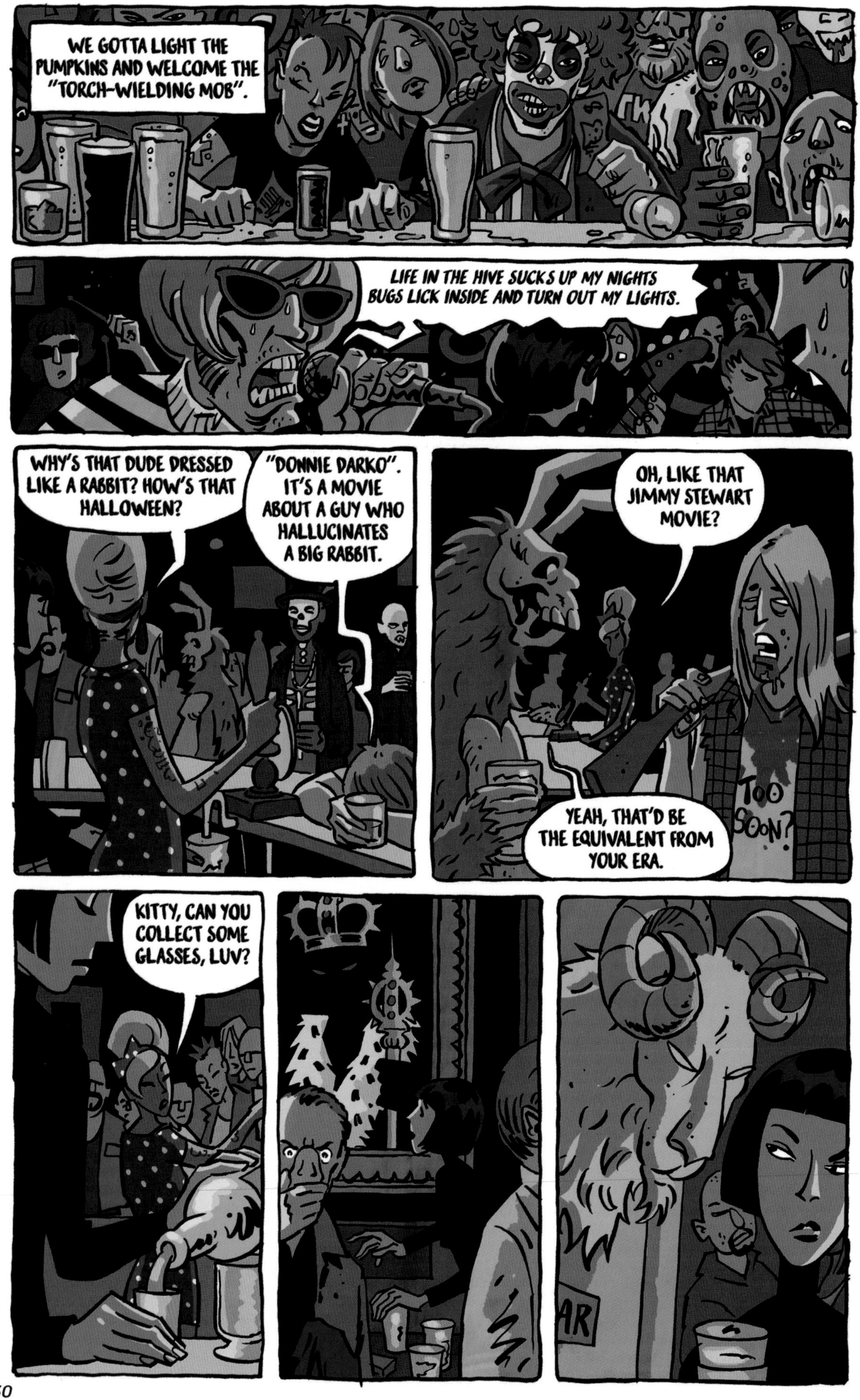
WE GOTTA LIGHT THE PUMPKINS AND WELCOME THE "TORCH-WIELDING MOB".
LIFE IN THE HIVE SUCKS UP MY NIGHTS BUGS LICK INSIDE AND TURN OUT MY LIGHTS.
WHY'S THAT DUDE DRESSED LIKE A RABBIT? HOW'S THAT HALLOWEEN?
"DONNIE DARKO". IT'S A MOVIE ABOUT A GUY WHO HALLUCINATES A BIG RABBIT.
OH, LIKE THAT JIMMY STEWART MOVIE?
TOO SOON?
YEAH, THAT'D BE THE EQUIVALENT FROM YOUR ERA.
KITTY, CAN YOU COLLECT SOME GLASSES, LUV?

THERE'S A GHOST IN MY HOUSE, A HAUNTOLOGY OF MY WIFE...

THESE EMPTY?

CLICK!

RAM? MY MEDICINE... WHERE ISSS IT?

WHICH NEWSPAPER DO YOU WORK FOR, KITTY? I'M GUESSING IT'S NOT THE CONVIVIAL TIMES...

MY CELLAR DOOR IS ALWAYS LOCKED. UNLESS I'M LOOKING TO CATCH THE CURIOUS.

A FEW MORE STEPS AND YOU'LL BE IN THE BELLY OF THE BLACK CROWN. IS IT WORTH GETTING EATEN JUST TO FIND OUT WHAT'S INSIDE?

I APPRECIATE YOUR INTEREST, OF COURSE. YOU'VE COME TO THE RIGHT PLACE IF YOU'RE LOOKING FOR A STORY. THE BLACK CROWN HOLDS SO MANY. SOME GO DEEPER THAN OTHERS. AND SOME IT WOULD RATHER NOT GIVE UP AT ALL.

I—I CAME FOR THE BARMAID'S JOB...

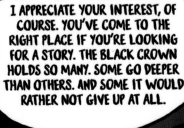

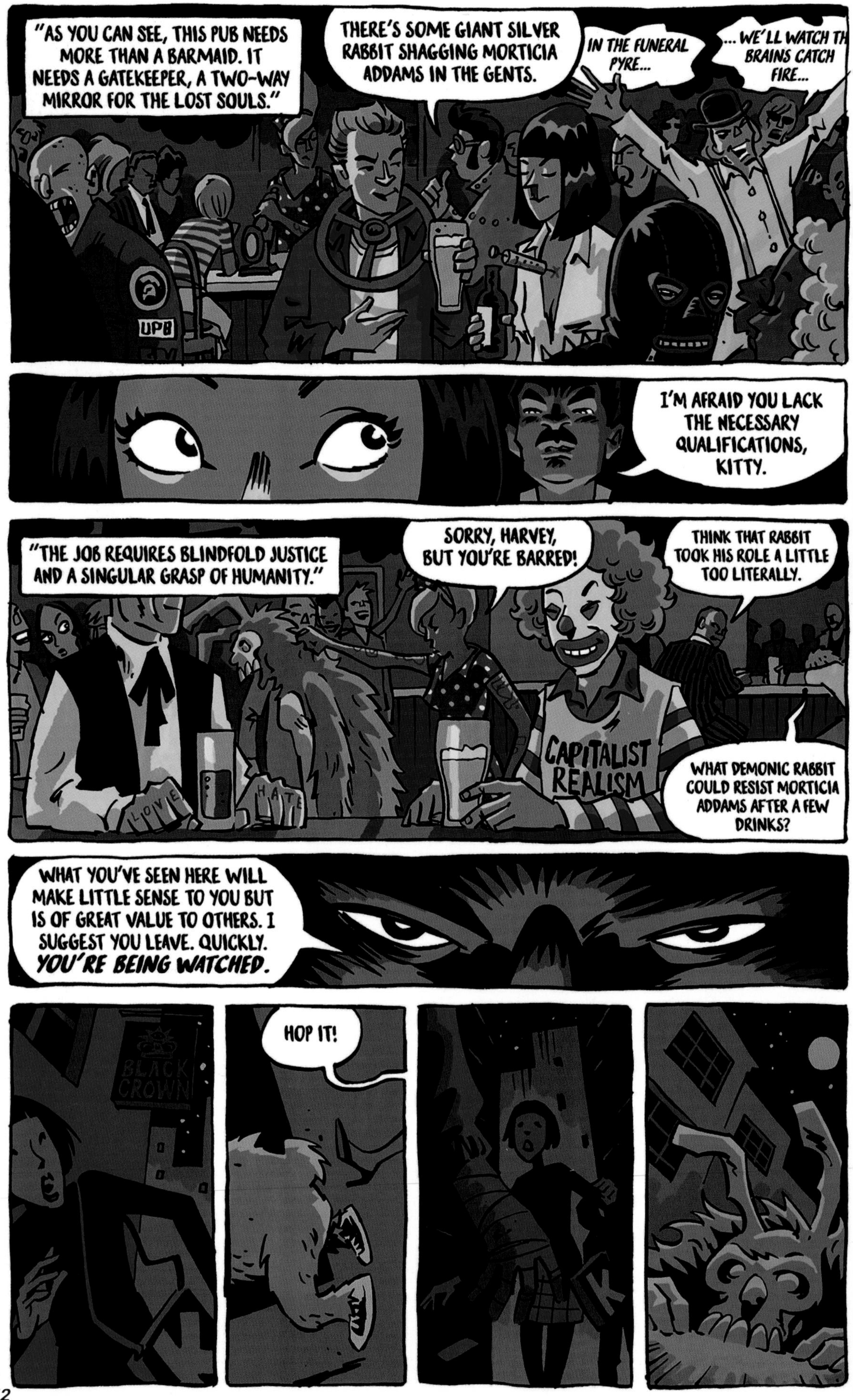
"AS YOU CAN SEE, THIS PUB NEEDS MORE THAN A BARMAID. IT NEEDS A GATEKEEPER, A TWO-WAY MIRROR FOR THE LOST SOULS."
THERE'S SOME GIANT SILVER RABBIT SHAGGING MORTICIA ADDAMS IN THE GENTS.
IN THE FUNERAL PYRE...
...WE'LL WATCH TH BRAINS CATCH FIRE...
UPB
I'M AFRAID YOU LACK THE NECESSARY QUALIFICATIONS, KITTY.
"THE JOB REQUIRES BLINDFOLD JUSTICE AND A SINGULAR GRASP OF HUMANITY."
SORRY, HARVEY, BUT YOU'RE BARRED!
THINK THAT RABBIT TOOK HIS ROLE A LITTLE TOO LITERALLY.
CAPITALIST REALISM
LOVE
HATE
WHAT DEMONIC RABBIT COULD RESIST MORTICIA ADDAMS AFTER A FEW DRINKS?
WHAT YOU'VE SEEN HERE WILL MAKE LITTLE SENSE TO YOU BUT IS OF GREAT VALUE TO OTHERS. I SUGGEST YOU LEAVE. QUICKLY. *YOU'RE BEING WATCHED.*
BLACK CROWN
HOP IT!

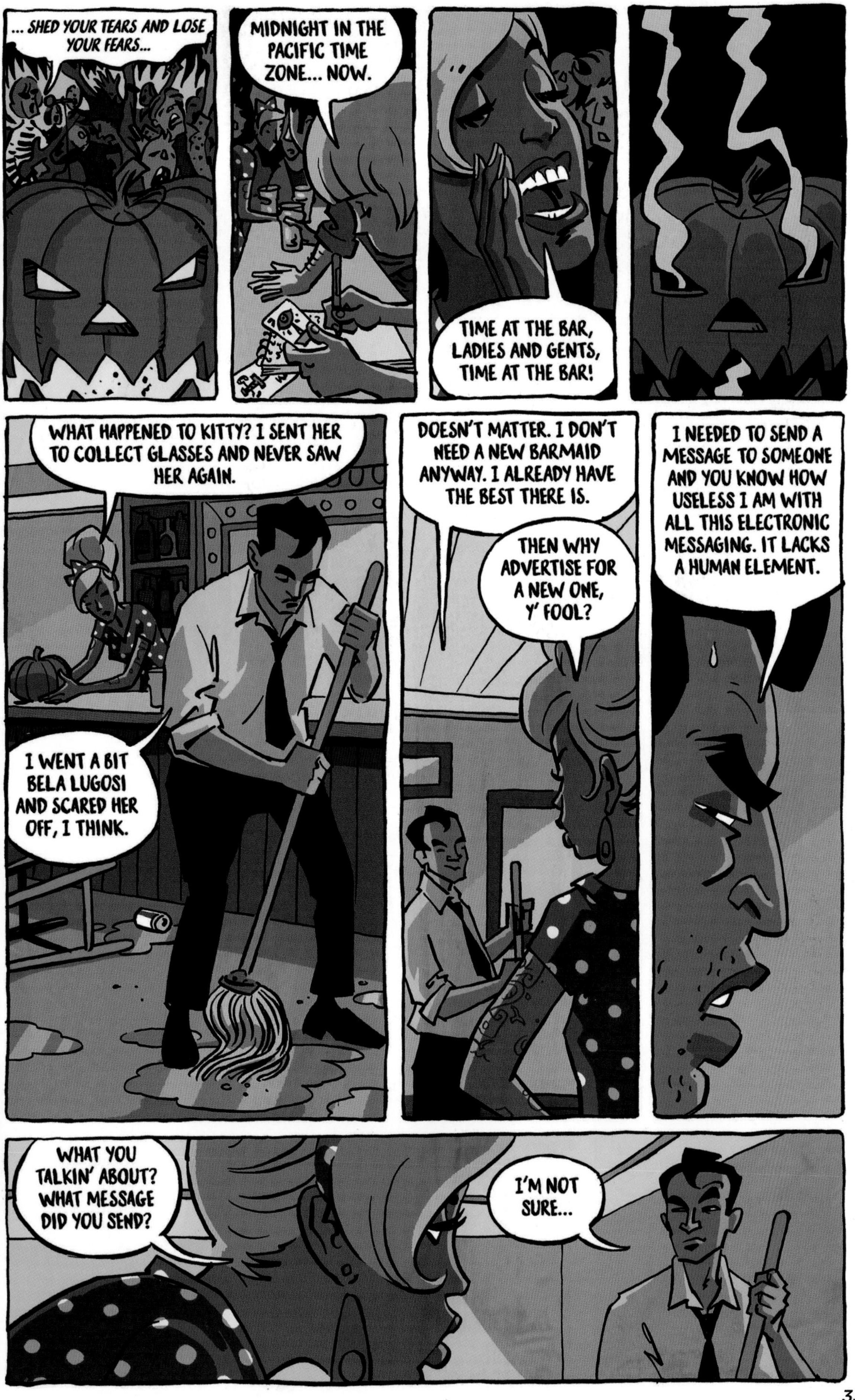
... SHED YOUR TEARS AND LOSE YOUR FEARS...
MIDNIGHT IN THE PACIFIC TIME ZONE... NOW.
TIME AT THE BAR, LADIES AND GENTS, TIME AT THE BAR!
WHAT HAPPENED TO KITTY? I SENT HER TO COLLECT GLASSES AND NEVER SAW HER AGAIN.
I WENT A BIT BELA LUGOSI AND SCARED HER OFF, I THINK.
DOESN'T MATTER. I DON'T NEED A NEW BARMAID ANYWAY. I ALREADY HAVE THE BEST THERE IS.
THEN WHY ADVERTISE FOR A NEW ONE, Y' FOOL?
I NEEDED TO SEND A MESSAGE TO SOMEONE AND YOU KNOW HOW USELESS I AM WITH ALL THIS ELECTRONIC MESSAGING. IT LACKS A HUMAN ELEMENT.
WHAT YOU TALKIN' ABOUT? WHAT MESSAGE DID YOU SEND?
I'M NOT SURE...

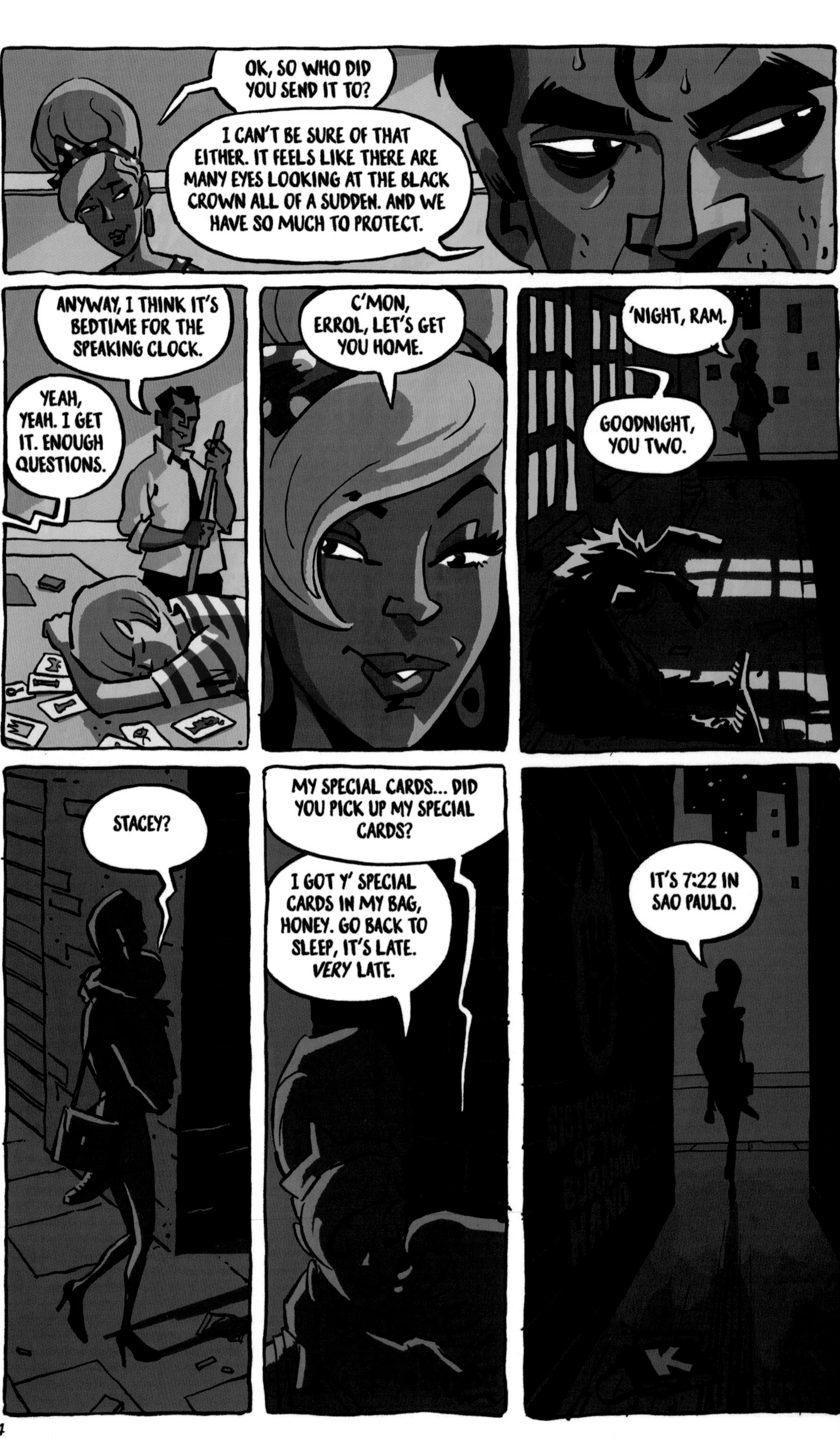
OK, SO WHO DID YOU SEND IT TO?
I CAN'T BE SURE OF THAT EITHER. IT FEELS LIKE THERE ARE MANY EYES LOOKING AT THE BLACK CROWN ALL OF A SUDDEN. AND WE HAVE SO MUCH TO PROTECT.
ANYWAY, I THINK IT'S BEDTIME FOR THE SPEAKING CLOCK.
YEAH, YEAH. I GET IT. ENOUGH QUESTIONS.
C'MON, ERROL, LET'S GET YOU HOME.
'NIGHT, RAM.
GOODNIGHT, YOU TWO.
STACEY?
MY SPECIAL CARDS... DID YOU PICK UP MY SPECIAL CARDS?
I GOT Y' SPECIAL CARDS IN MY BAG, HONEY. GO BACK TO SLEEP, IT'S LATE. *VERY* LATE.
IT'S 7:22 IN SAO PAULO.

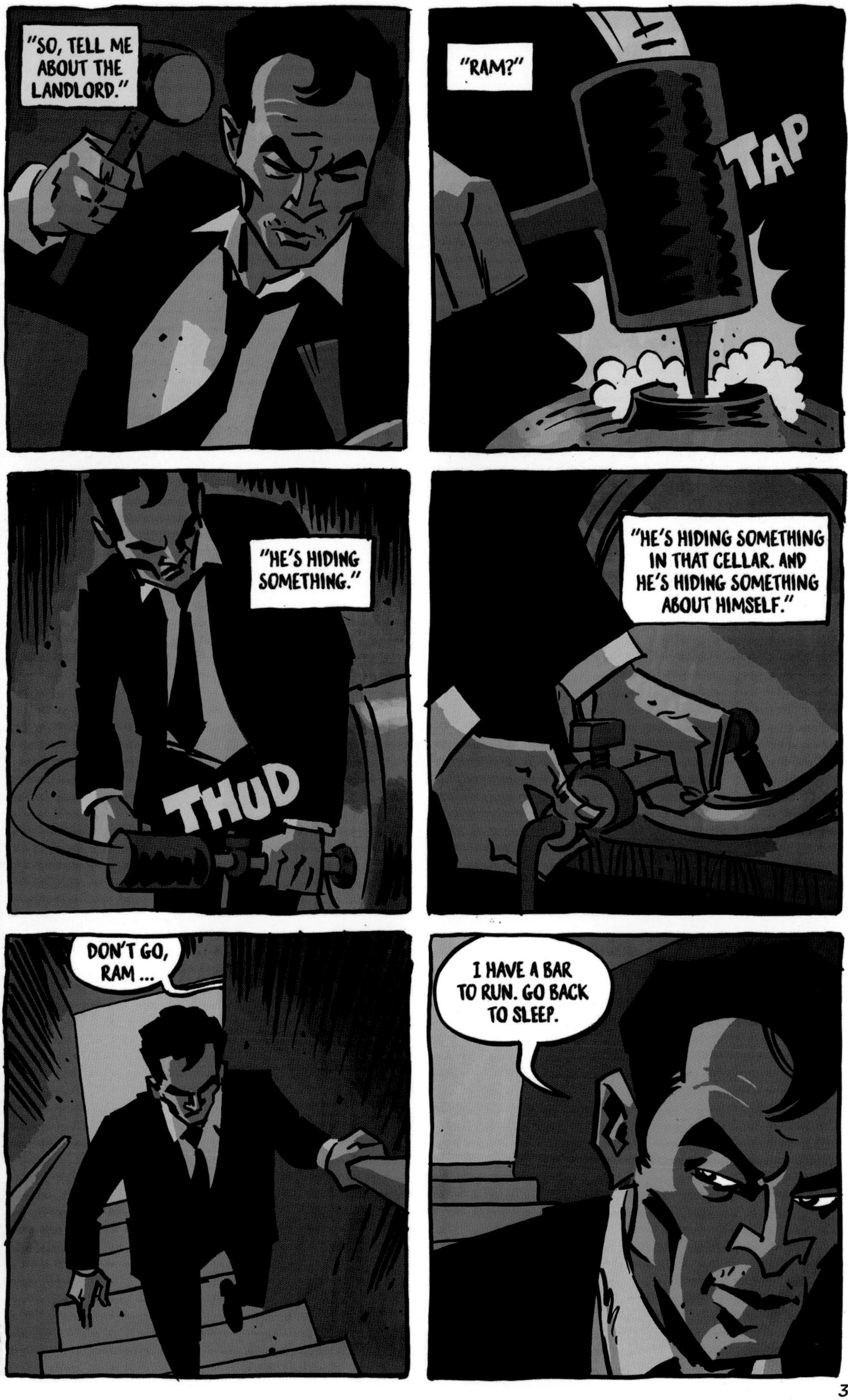
"SO, TELL ME ABOUT THE LANDLORD."
"RAM?"
TAP
"HE'S HIDING SOMETHING."
THUD
"HE'S HIDING SOMETHING IN THAT CELLAR. AND HE'S HIDING SOMETHING ABOUT HIMSELF."
DON'T GO, RAM ...
I HAVE A BAR TO RUN. GO BACK TO SLEEP.

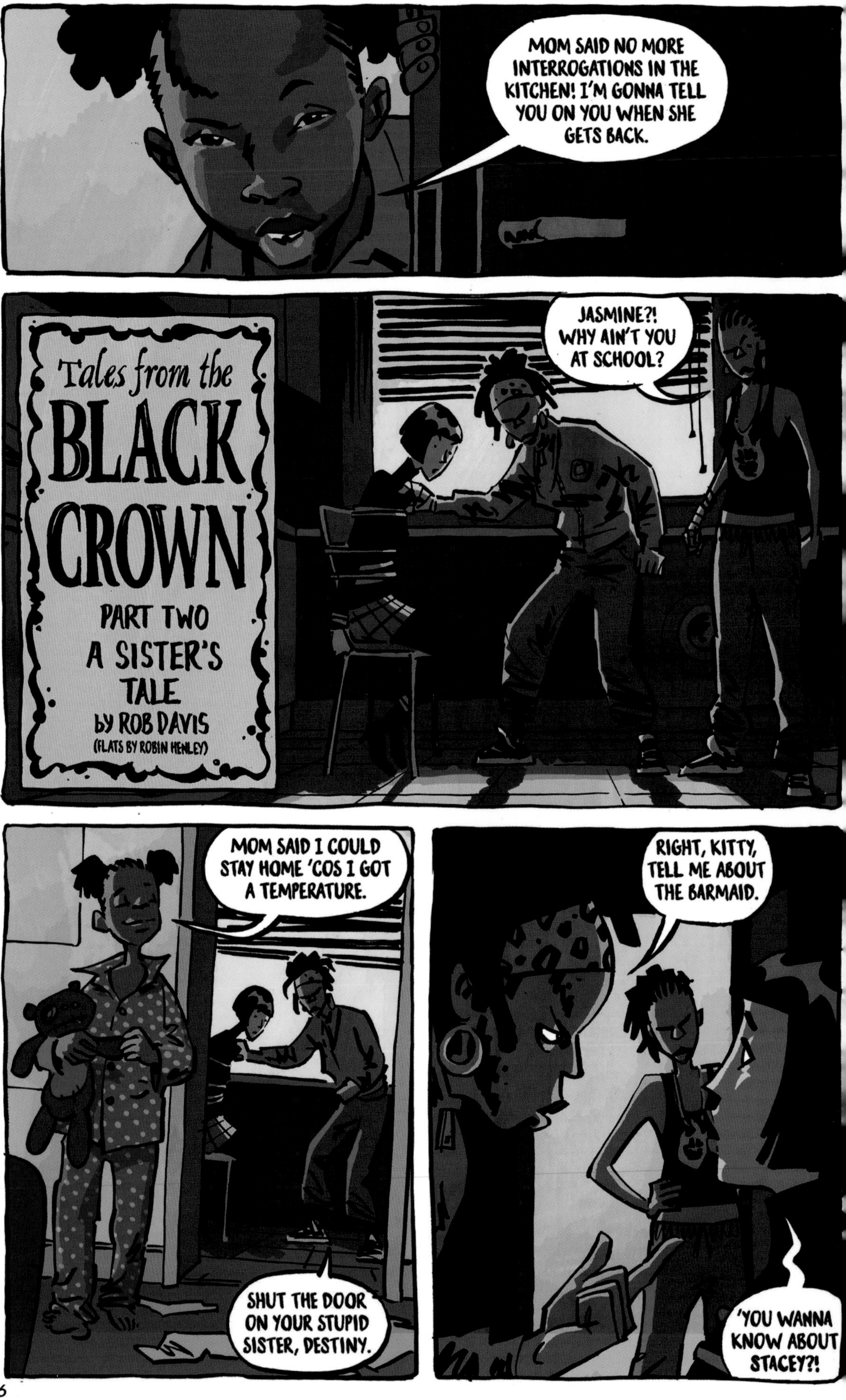
MOM SAID NO MORE INTERROGATIONS IN THE KITCHEN! I'M GONNA TELL YOU ON YOU WHEN SHE GETS BACK.
Tales from the BLACK CROWN
PART TWO A SISTER'S TALE
by ROB DAVIS
(FLATS BY ROBIN HENLEY)
JASMINE?! WHY AIN'T YOU AT SCHOOL?
MOM SAID I COULD STAY HOME 'COS I GOT A TEMPERATURE.
SHUT THE DOOR ON YOUR STUPID SISTER, DESTINY.
RIGHT, KITTY, TELL ME ABOUT THE BARMAID.
'YOU WANNA KNOW ABOUT STACEY?!

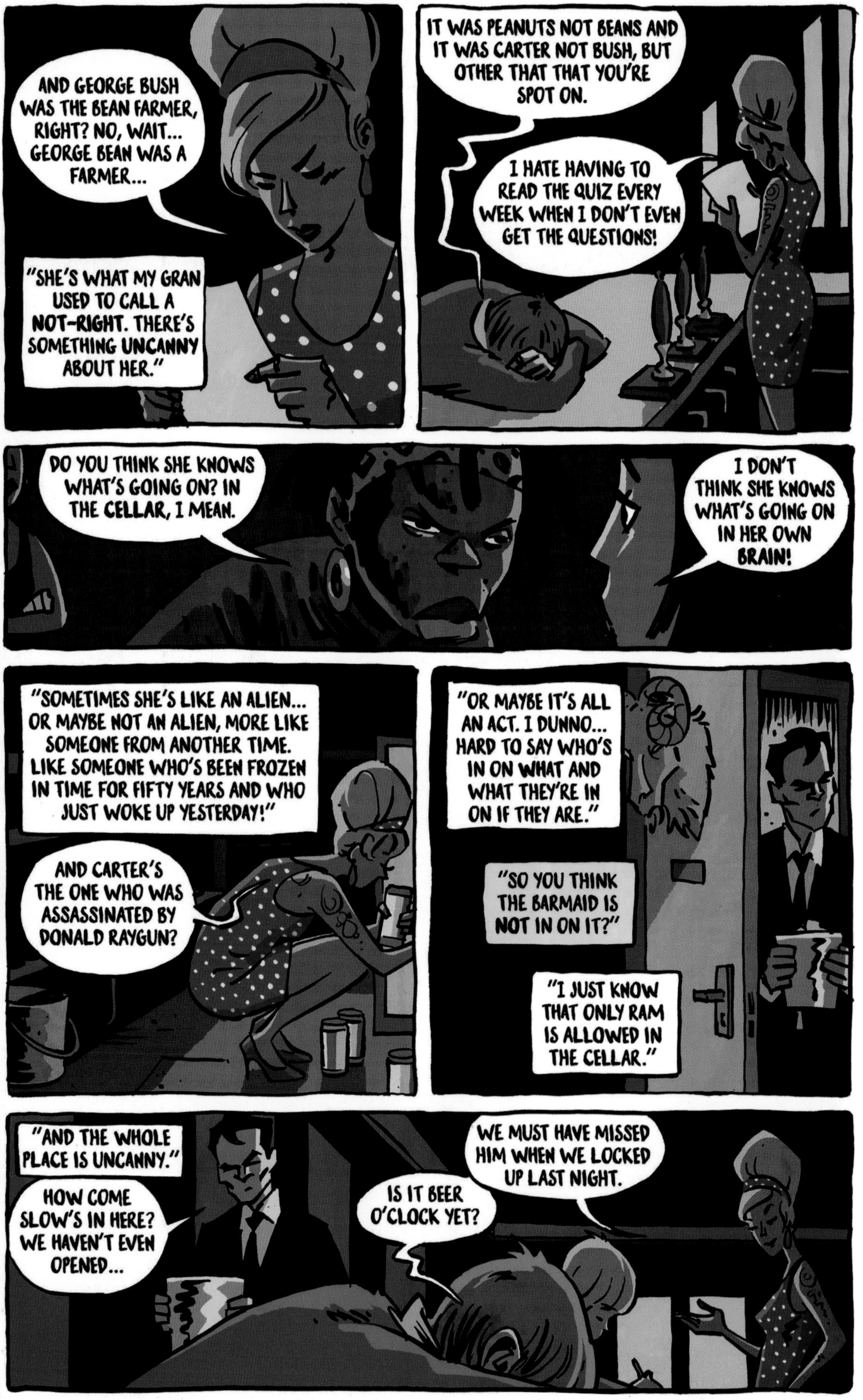
AND GEORGE BUSH WAS THE BEAN FARMER, RIGHT? NO, WAIT... GEORGE BEAN WAS A FARMER...
"SHE'S WHAT MY GRAN USED TO CALL A NOT-RIGHT. THERE'S SOMETHING UNCANNY ABOUT HER."
IT WAS PEANUTS NOT BEANS AND IT WAS CARTER NOT BUSH, BUT OTHER THAT THAT YOU'RE SPOT ON.
I HATE HAVING TO READ THE QUIZ EVERY WEEK WHEN I DON'T EVEN GET THE QUESTIONS!
DO YOU THINK SHE KNOWS WHAT'S GOING ON? IN THE CELLAR, I MEAN.
I DON'T THINK SHE KNOWS WHAT'S GOING ON IN HER OWN BRAIN!
"SOMETIMES SHE'S LIKE AN ALIEN... OR MAYBE NOT AN ALIEN, MORE LIKE SOMEONE FROM ANOTHER TIME. LIKE SOMEONE WHO'S BEEN FROZEN IN TIME FOR FIFTY YEARS AND WHO JUST WOKE UP YESTERDAY!"
AND CARTER'S THE ONE WHO WAS ASSASSINATED BY DONALD RAYGUN?
"OR MAYBE IT'S ALL AN ACT. I DUNNO... HARD TO SAY WHO'S IN ON WHAT AND WHAT THEY'RE IN ON IF THEY ARE."
"SO YOU THINK THE BARMAID IS NOT IN ON IT?"
"I JUST KNOW THAT ONLY RAM IS ALLOWED IN THE CELLAR."
"AND THE WHOLE PLACE IS UNCANNY."
HOW COME SLOW'S IN HERE? WE HAVEN'T EVEN OPENED...
IS IT BEER O'CLOCK YET?
WE MUST HAVE MISSED HIM WHEN WE LOCKED UP LAST NIGHT.

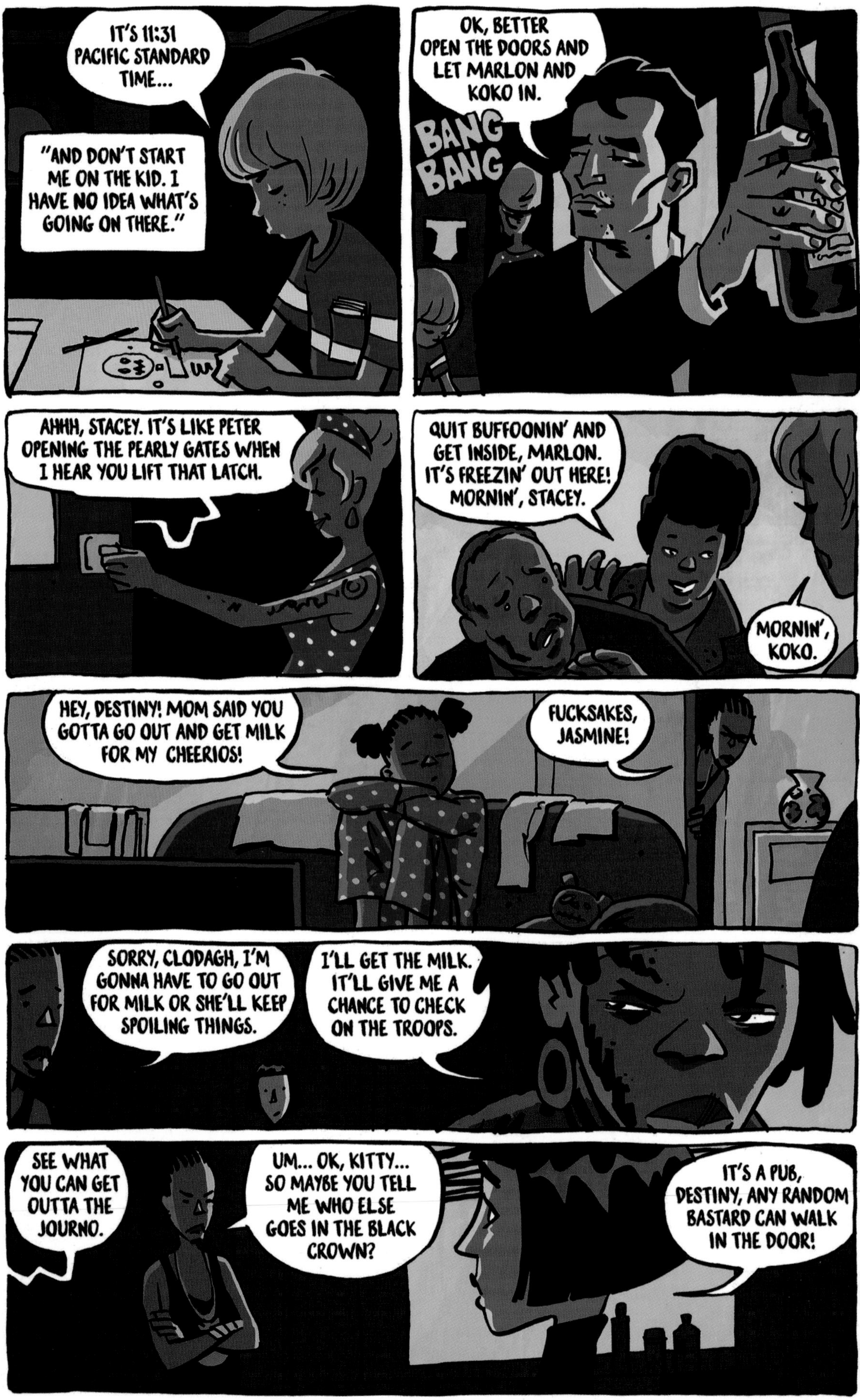
IT'S 11:31 PACIFIC STANDARD TIME...
"AND DON'T START ME ON THE KID. I HAVE NO IDEA WHAT'S GOING ON THERE."
OK, BETTER OPEN THE DOORS AND LET MARLON AND KOKO IN.
BANG BANG
AHHH, STACEY. IT'S LIKE PETER OPENING THE PEARLY GATES WHEN I HEAR YOU LIFT THAT LATCH.
QUIT BUFFOONIN' AND GET INSIDE, MARLON. IT'S FREEZIN' OUT HERE! MORNIN', STACEY.
MORNIN', KOKO.
HEY, DESTINY! MOM SAID YOU GOTTA GO OUT AND GET MILK FOR MY CHEERIOS!
FUCKSAKES, JASMINE!
SORRY, CLODAGH, I'M GONNA HAVE TO GO OUT FOR MILK OR SHE'LL KEEP SPOILING THINGS.
I'LL GET THE MILK. IT'LL GIVE ME A CHANCE TO CHECK ON THE TROOPS.
SEE WHAT YOU CAN GET OUTTA THE JOURNO.
UM... OK, KITTY... SO MAYBE YOU TELL ME WHO ELSE GOES IN THE BLACK CROWN?
IT'S A PUB, DESTINY, ANY RANDOM BASTARD CAN WALK IN THE DOOR!

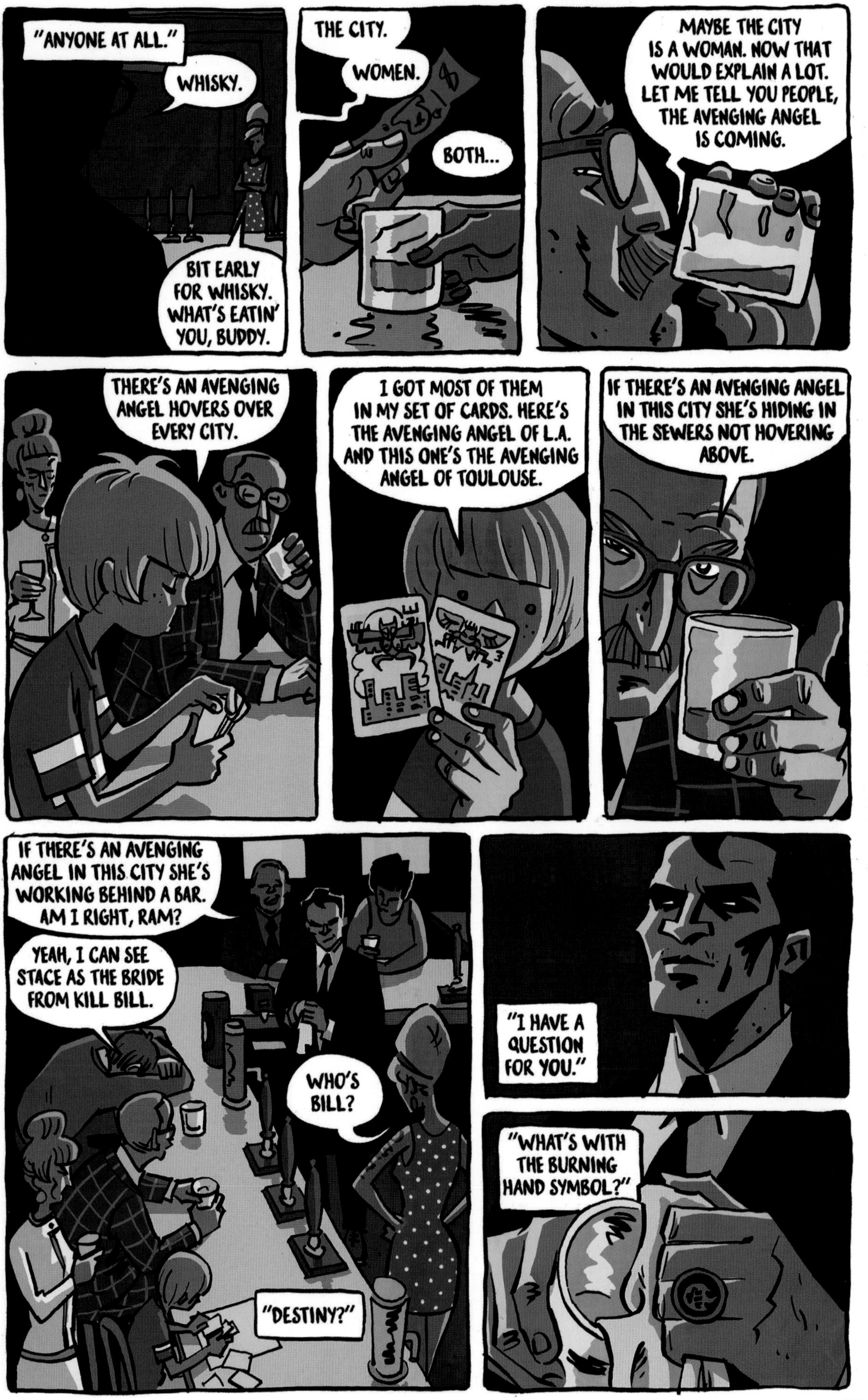
"ANYONE AT ALL."
WHISKY.
BIT EARLY FOR WHISKY. WHAT'S EATIN' YOU, BUDDY.
THE CITY.
WOMEN.
BOTH...
MAYBE THE CITY IS A WOMAN. NOW THAT WOULD EXPLAIN A LOT. LET ME TELL YOU PEOPLE, THE AVENGING ANGEL IS COMING.
THERE'S AN AVENGING ANGEL HOVERS OVER EVERY CITY.
I GOT MOST OF THEM IN MY SET OF CARDS. HERE'S THE AVENGING ANGEL OF L.A. AND THIS ONE'S THE AVENGING ANGEL OF TOULOUSE.
IF THERE'S AN AVENGING ANGEL IN THIS CITY SHE'S HIDING IN THE SEWERS NOT HOVERING ABOVE.
IF THERE'S AN AVENGING ANGEL IN THIS CITY SHE'S WORKING BEHIND A BAR. AM I RIGHT, RAM?
YEAH, I CAN SEE STACE AS THE BRIDE FROM KILL BILL.
WHO'S BILL?
"DESTINY?"
"I HAVE A QUESTION FOR YOU."
"WHAT'S WITH THE BURNING HAND SYMBOL?"

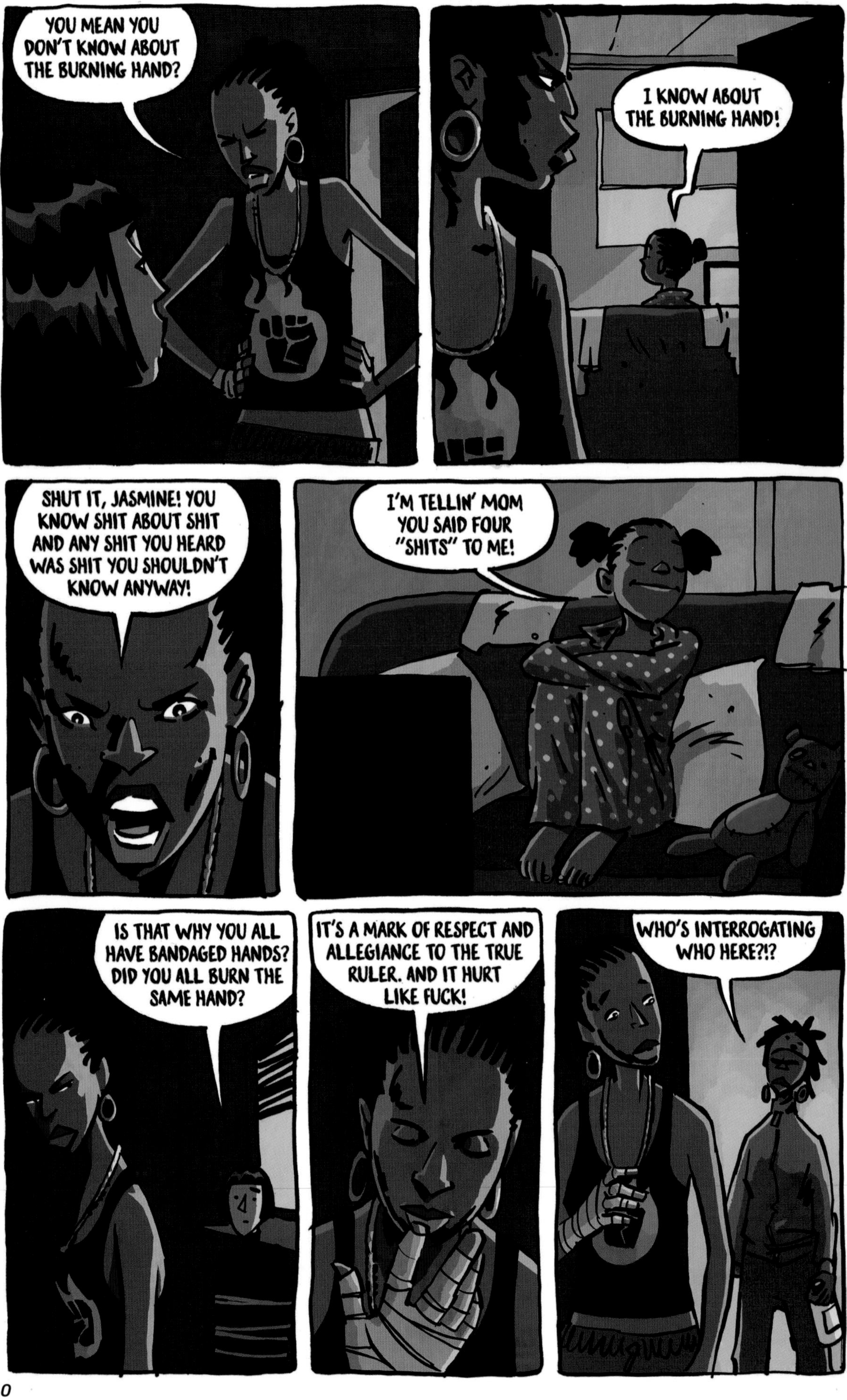
YOU MEAN YOU DON'T KNOW ABOUT THE BURNING HAND?
I KNOW ABOUT THE BURNING HAND!
SHUT IT, JASMINE! YOU KNOW SHIT ABOUT SHIT AND ANY SHIT YOU HEARD WAS SHIT YOU SHOULDN'T KNOW ANYWAY!
I'M TELLIN' MOM YOU SAID FOUR "SHITS" TO ME!
IS THAT WHY YOU ALL HAVE BANDAGED HANDS? DID YOU ALL BURN THE SAME HAND?
IT'S A MARK OF RESPECT AND ALLEGIANCE TO THE TRUE RULER. AND IT HURT LIKE FUCK!
WHO'S INTERROGATING WHO HERE?!?

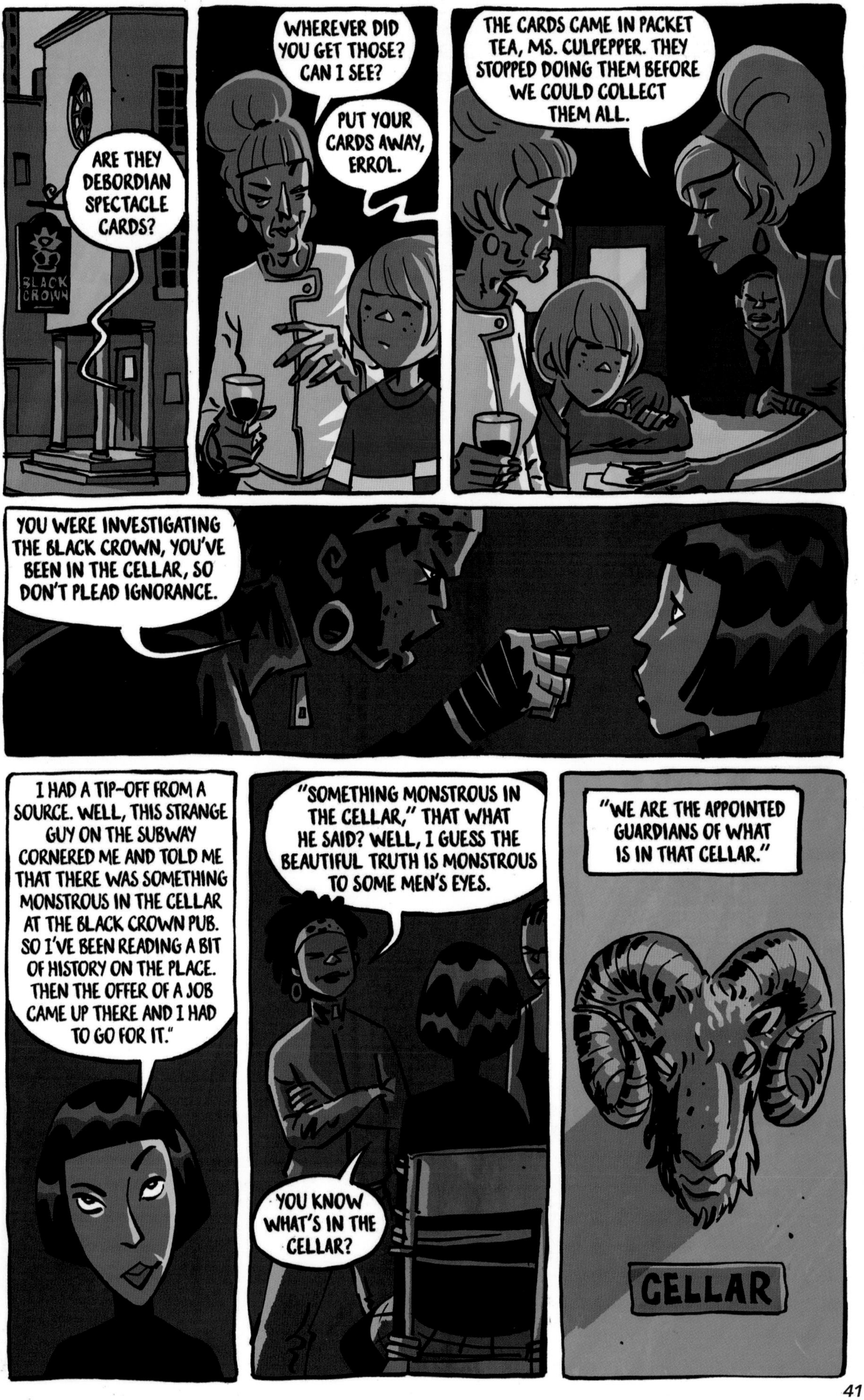
ARE THEY DEBORDIAN SPECTACLE CARDS?
BLACK CROWN
WHEREVER DID YOU GET THOSE? CAN I SEE?
PUT YOUR CARDS AWAY, ERROL.
THE CARDS CAME IN PACKET TEA, MS. CULPEPPER. THEY STOPPED DOING THEM BEFORE WE COULD COLLECT THEM ALL.
YOU WERE INVESTIGATING THE BLACK CROWN, YOU'VE BEEN IN THE CELLAR, SO DON'T PLEAD IGNORANCE.
I HAD A TIP-OFF FROM A SOURCE. WELL, THIS STRANGE GUY ON THE SUBWAY CORNERED ME AND TOLD ME THAT THERE WAS SOMETHING MONSTROUS IN THE CELLAR AT THE BLACK CROWN PUB. SO I'VE BEEN READING A BIT OF HISTORY ON THE PLACE. THEN THE OFFER OF A JOB CAME UP THERE AND I HAD TO GO FOR IT."
"SOMETHING MONSTROUS IN THE CELLAR," THAT WHAT HE SAID? WELL, I GUESS THE BEAUTIFUL TRUTH IS MONSTROUS TO SOME MEN'S EYES.
YOU KNOW WHAT'S IN THE CELLAR?
"WE ARE THE APPOINTED GUARDIANS OF WHAT IS IN THAT CELLAR."
CELLAR

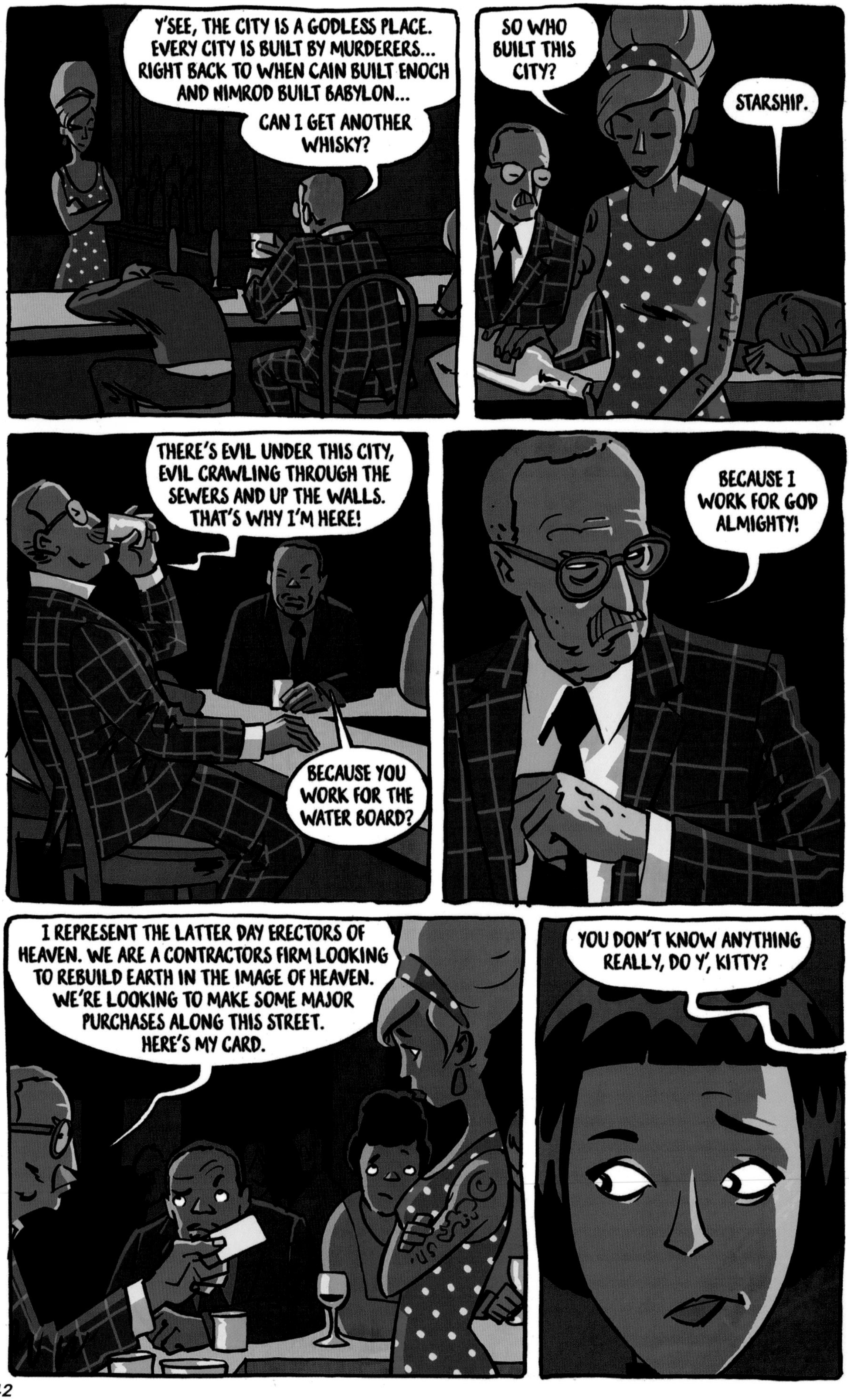
Y'SEE, THE CITY IS A GODLESS PLACE. EVERY CITY IS BUILT BY MURDERERS... RIGHT BACK TO WHEN CAIN BUILT ENOCH AND NIMROD BUILT BABYLON...
CAN I GET ANOTHER WHISKY?
SO WHO BUILT THIS CITY?
STARSHIP.
THERE'S EVIL UNDER THIS CITY, EVIL CRAWLING THROUGH THE SEWERS AND UP THE WALLS. THAT'S WHY I'M HERE!
BECAUSE YOU WORK FOR THE WATER BOARD?
BECAUSE I WORK FOR GOD ALMIGHTY!
I REPRESENT THE LATTER DAY ERECTORS OF HEAVEN. WE ARE A CONTRACTORS FIRM LOOKING TO REBUILD EARTH IN THE IMAGE OF HEAVEN. WE'RE LOOKING TO MAKE SOME MAJOR PURCHASES ALONG THIS STREET. HERE'S MY CARD.
YOU DON'T KNOW ANYTHING REALLY, DO Y', KITTY?

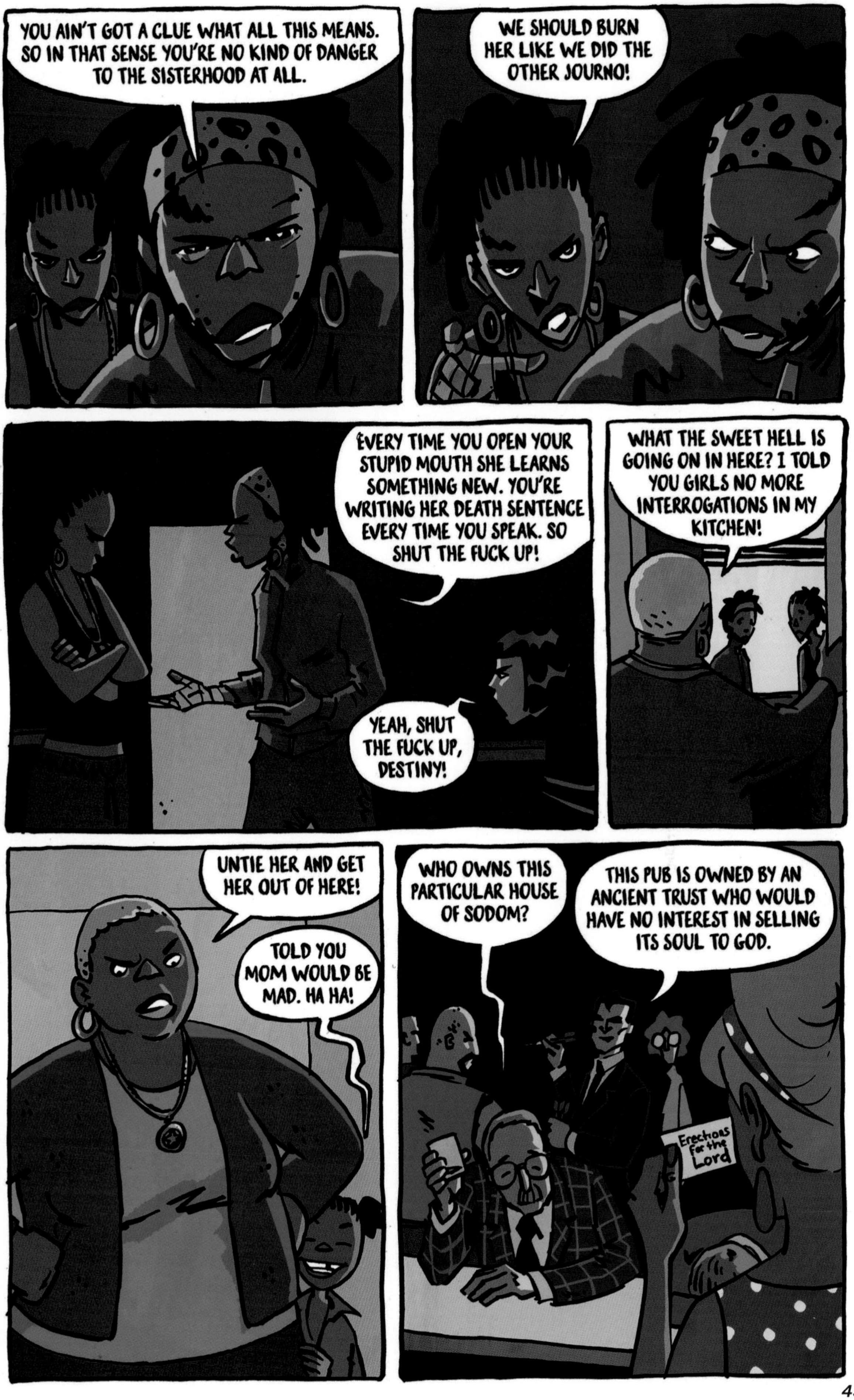
YOU AIN'T GOT A CLUE WHAT ALL THIS MEANS. SO IN THAT SENSE YOU'RE NO KIND OF DANGER TO THE SISTERHOOD AT ALL.
WE SHOULD BURN HER LIKE WE DID THE OTHER JOURNO!
EVERY TIME YOU OPEN YOUR STUPID MOUTH SHE LEARNS SOMETHING NEW. YOU'RE WRITING HER DEATH SENTENCE EVERY TIME YOU SPEAK. SO SHUT THE FUCK UP!
YEAH, SHUT THE FUCK UP, DESTINY!
WHAT THE SWEET HELL IS GOING ON IN HERE? I TOLD YOU GIRLS NO MORE INTERROGATIONS IN MY KITCHEN!
UNTIE HER AND GET HER OUT OF HERE!
TOLD YOU MOM WOULD BE MAD. HA HA!
WHO OWNS THIS PARTICULAR HOUSE OF SODOM?
THIS PUB IS OWNED BY AN ANCIENT TRUST WHO WOULD HAVE NO INTEREST IN SELLING ITS SOUL TO GOD.
Erections for the Lord

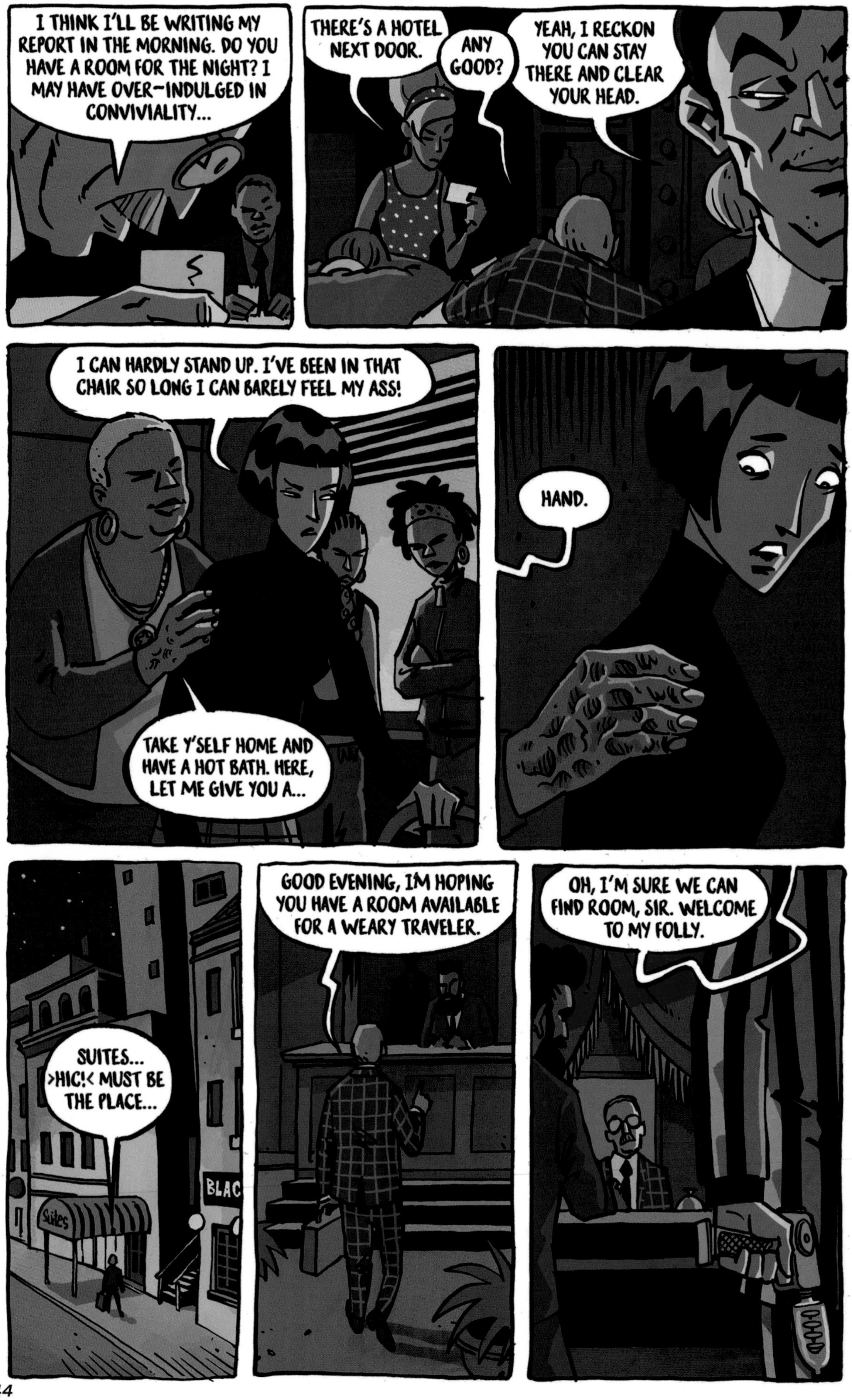
I THINK I'LL BE WRITING MY REPORT IN THE MORNING. DO YOU HAVE A ROOM FOR THE NIGHT? I MAY HAVE OVER-INDULGED IN CONVIVIALITY...
THERE'S A HOTEL NEXT DOOR.
ANY GOOD?
YEAH, I RECKON YOU CAN STAY THERE AND CLEAR YOUR HEAD.
I CAN HARDLY STAND UP. I'VE BEEN IN THAT CHAIR SO LONG I CAN BARELY FEEL MY ASS!
TAKE Y'SELF HOME AND HAVE A HOT BATH. HERE, LET ME GIVE YOU A...
HAND.
SUITES... >HIC!< MUST BE THE PLACE...
Suites
BLAC
GOOD EVENING, I'M HOPING YOU HAVE A ROOM AVAILABLE FOR A WEARY TRAVELER.
OH, I'M SURE WE CAN FIND ROOM, SIR. WELCOME TO MY FOLLY.

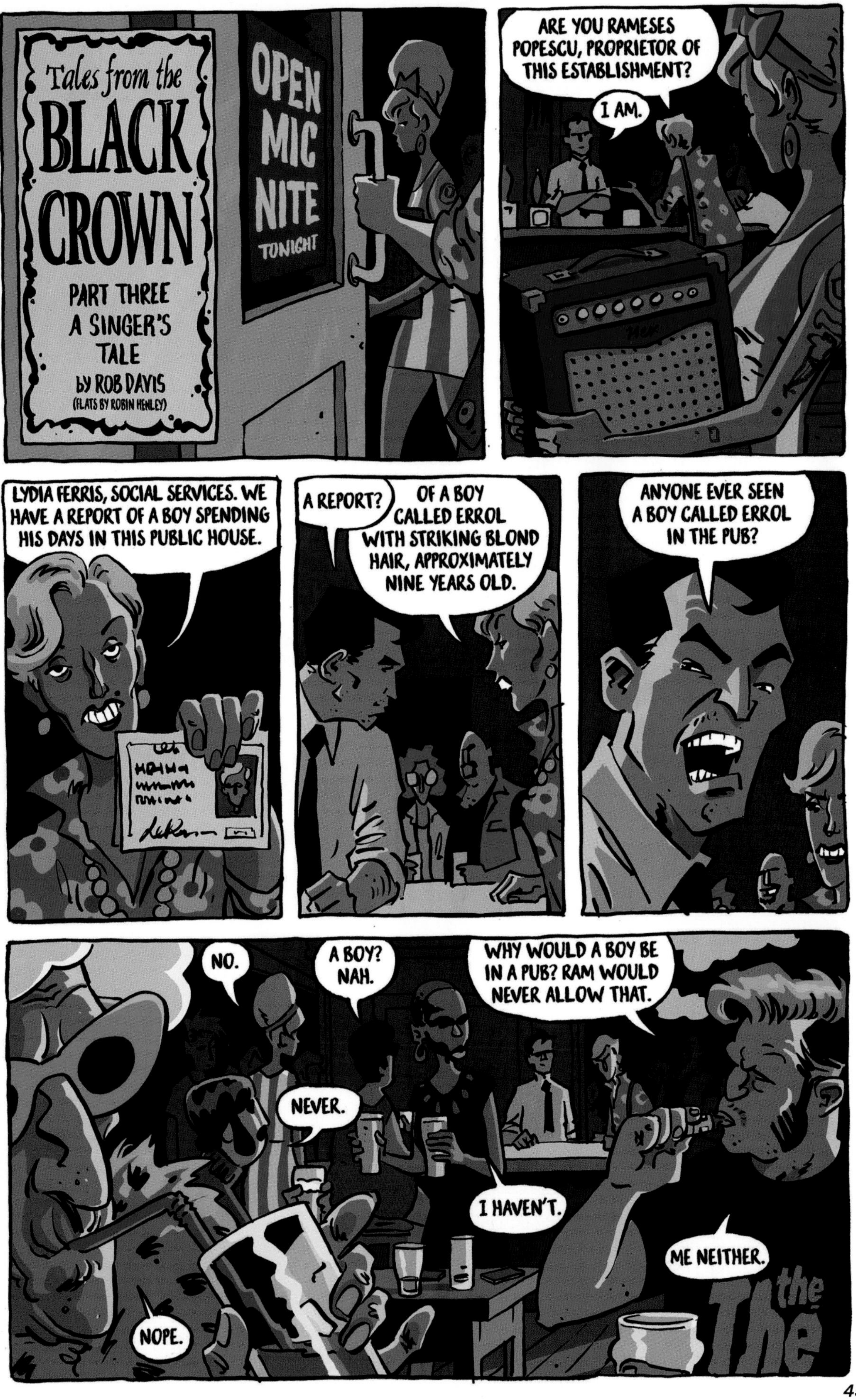

Tales from the
BLACK CROWN
PART THREE
A SINGER'S TALE
by ROB DAVIS
(FLATS BY ROBIN HENLEY)
OPEN MIC NITE TONIGHT
ARE YOU RAMESES POPESCU, PROPRIETOR OF THIS ESTABLISHMENT?
I AM.
LYDIA FERRIS, SOCIAL SERVICES. WE HAVE A REPORT OF A BOY SPENDING HIS DAYS IN THIS PUBLIC HOUSE.
A REPORT?
OF A BOY CALLED ERROL WITH STRIKING BLOND HAIR, APPROXIMATELY NINE YEARS OLD.
ANYONE EVER SEEN A BOY CALLED ERROL IN THE PUB?
NO.
A BOY? NAH.
WHY WOULD A BOY BE IN A PUB? RAM WOULD NEVER ALLOW THAT.
NEVER.
I HAVEN'T.
ME NEITHER.
NOPE.
the The

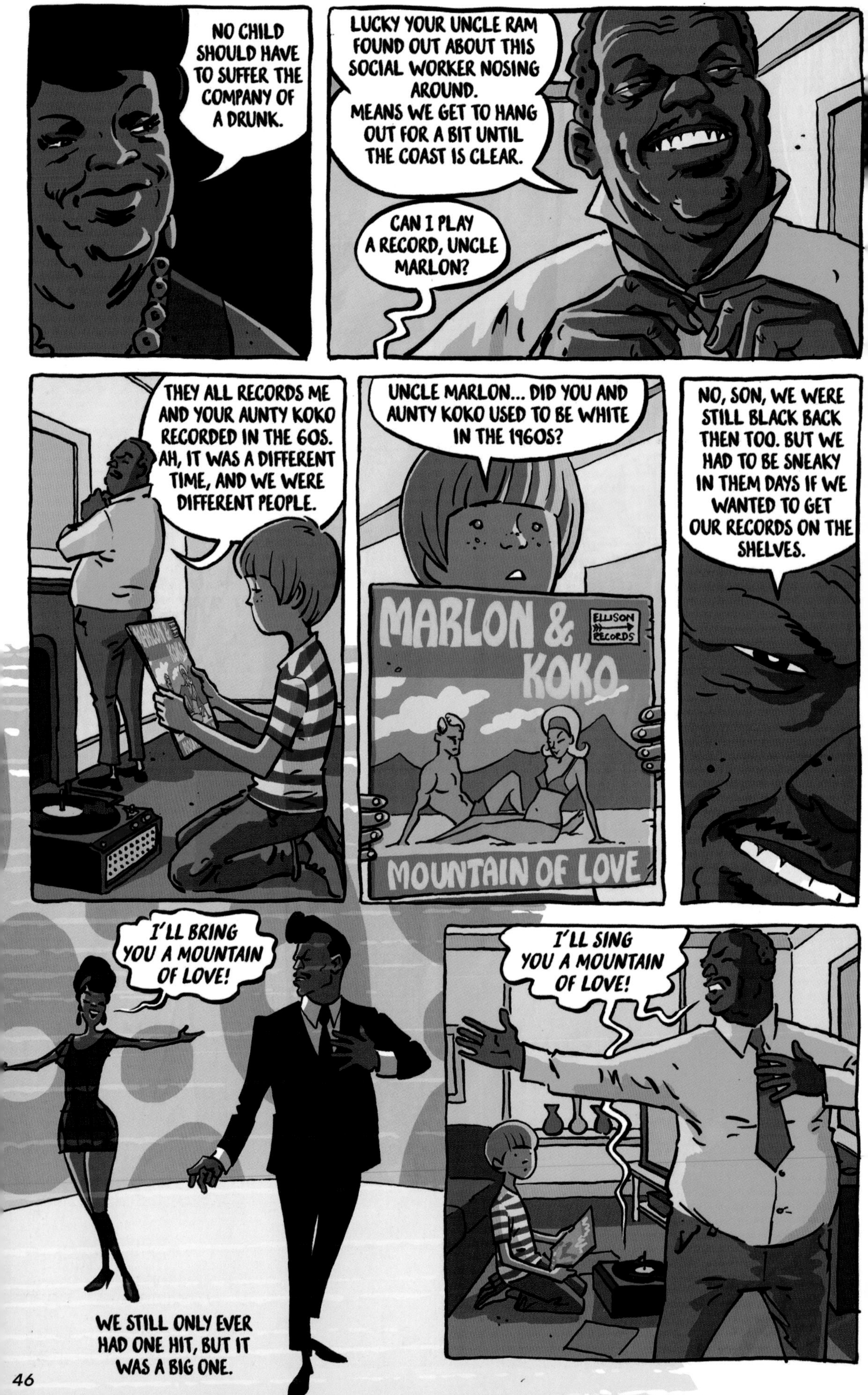
NO CHILD SHOULD HAVE TO SUFFER THE COMPANY OF A DRUNK.
LUCKY YOUR UNCLE RAM FOUND OUT ABOUT THIS SOCIAL WORKER NOSING AROUND. MEANS WE GET TO HANG OUT FOR A BIT UNTIL THE COAST IS CLEAR.
CAN I PLAY A RECORD, UNCLE MARLON?
THEY ALL RECORDS ME AND YOUR AUNTY KOKO RECORDED IN THE 60S. AH, IT WAS A DIFFERENT TIME, AND WE WERE DIFFERENT PEOPLE.
UNCLE MARLON... DID YOU AND AUNTY KOKO USED TO BE WHITE IN THE 1960S?
MARLON & KOKO
ELLISON RECORDS
MOUNTAIN OF LOVE
NO, SON, WE WERE STILL BLACK BACK THEN TOO. BUT WE HAD TO BE SNEAKY IN THEM DAYS IF WE WANTED TO GET OUR RECORDS ON THE SHELVES.
I'LL BRING YOU A MOUNTAIN OF LOVE!
WE STILL ONLY EVER HAD ONE HIT, BUT IT WAS A BIG ONE.
I'LL SING YOU A MOUNTAIN OF LOVE!

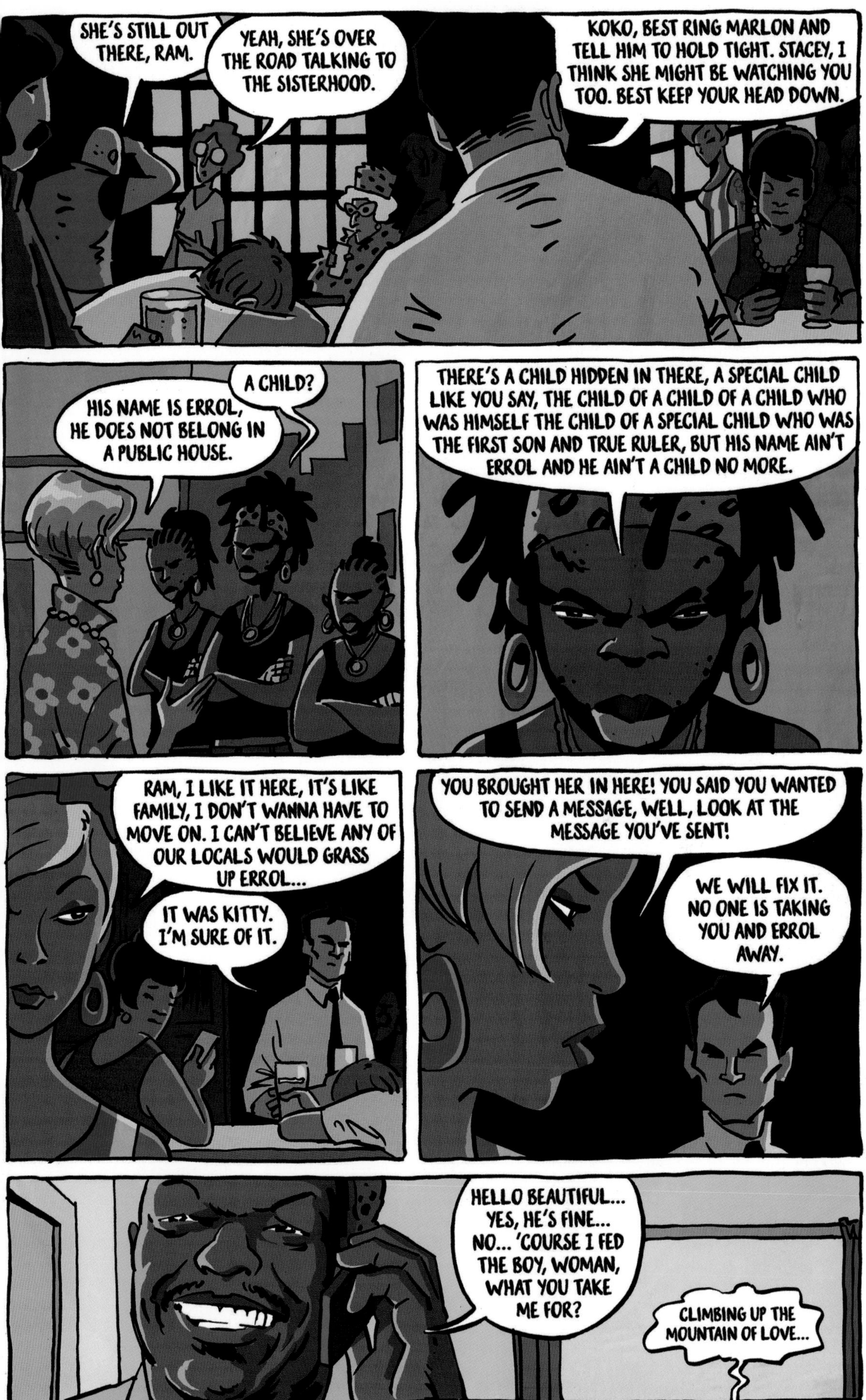
SHE'S STILL OUT THERE, RAM.
YEAH, SHE'S OVER THE ROAD TALKING TO THE SISTERHOOD.
KOKO, BEST RING MARLON AND TELL HIM TO HOLD TIGHT. STACEY, I THINK SHE MIGHT BE WATCHING YOU TOO. BEST KEEP YOUR HEAD DOWN.
HIS NAME IS ERROL, HE DOES NOT BELONG IN A PUBLIC HOUSE.
A CHILD?
THERE'S A CHILD HIDDEN IN THERE, A SPECIAL CHILD LIKE YOU SAY, THE CHILD OF A CHILD OF A CHILD WHO WAS HIMSELF THE CHILD OF A SPECIAL CHILD WHO WAS THE FIRST SON AND TRUE RULER, BUT HIS NAME AIN'T ERROL AND HE AIN'T A CHILD NO MORE.
RAM, I LIKE IT HERE, IT'S LIKE FAMILY, I DON'T WANNA HAVE TO MOVE ON. I CAN'T BELIEVE ANY OF OUR LOCALS WOULD GRASS UP ERROL...
IT WAS KITTY. I'M SURE OF IT.
YOU BROUGHT HER IN HERE! YOU SAID YOU WANTED TO SEND A MESSAGE, WELL, LOOK AT THE MESSAGE YOU'VE SENT!
WE WILL FIX IT. NO ONE IS TAKING YOU AND ERROL AWAY.
HELLO BEAUTIFUL... YES, HE'S FINE... NO... 'COURSE I FED THE BOY, WOMAN, WHAT YOU TAKE ME FOR?
CLIMBING UP THE MOUNTAIN OF LOVE...

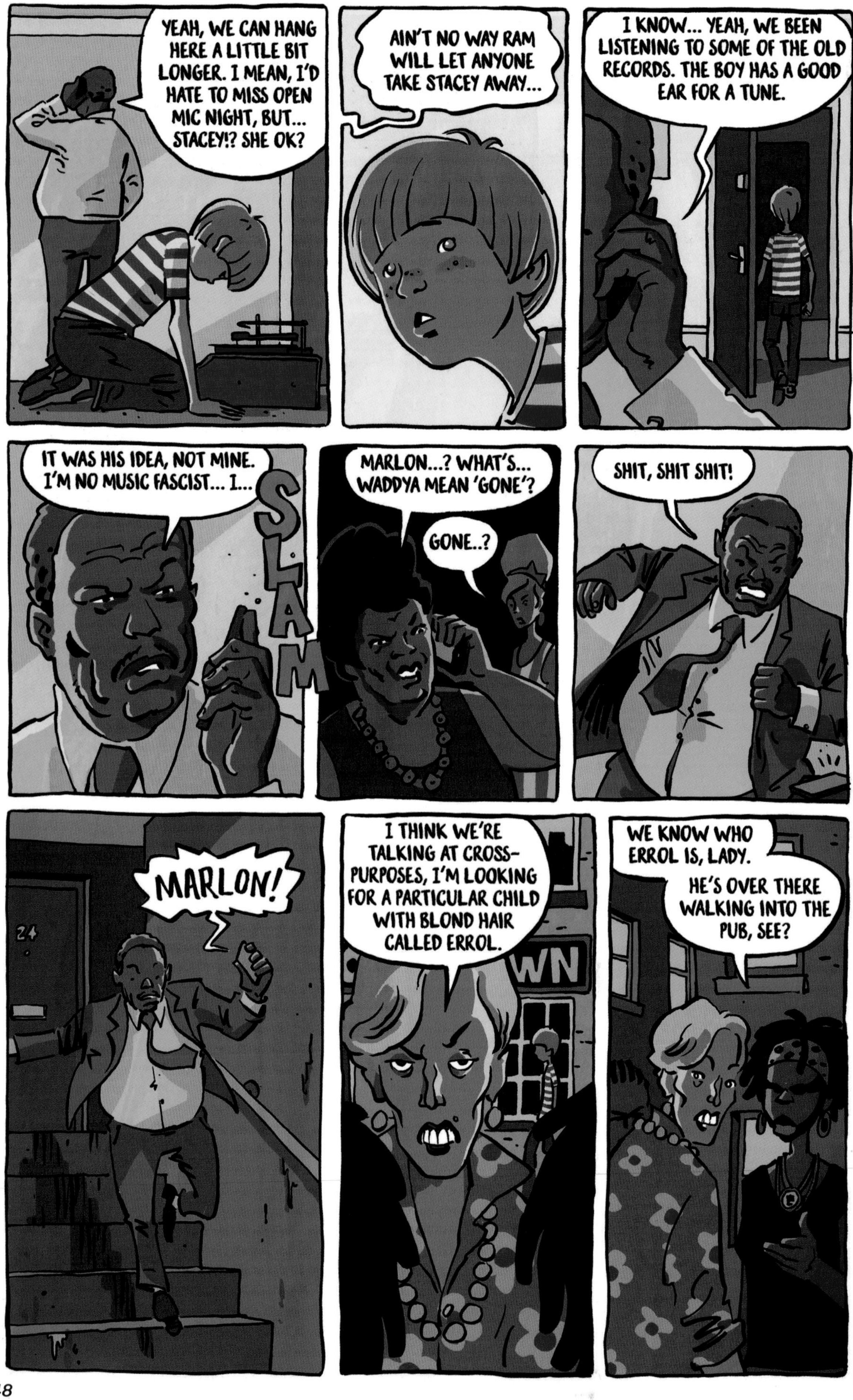
YEAH, WE CAN HANG HERE A LITTLE BIT LONGER. I MEAN, I'D HATE TO MISS OPEN MIC NIGHT, BUT... STACEY!? SHE OK?
AIN'T NO WAY RAM WILL LET ANYONE TAKE STACEY AWAY...
I KNOW... YEAH, WE BEEN LISTENING TO SOME OF THE OLD RECORDS. THE BOY HAS A GOOD EAR FOR A TUNE.
IT WAS HIS IDEA, NOT MINE. I'M NO MUSIC FASCIST... I...
SLAM
MARLON...? WHAT'S... WADDYA MEAN 'GONE'?
GONE..?
SHIT, SHIT SHIT!
MARLON!
I THINK WE'RE TALKING AT CROSS-PURPOSES, I'M LOOKING FOR A PARTICULAR CHILD WITH BLOND HAIR CALLED ERROL.
WN
WE KNOW WHO ERROL IS, LADY.
HE'S OVER THERE WALKING INTO THE PUB, SEE?

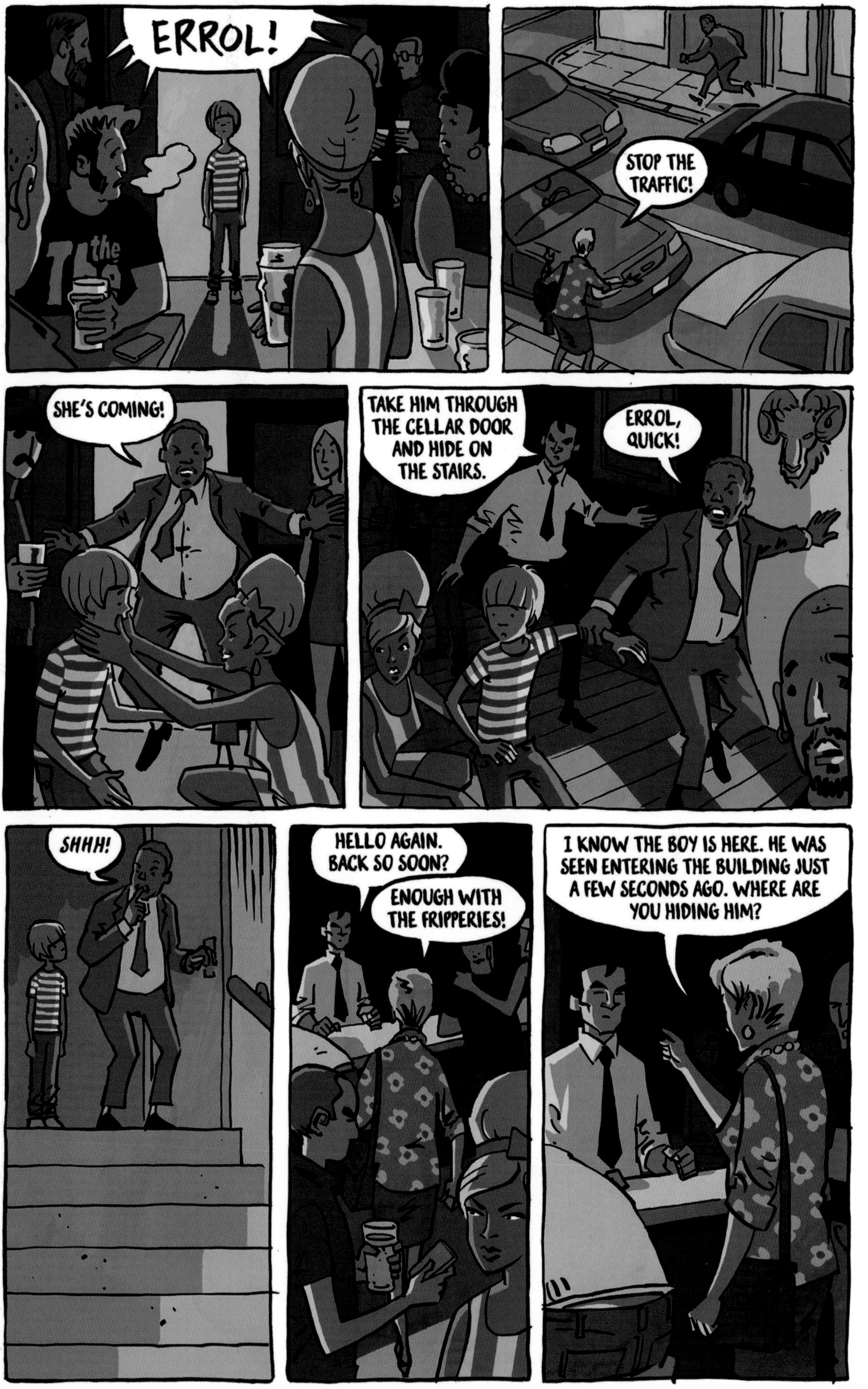
ERROL!
STOP THE TRAFFIC!
SHE'S COMING!
TAKE HIM THROUGH THE CELLAR DOOR AND HIDE ON THE STAIRS.
ERROL, QUICK!
SHHH!
HELLO AGAIN. BACK SO SOON?
ENOUGH WITH THE FRIPPERIES!
I KNOW THE BOY IS HERE. HE WAS SEEN ENTERING THE BUILDING JUST A FEW SECONDS AGO. WHERE ARE YOU HIDING HIM?

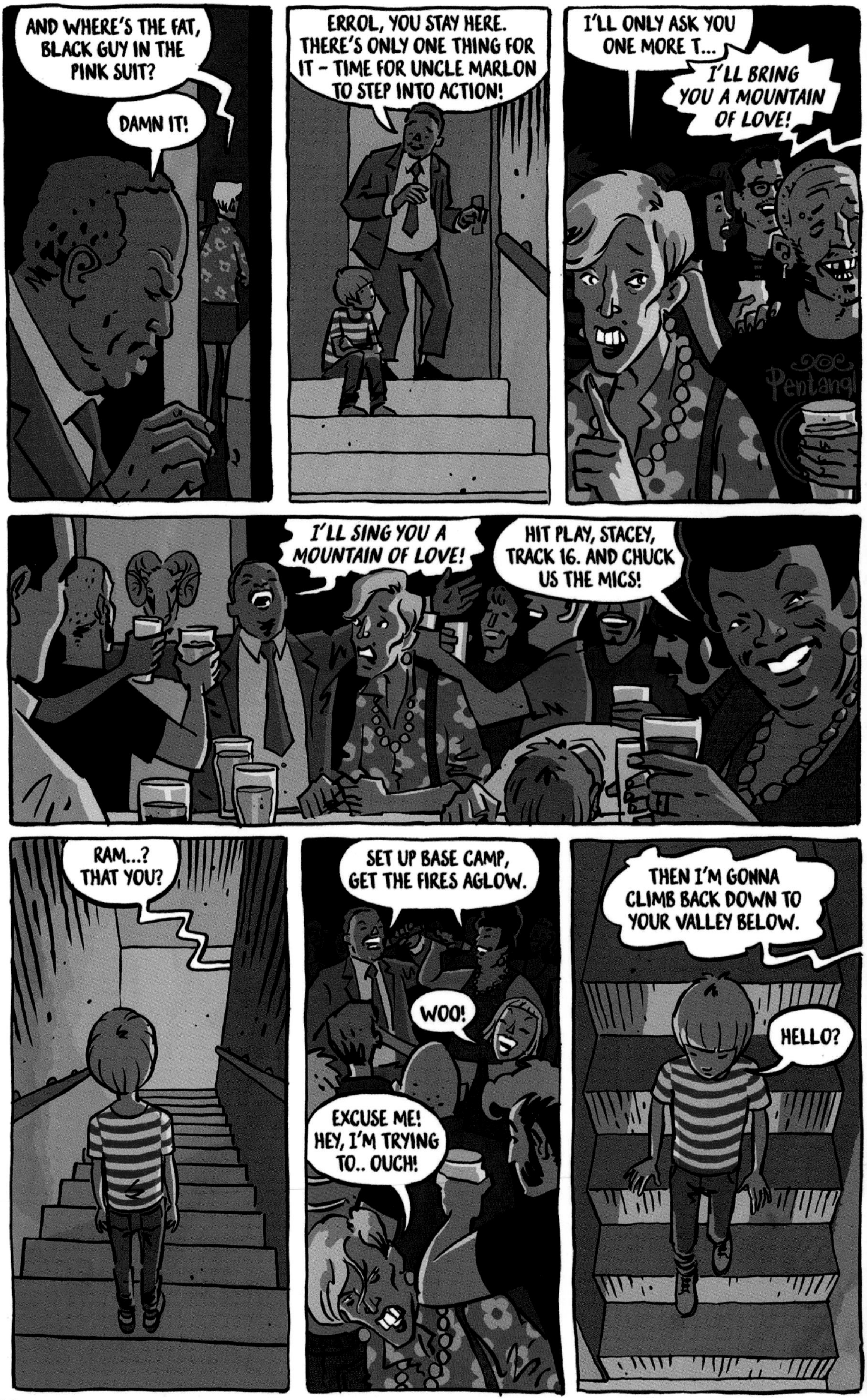
AND WHERE'S THE FAT, BLACK GUY IN THE PINK SUIT?
DAMN IT!
ERROL, YOU STAY HERE. THERE'S ONLY ONE THING FOR IT – TIME FOR UNCLE MARLON TO STEP INTO ACTION!
I'LL ONLY ASK YOU ONE MORE T...
I'LL BRING YOU A MOUNTAIN OF LOVE!
Pentangl
I'LL SING YOU A MOUNTAIN OF LOVE!
HIT PLAY, STACEY, TRACK 16. AND CHUCK US THE MICS!
RAM...? THAT YOU?
SET UP BASE CAMP, GET THE FIRES AGLOW.
WOO!
EXCUSE ME! HEY, I'M TRYING TO.. OUCH!
THEN I'M GONNA CLIMB BACK DOWN TO YOUR VALLEY BELOW.
HELLO?

EXCUSE ME...
HEY! I'M LOOKING
FOR A...

YOU START AT THE BOTTOM AND CLIMB UP TO THE TOP.
WHEN YOU REACH THE PEAK BABY PLEASE DON'T STOP...

'LIKE HILLARY, MALLORY AND

TENSING, IT'S MY LOVE FOR YOU

THAT I'M SENSING...

CLIMBING UP, UP, UP TO THE MOUNTAIN OF LOVE, UP, UP, UP TO THE MOUNTAIN OF LOVE...

WHO ARE
YOU?

I'M
ERROL.

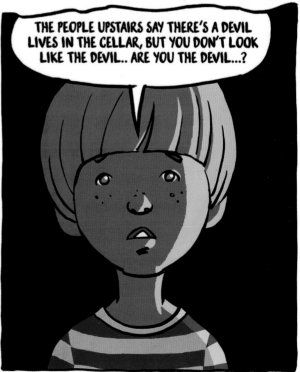

THE PEOPLE UPSTAIRS SAY THERE'S A DEVIL
LIVES IN THE CELLAR, BUT YOU DON'T LOOK
LIKE THE DEVIL.. ARE YOU THE DEVIL...?

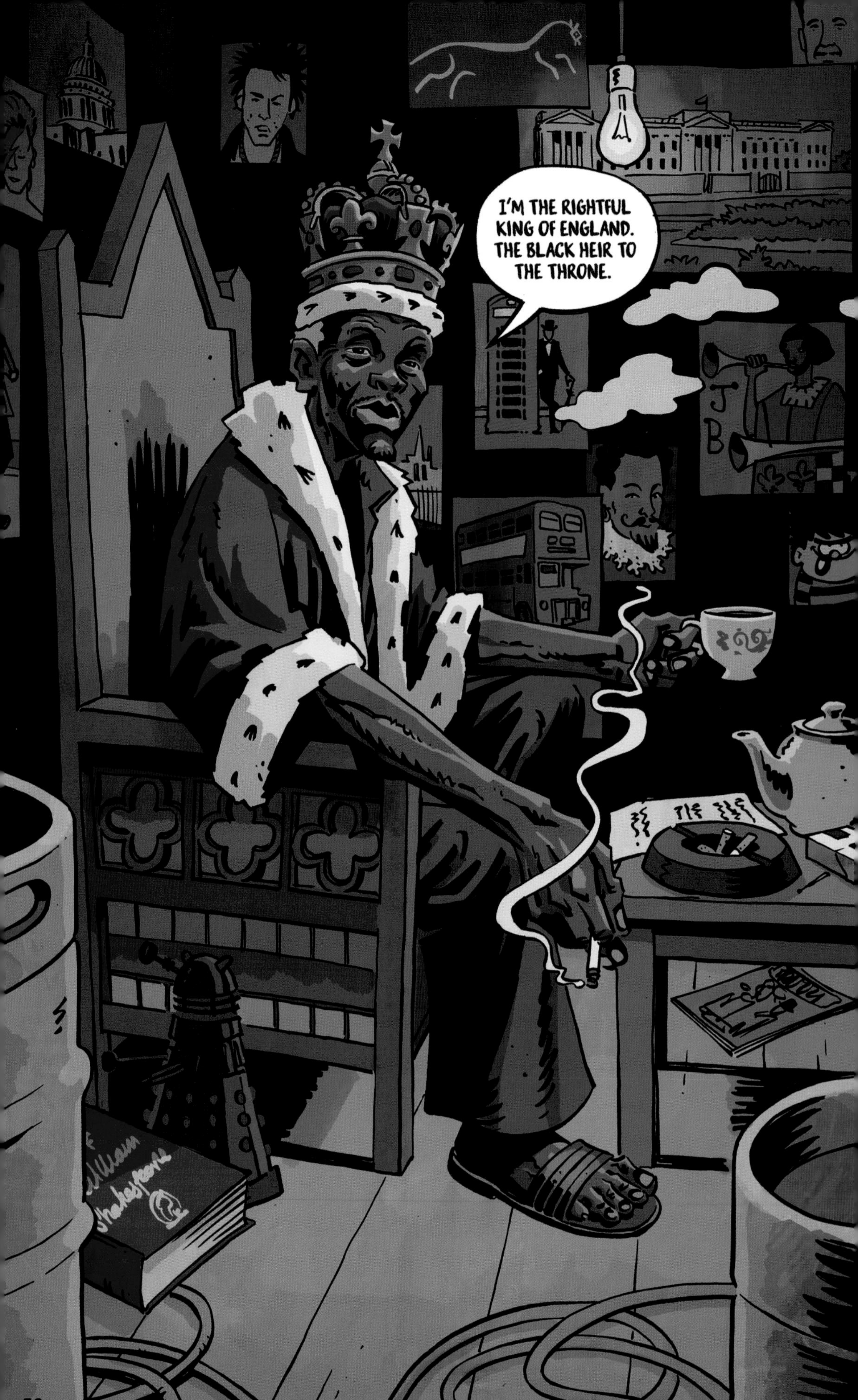
I'M THE RIGHTFUL KING OF ENGLAND. THE BLACK HEIR TO THE THRONE.

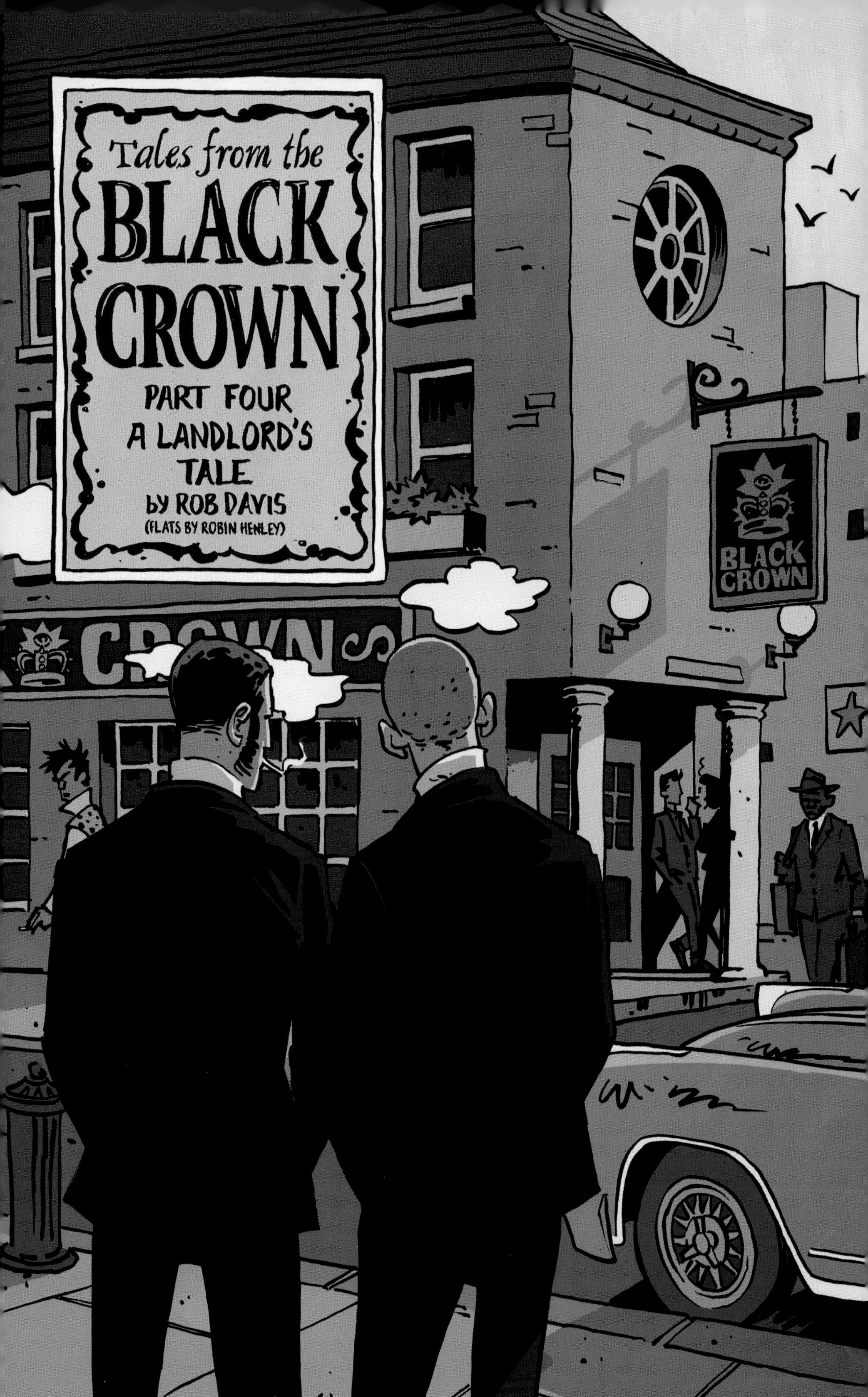

Tales from the
BLACK
CROWN
PART FOUR
A LANDLORD'S
TALE
by ROB DAVIS
(FLATS BY ROBIN HENLEY)
BLACK
CROWN

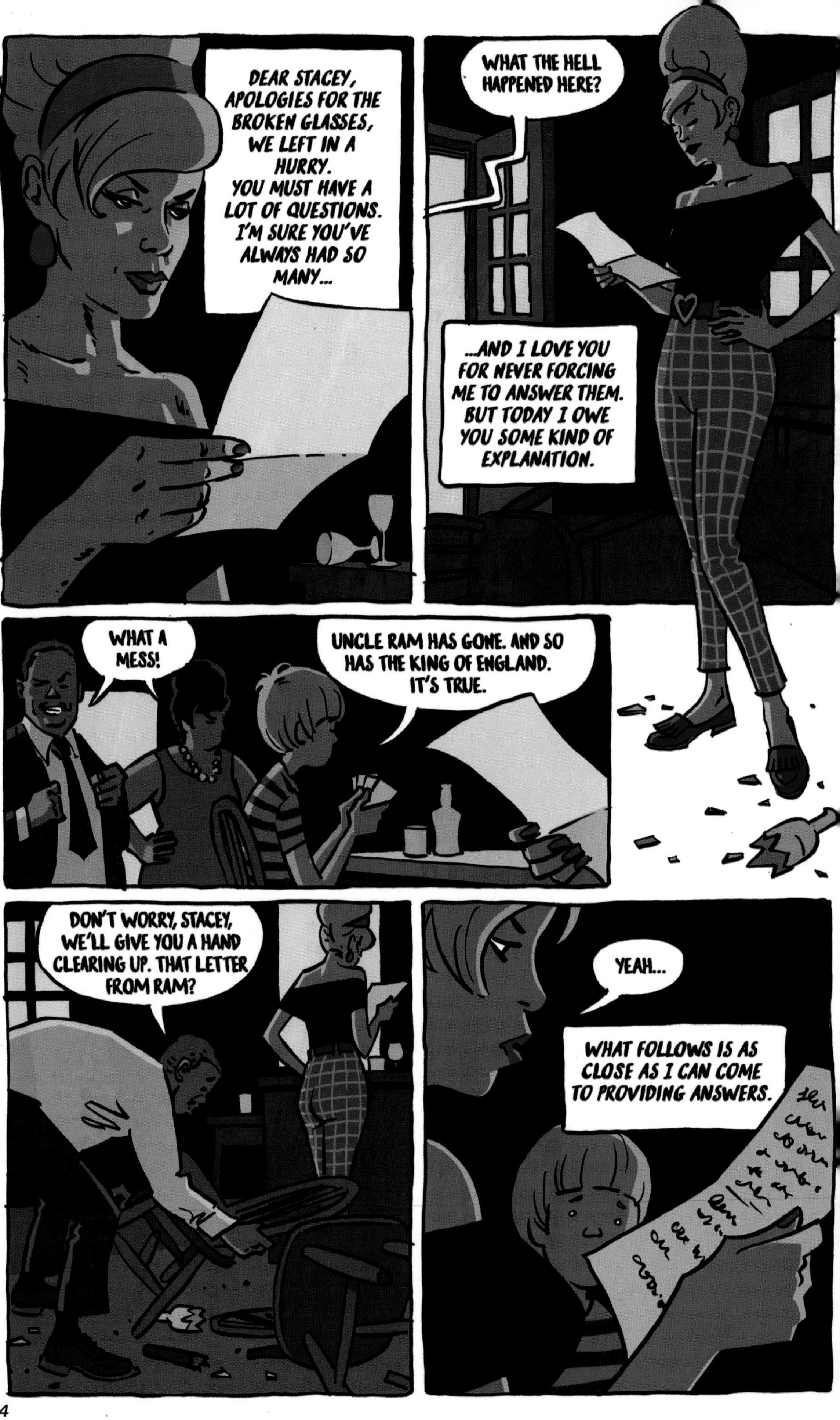
DEAR STACEY,
APOLOGIES FOR THE BROKEN GLASSES, WE LEFT IN A HURRY.
YOU MUST HAVE A LOT OF QUESTIONS. I'M SURE YOU'VE ALWAYS HAD SO MANY...
WHAT THE HELL HAPPENED HERE?
...AND I LOVE YOU FOR NEVER FORCING ME TO ANSWER THEM. BUT TODAY I OWE YOU SOME KIND OF EXPLANATION.
WHAT A MESS!
UNCLE RAM HAS GONE. AND SO HAS THE KING OF ENGLAND. IT'S TRUE.
DON'T WORRY, STACEY, WE'LL GIVE YOU A HAND CLEARING UP. THAT LETTER FROM RAM?
YEAH...
WHAT FOLLOWS IS AS CLOSE AS I CAN COME TO PROVIDING ANSWERS.

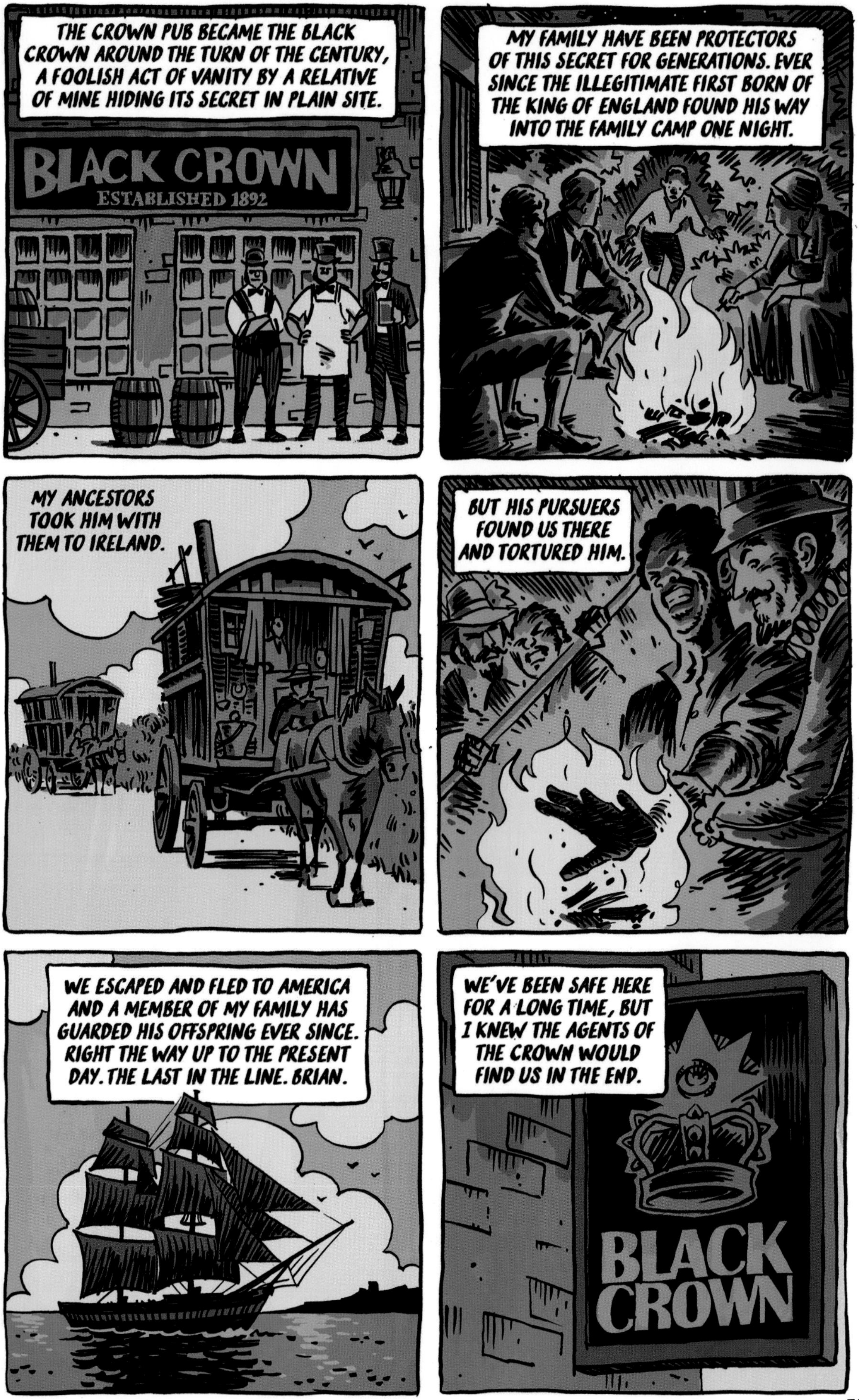
THE CROWN PUB BECAME THE BLACK CROWN AROUND THE TURN OF THE CENTURY, A FOOLISH ACT OF VANITY BY A RELATIVE OF MINE HIDING ITS SECRET IN PLAIN SITE.
BLACK CROWN
ESTABLISHED 1892
MY FAMILY HAVE BEEN PROTECTORS OF THIS SECRET FOR GENERATIONS. EVER SINCE THE ILLEGITIMATE FIRST BORN OF THE KING OF ENGLAND FOUND HIS WAY INTO THE FAMILY CAMP ONE NIGHT.
MY ANCESTORS TOOK HIM WITH THEM TO IRELAND.
BUT HIS PURSUERS FOUND US THERE AND TORTURED HIM.
WE ESCAPED AND FLED TO AMERICA AND A MEMBER OF MY FAMILY HAS GUARDED HIS OFFSPRING EVER SINCE. RIGHT THE WAY UP TO THE PRESENT DAY. THE LAST IN THE LINE. BRIAN.
WE'VE BEEN SAFE HERE FOR A LONG TIME, BUT I KNEW THE AGENTS OF THE CROWN WOULD FIND US IN THE END.
BLACK CROWN

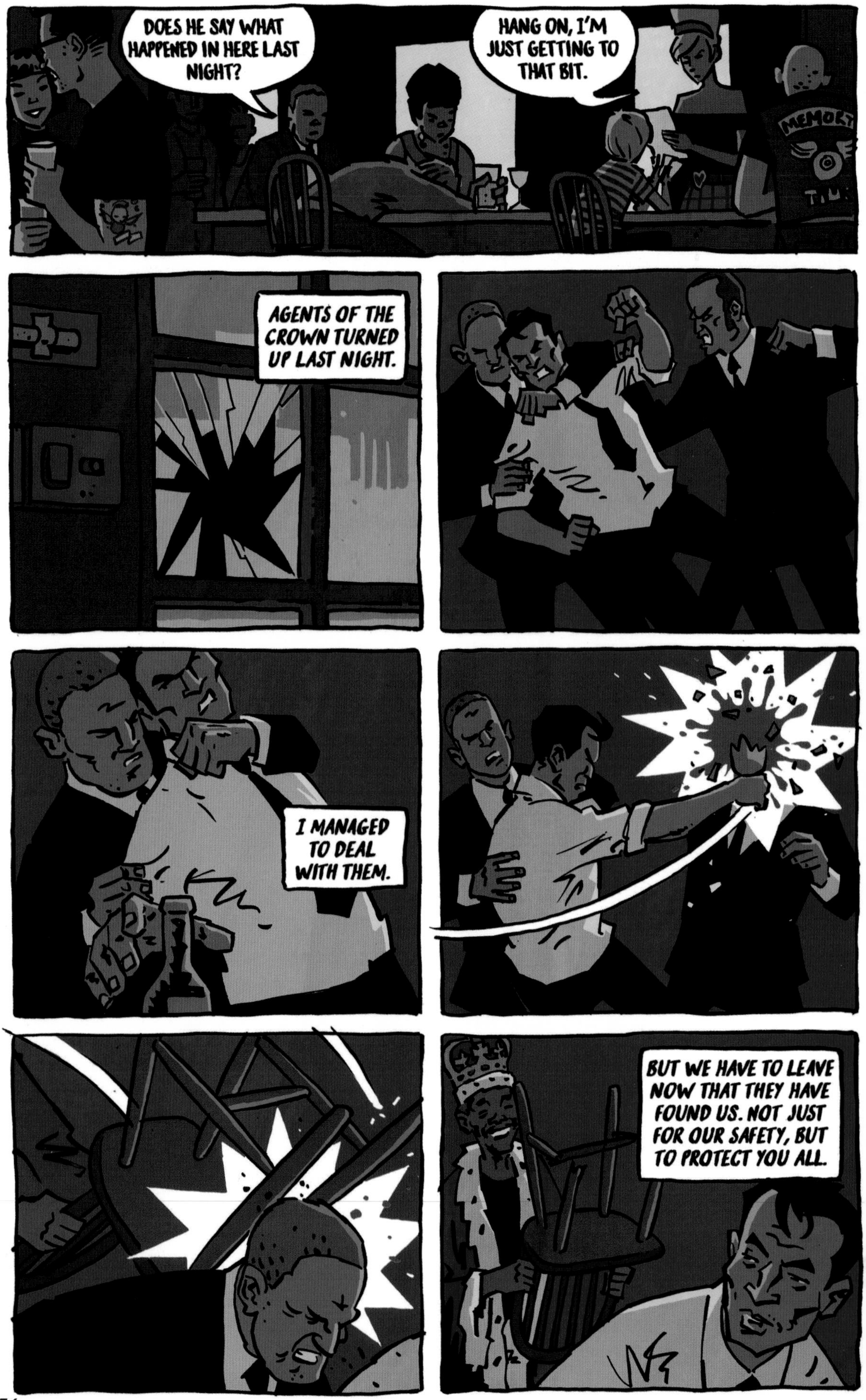
DOES HE SAY WHAT HAPPENED IN HERE LAST NIGHT?
HANG ON, I'M JUST GETTING TO THAT BIT.
AGENTS OF THE CROWN TURNED UP LAST NIGHT.
I MANAGED TO DEAL WITH THEM.
BUT WE HAVE TO LEAVE NOW THAT THEY HAVE FOUND US. NOT JUST FOR OUR SAFETY, BUT TO PROTECT YOU ALL.

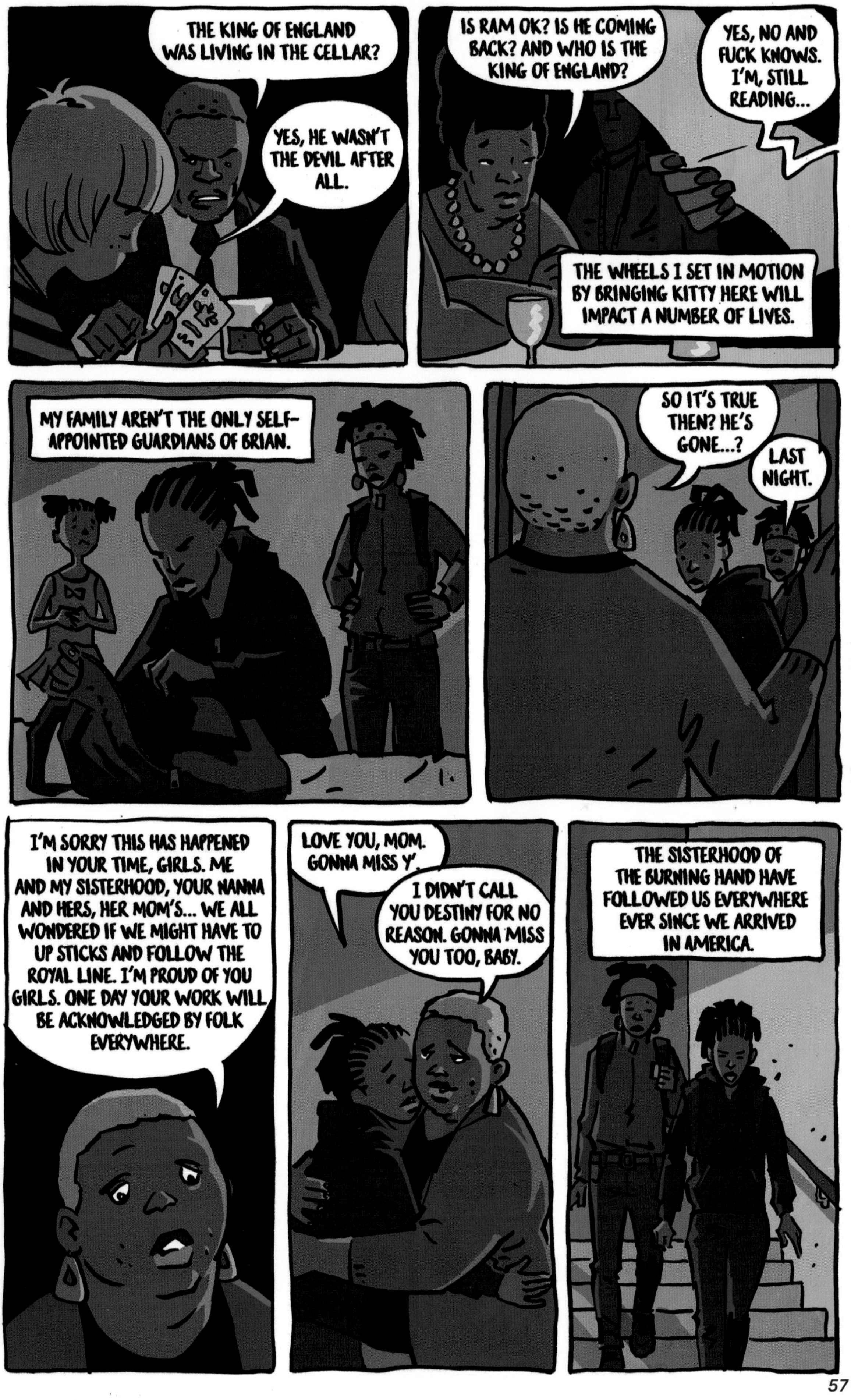
THE KING OF ENGLAND WAS LIVING IN THE CELLAR?
YES, HE WASN'T THE DEVIL AFTER ALL.
IS RAM OK? IS HE COMING BACK? AND WHO IS THE KING OF ENGLAND?
YES, NO AND FUCK KNOWS. I'M, STILL READING...
THE WHEELS I SET IN MOTION BY BRINGING KITTY HERE WILL IMPACT A NUMBER OF LIVES.
MY FAMILY AREN'T THE ONLY SELF-APPOINTED GUARDIANS OF BRIAN.
SO IT'S TRUE THEN? HE'S GONE...?
LAST NIGHT.
I'M SORRY THIS HAS HAPPENED IN YOUR TIME, GIRLS. ME AND MY SISTERHOOD, YOUR NANNA AND HERS, HER MOM'S... WE ALL WONDERED IF WE MIGHT HAVE TO UP STICKS AND FOLLOW THE ROYAL LINE. I'M PROUD OF YOU GIRLS. ONE DAY YOUR WORK WILL BE ACKNOWLEDGED BY FOLK EVERYWHERE.
LOVE YOU, MOM. GONNA MISS Y'.
I DIDN'T CALL YOU DESTINY FOR NO REASON. GONNA MISS YOU TOO, BABY.
THE SISTERHOOD OF THE BURNING HAND HAVE FOLLOWED US EVERYWHERE EVER SINCE WE ARRIVED IN AMERICA.

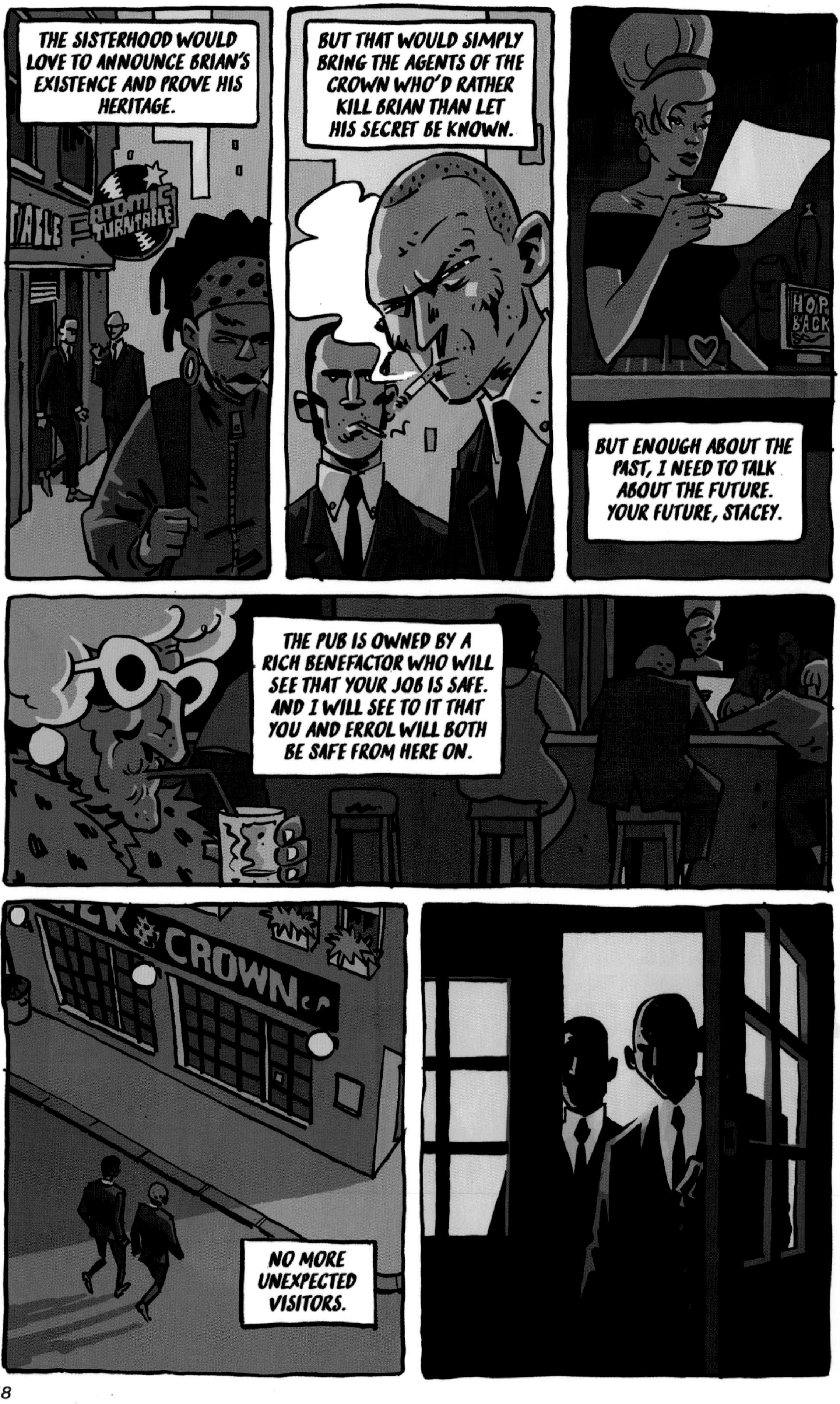
THE SISTERHOOD WOULD LOVE TO ANNOUNCE BRIAN'S EXISTENCE AND PROVE HIS HERITAGE.
ATOMIC TURNTABLE
BUT THAT WOULD SIMPLY BRING THE AGENTS OF THE CROWN WHO'D RATHER KILL BRIAN THAN LET HIS SECRET BE KNOWN.
BUT ENOUGH ABOUT THE PAST, I NEED TO TALK ABOUT THE FUTURE. YOUR FUTURE, STACEY.
THE PUB IS OWNED BY A RICH BENEFACTOR WHO WILL SEE THAT YOUR JOB IS SAFE. AND I WILL SEE TO IT THAT YOU AND ERROL WILL BOTH BE SAFE FROM HERE ON.
CROWN
NO MORE UNEXPECTED VISITORS.

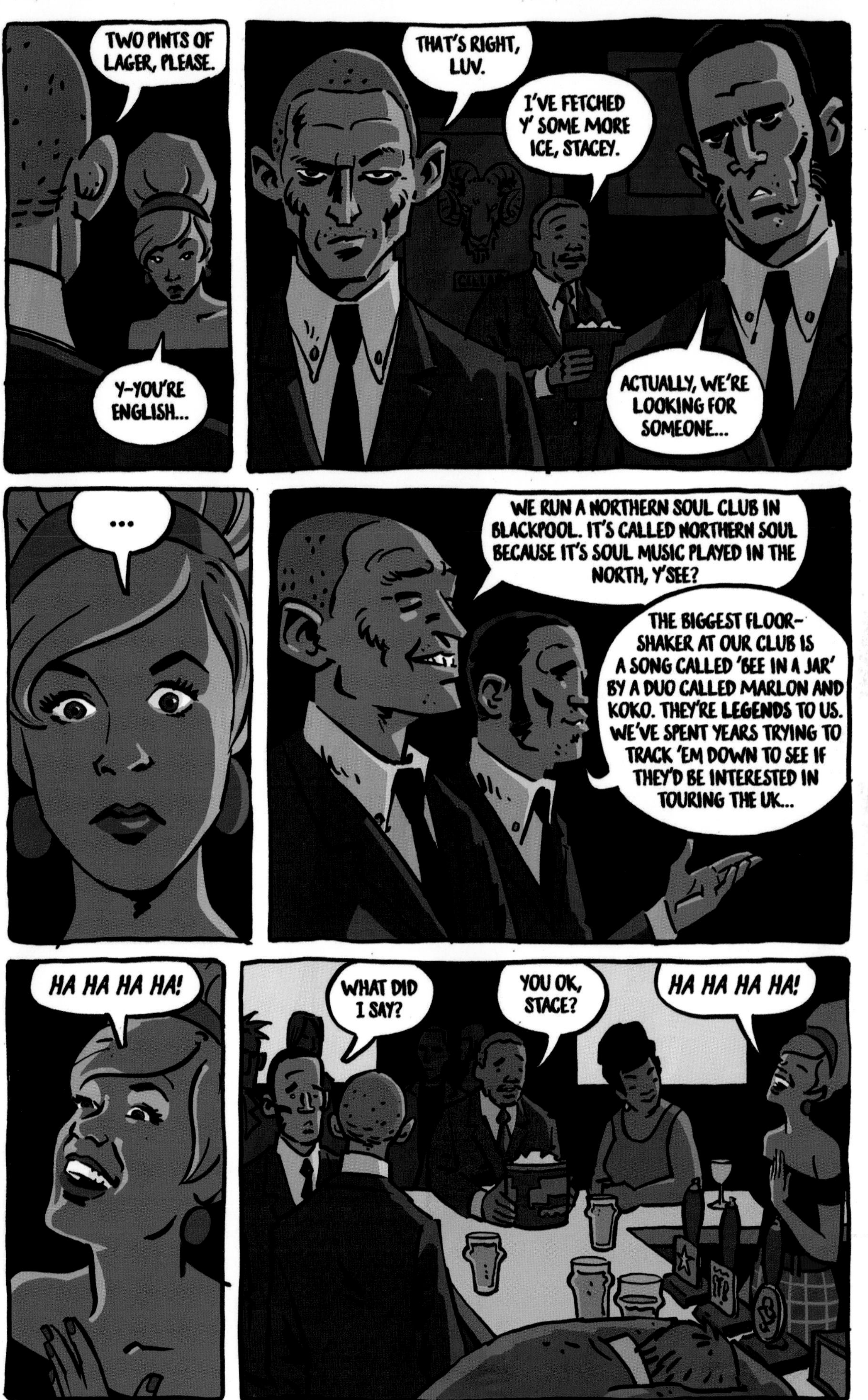
TWO PINTS OF LAGER, PLEASE.
Y-YOU'RE ENGLISH...
THAT'S RIGHT, LUV.
I'VE FETCHED Y' SOME MORE ICE, STACEY.
ACTUALLY, WE'RE LOOKING FOR SOMEONE...
...
WE RUN A NORTHERN SOUL CLUB IN BLACKPOOL. IT'S CALLED NORTHERN SOUL BECAUSE IT'S SOUL MUSIC PLAYED IN THE NORTH, Y'SEE?
THE BIGGEST FLOOR-SHAKER AT OUR CLUB IS A SONG CALLED 'BEE IN A JAR' BY A DUO CALLED MARLON AND KOKO. THEY'RE LEGENDS TO US. WE'VE SPENT YEARS TRYING TO TRACK 'EM DOWN TO SEE IF THEY'D BE INTERESTED IN TOURING THE UK...
HA HA HA HA!
WHAT DID I SAY?
YOU OK, STACE?
HA HA HA HA!

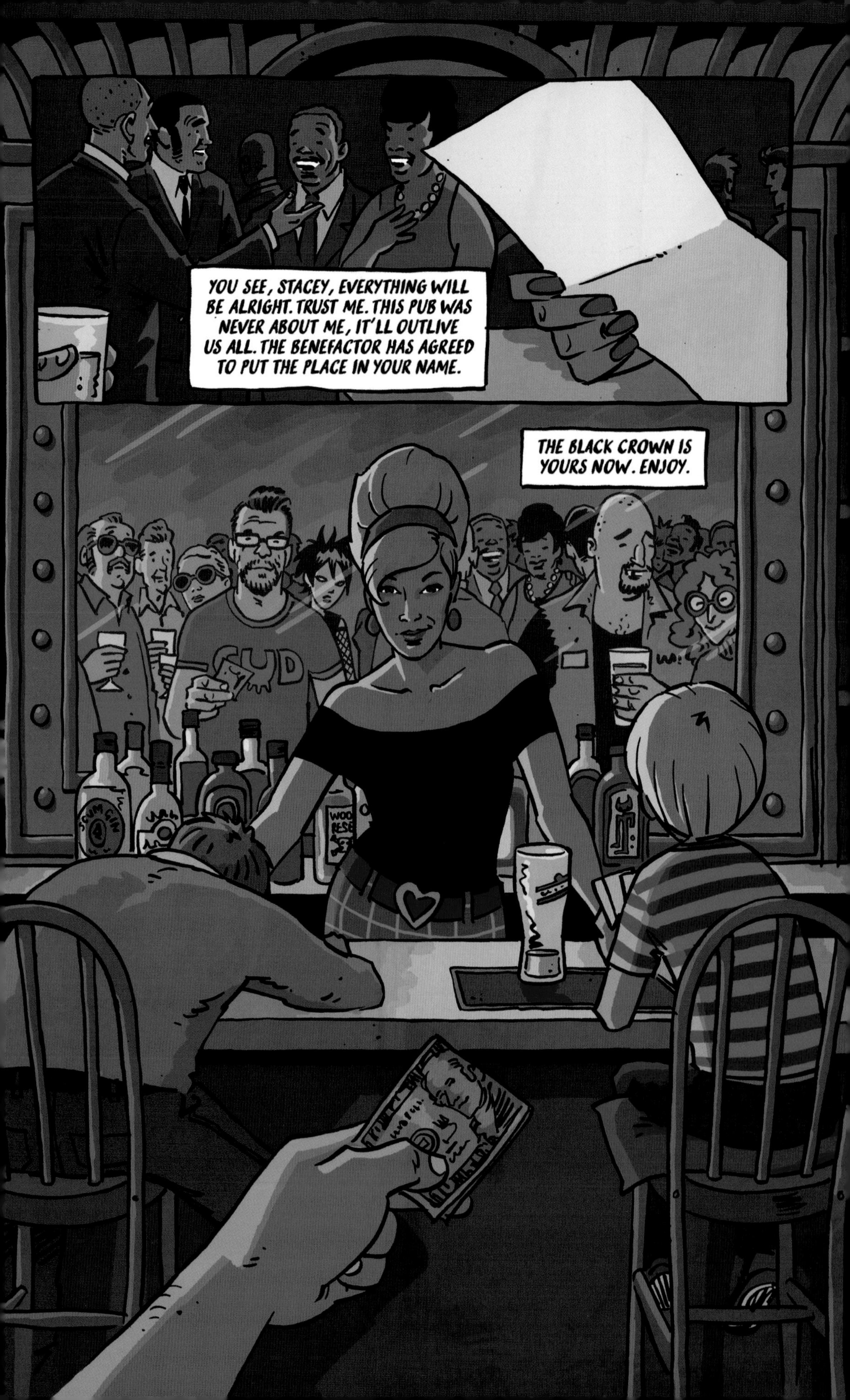
YOU SEE, STACEY, EVERYTHING WILL BE ALRIGHT. TRUST ME. THIS PUB WAS NEVER ABOUT ME, IT'LL OUTLIVE US ALL. THE BENEFACTOR HAS AGREED TO PUT THE PLACE IN YOUR NAME.
THE BLACK CROWN IS YOURS NOW. ENJOY.

Four Chambers

with ROB DAVIS, writer / artist of *TALES FROM THE BLACK CROWN PUB*

The Quartet Directive

Upper left: Your bookshelf
Upper right: An image with an unexpected backstory
Lower left: A favorite band/album cover art
Lower right: A storefront that inspires

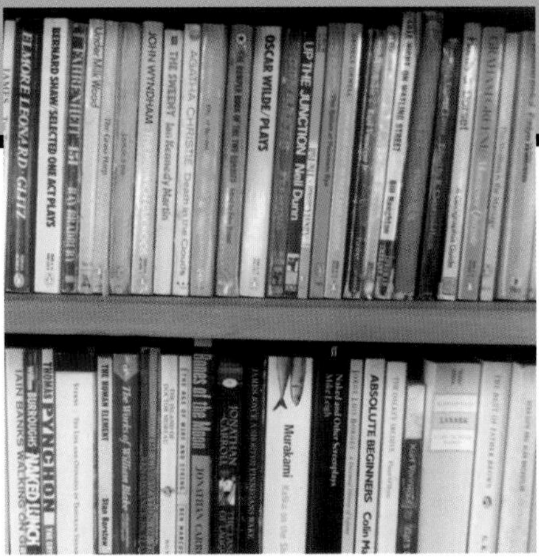
JOHN WYNDHAM
AGATHA CHRISTIE
OSCAR WILDE / PLAYS
UP THE JUNCTION Nell Dunn
Murakami
ABSOLUTE BEGINNERS

I didn't do education at school. I couldn't read or write very well until much later. On my last day at school I broke into the store cupboard and took a copy of every book I hadn't read. I've read them all now. I still have many of the books I took that day. I can see four of them in the picture, including Kes and Under Milk Wood.

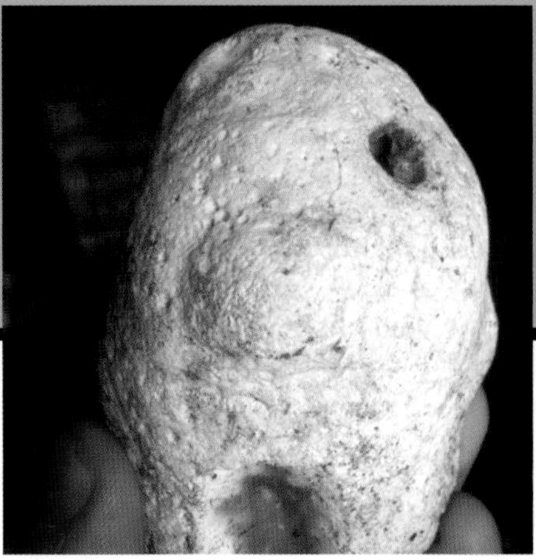

During a period of unemployment and black depression I lived in a village called Puddletown in Dorset. The only thing that gave me joy during this time was going out walking through the woods and across the fields with my eldest son who was 4 at the time. On one of these walks I was explaining to him the ancient belief that the flint stones turned over during ploughing were the captured souls of the dead. "Like that one-eyed man there?" said my son, pointing at the ground. I bent down and this is what I picked up. Wonder who he was? Looks like he died a horrible death.

I think this was the first album I bought on vinyl in 1982. All my previous purchases had been on cassette, but I had to own a full-scale version of this. It was a major influence on me. The Uffington Horse on the front captures the chalkhills I associate with where I come from, and the prehistoric design is up there with Picasso. The lyrics inside were handwritten in a vaguely Celtic style that I copied and adopted as my handwriting style for a few years.

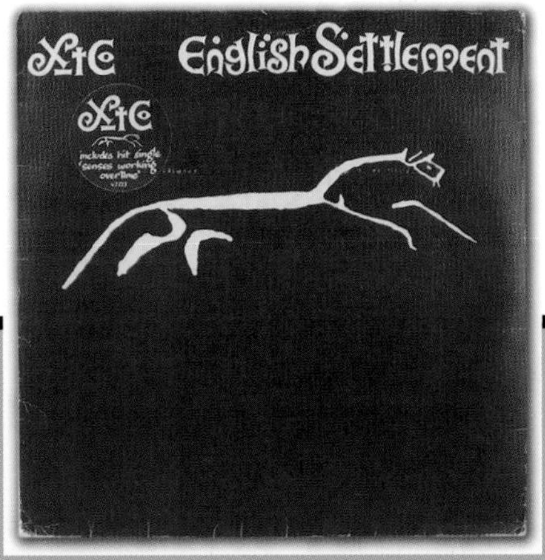
XTC English Settlement
XTC

In the 1980s Westbourne (near Bournemouth) had a seedy edge to it. And the edge of the seedy was Queens Road where Armadillo Records sold the kind of things you didn't see anywhere else (including alternative U.S. comics by Crumb and the like). Don't know what age I was when I first braved the terrifying frontage with its punk and psychedelia images. Can't find an image of the front, but here's the inside.

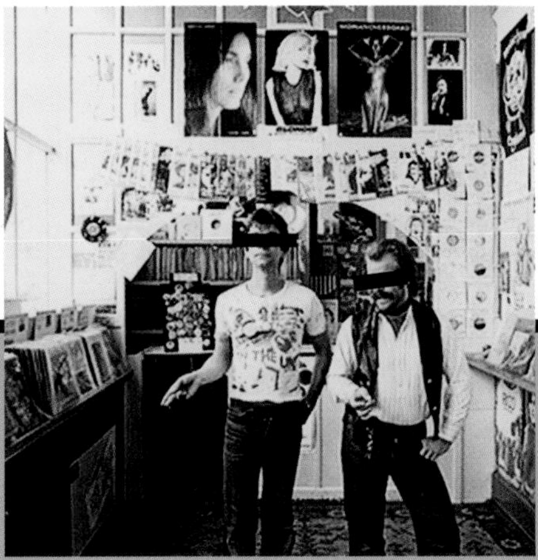

swell maps

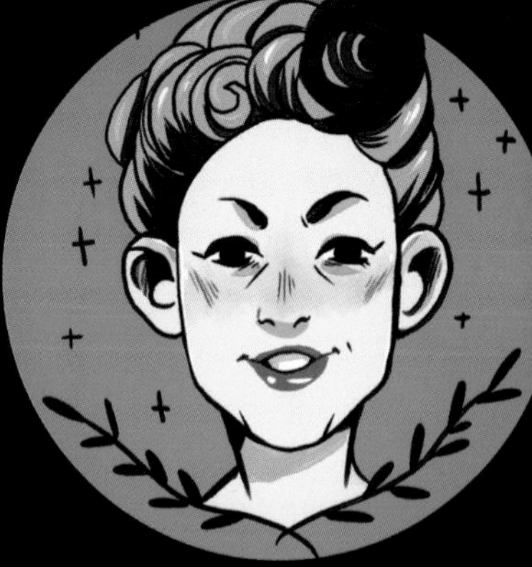

Welcome to NEWCASTLE, with your musical tour guide Cathi Unsworth

Illustrations by Cara McGee

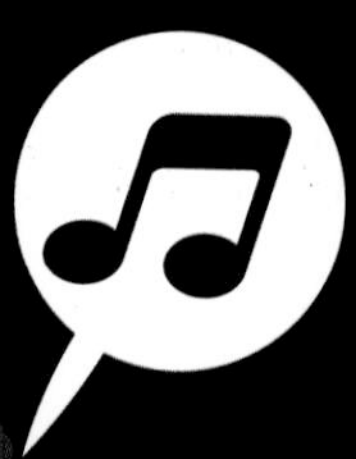

There has been a settlement on the north bank of the River Tyne since the **Emperor Hadrian** visited the edge of Britannia in A.D. 122 and saw marauding Picts across the frontier. Pons Aelius was a fort on the original eastern end of the resultant Hadrian's Wall, meaning Aelian Bridge. On its site now stands The Castle, built by **Robert Curthose**, eldest son of **William the Conqueror**, for very similar reasons in 1172. From this the city takes its name and the triple-castle shield on its coat of arms. The motto: Fortiter Defendit Triumphans (Triumphing by Brave Defence) sums up the spirit that built the city, its football team "The Magpies" and most famous son, **Viz** comics' **Biffa Bacon**. Its skyline remains synonymous with the iron bridge used to iconic effect in **Mike Hodges'** cinematic ode to the Toon, *Get Carter*, despite the fact that his source material, Ted Lewis' *Jack's Return Home*, was set 130 miles down the road in Scunthorpe and his leading man, a Cockney who couldn't say, "Hadaway an' shite, ya bastad," if Biffa was offering him outside.

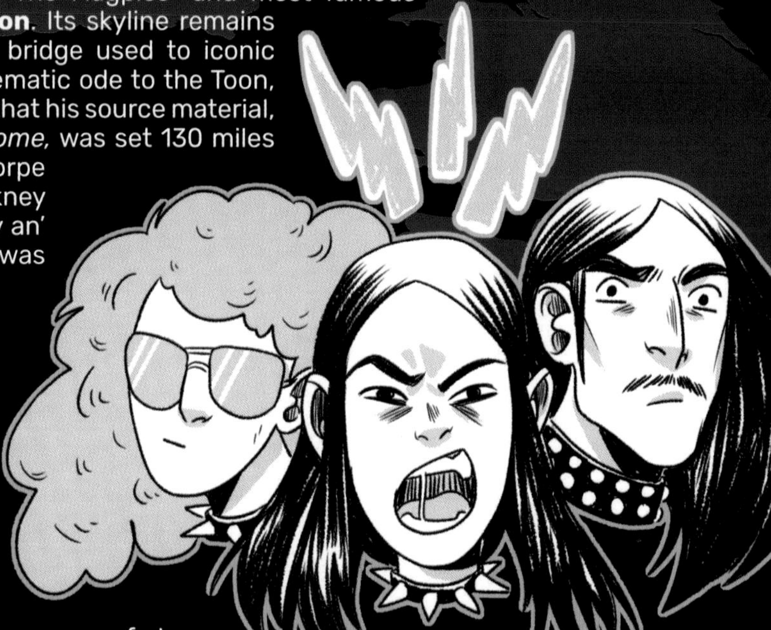

It was in Newcastle that the power of steam was harnessed to an iron horse by handyman **George Stephenson**, who designed his first locomotive in 1814, created the rail gauge and constructed the first public line, from Stockton to Darlington, in 1825. Around the same time, local lad **John Martin** made his name as a painter of vast, apocalyptic landscapes, inspired by the surrounding terrain of the Wallsend Colliery and the new world of Stephenson's achievements. A century and a half later, Martin's *oeuvre* would have made the ideal adornment for the album covers of **Venom**, the Newcastle band who alchemized the inferno into sonic form and labeled it **Black Metal**. All that smelting in the atmosphere also forged **AC/DC**'s **Brian Johnson** (in native flat cap), and **The Tygers of Pan Tang**, named after one of the fantastical lands of seer **Michael Moorcock**.

NEWCASTLE UNITED

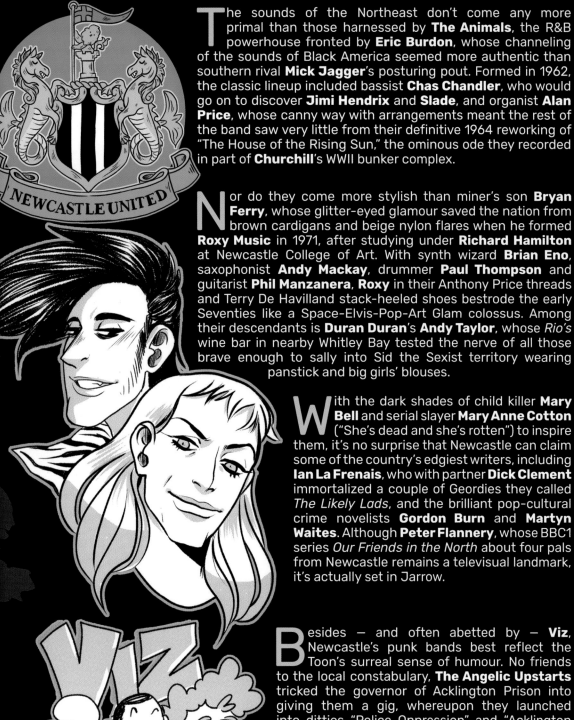

The sounds of the Northeast don't come any more primal than those harnessed by **The Animals**, the R&B powerhouse fronted by **Eric Burdon**, whose channeling of the sounds of Black America seemed more authentic than southern rival **Mick Jagger**'s posturing pout. Formed in 1962, the classic lineup included bassist **Chas Chandler**, who would go on to discover **Jimi Hendrix** and **Slade**, and organist **Alan Price**, whose canny way with arrangements meant the rest of the band saw very little from their definitive 1964 reworking of "The House of the Rising Sun," the ominous ode they recorded in part of **Churchill**'s WWII bunker complex.

Nor do they come more stylish than miner's son **Bryan Ferry**, whose glitter-eyed glamour saved the nation from brown cardigans and beige nylon flares when he formed **Roxy Music** in 1971, after studying under **Richard Hamilton** at Newcastle College of Art. With synth wizard **Brian Eno**, saxophonist **Andy Mackay**, drummer **Paul Thompson** and guitarist **Phil Manzanera**, **Roxy** in their Anthony Price threads and Terry De Havilland stack-heeled shoes bestrode the early Seventies like a Space-Elvis-Pop-Art Glam colossus. Among their descendants is **Duran Duran**'s **Andy Taylor**, whose *Rio's* wine bar in nearby Whitley Bay tested the nerve of all those brave enough to sally into Sid the Sexist territory wearing panstick and big girls' blouses.

With the dark shades of child killer **Mary Bell** and serial slayer **Mary Anne Cotton** ("She's dead and she's rotten") to inspire them, it's no surprise that Newcastle can claim some of the country's edgiest writers, including **Ian La Frenais**, who with partner **Dick Clement** immortalized a couple of Geordies they called *The Likely Lads*, and the brilliant pop-cultural crime novelists **Gordon Burn** and **Martyn Waites**. Although **Peter Flannery**, whose BBC1 series *Our Friends in the North* about four pals from Newcastle remains a televisual landmark, it's actually set in Jarrow.

VIZ
BOLLOCKS!

Besides – and often abetted by – **Viz**, Newcastle's punk bands best reflect the Toon's surreal sense of humour. No friends to the local constabulary, **The Angelic Upstarts** tricked the governor of Acklington Prison into giving them a gig, whereupon they launched into ditties "Police Oppression" and "Acklington Breakout." Some of their audience asked to be let back into their cells. Toon punks also include **The Toy Dolls**, **Punishment of Luxury**, **Pigs, Pigs, Pigs etc.** and the legendary **Arthur Two-Stroke and the Chart Commandos** (AKA *Tony O'Diamond & Top Group Fantastic*, AKA *Arthur Two-Stroke's Big Black Bomb*) whose promotional posters were designed by **Viz** founder **Chris Donald** himself. Howay the lads!

Raised in a field in Outer Norfolk, CATHI UNSWORTH was a teenage goth whose spells actually worked when she made her way to London and became a journalist on *Sounds* at the age of 19. Before the weekly music press became extinct, she also worked for *Melody Maker*, then went on to co-create *Purr* and write reams more about music, film, fashion, noir fiction and general weirdness for everyone from the *Fortean Times* to the *Financial Times*. Over the past decade she has written five noir novels into which she pours all her obsessions with secret histories and pop culture. You can find out more at www.cathiunsworth.co.uk

FROM THEORY TO REVOLUTION

OCTOBER 2017
NEW YORK COMIC CON

The first title from the BLACK CROWN imprint, Peter Milligan and Tess Fowler's KID LOBOTOMY is finally released.

BLACK CROWN launches at New York Comic Con. IDW brings Milligan and Fowler to NYC to celebrate the release of KID LOBOTOMY.

"DEFIANT REBELLIOUS DISOBEDIENT +UTTERLY BADASS."
—GEEK.COM

In addition to booth signings, St. Mark's Comics in the East Village hosts the major signing event which couldn't have been more apropos considering that St. Mark's is the inspiration for BLACK CROWN's Canon Street, a shared landscape with eclectic storefronts that correlate to each miniseries.

The first BLACK CROWN QUARTERLY is released two weeks later.

IDW

BLACKCROWN BOOTH BAES
[illegible]NYORK COMIC CON 10/7/17

FRIDAY NIGHT
@ ST. MARK'S COMICS
NYC 10/6/17

BC REPLACES 'SUPREME'
AS DE REGEUR DECK LOGO

KID LOBOTOMY
#1
BLACK CROWN
kidlobotomy
#1
oct2017
MILLIGAN
FOWLER
LOUGHRIDGE
BIDIKAR
IDW

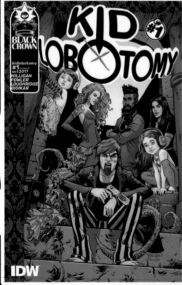

"So many favorite moments. The day Shelly Bond called me on the phone is a favourite, but I think I have to go with the magical weekend that was New York Comic Con, where she and Peter Milligan gave me the plague. If you've never herded a coughing, bleary-eyed British comics writer through a Duane Reade, I highly recommend it."
—Tini Howard, writer of ASSASSINISTAS

2017
OCTOBER

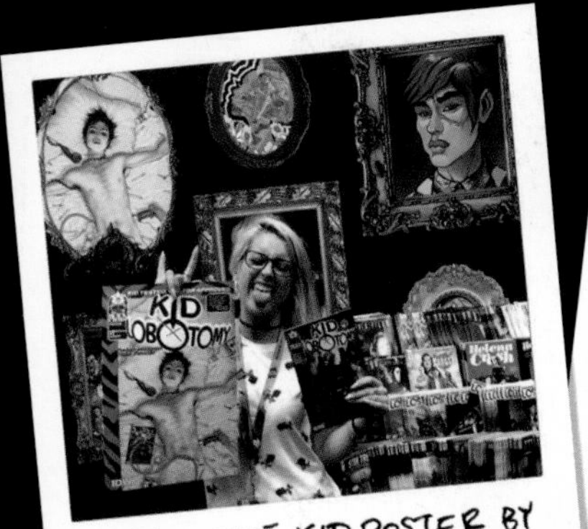

EXCLUSIVE KID POSTER BY FRANK QUITELY — NYCC

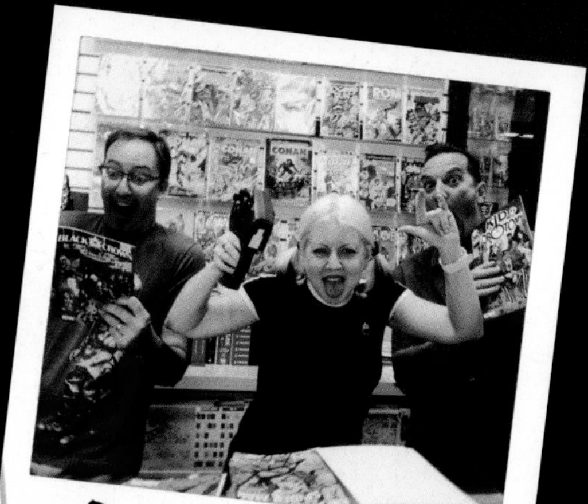

BC TAKEOVER
LCBS HOUSE OF SECRETS

"The highlight of 365 dreamy days in the Black Crown Family was the surreal first sighting of Philip Bond's Dying Embers duo, confirming that the comic wasn't just a hallucinatory side-effect of my medication but a benefit."
—Will Potter, writer of CUD: RICH & STRANGE

NOVEMBER
The first BLACK CROWN QUARTERLY is released two weeks later.

PUNKS NOT DEAD co-creators David Barnett and Martin Simmonds, BCQ contributors Jamie Coe, Will Potter and Carl Puttnam, and returning KID LOBOTOMY hero Peter Milligan sign at London's Forbidden Planet.

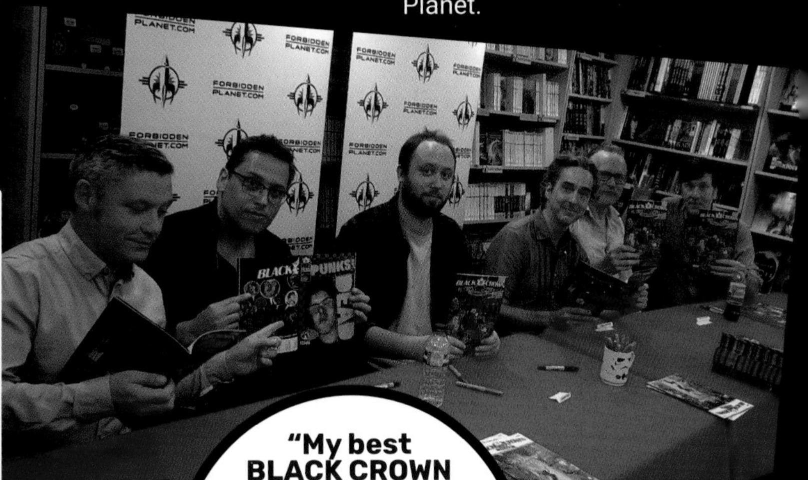

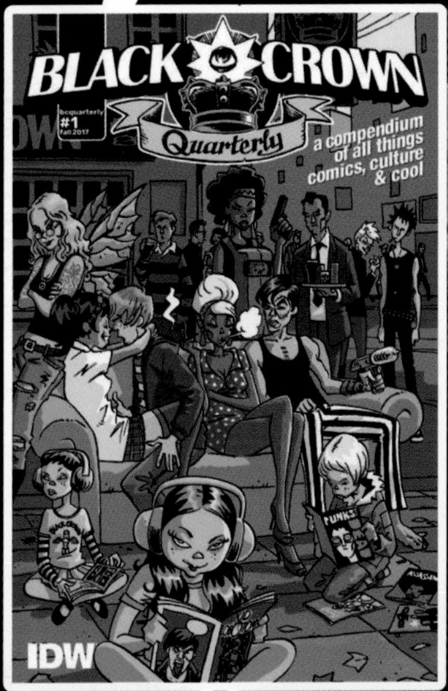
BLACK CROWN
Quarterly
bcquarterly #1 fall 2017
a compendium of all things comics, culture & cool
IDW

"My best BLACK CROWN experience? Probably seeing KID LOBOTOMY #1 for the first time and thinking, this has the authentic stamp of weirdness."
— Peter Milligan, writer of KID LOBOTOMY

NOVEMBER

Canon Street
Hypothetical Place

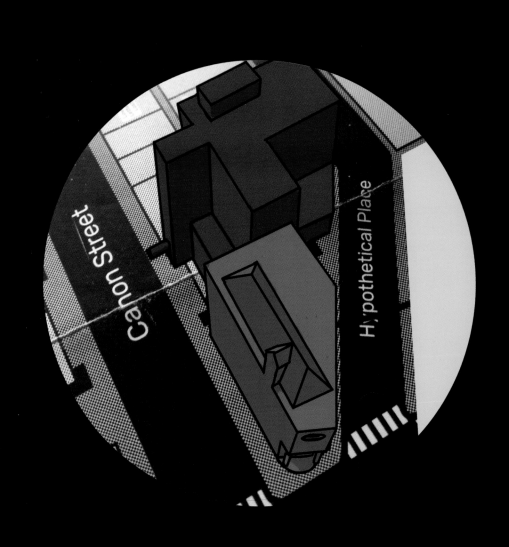

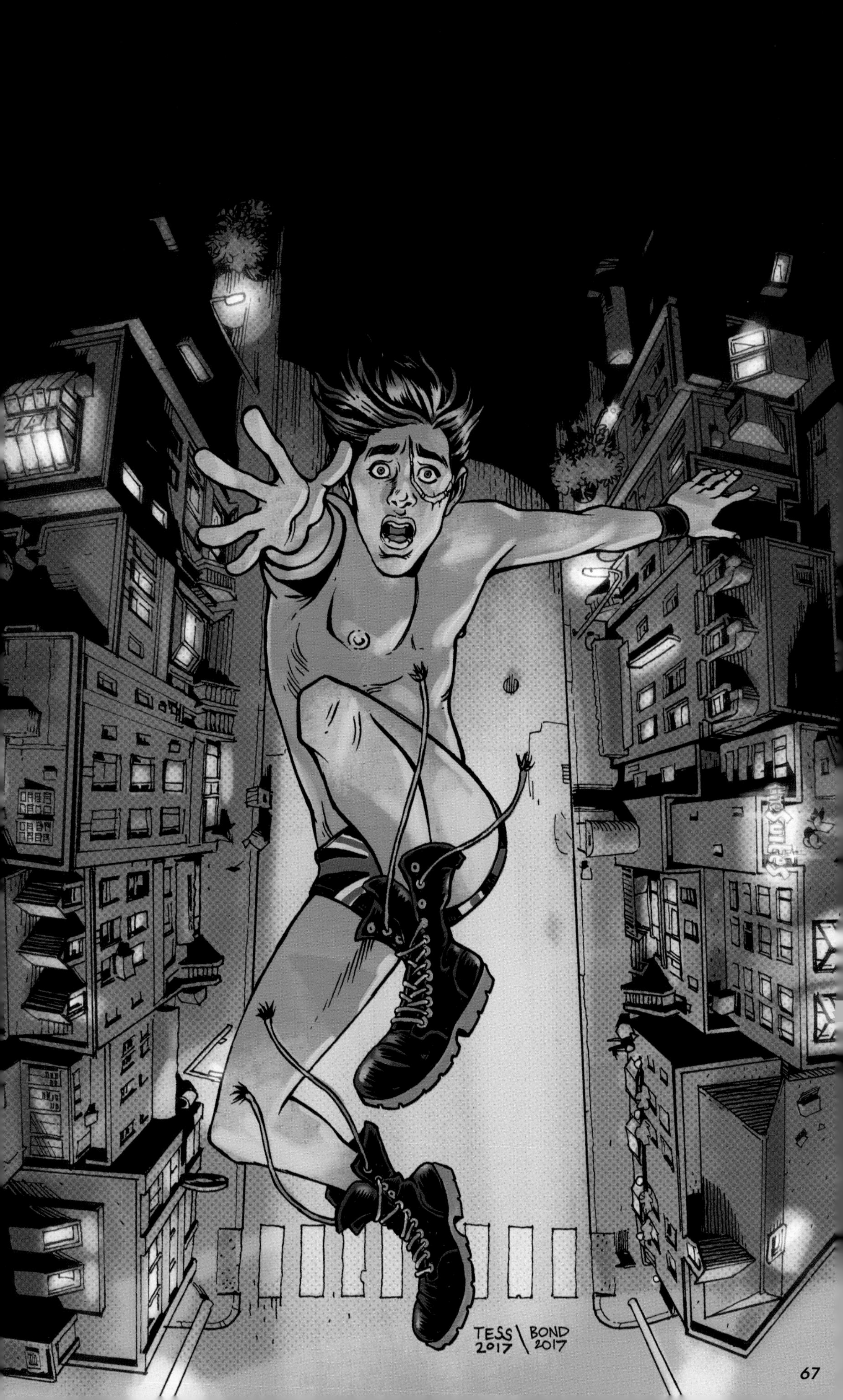
TESS 2017
BOND 2017

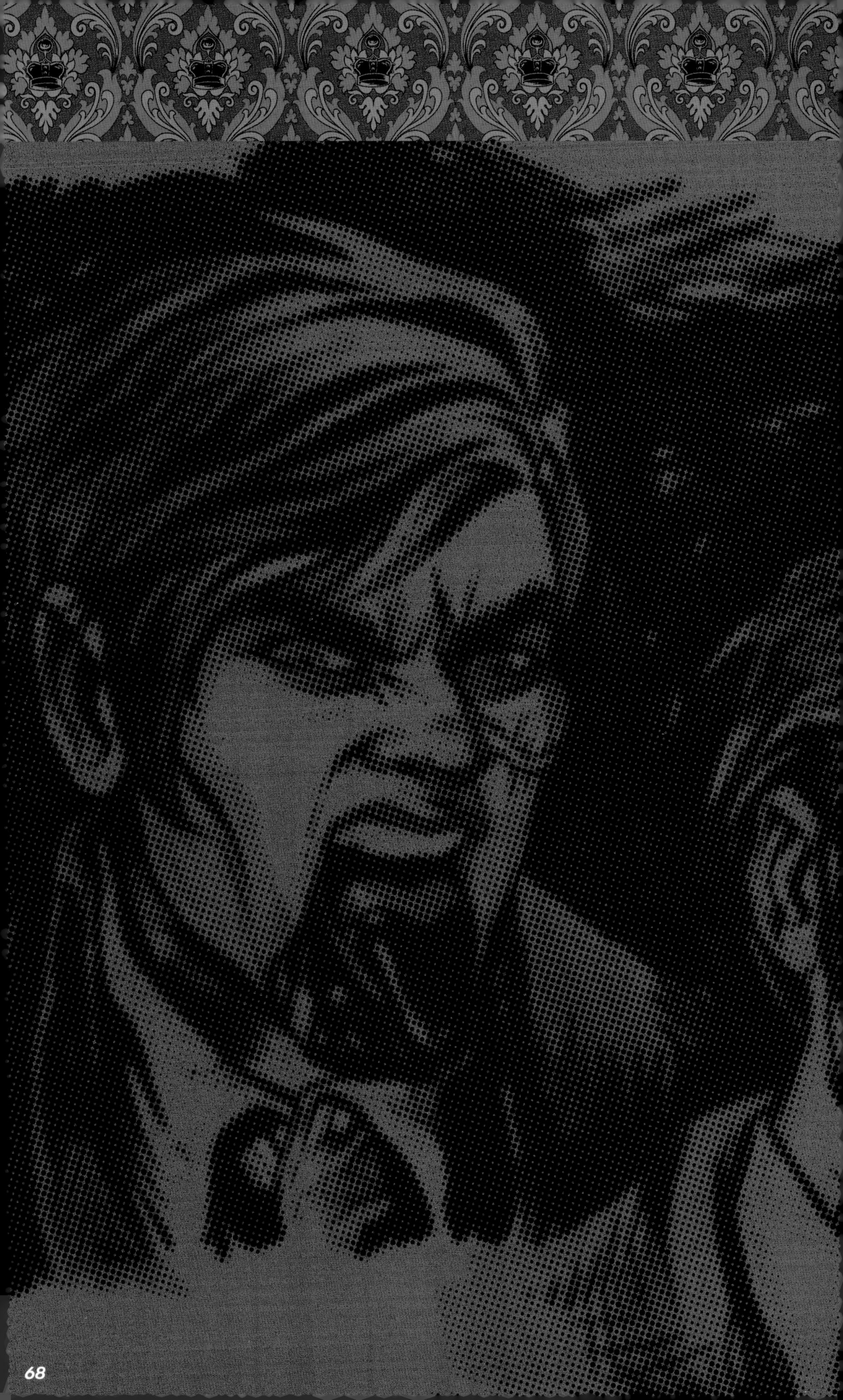

KID LOBOTOMY

created by PETER MILLIGAN & TESS FOWLER

SPILLED TRADE SECRET:

THE BLUE-HAIRED MAIDEN

Not unlike a band's debut album, the first comic book to usher in a new imprint is a statement of intent. Its mission: to set the tone for every BLACK CROWN series that follows. KID LOBOTOMY is dark and demented like its writer and captures the beauty and bleakness of our times with a hearty dose of black humour.

THE HIEROPHANT + THE HYENA

Tess Fowler was the first writer/artist I hired in the fall of 2016 for FEMME MAGNIFIQUE, a comic book anthology that salutes powerful women in pop, politics, art and science. I wanted to continue my working relationship with Tess and thought she would make a great visual accomplice for writer Peter Milligan. And I had a sneaking suspicion she'd draw one mean cockroach (or one million).

Milligan, for the uninitiated, is one of the original postmodern masters of comics. He was part of a British Invasion of writers published stateside in the early '90s who showed us young Americans a thing or two about the human condition. But Milligan was always a few brain cells apart from the rest. He would find wholly original ways to deconstruct and bend the comics medium to his sick, twisted literary pleasures.

THE SANGUINE SALUTATION

As for how I convinced this sultan of the surreal to drop everything and write for me again? It began, as it usually does, with an impetuous decision (on Valentine's Day no less) and a 2-word e-mail subject header separated by a comma, a continent and a crass commercial holiday.

"HEY, LOBOTOMY!"

I'm sure his wife was thrilled to be interrupted by this sort of madness over cheap roses and *crème brûlée*. Twenty-four hours later, buried beneath dead rose petals, the KID came to life.

—With apologies to Milligan's wife

BLACK CROWN
kidlobotomy
#1 cover A
oct2017
MILLIGAN
FOWLER
LOUGHRIDGE
BIDIKAR
KID LOBOTOMY
#1
IDW

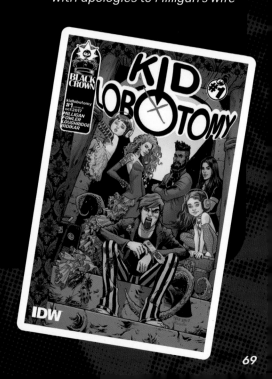

"Eponymous Kid. Failed rock star, failed hotel manager, very successful madman. Due to his strange therapies and brain ops, his inner demons seem to be running amok. Which is probably one reason why he agreed to manage the family hotel, The Suites. Racked with guilt and desire over his incestuous feelings for his sister, Kid is our very flawed hero."

—Peter Milligan, co-creator/writer

"I'm on trial and I can't win, baby."

—Randall van de Post, psycho killer

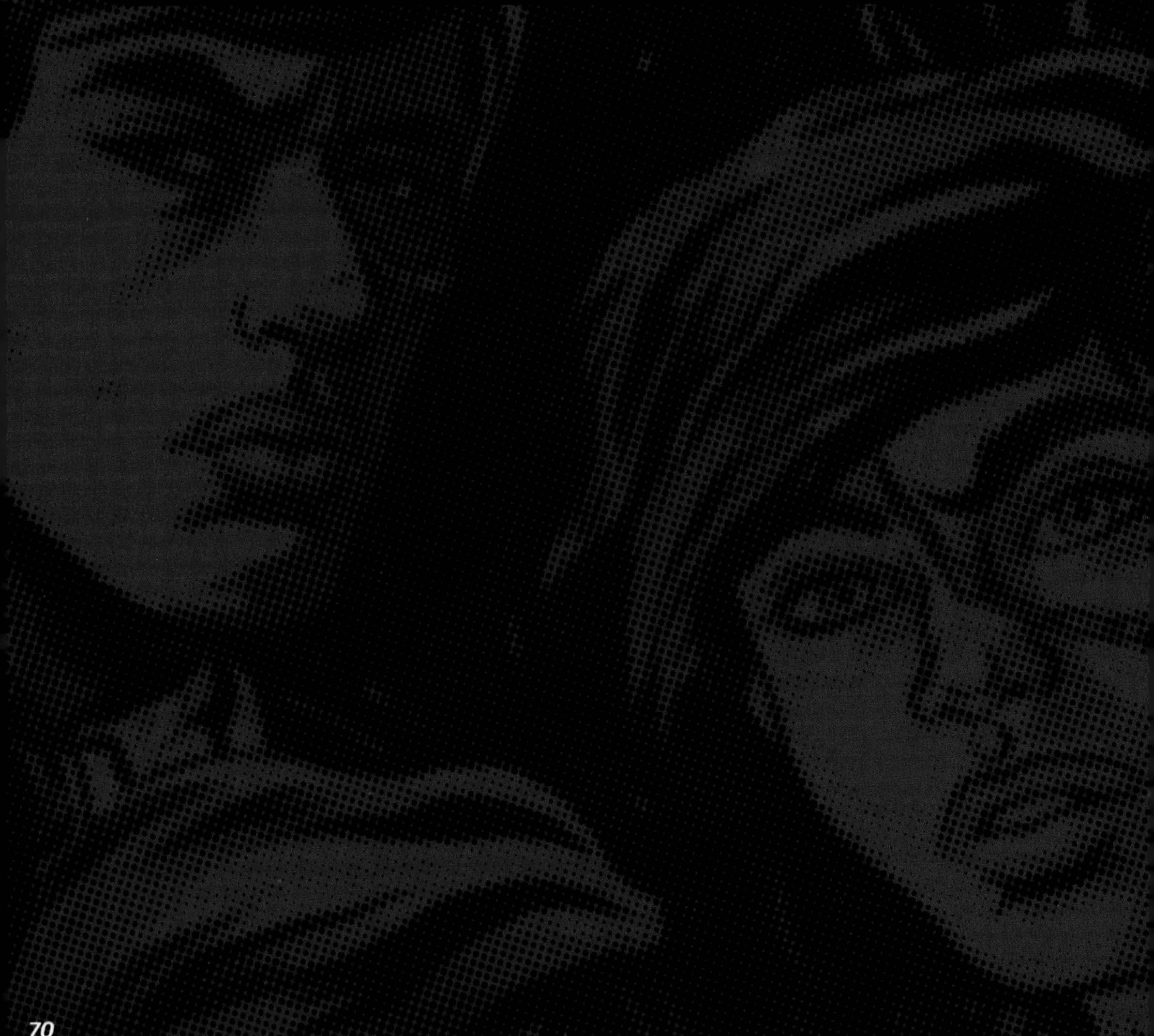

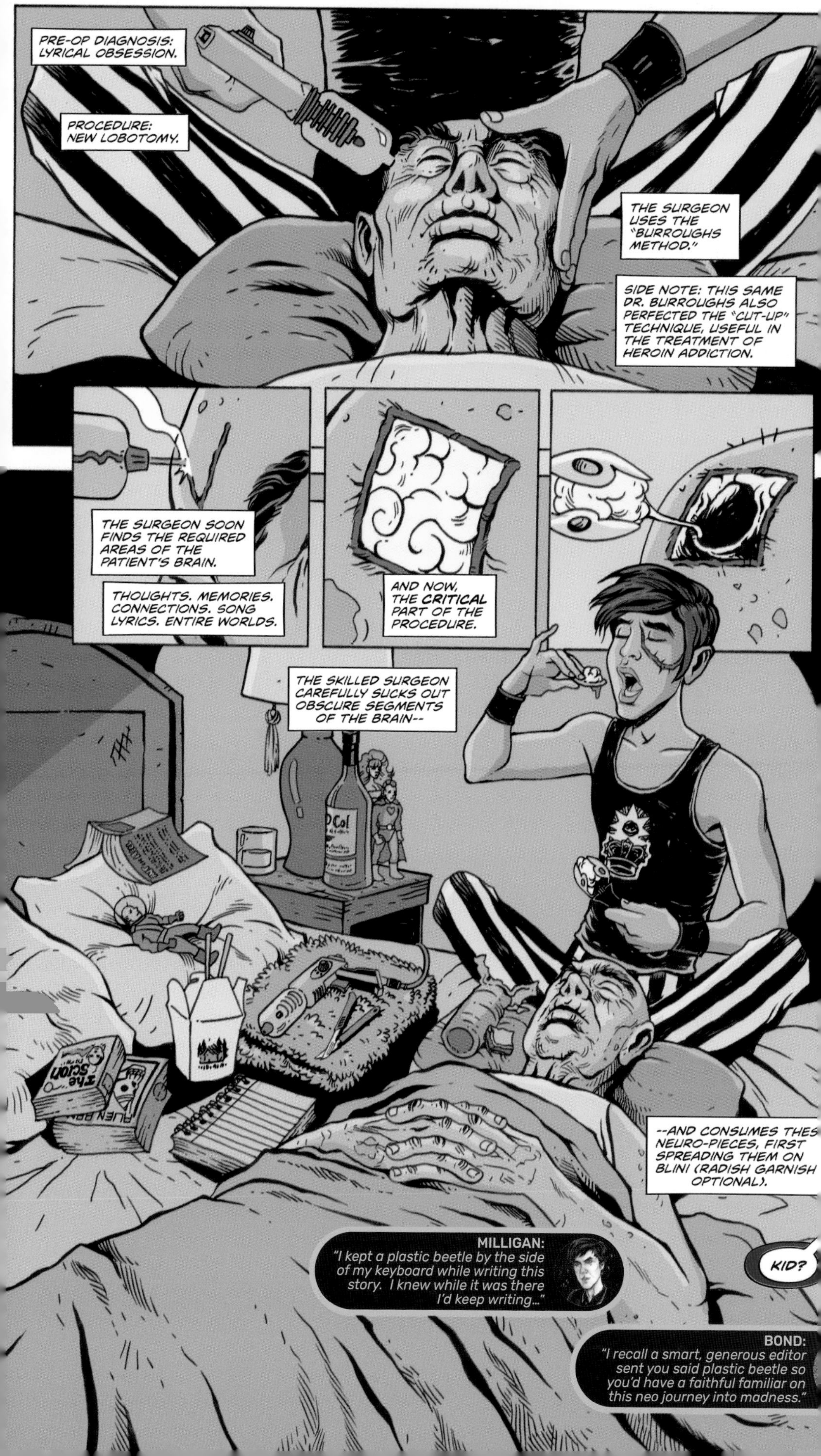
PRE-OP DIAGNOSIS: LYRICAL OBSESSION.
PROCEDURE: NEW LOBOTOMY.
THE SURGEON USES THE "BURROUGHS METHOD."
SIDE NOTE: THIS SAME DR. BURROUGHS ALSO PERFECTED THE "CUT-UP" TECHNIQUE, USEFUL IN THE TREATMENT OF HEROIN ADDICTION.
THE SURGEON SOON FINDS THE REQUIRED AREAS OF THE PATIENT'S BRAIN.
THOUGHTS. MEMORIES. CONNECTIONS. SONG LYRICS. ENTIRE WORLDS.
AND NOW, THE CRITICAL PART OF THE PROCEDURE.
THE SKILLED SURGEON CAREFULLY SUCKS OUT OBSCURE SEGMENTS OF THE BRAIN--
--AND CONSUMES THES NEURO-PIECES, FIRST SPREADING THEM ON BLINI (RADISH GARNISH OPTIONAL).
KID?
MILLIGAN: "I kept a plastic beetle by the side of my keyboard while writing this story. I knew while it was there I'd keep writing..."
BOND: "I recall a smart, generous editor sent you said plastic beetle so you'd have a faithful familiar on this neo journey into madness."

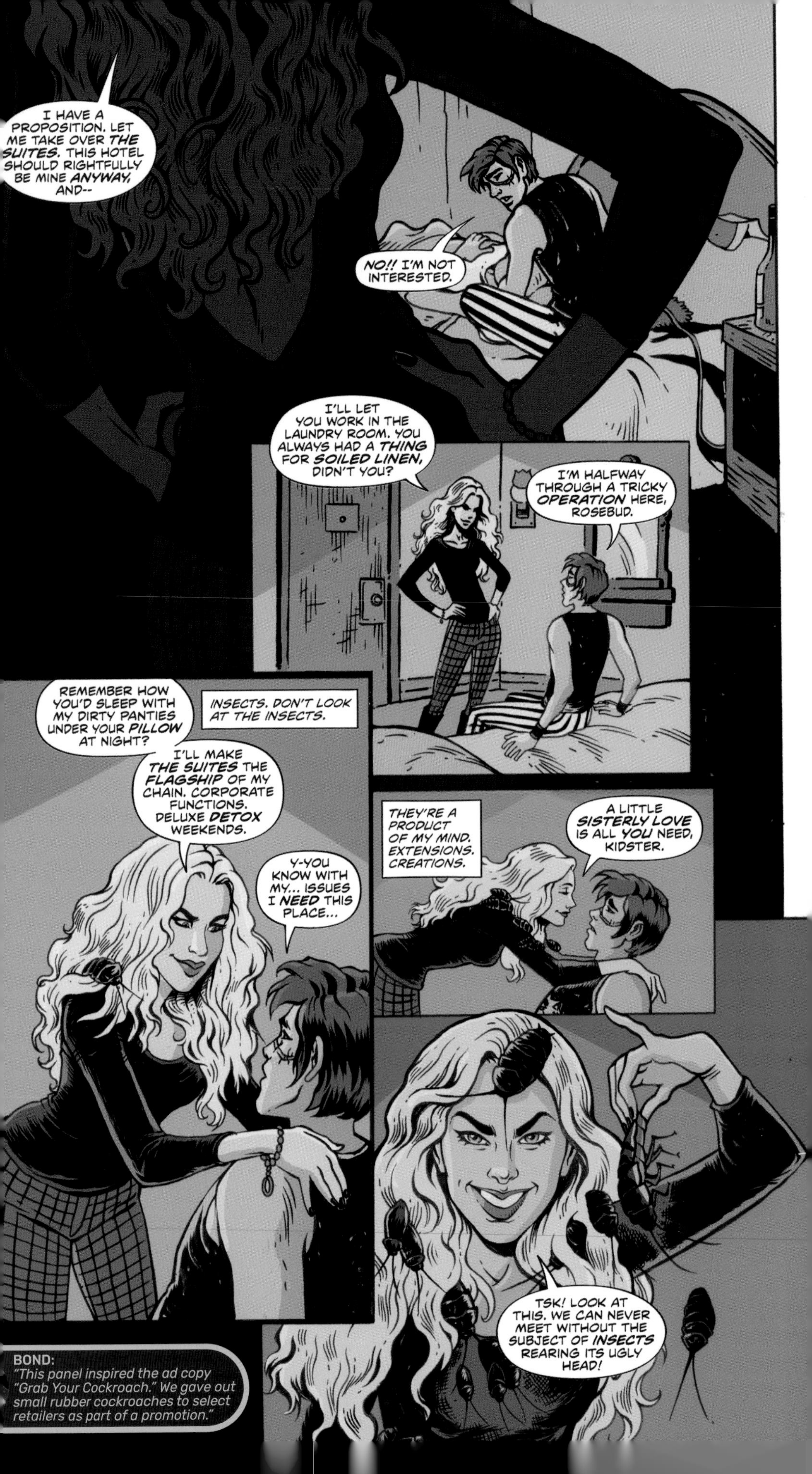

I HAVE A PROPOSITION. LET ME TAKE OVER THE SUITES. THIS HOTEL SHOULD RIGHTFULLY BE MINE ANYWAY, AND--
NO!! I'M NOT INTERESTED.
I'LL LET YOU WORK IN THE LAUNDRY ROOM. YOU ALWAYS HAD A THING FOR SOILED LINEN, DIDN'T YOU?
I'M HALFWAY THROUGH A TRICKY OPERATION HERE, ROSEBUD.
REMEMBER HOW YOU'D SLEEP WITH MY DIRTY PANTIES UNDER YOUR PILLOW AT NIGHT?
INSECTS. DON'T LOOK AT THE INSECTS.
I'LL MAKE THE SUITES THE FLAGSHIP OF MY CHAIN. CORPORATE FUNCTIONS. DELUXE DETOX WEEKENDS.
Y-YOU KNOW WITH MY... ISSUES I NEED THIS PLACE...
THEY'RE A PRODUCT OF MY MIND. EXTENSIONS. CREATIONS.
A LITTLE SISTERLY LOVE IS ALL YOU NEED, KIDSTER.
TSK! LOOK AT THIS. WE CAN NEVER MEET WITHOUT THE SUBJECT OF INSECTS REARING ITS UGLY HEAD!

BOND:
"This panel inspired the ad copy "Grab Your Cockroach." We gave out small rubber cockroaches to select retailers as part of a promotion."

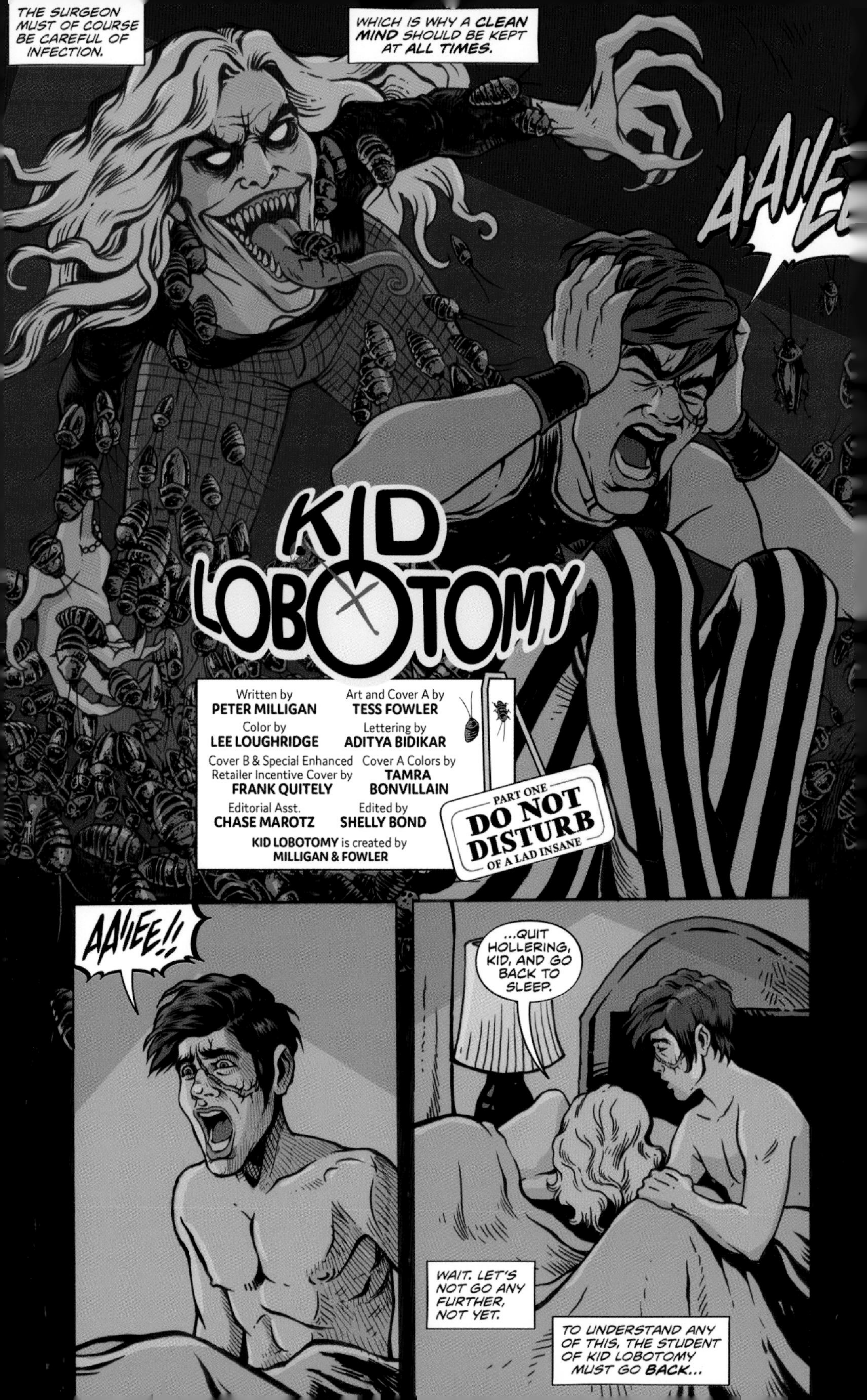

THE SURGEON MUST OF COURSE BE CAREFUL OF INFECTION.
WHICH IS WHY A CLEAN MIND SHOULD BE KEPT AT ALL TIMES.
AAIIEE
KID LOBOTOMY
Written by PETER MILLIGAN
Art and Cover A by TESS FOWLER
Color by LEE LOUGHRIDGE
Lettering by ADITYA BIDIKAR
Cover B & Special Enhanced Retailer Incentive Cover by FRANK QUITELY
Cover A Colors by TAMRA BONVILLAIN
Editorial Asst. CHASE MAROTZ
Edited by SHELLY BOND
KID LOBOTOMY is created by MILLIGAN & FOWLER
PART ONE
DO NOT DISTURB
OF A LAD INSANE
AAIIEE!!
...QUIT HOLLERING, KID, AND GO BACK TO SLEEP.
WAIT. LET'S NOT GO ANY FURTHER, NOT YET.
TO UNDERSTAND ANY OF THIS, THE STUDENT OF KID LOBOTOMY MUST GO BACK...

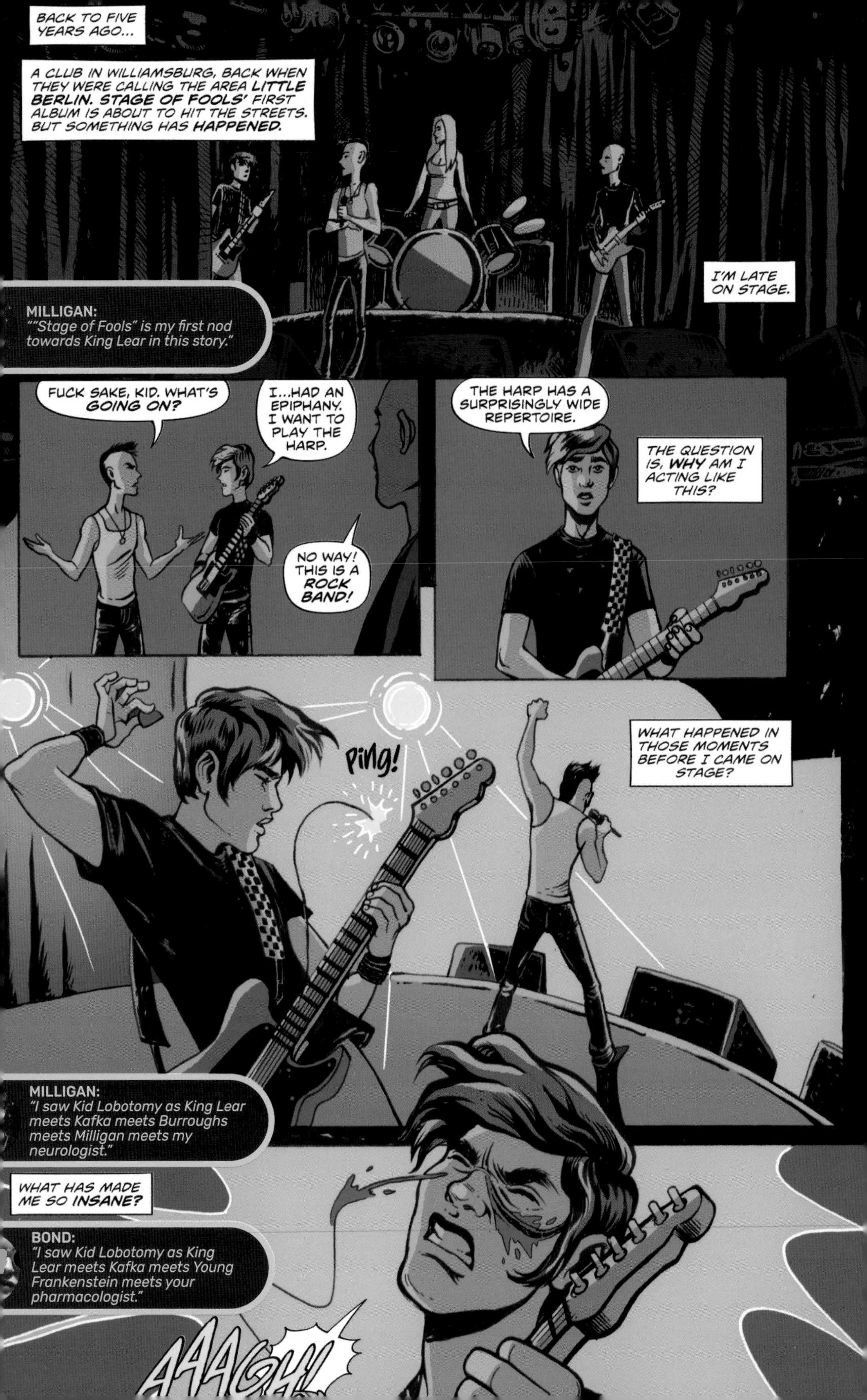
BACK TO FIVE YEARS AGO...
A CLUB IN WILLIAMSBURG, BACK WHEN THEY WERE CALLING THE AREA LITTLE BERLIN. STAGE OF FOOLS' FIRST ALBUM IS ABOUT TO HIT THE STREETS. BUT SOMETHING HAS HAPPENED.
I'M LATE ON STAGE.
MILLIGAN:
""Stage of Fools" is my first nod towards King Lear in this story."
FUCK SAKE, KID. WHAT'S GOING ON?
I...HAD AN EPIPHANY. I WANT TO PLAY THE HARP.
NO WAY! THIS IS A ROCK BAND!
THE HARP HAS A SURPRISINGLY WIDE REPERTOIRE.
THE QUESTION IS, WHY AM I ACTING LIKE THIS?
PING!
WHAT HAPPENED IN THOSE MOMENTS BEFORE I CAME ON STAGE?
MILLIGAN:
"I saw Kid Lobotomy as King Lear meets Kafka meets Burroughs meets Milligan meets my neurologist."
WHAT HAS MADE ME SO INSANE?
BOND:
"I saw Kid Lobotomy as King Lear meets Kafka meets Young Frankenstein meets your pharmacologist."
AAAGH!

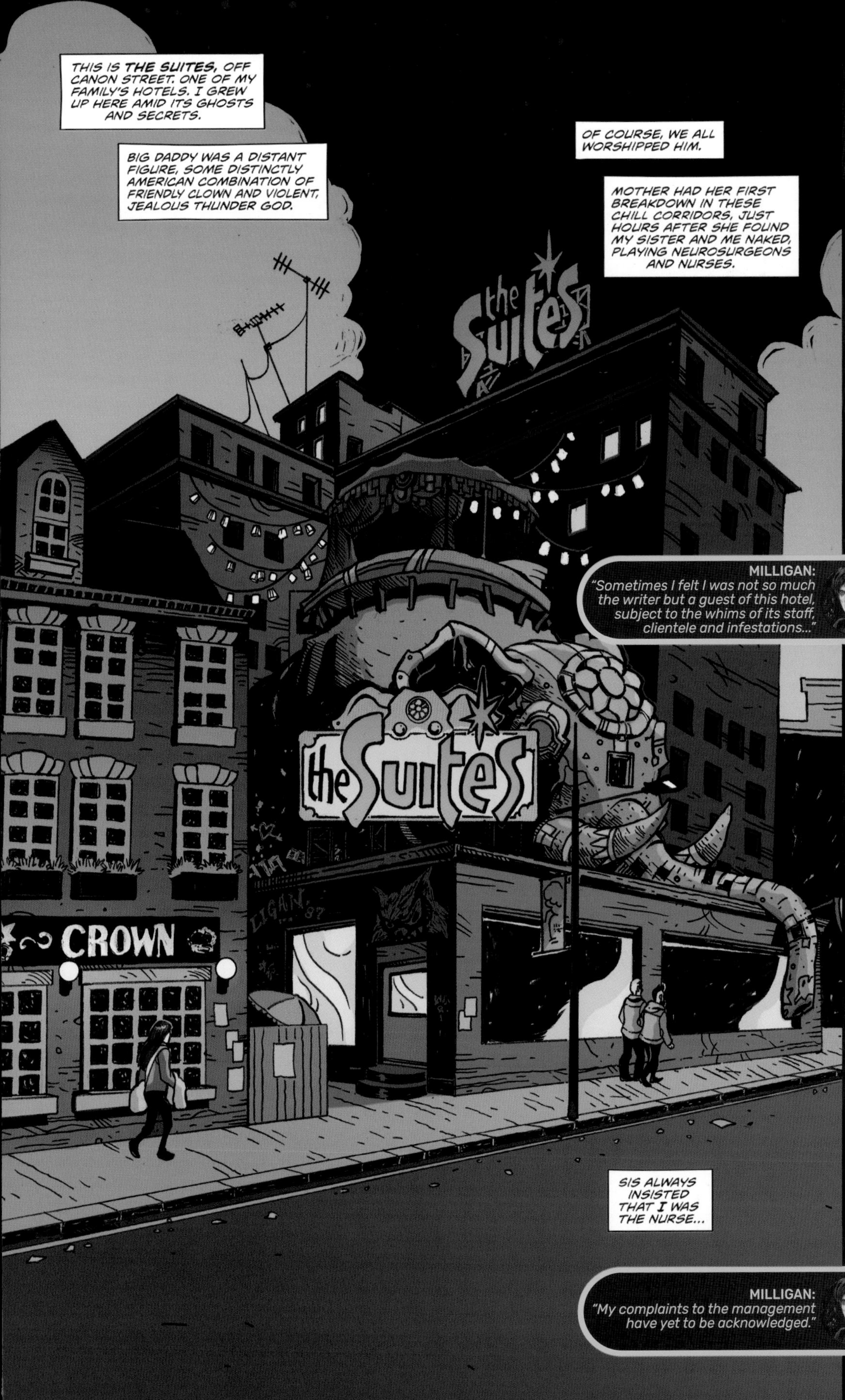

THIS IS **THE SUITES,** OFF CANON STREET. ONE OF MY FAMILY'S HOTELS. I GREW UP HERE AMID ITS GHOSTS AND SECRETS.
BIG DADDY WAS A DISTANT FIGURE, SOME DISTINCTLY AMERICAN COMBINATION OF FRIENDLY CLOWN AND VIOLENT, JEALOUS THUNDER GOD.
OF COURSE, WE ALL WORSHIPPED HIM.
MOTHER HAD HER FIRST BREAKDOWN IN THESE CHILL CORRIDORS, JUST HOURS AFTER SHE FOUND MY SISTER AND ME NAKED, PLAYING NEUROSURGEONS AND NURSES.
the Suites
MILLIGAN: "Sometimes I felt I was not so much the writer but a guest of this hotel, subject to the whims of its staff, clientele and infestations..."
the Suites
CROWN
SIS ALWAYS INSISTED THAT *I* WAS THE NURSE...
MILLIGAN: "My complaints to the management have yet to be acknowledged."

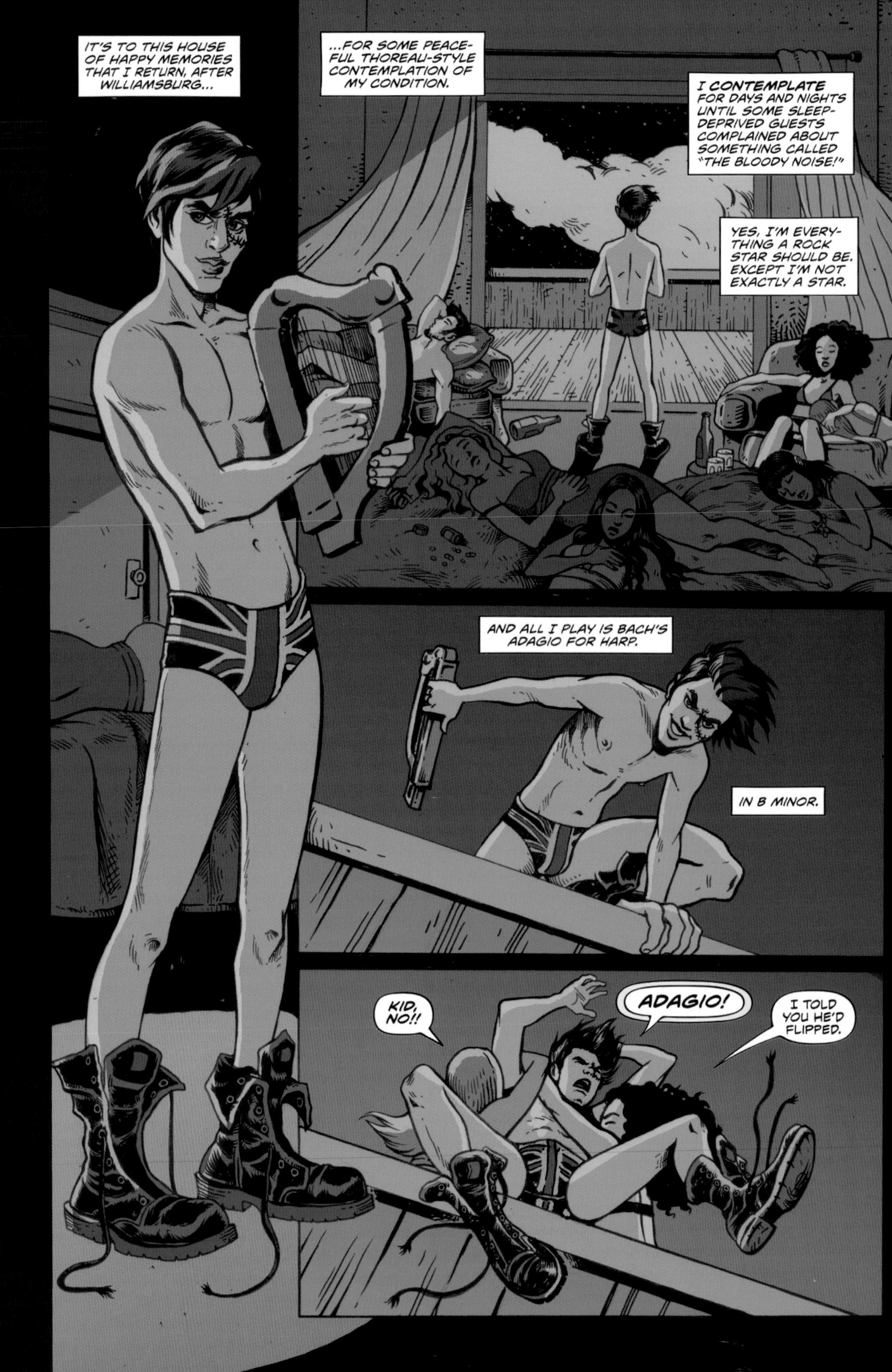
IT'S TO THIS HOUSE OF HAPPY MEMORIES THAT I RETURN, AFTER WILLIAMSBURG...
...FOR SOME PEACEFUL THOREAU-STYLE CONTEMPLATION OF MY CONDITION.
I CONTEMPLATE FOR DAYS AND NIGHTS UNTIL SOME SLEEP-DEPRIVED GUESTS COMPLAINED ABOUT SOMETHING CALLED "THE BLOODY NOISE!"
YES, I'M EVERYTHING A ROCK STAR SHOULD BE. EXCEPT I'M NOT EXACTLY A STAR.
AND ALL I PLAY IS BACH'S ADAGIO FOR HARP.
IN B MINOR.
KID, NO!!
ADAGIO!
I TOLD YOU HE'D FLIPPED.

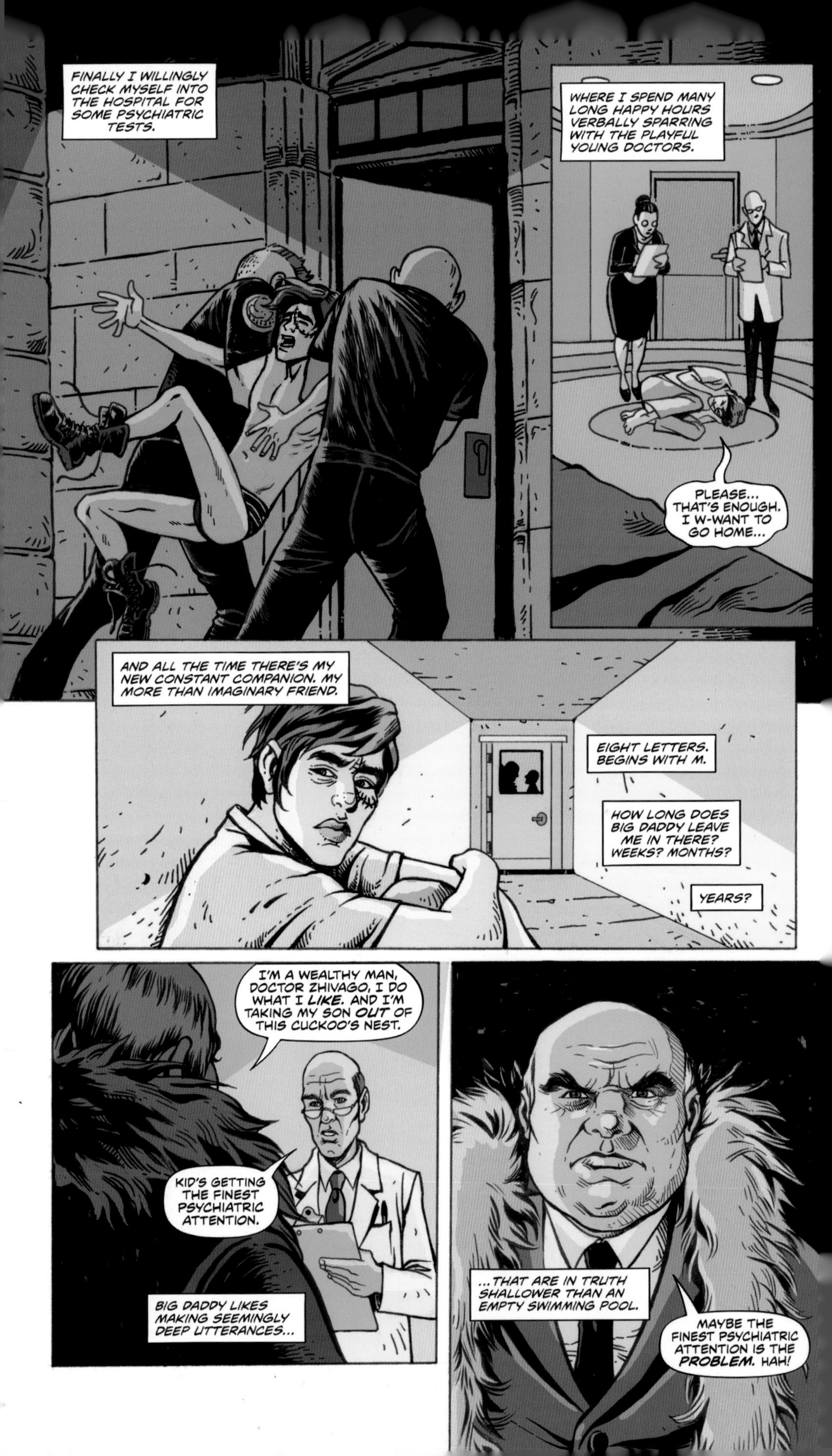
FINALLY I WILLINGLY CHECK MYSELF INTO THE HOSPITAL FOR SOME PSYCHIATRIC TESTS.
WHERE I SPEND MANY LONG HAPPY HOURS VERBALLY SPARRING WITH THE PLAYFUL YOUNG DOCTORS.
PLEASE... THAT'S ENOUGH. I W-WANT TO GO HOME...
AND ALL THE TIME THERE'S MY NEW CONSTANT COMPANION. MY MORE THAN IMAGINARY FRIEND.
EIGHT LETTERS. BEGINS WITH M.
HOW LONG DOES BIG DADDY LEAVE ME IN THERE? WEEKS? MONTHS?
YEARS?
I'M A WEALTHY MAN, DOCTOR ZHIVAGO, I DO WHAT I LIKE. AND I'M TAKING MY SON OUT OF THIS CUCKOO'S NEST.
KID'S GETTING THE FINEST PSYCHIATRIC ATTENTION.
BIG DADDY LIKES MAKING SEEMINGLY DEEP UTTERANCES...
...THAT ARE IN TRUTH SHALLOWER THAN AN EMPTY SWIMMING POOL.
MAYBE THE FINEST PSYCHIATRIC ATTENTION IS THE PROBLEM. HAH!

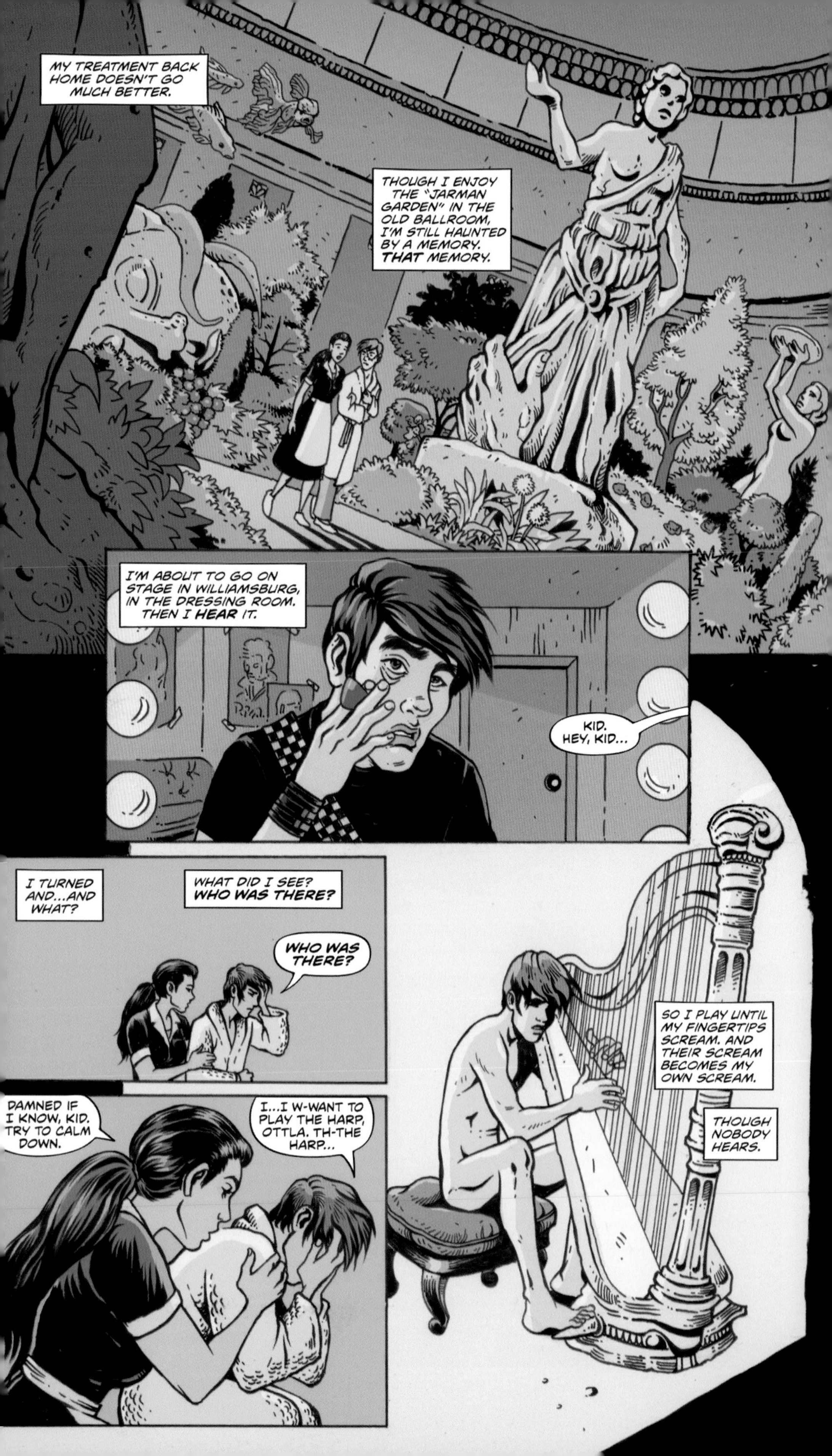
MY TREATMENT BACK HOME DOESN'T GO MUCH BETTER.
THOUGH I ENJOY THE "JARMAN GARDEN" IN THE OLD BALLROOM, I'M STILL HAUNTED BY A MEMORY. THAT MEMORY.
I'M ABOUT TO GO ON STAGE IN WILLIAMSBURG, IN THE DRESSING ROOM. THEN I HEAR IT.
KID. HEY, KID...
I TURNED AND...AND WHAT?
WHAT DID I SEE? WHO WAS THERE?
WHO WAS THERE?
DAMNED IF I KNOW, KID. TRY TO CALM DOWN.
I...I W-WANT TO PLAY THE HARP, OTTLA. TH-THE HARP...
SO I PLAY UNTIL MY FINGERTIPS SCREAM. AND THEIR SCREAM BECOMES MY OWN SCREAM.
THOUGH NOBODY HEARS.

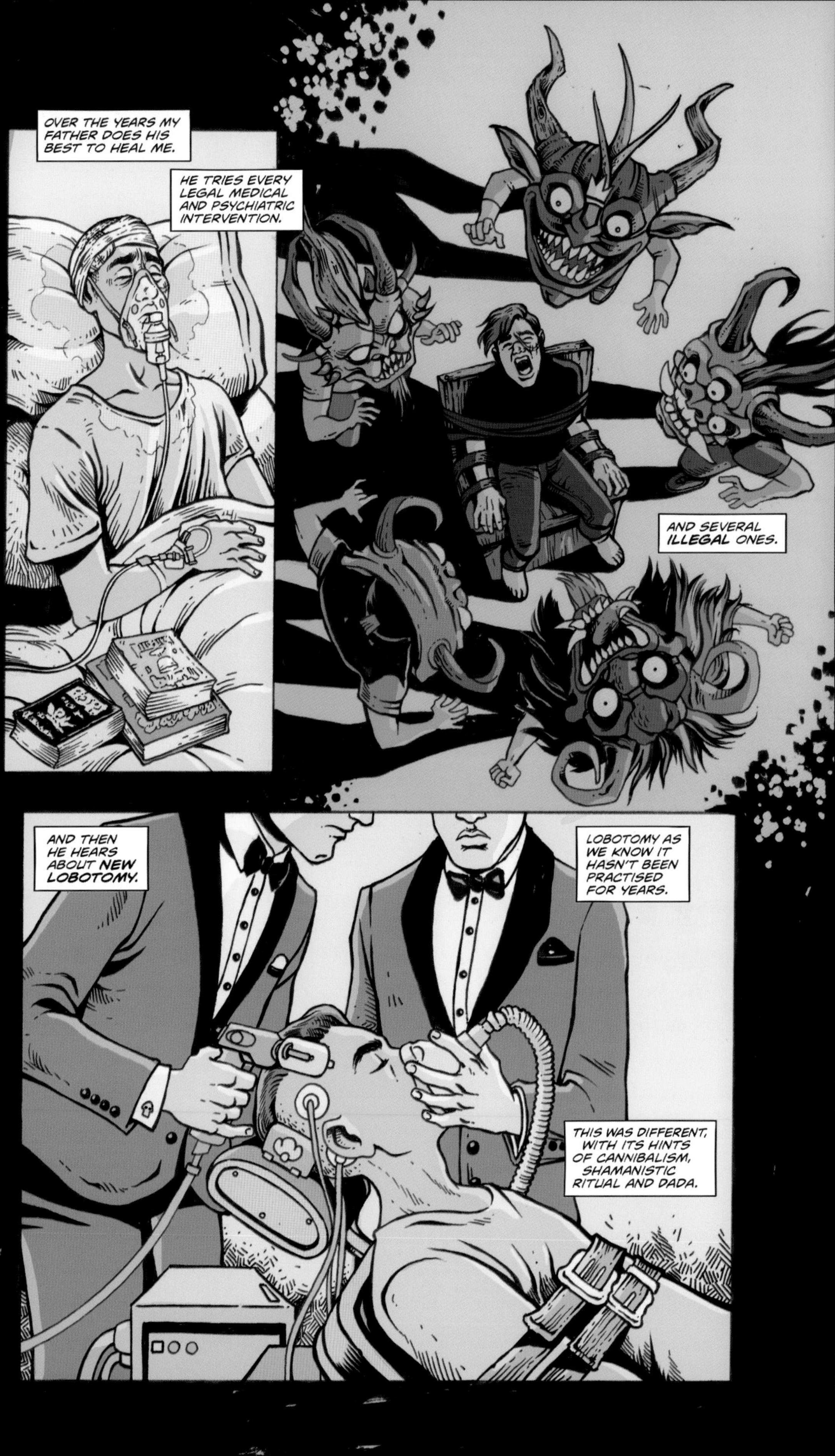
OVER THE YEARS MY FATHER DOES HIS BEST TO HEAL ME.
HE TRIES EVERY LEGAL MEDICAL AND PSYCHIATRIC INTERVENTION.
AND SEVERAL ILLEGAL ONES.
AND THEN HE HEARS ABOUT NEW LOBOTOMY.
LOBOTOMY AS WE KNOW IT HASN'T BEEN PRACTISED FOR YEARS.
THIS WAS DIFFERENT, WITH ITS HINTS OF CANNIBALISM, SHAMANISTIC RITUAL AND DADA.

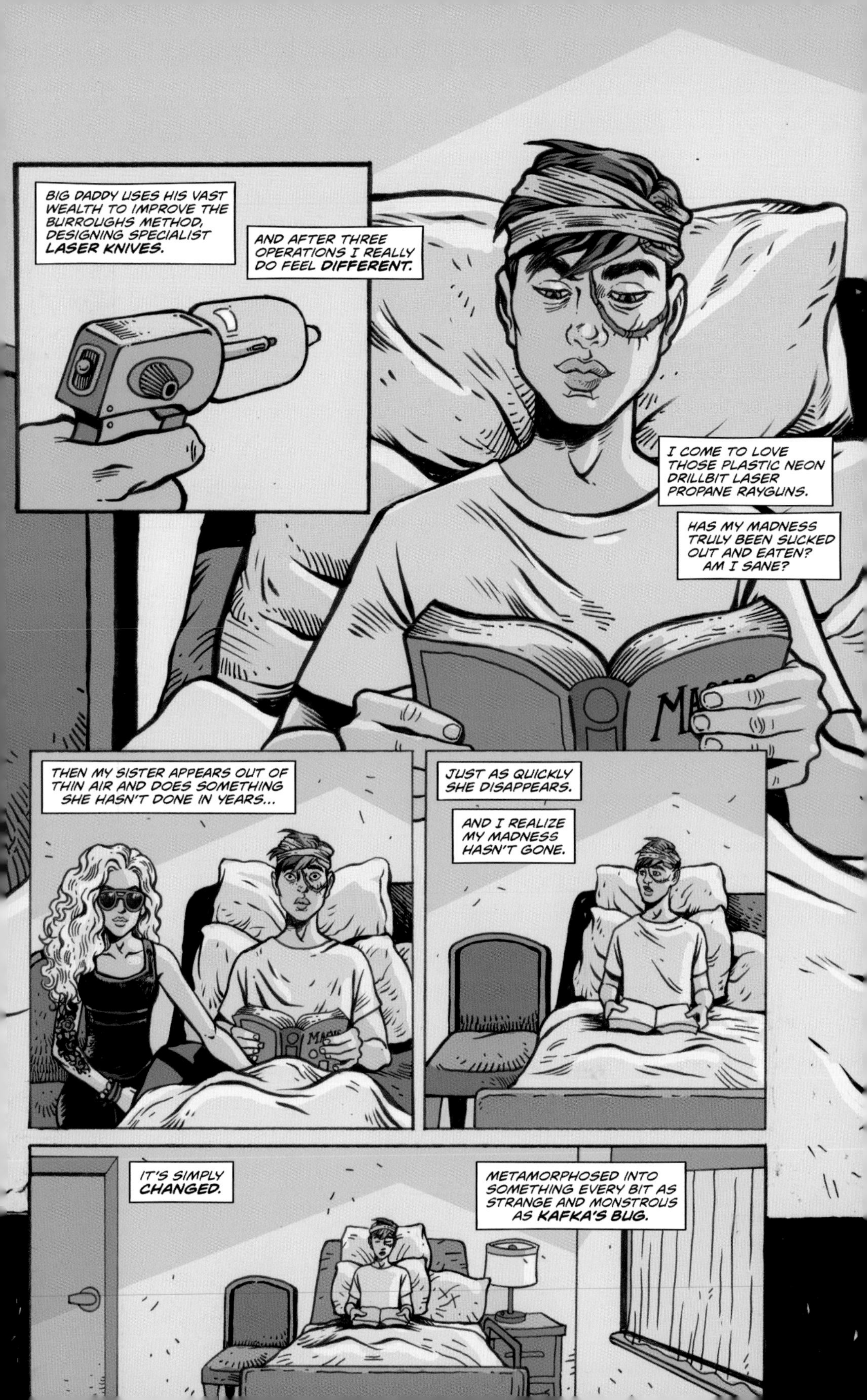

BIG DADDY USES HIS VAST WEALTH TO IMPROVE THE BURROUGHS METHOD, DESIGNING SPECIALIST **LASER KNIVES.**
AND AFTER THREE OPERATIONS I REALLY DO FEEL **DIFFERENT.**
I COME TO LOVE THOSE PLASTIC NEON DRILLBIT LASER PROPANE RAYGUNS.
HAS MY MADNESS TRULY BEEN SUCKED OUT AND EATEN? AM I SANE?
THEN MY SISTER APPEARS OUT OF THIN AIR AND DOES SOMETHING SHE HASN'T DONE IN YEARS...
JUST AS QUICKLY SHE DISAPPEARS.
AND I REALIZE MY MADNESS HASN'T GONE.
IT'S SIMPLY **CHANGED.**
METAMORPHOSED INTO SOMETHING EVERY BIT AS STRANGE AND MONSTROUS AS **KAFKA'S BUG.**

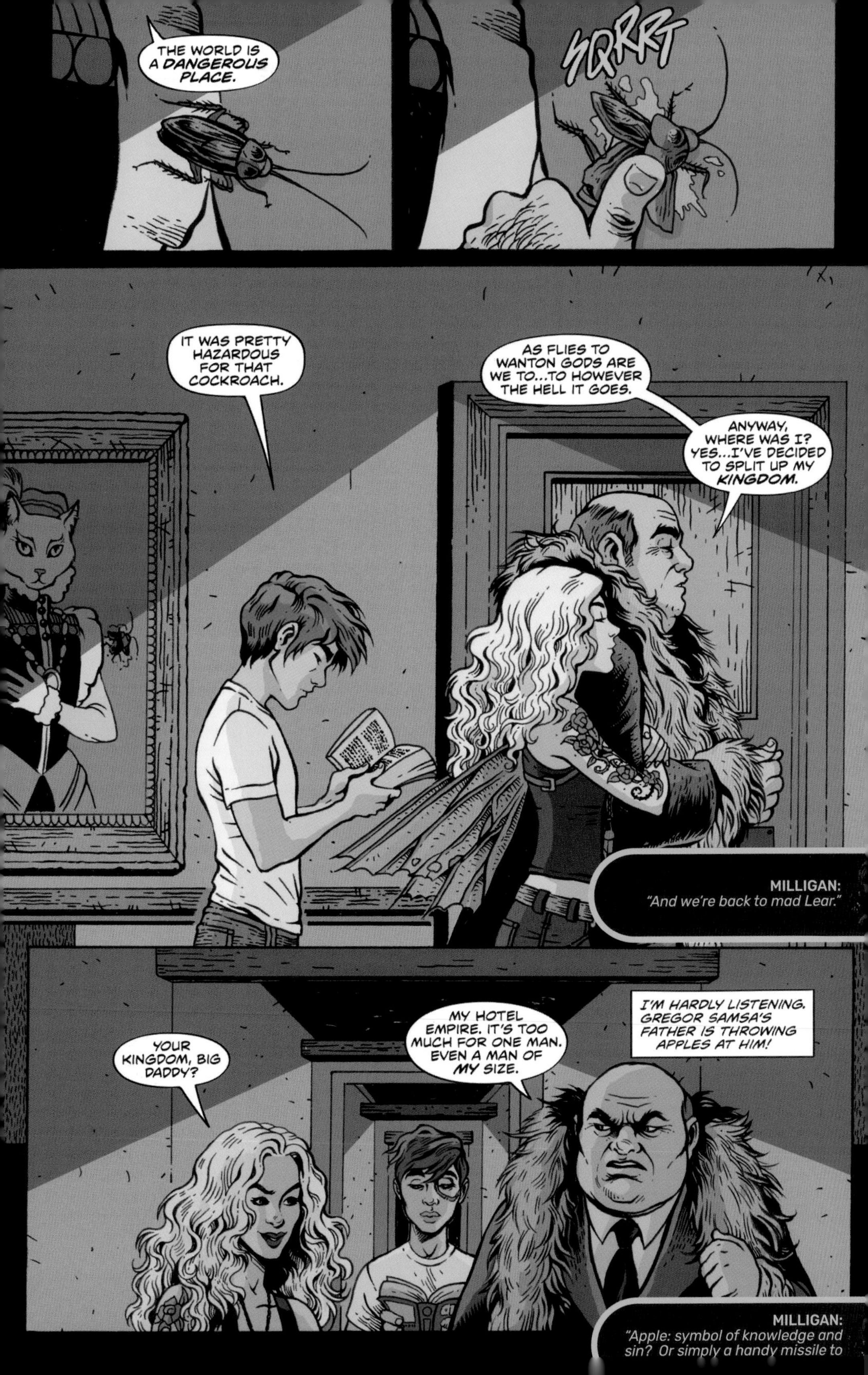
THE WORLD IS A DANGEROUS PLACE.
SQRRT
IT WAS PRETTY HAZARDOUS FOR THAT COCKROACH.
AS FLIES TO WANTON GODS ARE WE TO...TO HOWEVER THE HELL IT GOES.
ANYWAY, WHERE WAS I? YES...I'VE DECIDED TO SPLIT UP MY KINGDOM.
YOUR KINGDOM, BIG DADDY?
MY HOTEL EMPIRE. IT'S TOO MUCH FOR ONE MAN. EVEN A MAN OF MY SIZE.
I'M HARDLY LISTENING. GREGOR SAMSA'S FATHER IS THROWING APPLES AT HIM!

MILLIGAN:
"And we're back to mad Lear."

MILLIGAN:
"Apple: symbol of knowledge and sin? Or simply a handy missile to

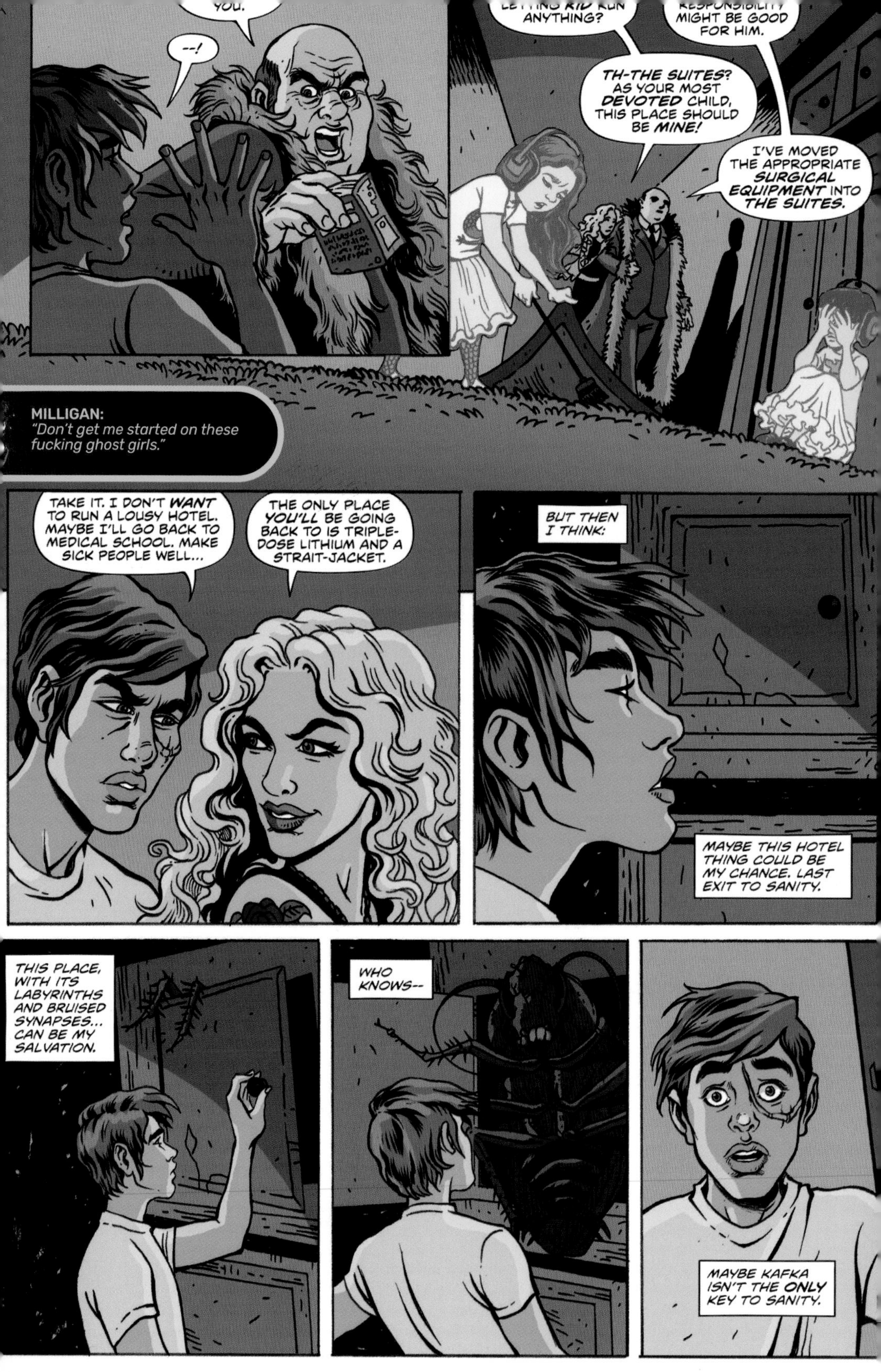
YOU.
--!
ANYTHING?
MIGHT BE GOOD FOR HIM.
TH-THE SUITES? AS YOUR MOST DEVOTED CHILD, THIS PLACE SHOULD BE MINE!
I'VE MOVED THE APPROPRIATE SURGICAL EQUIPMENT INTO THE SUITES.
TAKE IT. I DON'T WANT TO RUN A LOUSY HOTEL. MAYBE I'LL GO BACK TO MEDICAL SCHOOL. MAKE SICK PEOPLE WELL...
THE ONLY PLACE YOU'LL BE GOING BACK TO IS TRIPLE-DOSE LITHIUM AND A STRAIT-JACKET.
BUT THEN I THINK:
MAYBE THIS HOTEL THING COULD BE MY CHANCE. LAST EXIT TO SANITY.
THIS PLACE, WITH ITS LABYRINTHS AND BRUISED SYNAPSES... CAN BE MY SALVATION.
WHO KNOWS--
MAYBE KAFKA ISN'T THE ONLY KEY TO SANITY.

MILLIGAN:
"Don't get me started on these fucking ghost girls."

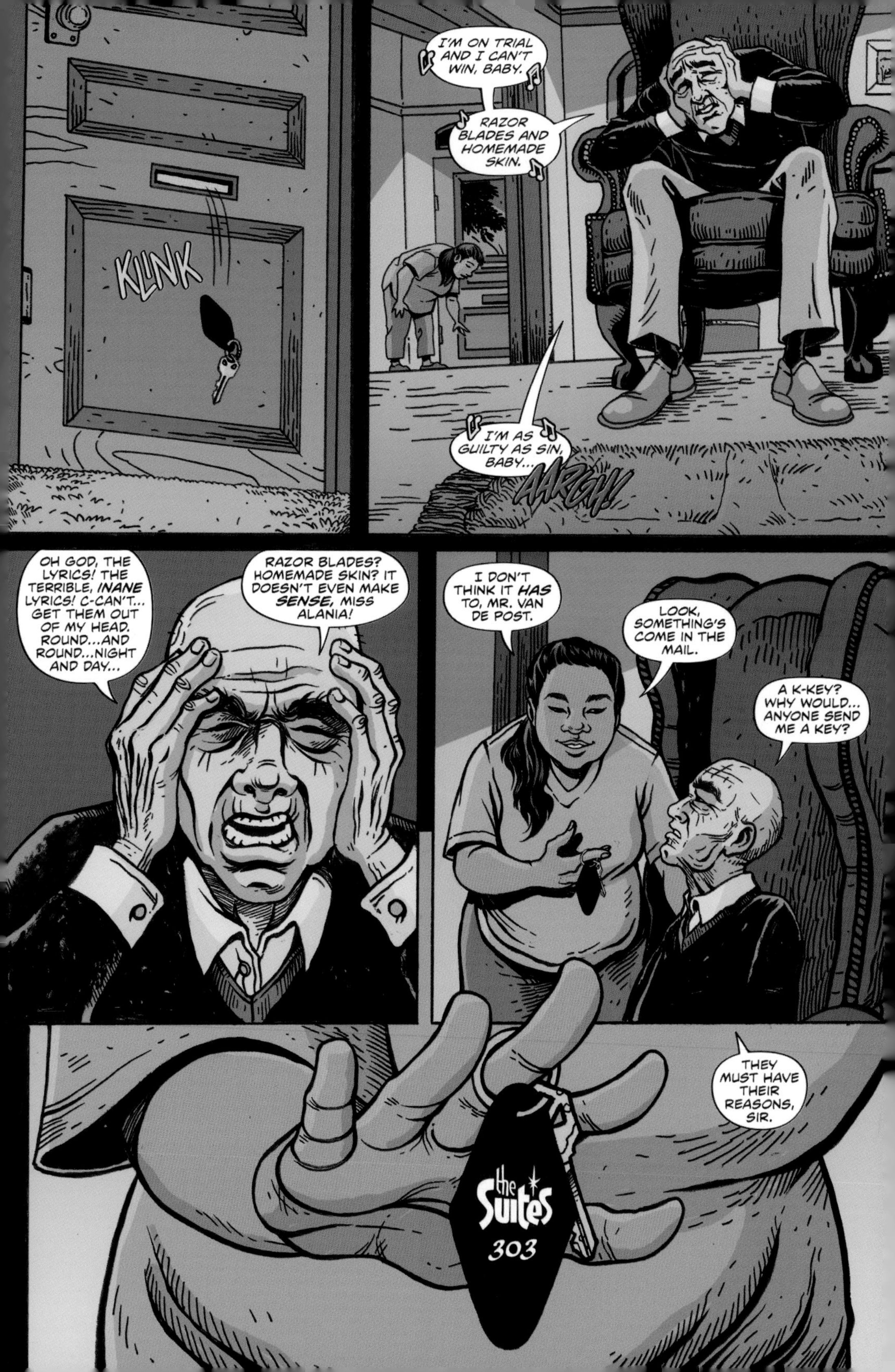
KLINK
I'M ON TRIAL AND I CAN'T WIN, BABY.
RAZOR BLADES AND HOMEMADE SKIN.
I'M AS GUILTY AS SIN, BABY...
AARGH!
OH GOD, THE LYRICS! THE TERRIBLE, INANE LYRICS! C-CAN'T... GET THEM OUT OF MY HEAD. ROUND...AND ROUND...NIGHT AND DAY...
RAZOR BLADES? HOMEMADE SKIN? IT DOESN'T EVEN MAKE SENSE, MISS ALANIA!
I DON'T THINK IT HAS TO, MR. VAN DE POST.
LOOK, SOMETHING'S COME IN THE MAIL.
A K-KEY? WHY WOULD... ANYONE SEND ME A KEY?
THEY MUST HAVE THEIR REASONS, SIR.
the Suites
303

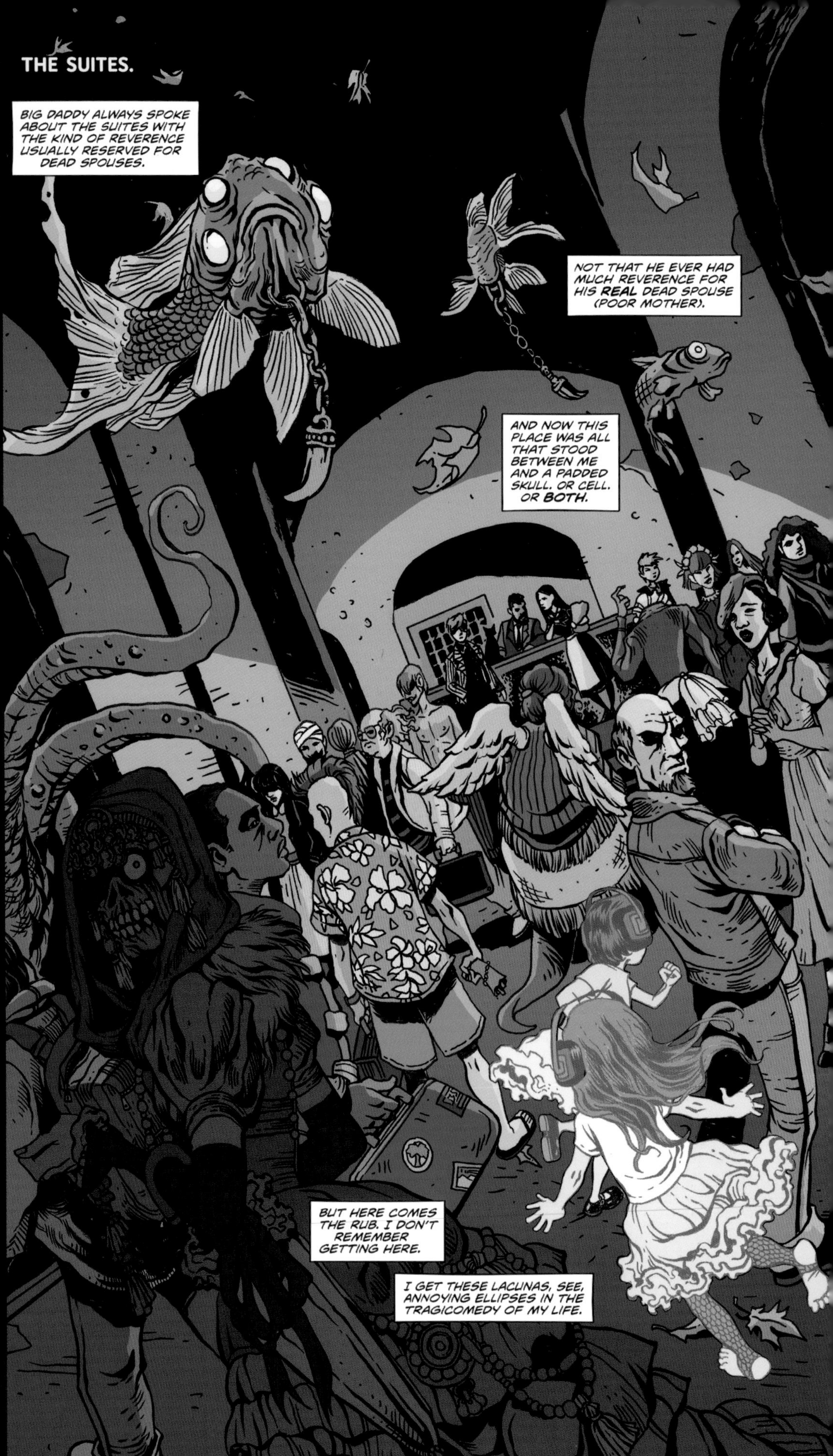
THE SUITES.
BIG DADDY ALWAYS SPOKE ABOUT THE SUITES WITH THE KIND OF REVERENCE USUALLY RESERVED FOR DEAD SPOUSES.
NOT THAT HE EVER HAD MUCH REVERENCE FOR HIS REAL DEAD SPOUSE (POOR MOTHER).
AND NOW THIS PLACE WAS ALL THAT STOOD BETWEEN ME AND A PADDED SKULL. OR CELL. OR BOTH.
BUT HERE COMES THE RUB. I DON'T REMEMBER GETTING HERE.
I GET THESE LACUNAS, SEE, ANNOYING ELLIPSES IN THE TRAGICOMEDY OF MY LIFE.

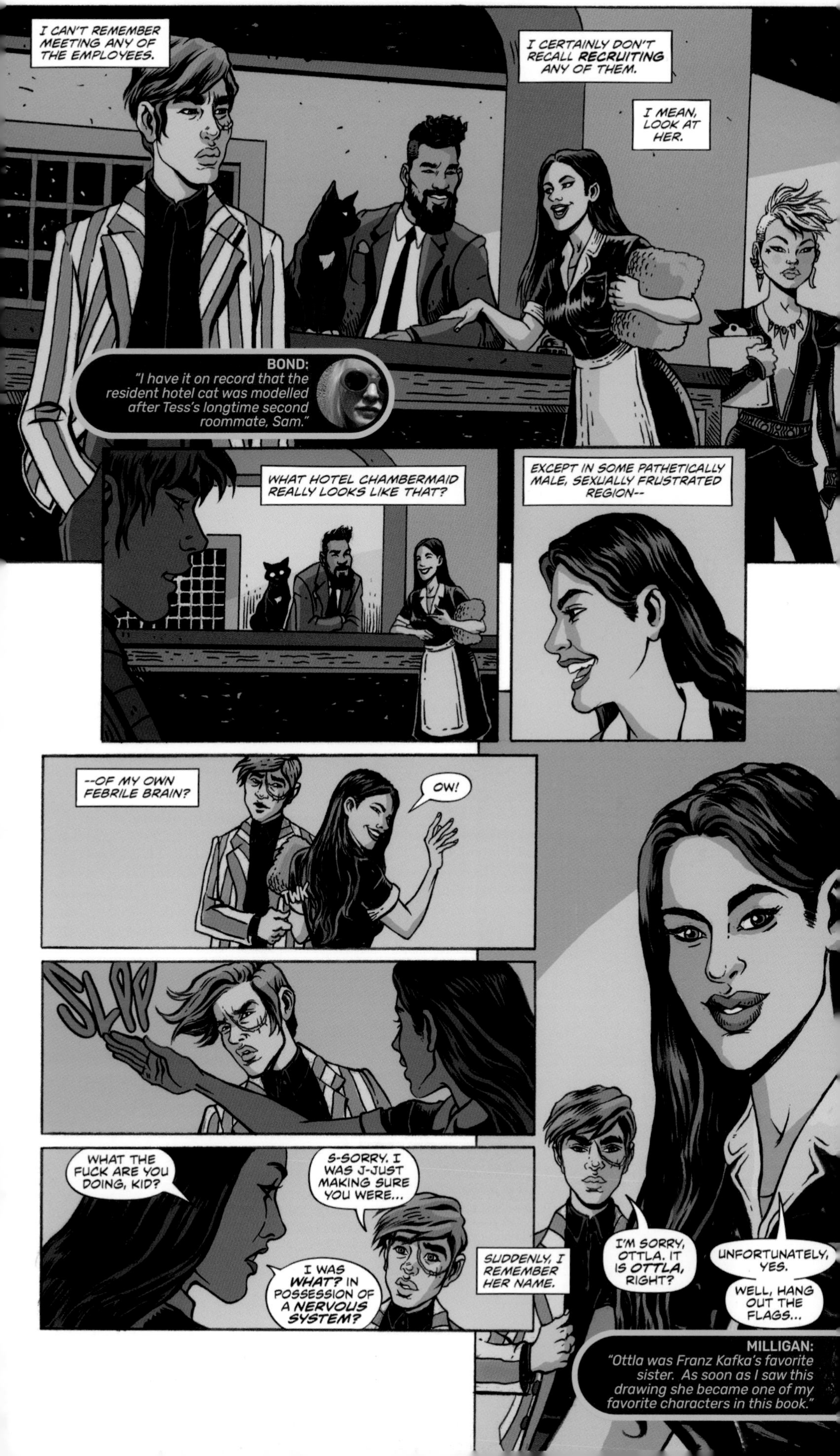
I CAN'T REMEMBER MEETING ANY OF THE EMPLOYEES.
I CERTAINLY DON'T RECALL **RECRUITING** ANY OF THEM.
I MEAN, LOOK AT HER.
BOND:
"I have it on record that the resident hotel cat was modelled after Tess's longtime second roommate, Sam."
WHAT HOTEL CHAMBERMAID REALLY LOOKS LIKE THAT?
EXCEPT IN SOME PATHETICALLY MALE, SEXUALLY FRUSTRATED REGION--
--OF MY OWN FEBRILE BRAIN?
OW!
TWK
SLAP
WHAT THE FUCK ARE YOU DOING, KID?
S-SORRY. I WAS J-JUST MAKING SURE YOU WERE...
I WAS **WHAT?** IN POSSESSION OF A **NERVOUS SYSTEM?**
SUDDENLY, I REMEMBER HER NAME.
I'M SORRY, OTTLA. IT IS **OTTLA**, RIGHT?
UNFORTUNATELY, YES.
WELL, HANG OUT THE FLAGS...
MILLIGAN:
"Ottla was Franz Kafka's favorite sister. As soon as I saw this drawing she became one of my favorite characters in this book."

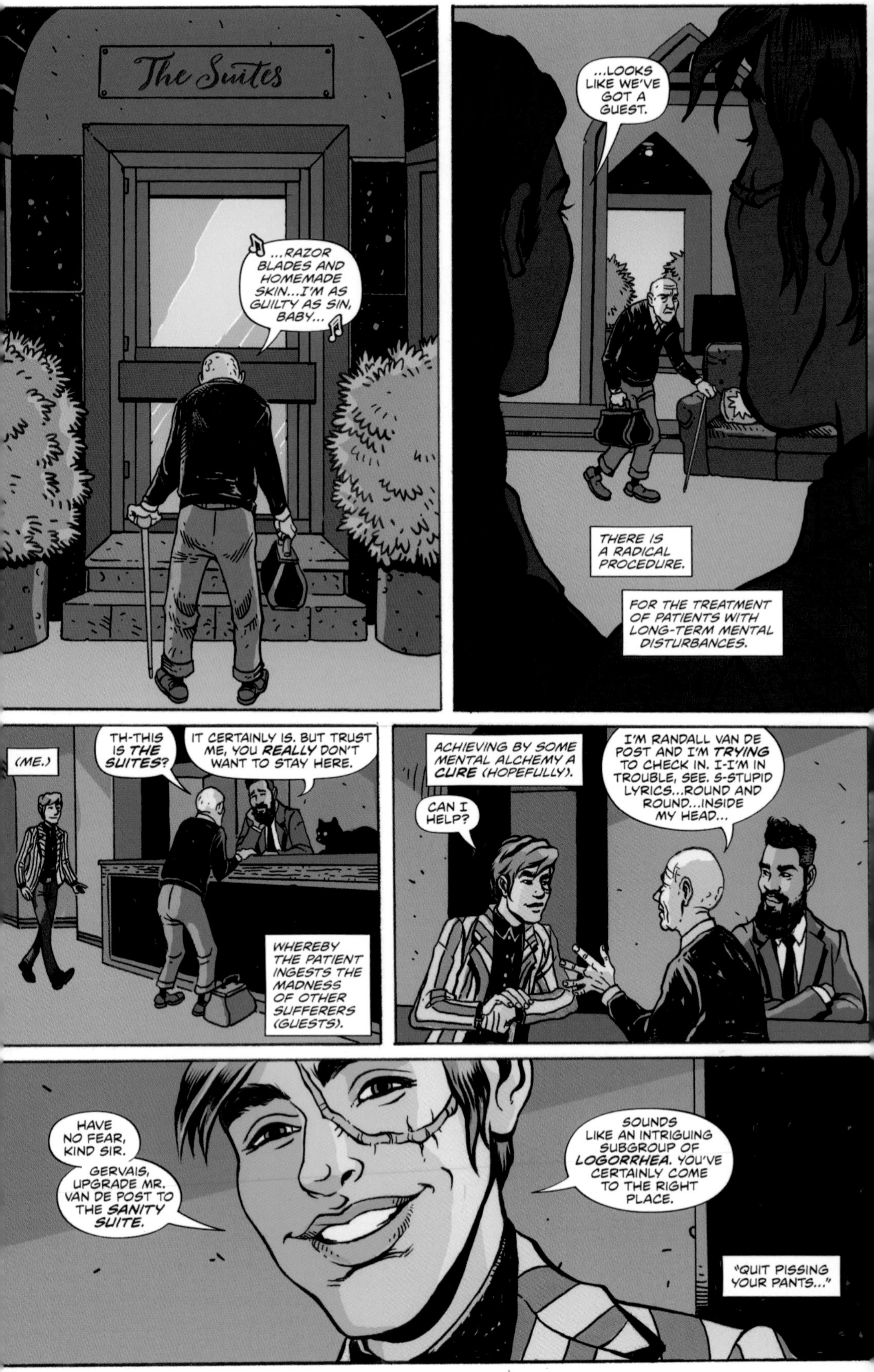
The Suites
...RAZOR BLADES AND HOMEMADE SKIN...I'M AS GUILTY AS SIN, BABY...
...LOOKS LIKE WE'VE GOT A GUEST.
THERE IS A RADICAL PROCEDURE.
FOR THE TREATMENT OF PATIENTS WITH LONG-TERM MENTAL DISTURBANCES.
(ME.)
TH-THIS IS THE SUITES?
IT CERTAINLY IS. BUT TRUST ME, YOU REALLY DON'T WANT TO STAY HERE.
WHEREBY THE PATIENT INGESTS THE MADNESS OF OTHER SUFFERERS (GUESTS).
ACHIEVING BY SOME MENTAL ALCHEMY A CURE (HOPEFULLY).
CAN I HELP?
I'M RANDALL VAN DE POST AND I'M TRYING TO CHECK IN. I-I'M IN TROUBLE, SEE. S-STUPID LYRICS...ROUND AND ROUND...INSIDE MY HEAD...
SOUNDS LIKE AN INTRIGUING SUBGROUP OF LOGORRHEA. YOU'VE CERTAINLY COME TO THE RIGHT PLACE.
HAVE NO FEAR, KIND SIR.
GERVAIS, UPGRADE MR. VAN DE POST TO THE SANITY SUITE.
"QUIT PISSING YOUR PANTS..."

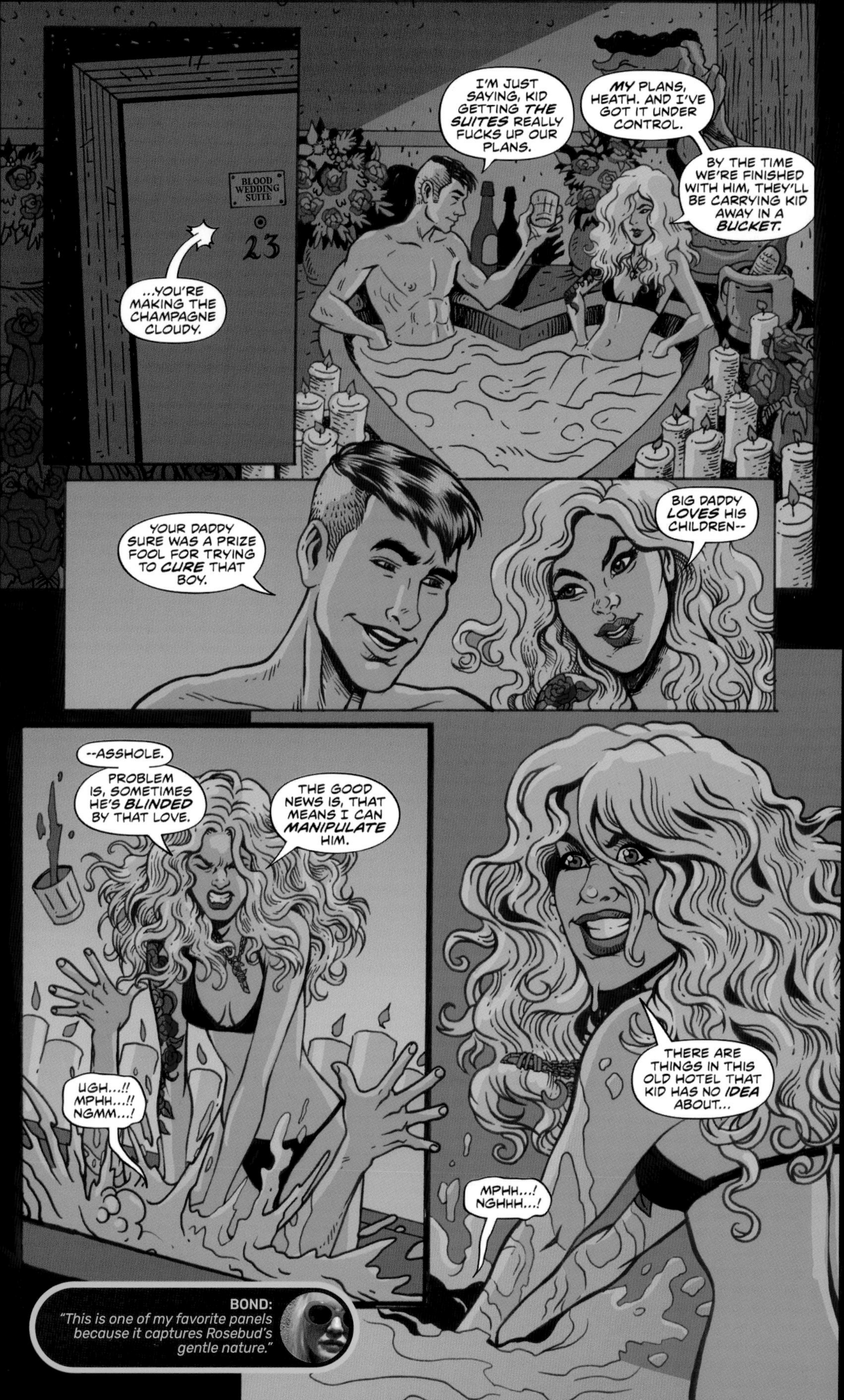
BLOOD WEDDING SUITE
23
...YOU'RE MAKING THE CHAMPAGNE CLOUDY.
I'M JUST SAYING, KID GETTING THE SUITES REALLY FUCKS UP OUR PLANS.
MY PLANS, HEATH. AND I'VE GOT IT UNDER CONTROL.
BY THE TIME WE'RE FINISHED WITH HIM, THEY'LL BE CARRYING KID AWAY IN A BUCKET.
YOUR DADDY SURE WAS A PRIZE FOOL FOR TRYING TO CURE THAT BOY.
BIG DADDY LOVES HIS CHILDREN--
--ASSHOLE.
PROBLEM IS, SOMETIMES HE'S BLINDED BY THAT LOVE.
THE GOOD NEWS IS, THAT MEANS I CAN MANIPULATE HIM.
UGH...!! MPHH...!! NGMM...!
THERE ARE THINGS IN THIS OLD HOTEL THAT KID HAS NO IDEA ABOUT...
MPHH...! NGHHH...!

BOND:
"This is one of my favorite panels because it captures Rosebud's gentle nature."

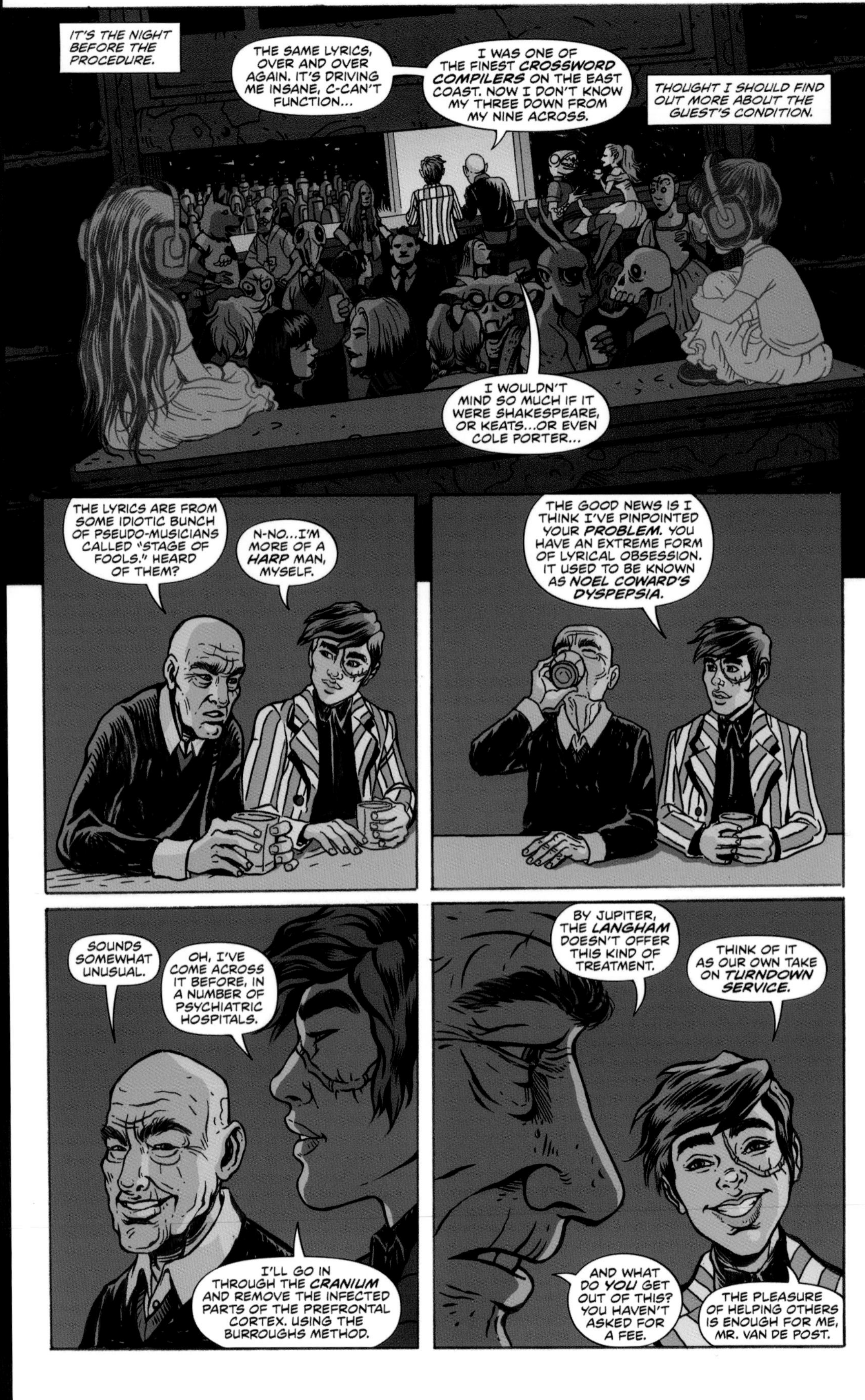
IT'S THE NIGHT BEFORE THE PROCEDURE.
THE SAME LYRICS, OVER AND OVER AGAIN. IT'S DRIVING ME INSANE, C-CAN'T FUNCTION...
I WAS ONE OF THE FINEST CROSSWORD COMPILERS ON THE EAST COAST. NOW I DON'T KNOW MY THREE DOWN FROM MY NINE ACROSS.
THOUGHT I SHOULD FIND OUT MORE ABOUT THE GUEST'S CONDITION.
I WOULDN'T MIND SO MUCH IF IT WERE SHAKESPEARE, OR KEATS...OR EVEN COLE PORTER...
THE LYRICS ARE FROM SOME IDIOTIC BUNCH OF PSEUDO-MUSICIANS CALLED "STAGE OF FOOLS." HEARD OF THEM?
N-NO...I'M MORE OF A HARP MAN, MYSELF.
THE GOOD NEWS IS I THINK I'VE PINPOINTED YOUR PROBLEM. YOU HAVE AN EXTREME FORM OF LYRICAL OBSESSION. IT USED TO BE KNOWN AS NOEL COWARD'S DYSPEPSIA.
SOUNDS SOMEWHAT UNUSUAL.
OH, I'VE COME ACROSS IT BEFORE, IN A NUMBER OF PSYCHIATRIC HOSPITALS.
I'LL GO IN THROUGH THE CRANIUM AND REMOVE THE INFECTED PARTS OF THE PREFRONTAL CORTEX. USING THE BURROUGHS METHOD.
BY JUPITER, THE LANGHAM DOESN'T OFFER THIS KIND OF TREATMENT.
THINK OF IT AS OUR OWN TAKE ON TURNDOWN SERVICE.
AND WHAT DO YOU GET OUT OF THIS? YOU HAVEN'T ASKED FOR A FEE.
THE PLEASURE OF HELPING OTHERS IS ENOUGH FOR ME, MR. VAN DE POST.

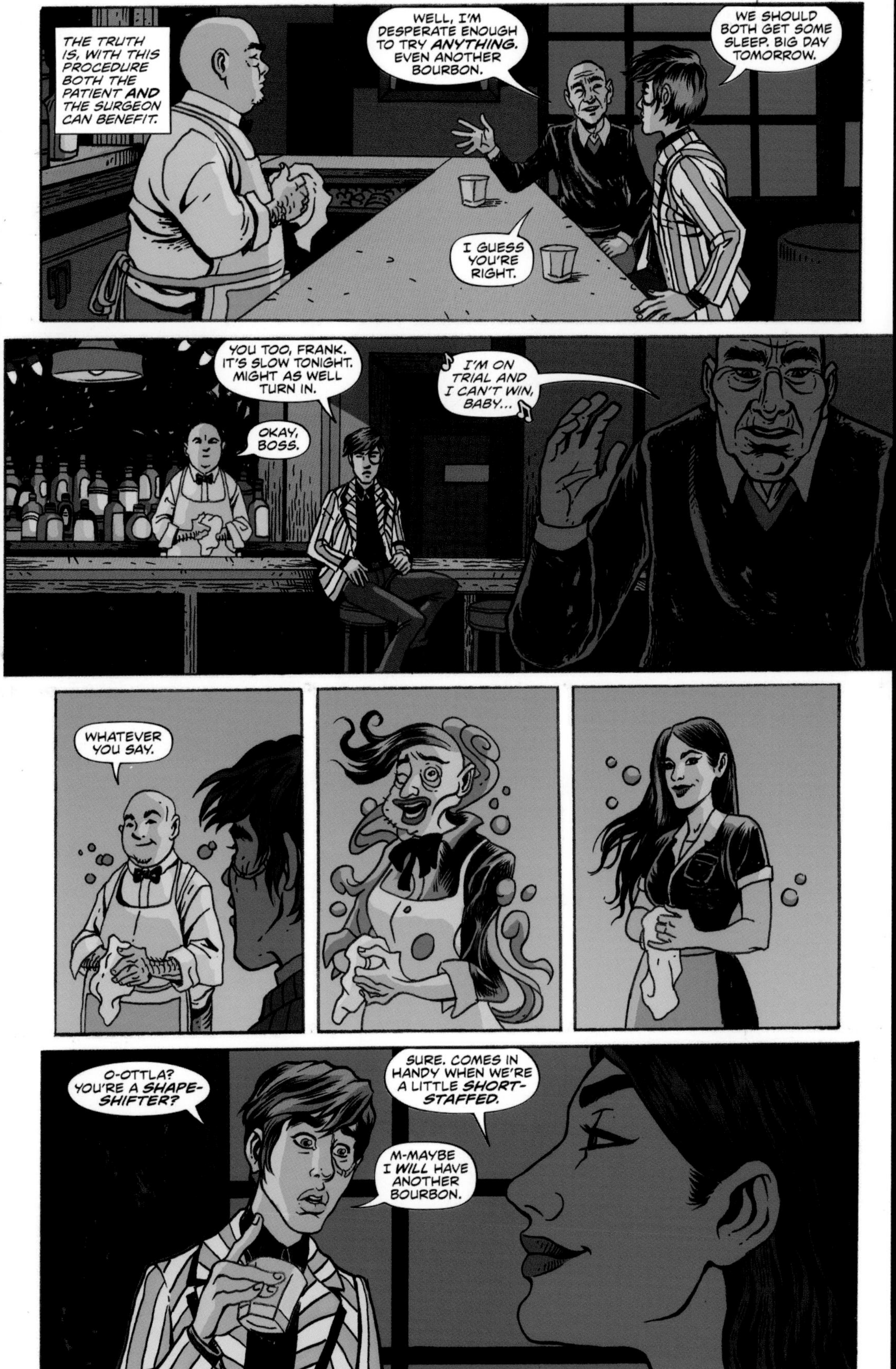
THE TRUTH IS, WITH THIS PROCEDURE BOTH THE PATIENT AND THE SURGEON CAN BENEFIT.
WELL, I'M DESPERATE ENOUGH TO TRY ANYTHING. EVEN ANOTHER BOURBON.
WE SHOULD BOTH GET SOME SLEEP. BIG DAY TOMORROW.
I GUESS YOU'RE RIGHT.
YOU TOO, FRANK. IT'S SLOW TONIGHT. MIGHT AS WELL TURN IN.
OKAY, BOSS.
I'M ON TRIAL AND I CAN'T WIN, BABY...
WHATEVER YOU SAY.
O-OTTLA? YOU'RE A SHAPE-SHIFTER?
SURE. COMES IN HANDY WHEN WE'RE A LITTLE SHORT-STAFFED.
M-MAYBE I WILL HAVE ANOTHER BOURBON.

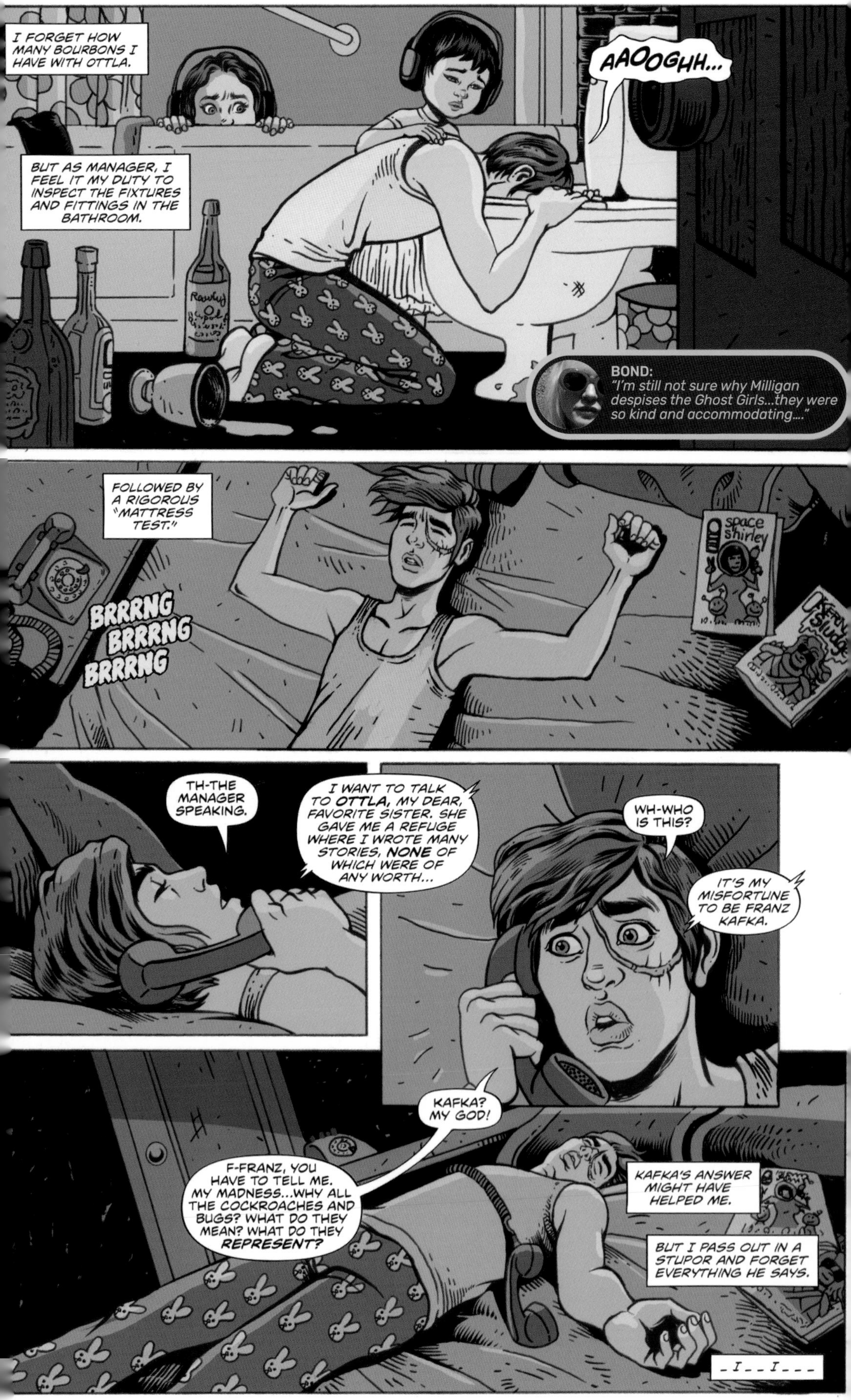
I FORGET HOW MANY BOURBONS I HAVE WITH OTTLA.
AAOOGHH...
BUT AS MANAGER, I FEEL IT MY DUTY TO INSPECT THE FIXTURES AND FITTINGS IN THE BATHROOM.
BOND:
"I'm still not sure why Milligan despises the Ghost Girls...they were so kind and accommodating...."
FOLLOWED BY A RIGOROUS "MATTRESS TEST."
BRRRNG BRRRNG BRRRNG
space shirley
TH-THE MANAGER SPEAKING.
I WANT TO TALK TO OTTLA, MY DEAR, FAVORITE SISTER. SHE GAVE ME A REFUGE WHERE I WROTE MANY STORIES, NONE OF WHICH WERE OF ANY WORTH...
WH-WHO IS THIS?
IT'S MY MISFORTUNE TO BE FRANZ KAFKA.
KAFKA? MY GOD!
F-FRANZ, YOU HAVE TO TELL ME. MY MADNESS...WHY ALL THE COCKROACHES AND BUGS? WHAT DO THEY MEAN? WHAT DO THEY REPRESENT?
KAFKA'S ANSWER MIGHT HAVE HELPED ME.
BUT I PASS OUT IN A STUPOR AND FORGET EVERYTHING HE SAYS.
_I_ _I_ _ _

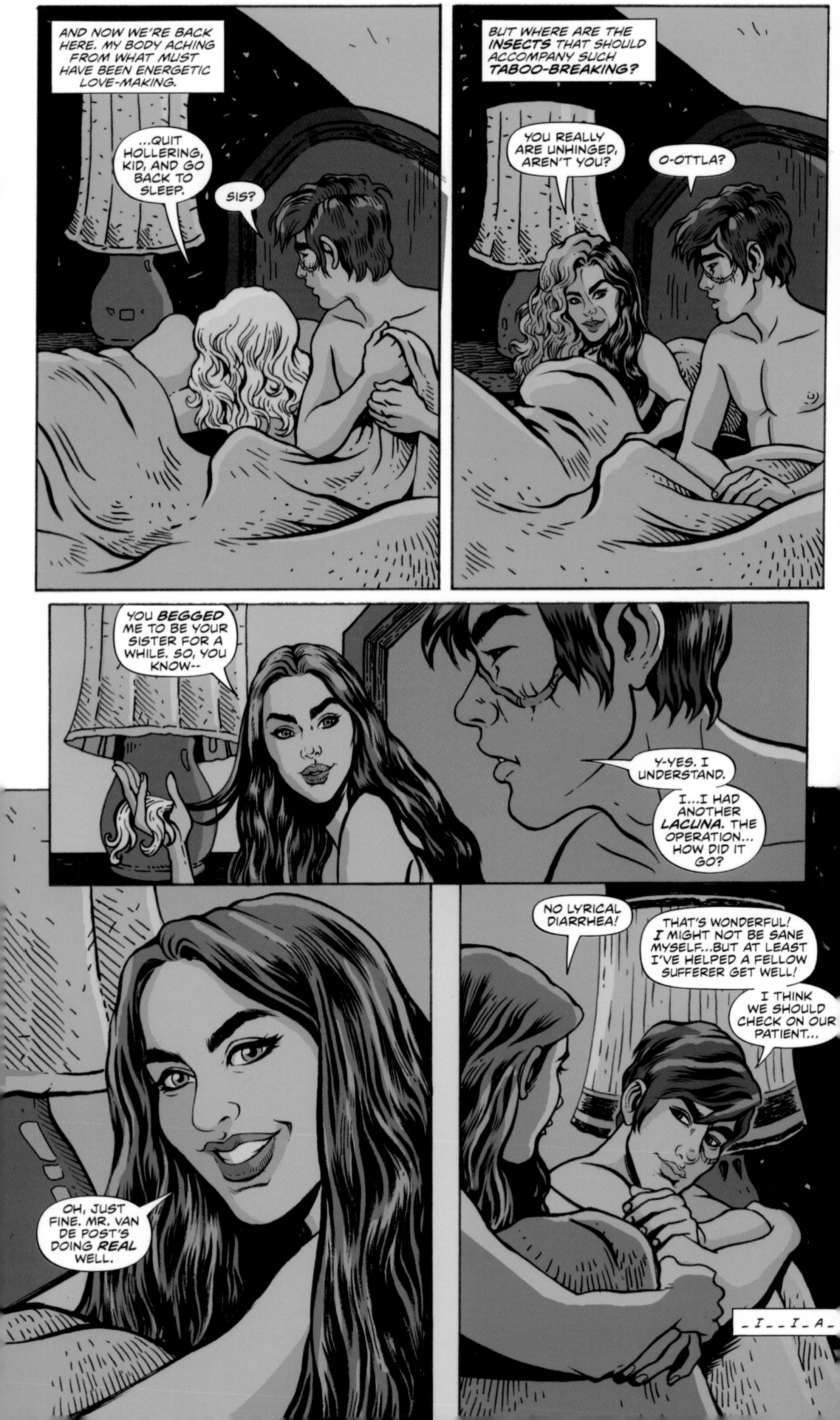
AND NOW WE'RE BACK HERE. MY BODY ACHING FROM WHAT MUST HAVE BEEN ENERGETIC LOVE-MAKING.
...QUIT HOLLERING, KID, AND GO BACK TO SLEEP.
SIS?
BUT WHERE ARE THE INSECTS THAT SHOULD ACCOMPANY SUCH TABOO-BREAKING?
YOU REALLY ARE UNHINGED, AREN'T YOU?
O-OTTLA?
YOU BEGGED ME TO BE YOUR SISTER FOR A WHILE. SO, YOU KNOW--
Y-YES. I UNDERSTAND.
I...I HAD ANOTHER LACUNA. THE OPERATION... HOW DID IT GO?
OH, JUST FINE. MR. VAN DE POST'S DOING REAL WELL.
NO LYRICAL DIARRHEA!
THAT'S WONDERFUL! I MIGHT NOT BE SANE MYSELF...BUT AT LEAST I'VE HELPED A FELLOW SUFFERER GET WELL!
I THINK WE SHOULD CHECK ON OUR PATIENT...
_ I _ _ I _ A _

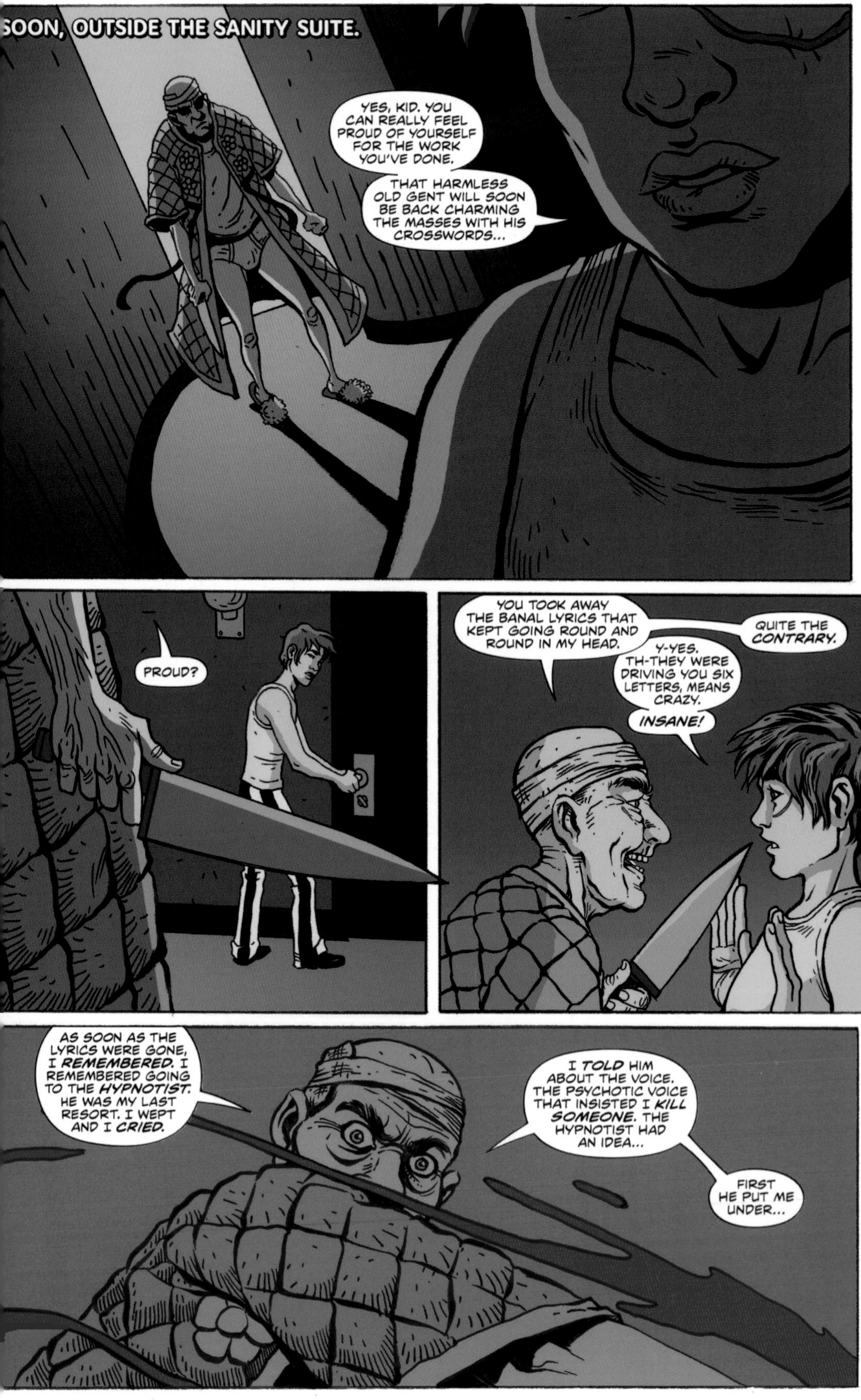
SOON, OUTSIDE THE SANITY SUITE.
YES, KID. YOU CAN REALLY FEEL PROUD OF YOURSELF FOR THE WORK YOU'VE DONE.
THAT HARMLESS OLD GENT WILL SOON BE BACK CHARMING THE MASSES WITH HIS CROSSWORDS...
PROUD?
YOU TOOK AWAY THE BANAL LYRICS THAT KEPT GOING ROUND AND ROUND IN MY HEAD.
QUITE THE *CONTRARY.*
Y-YES. TH-THEY WERE DRIVING YOU SIX LETTERS, MEANS CRAZY.
INSANE!
AS SOON AS THE LYRICS WERE GONE, I *REMEMBERED.* I REMEMBERED GOING TO THE *HYPNOTIST.* HE WAS MY LAST RESORT. I WEPT AND I *CRIED.*
I *TOLD* HIM ABOUT THE VOICE. THE PSYCHOTIC VOICE THAT INSISTED I *KILL SOMEONE.* THE HYPNOTIST HAD AN IDEA...
FIRST HE PUT ME UNDER...

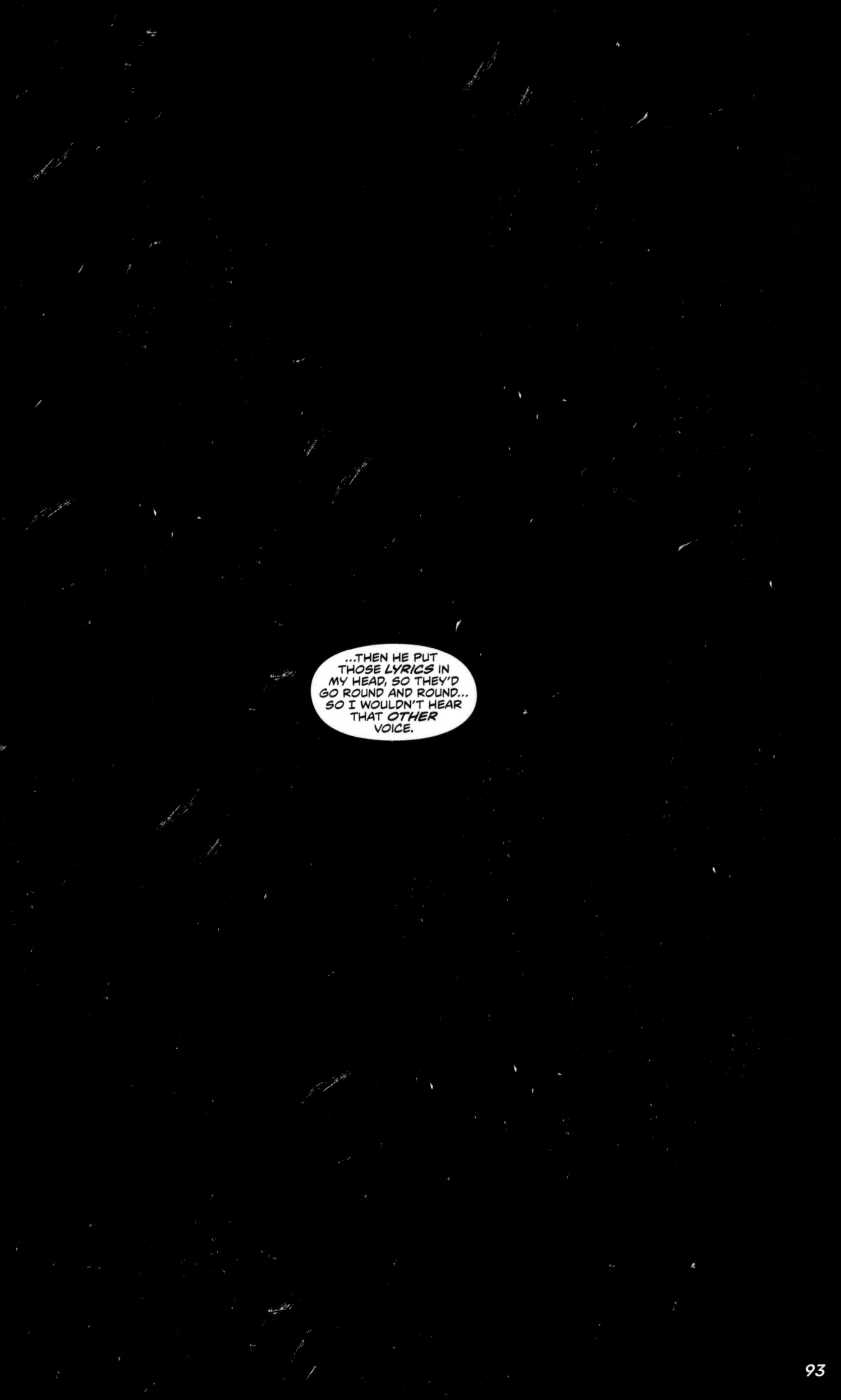
...THEN HE PUT THOSE *LYRICS* IN MY HEAD, SO THEY'D GO ROUND AND ROUND... SO I WOULDN'T HEAR THAT *OTHER* VOICE.

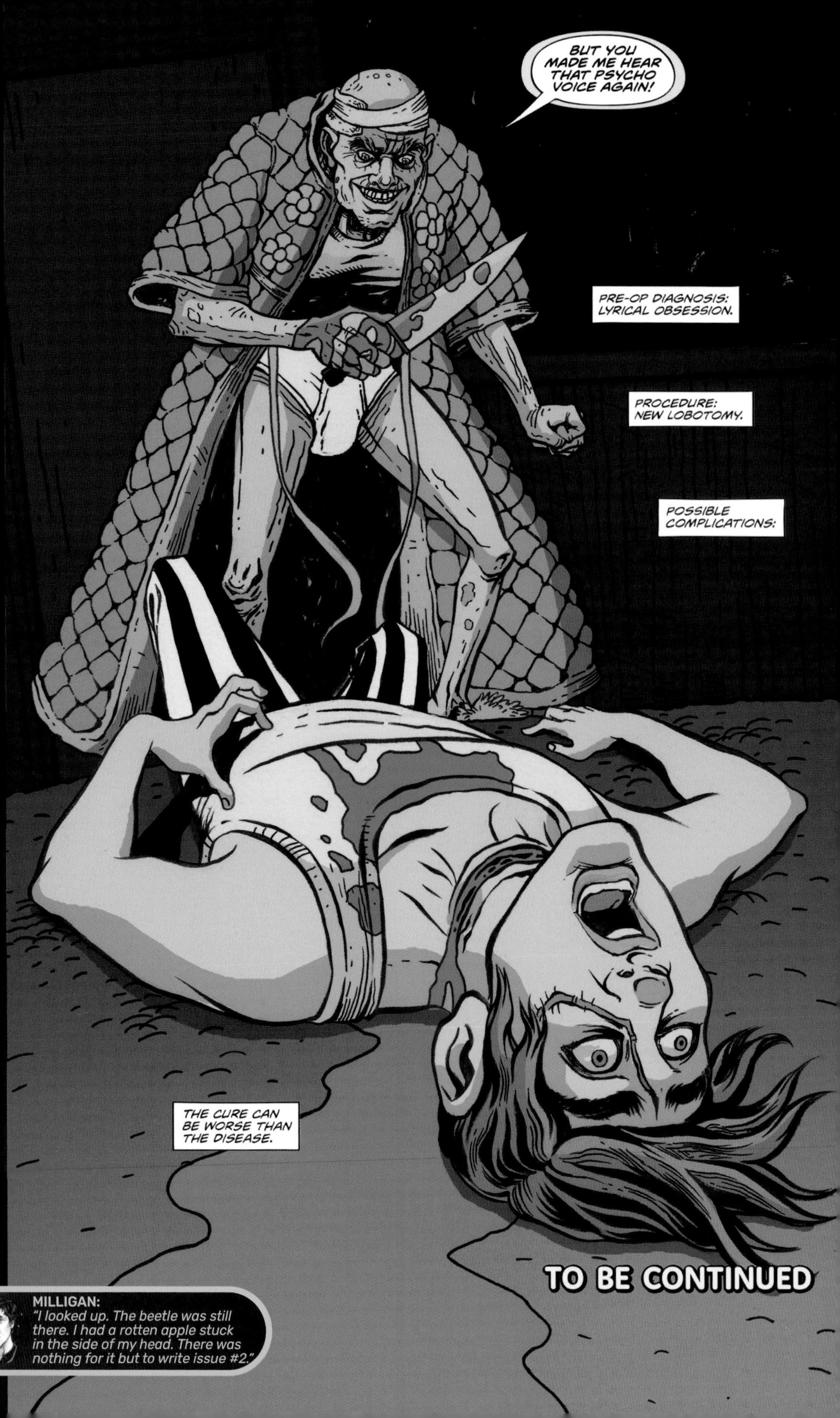
BUT YOU MADE ME HEAR THAT PSYCHO VOICE AGAIN!
PRE-OP DIAGNOSIS: LYRICAL OBSESSION.
PROCEDURE: NEW LOBOTOMY.
POSSIBLE COMPLICATIONS:
THE CURE CAN BE WORSE THAN THE DISEASE.
TO BE CONTINUED

MILLIGAN:
"I looked up. The beetle was still there. I had a rotten apple stuck in the side of my head. There was nothing for it but to write issue #2."

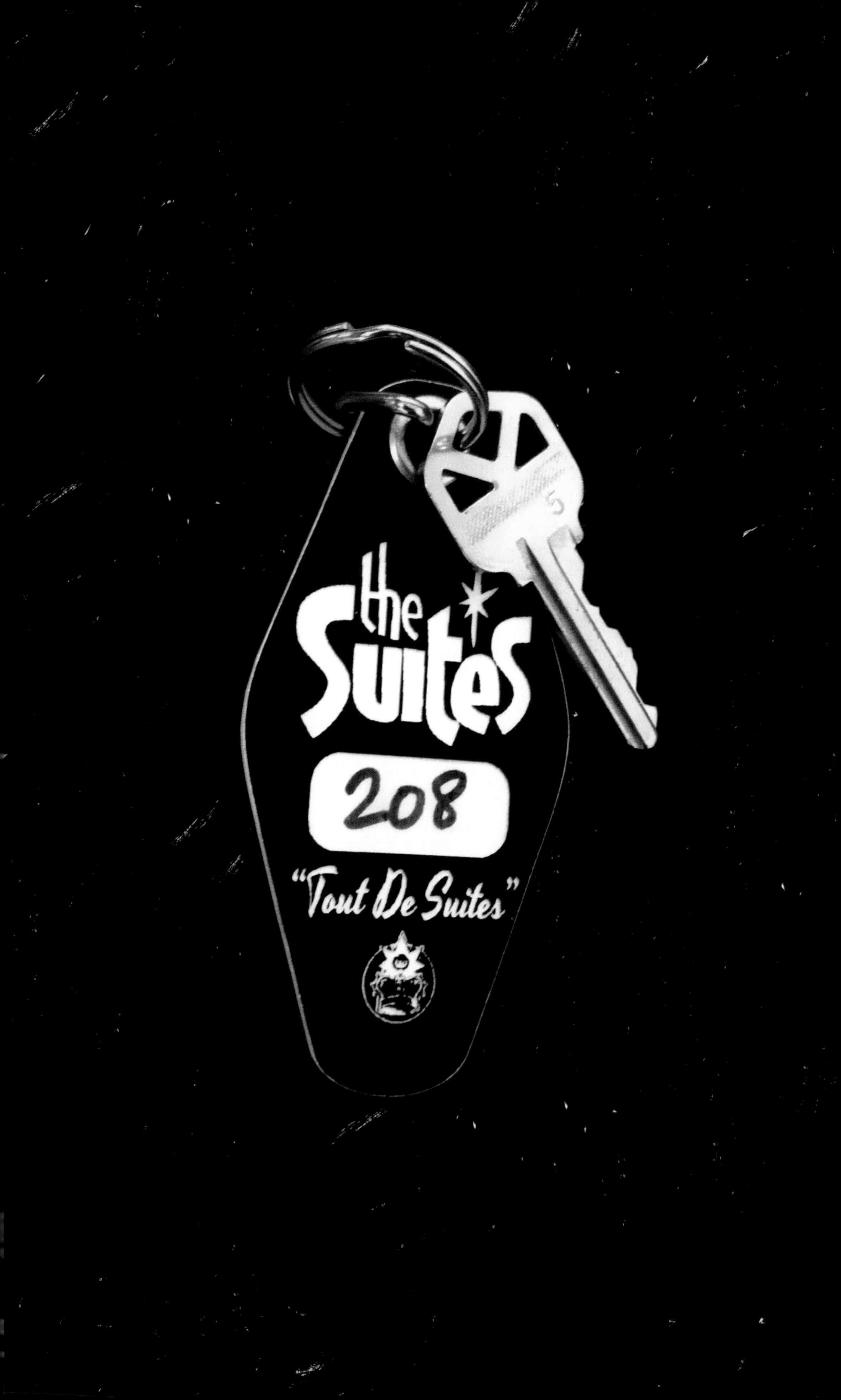
the Suites
208
"Tout De Suites"

KID COMMANDO

The original prolific provocateur, **KID LOBOTOMY** scribe **PETER MILLIGAN** waxes nostalgic with **SHELLY BOND** on the writer's craft, his privates, and the color that clashes with his metaphors.

artwork by Tess Fowler & Tamra Bonvillain

BOND: What's the secret behind your compulsive discipline?

MILLIGAN: I'm not sure if it is discipline, though there is a bit of a compulsion to always having to have a notebook and be thinking and scribbling ideas. That's the way I like it. Noel Coward once said that work is more fun than fun. And I think I pretty much agree with that — at least, that should be the aim.

BOND: Ever try your hand at drawing?

MILLIGAN: Now? Not so much. I started to do a bit more last year. There's an amazing old oak tree at the bottom of my garden and I was interested in drawing and gazing at that. It's pleasant to study something even more gnarled and twisted than one's self.

BOND: If you could rewrite the ending of a comic you've written, which would it be, what would it be, and why?

MILLIGAN: Not so much an ending but a particular scene. It was in *Enigma* when Titus Bird makes a very subtle pass at our hero, Michael. Michael punches Titus, who then apologizes for the pass. I wanted to show how deeply engrained shame and societal bias is even in a gay man like Titus, but I'm not sure if that comes across. Michael should have been apologizing to Titus.

BOND: Name one comic you've written that the US President would appreciate or abhor.

MILLIGAN: I sincerely hope that the current US President abhors everything I write.

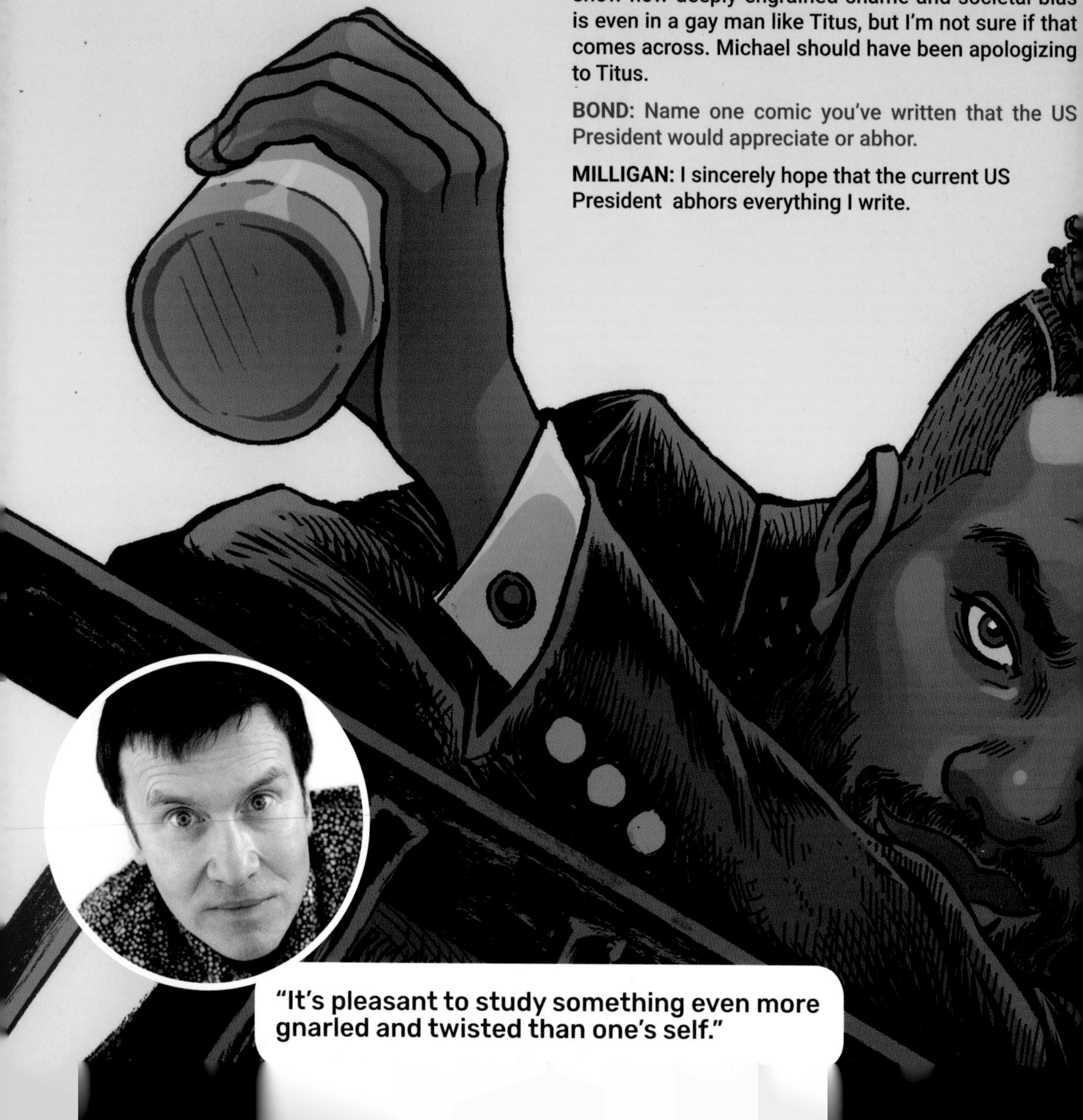

"It's pleasant to study something even more gnarled and twisted than one's self."

BOND: What advice would you like to give to your 12-year-old self? 15-year-old self? 20-year-old self?

MILLIGAN: Bloody hell. 12-year-old self; Stop fucking around. 15-year-old self: stop fucking around, you idiot you're 15 now! 22-year old-self. Don't get married to the first girlfriend you have after your father dies. It's not good for either of you.

BOND: You have four brothers and one sister. Do you all call yourselves Milligan, and, if so, how do you tell each other apart?

MILLIGAN: No. One is known as Spike (after the Irish comedian Spike Milligan), and we rarely tell each other apart. We've had plastic surgery so we look identical.

BOND: You're running in the forest in Union Jack underwear. Boxers, briefs or thong? Platforms, kitten heels or ballerina flats?

MILLIGAN: Please. I don't wear any political or national symbol within half an inch of my genitals. And I don't wear anything with a Union Jack, for me that doesn't represent so much Cool Britannia but Empire. Black boxers, and Church's loafers.

BOND: Which comes first: The title or the idea?

MILLIGAN: Sometimes both but it depends what you mean by "idea". I'm always anxious to home in on theme or themes.

BOND: The contemplative monologue or the zinger?

MILLIGAN: One has to be careful where your zingers come from. They can too easily be cheap reproductions. So probably if I had to choose it'd be contemplative monologue. That said, the best Groucho Marx one-liner is probably worth pages of agonized navel-gazing.

BOND: The hero or the villain?

MILLIGAN: In an ideal world or story they're probably the same person or thing.

BOND: The quiet or the riot?

MILLIGAN: You need both to appreciate either.

BOND: The chicken or the egg?

MILLIGAN: Bicycle.

BOND: First time it blew your mind:

A Comic book:

MILLIGAN: I read books that made me want to write, saw paintings that made me want to paint. As a kid I didn't really read comics that way. It's been a slow appreciation of what they can do. A few of my own comics have had a deep impression. At the risk of sounding self-obsessed, the first comics I produced with Brendan McCarthy and the late Brett Ewins kind of turned my life round. The first issue of *Shade, the Changing Man*, my first ongoing series [with artist Chris Bachalo] was really something. Something for me, that is.

A Renaissance painter:

MILLIGAN: Caravaggio

A Modern playwright:

MILLIGAN: Samuel Beckett

A lemon-colored poet's shirt:

MILLIGAN: Is probably going to clash with my metaphors.

"Hot Tramp, I Love You So":

MILLIGAN: But I want you to sign a pre-nuptial.

Peter Milligan has been writing comic books since The Smiths released ***Hatful of Hollow.***

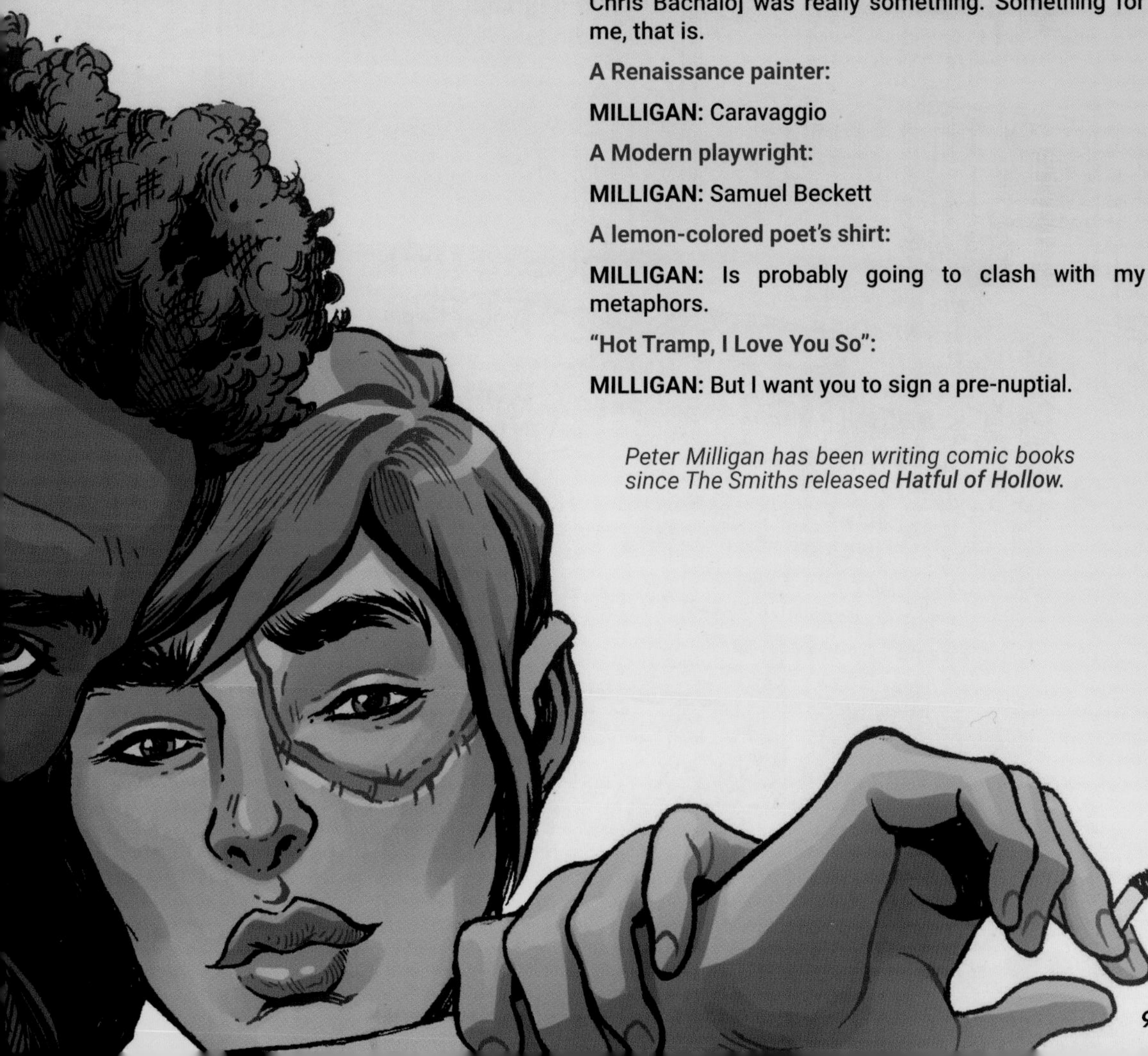

e sent to my sister R

ver had a chance t

hanges its surna

TESS
2017

DO NOT DISTURB

'But as I die I hope my

ROOM 211. Milligan, Peter
Wake-up call 6:00am

I get up early, go through a number of complex exercises that are illegal in five states of America, breakfast on a bowl of fried cockroaches, clear my head, gird my loins, sharpen my pituitary gland and get down to work. With a cup of coffee.

Favorite SFX: SPLLLT, the sound a rotten apple makes when falling on Isaac Newton's head.

Room 823. Fowler, Tess
Wake-up call 12:30pm

8am: Wake to the sound of existential dread.
9am: Anxiety settles in for daily stranglehold. Hullo, Old Chum.
11am: Hook self up to caffeine drip.
1pm: Inking pages taped to art table. Internal engine chugging. Podcast playing via Xbox in background.
3pm: E-mail from Boss lady. Usually haha funny. Usually full of updates and good ideas. Sometimes scary. Always intimidating.
5pm: Feed cat. He's biting my ankles.
7pm: More inking.
8pm: Dinner. Usually takeout. Often sushi or ramen. Sometimes sammiches.
10pm: Engine dies.
(During deadlines schedule flips, i.e., Night owl monster-mode activate)

Favorite SFX: In real life: velcro. In comics: thunder.

BRIAN SPOONER

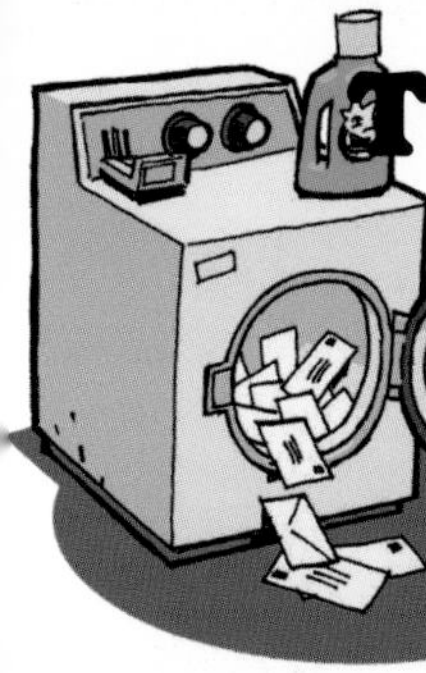

THE LAUNDRY ROOM

Address your complaints or compliments to
suiteslaundry@blackcrown.pub

By popular demand! A non-Internet old school forum wherein you can step up to the podium and swing that mic like a rock star.
But first, a word from our sponsors:

Peter Milligan here, sometime figment of Kid Lobotomy's distressed imagination, perennial disruptor of turn-down services. Writing a book like this makes you feel a little like a ghost, inhabiting the hotel and listening in on its guests. I am, though, an unusual kind of hotel ghost. Talk to me… and I'll talk right back.

Peter M, London

Thank you, Mr. M, for tearing yourself away from the upper crust art galleries and elite schisms of London high society!
Your input back here in the verdant trenches of other people's laundry is not just appreciated, it's a social imperative! Thank you, Sir! Thank you kindly!

Hello From Inside The Dryer On The Left. I hope this note finds you well and in one piece after wandering the halls of this dark place. If you're reading this you know my heart lives here under the floorboards now. Just one more wailing voice among the echoes.
Truthfully, Traveler: there's no place I'd rather be. For you see, the darkest shadow is sister to light. I have found hope here, with the freakish staff and bumps in the night.
Please. Stay awhile. Let's chat. :)

Tess F, Los Angeles

Tess, we are honored to have such a thoughtful, adroit artist lounging around with us while those pencils grow old and gray sans ink on your drawing table. Have some top shelf whiskey and share your insights on issues great, small and maddening!

Dear Laundry People,
What the living hell happened to the buttons on my best dress shirt??!! I'm supposed to be getting married next weekend!

Dave G, Room 616

That depends. If they were your average cheap shirt button variety, they crack easily and we'd be happy to replace them. If they were Swarovski crystal buttons taken from your mother's cashmere sweater, you should have bloody well said something. We would have removed said buttons before washing and sewn them back on. It's all part of the goddamn personal service, Dave.

MUSIC TO WATCH TOWELS TUMBLE DRY

Roxy Music - Street Life
David Bowie - Speed of Life
Moloko - The Only Ones
Suede - Trash
The Clash - Somebody Got Murdered
Gang Of Four - Call Me Up
The Smiths - Shakespeare's Sister
the The - Sweet Bird Of Truth
Heaven 17 - Penthouse And Pavement

send your playlist to the Laundry Room!

To be sent to my sister ROSEBUD on the event of my DEATH:

We never had a chance to be normal, did we Sis? I mean, what family changes its surname from SAMSA to LOBOTOMY? Might as well have changed it to LIPOSUCTION - That at least sounds modern. Though going through school as 'KID LIPOSUCTION' might have had challenges.
What family forces its two highly intelligent and sensitive children (you & me) to grow up in The Suites?

You and I have been at war recently, Sis. But as I die I hope my last thoughts are of those two frightened, traumatized, INCREDIBLY ATTRACTIVE kids clinging hold of each other for comfort.

There was so much for the doctors to work on with me, but none of them ever got to the bottom of my problems. I can't help thinking the secret to who I am is right here, in the lower depths of The Suites. I know there are skeletons buried in this place. If you want to find out what made me and who I am, go down there. WAY DOWN. There's something special I left for you that's worth some SERIOUS COIN.

Your loving DEAD brother, Kid

PS Be kind to Ottla & Gervais or my vengeful GHOST will return to the hotel to FUCK UP your corporate lunches and executive detox!

CASE FILE: BCPD#KL00124b

Evidence control reveals document found at crime scene. Need to obtain an exemplar to confirm note was written by deceased and was written voluntarily by deceased.

Detective Thomas Gunnakowski, BCPD

COME AS YOU ARE
Leave as Someone Else

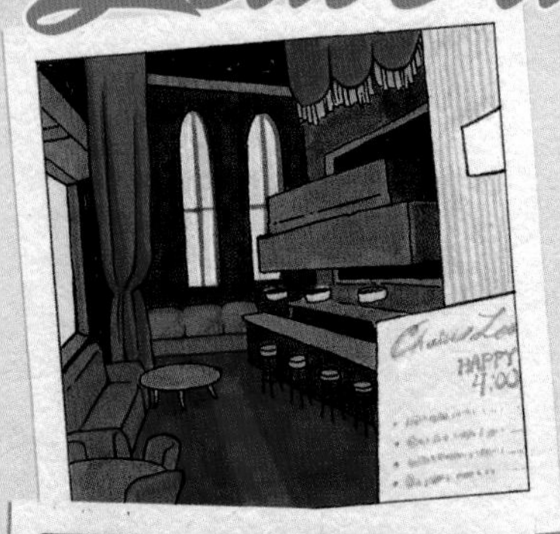
HAPPY
4:00

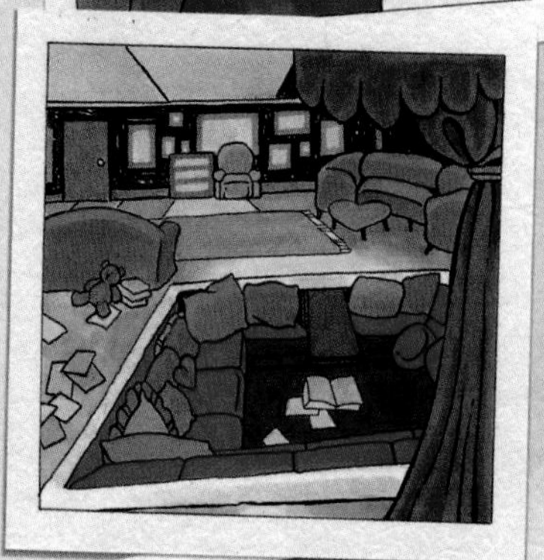

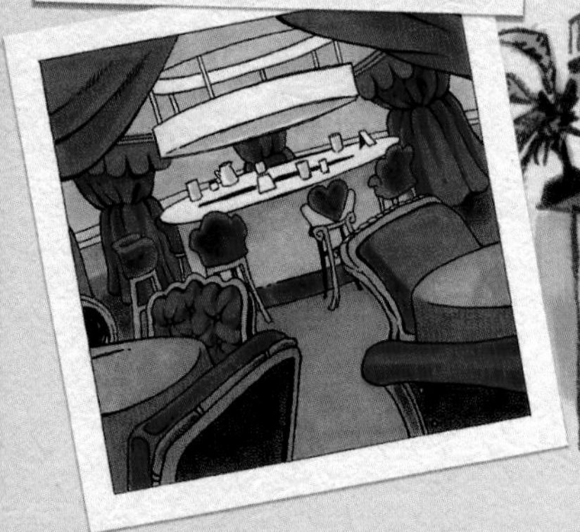

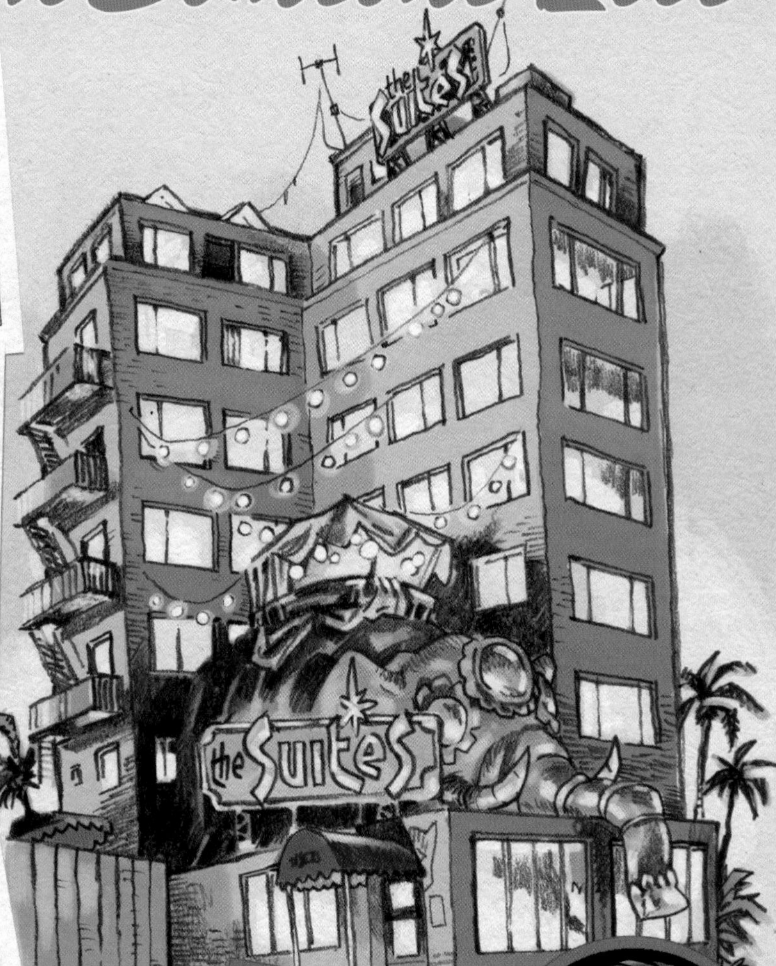
the Suites
the Suites

Meet our host, the manager with the most: KID

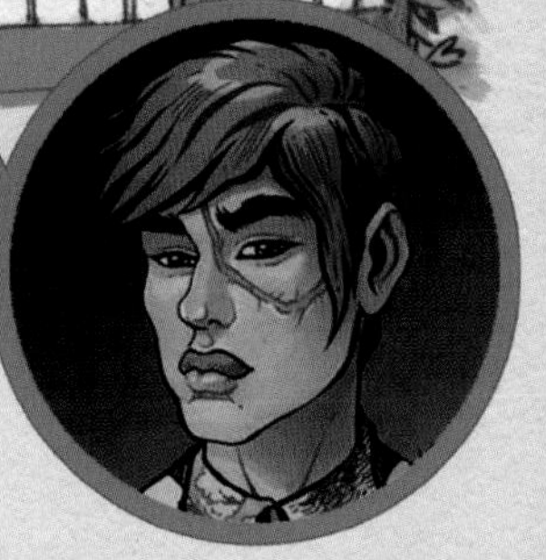

When you're in the naked city you need consider only one place for your stay: THE SUITES, at the corner of Great Yarn and Canon behind The BLACK CROWN Pub.

Win a Free drink coupon* by telling us why you're here!

I need a night away because (check YOUR reason below):

☐ I need a change of scenery.
☐ I need a change of identity.
☐ I could murder my husband.
☐ The bastard won't stop snoring!
☐ I want time to shop.
☐ I want time to shop for a neon plastic propane drillbit laser raygun—for special occasions.

ACT NOW! If you qualify, free LOBOTOMY in OCTOBER.

Tout de Suites!

*Excluding top shelf, European spirits, anything the color of caramel or cardboard, sans rocks, between the hours of 3 and 4 every other Thursday or during happy hour on Fridays.

COMIC-BOOK Writer
24 hour TIP LINE
0800-MILLIGAN

cockroach!!

Realistic, manmade, rubber cockroach! Scare your friends! Impress future employers!

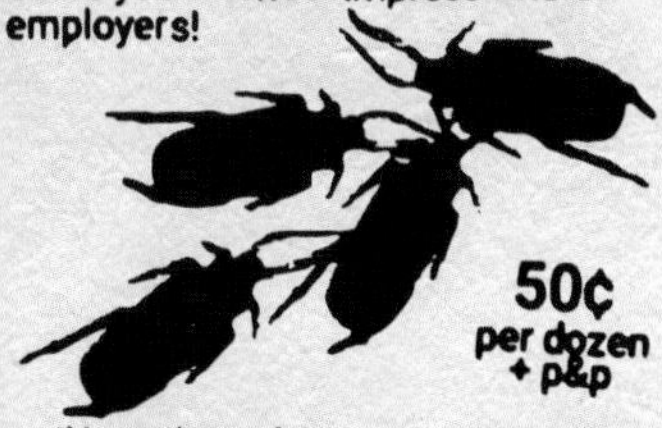

50¢
per dozen
+ p&p

*Manmade out of actual rubber, not actual cockroaches, live or otherwise. All sales final.

Item No. 112010

I Spy with my...Third eye?

A most devilish deception. It looks so real it makes one shudder! Adhere between right eye and left eye respectively and magickally peer into the very souls of friends... and enemies!

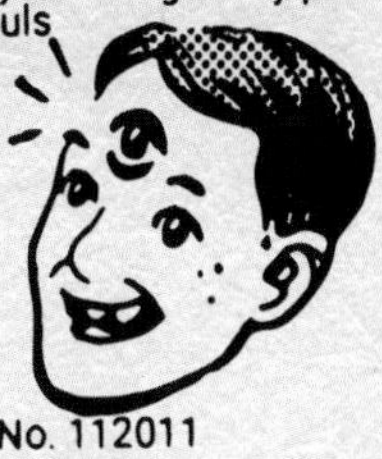

just
$4.99

Item No. 112011

CAN'T WRITE? CAN'T DRAW?

LEARN TO EDIT!

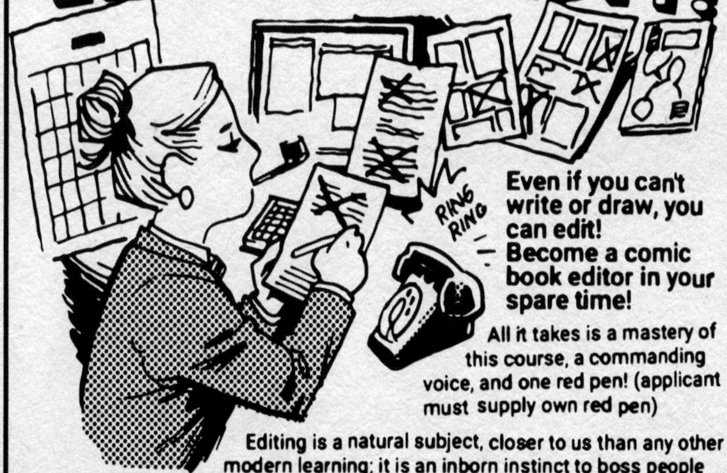
RING
RING

Even if you can't write or draw, you can edit! Become a comic book editor in your spare time!

All it takes is a mastery of this course, a commanding voice, and one red pen! (applicant must supply own red pen)

Editing is a natural subject, closer to us than any other modern learning; it is an inborn instinct to boss people around, deprive them of any/all confidence. Be the ice skate blade that glides over an artist's fingers! You know you want to! No filter necessary! Be the first on your block to kick someone in the proverbial darlings! Method can be applied in writing or orally!

1. Still - Life Editing
2. Perspective - only yours applies. You are the rule and the exception.
4. Figure Editing - it figures you have to play both good cop and bad cop. Turn on a dime! Show those freeloaders who's the boss.
5. Composition Editing - tangents be damned!

Yes! Sign me up!
Send name, address and credit card details to Roeberg & Son Publishing House, 643 E Canon St. Suite #208

Introducing

The neon laser drill-bit propane raygun!

-for everyday special occasions!

After years of deep space thinking we've made it a reality! Incredible detail! Authentic lights, sounds and smells!
Officially licensed toy replica as seen in the KID LOBOTOMY™ comics from Black Crown!

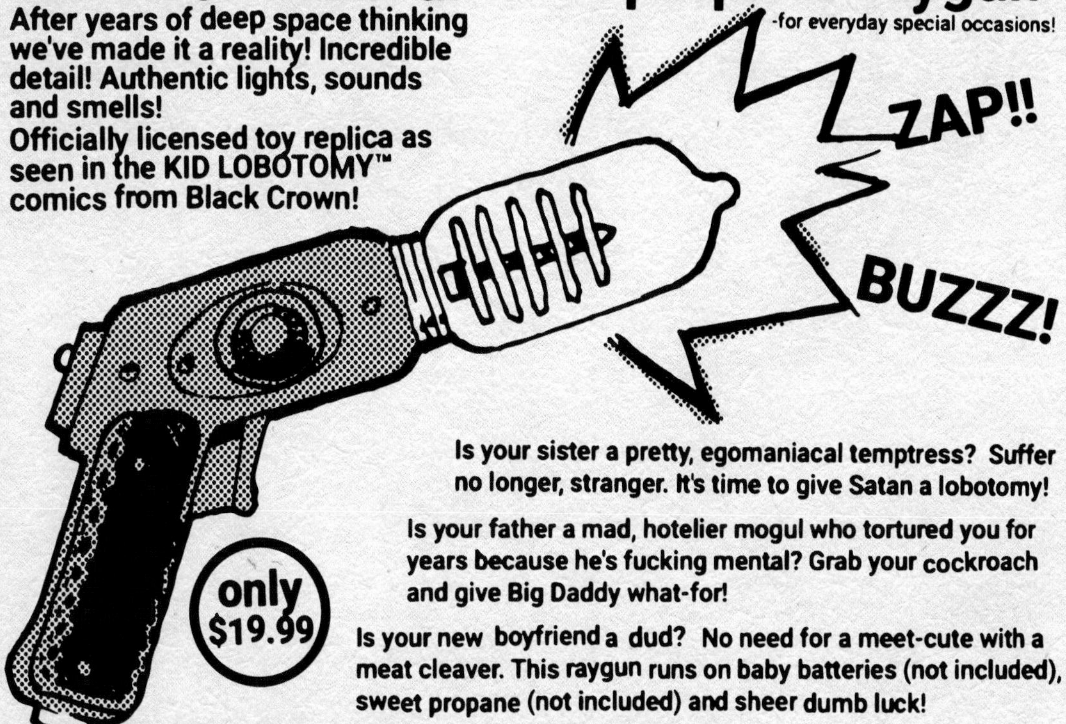
ZAP!!
BUZZZ!

only
$19.99

Is your sister a pretty, egomaniacal temptress? Suffer no longer, stranger. It's time to give Satan a lobotomy!

Is your father a mad, hotelier mogul who tortured you for years because he's fucking mental? Grab your cockroach and give Big Daddy what-for!

Is your new boyfriend a dud? No need for a meet-cute with a meat cleaver. This raygun runs on baby batteries (not included), sweet propane (not included) and sheer dumb luck!

Don't delay, order yours today!

Item No.112017/kid2

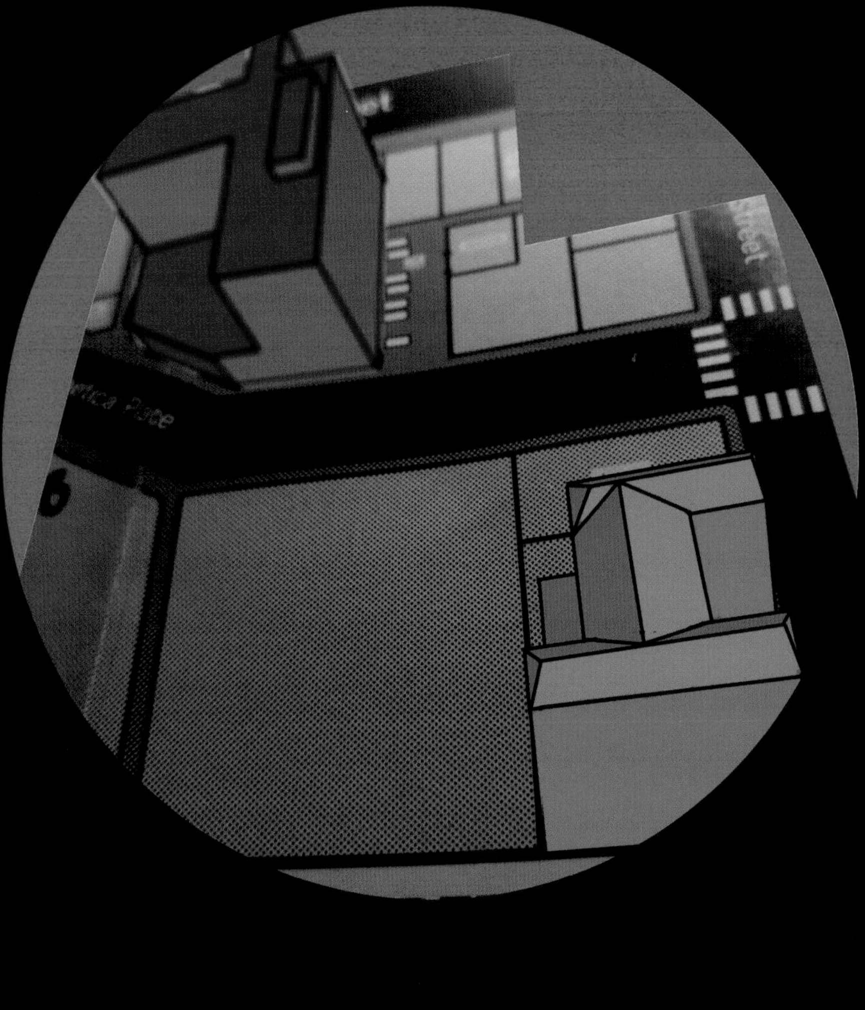
Street

The Definite Article

SPILLED TRADE SECRET:

CUD or NOTHING!

Sure, Philip Bond, my esteemed partner in all things life-related since 1999, has exposed me to a few bands I'd follow into a bubbling volcano. But my introduction to CUD a few years back needed no puffed-up persuasion: This band charmed me from the get-go. In the early '90s Philip and his roommates/art comrades-in-arms, Glyn Dillon and Jamie Hewlett, hung out with the band, saw many live shows and collaborated on a poster for their 1992 album, *Asquarius*. If that's not enough, there's this: CUD crossed the radar of noted musical dignitary John Peel. They must be fucking great. Led by Carl Puttnam, a torched crooner in a tight shirt with his soul on his back and nothing up his sleeve with fellow bandmates Mike Dunphy on guitar, Will Potter on bass, and Steve Goodwin on drums, made absurd art house videos and looked like comic book readers. And they had the balls to write and record a song called "*(Only) A Prawn In Whitby*," ripped from a tabloid headline that "allegedly" outed vegan poster-prince Morrissey concerning a singular culinary indulgence.

Philip once mentioned that CUD's bass player, Will Potter, was into comics and actually did a bit of writing and drawing for Deadline magazine. I didn't think much of it until the end of last winter. I was in the early stages of curating the BLACK CROWN QUARTERLY and in the final clutches of a Kickstarter campaign for (shameless plug alert) FEMME MAGNIFIQUE, a comic book anthology salute to 50 women in pop, politics, art and science. It was at this juncture, while I'm on my phone, in the car, that a person with the twitter handle @willcud tweeted a question at me: "Why was this incredible hardcover so bloody expensive?" "It's the shipping to the U.K.," I assured him. To Will, that was the ultimate deal-breaker. Since he phrased this fair question so politely, I decided to comp him the book — once I confirmed that he was, in fact, the Will Potter who plays a mean bass in CUD. So like most things you don't see coming (note: It's always a good thing that I'm not driving but in this case, it's a very good thing) it hits me hard and fast: the BCQ is a compendium of all things comics, culture + cool.

I need something solid by way of musical representation that's more than a suggested soundtrack but less than a self-indulgent satire through the rise and fall and rise of a favorite band that only elitest mid-century Brits and one Anglophile in Los Angeles know about.

So we're in the car and I'm giggling — not a "tee hee" but I'm grinning and chortling in a cool, respectable way like when you know you're crafting something behind your partner's back and he doesn't know it yet but he's going to acquiesce and admit defeat. I asked Will to pitch me a regular short feature about CUD for the BCQ. I knew he could play bass. I knew he was well mannered. But did he possess the tempo and tenacity to write a lean, mean comic? One week and a one-sheet pitch later, I was in. And so was lead singer/songwriter turned comics writer Carl Puttnam. It was one of the funniest pitches I'd ever read, and I knew it needed one final component: a phenomenal artist who was devoted to the band, who could give it the verve and velocity it not only demanded but deserved. Will, Carl and I agreed that there was (only) one prawn for the job. That guy was unavailable so we hired Philip Bond, who is also a vegetarian but was once spotted taking a bite out of a bean burrito that had the strange taste of cow and cud. Let me know if we've sold you on the gospel of CUD, the darlings of Leeds, U.K., who should have tripped American grunge onto its pretty face and taken the states by storm. Never say never.

Shelly Bond
BLACK CROWN HQ
Editor. Curator. Time Traveler

CUD: RICH AND STRANGE is a regular feature in the ***BLACK CROWN QUARTERLY.***

Philip Bond sent the "alleged" veggie burrito back to the kitchen for a sound check.

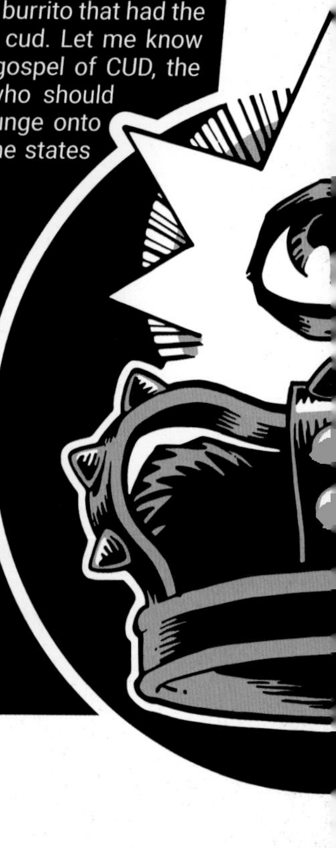

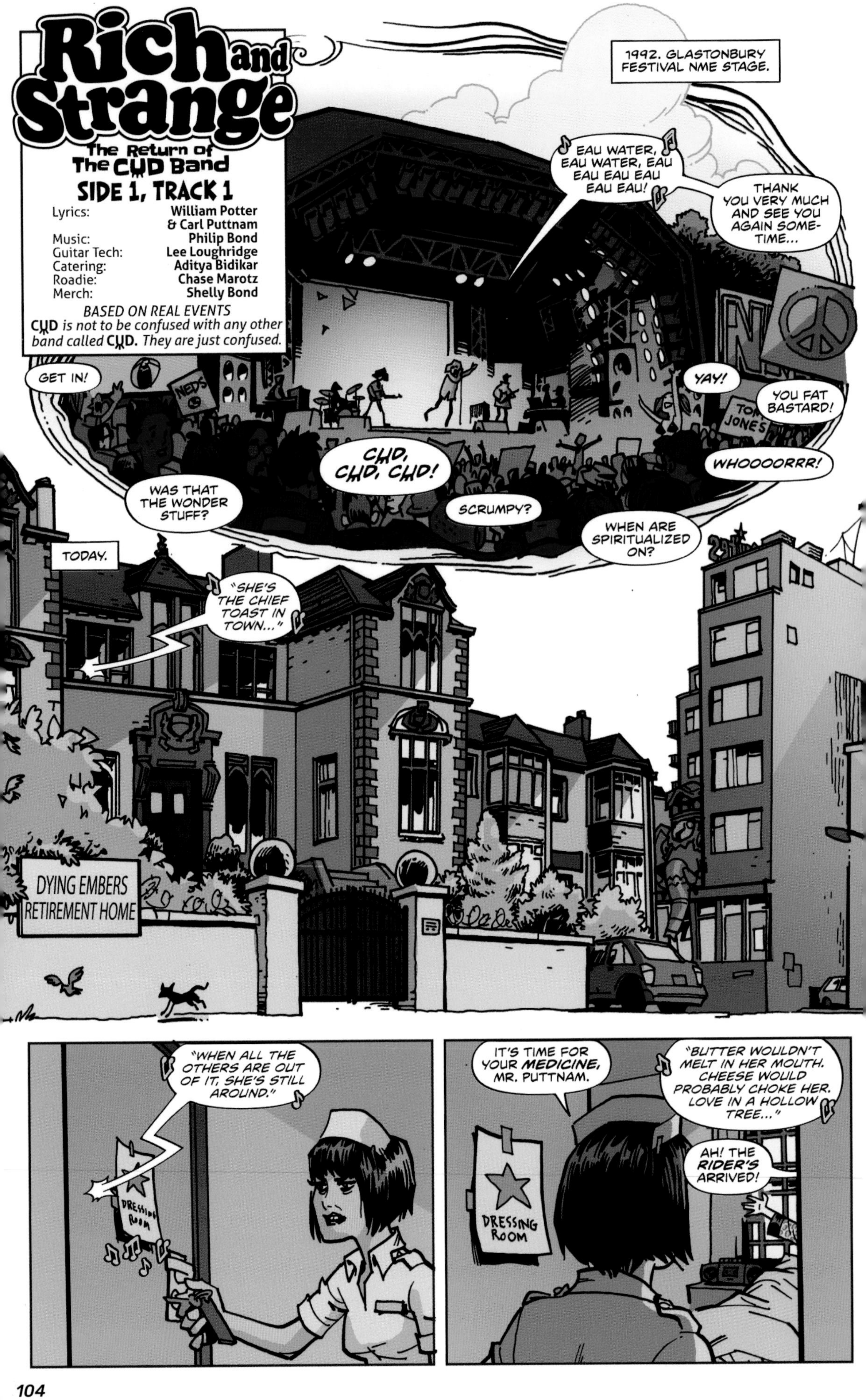
Rich and Strange
The Return of The CUD Band
SIDE 1, TRACK 1
Lyrics: William Potter & Carl Puttnam
Music: Philip Bond
Guitar Tech: Lee Loughridge
Catering: Aditya Bidikar
Roadie: Chase Marotz
Merch: Shelly Bond
BASED ON REAL EVENTS
CUD is not to be confused with any other band called CUD. They are just confused.
1992. GLASTONBURY FESTIVAL NME STAGE.
EAU WATER, EAU WATER, EAU EAU EAU EAU EAU EAU!
THANK YOU VERY MUCH AND SEE YOU AGAIN SOMETIME...
GET IN!
NED'S
YAY!
YOU FAT BASTARD!
TOM JONES
CUD, CUD, CUD!
WHOOOORRR!
WAS THAT THE WONDER STUFF?
SCRUMPY?
WHEN ARE SPIRITUALIZED ON?
TODAY.
"SHE'S THE CHIEF TOAST IN TOWN..."
DYING EMBERS RETIREMENT HOME
"WHEN ALL THE OTHERS ARE OUT OF IT, SHE'S STILL AROUND."
DRESSING ROOM
IT'S TIME FOR YOUR MEDICINE, MR. PUTTNAM.
"BUTTER WOULDN'T MELT IN HER MOUTH. CHEESE WOULD PROBABLY CHOKE HER. LOVE IN A HOLLOW TREE..."
DRESSING ROOM
AH! THE RIDER'S ARRIVED!

WOULDN'T YOU RATHER BE LISTENING TO *TWILIGHT FM*? THE OTHER INMATES--I MEAN *RESIDENTS*--PREFER IT...

"...NING TO THE MELLOW HOUR. THIS NEXT SONG GOES OUT TO GARY, SEEING OUT HIS FINAL DAYS AT *DYING EMBERS*. JUST FOR YOU, GAZZA, HERE'S '(DON'T FEAR) THE REAPER'..."

CLICK

AH, AH! *A DUBAND, VOSNE ROMANÉE 2002.* A VILLAGE WINE, MAYBE. IT'S NOT *GRAND CRU*, BUT MORE THAN CAPABLE OF LASTING IF IT'S BEEN CELLARED CORRECTLY...AND IT *HAS!* IT'S *MINE!*

IF YOU SAY SO, MR. PUTTNAM. NOW IF YOU'LL JUST ROLL UP YOUR SLEEVE...

THE *ST. JULIEN '94?* IS IT *YOURS?* I CAN'T IMAGINE IT'S EVEN WORTH *OPENING.* IF IT'S NOT ALREADY *BUGGERED* THEN *I* AM.

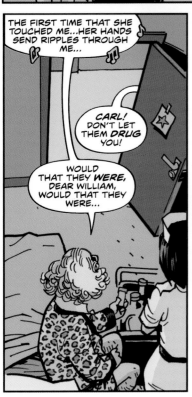

THE FIRST TIME THAT SHE TOUCHED ME...HER HANDS SEND RIPPLES THROUGH ME...

CARL! DON'T LET THEM *DRUG* YOU!

WOULD THAT THEY *WERE*, DEAR WILLIAM, WOULD THAT THEY *WERE*...

MR. POTTER! WILL YOU *STOP* INTERRUPTING MY *ROUNDS*...AND RETURN THAT WHEELCHAIR TO MR. CHESLIN!

POTTER!!

CHUNK

AGH!

NURSE MANGAL, I *LOVE* HOW YOUR CHEEKS FLUSH WHEN YOU'RE ANGRY.

RIGHT, I'M FETCHING *SEAN!*

OOH, SEAN THE *BRAWN*, WHY DON'T YOU!

DID YOU SEE HOW SHE LOOKED AT ME, WITH THAT *TWINKLE* IN HER EYE?

SHE HAS A GLASS EYE.

CARL, WE *HAVE* TO GET OUT OF HERE!

IS IT *SHOW-TIME?*

YES, IT'S *SHOW-TIME.*

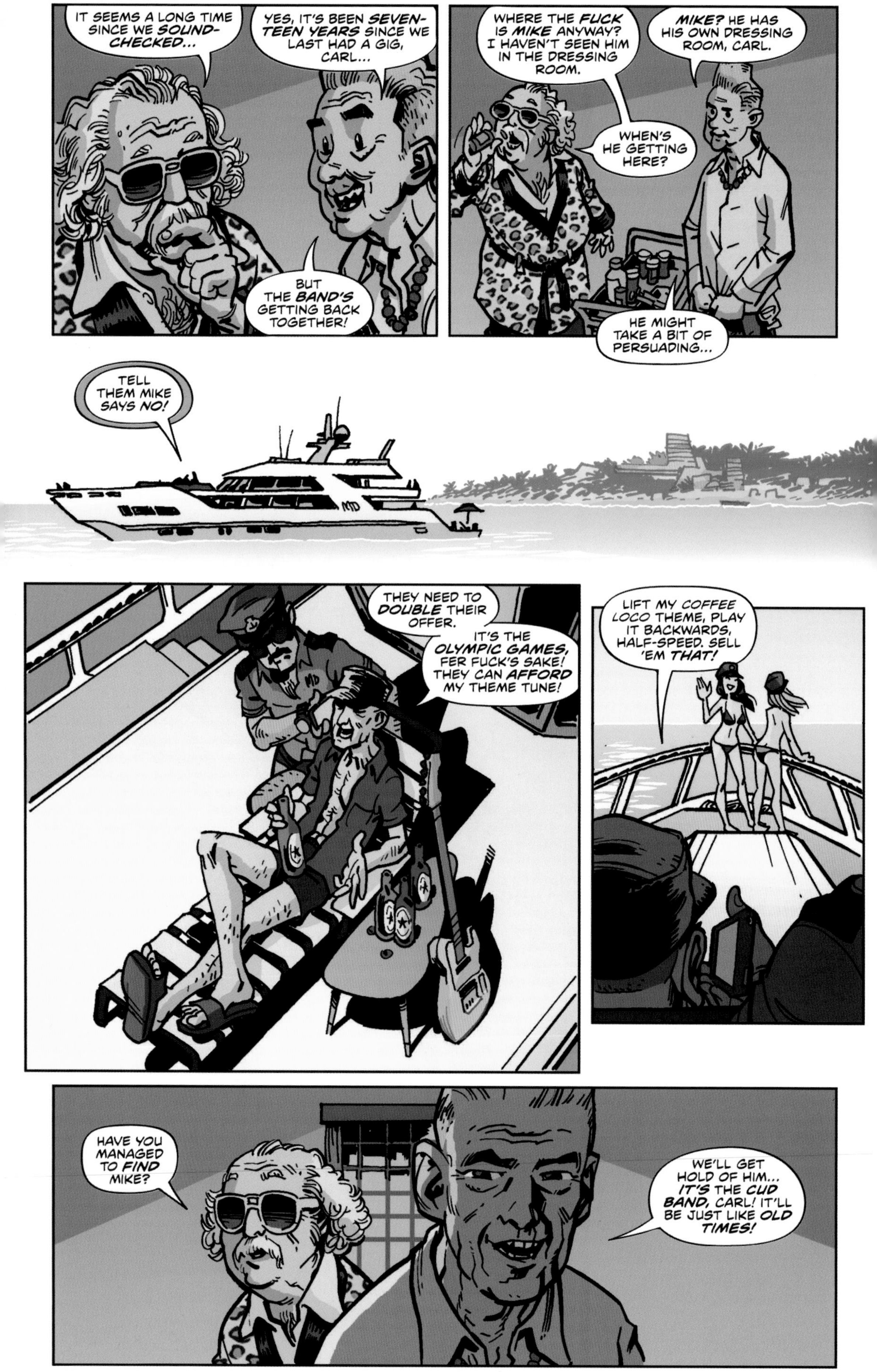
IT SEEMS A LONG TIME SINCE WE SOUND-CHECKED...
YES, IT'S BEEN SEVEN-TEEN YEARS SINCE WE LAST HAD A GIG, CARL...
BUT THE BAND'S GETTING BACK TOGETHER!
WHERE THE FUCK IS MIKE ANYWAY? I HAVEN'T SEEN HIM IN THE DRESSING ROOM.
MIKE? HE HAS HIS OWN DRESSING ROOM, CARL.
WHEN'S HE GETTING HERE?
HE MIGHT TAKE A BIT OF PERSUADING...
TELL THEM MIKE SAYS NO!
MD
THEY NEED TO DOUBLE THEIR OFFER.
IT'S THE OLYMPIC GAMES, FER FUCK'S SAKE! THEY CAN AFFORD MY THEME TUNE!
LIFT MY COFFEE LOCO THEME, PLAY IT BACKWARDS, HALF-SPEED. SELL 'EM THAT!
HAVE YOU MANAGED TO FIND MIKE?
WE'LL GET HOLD OF HIM... IT'S THE CUD BAND, CARL! IT'LL BE JUST LIKE OLD TIMES!

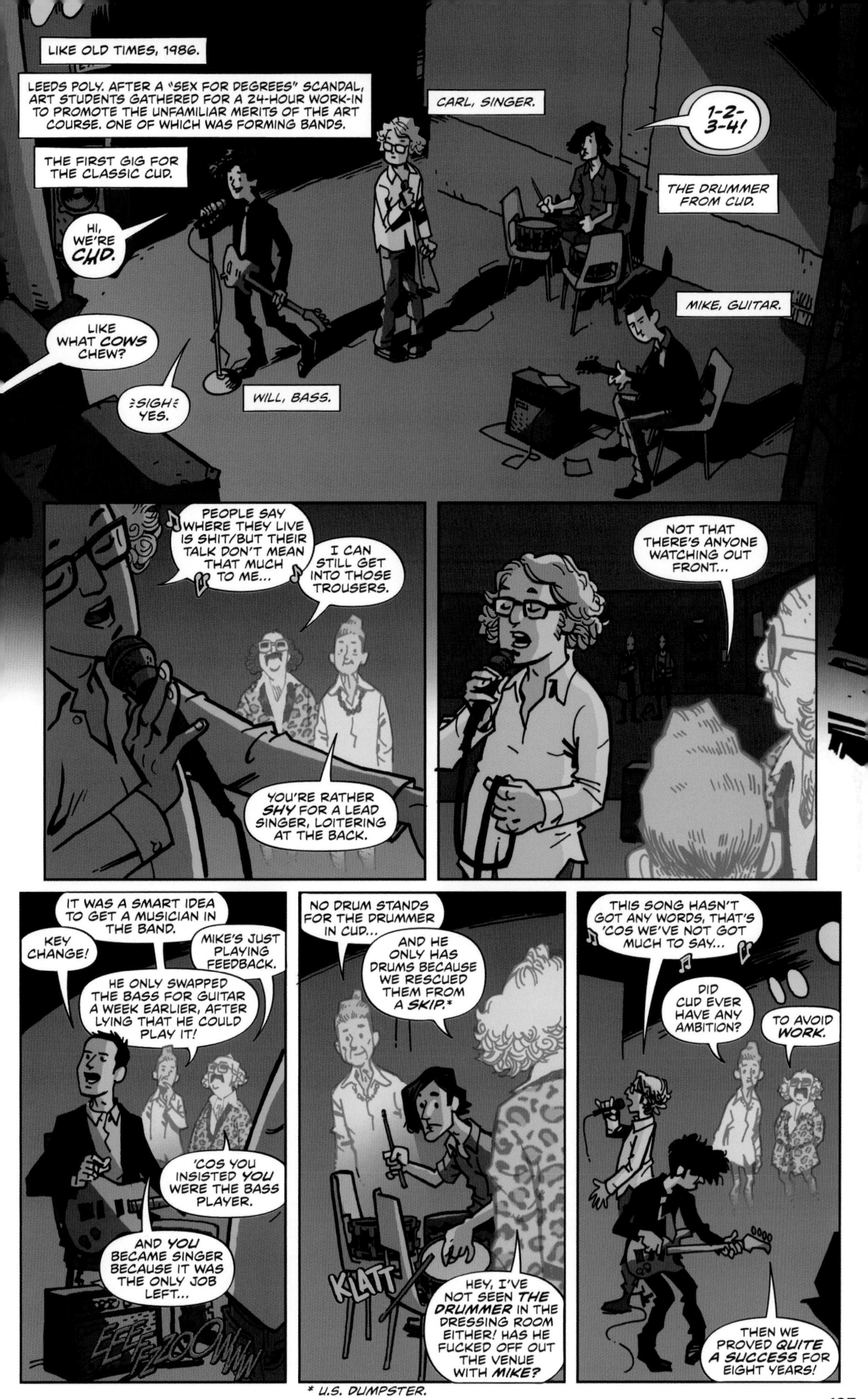
LIKE OLD TIMES, 1986.
LEEDS POLY. AFTER A "SEX FOR DEGREES" SCANDAL, ART STUDENTS GATHERED FOR A 24-HOUR WORK-IN TO PROMOTE THE UNFAMILIAR MERITS OF THE ART COURSE. ONE OF WHICH WAS FORMING BANDS.
THE FIRST GIG FOR THE CLASSIC CUD.
CARL, SINGER.
1-2-3-4!
THE DRUMMER FROM CUD.
HI, WE'RE CUD.
MIKE, GUITAR.
LIKE WHAT COWS CHEW?
SIGH YES.
WILL, BASS.
PEOPLE SAY WHERE THEY LIVE IS SHIT/BUT THEIR TALK DON'T MEAN THAT MUCH TO ME...
I CAN STILL GET INTO THOSE TROUSERS.
YOU'RE RATHER SHY FOR A LEAD SINGER, LOITERING AT THE BACK.
NOT THAT THERE'S ANYONE WATCHING OUT FRONT...
IT WAS A SMART IDEA TO GET A MUSICIAN IN THE BAND.
KEY CHANGE!
MIKE'S JUST PLAYING FEEDBACK.
HE ONLY SWAPPED THE BASS FOR GUITAR A WEEK EARLIER, AFTER LYING THAT HE COULD PLAY IT!
'COS YOU INSISTED YOU WERE THE BASS PLAYER.
AND YOU BECAME SINGER BECAUSE IT WAS THE ONLY JOB LEFT...
EEEEFZOOWWW
NO DRUM STANDS FOR THE DRUMMER IN CUD...
AND HE ONLY HAS DRUMS BECAUSE WE RESCUED THEM FROM A SKIP.*
KLATT
HEY, I'VE NOT SEEN THE DRUMMER IN THE DRESSING ROOM EITHER! HAS HE FUCKED OFF OUT THE VENUE WITH MIKE?
THIS SONG HASN'T GOT ANY WORDS, THAT'S 'COS WE'VE NOT GOT MUCH TO SAY...
DID CUD EVER HAVE ANY AMBITION?
TO AVOID WORK.
THEN WE PROVED QUITE A SUCCESS FOR EIGHT YEARS!

* U.S. DUMPSTER.

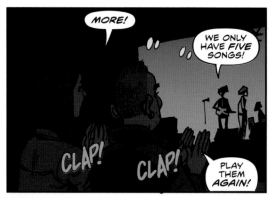

MORE!

WE ONLY HAVE *FIVE* SONGS!

CLAP!

CLAP!

PLAY THEM *AGAIN!*

AND *THAT,* CARL, IS WHY WE NEED TO GET THE BAND BACK TOGETHER!

THAT WAS THE VINTAGE SOUND OF *MIKE DUNPHY AND CUD.* PUT THEM IN THE *"WHERE ARE THEY NOW?"* FILE...

AND WE HAVE A *CALLER...*

...HI, CARLY, YOU'RE LIVE ON TWILIGHT FM...

LET'S DO IT AGAIN, BUT *BETTER* THIS TIME. THIS TIME...

...WE'LL HIT THE *BIG TIME!*

I HAVE A *SECRET WEAPON...*

YOU IN *TROUBLE,* POTTER, AND YOU KNOW SEAN *LIKES* HITTING THINGS!

...MEET OUR NEW *DRUMMER!*

SEAN *LIKES* HITTING THINGS!

YES, YOU *SAID.* CAN YOU ALSO COUNT UP TO *FOUR?*

AS FOR *YOU,* MR. PUTTNAM, YOU HAVE A *VISITOR...*

YOUNG *LADY!* YOU LOOK STRIKINGLY *FAMILIAR...*

FADEOUT.

NEXT: WHO IS CARL'S SURPRISE VISITOR? AND WHY THE STUPID NAME?

108

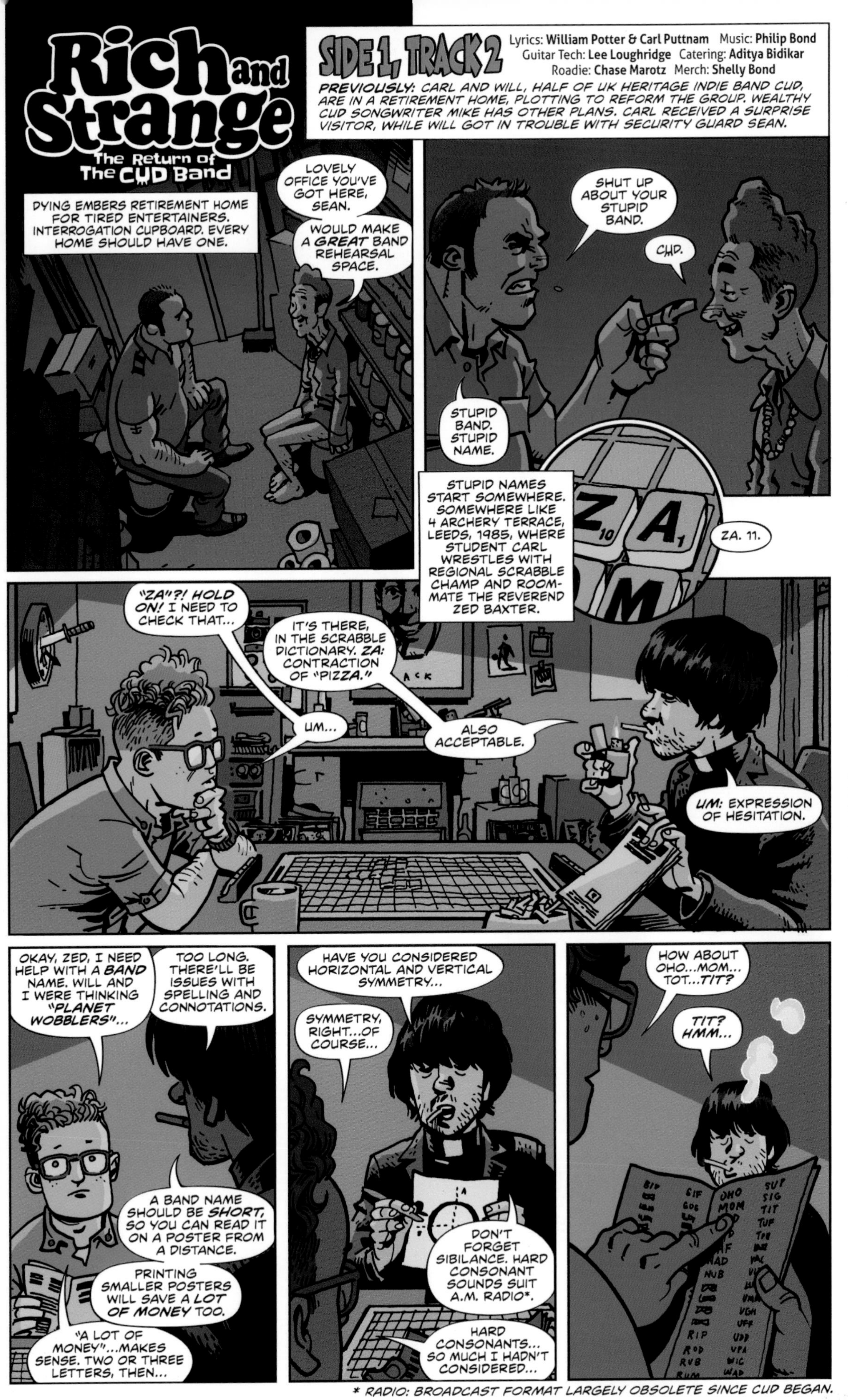

Rich and Strange
The Return of The CUD Band
SIDE 1, TRACK 2
Lyrics: William Potter & Carl Puttnam Music: Philip Bond
Guitar Tech: Lee Loughridge Catering: Aditya Bidikar
Roadie: Chase Marotz Merch: Shelly Bond
PREVIOUSLY: CARL AND WILL, HALF OF UK HERITAGE INDIE BAND CUD, ARE IN A RETIREMENT HOME, PLOTTING TO REFORM THE GROUP. WEALTHY CUD SONGWRITER MIKE HAS OTHER PLANS. CARL RECEIVED A SURPRISE VISITOR, WHILE WILL GOT IN TROUBLE WITH SECURITY GUARD SEAN.
DYING EMBERS RETIREMENT HOME FOR TIRED ENTERTAINERS. INTERROGATION CUPBOARD. EVERY HOME SHOULD HAVE ONE.
LOVELY OFFICE YOU'VE GOT HERE, SEAN.
WOULD MAKE A GREAT BAND REHEARSAL SPACE.
SHUT UP ABOUT YOUR STUPID BAND.
CUD.
STUPID BAND. STUPID NAME.
STUPID NAMES START SOMEWHERE. SOMEWHERE LIKE 4 ARCHERY TERRACE, LEEDS, 1985, WHERE STUDENT CARL WRESTLES WITH REGIONAL SCRABBLE CHAMP AND ROOM-MATE THE REVEREND ZED BAXTER.
Z10 A1
ZA. 11.
"ZA"?! HOLD ON! I NEED TO CHECK THAT...
IT'S THERE, IN THE SCRABBLE DICTIONARY. ZA: CONTRACTION OF "PIZZA."
UM...
ALSO ACCEPTABLE.
UM: EXPRESSION OF HESITATION.
OKAY, ZED, I NEED HELP WITH A BAND NAME. WILL AND I WERE THINKING "PLANET WOBBLERS"...
TOO LONG. THERE'LL BE ISSUES WITH SPELLING AND CONNOTATIONS.
A BAND NAME SHOULD BE SHORT, SO YOU CAN READ IT ON A POSTER FROM A DISTANCE.
PRINTING SMALLER POSTERS WILL SAVE A LOT OF MONEY TOO.
"A LOT OF MONEY"...MAKES SENSE. TWO OR THREE LETTERS, THEN...
HAVE YOU CONSIDERED HORIZONTAL AND VERTICAL SYMMETRY...
SYMMETRY, RIGHT...OF COURSE...
DON'T FORGET SIBILANCE. HARD CONSONANT SOUNDS SUIT A.M. RADIO*.
HARD CONSONANTS... SO MUCH I HADN'T CONSIDERED...
HOW ABOUT OHO...MOM... TOT...TIT?
TIT? HMM...
OHO MOM TIT TUF NUB RIP RUB

* RADIO: BROADCAST FORMAT LARGELY OBSOLETE SINCE CUD BEGAN.

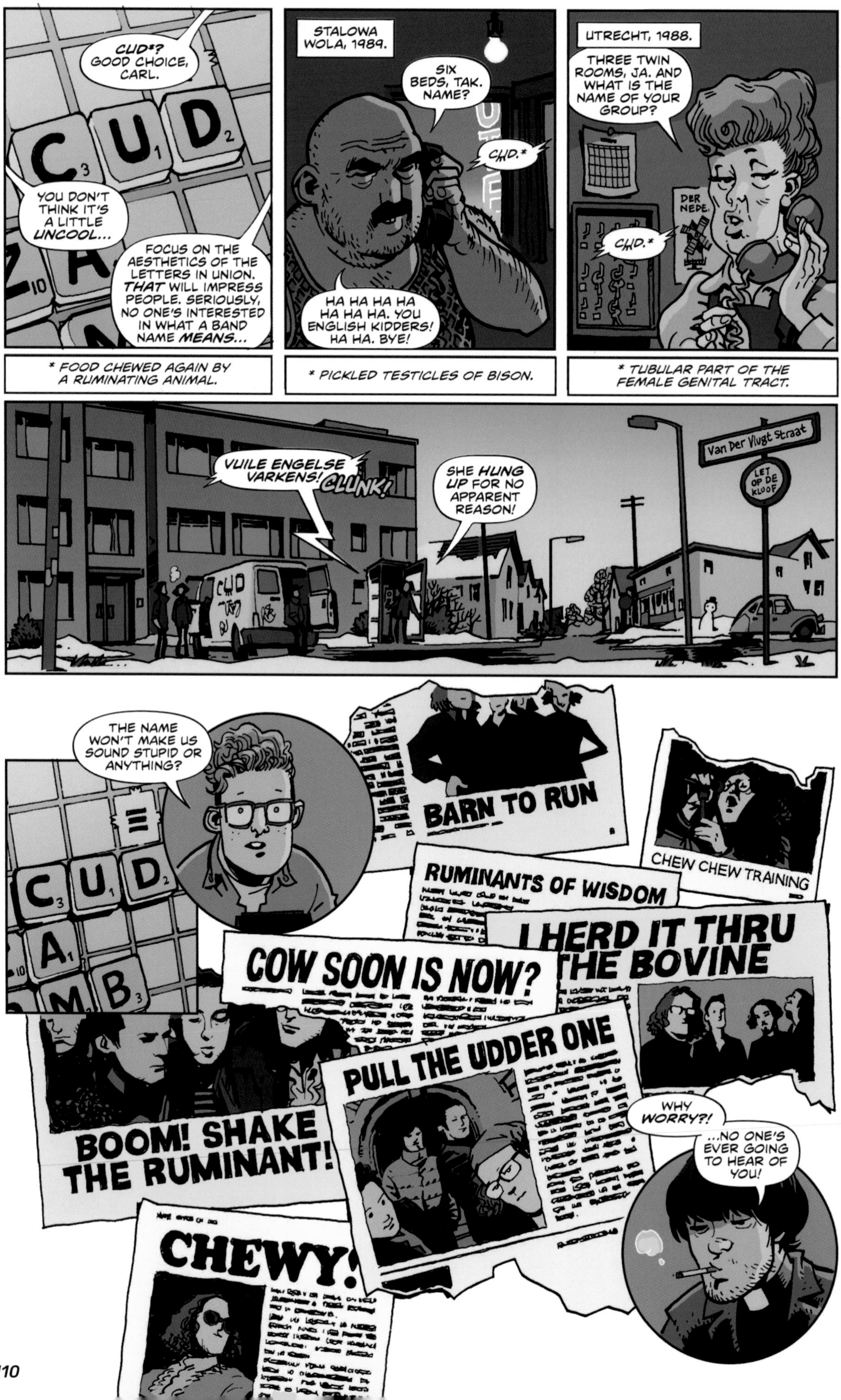
CUD*? GOOD CHOICE, CARL.
YOU DON'T THINK IT'S A LITTLE UNCOOL...
FOCUS ON THE AESTHETICS OF THE LETTERS IN UNION. THAT WILL IMPRESS PEOPLE. SERIOUSLY, NO ONE'S INTERESTED IN WHAT A BAND NAME MEANS...
* FOOD CHEWED AGAIN BY A RUMINATING ANIMAL.
STALOWA WOLA, 1989.
SIX BEDS, TAK. NAME?
CUD.*
HA HA HA HA HA HA HA. YOU ENGLISH KIDDERS! HA HA. BYE!
* PICKLED TESTICLES OF BISON.
UTRECHT, 1988.
THREE TWIN ROOMS, JA. AND WHAT IS THE NAME OF YOUR GROUP?
DER NEDE.
CUD.*
* TUBULAR PART OF THE FEMALE GENITAL TRACT.
VUILE ENGELSE VARKENS!
CLUNK!
SHE HUNG UP FOR NO APPARENT REASON!
Van Der Vlugt Straat
LET OP DE KLOOF
CUD
THE NAME WON'T MAKE US SOUND STUPID OR ANYTHING?
BARN TO RUN
CHEW CHEW TRAINING
RUMINANTS OF WISDOM
I HERD IT THRU THE BOVINE
COW SOON IS NOW?
PULL THE UDDER ONE
BOOM! SHAKE THE RUMINANT!
CHEWY!
WHY WORRY?!
...NO ONE'S EVER GOING TO HEAR OF YOU!

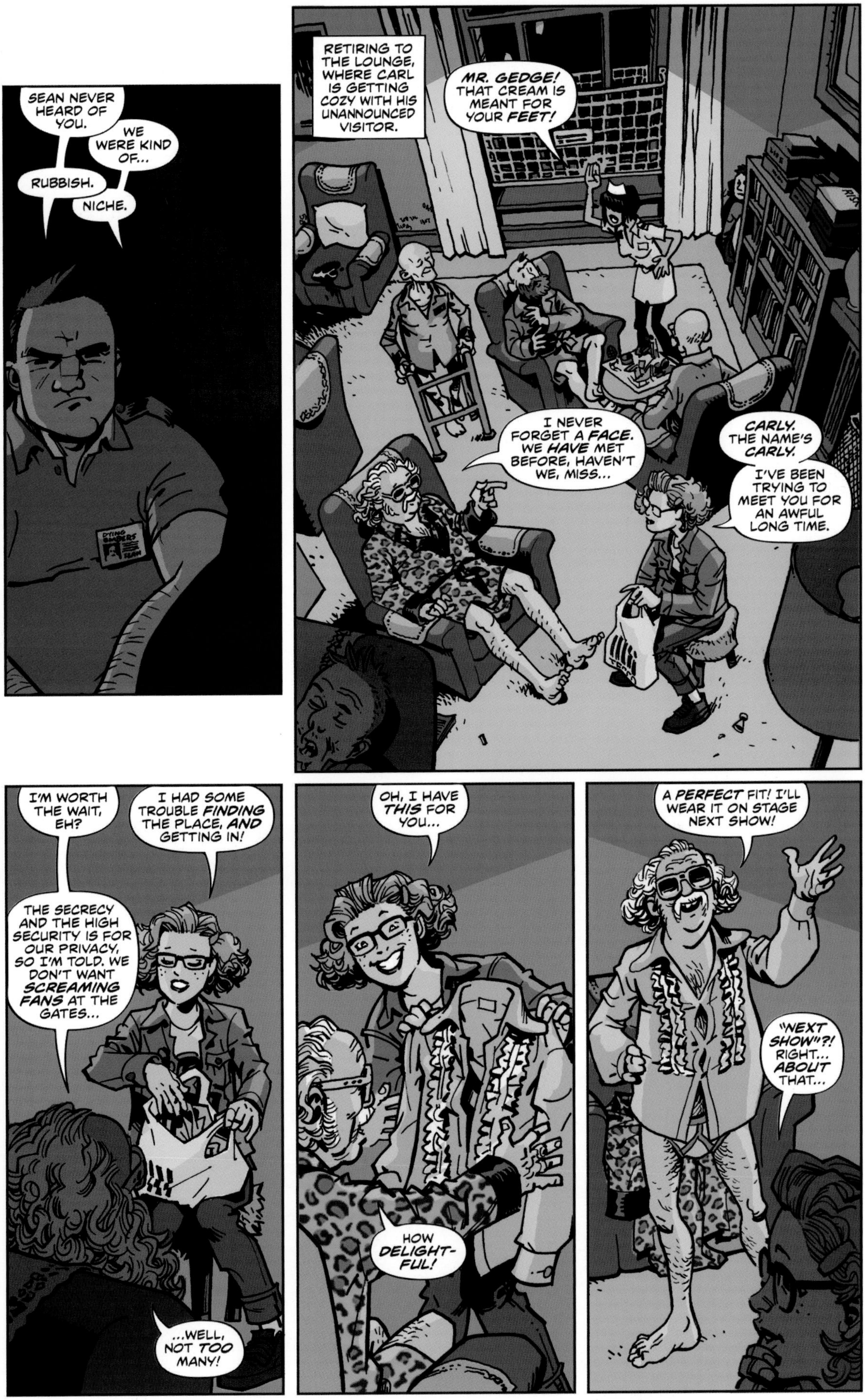

SEAN NEVER HEARD OF YOU.
WE WERE KIND OF...
RUBBISH.
NICHE.
RETIRING TO THE LOUNGE, WHERE CARL IS GETTING COZY WITH HIS UNANNOUNCED VISITOR.
MR. GEDGE! THAT CREAM IS MEANT FOR YOUR FEET!
I NEVER FORGET A FACE. WE HAVE MET BEFORE, HAVEN'T WE, MISS...
CARLY. THE NAME'S CARLY.
I'VE BEEN TRYING TO MEET YOU FOR AN AWFUL LONG TIME.
I'M WORTH THE WAIT, EH?
I HAD SOME TROUBLE FINDING THE PLACE, AND GETTING IN!
THE SECRECY AND THE HIGH SECURITY IS FOR OUR PRIVACY, SO I'M TOLD. WE DON'T WANT SCREAMING FANS AT THE GATES...
...WELL, NOT TOO MANY!
OH, I HAVE THIS FOR YOU...
HOW DELIGHT-FUL!
A PERFECT FIT! I'LL WEAR IT ON STAGE NEXT SHOW!
"NEXT SHOW"?! RIGHT... ABOUT THAT...

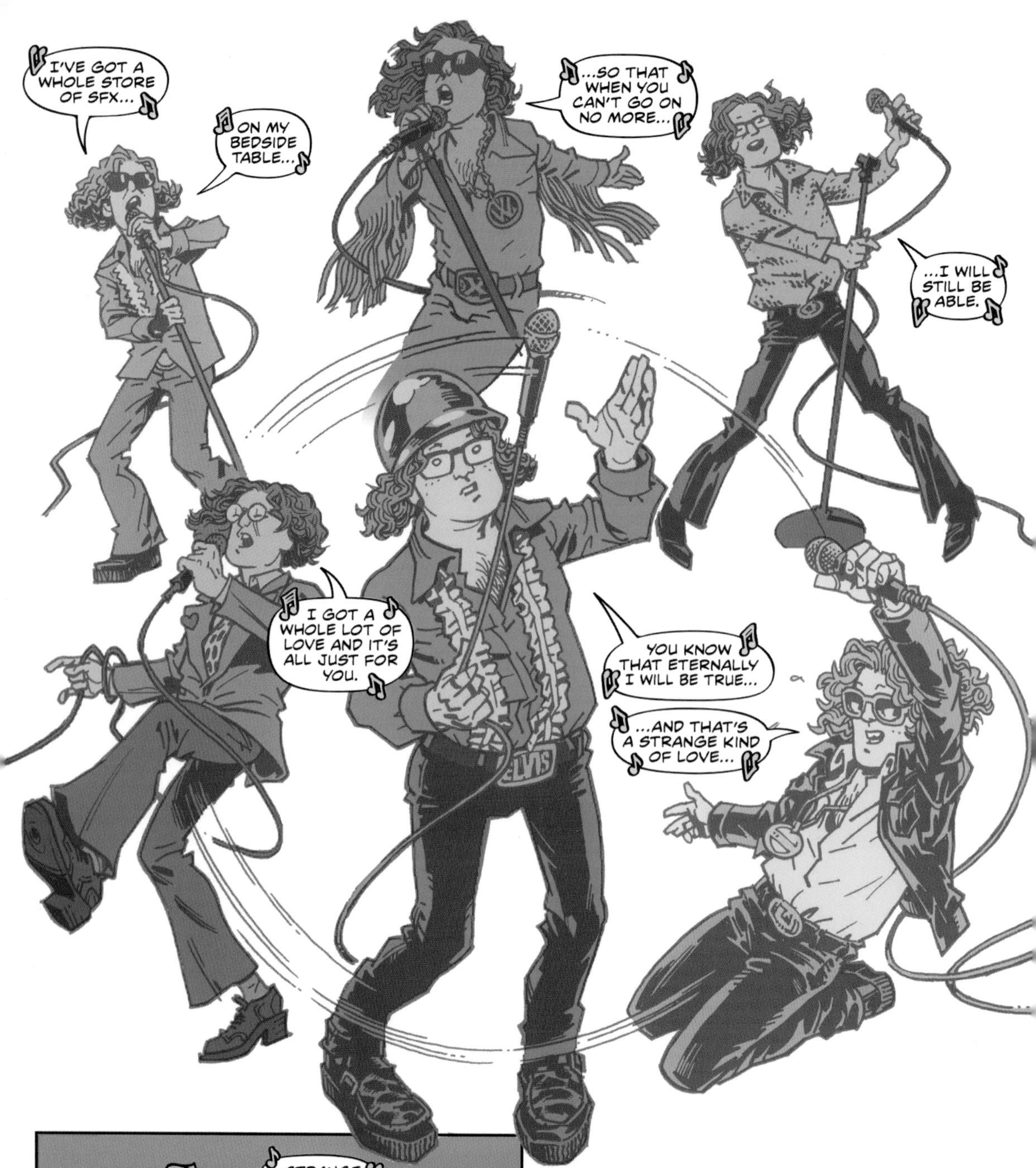
I'VE GOT A WHOLE STORE OF SFX...
ON MY BEDSIDE TABLE...
...SO THAT WHEN YOU CAN'T GO ON NO MORE...
...I WILL STILL BE ABLE.
I GOT A WHOLE LOT OF LOVE AND IT'S ALL JUST FOR YOU.
YOU KNOW THAT ETERNALLY I WILL BE TRUE...
...AND THAT'S A STRANGE KIND OF LOVE...

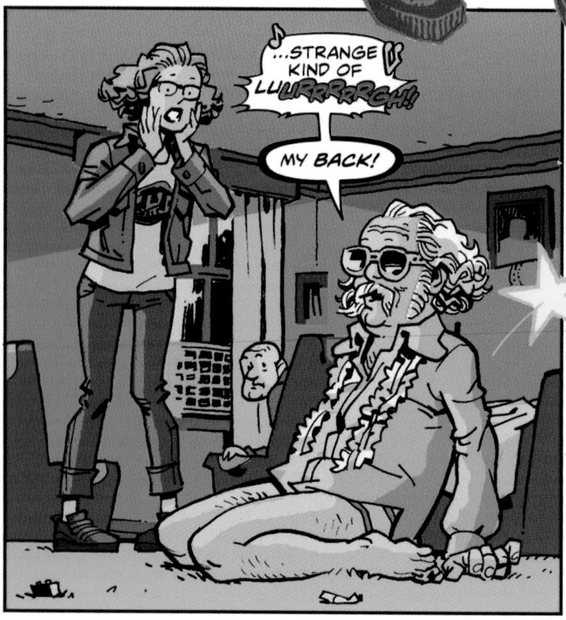
...STRANGE KIND OF LUURRRRRGH!!
MY BACK!

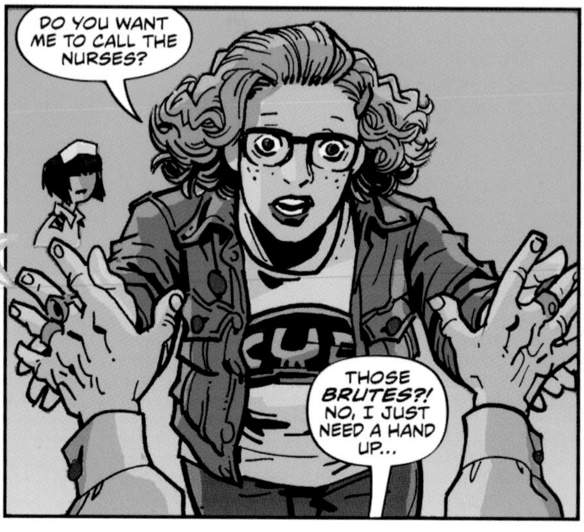
DO YOU WANT ME TO CALL THE NURSES?
THOSE BRUTES?! NO, I JUST NEED A HAND UP...

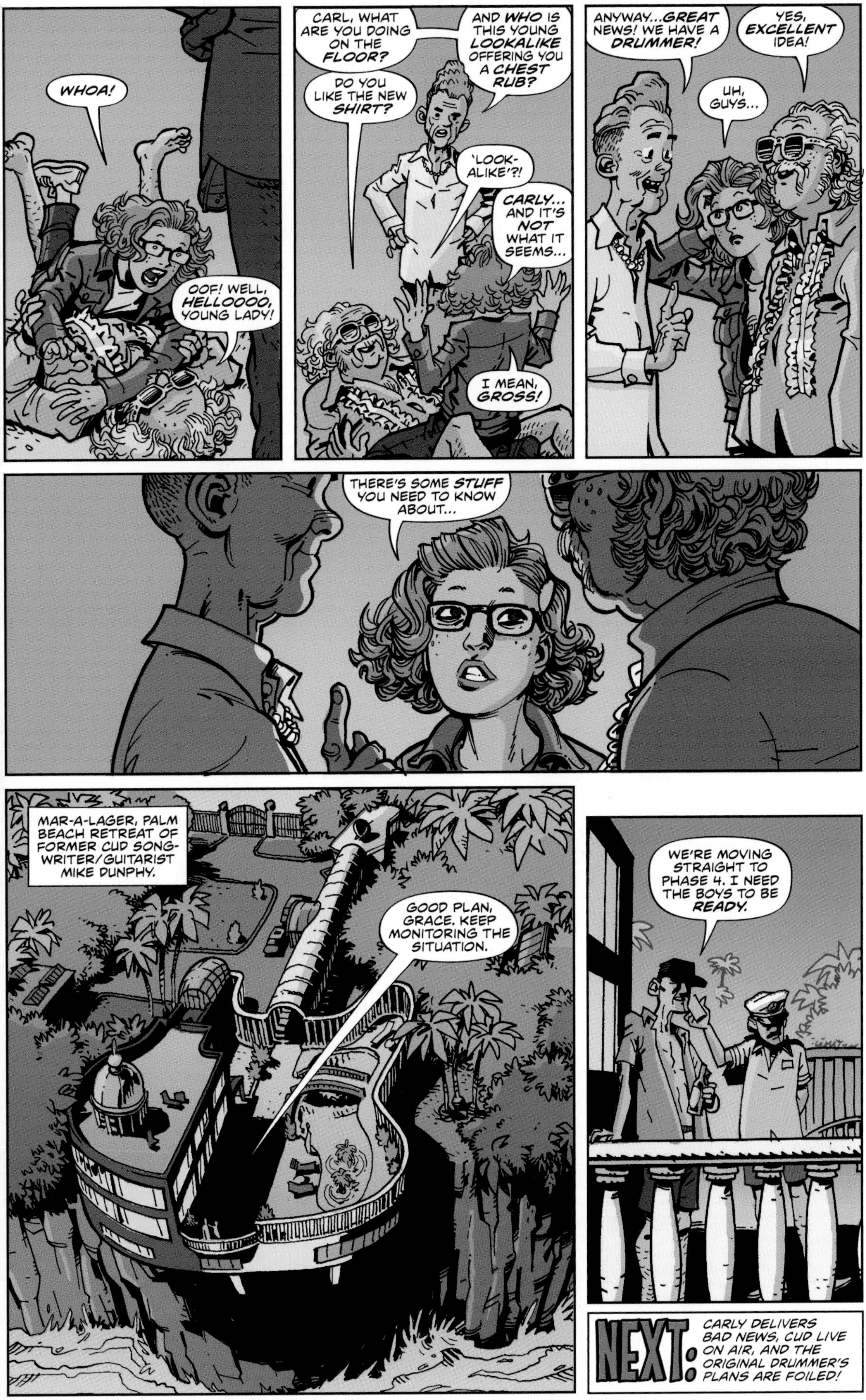
WHOA!
OOF! WELL, HELLOOOO, YOUNG LADY!
CARL, WHAT ARE YOU DOING ON THE FLOOR?
AND WHO IS THIS YOUNG LOOKALIKE OFFERING YOU A CHEST RUB?
DO YOU LIKE THE NEW SHIRT?
'LOOK-ALIKE'?!
CARLY... AND IT'S NOT WHAT IT SEEMS...
I MEAN, GROSS!
ANYWAY...GREAT NEWS! WE HAVE A DRUMMER!
YES, EXCELLENT IDEA!
UH, GUYS...
THERE'S SOME STUFF YOU NEED TO KNOW ABOUT...
MAR-A-LAGER, PALM BEACH RETREAT OF FORMER CUD SONG-WRITER/GUITARIST MIKE DUNPHY.
GOOD PLAN, GRACE. KEEP MONITORING THE SITUATION.
WE'RE MOVING STRAIGHT TO PHASE 4. I NEED THE BOYS TO BE READY.
NEXT:
CARLY DELIVERS BAD NEWS, CUD LIVE ON AIR, AND THE ORIGINAL DRUMMER'S PLANS ARE FOILED!

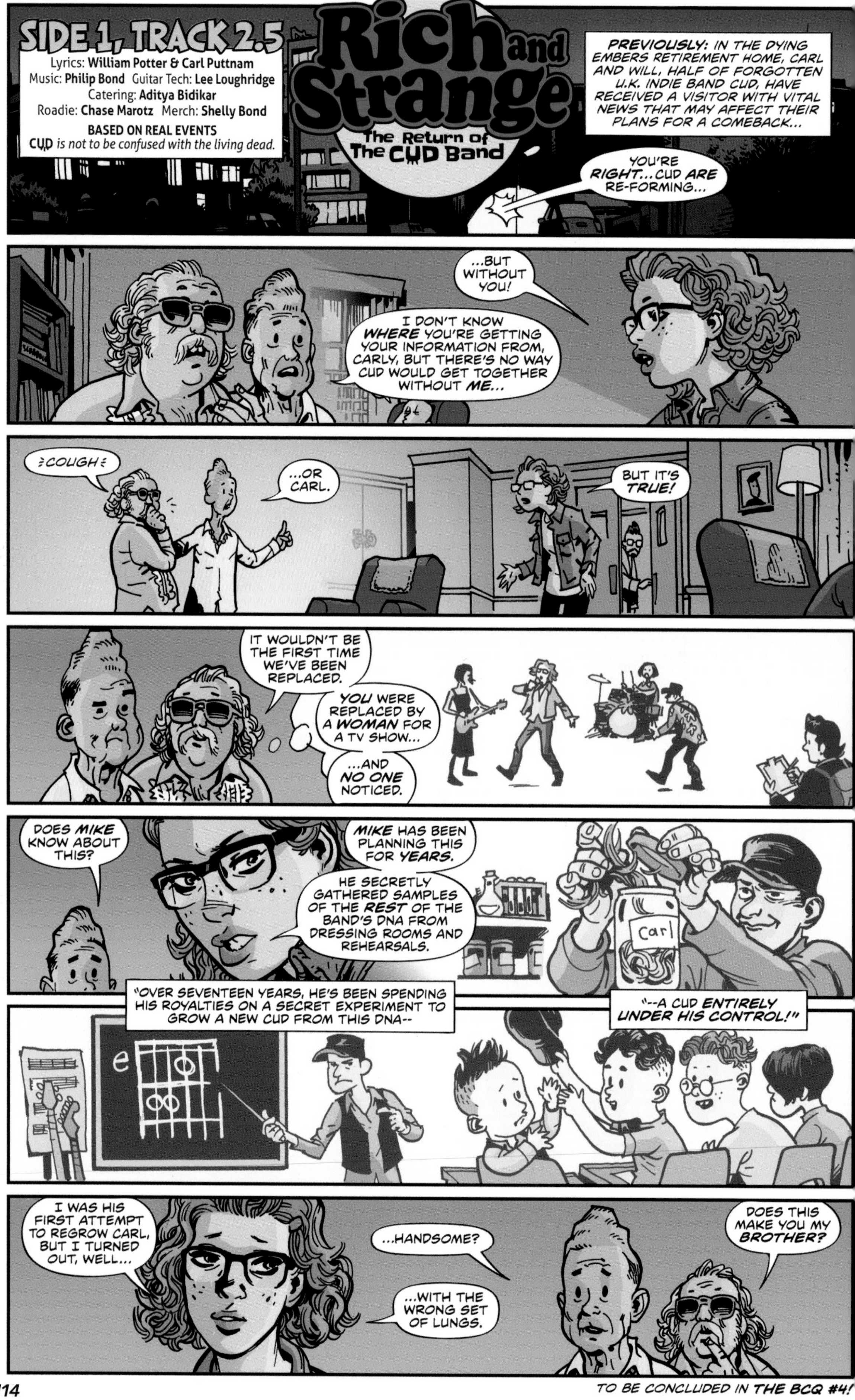
SIDE 1, TRACK 2.5
Lyrics: William Potter & Carl Puttnam
Music: Philip Bond Guitar Tech: Lee Loughridge
Catering: Aditya Bidikar
Roadie: Chase Marotz Merch: Shelly Bond
BASED ON REAL EVENTS
CUD is not to be confused with the living dead.
Rich and Strange
The Return of The CUD Band
PREVIOUSLY: IN THE DYING EMBERS RETIREMENT HOME, CARL AND WILL, HALF OF FORGOTTEN U.K. INDIE BAND CUD, HAVE RECEIVED A VISITOR WITH VITAL NEWS THAT MAY AFFECT THEIR PLANS FOR A COMEBACK...
YOU'RE RIGHT... CUD ARE RE-FORMING...
...BUT WITHOUT YOU!
I DON'T KNOW WHERE YOU'RE GETTING YOUR INFORMATION FROM, CARLY, BUT THERE'S NO WAY CUD WOULD GET TOGETHER WITHOUT ME...
COUGH
...OR CARL.
BUT IT'S TRUE!
IT WOULDN'T BE THE FIRST TIME WE'VE BEEN REPLACED.
YOU WERE REPLACED BY A WOMAN FOR A TV SHOW...
...AND NO ONE NOTICED.
DOES MIKE KNOW ABOUT THIS?
MIKE HAS BEEN PLANNING THIS FOR YEARS.
HE SECRETLY GATHERED SAMPLES OF THE REST OF THE BAND'S DNA FROM DRESSING ROOMS AND REHEARSALS.
Carl
"OVER SEVENTEEN YEARS, HE'S BEEN SPENDING HIS ROYALTIES ON A SECRET EXPERIMENT TO GROW A NEW CUD FROM THIS DNA--
"--A CUD ENTIRELY UNDER HIS CONTROL!"
e
I WAS HIS FIRST ATTEMPT TO REGROW CARL, BUT I TURNED OUT, WELL...
...HANDSOME?
...WITH THE WRONG SET OF LUNGS.
DOES THIS MAKE YOU MY BROTHER?

TO BE CONCLUDED IN THE BCQ #4!

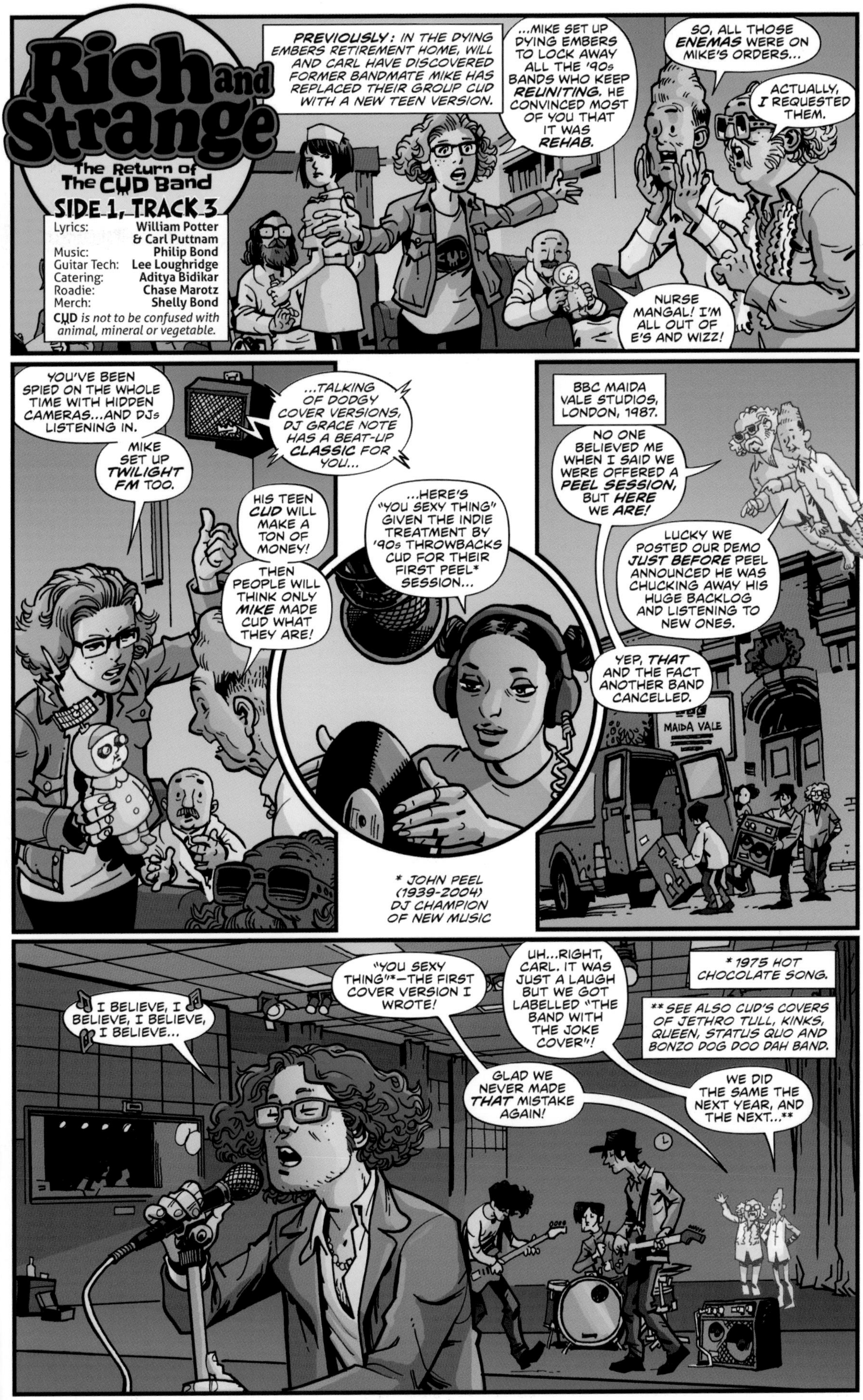
Rich and Strange
The Return of The CUD Band
SIDE 1, TRACK 3
Lyrics: William Potter & Carl Puttnam
Music: Philip Bond
Guitar Tech: Lee Loughridge
Catering: Aditya Bidikar
Roadie: Chase Marotz
Merch: Shelly Bond
CUD is not to be confused with animal, mineral or vegetable.
PREVIOUSLY: IN THE DYING EMBERS RETIREMENT HOME, WILL AND CARL HAVE DISCOVERED FORMER BANDMATE MIKE HAS REPLACED THEIR GROUP CUD WITH A NEW TEEN VERSION.
...MIKE SET UP DYING EMBERS TO LOCK AWAY ALL THE '90s BANDS WHO KEEP REUNITING. HE CONVINCED MOST OF YOU THAT IT WAS REHAB.
SO, ALL THOSE ENEMAS WERE ON MIKE'S ORDERS...
ACTUALLY, I REQUESTED THEM.
NURSE MANGAL! I'M ALL OUT OF E'S AND WIZZ!
YOU'VE BEEN SPIED ON THE WHOLE TIME WITH HIDDEN CAMERAS...AND DJs LISTENING IN.
MIKE SET UP TWILIGHT FM TOO.
...TALKING OF DODGY COVER VERSIONS, DJ GRACE NOTE HAS A BEAT-UP CLASSIC FOR YOU...
HIS TEEN CUD WILL MAKE A TON OF MONEY!
THEN PEOPLE WILL THINK ONLY MIKE MADE CUD WHAT THEY ARE!
...HERE'S "YOU SEXY THING" GIVEN THE INDIE TREATMENT BY '90s THROWBACKS CUD FOR THEIR FIRST PEEL* SESSION...
* JOHN PEEL (1939-2004) DJ CHAMPION OF NEW MUSIC
BBC MAIDA VALE STUDIOS, LONDON, 1987.
NO ONE BELIEVED ME WHEN I SAID WE WERE OFFERED A PEEL SESSION, BUT HERE WE ARE!
LUCKY WE POSTED OUR DEMO JUST BEFORE PEEL ANNOUNCED HE WAS CHUCKING AWAY HIS HUGE BACKLOG AND LISTENING TO NEW ONES.
YEP, THAT AND THE FACT ANOTHER BAND CANCELLED.
MAIDA VALE
I BELIEVE, I BELIEVE, I BELIEVE, I BELIEVE...
"YOU SEXY THING"*—THE FIRST COVER VERSION I WROTE!
UH...RIGHT, CARL. IT WAS JUST A LAUGH BUT WE GOT LABELLED "THE BAND WITH THE JOKE COVER"!
GLAD WE NEVER MADE THAT MISTAKE AGAIN!
* 1975 HOT CHOCOLATE SONG.
** SEE ALSO CUD'S COVERS OF JETHRO TULL, KINKS, QUEEN, STATUS QUO AND BONZO DOG DOO DAH BAND.
WE DID THE SAME THE NEXT YEAR, AND THE NEXT...**

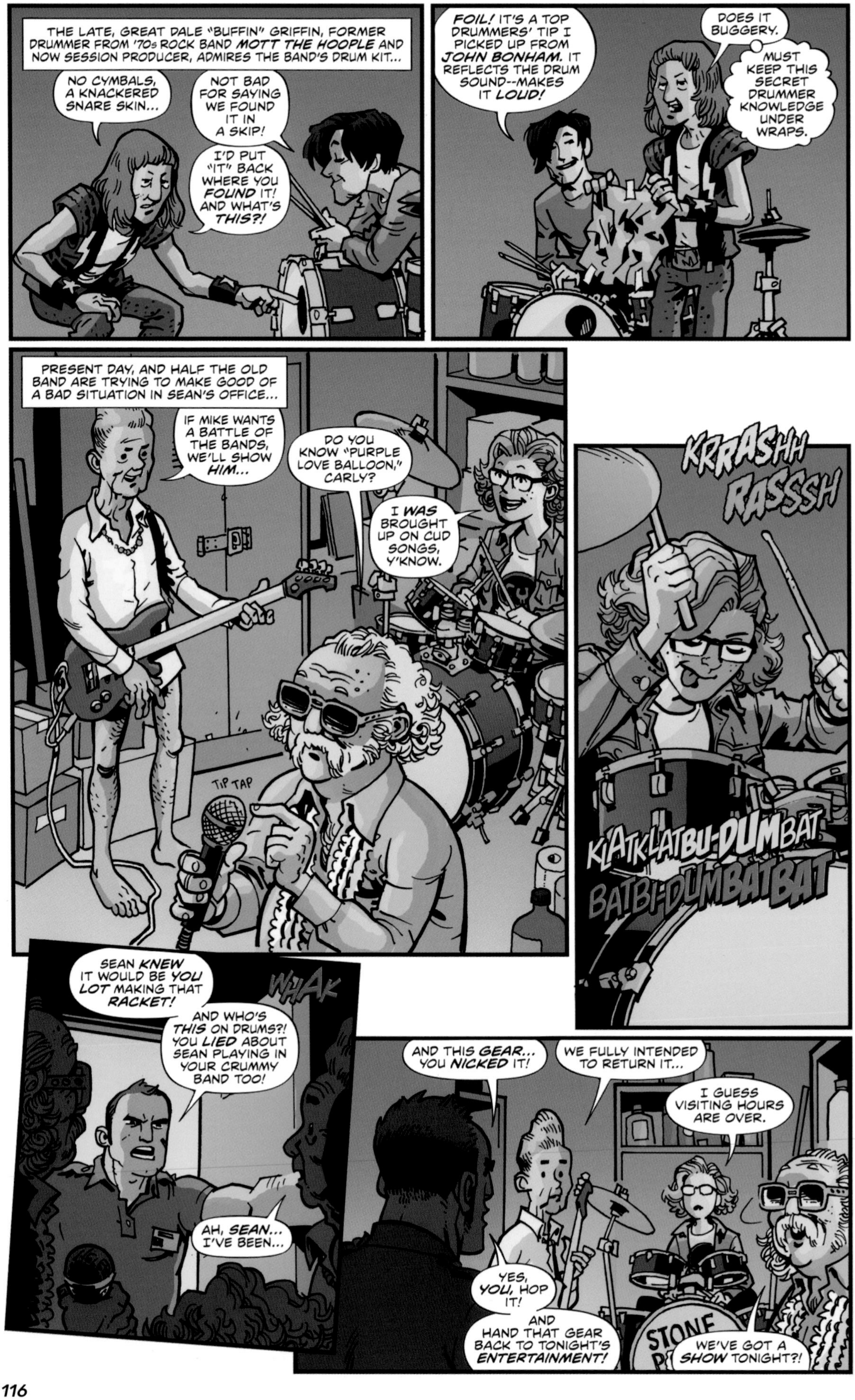
THE LATE, GREAT DALE "BUFFIN" GRIFFIN, FORMER DRUMMER FROM '70s ROCK BAND *MOTT THE HOOPLE* AND NOW SESSION PRODUCER, ADMIRES THE BAND'S DRUM KIT...
NO CYMBALS, A KNACKERED SNARE SKIN...
NOT BAD FOR SAYING WE FOUND IT IN A SKIP!
I'D PUT "IT" BACK WHERE YOU *FOUND* IT! AND WHAT'S *THIS?!*
FOIL! IT'S A TOP DRUMMERS' TIP I PICKED UP FROM *JOHN BONHAM.* IT REFLECTS THE DRUM SOUND--MAKES IT *LOUD!*
DOES IT BUGGERY.
MUST KEEP THIS SECRET DRUMMER KNOWLEDGE UNDER WRAPS.
PRESENT DAY, AND HALF THE OLD BAND ARE TRYING TO MAKE GOOD OF A BAD SITUATION IN SEAN'S OFFICE...
IF MIKE WANTS A BATTLE OF THE BANDS, WE'LL SHOW *HIM...*
DO YOU KNOW "PURPLE LOVE BALLOON," CARLY?
I *WAS* BROUGHT UP ON CUD SONGS, Y'KNOW.
TIP TAP
KRRASHH
RASSSH
KLATKLATBU-DUMBAT
BATBI-DUMBATBAT
SEAN *KNEW* IT WOULD BE *YOU LOT* MAKING THAT *RACKET!*
WHAK
AND WHO'S *THIS* ON DRUMS?! YOU *LIED* ABOUT SEAN PLAYING IN YOUR CRUMMY BAND TOO!
AH, *SEAN...* I'VE BEEN...
AND THIS *GEAR...* YOU *NICKED* IT!
WE FULLY INTENDED TO RETURN IT...
I GUESS VISITING HOURS ARE OVER.
YES, *YOU,* HOP IT!
AND HAND THAT GEAR BACK TO TONIGHT'S *ENTERTAINMENT!*
STONE
WE'VE GOT A *SHOW* TONIGHT?!

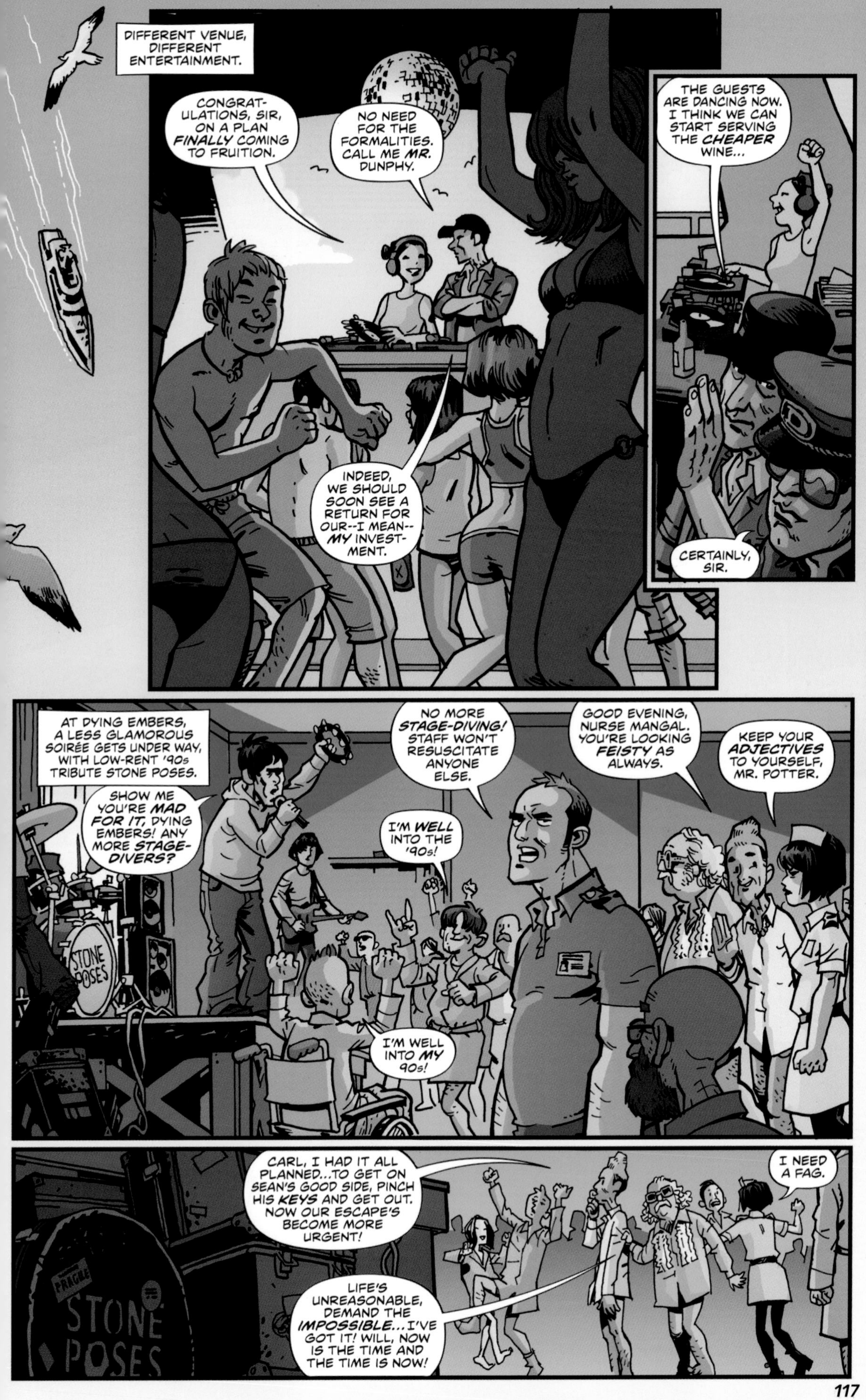
DIFFERENT VENUE, DIFFERENT ENTERTAINMENT.
CONGRAT-ULATIONS, SIR, ON A PLAN FINALLY COMING TO FRUITION.
NO NEED FOR THE FORMALITIES. CALL ME MR. DUNPHY.
INDEED, WE SHOULD SOON SEE A RETURN FOR OUR--I MEAN--MY INVEST-MENT.
THE GUESTS ARE DANCING NOW. I THINK WE CAN START SERVING THE CHEAPER WINE...
CERTAINLY, SIR.
AT DYING EMBERS, A LESS GLAMOROUS SOIRÉE GETS UNDER WAY, WITH LOW-RENT '90s TRIBUTE STONE POSES.
SHOW ME YOU'RE MAD FOR IT, DYING EMBERS! ANY MORE STAGE-DIVERS?
NO MORE STAGE-DIVING! STAFF WON'T RESUSCITATE ANYONE ELSE.
I'M WELL INTO THE '90s!
I'M WELL INTO MY 90s!
GOOD EVENING, NURSE MANGAL. YOU'RE LOOKING FEISTY AS ALWAYS.
KEEP YOUR ADJECTIVES TO YOURSELF, MR. POTTER.
STONE POSES
CARL, I HAD IT ALL PLANNED...TO GET ON SEAN'S GOOD SIDE, PINCH HIS KEYS AND GET OUT. NOW OUR ESCAPE'S BECOME MORE URGENT!
I NEED A FAG.
LIFE'S UNREASONABLE, DEMAND THE IMPOSSIBLE... I'VE GOT IT! WILL, NOW IS THE TIME AND THE TIME IS NOW!
FRAGILE
STONE POSES

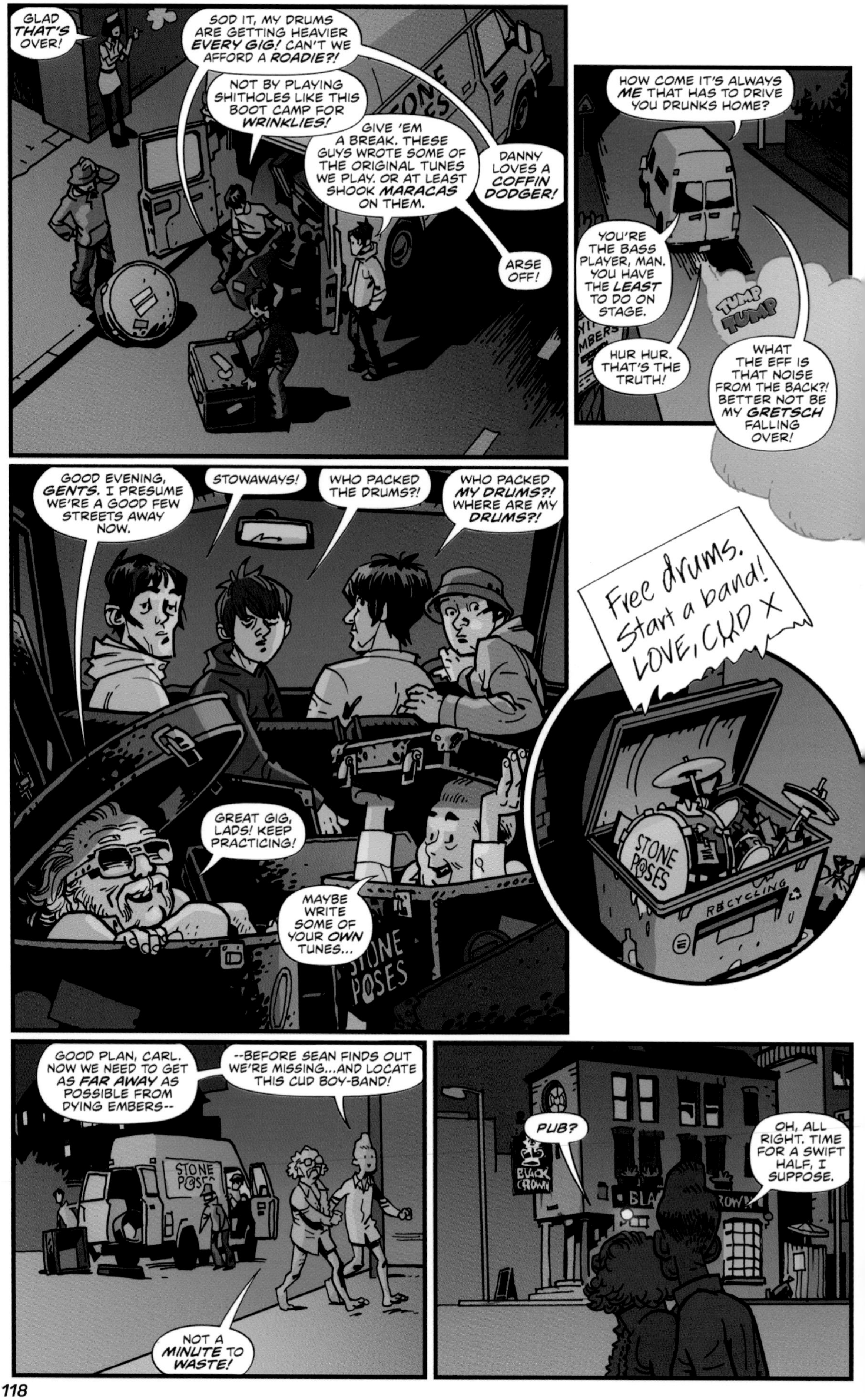
GLAD THAT'S OVER!
SOD IT, MY DRUMS ARE GETTING HEAVIER EVERY GIG! CAN'T WE AFFORD A ROADIE?!
NOT BY PLAYING SHITHOLES LIKE THIS BOOT CAMP FOR WRINKLIES!
GIVE 'EM A BREAK. THESE GUYS WROTE SOME OF THE ORIGINAL TUNES WE PLAY. OR AT LEAST SHOOK MARACAS ON THEM.
DANNY LOVES A COFFIN DODGER!
ARSE OFF!
HOW COME IT'S ALWAYS ME THAT HAS TO DRIVE YOU DRUNKS HOME?
YOU'RE THE BASS PLAYER, MAN. YOU HAVE THE LEAST TO DO ON STAGE.
HUR HUR. THAT'S THE TRUTH!
TUMP TUMP
WHAT THE EFF IS THAT NOISE FROM THE BACK?! BETTER NOT BE MY GRETSCH FALLING OVER!
GOOD EVENING, GENTS. I PRESUME WE'RE A GOOD FEW STREETS AWAY NOW.
STOWAWAYS!
WHO PACKED THE DRUMS?!
WHO PACKED MY DRUMS?! WHERE ARE MY DRUMS?!
GREAT GIG, LADS! KEEP PRACTICING!
MAYBE WRITE SOME OF YOUR OWN TUNES...
STONE POSES
Free drums. Start a band! LOVE, CUD X
STONE POSES
RECYCLING
GOOD PLAN, CARL. NOW WE NEED TO GET AS FAR AWAY AS POSSIBLE FROM DYING EMBERS--
--BEFORE SEAN FINDS OUT WE'RE MISSING...AND LOCATE THIS CUD BOY-BAND!
STONE POSES
NOT A MINUTE TO WASTE!
BLACK CROWN
PUB?
OH, ALL RIGHT. TIME FOR A SWIFT HALF, I SUPPOSE.

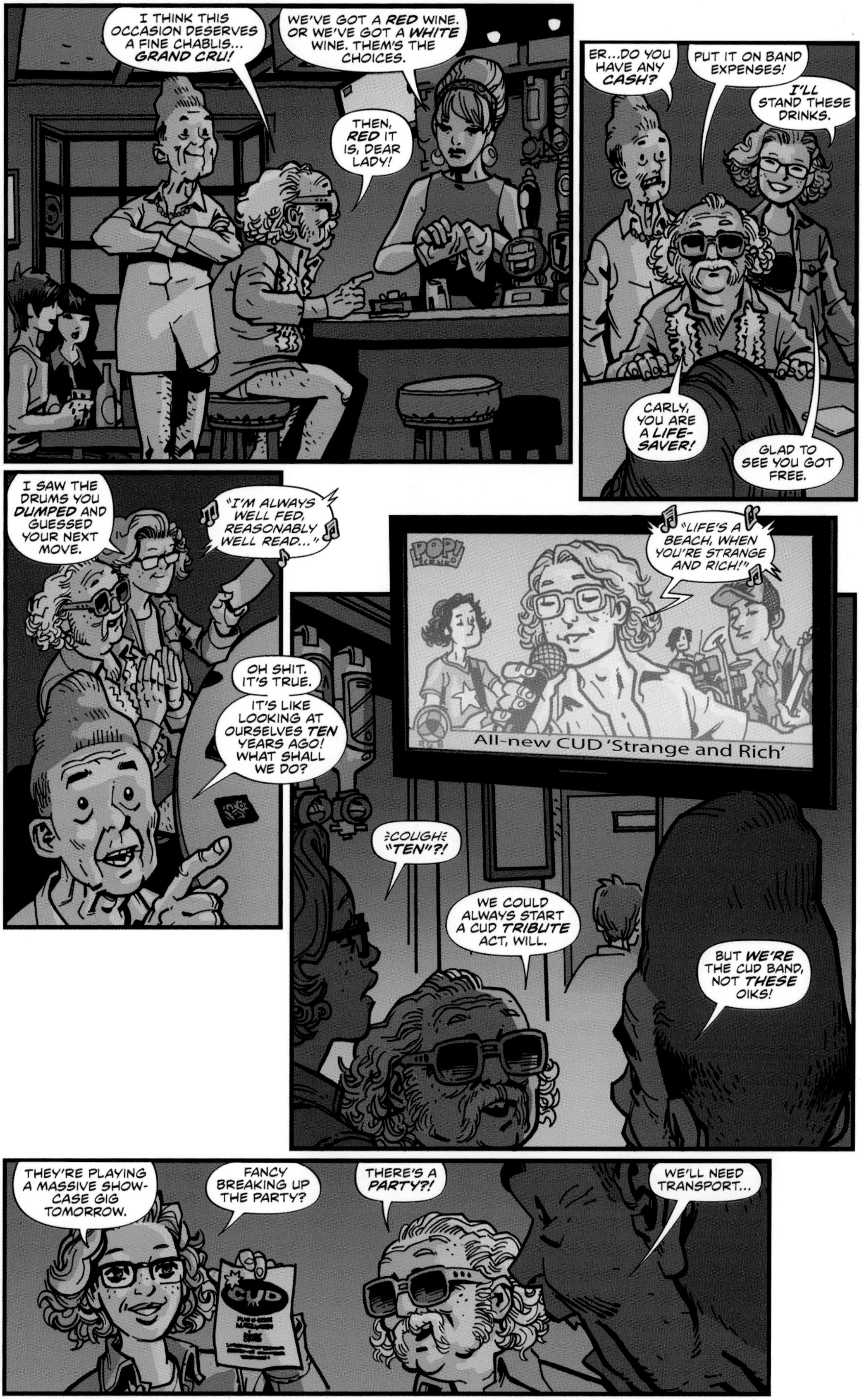
I THINK THIS OCCASION DESERVES A FINE CHABLIS... GRAND CRU!
WE'VE GOT A RED WINE. OR WE'VE GOT A WHITE WINE. THEM'S THE CHOICES.
THEN, RED IT IS, DEAR LADY!
ER...DO YOU HAVE ANY CASH?
PUT IT ON BAND EXPENSES!
I'LL STAND THESE DRINKS.
CARLY, YOU ARE A LIFE-SAVER!
GLAD TO SEE YOU GOT FREE.
I SAW THE DRUMS YOU DUMPED AND GUESSED YOUR NEXT MOVE.
"I'M ALWAYS WELL FED, REASONABLY WELL READ..."
OH SHIT. IT'S TRUE.
IT'S LIKE LOOKING AT OURSELVES TEN YEARS AGO! WHAT SHALL WE DO?
"LIFE'S A BEACH, WHEN YOU'RE STRANGE AND RICH!"
POP! SCENE
All-new CUD 'Strange and Rich'
RGB
COUGH "TEN"?!
WE COULD ALWAYS START A CUD TRIBUTE ACT, WILL.
BUT WE'RE THE CUD BAND, NOT THESE OIKS!
THEY'RE PLAYING A MASSIVE SHOW-CASE GIG TOMORROW.
FANCY BREAKING UP THE PARTY?
CUD
THERE'S A PARTY?!
WE'LL NEED TRANSPORT...

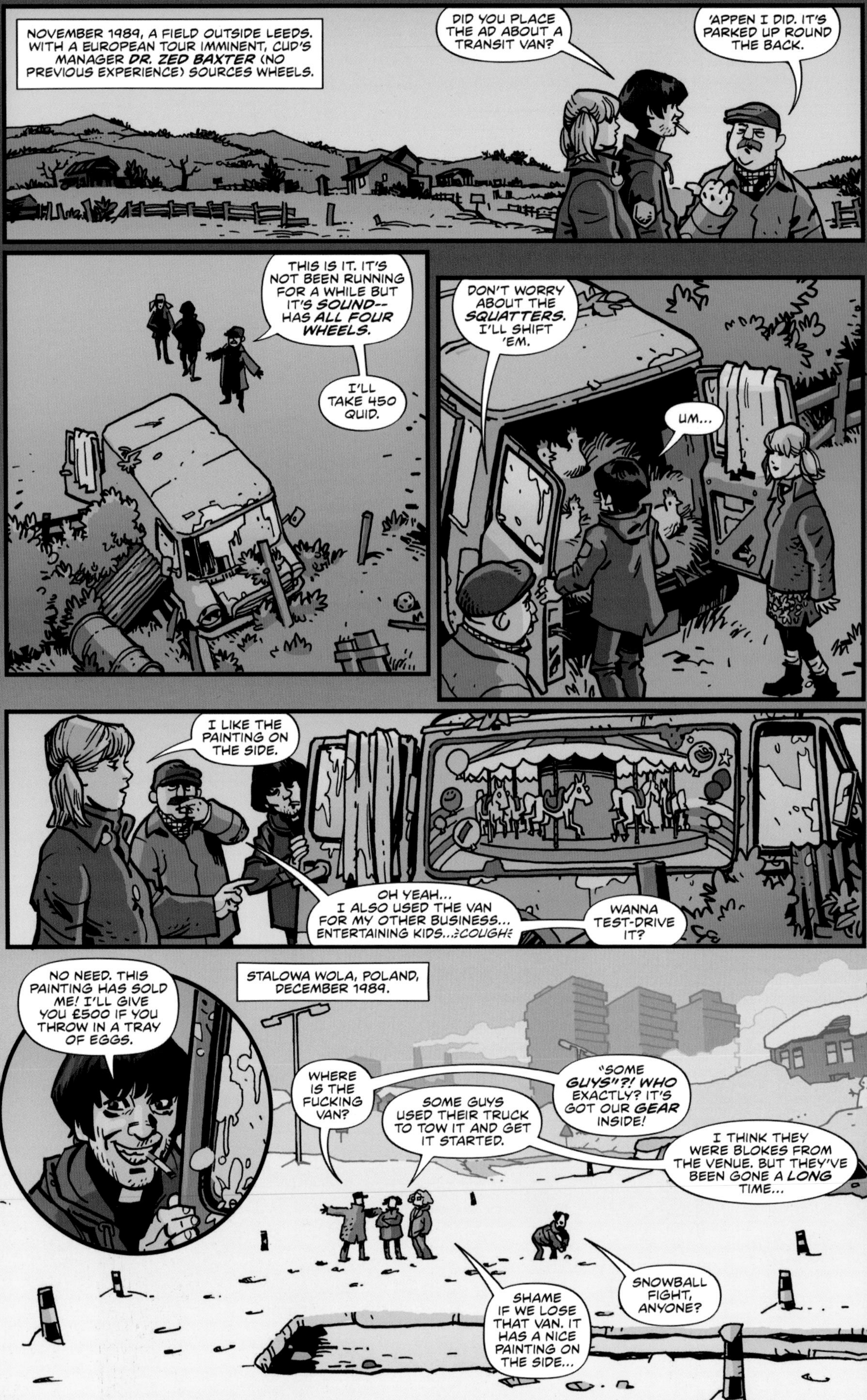
NOVEMBER 1989, A FIELD OUTSIDE LEEDS. WITH A EUROPEAN TOUR IMMINENT, CUD'S MANAGER DR. ZED BAXTER (NO PREVIOUS EXPERIENCE) SOURCES WHEELS.
DID YOU PLACE THE AD ABOUT A TRANSIT VAN?
'APPEN I DID. IT'S PARKED UP ROUND THE BACK.
THIS IS IT. IT'S NOT BEEN RUNNING FOR A WHILE BUT IT'S SOUND-- HAS ALL FOUR WHEELS.
I'LL TAKE 450 QUID.
DON'T WORRY ABOUT THE SQUATTERS. I'LL SHIFT 'EM.
UM...
I LIKE THE PAINTING ON THE SIDE.
OH YEAH... I ALSO USED THE VAN FOR MY OTHER BUSINESS... ENTERTAINING KIDS... *COUGH*
WANNA TEST-DRIVE IT?
NO NEED. THIS PAINTING HAS SOLD ME! I'LL GIVE YOU £500 IF YOU THROW IN A TRAY OF EGGS.
STALOWA WOLA, POLAND, DECEMBER 1989.
WHERE IS THE FUCKING VAN?
SOME GUYS USED THEIR TRUCK TO TOW IT AND GET IT STARTED.
"SOME GUYS"?! WHO EXACTLY? IT'S GOT OUR GEAR INSIDE!
I THINK THEY WERE BLOKES FROM THE VENUE. BUT THEY'VE BEEN GONE A LONG TIME...
SHAME IF WE LOSE THAT VAN. IT HAS A NICE PAINTING ON THE SIDE...
SNOWBALL FIGHT, ANYONE?

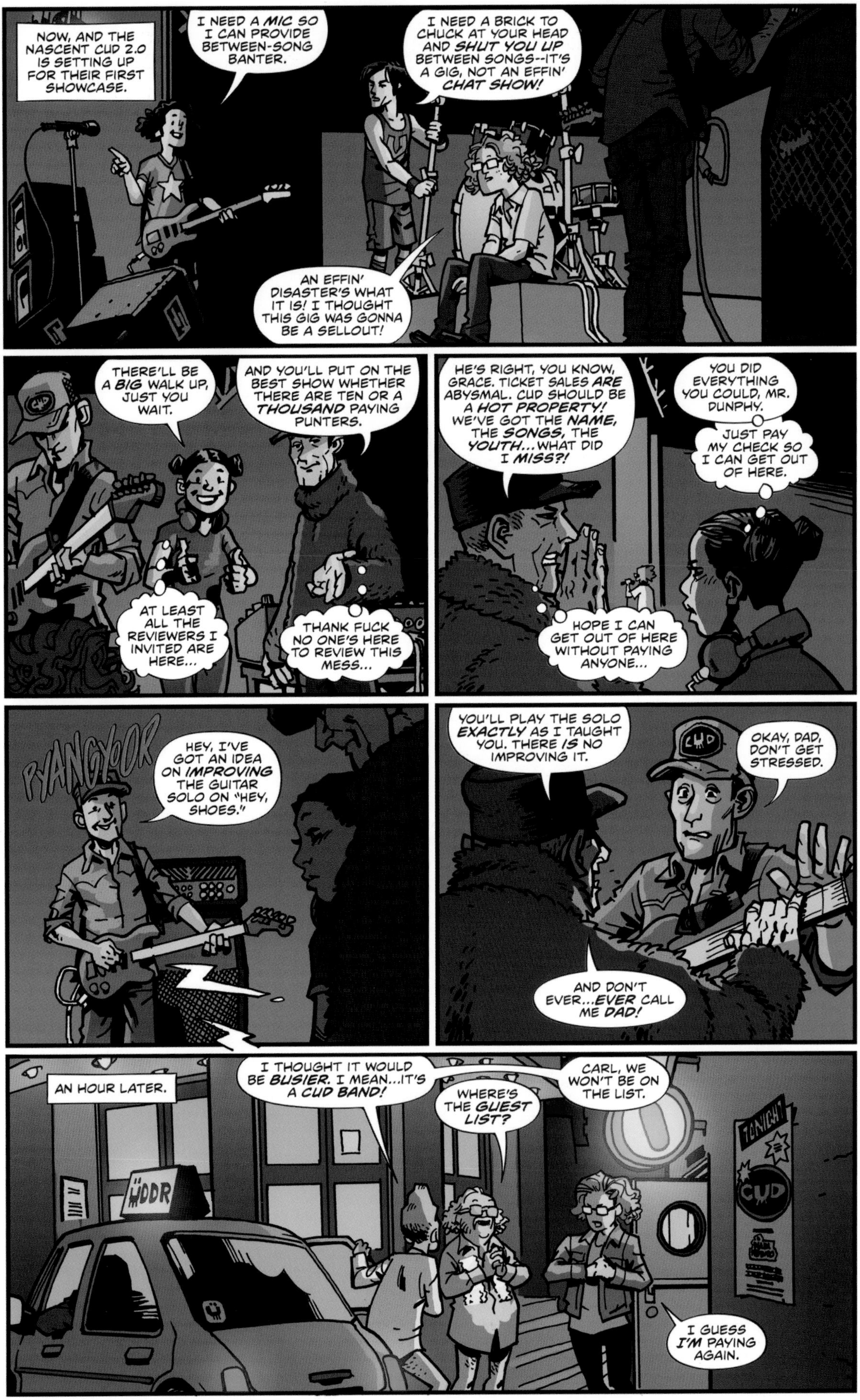
NOW, AND THE NASCENT CUD 2.0 IS SETTING UP FOR THEIR FIRST SHOWCASE.
I NEED A MIC SO I CAN PROVIDE BETWEEN-SONG BANTER.
I NEED A BRICK TO CHUCK AT YOUR HEAD AND SHUT YOU UP BETWEEN SONGS--IT'S A GIG, NOT AN EFFIN' CHAT SHOW!
AN EFFIN' DISASTER'S WHAT IT IS! I THOUGHT THIS GIG WAS GONNA BE A SELLOUT!
THERE'LL BE A BIG WALK UP, JUST YOU WAIT.
AND YOU'LL PUT ON THE BEST SHOW WHETHER THERE ARE TEN OR A THOUSAND PAYING PUNTERS.
AT LEAST ALL THE REVIEWERS I INVITED ARE HERE...
THANK FUCK NO ONE'S HERE TO REVIEW THIS MESS...
HE'S RIGHT, YOU KNOW, GRACE. TICKET SALES ARE ABYSMAL. CUD SHOULD BE A HOT PROPERTY! WE'VE GOT THE NAME, THE SONGS, THE YOUTH... WHAT DID I MISS?!
YOU DID EVERYTHING YOU COULD, MR. DUNPHY.
JUST PAY MY CHECK SO I CAN GET OUT OF HERE.
HOPE I CAN GET OUT OF HERE WITHOUT PAYING ANYONE...
PYANGYOOR
HEY, I'VE GOT AN IDEA ON IMPROVING THE GUITAR SOLO ON "HEY, SHOES."
YOU'LL PLAY THE SOLO EXACTLY AS I TAUGHT YOU. THERE IS NO IMPROVING IT.
OKAY, DAD, DON'T GET STRESSED.
AND DON'T EVER...EVER CALL ME DAD!
AN HOUR LATER.
I THOUGHT IT WOULD BE BUSIER. I MEAN...IT'S A CUD BAND!
WHERE'S THE GUEST LIST?
CARL, WE WON'T BE ON THE LIST.
TONIGHT
CUD
I GUESS I'M PAYING AGAIN.

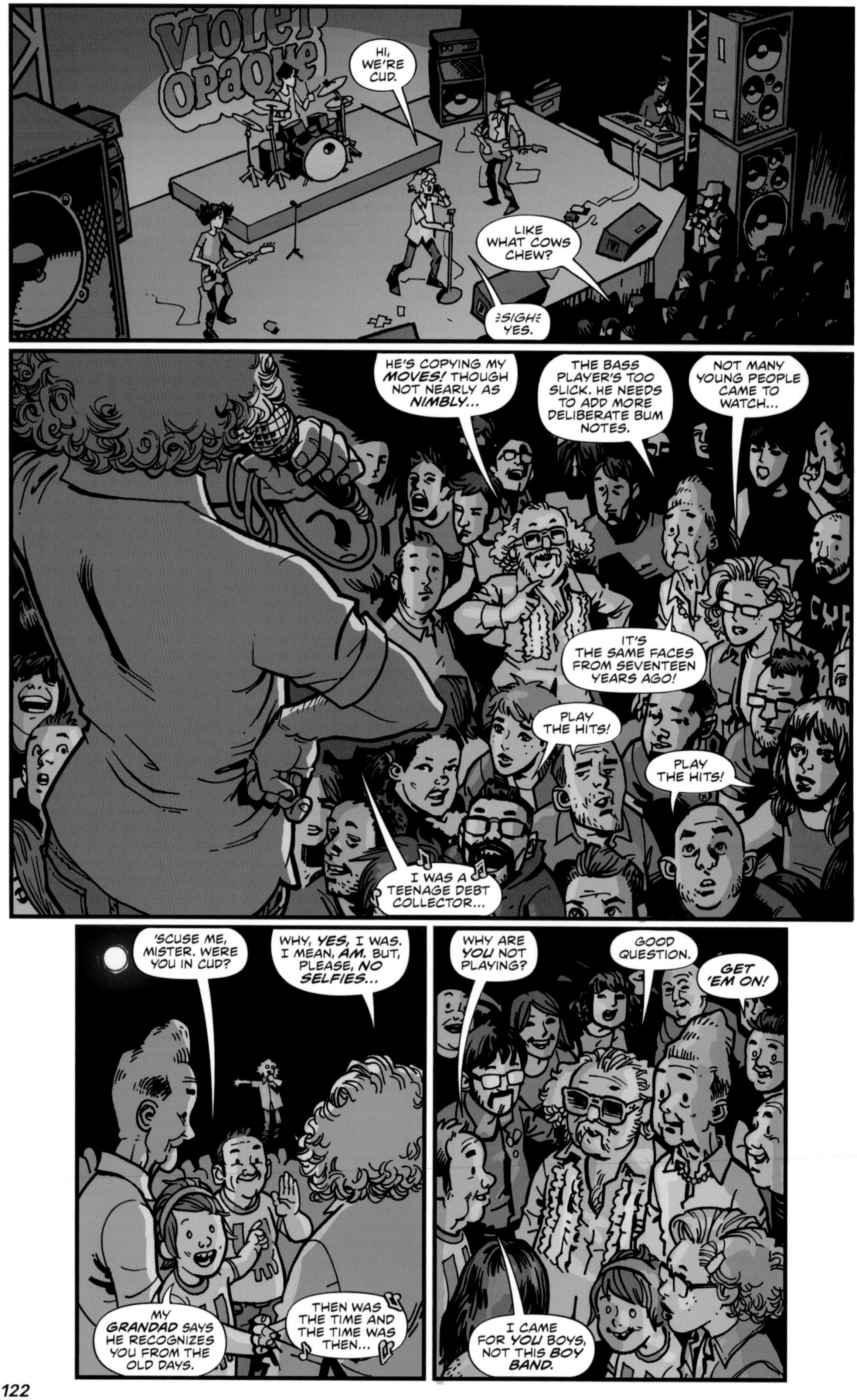

HI, WE'RE CUD.
LIKE WHAT COWS CHEW?
SIGH YES.
HE'S COPYING MY *MOVES!* THOUGH NOT NEARLY AS *NIMBLY...*
THE BASS PLAYER'S TOO SLICK. HE NEEDS TO ADD MORE DELIBERATE BUM NOTES.
NOT MANY YOUNG PEOPLE CAME TO WATCH...
IT'S THE SAME FACES FROM SEVENTEEN YEARS AGO!
PLAY THE HITS!
PLAY THE HITS!
I WAS A TEENAGE DEBT COLLECTOR...
'SCUSE ME, MISTER. WERE YOU IN CUD?
WHY, *YES,* I WAS. I MEAN, *AM.* BUT, PLEASE, *NO SELFIES...*
MY *GRANDAD* SAYS HE RECOGNIZES YOU FROM THE OLD DAYS.
THEN WAS THE TIME AND THE TIME WAS THEN...
WHY ARE *YOU* NOT PLAYING?
GOOD QUESTION.
GET 'EM ON!
I CAME FOR *YOU* BOYS, NOT THIS *BOY BAND.*

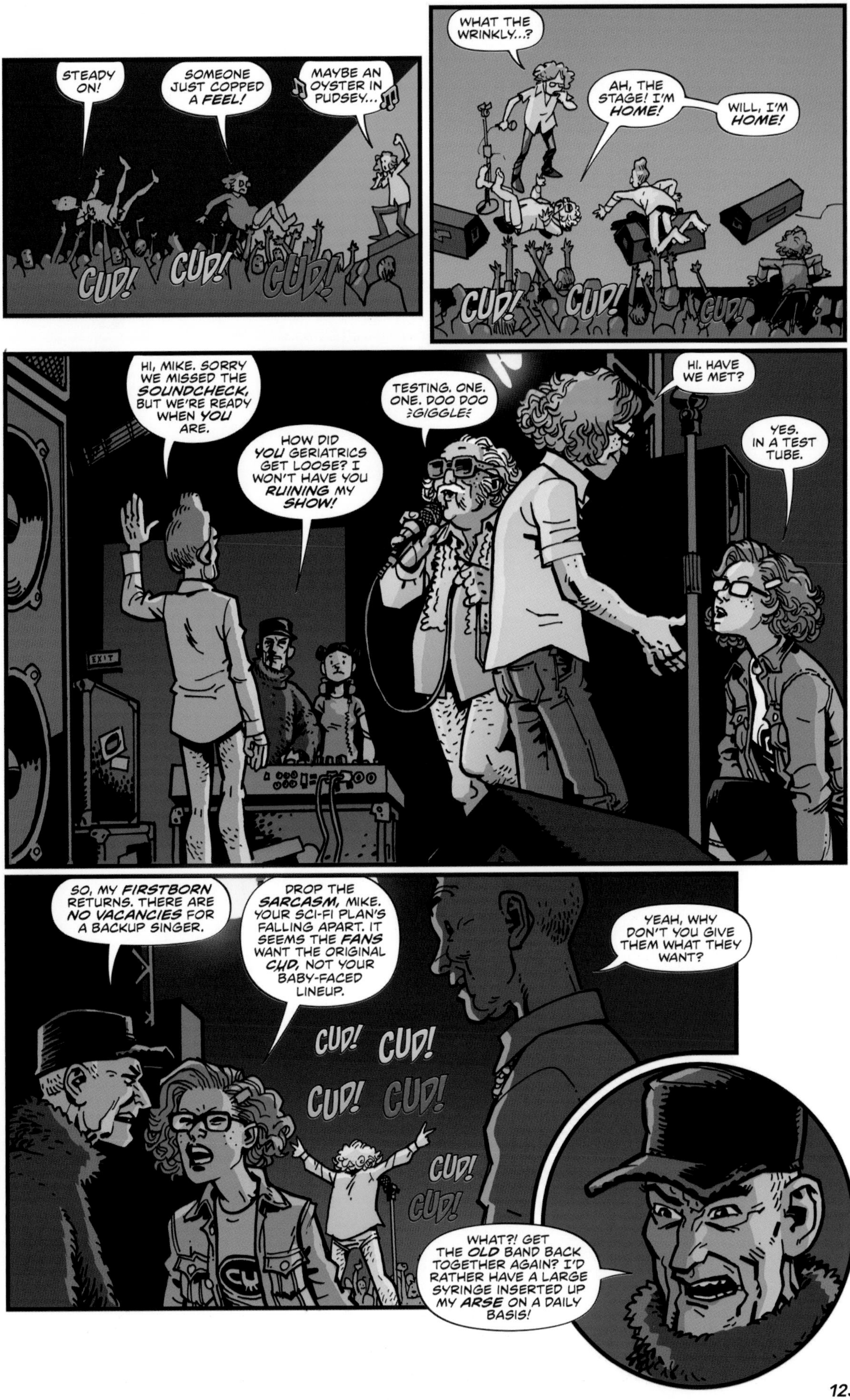

STEADY ON!
SOMEONE JUST COPPED A FEEL!
MAYBE AN OYSTER IN PUDSEY...
CUD! CUD! CUD!
WHAT THE WRINKLY...?
AH, THE STAGE! I'M HOME!
WILL, I'M HOME!
CUD! CUD! CUD!
HI, MIKE. SORRY WE MISSED THE SOUNDCHECK, BUT WE'RE READY WHEN YOU ARE.
HOW DID YOU GERIATRICS GET LOOSE? I WON'T HAVE YOU RUINING MY SHOW!
TESTING. ONE. ONE. DOO DOO GIGGLE
HI. HAVE WE MET?
YES. IN A TEST TUBE.
EXIT
SO, MY FIRSTBORN RETURNS. THERE ARE NO VACANCIES FOR A BACKUP SINGER.
DROP THE SARCASM, MIKE. YOUR SCI-FI PLAN'S FALLING APART. IT SEEMS THE FANS WANT THE ORIGINAL CUD, NOT YOUR BABY-FACED LINEUP.
YEAH, WHY DON'T YOU GIVE THEM WHAT THEY WANT?
CUD! CUD! CUD! CUD! CUD! CUD!
WHAT?! GET THE OLD BAND BACK TOGETHER AGAIN? I'D RATHER HAVE A LARGE SYRINGE INSERTED UP MY ARSE ON A DAILY BASIS!

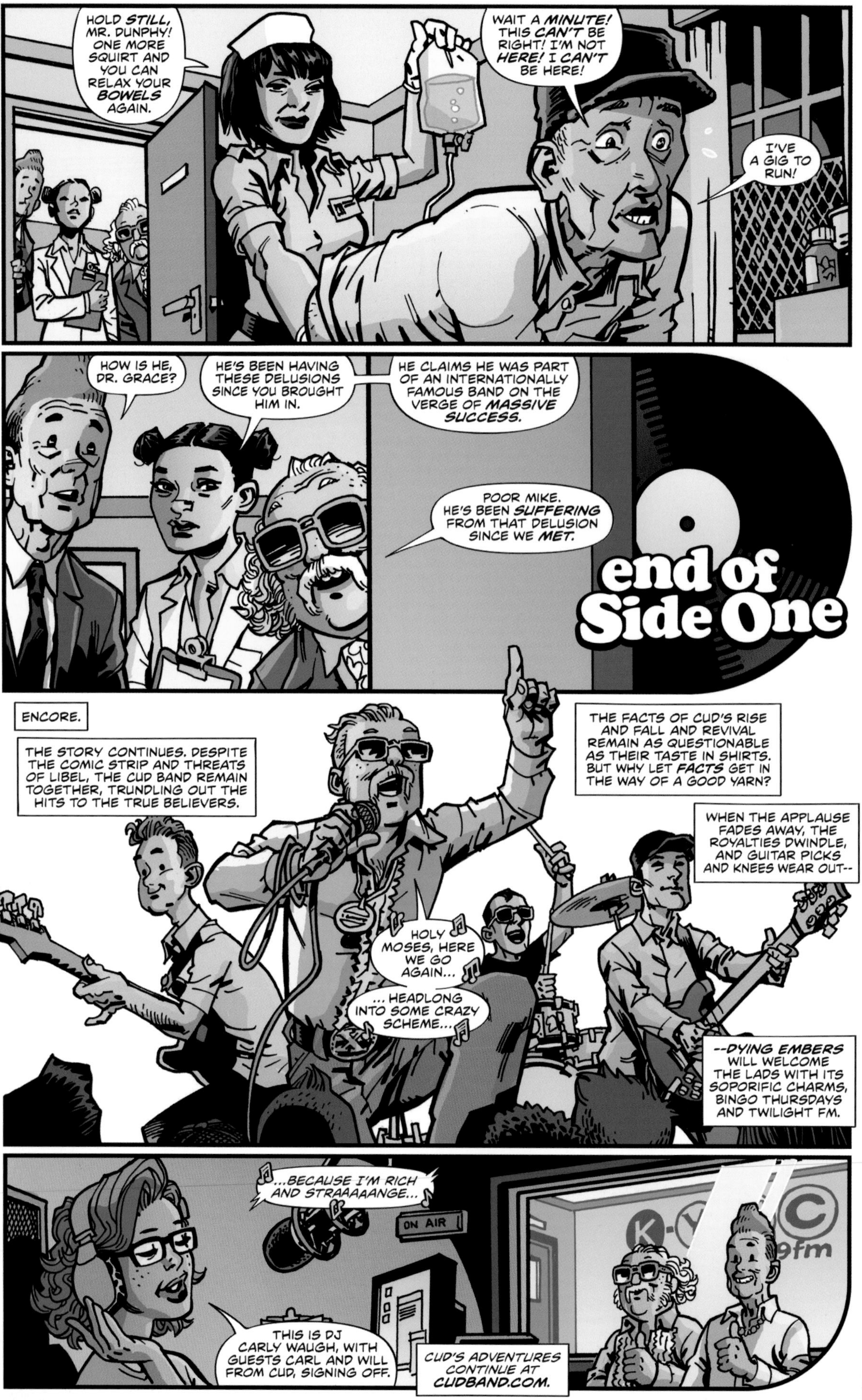
HOLD STILL, MR. DUNPHY! ONE MORE SQUIRT AND YOU CAN RELAX YOUR BOWELS AGAIN.
WAIT A MINUTE! THIS CAN'T BE RIGHT! I'M NOT HERE! I CAN'T BE HERE!
I'VE A GIG TO RUN!
HOW IS HE, DR. GRACE?
HE'S BEEN HAVING THESE DELUSIONS SINCE YOU BROUGHT HIM IN.
HE CLAIMS HE WAS PART OF AN INTERNATIONALLY FAMOUS BAND ON THE VERGE OF MASSIVE SUCCESS.
POOR MIKE. HE'S BEEN SUFFERING FROM THAT DELUSION SINCE WE MET.
end of Side One
ENCORE.
THE STORY CONTINUES. DESPITE THE COMIC STRIP AND THREATS OF LIBEL, THE CUD BAND REMAIN TOGETHER, TRUNDLING OUT THE HITS TO THE TRUE BELIEVERS.
THE FACTS OF CUD'S RISE AND FALL AND REVIVAL REMAIN AS QUESTIONABLE AS THEIR TASTE IN SHIRTS. BUT WHY LET FACTS GET IN THE WAY OF A GOOD YARN?
WHEN THE APPLAUSE FADES AWAY, THE ROYALTIES DWINDLE, AND GUITAR PICKS AND KNEES WEAR OUT--
HOLY MOSES, HERE WE GO AGAIN...
... HEADLONG INTO SOME CRAZY SCHEME...
--DYING EMBERS WILL WELCOME THE LADS WITH ITS SOPORIFIC CHARMS, BINGO THURSDAYS AND TWILIGHT FM.
...BECAUSE I'M RICH AND STRAAAAANGE...
ON AIR
THIS IS DJ CARLY WAUGH, WITH GUESTS CARL AND WILL FROM CUD, SIGNING OFF.
CUD'S ADVENTURES CONTINUE AT CUDBAND.COM.

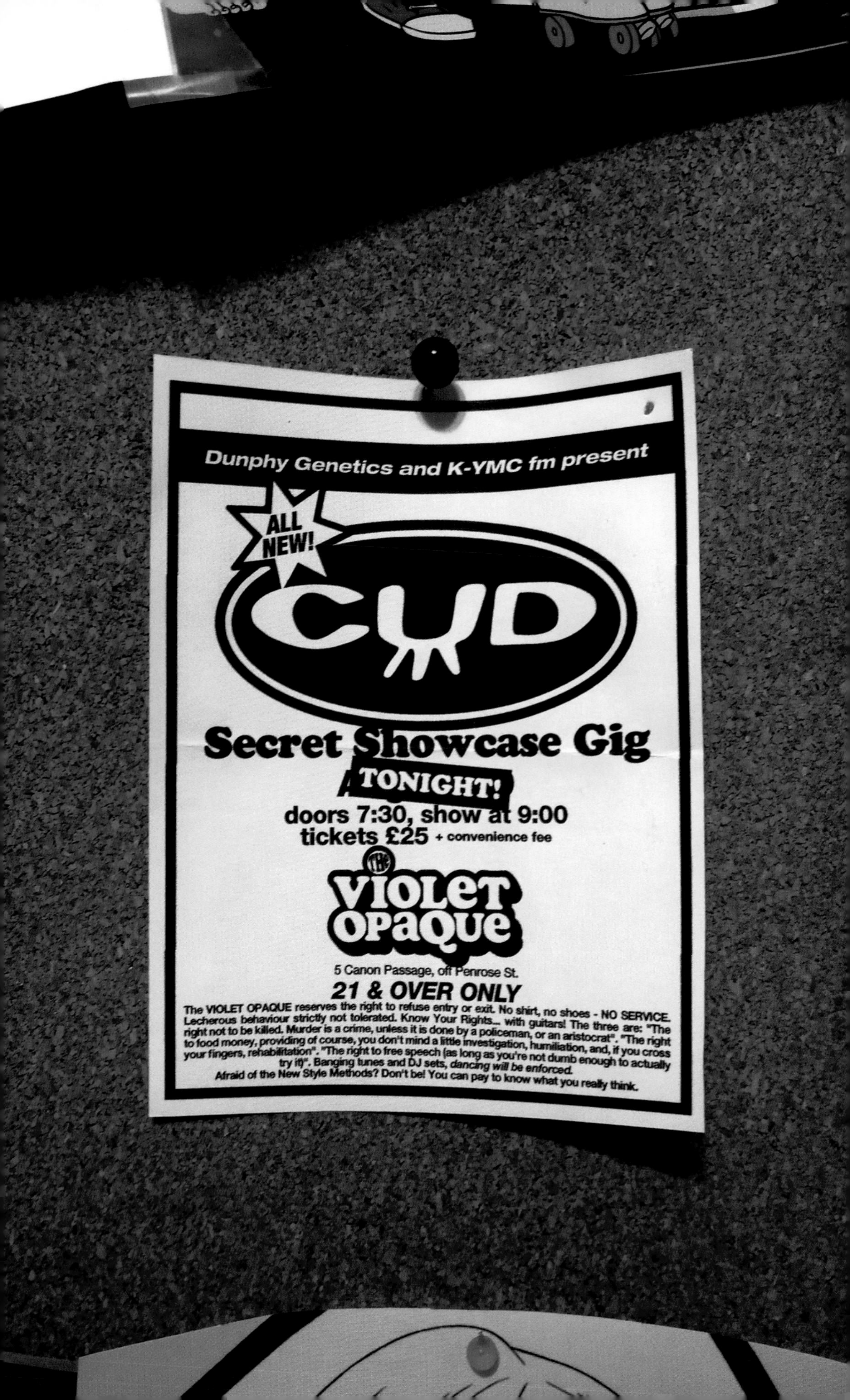
Dunphy Genetics and K-YMC fm present
ALL NEW!
CUD
Secret Showcase Gig
TONIGHT!
doors 7:30, show at 9:00
tickets £25 + convenience fee
THE
VIOLET
OPAQUE
5 Canon Passage, off Penrose St.
21 & OVER ONLY
The VIOLET OPAQUE reserves the right to refuse entry or exit. No shirt, no shoes - NO SERVICE.
Lecherous behaviour strictly not tolerated. Know Your Rights... with guitars! The three are: "The
right not to be killed. Murder is a crime, unless it is done by a policeman, or an aristocrat". "The right
to food money, providing of course, you don't mind a little investigation, humiliation, and, if you cross
your fingers, rehabilitation". "The right to free speech (as long as you're not dumb enough to actually
try it)". Banging tunes and DJ sets, dancing will be enforced.
Afraid of the New Style Methods? Don't be! You can pay to know what you really think.

Rich and Strange

– sleeve notes by William Potter

RICH AND STRANGE had a nebulous aim to tell the tale of British indie combo CUD's unmeteoric rise to renown, subsequent slump and accidental revival. But where does fact become fiction? This commentary promises to confuse the subject even further.

Page 1, Panel 1. We stake our claim that CUD were a successful band, despite our efforts to sabotage our career. Praise due to letterer Aditya Bidikar for adding the lines under the U in CUD. This harks back to an early logo when the U was a cow's udder, complete with three teats. (Cue joke: How many tits are in CUD?) Lyrics: *Eau Water*

Panels 2-3. The original script had Carl listening to prog. For legal reasons, we switched it to CUD's *Love in a Hollow Tree.*

Page 2, Panels 1-2. Carl is particular about his tipple, having spent some years in the wine trade. The seated doll in panel 1 is Space Baby, picked up on a tour of Poland, cover star of our 1990 *Leggy Mambo* LP and an unpopular T-shirt. He reappears later.

Panel 3. Lyrics: *Purple Love Balloon*

Panel 4. There are hints throughout that other British indie bands ended up in Dying Embers. Matt Cheslin plays bass in *Ned's Atomic Dustbin*. I wrote a scene with him, which had to be cut, involving me leaving my used colostomy bag as an exploding cushion on his seat.

Panel 5. I love the fact that old Carl and I spend the whole adventure without trousers. And me without undies either.

Page 3, Panel 4. We got Mike to contribute here, choosing his favourite yellow Telecaster, bottled Newkie Brown ale and cuss words.

Page 4, Panel 1. There is filmed footage of our first gig online, at youtube.com/CUDvideos. At the time, Carl and I were Fine Art students. Mike studied Graphic Design (alongside comics ace Duncan Fegredo).

Panel 2. Carl believes that a key theme of Rich & Strange is misremembering, with him recollecting our CUD adventures differently to me. That's not how I remember it. Lyrics: *Mind the Gap*

Panel 4. True! Mike offered his services as a bass player. We put him on guitar and he bought one next week for 50 quid, mail-order.

Panel 5. True! We rescued bits of a drum kit before another bunch of kids smashed them to pieces.

Panel 6. Lyrics: *Art!*

Page 6, Panel 1. Kudos to colourist Lee Loughridge for his cool cupboard blues, cigarette-tinted tawny greys and the fawn and yellow splendor of Dying Embers.

Panel 3. First manager Zed Baxter was indeed a Scrabble guru and enjoyed 30 mins of fame as a contestant on anagram-busting TV gameshow Countdown. He was also an ordained minister for the Church of Subgenius, subject to a fee of $35.

Panel 4. *Planet Wobblers* was the name of a synth-pop duo that Carl and I once performed as.

Page 7, Panel 3. A genuine issue in the Netherlands, and probably why we rarely toured the Continent. That, and the fact no one wanted us.

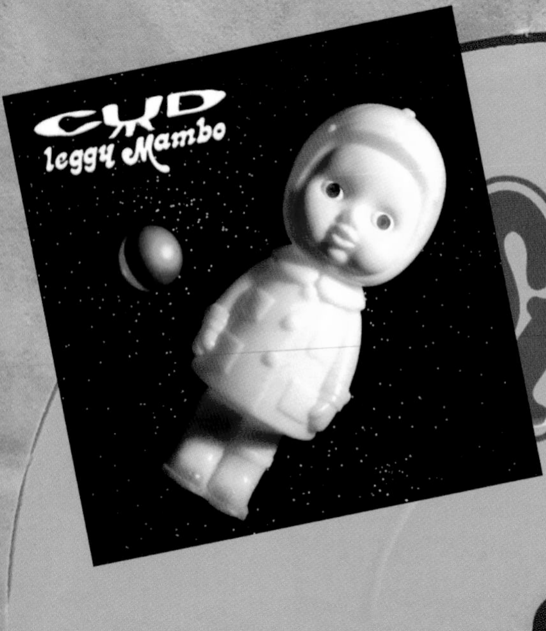
CUD
leggy Mambo

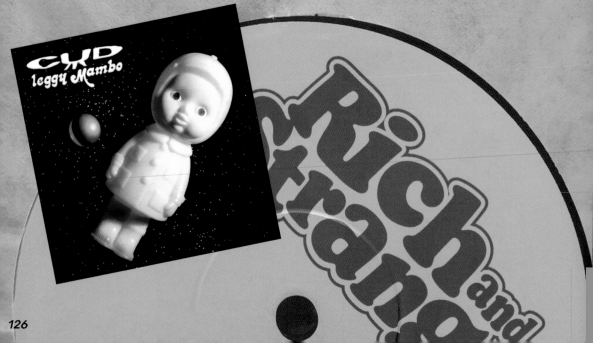

Panel 5. Headlines from genuine press clippings. Others that missed the cut include Popular Chewnes, Cow Soon Is Now? and Udderly Fab-tastic!

Page 8, Panel 2. Another indie band name drop, David Gedge of *The Wedding Present*, who writes his own line of biographical comic books.

Page 9, Panel 1. We were stoked to have Philip Bond draw this strip. But this isn't the first time Philip has drawn CUD. In the heyday, he worked on several single inserts and an amazing poster for the album *Asquarius*, along with genii Glyn Dillon and Jamie Hewlett. Lyrics: *Strange Kind of Love*

Page 11, Panel 4. I was on a U.S. road trip when CUD played on music/comedy show Popadoodledandy. Jessica mimed my part too well.

Page 12, Panel 2. Space Baby, the traitor!

Panel 4. In 1987, Carl sent our first demo to Peel and he got the offer of a session within the week! We didn't believe him 'til he picked up the phone and called the BBC…

Page 13, Panel 1. Ex-Mott drummer Dale Griffin worked as a BBC Radio 1 session producer from 1981 to 1994.

Panel 2. I knew our drummer tried this but only recently confirmed the rumour that Bonham did the same.

Page 14, Panel 5. Here, I reveal the original plot, had the series lived on for several more episodes, while Carl quotes lyrics from *Now*.

Page 15, Panel 4. CUD found their drums in a skip, and now we're full circle. Almost like it was planned.

Page 16, Panel 4. Carl came up with the idea that the "new" CUD should sing twisted versions of our old tunes. This, of course, is a play on *Rich and Strange*.

Page 17, Panel 6. That bloody blue van had to be tow-started every time. We drove it all the way from Leeds, U.K. to Poland. In winter. Even during this period of communism and empty shelves, the locals found our vehicle lacking.

Page 18, Panel 5. A play on our tune *Hey, Boots*.

Page 19, Panel 1. See what we did there? (Check page 4).

Panel 2. We play to the same faces from 25 years ago now. Don't see why this would change. Lyrics, a spin on *I've Had It with Blondes*.

Panel 3. Lyrics a spin on *Now*

Page 20, Panel 1. Lyrics a spin on *Only (A Prawn in Whitby)*

Page 21, Panel 2. Will there be a Side Two? I had a sequel idea involving a quest to find the drummers from CUD but, for now, it's a wrap.

Panel 3. Current drummer, Gogs, finally gets a look-in. I wrote a scene for him, as a scalper selling worthless CUD show tickets, but it didn't make the cut. Sorry, Gogs. And we end, where we began, singing our hit.

CUD's sleeve notes and adventures
continue at **cudband.com**

Four Chambers

with CARL PUTTNAM, co-writer/lead singer of *CUD: RICH AND STRANGE*

The Quartet Directive

Upper left: Your bookshelf
Upper right: An image with an unexpected backstory
Lower left: A favorite band/album cover art
Lower right: A storefront that inspires

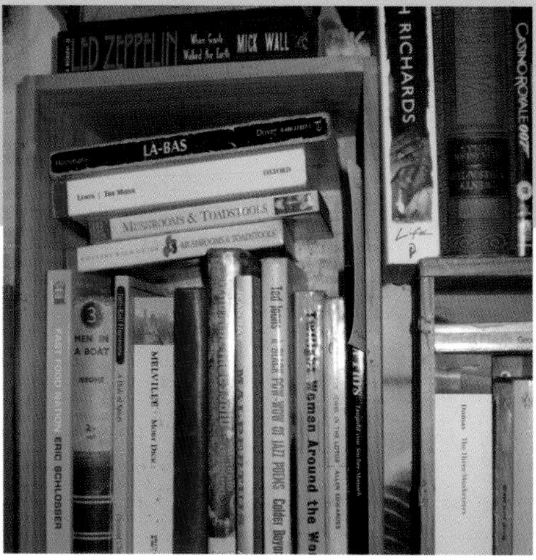

LED ZEPPELIN
MICK WALL
RICHARDS
CASINO ROYALE 007
LA-BAS
MUSHROOMS & TOADSTOOLS
FAST FOOD NATION ERIC SCHLOSSER
MELVILLE Moby Dick

My year 8 (13 -14 years old) teacher had me reading Camus and "The White Hotel" (an odd recommendation with its "adult" content), and my Art History tutor at art college introduced me to Huysmans, and then Huysmans (via "A Rebours") took me to obscure-ish Greek and Roman literature. The leather bound book is "City of Night" by John Rechy, surely one of the most sordid books ever written.The leather binding is the cover of an old Bible. A character in "A Rebours" uses this method to smuggle Sade into church each Sunday.

The first record I bought was "Songs in the Key Of Life" by Stevie Wonder. I never got to listen to it for maybe five years, because my dad never let us play records. He would unplug and replug the stereo in ways that only he knew, ensuring only he used it. A friend's dad would let us play stuff from his collection and make recommendations. He played me Hawkwind, The Doors , The Byrds and Amon Duul. Amon Duul's "Yeti" fascinated and frightened me. When I plucked up the courage, I fell in love. I still use his collection as a measure of an unknown record's worth.

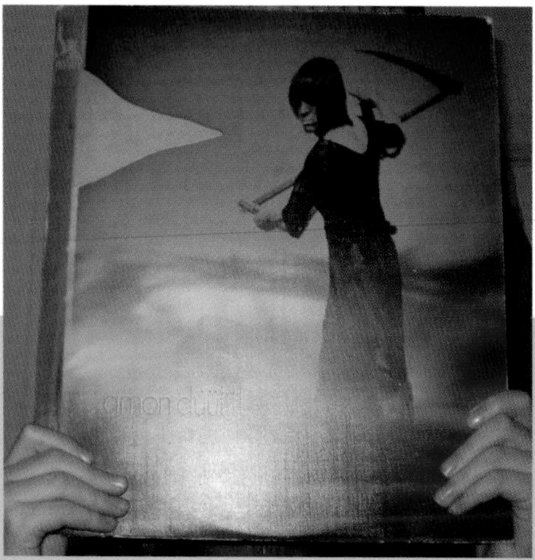

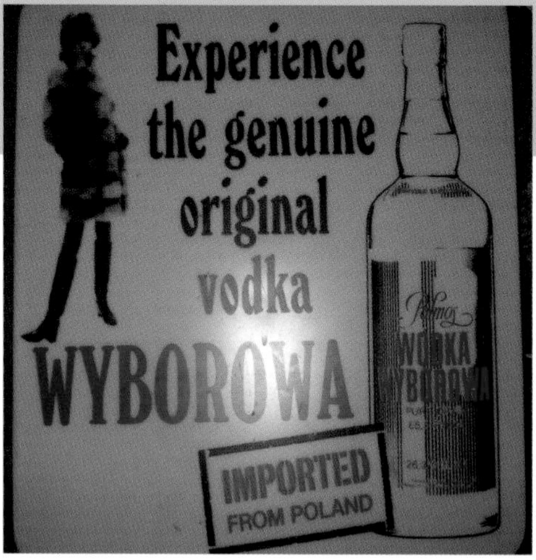

Experience the genuine original vodka
WYBOROWA
IMPORTED FROM POLAND

Milan's was a Polish bar operated by a Serb (yep!) just 'round the corner from where I live. He served drinks to my partner, me, one or two of our friends, and the remains of the area's East European community. I always coveted this rather cool bar decoration. The bar burnt down — suspiciously, by Milan's reckoning. I found this in the wreckage — he let me keep it.

There's no way I'm telling you my favourite thrift store or secondhand record shop! We're "friends," I suppose, but it's like when you're in the the dentist's office and you read an article about "this wonderful little unspoilt coastal village...last summer." It won't be for much longer! But here's somewhere I'd love to share: Kirkgate Market in Leeds has an egg shop. Sells eggs. Eggs and egg-related products. Lots of different sizes and types. The gent who owns the store knows his eggs.You're getting the gist...

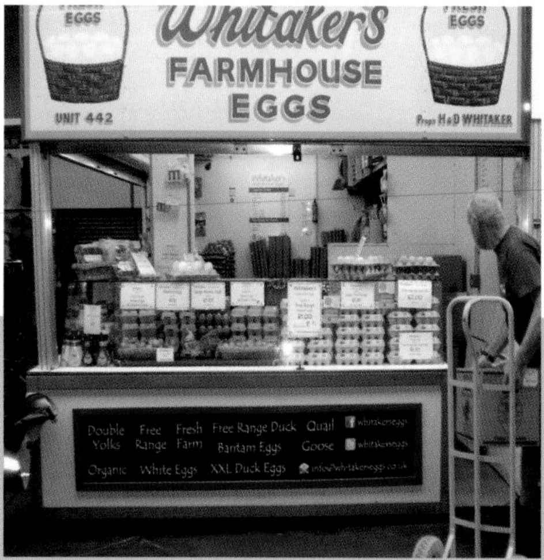

EGGS
Whitaker's
FARMHOUSE EGGS
UNIT 442
Props H&D WHITAKER
Double Yolks
Free Range
Fresh Farm
Free Range Duck
Bantam Eggs
Quail
Goose
Organic
White Eggs
XXL Duck Eggs

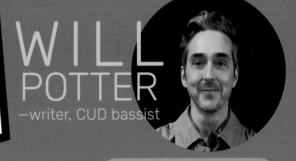

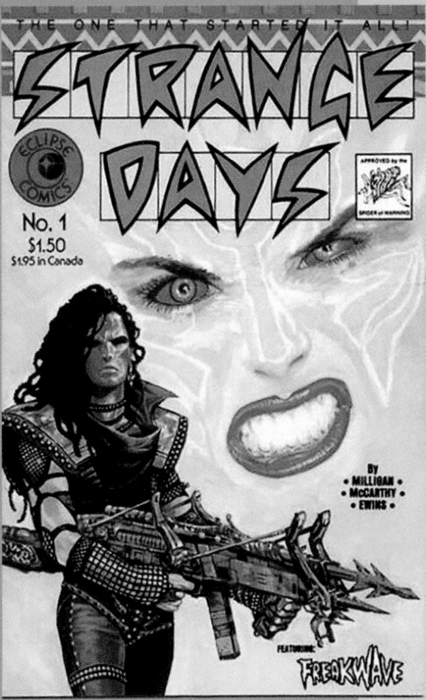
THE ONE THAT STARTED IT ALL!
STRANGE DAYS
ECLIPSE COMICS
No. 1
$1.50
$1.95 in Canada
By
MILLIGAN
McCARTHY
EWINS
FEATURING
FREAKWAVE

Strange Days #1 (Eclipse Comics, Nov 1984) by Peter Milligan, Brendan McCarthy, Brett Ewins

................................COMIC

*I was already a fan of Brett Ewins, Peter Milligan and Brendan McCarthy for their work in the UK weekly **2000AD** but **Strange Days** was a revelation. This US anthology gave them unbridled freedom with their own creations and the light poured out of them.*

***Freakwave** tells of the Drifter, a windsurfing Pete Burns look-alike negotiating a washed-up world where militants and dilettantes populate hovering iconic heads. Milligan channels Lear and Lennon into a **Mad Max**-world, while McCarthy's sexy figure work, extraordinary designs and luminous colours are in full flow.*

*The late great Brett Ewins' ace detective **Johnny Nemo** steers a trail of nicotine and blood through a future London, and would later launch the UK monthly **Deadline** in 1989 (which gave a break to a new wave of hot writers and artists).*

*Milligan and McCarthy's **Paradax!** was my favourite, starring a louche, boozy accidental superhero with a lazy panache and a gorgeous girlfriend.*

*For art, attitude, skill, and style, **Strange Days** was a template. It was all I wanted to be and see in comics, beyond my capability, an aspiration and inspiration.*

BEAT SURRENDER

Wherein we wax nostalgic on the comic + record that made us drop to our knees.

WILL POTTER

—writer, CUD bassist

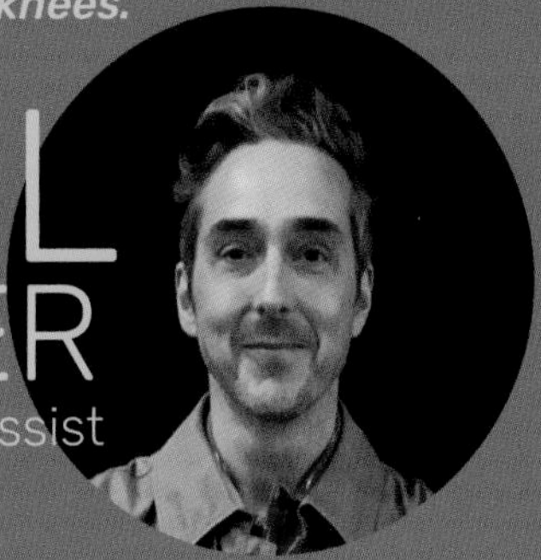

RECORD................................

*I remember exactly where I was when I heard this the first time: Waiting in Dave Gregory's car on Albion St, Leeds. Dave Gregory was the guitarist in arch-pop, post-punk band XTC and was producing CUD's LP **Leggy Mambo** in summer 1990. As such he was an arbiter of taste.*

*Like most, I'd filed The Beach Boys away in a drawer labelled "surf party pop" and never explored beyond my cassette of **20 Golden Greats**. The track Dave played from his Boys bootleg was a revelation – an unfinished song with downbeat, mournful harmonies, odd juxtapositions, fuzzed bass, glockenspiel and a handful of words, which built into a hypnotic repeated refrain. Of course, it was Brian Wilson at his best, bathing tape in layers of honey and wonder. A whole world of Wilson's most offbeat output awaited, a love affair that lasted.*

Beach Boys
Can't Wait Too Long (1967)
(Bonus track on *Smiley Smile/Wild Honey* CD, 1990)

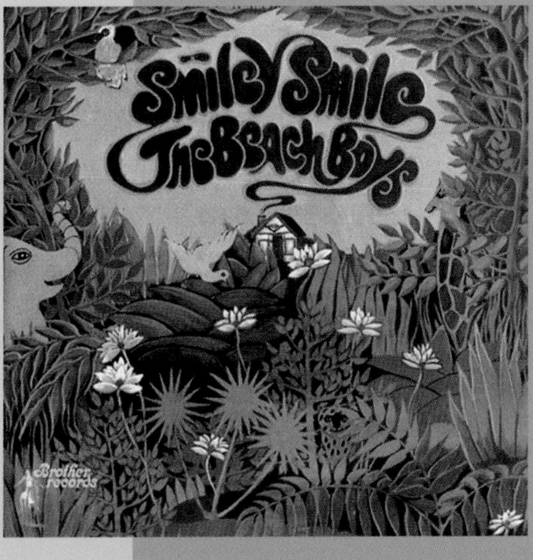
Smiley Smile
The Beach Boys
Brother records

swell maps

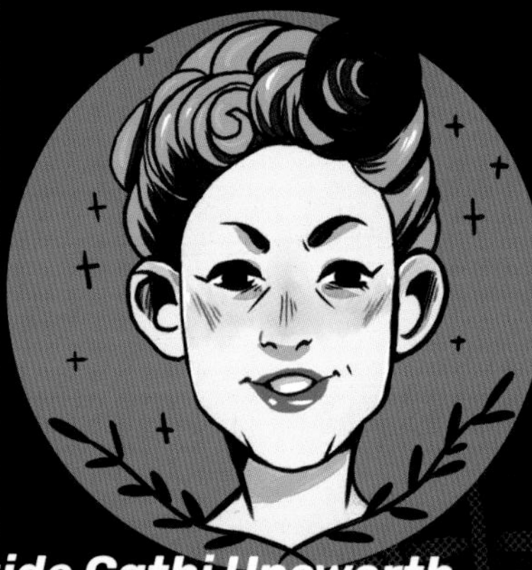

Welcome to LEEDS, with your musical tour guide Cathi Unsworth
Illustrations by Cara McGee

LEEDS is a city in West Yorkshire. Its coat of arms is designed around three silver owls taken from the heraldry of Sir John Savile, the city's first Alderman. Its motto is *Pro Rege et Lege*, meaning "For King and the Law"— which will come as a surprise to readers of David Peace's *Red Riding Quartet* in which the police of Leeds are a law unto themselves, with real-life connections to Sir Jimmy Savile, the Monster of Leeds.

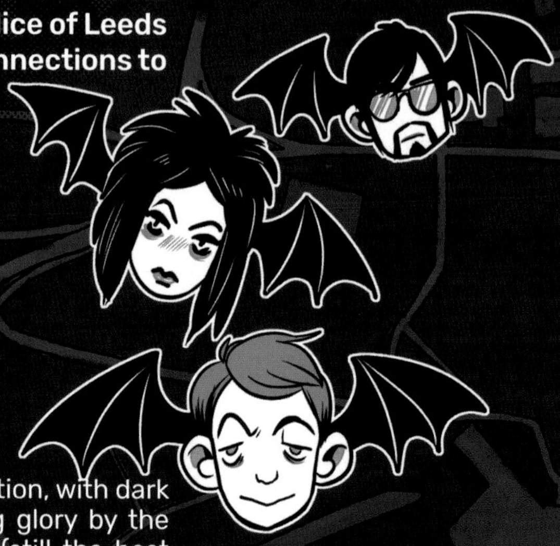

Leeds was rebuilt during the Industrial Revolution, with dark Satanic mills captured in all their glowering glory by the Victorian painter John Atkinson Grimshaw (still the best name of any artist born in Yorkshire). Statues were erected to local dignitaries like brewer Joshua Tetley, PM Sir Robert Walpole and chip shop impresario Harry Ramsden that would come to life at night and cavort with the nymphs on neighbouring municipal fountains. This phenomenon was recorded in song by Leeds' Poet Laureate, Jake Thackray, whose own statue now looks out over the city centre, keeping a stern eye out for that sort of thing.

Leeds is a city of alchemists, turning industrial smog into lyrical gold. Playwright and National Treasure **Alan Bennett** was born here in 1934 and his brand of wry, observational humour is the foundation of another Leeds-minted genre of music, **Indie**. This was invented when members of **The Wedding Present** reenacted the bicycle ride to Fountains Abbey from Bennett's 1972 play *A Day Out* and, after consuming lashings of ginger beer, made up the songs to their first album, *Thora Hird*, on the way home, using their bells to initiate the distinctive "jingle-jangle" Indie sound. Soon, the student bars of Headingly resounded to the yearning ditties of **The Bridewell Taxis**, **The Edsel Auctioneer**, **The Pale Saints**, **The Parachute Men** and **CUD**. (**The Kaiser Chiefs** were the same sort of thing, only about ten years later.)

Leeds is renowned for its Gothic architecture, the foremost example of which is the Medieval Kirkstall Abby. Inside these picturesque ruins a genre of music, also known as **Gothic**, incubated and emerged on leathery wings as the light faded over the rooftops in the early 1980s. Fluttering out of the turrets came **The Sisters of Mercy**, **Soft Cell**, **The March Violets**, **Gang of Four**, **The Mekons**, **The Three Johns** and **Red Lorry Yellow Lorry**, whose mournful tunes, electro refashioning of Northern Soul standards and plaintive Country & Western cover versions lured generations of young people into hairspray abuse, the consumption of snakebite-and-black and early, unconsecrated graves. The bats haven't left the belfry yet—the Abbey is currently inhabited by **Cronin**.

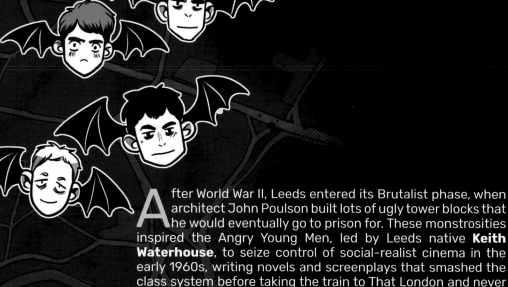

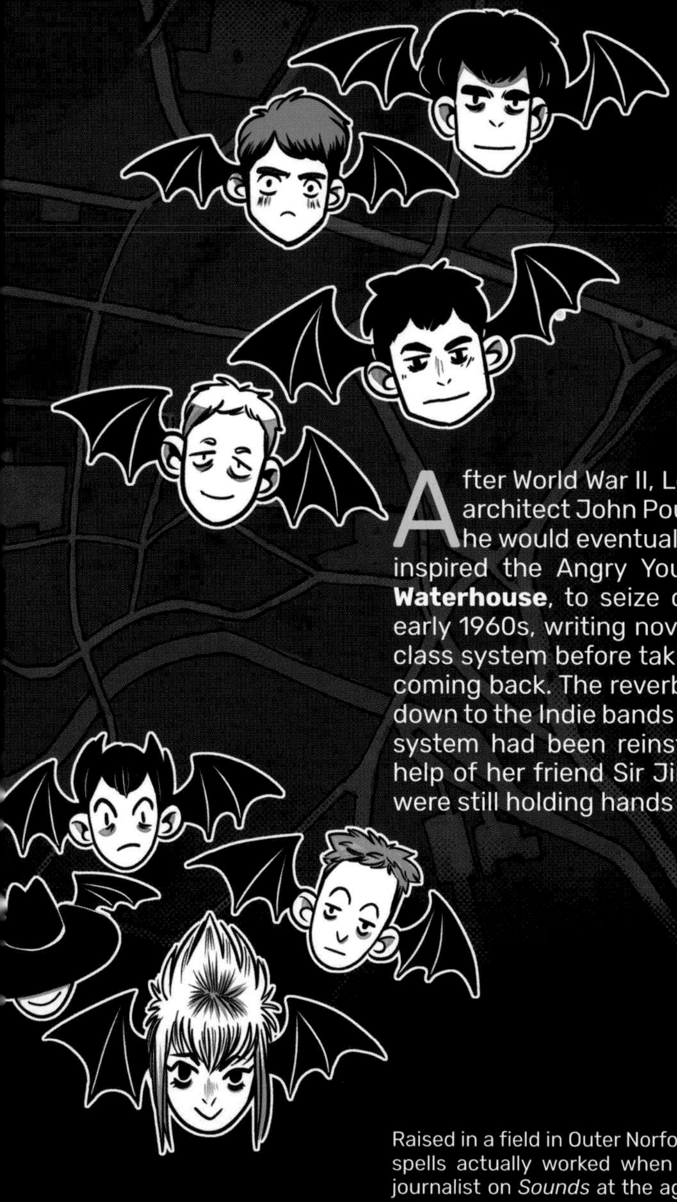

After World War II, Leeds entered its Brutalist phase, when architect John Poulson built lots of ugly tower blocks that he would eventually go to prison for. These monstrosities inspired the Angry Young Men, led by Leeds native **Keith Waterhouse**, to seize control of social-realist cinema in the early 1960s, writing novels and screenplays that smashed the class system before taking the train to That London and never coming back. The reverberations of the *Billy Liar* years chimed down to the Indie bands well into the 1980s, long after the class system had been reinstated by Margaret Thatcher (with the help of her friend Sir Jimmy Savile) and **The Parachute Men** were still holding hands on a platform in Leeds Station.

Raised in a field in Outer Norfolk, CATHI UNSWORTH was a teenage goth whose spells actually worked when she made her way to London and became a journalist on *Sounds* at the age of 19. Before the weekly music press became extinct, she also worked for *Melody Maker*, then went on to co-create *Purr* and write reams more about music, film, fashion, noir fiction and general weirdness for everyone from the *Fortean Times* to the *Financial Times*. Over the past decade she has written five noir novels into which she pours all her obsessions with secret histories and pop culture. You can find out more at www.cathiunsworth.co.uk

Hey, AMATEUR!

HOW TO ROCK BARRE CHORDS

by WILL POTTER and KATIE SKELLY

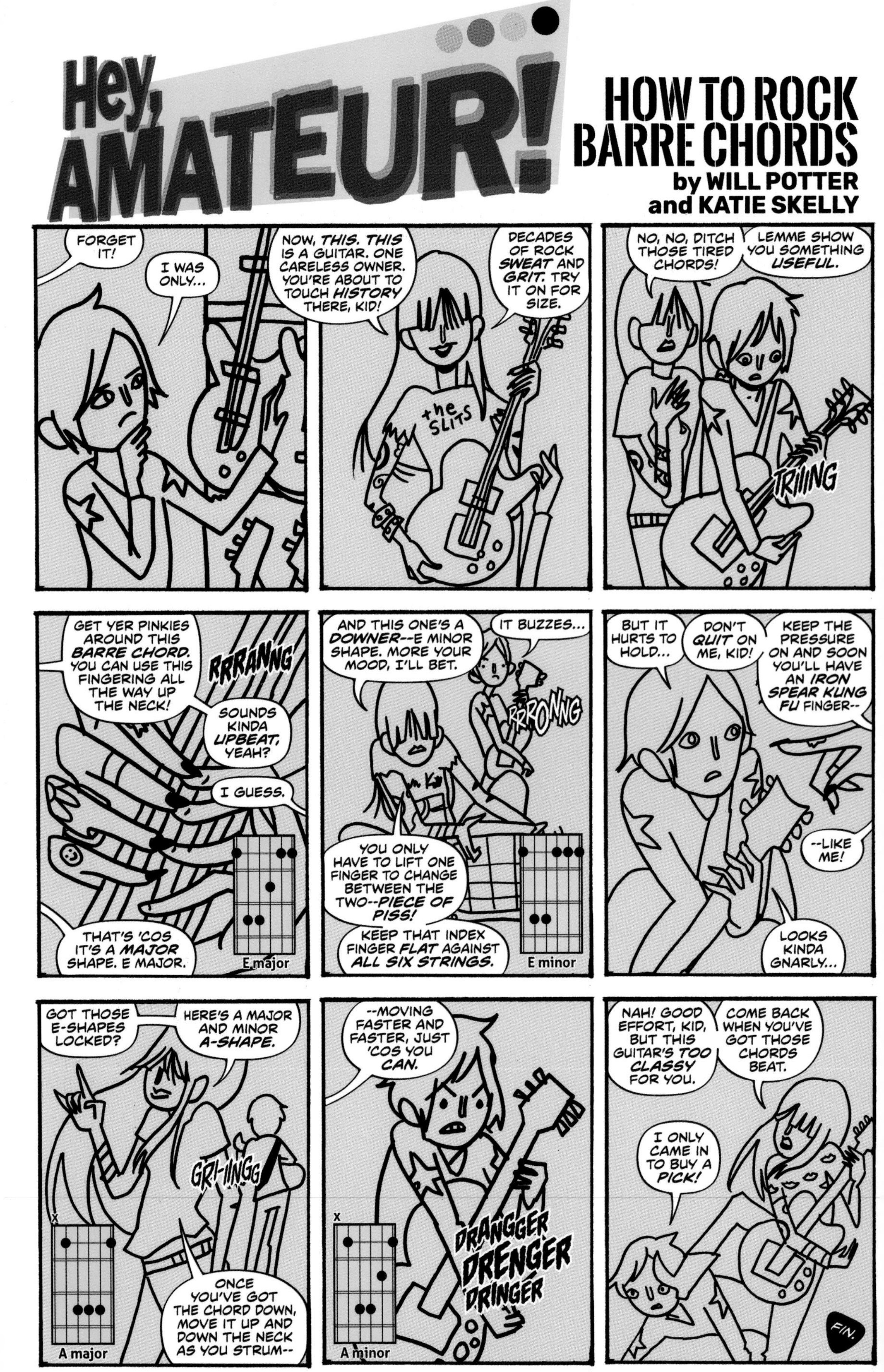

FORGET IT!
I WAS ONLY...
NOW, THIS. THIS IS A GUITAR. ONE CARELESS OWNER. YOU'RE ABOUT TO TOUCH HISTORY THERE, KID!
DECADES OF ROCK SWEAT AND GRIT. TRY IT ON FOR SIZE.
the SLITS
NO, NO, DITCH THOSE TIRED CHORDS!
LEMME SHOW YOU SOMETHING USEFUL.
TRIIING
GET YER PINKIES AROUND THIS BARRE CHORD. YOU CAN USE THIS FINGERING ALL THE WAY UP THE NECK!
RRRANNG
SOUNDS KINDA UPBEAT, YEAH?
I GUESS.
THAT'S 'COS IT'S A MAJOR SHAPE. E MAJOR.
E major
AND THIS ONE'S A DOWNER--E MINOR SHAPE. MORE YOUR MOOD, I'LL BET.
IT BUZZES...
RRRONNG
YOU ONLY HAVE TO LIFT ONE FINGER TO CHANGE BETWEEN THE TWO--PIECE OF PISS!
KEEP THAT INDEX FINGER FLAT AGAINST ALL SIX STRINGS.
E minor
BUT IT HURTS TO HOLD...
DON'T QUIT ON ME, KID!
KEEP THE PRESSURE ON AND SOON YOU'LL HAVE AN IRON SPEAR KUNG FU FINGER--
--LIKE ME!
LOOKS KINDA GNARLY...
GOT THOSE E-SHAPES LOCKED?
HERE'S A MAJOR AND MINOR A-SHAPE.
GRI-IINGG
ONCE YOU'VE GOT THE CHORD DOWN, MOVE IT UP AND DOWN THE NECK AS YOU STRUM--
A major
--MOVING FASTER AND FASTER, JUST 'COS YOU CAN.
DRANGGER DRENGER DRINGER
A minor
NAH! GOOD EFFORT, KID, BUT THIS GUITAR'S TOO CLASSY FOR YOU.
COME BACK WHEN YOU'VE GOT THOSE CHORDS BEAT.
I ONLY CAME IN TO BUY A PICK!
FIN.

Will Potter writes comics and plays bass for UK indie survivors CUD. His fave chord is G7add9sus4.
Katie Skelly is the creator of *My Pretty Vampire*. She just learned how a guitar works!

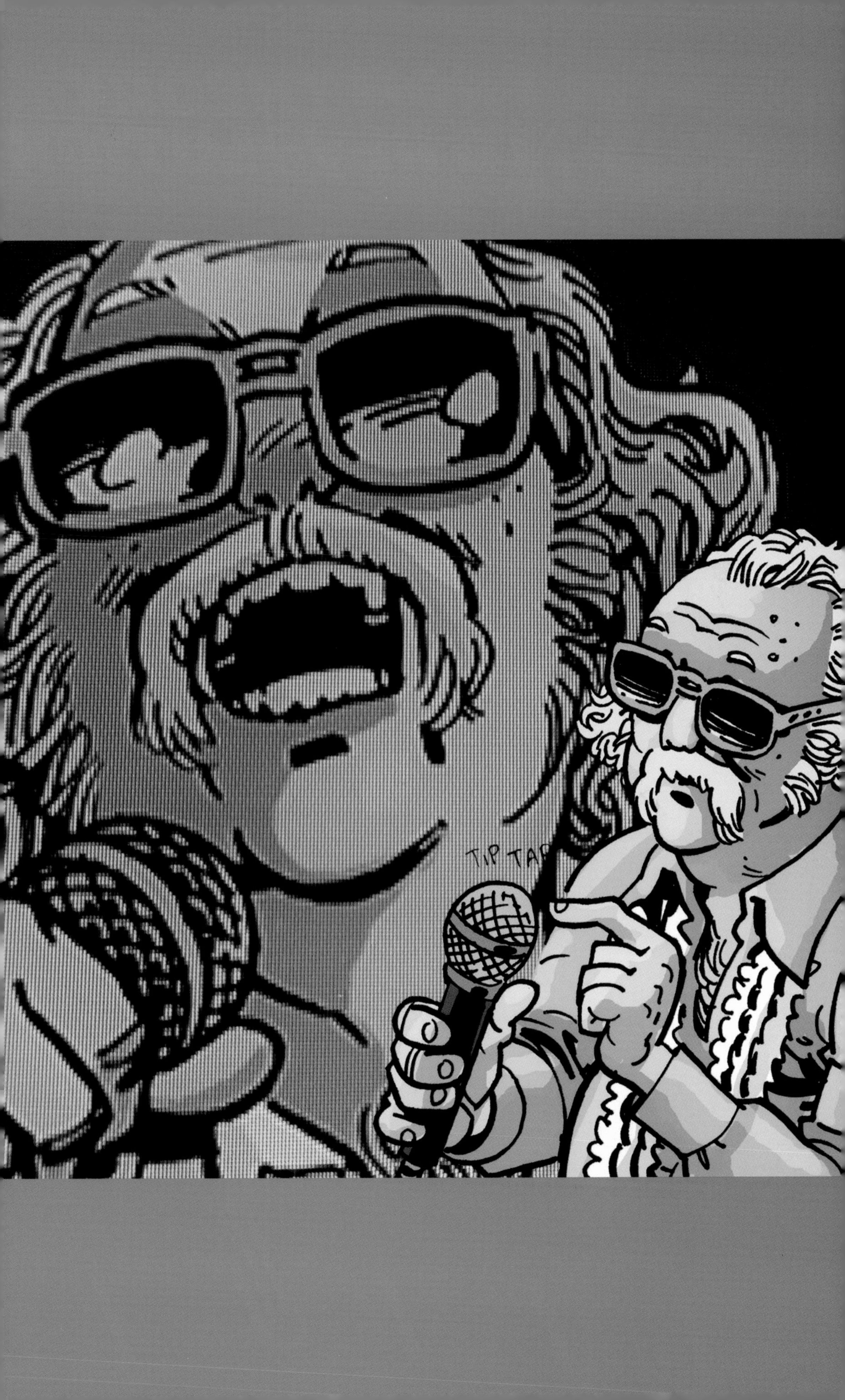
TIP TAP

FROM THEORY TO REVOLUTION

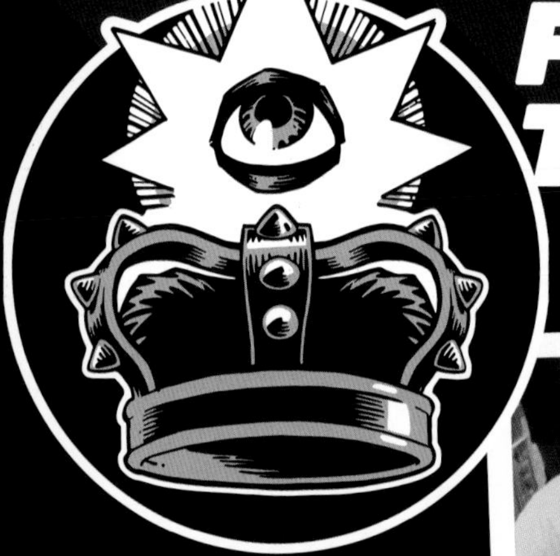

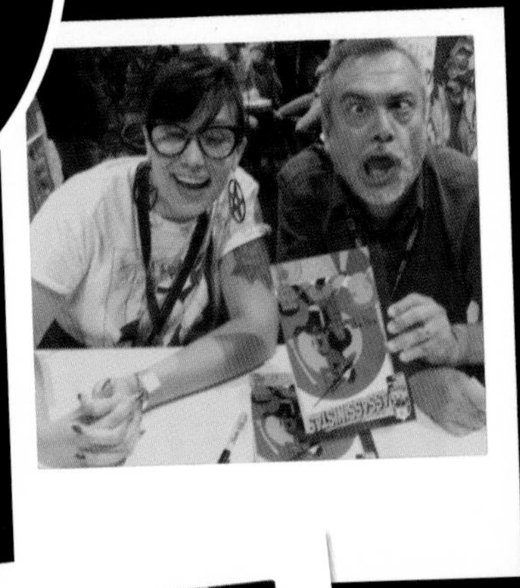

NOVEMBER 2017
Shelly Bond and Tini Howard appear as guests of the Bull City Comicon in Durham, North Carolina to talk about BLACK CROWN and ASSASSINISTAS.

DECEMBER
ASSASSINISTAS debuts to great acclaim.

"Howard weaves a complex network of race, class, and gender dynamics into the relationships at the core of the series that sit like tripwires between them... a complex engine of performance parts that took careful consideration and a fearless attitude to assemble." 10/10

—Comicosity

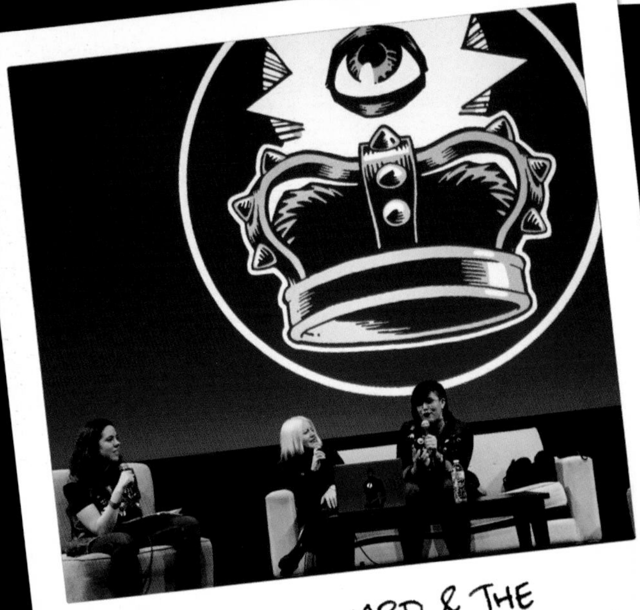

BOND, HOWARD & THE ALL-SEEING-EYE, NCCON

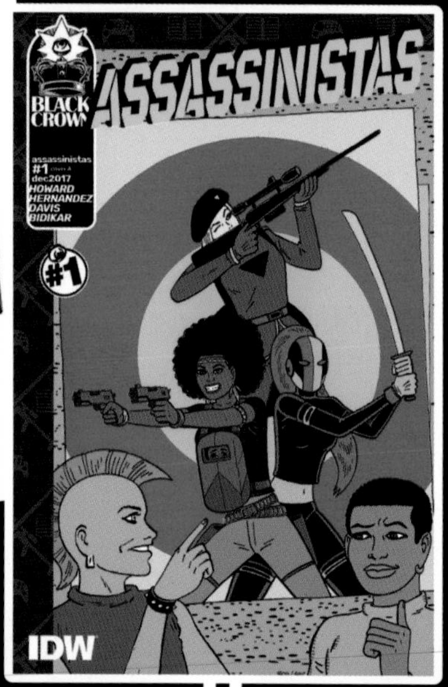
BLACK CROWN
ASSASSINISTAS
assassinistas #1 dec2017
HOWARD
HERNANDEZ
DAVIS
BIDIKAR
#1
IDW

2017 NOVEMBER **DECEMBER**

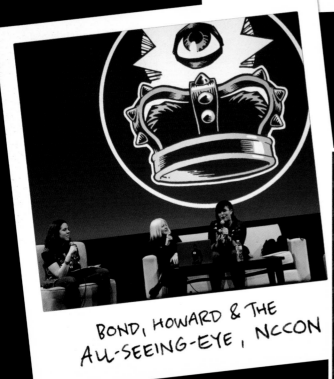

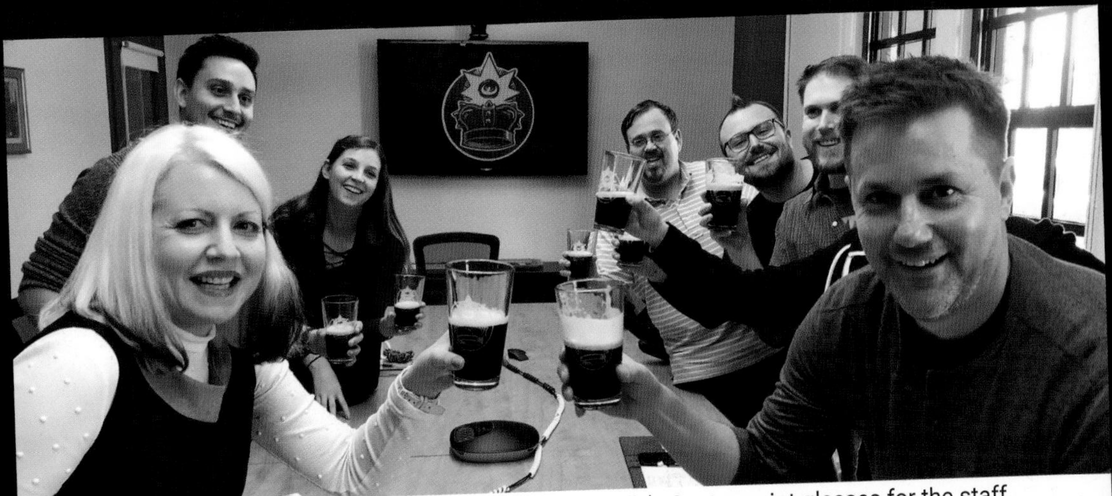

Xmas from the Crown (ahem: IDW conference room actually). Custom pint glasses for the staff.
L to R: Shelly Bond, Kahlil Schweitzer, Alex Goldstein, Joel Elad, Chase Marotz, Steven Scott, Chris Ryall

JANUARY 2018
BLACK CROWN QUARTERLY
#2 debuts

"Martin Simmonds' wraparound cover arrived slick with beer, backwash and saliva. We dried it out in the sun for 3 days before scanning."

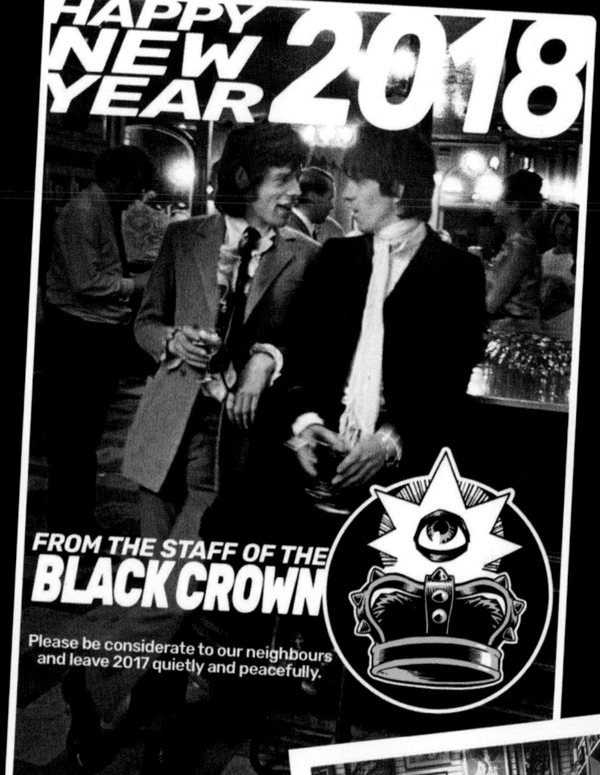

HAPPY NEW YEAR 2018
FROM THE STAFF OF THE
BLACK CROWN
Please be considerate to our neighbours and leave 2017 quietly and peacefully.

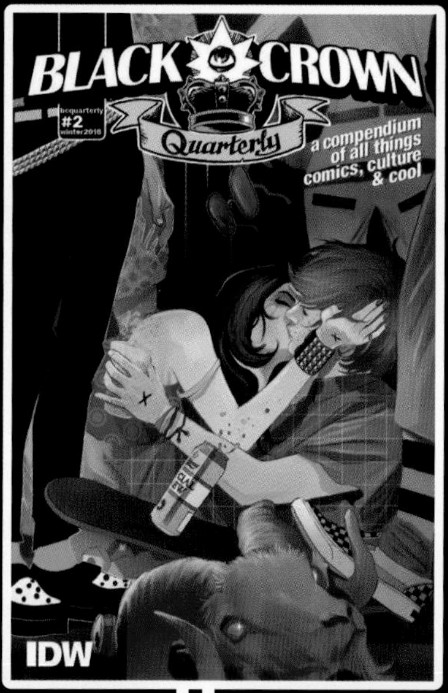

BLACK CROWN
#2
Quarterly
a compendium of all things comics, culture & cool
IDW

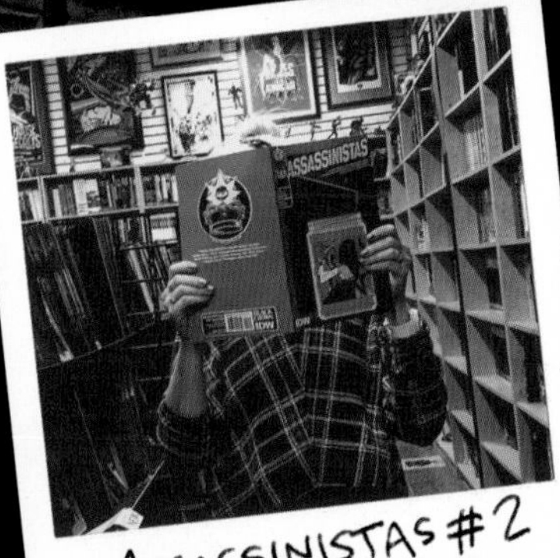

ASSASSINISTAS #2
OUT IN THE WILD

2018 JANUARY

Recursion Street
Penrose Street

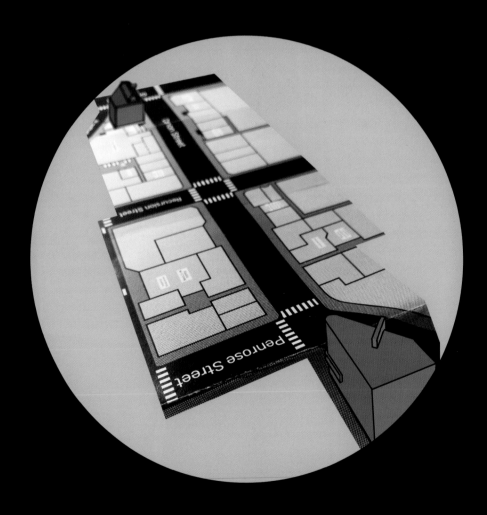

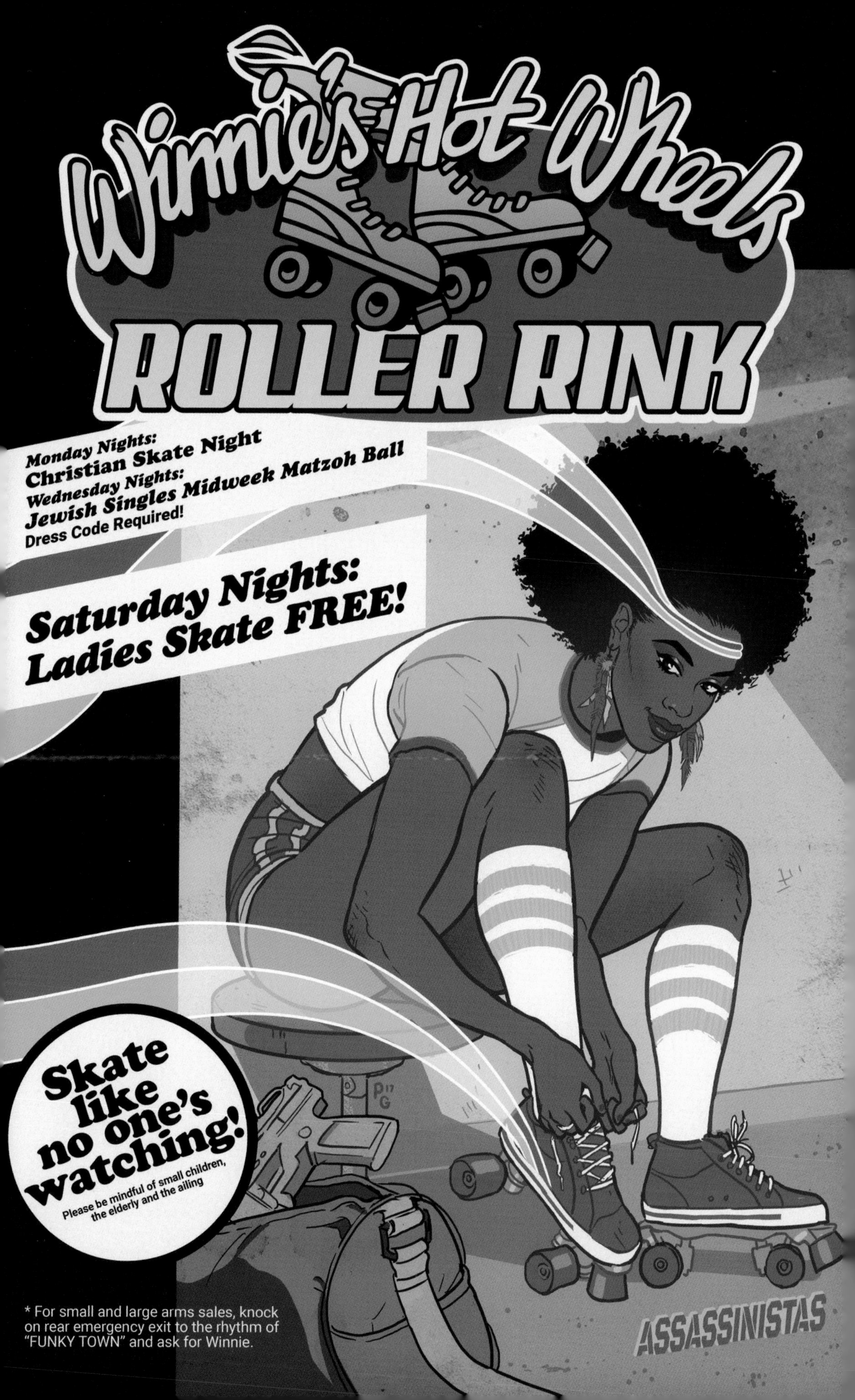
Winnie's Hot Wheels
ROLLER RINK
Monday Nights:
Christian Skate Night
Wednesday Nights:
Jewish Singles Midweek Matzoh Ball
Dress Code Required!
Saturday Nights:
Ladies Skate FREE!
Skate like no one's watching!
Please be mindful of small children, the elderly and the ailing
* For small and large arms sales, knock on rear emergency exit to the rhythm of "FUNKY TOWN" and ask for Winnie.
ASSASSINISTAS

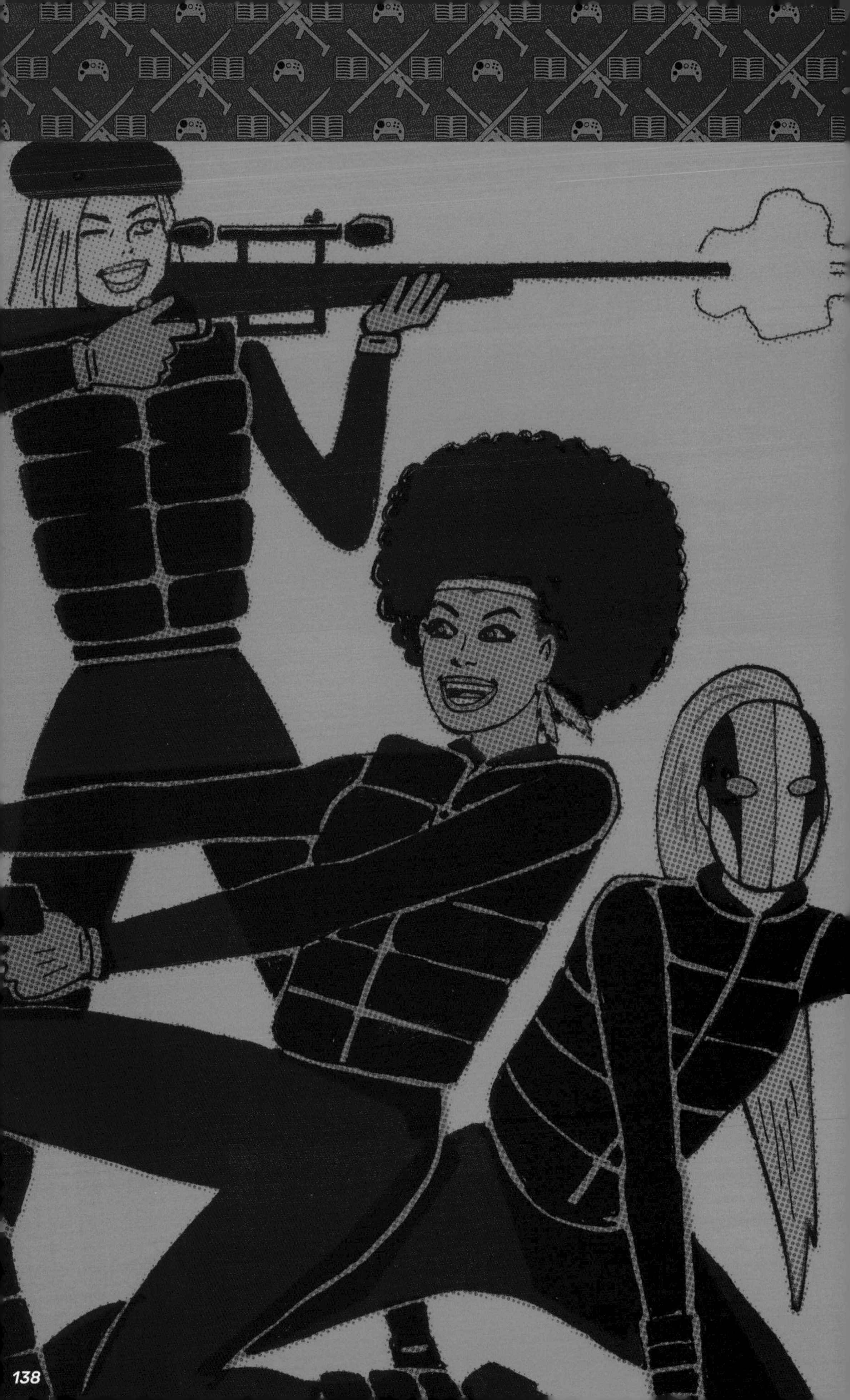

ASSASSINISTAS

created by TINI HOWARD & GILBERT HERNANDEZ

MARTINI KILL + CLASSIC

I discovered Tini Howard's work one rare, rainy Saturday night in bed in the fall of 2016 when I read the entirety of *The Secret Loves of Geek Girls* anthology. Many of the stories were impressive but only Tini's narrator grabbed me by the pajama collar and refused to let go. I sent Tini an e-mail the following day, hoping to persuade her to write comics.

A phone conversation would follow:

Overeager editor on phone:
"Hi, is this "Tiny"?

Future Black Crown star writer:
"It's Tini, as in Martini."

Idiot editor drops phone:
SFX: clunk

Three hours later, to a black mascara & glitter glob soundtrack of Siouxie and the Banshees, Bauhaus and Bat for Lashes, Tini sent me PDFs of her Blackmask series *The Skeptics* and a short superhero story.

She had me at the first panel/first caption/ first page.

Five stellar creator-owned comic book pitches later, I wanted to buy four; We settled on two.

ATTN GLAM ROCKERS: SEE YOU AT THE ILLEGAL WEAPONS FRONT THAT DOUBLES AS A ROLLER DISCO!

Upon first glance at the ASSASSINISTAS proposal I instantly — and only — saw Gilbert Hernandez's exultant ink lines on those badass female bounty hunters. I've been fortunate to work with Gilbert (and adore his family!) somewhat regularly since the late '90s, and I owe him for a good chunk of my career. If I hadn't discovered the unparalleled punk opus that is *Love And Rockets* in 1987 when I was in college, I wouldn't know that black & white indie comics were a thing in general, written for me specifically — much less a career option. I couldn't write or draw, but when it came to the comics industry and picaresque stories starring strong women like Gilbert's from Palomar, I wanted in.

BLACK CROWN
ASSASSINISTAS
assassinistas
#1
dec2017
HOWARD
HERNANDEZ
DAVIS
BIDIKAR
#1
IDW

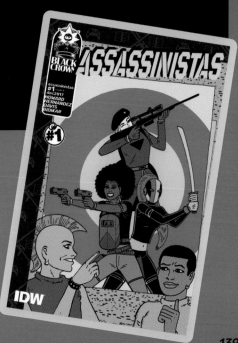

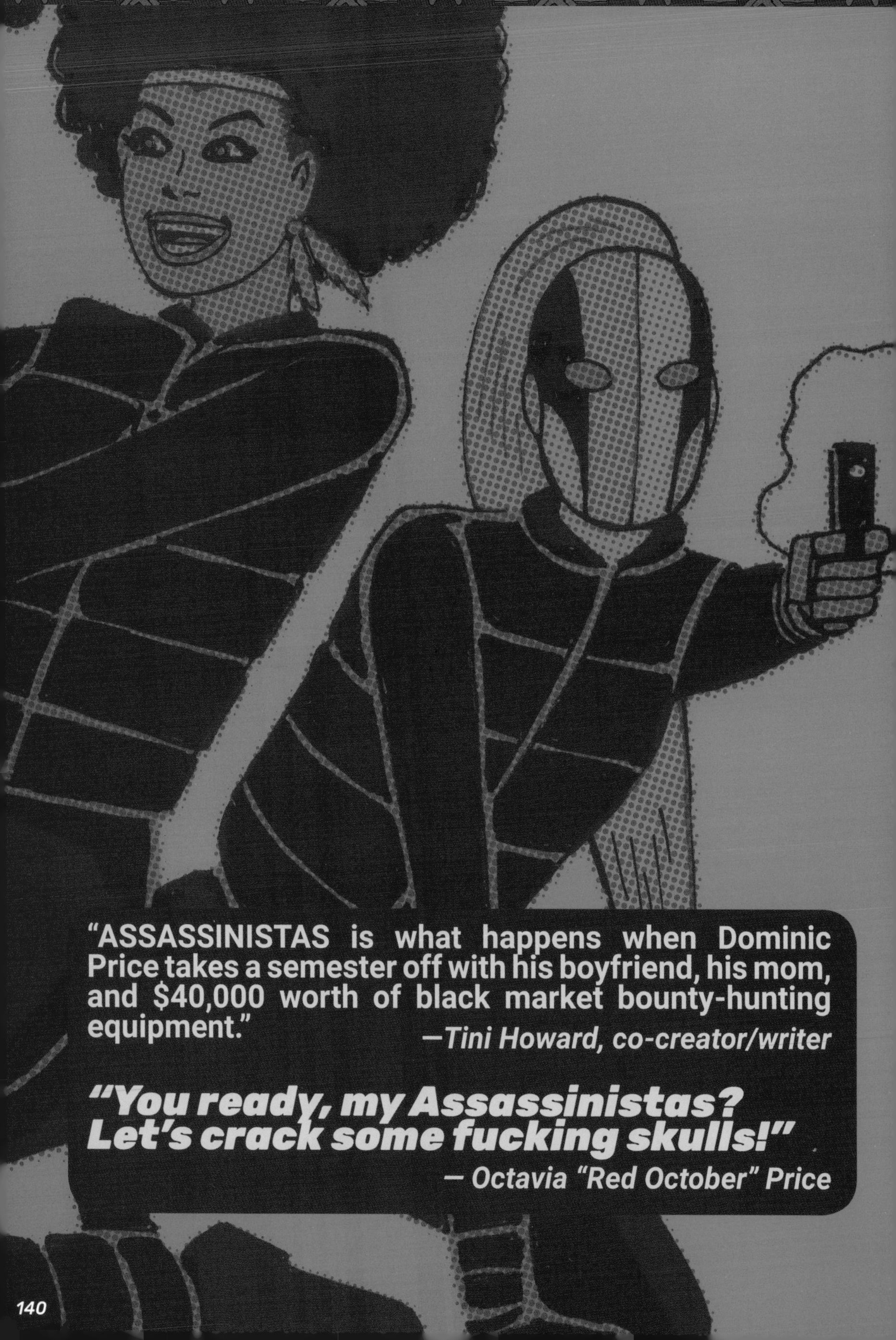

"ASSASSINISTAS is what happens when Dominic Price takes a semester off with his boyfriend, his mom, and $40,000 worth of black market bounty-hunting equipment."

—Tini Howard, co-creator/writer

"You ready, my Assassinistas? Let's crack some fucking skulls!"

– Octavia "Red October" Price

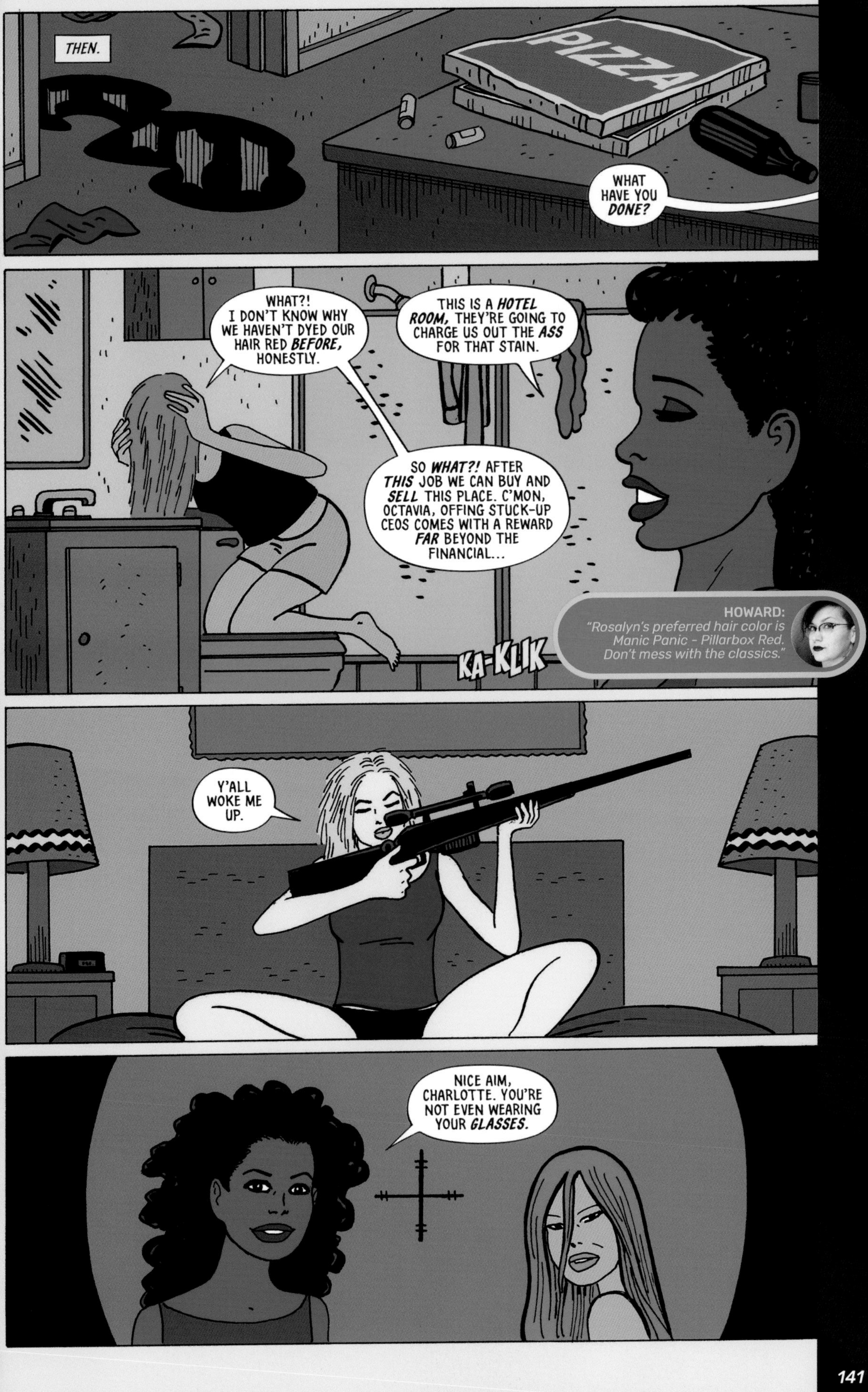

THEN.
PIZZA
WHAT HAVE YOU DONE?
WHAT?! I DON'T KNOW WHY WE HAVEN'T DYED OUR HAIR RED BEFORE, HONESTLY.
THIS IS A HOTEL ROOM, THEY'RE GOING TO CHARGE US OUT THE ASS FOR THAT STAIN.
SO WHAT?! AFTER THIS JOB WE CAN BUY AND SELL THIS PLACE. C'MON, OCTAVIA, OFFING STUCK-UP CEOS COMES WITH A REWARD FAR BEYOND THE FINANCIAL...
KA-KLIK
HOWARD:
"Rosalyn's preferred hair color is Manic Panic - Pillarbox Red. Don't mess with the classics."
Y'ALL WOKE ME UP.
NICE AIM, CHARLOTTE. YOU'RE NOT EVEN WEARING YOUR GLASSES.

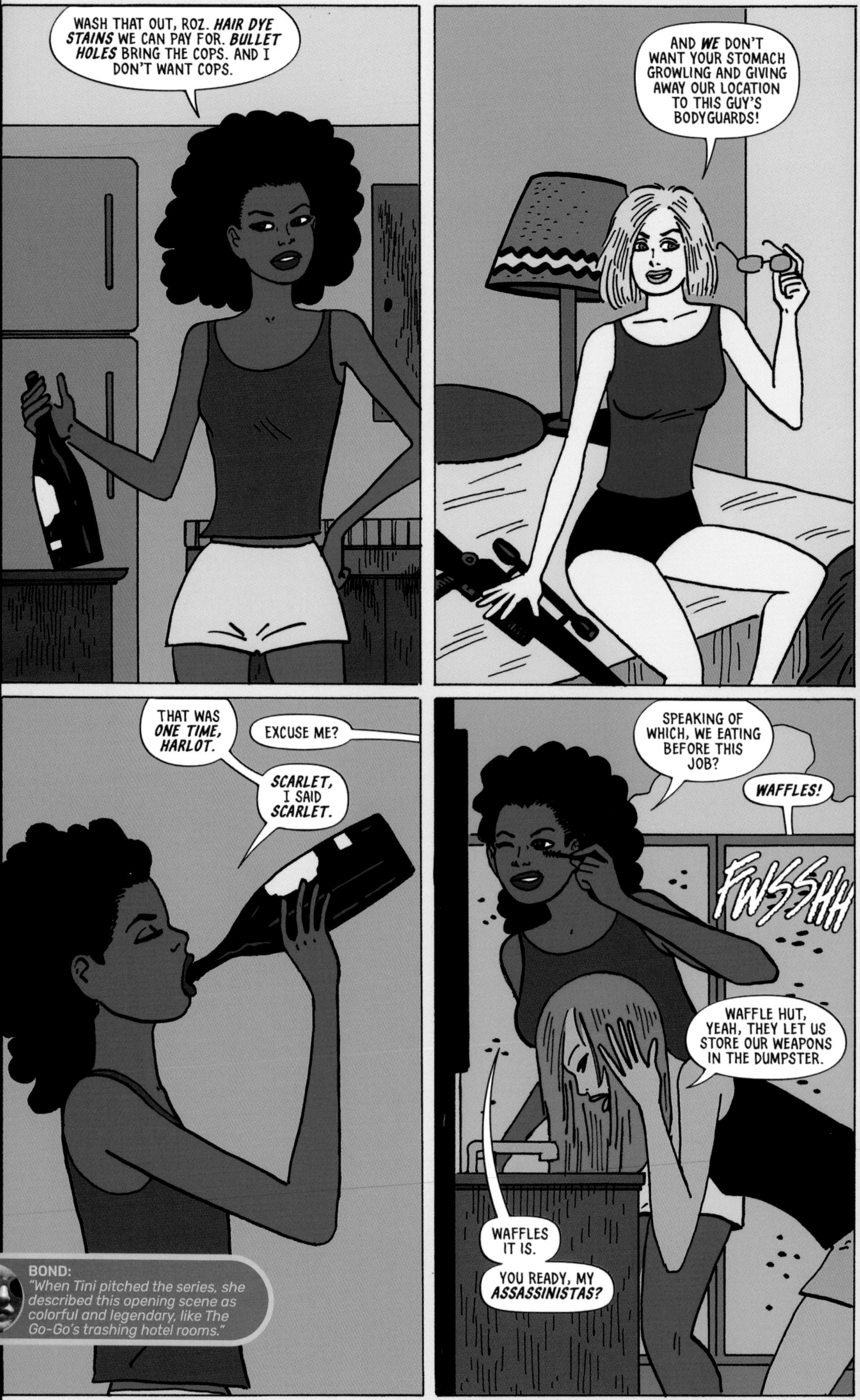
WASH THAT OUT, ROZ. HAIR DYE STAINS WE CAN PAY FOR. BULLET HOLES BRING THE COPS. AND I DON'T WANT COPS.
AND WE DON'T WANT YOUR STOMACH GROWLING AND GIVING AWAY OUR LOCATION TO THIS GUY'S BODYGUARDS!
THAT WAS ONE TIME, HARLOT.
EXCUSE ME?
SCARLET, I SAID SCARLET.
SPEAKING OF WHICH, WE EATING BEFORE THIS JOB?
WAFFLES!
FWSSHH
WAFFLE HUT, YEAH, THEY LET US STORE OUR WEAPONS IN THE DUMPSTER.
WAFFLES IT IS.
YOU READY, MY ASSASSINISTAS?

BOND:
"When Tini pitched the series, she described this opening scene as colorful and legendary, like The Go-Go's trashing hotel rooms."

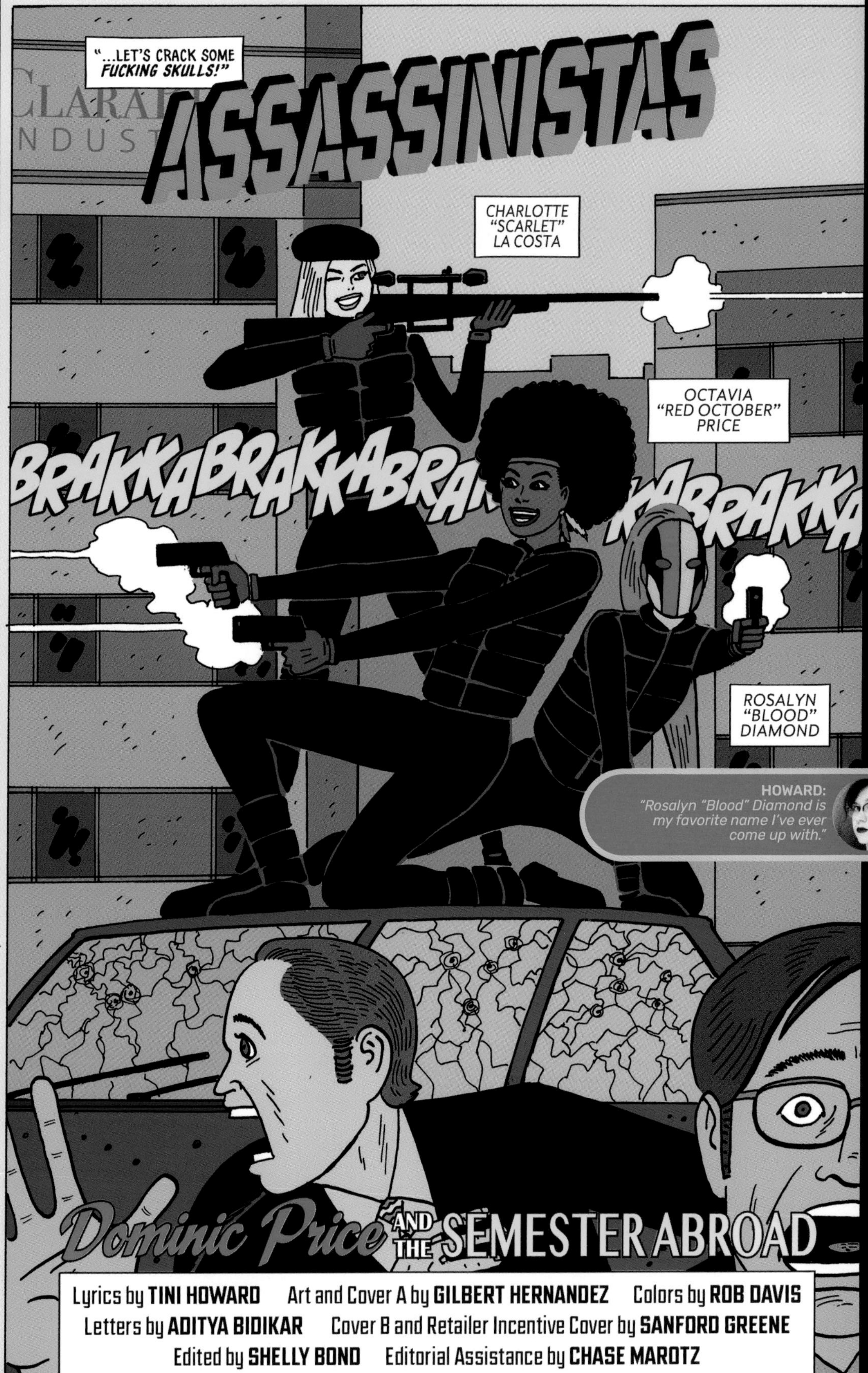
"...LET'S CRACK SOME FUCKING SKULLS!"
ASSASSINISTAS
CHARLOTTE "SCARLET" LA COSTA
OCTAVIA "RED OCTOBER" PRICE
BRAKKABRAKKABRAK
KABRAKKA
ROSALYN "BLOOD" DIAMOND
Dominic Price AND THE SEMESTER ABROAD
Lyrics by TINI HOWARD Art and Cover A by GILBERT HERNANDEZ Colors by ROB DAVIS
Letters by ADITYA BIDIKAR Cover B and Retailer Incentive Cover by SANFORD GREENE
Edited by SHELLY BOND Editorial Assistance by CHASE MAROTZ
ASSASSINISTAS is created by Howard & Hernandez

HOWARD:
"Rosalyn "Blood" Diamond is my favorite name I've ever come up with."

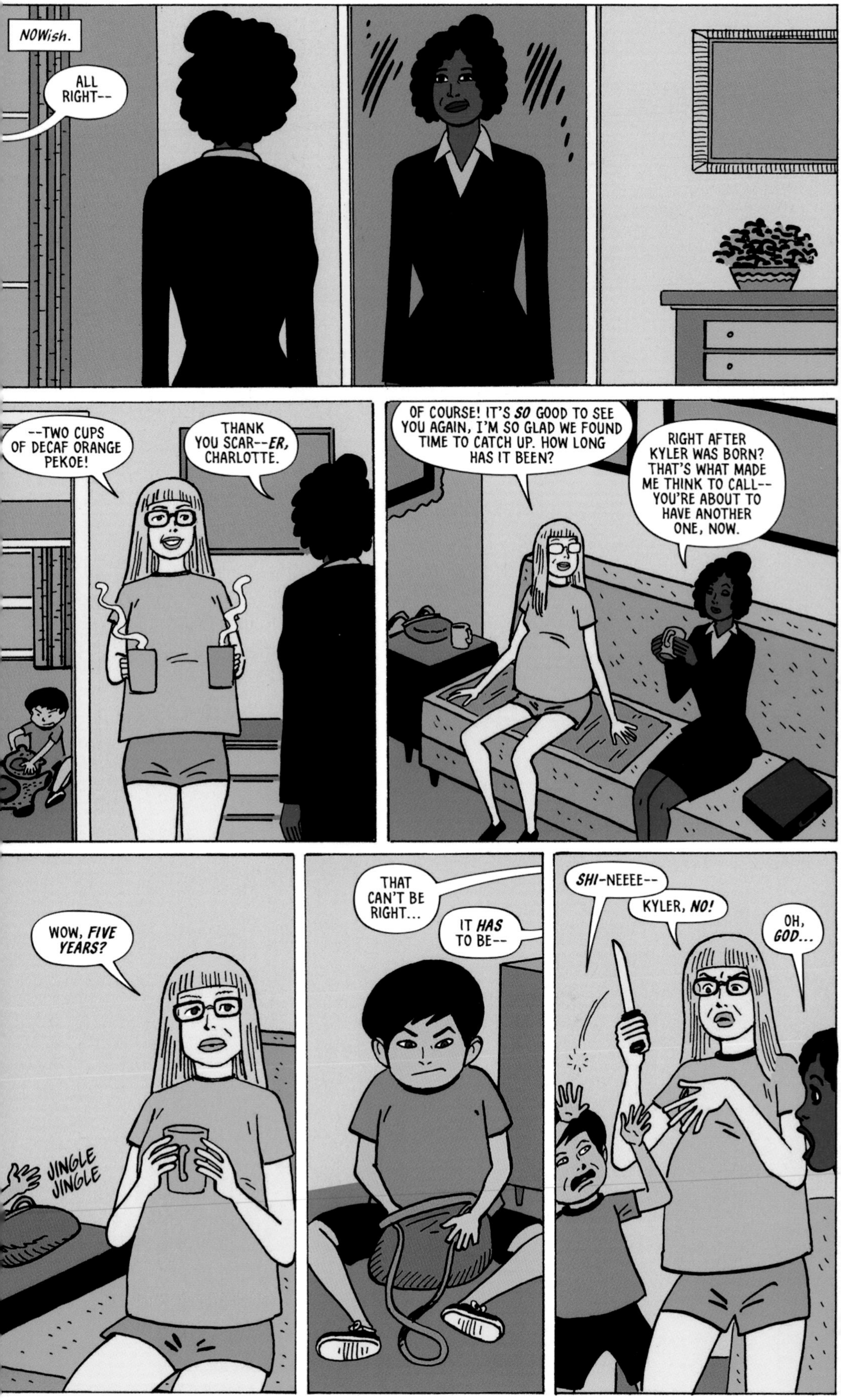
NOWish.
ALL RIGHT--
--TWO CUPS OF DECAF ORANGE PEKOE!
THANK YOU SCAR--*ER,* CHARLOTTE.
OF COURSE! IT'S *SO* GOOD TO SEE YOU AGAIN, I'M SO GLAD WE FOUND TIME TO CATCH UP. HOW LONG HAS IT BEEN?
RIGHT AFTER KYLER WAS BORN? THAT'S WHAT MADE ME THINK TO CALL--YOU'RE ABOUT TO HAVE ANOTHER ONE, NOW.
WOW, *FIVE YEARS?*
JINGLE JINGLE
THAT CAN'T BE RIGHT...
IT *HAS* TO BE--
SHI-NEEEE--
KYLER, *NO!*
OH, *GOD...*

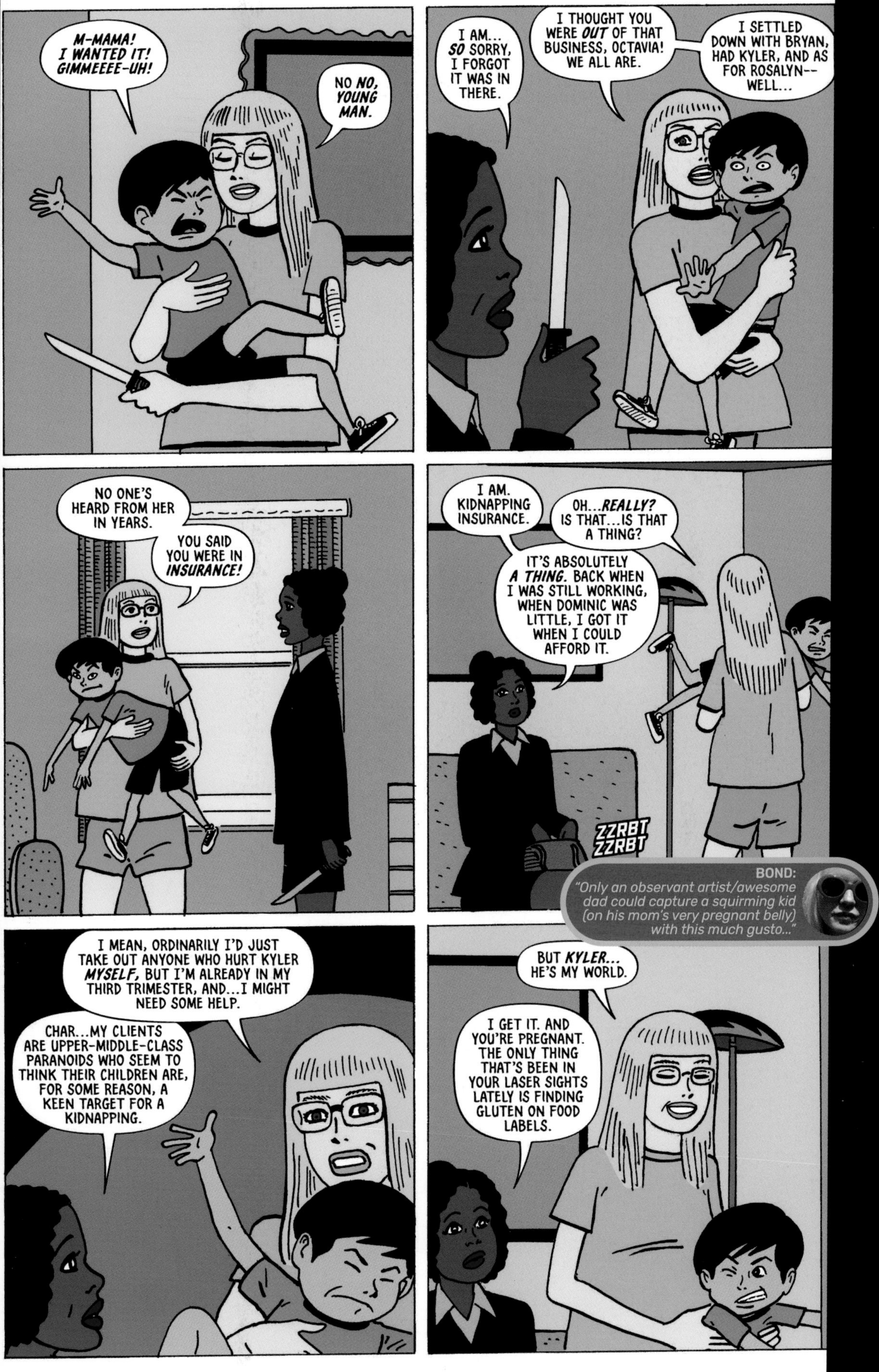
M-MAMA! I WANTED IT! GIMMEEEE-UH!
NO NO, YOUNG MAN.
I AM... SO SORRY, I FORGOT IT WAS IN THERE.
I THOUGHT YOU WERE OUT OF THAT BUSINESS, OCTAVIA! WE ALL ARE.
I SETTLED DOWN WITH BRYAN, HAD KYLER, AND AS FOR ROSALYN-- WELL...
NO ONE'S HEARD FROM HER IN YEARS.
YOU SAID YOU WERE IN INSURANCE!
I AM. KIDNAPPING INSURANCE.
OH...REALLY? IS THAT...IS THAT A THING?
IT'S ABSOLUTELY A THING. BACK WHEN I WAS STILL WORKING, WHEN DOMINIC WAS LITTLE, I GOT IT WHEN I COULD AFFORD IT.
ZZRBT ZZRBT
BOND:
"Only an observant artist/awesome dad could capture a squirming kid (on his mom's very pregnant belly) with this much gusto..."
I MEAN, ORDINARILY I'D JUST TAKE OUT ANYONE WHO HURT KYLER MYSELF, BUT I'M ALREADY IN MY THIRD TRIMESTER, AND...I MIGHT NEED SOME HELP.
CHAR...MY CLIENTS ARE UPPER-MIDDLE-CLASS PARANOIDS WHO SEEM TO THINK THEIR CHILDREN ARE, FOR SOME REASON, A KEEN TARGET FOR A KIDNAPPING.
BUT KYLER... HE'S MY WORLD.
I GET IT. AND YOU'RE PREGNANT. THE ONLY THING THAT'S BEEN IN YOUR LASER SIGHTS LATELY IS FINDING GLUTEN ON FOOD LABELS.

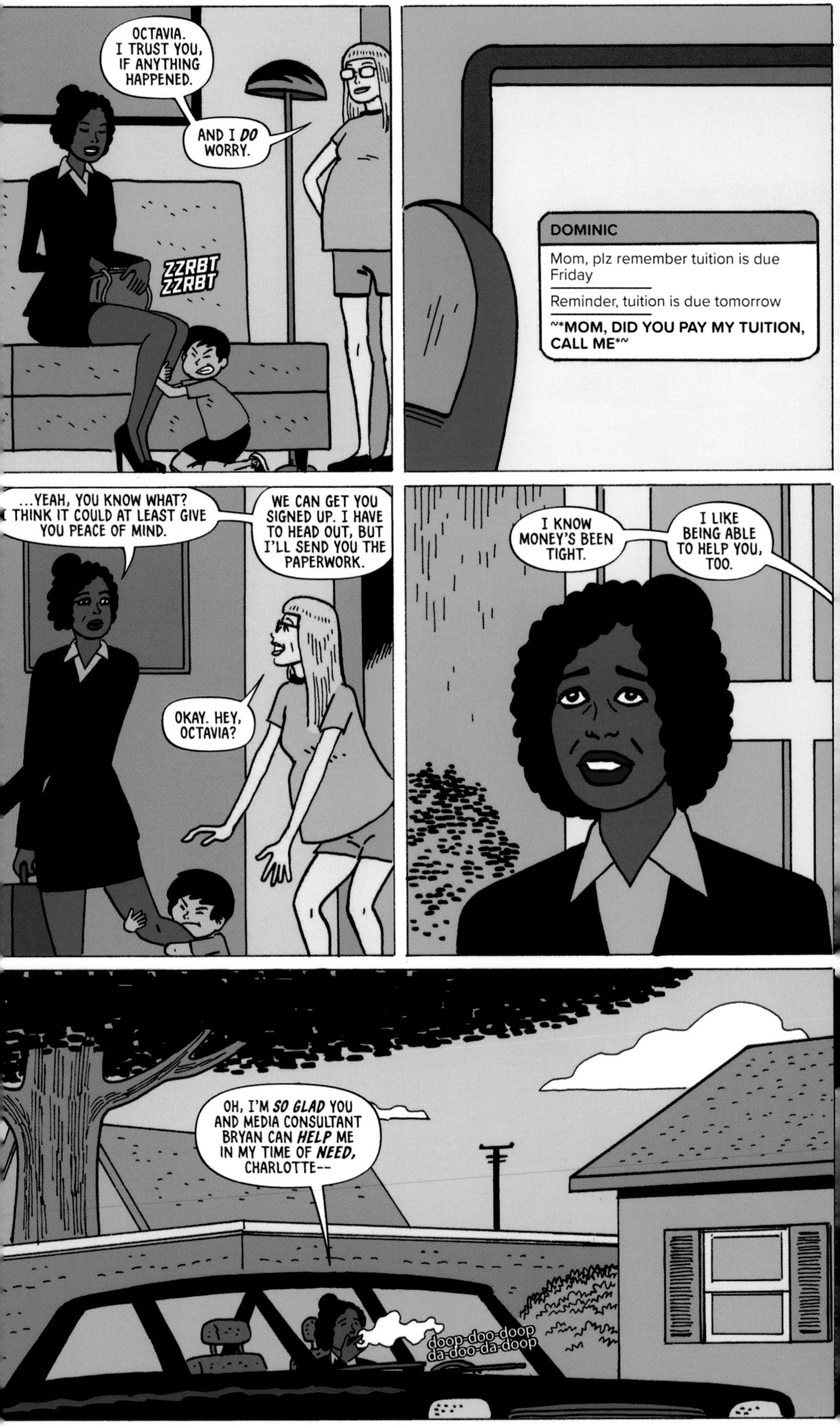
OCTAVIA. I TRUST YOU, IF ANYTHING HAPPENED.
AND I DO WORRY.
ZZRBT ZZRBT
DOMINIC
Mom, plz remember tuition is due Friday
Reminder, tuition is due tomorrow
~*MOM, DID YOU PAY MY TUITION, CALL ME*~
...YEAH, YOU KNOW WHAT? I THINK IT COULD AT LEAST GIVE YOU PEACE OF MIND.
WE CAN GET YOU SIGNED UP. I HAVE TO HEAD OUT, BUT I'LL SEND YOU THE PAPERWORK.
OKAY. HEY, OCTAVIA?
I KNOW MONEY'S BEEN TIGHT.
I LIKE BEING ABLE TO HELP YOU, TOO.
OH, I'M SO GLAD YOU AND MEDIA CONSULTANT BRYAN CAN HELP ME IN MY TIME OF NEED, CHARLOTTE--
doop-doo-doop da-doo-da-doop

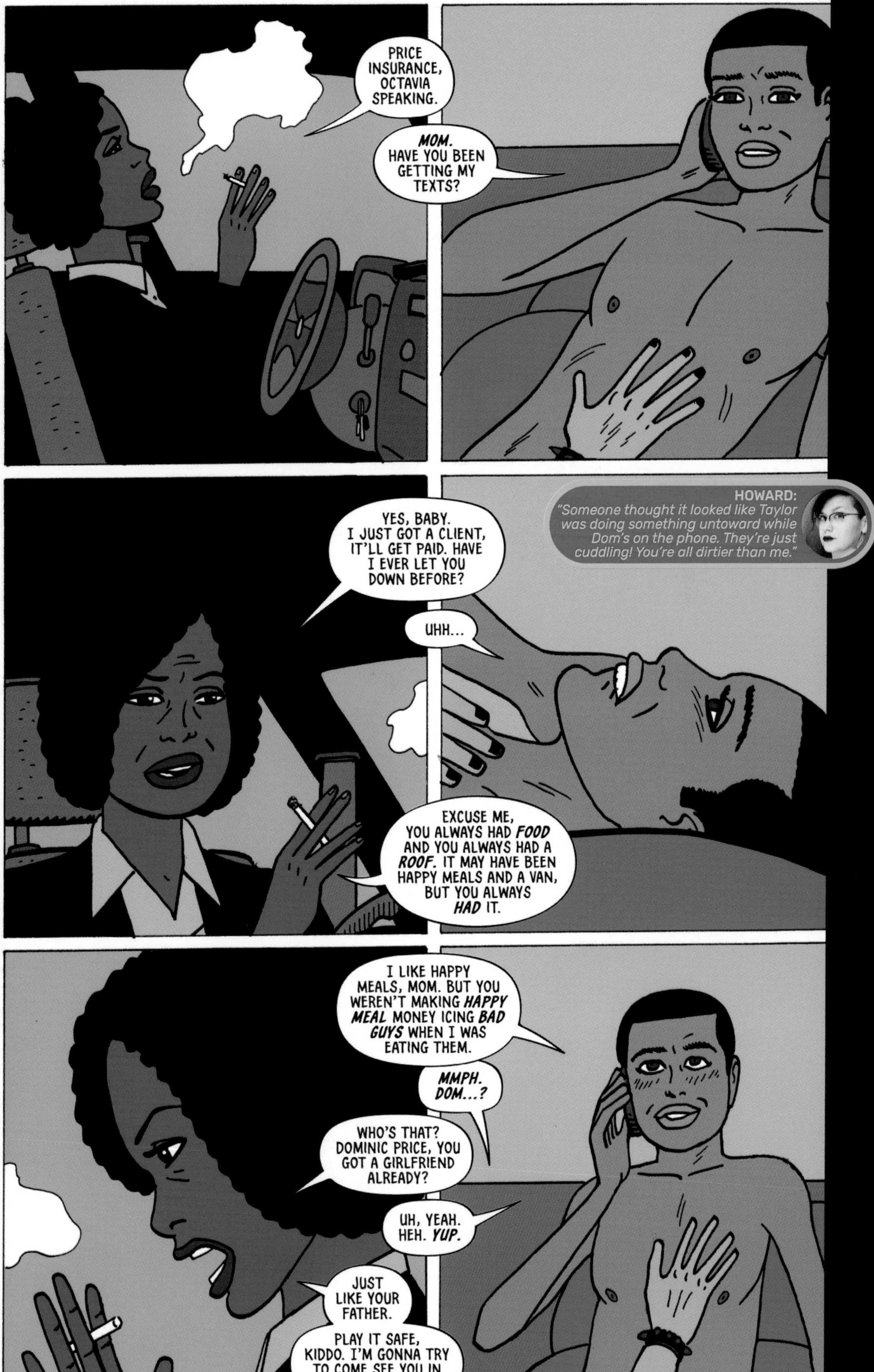

PRICE INSURANCE, OCTAVIA SPEAKING.
MOM. HAVE YOU BEEN GETTING MY TEXTS?
YES, BABY. I JUST GOT A CLIENT, IT'LL GET PAID. HAVE I EVER LET YOU DOWN BEFORE?
UHH...
HOWARD: "Someone thought it looked like Taylor was doing something untoward while Dom's on the phone. They're just cuddling! You're all dirtier than me."
EXCUSE ME, YOU ALWAYS HAD FOOD AND YOU ALWAYS HAD A ROOF. IT MAY HAVE BEEN HAPPY MEALS AND A VAN, BUT YOU ALWAYS HAD IT.
I LIKE HAPPY MEALS, MOM. BUT YOU WEREN'T MAKING HAPPY MEAL MONEY ICING BAD GUYS WHEN I WAS EATING THEM.
MMPH. DOM...?
WHO'S THAT? DOMINIC PRICE, YOU GOT A GIRLFRIEND ALREADY?
UH, YEAH. HEH. YUP.
JUST LIKE YOUR FATHER.
PLAY IT SAFE, KIDDO. I'M GONNA TRY TO COME SEE YOU IN A FEW WEEKS.

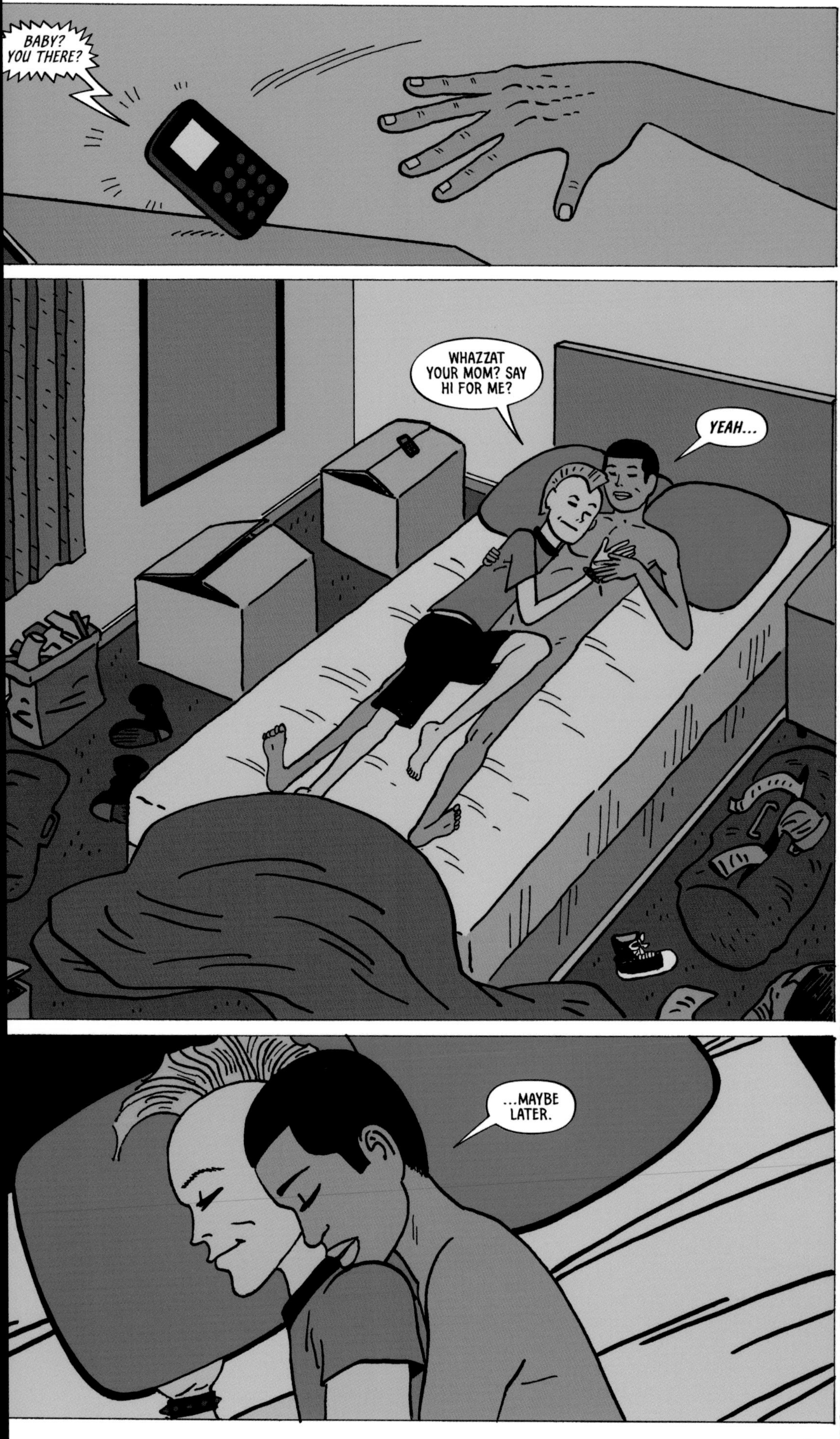
BABY? YOU THERE?
WHAZZAT YOUR MOM? SAY HI FOR ME?
YEAH...
...MAYBE LATER.

THAT NIGHT.

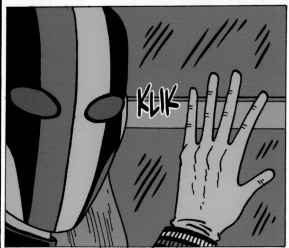

KLIK

SHHNK

BEEEP THE WINDOW IS AJAR. YOU HAVE THIRTY SECONDS TO CLOSE THE WINDOW.

FLIK

KYLER...?

BLOOD DIAMOND

HERNANDEZ:
"Kyler dreams of fried chicken..."

RATTLE RATTLE

...KYLER?!

THUNK

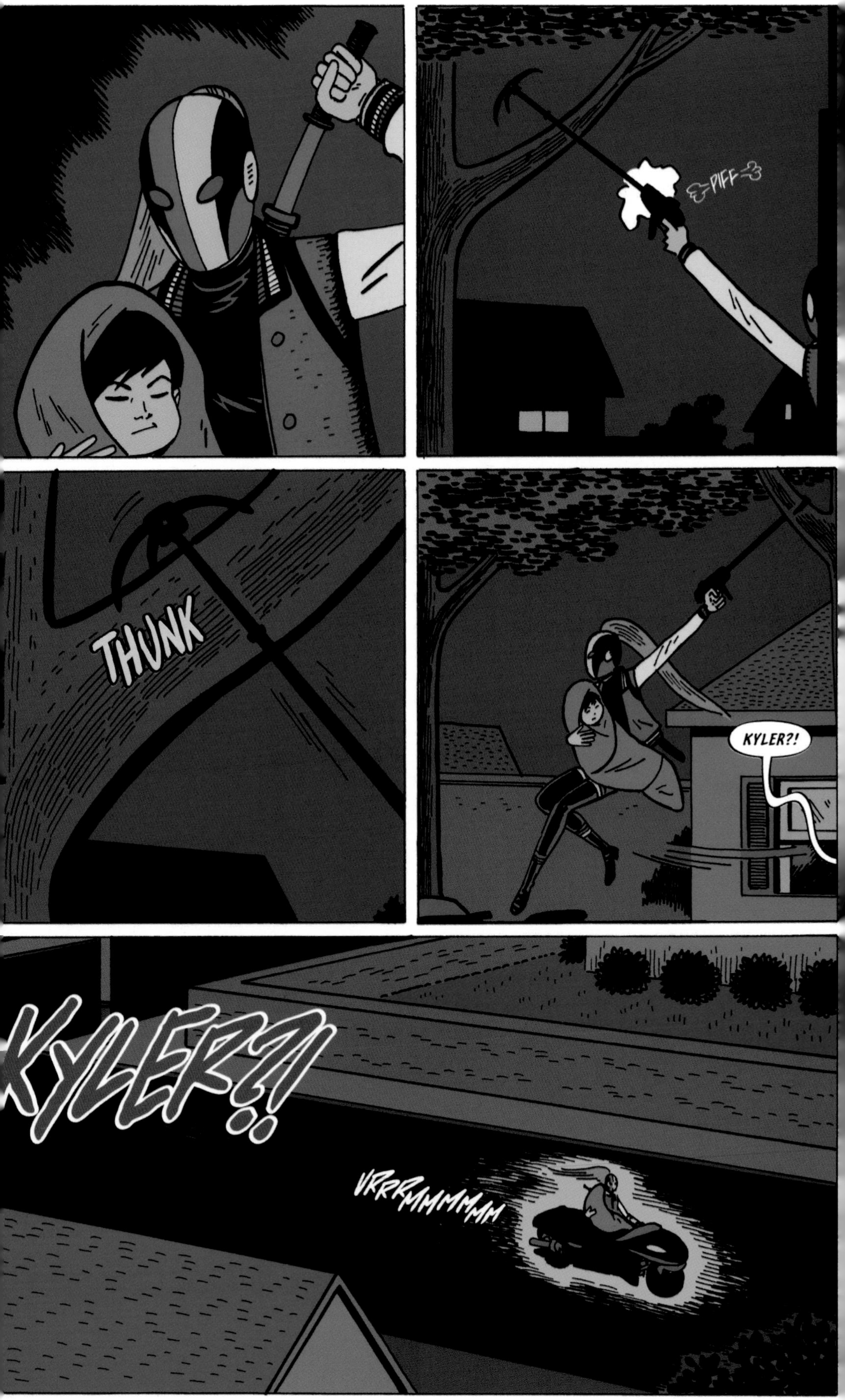
PIFF
THUNK
KYLER?!
KYLER?!
VRRRMMMMMM

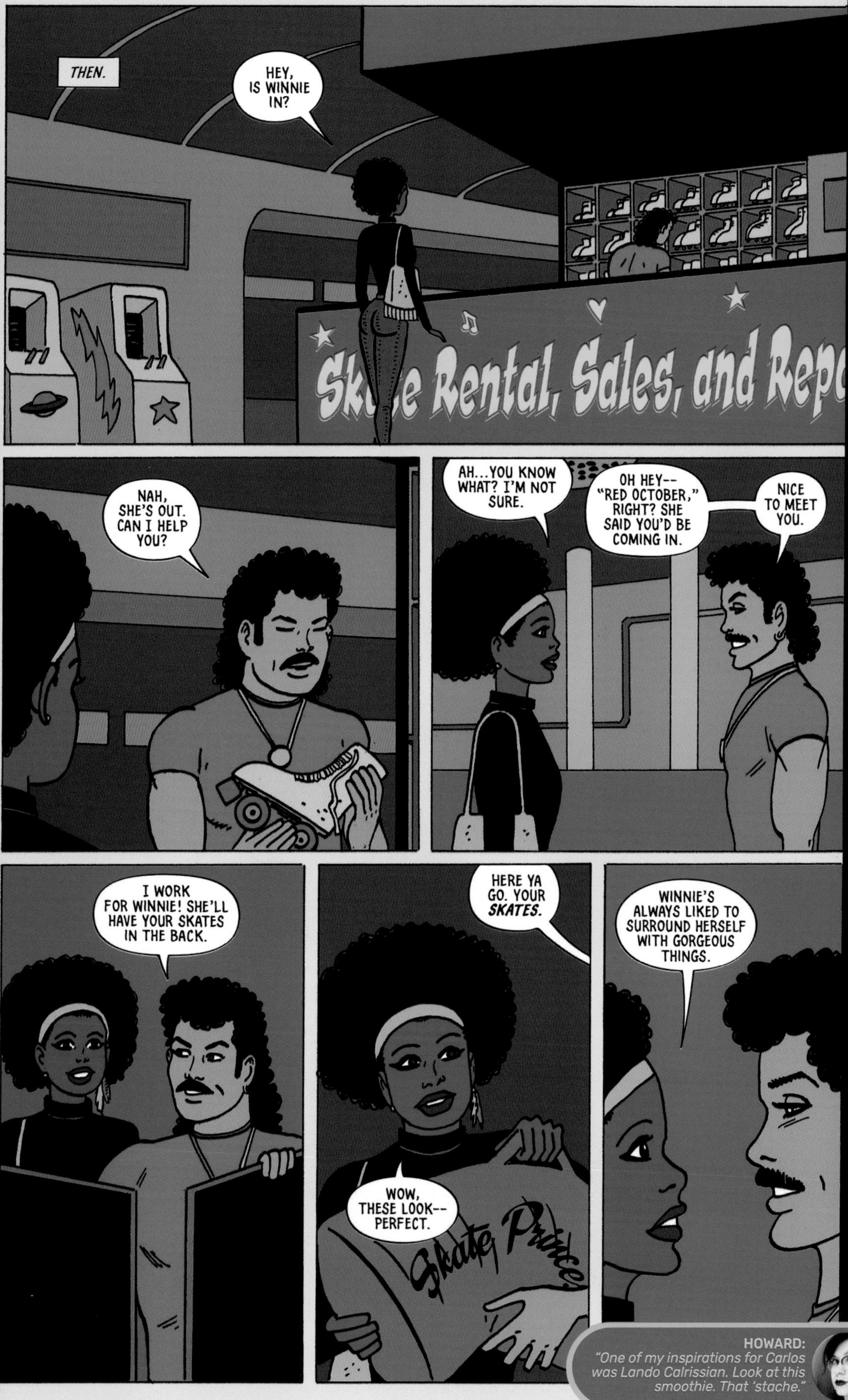
THEN.
HEY, IS WINNIE IN?
Rental, Sales, and
NAH, SHE'S OUT. CAN I HELP YOU?
AH...YOU KNOW WHAT? I'M NOT SURE.
OH HEY-- "RED OCTOBER," RIGHT? SHE SAID YOU'D BE COMING IN.
NICE TO MEET YOU.
I WORK FOR WINNIE! SHE'LL HAVE YOUR SKATES IN THE BACK.
HERE YA GO. YOUR *SKATES.*
WOW, THESE LOOK-- PERFECT.
Skate Prince
WINNIE'S ALWAYS LIKED TO SURROUND HERSELF WITH GORGEOUS THINGS.

HOWARD:
"One of my inspirations for Carlos was Lando Calrissian. Look at this smoothie. That 'stache."

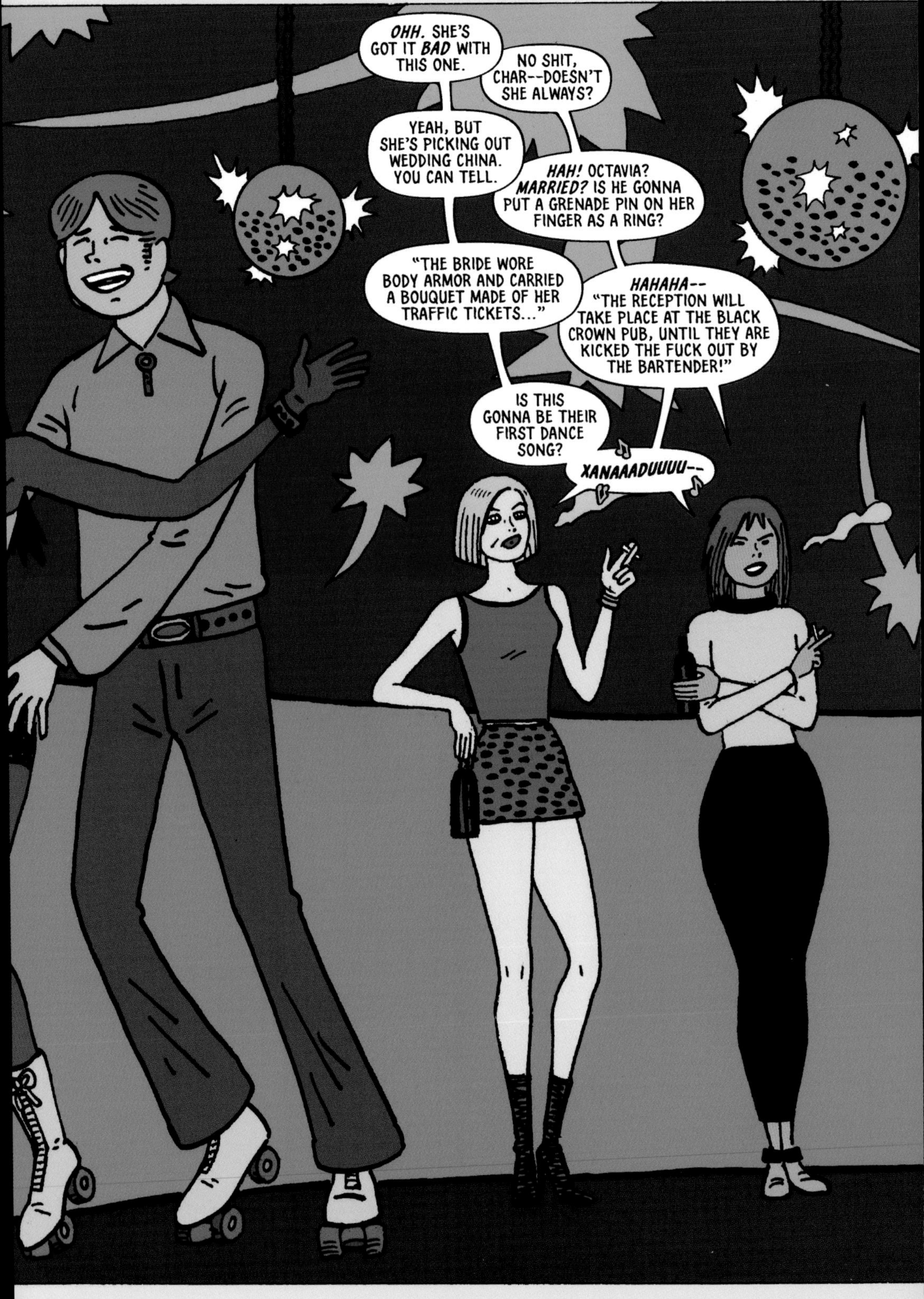

OHH. SHE'S GOT IT BAD WITH THIS ONE.
NO SHIT, CHAR--DOESN'T SHE ALWAYS?
YEAH, BUT SHE'S PICKING OUT WEDDING CHINA. YOU CAN TELL.
HAH! OCTAVIA? MARRIED? IS HE GONNA PUT A GRENADE PIN ON HER FINGER AS A RING?
"THE BRIDE WORE BODY ARMOR AND CARRIED A BOUQUET MADE OF HER TRAFFIC TICKETS..."
HAHAHA-- "THE RECEPTION WILL TAKE PLACE AT THE BLACK CROWN PUB, UNTIL THEY ARE KICKED THE FUCK OUT BY THE BARTENDER!"
IS THIS GONNA BE THEIR FIRST DANCE SONG?
XANAAADUUUU--

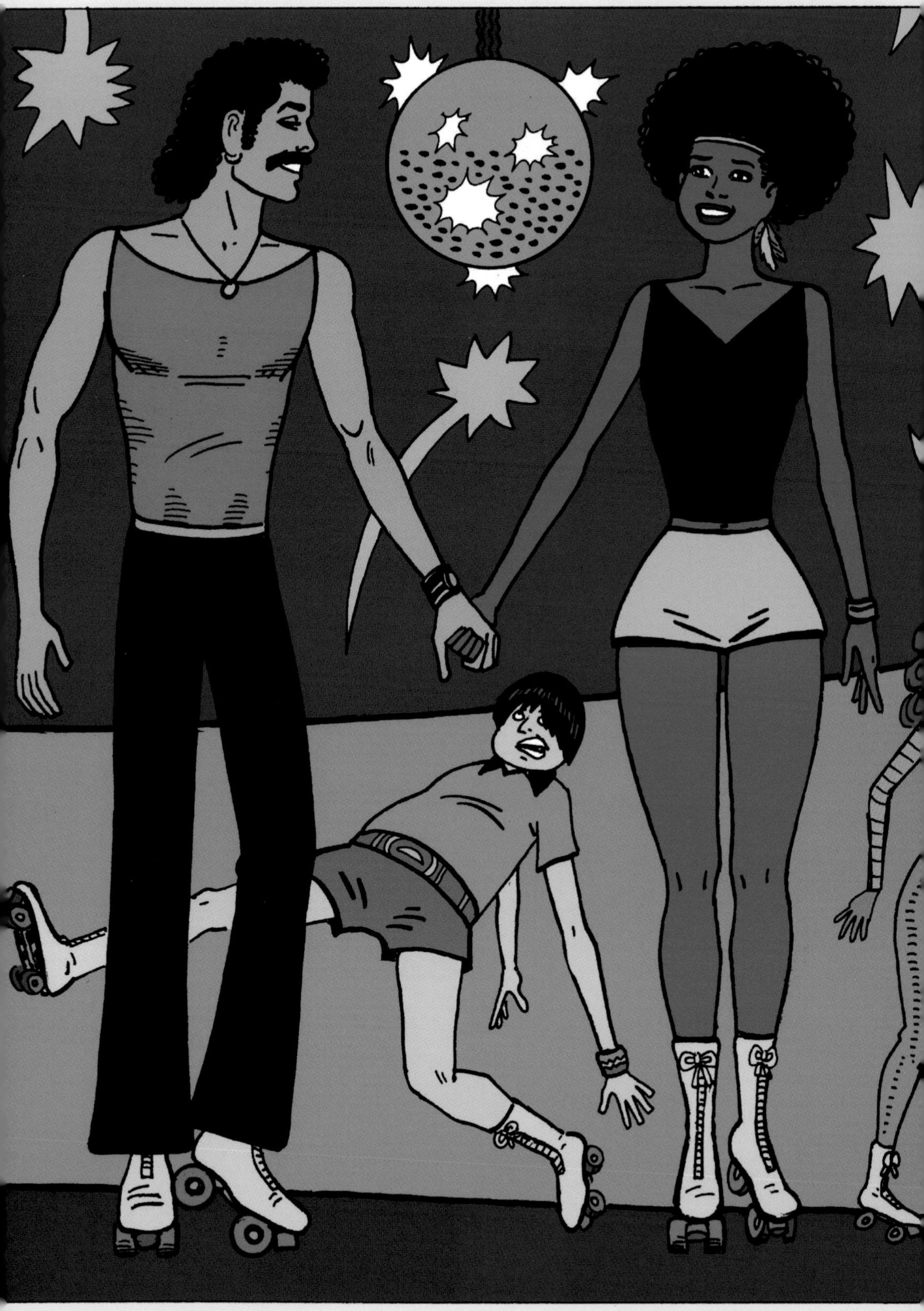

HERNANDEZ:
"We're a happy family, we're a happy family, we're a happy family, me, mom, and daddy."
—The Ramones

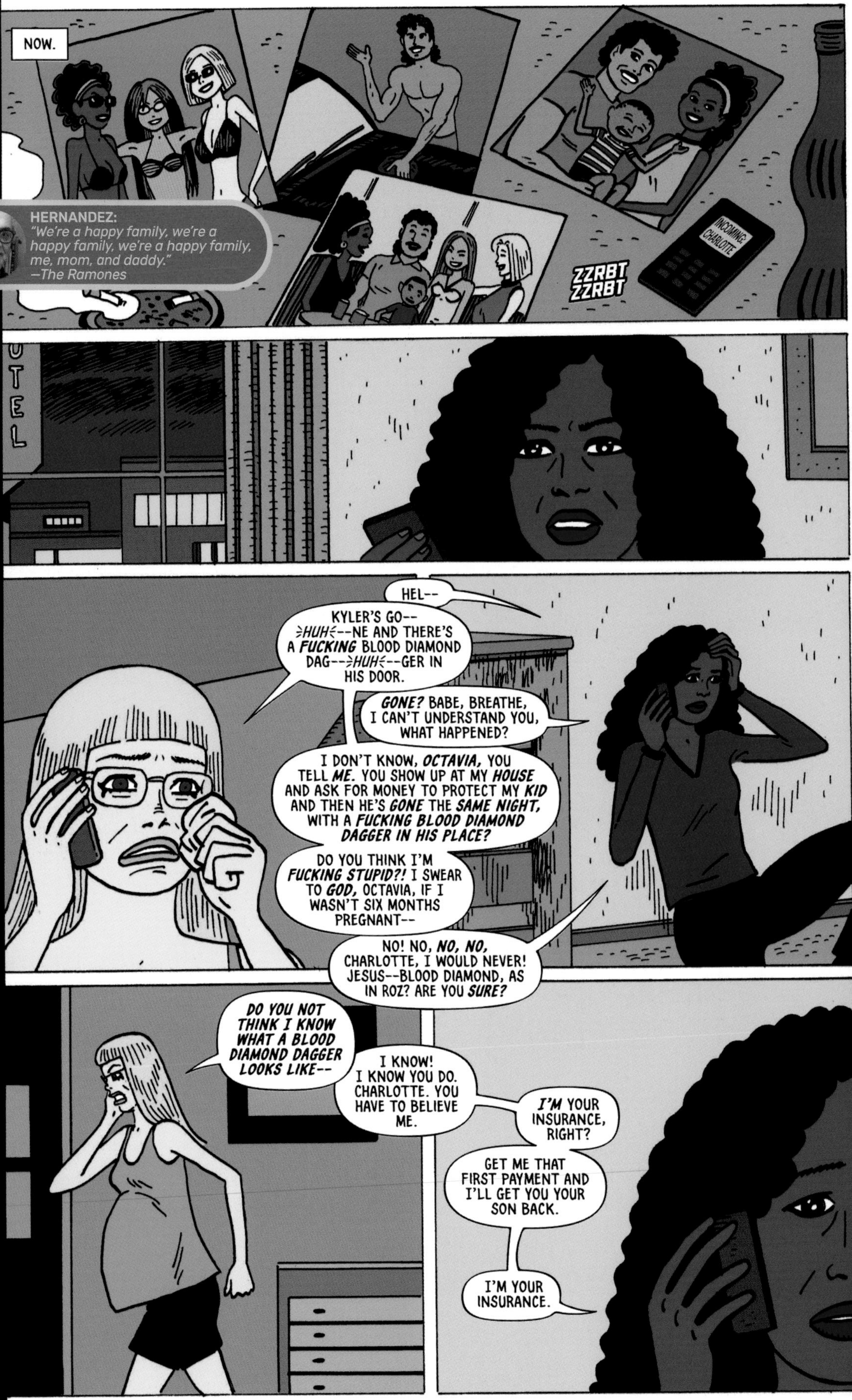

NOW.
INCOMING: CHARLOTTE
ZZRBT ZZRBT
HEL--
KYLER'S GO-- ⋟HUH⋞--NE AND THERE'S A FUCKING BLOOD DIAMOND DAG--⋟HUH⋞--GER IN HIS DOOR.
GONE? BABE, BREATHE, I CAN'T UNDERSTAND YOU, WHAT HAPPENED?
I DON'T KNOW, OCTAVIA, YOU TELL ME. YOU SHOW UP AT MY HOUSE AND ASK FOR MONEY TO PROTECT MY KID AND THEN HE'S GONE THE SAME NIGHT, WITH A FUCKING BLOOD DIAMOND DAGGER IN HIS PLACE?
DO YOU THINK I'M FUCKING STUPID?! I SWEAR TO GOD, OCTAVIA, IF I WASN'T SIX MONTHS PREGNANT--
NO! NO, NO, NO, CHARLOTTE, I WOULD NEVER! JESUS--BLOOD DIAMOND, AS IN ROZ? ARE YOU SURE?
DO YOU NOT THINK I KNOW WHAT A BLOOD DIAMOND DAGGER LOOKS LIKE--
I KNOW! I KNOW YOU DO. CHARLOTTE. YOU HAVE TO BELIEVE ME.
I'M YOUR INSURANCE, RIGHT?
GET ME THAT FIRST PAYMENT AND I'LL GET YOU YOUR SON BACK.
I'M YOUR INSURANCE.

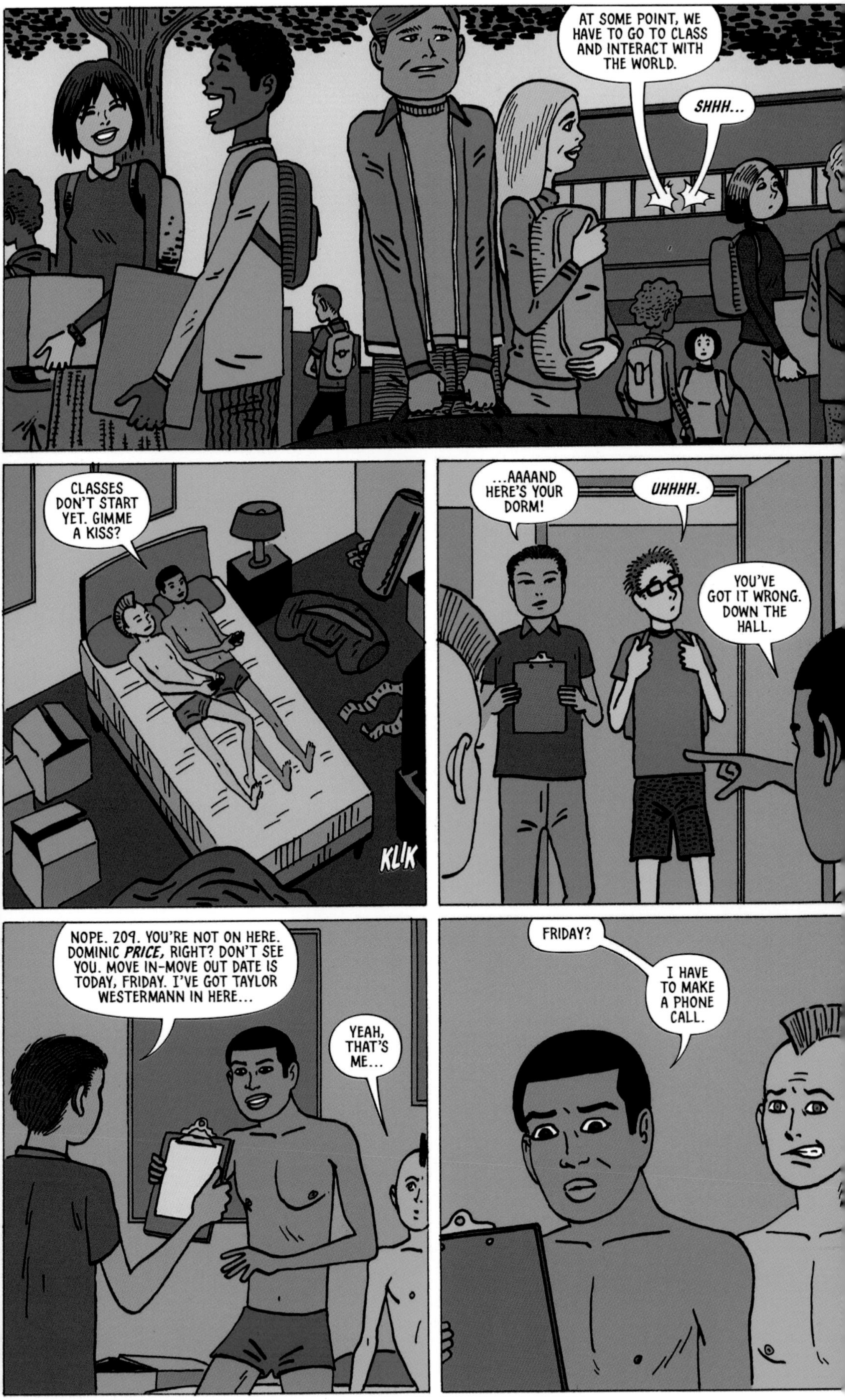
AT SOME POINT, WE HAVE TO GO TO CLASS AND INTERACT WITH THE WORLD.
SHHH...
CLASSES DON'T START YET. GIMME A KISS?
KLIK
...AAAAND HERE'S YOUR DORM!
UHHHH.
YOU'VE GOT IT WRONG. DOWN THE HALL.
NOPE. 209. YOU'RE NOT ON HERE. DOMINIC PRICE, RIGHT? DON'T SEE YOU. MOVE IN-MOVE OUT DATE IS TODAY, FRIDAY. I'VE GOT TAYLOR WESTERMANN IN HERE...
YEAH, THAT'S ME...
FRIDAY?
I HAVE TO MAKE A PHONE CALL.

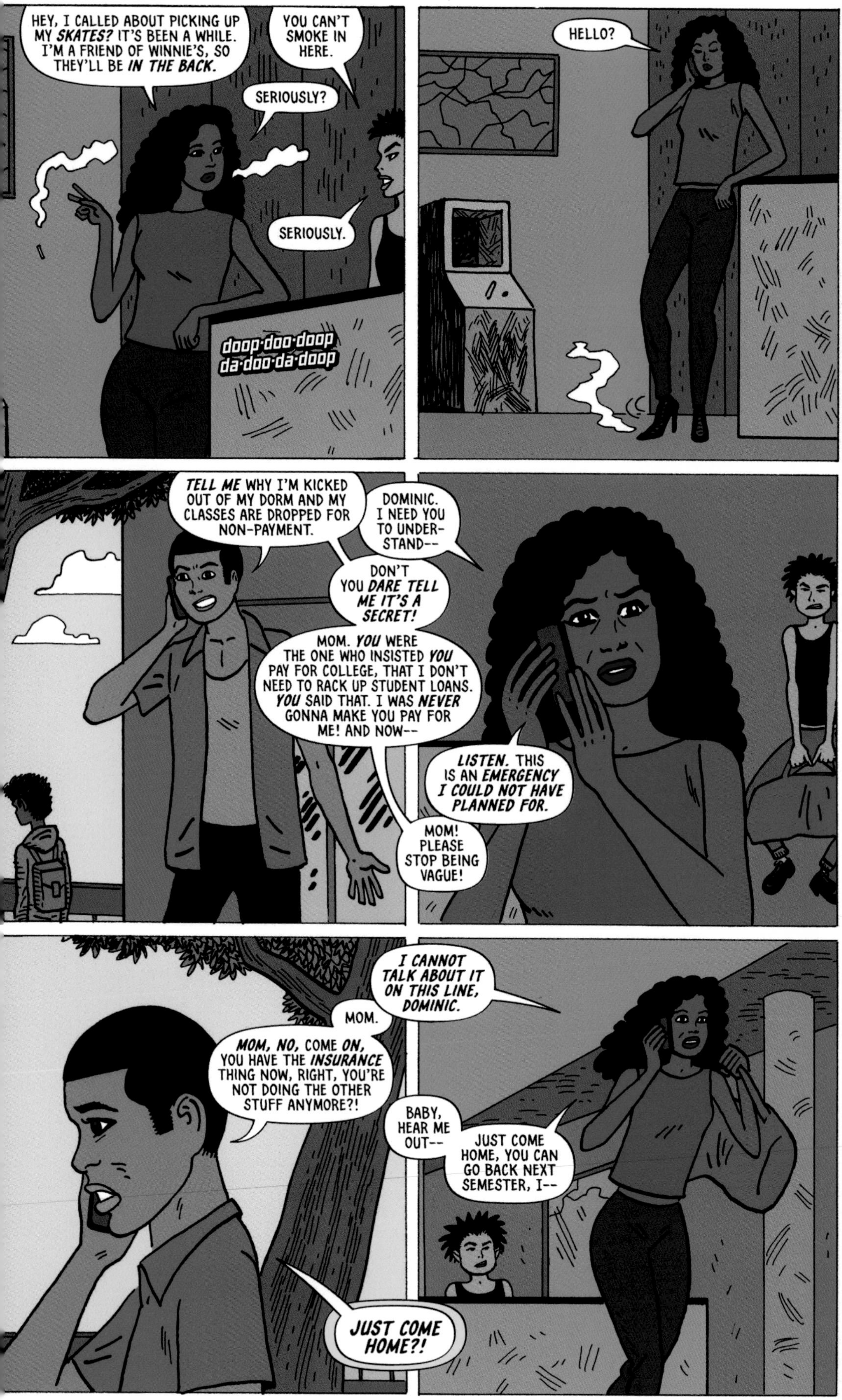

HEY, I CALLED ABOUT PICKING UP MY *SKATES?* IT'S BEEN A WHILE. I'M A FRIEND OF WINNIE'S, SO THEY'LL BE *IN THE BACK.*
YOU CAN'T SMOKE IN HERE.
SERIOUSLY?
SERIOUSLY.
doop·doo·doop da·doo·da·doop
HELLO?
TELL ME WHY I'M KICKED OUT OF MY DORM AND MY CLASSES ARE DROPPED FOR NON-PAYMENT.
DOMINIC. I NEED YOU TO UNDER-STAND--
DON'T YOU *DARE TELL ME IT'S A SECRET!*
MOM. *YOU* WERE THE ONE WHO INSISTED *YOU* PAY FOR COLLEGE, THAT I DON'T NEED TO RACK UP STUDENT LOANS. *YOU* SAID THAT. I WAS *NEVER* GONNA MAKE YOU PAY FOR ME! AND NOW--
LISTEN. THIS IS AN *EMERGENCY I COULD NOT HAVE PLANNED FOR.*
MOM! PLEASE STOP BEING VAGUE!
I CANNOT TALK ABOUT IT ON THIS LINE, DOMINIC.
MOM.
MOM, NO, COME *ON,* YOU HAVE THE *INSURANCE* THING NOW, RIGHT, YOU'RE NOT DOING THE OTHER STUFF ANYMORE?!
BABY, HEAR ME OUT--
JUST COME HOME, YOU CAN GO BACK NEXT SEMESTER, I--
JUST COME HOME?!

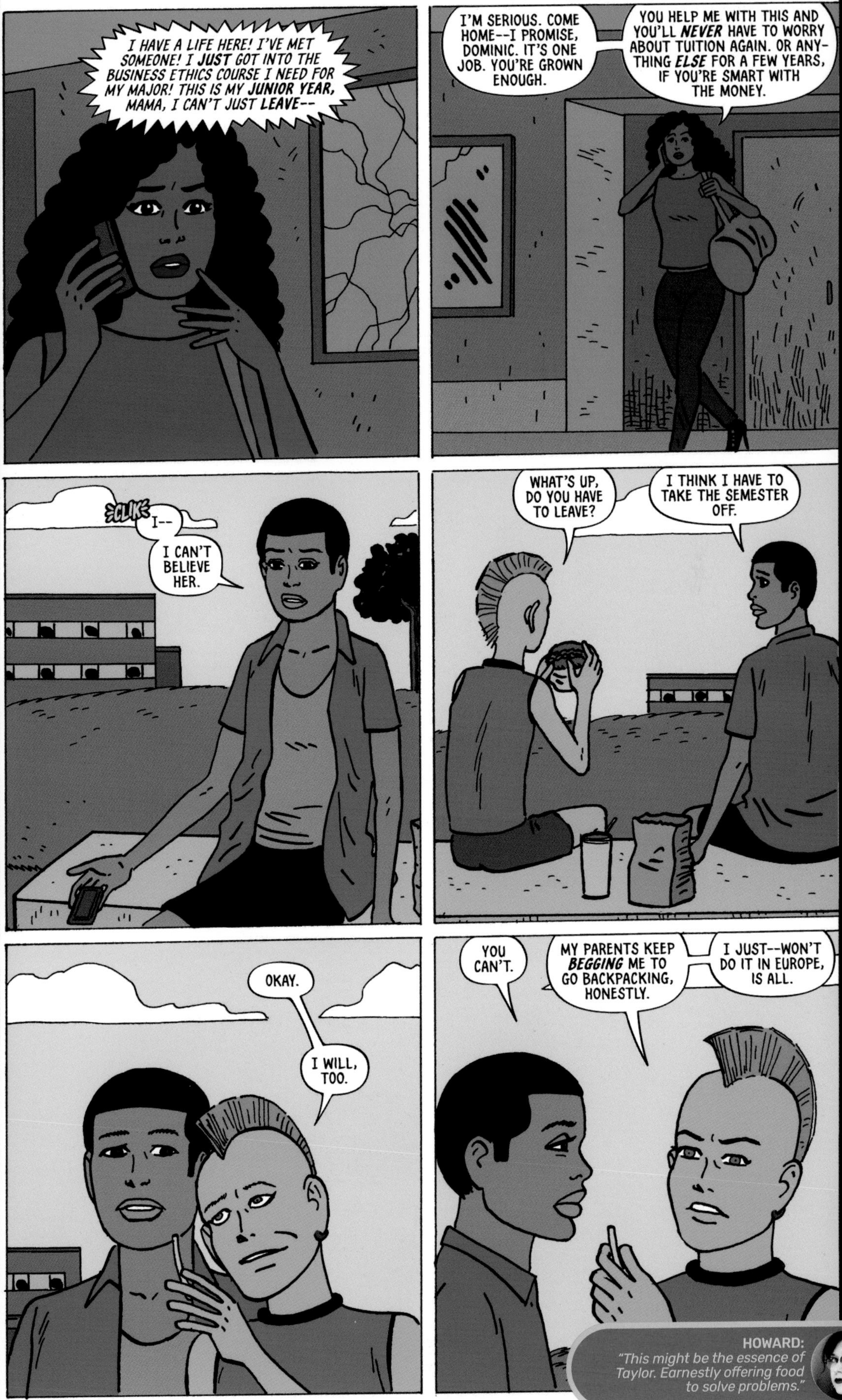
I HAVE A LIFE HERE! I'VE MET SOMEONE! I JUST GOT INTO THE BUSINESS ETHICS COURSE I NEED FOR MY MAJOR! THIS IS MY JUNIOR YEAR, MAMA, I CAN'T JUST LEAVE--
I'M SERIOUS. COME HOME--I PROMISE, DOMINIC. IT'S ONE JOB. YOU'RE GROWN ENOUGH.
YOU HELP ME WITH THIS AND YOU'LL NEVER HAVE TO WORRY ABOUT TUITION AGAIN. OR ANYTHING ELSE FOR A FEW YEARS, IF YOU'RE SMART WITH THE MONEY.
CLIK
I--
I CAN'T BELIEVE HER.
WHAT'S UP, DO YOU HAVE TO LEAVE?
I THINK I HAVE TO TAKE THE SEMESTER OFF.
OKAY.
I WILL, TOO.
YOU CAN'T.
MY PARENTS KEEP BEGGING ME TO GO BACKPACKING, HONESTLY.
I JUST--WON'T DO IT IN EUROPE, IS ALL.

HOWARD:
"This might be the essence of Taylor. Earnestly offering food to solve problems."

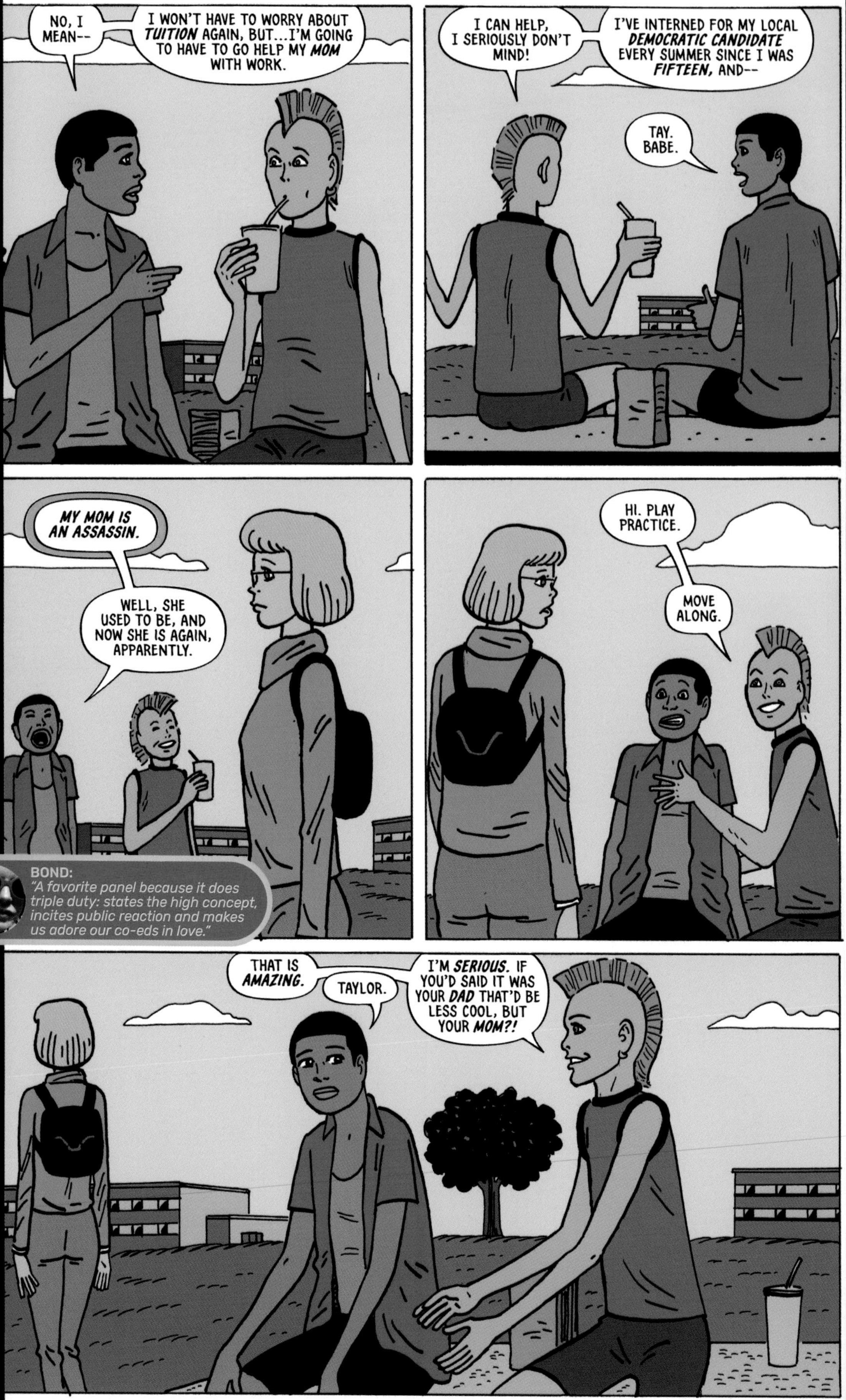
NO, I MEAN--
I WON'T HAVE TO WORRY ABOUT *TUITION* AGAIN, BUT...I'M GOING TO HAVE TO GO HELP MY *MOM* WITH WORK.
I CAN HELP, I SERIOUSLY DON'T MIND!
I'VE INTERNED FOR MY LOCAL *DEMOCRATIC CANDIDATE* EVERY SUMMER SINCE I WAS *FIFTEEN,* AND--
TAY. BABE.
MY MOM IS AN ASSASSIN.
WELL, SHE USED TO BE, AND NOW SHE IS AGAIN, APPARENTLY.
HI. PLAY PRACTICE.
MOVE ALONG.
THAT IS *AMAZING.*
TAYLOR.
I'M *SERIOUS.* IF YOU'D SAID IT WAS YOUR *DAD* THAT'D BE LESS COOL, BUT YOUR *MOM?!*

BOND:
"A favorite panel because it does triple duty: states the high concept, incites public reaction and makes us adore our co-eds in love."

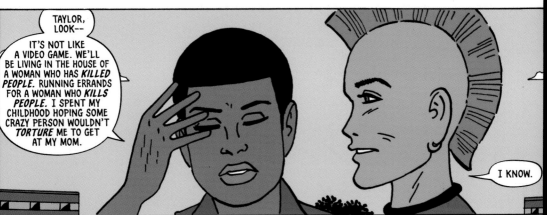

TAYLOR, LOOK-- IT'S NOT LIKE A VIDEO GAME. WE'LL BE LIVING IN THE HOUSE OF A WOMAN WHO HAS *KILLED PEOPLE.* RUNNING ERRANDS FOR A WOMAN WHO *KILLS PEOPLE.* I SPENT MY CHILDHOOD HOPING SOME CRAZY PERSON WOULDN'T *TORTURE* ME TO GET AT MY MOM.

I KNOW.

AND I DON'T WANT YOU TO HAVE TO GO BACK TO THAT ALONE.

I LIKE YOU A *LOT,* TAYLOR.

I WOULDN'T HAVE TOLD YOU THIS IF I DIDN'T.

I LIKE YOU A LOT, TOO. SO FAR THAT'S MOSTLY MEANT *MAKING OUT* AND PLAYING *VIDEO GAMES* EVERY WAKING MOMENT TOGETHER. WE'RE PROBABLY NO DIFFERENT FROM ANY OTHER HORNY COLLEGE COUPLE, BUT I...DON'T WANNA BE *WITHOUT* YOU. WE WERE APART ALL SUMMER. IT *SUCKED.*

I WANT YOU WITH ME.

THEN LET ME COME WITH YOU.

WE'RE NOT GOING TO HELP HER KILL PEOPLE.

YEAH, AGREED. WE CAN BE INTERNS!

HERNANDEZ: *"I guess you're looking for me to say, 'We can be interns! Just for one day!' You know, like Heroes!"*

159

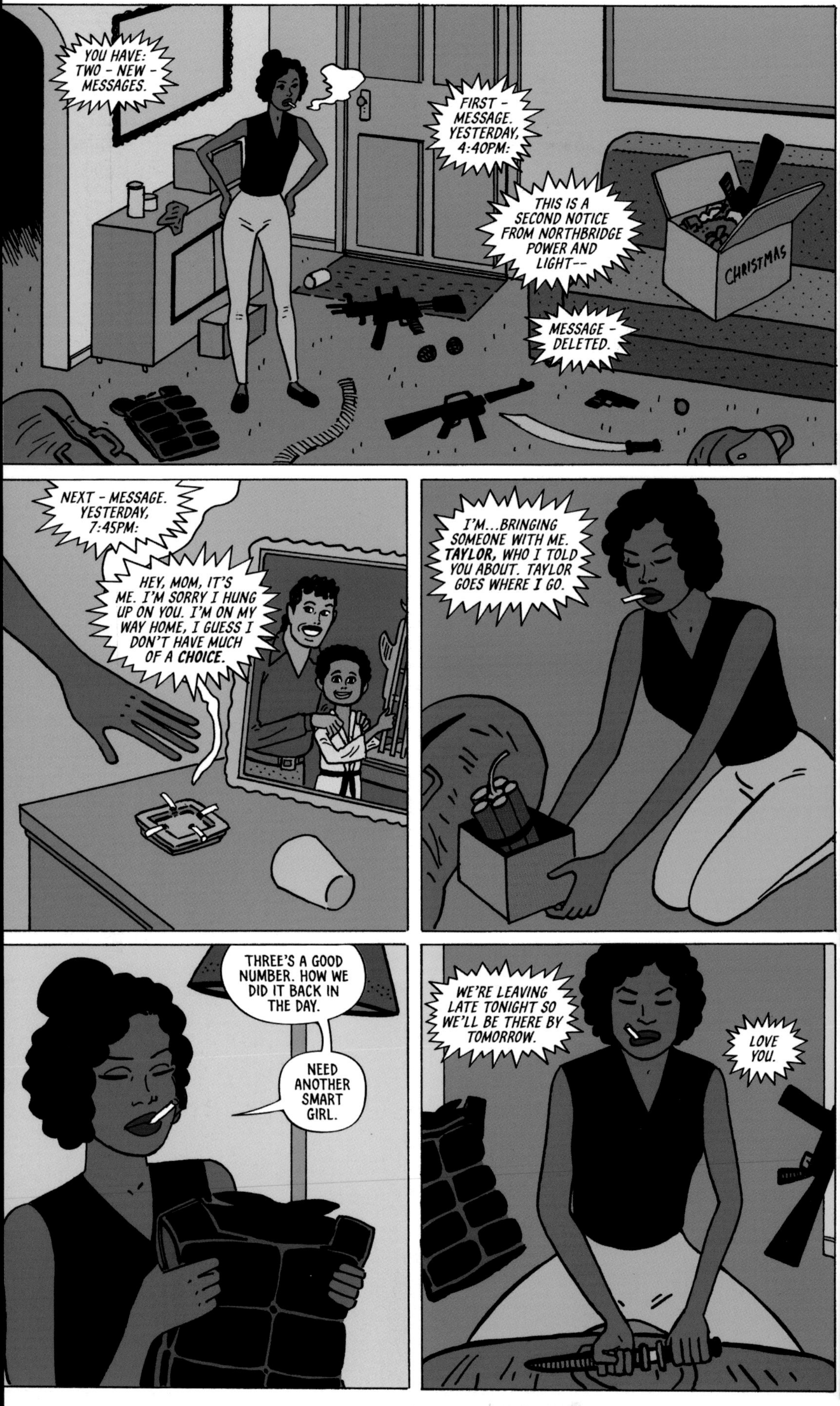
YOU HAVE: TWO - NEW - MESSAGES.
FIRST - MESSAGE. YESTERDAY, 4:40PM:
THIS IS A SECOND NOTICE FROM NORTHBRIDGE POWER AND LIGHT--
CHRISTMAS
MESSAGE - DELETED.
NEXT - MESSAGE. YESTERDAY, 7:45PM:
HEY, MOM, IT'S ME. I'M SORRY I HUNG UP ON YOU. I'M ON MY WAY HOME, I GUESS I DON'T HAVE MUCH OF A **CHOICE**.
I'M...BRINGING SOMEONE WITH ME. **TAYLOR**, WHO I TOLD YOU ABOUT. TAYLOR GOES WHERE **I** GO.
THREE'S A GOOD NUMBER. HOW WE DID IT BACK IN THE DAY.
NEED ANOTHER SMART GIRL.
WE'RE LEAVING LATE TONIGHT SO WE'LL BE THERE BY TOMORROW.
LOVE YOU.

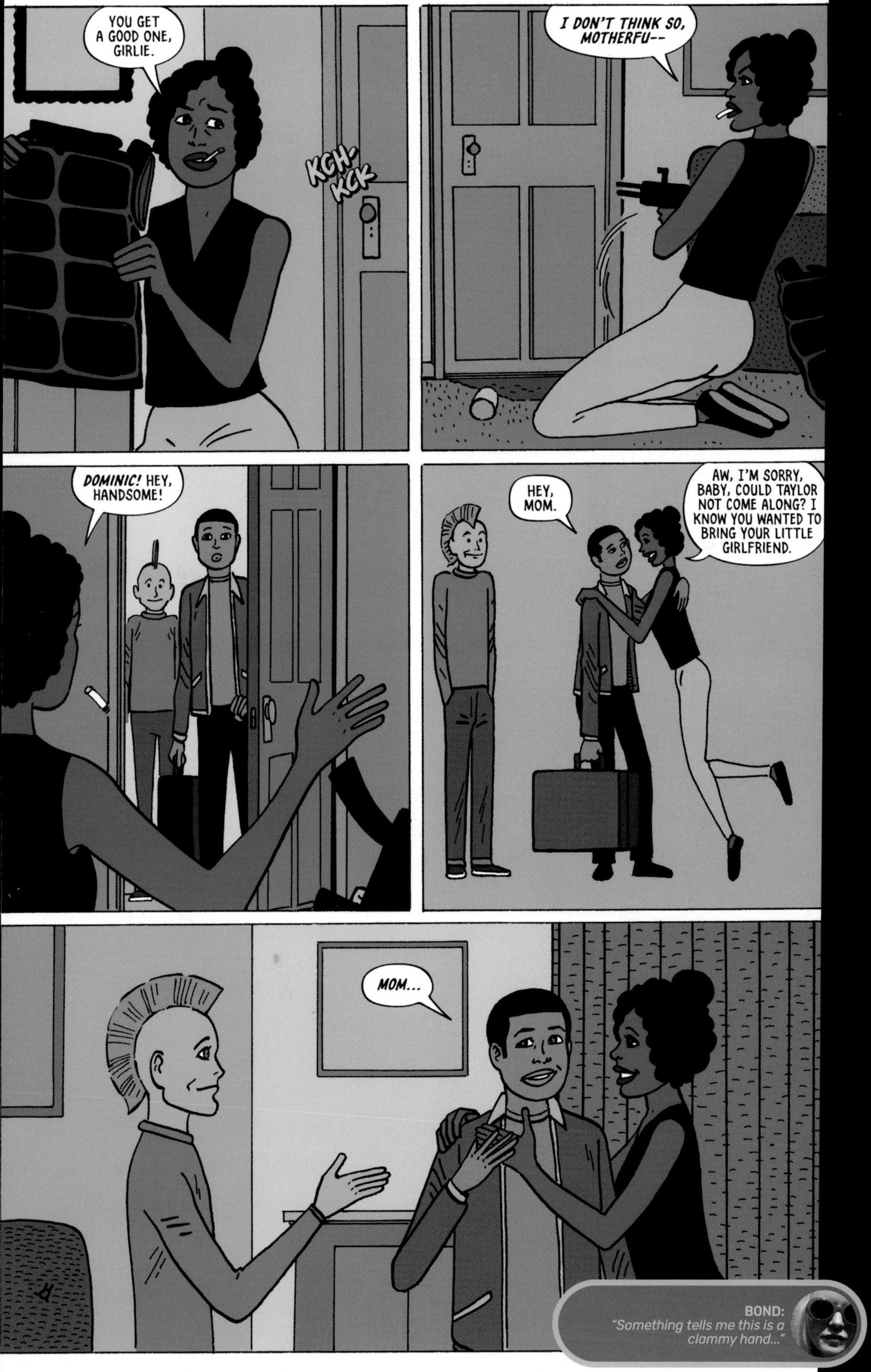
YOU GET A GOOD ONE, GIRLIE.
KCH-KCK
I DON'T THINK SO, MOTHERFU--
DOMINIC! HEY, HANDSOME!
HEY, MOM.
AW, I'M SORRY, BABY, COULD TAYLOR NOT COME ALONG? I KNOW YOU WANTED TO BRING YOUR LITTLE GIRLFRIEND.
MOM...
BOND:
"Something tells me this is a clammy hand..."

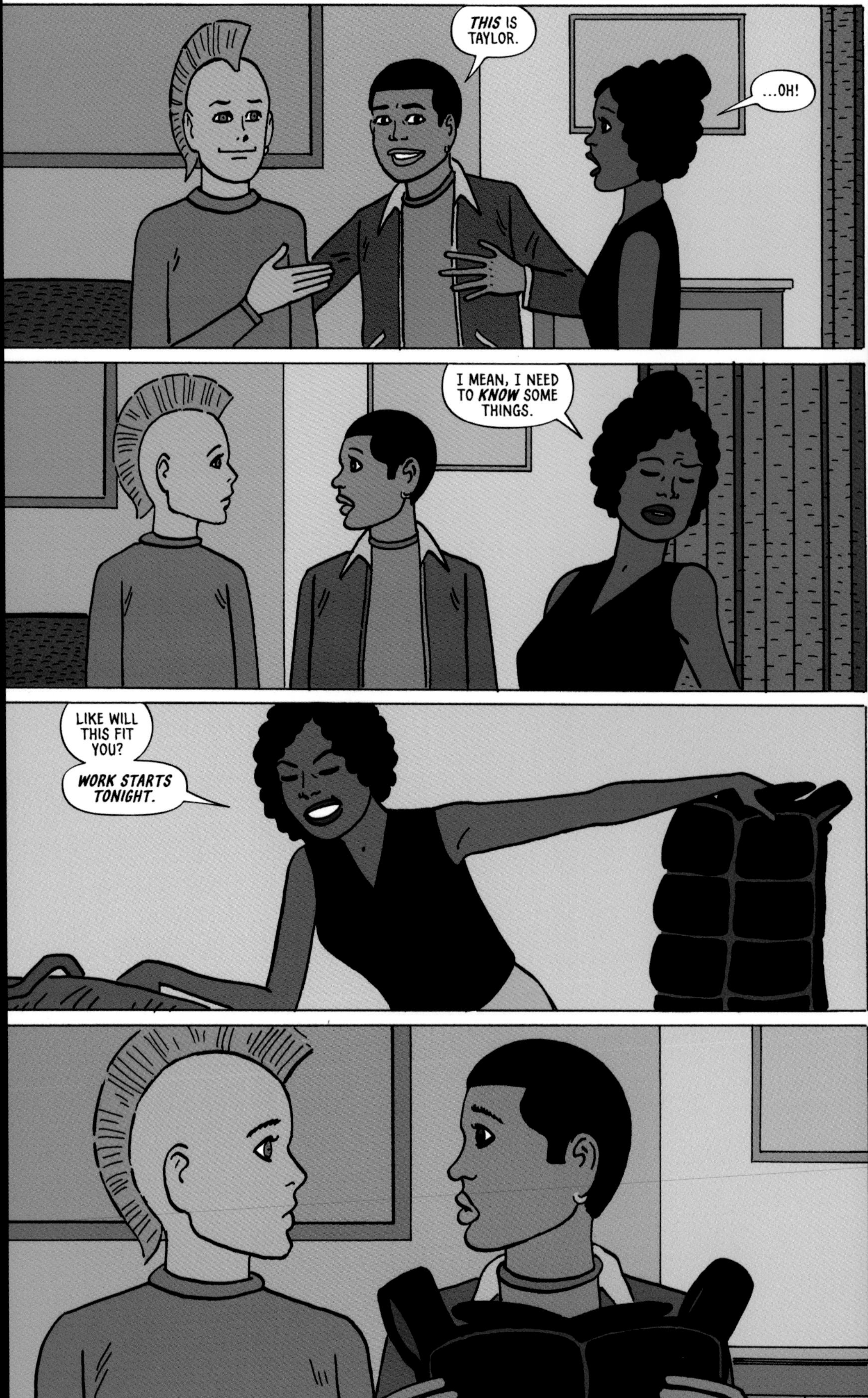
THIS IS TAYLOR.
...OH!
I MEAN, I NEED TO KNOW SOME THINGS.
LIKE WILL THIS FIT YOU?
WORK STARTS TONIGHT.

ADVERTISEMENT

MURDER-BASED

WORK STUDY / SEMESTER ABROAD

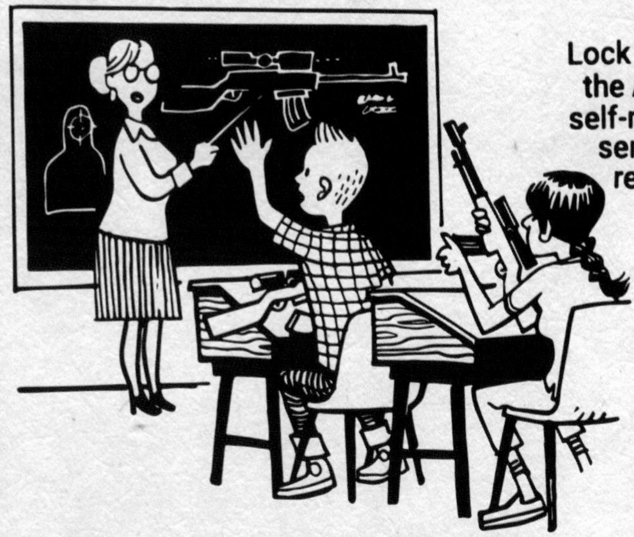

It's a hell of a SEMESTER!

Lock your dorms and Load your pistols - the **ASSASSINISTAS** are looking for self-motivated interns seeking to trade a semester of business courses for the realest real-life experience there is - **KIDNAPPING INSURANCE.**

We at **ASSASSINISTAS, INC**. are grateful for the opportunity to provide you with a MURDER-BASED WORK STUDY/SEMESTER ABROAD experience that will not only be fascinating, invigorating, and downright *bloody* - but also aid in y our academic goals while abetting your personal growth and development.

At **ASSASSINISTAS, INC.** we strive to make every student's MURDER-BASED WORK STUDY SEMESTER ABROAD experience as satisfying as possible. Our focus on the student experience is evident in the artillery we develop, in the targets we select, and in the planning and implementation of academic and cultural semi-automatic experiences. Our staff are fully equipped and trained to assist you in your MURDER-BASED WORK STUDY/SEMESTER ABROAD, and believe there's nothing quite like a hands-on experience.

Looking for your own semester away? Courses include:

- Wet Work
- Organized Crime
- Identity Theft
- Black Market
- Disorganized familial politics
- ...and more!

Call Now!!

applications c/o
Winnie's Hot Wheels Roller Rink
840 E Canon St.
include $75 processing fee

Item No.122017/ass1

Are you a secret sniper or an intrepid bounty hunter?
Can't find last-minute childcare?
Bundle up baby and safely take him/her on the job.

Introducing the

BULLETPROOF BABY-POD

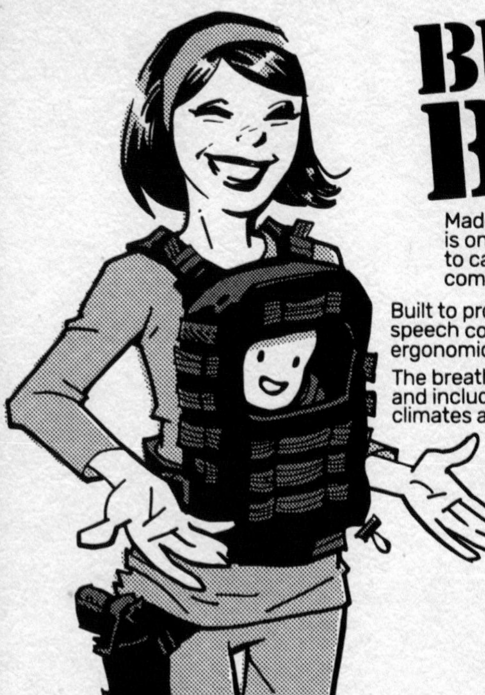

Made from 100% certified Kevlar XP, the **Bulletproof Baby Bodypod®** is one of few ergonomic soft structured tactical baby carriers designed to cater to newborns as well as toddlers without the need for any complex or bulky add-ons.

Built to provide ample neck support for infants that have yet to gain neck and speech control, it's one of the most versatile infant-baby-toddler bulletproof ergonomic carriers available.

The breathable woven cotton front panel is soft and durable and beautiful and includes a removable shield for nap time and diaper changes in all climates and terrain.

Tested and safe
Our fabric is kind to your baby's skin and safe to taste, free from hazardous substances and certified according to Class 1 standards for baby products.
Main fabric: 100% Kevlar XP
Other fabric: 100% polyester
MOLLE straps and Velcro allow customization of your Bulletproof Baby Bodypod
Add $2.99 for a target or £4.99 for your favorite band logo!

Care instructions
Machine wash warm. Wash separately. We recommend an environmentally friendly, mild and bleach-free detergent. Do not tumble dry. If the Baby Bodypod needs more than a simple cleaning due to blood, sweat, tears or gunpowder burns take to your local dry cleaners for more aggressive techniques.

Available in black, jungle camo, blue or pink.

Orders: NATIONAL UNIFORM, BOX 0043, LOVE'S LETTERS LOST, 18 CANON STREET
We ship worldwide!

Octavia

Charlotte

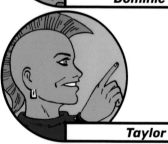
Rosalyn

Dominic

Taylor

Gilbert

Tini

MODERN FAMILY RETRO SASS HIGHLY TRAINED TO KICK YOUR ASS!

Co-creator/writer TINI HOWARD (*The Skeptics*), collector of cat toys, and co-creator/artist GILBERT HERNANDEZ (*Love And Rockets*), collector of straws, dish on desire, troubled sleep and strange plants.

Finish the following sentences: I wanted to be...
TH: A fighter pilot. I got too tall, though, and didn't want to kill anyone!
GH: Joan Crawford.

I suck at...
TH: Being normal, thank god. I'm loud and strange and so, so grateful that I failed at complacency and normalcy.
GH: Straws.

Trouble and desire...
TH: Sleep is so seductive to me, but when I do it too much I panic and hate myself.
GH: Trouble and desire and pizza.

I collect...
TH: Nightwing figurines, strange plants for my garden, interesting garments that I never wear, cat toys on behalf of the cat.
GH: Food into my body.

Famous quote that explains your *raisons d'être*?
TH: "When the muse comes to your bedside, don't tell her you'll fuck her later." — Allen Ginsberg
GH: "We're millionaires, boys! I'll share it with all of you!" — *King Kong*, 1933

What's your favorite comic book of all time?
TH: I think I have to say *The Sandman*. I know it's everyone's answer, but there's a reason for that.
GH: *Little Archie* #20. It inspired me to be the cartoonist I am now.

When my mother was a little girl, she had kidnapping insurance on her.

It's true — my grandfather (rest his soul) was a somewhat high-profile CIA agent, and her being kidnapped was a very real possibility, I suppose. She's going to hate me for saying this. I don't know if I blame her; a childhood spent with things like "kidnapping insurance" hanging over one's head can lead to a sort of craving for normalcy, a life as far from the "badass" and "fantastic" as one can imagine. Ultimately, that's what ASSASSINISTAS is all about.

Most of us, I think, are pretty mundane. We crave adventure in the great wide somewhere, to paraphrase a French peasant girl and a litigious mouse, because for most of us, it's just a fantasy. Adventure, for most of us, means a carefully planned weekend at a beachside resort, or a backpacking trip through some of the world's most populated cities. An unplanned drive down a planned and maintained highway.

The trade-off for real adventure is danger, and while most of us are eager to say we'd make the trade any day (I sure am), I have the strange privilege of being raised by someone who wouldn't. Perhaps real danger makes us crave normalcy the way normalcy makes us crave adventure.

Dominic and Octavia are the opposite of my mother and me, that way. She's very safe, and always kept me very safe. As a result, I have adopted one of the world's most dangerous lifestyles: freelance writer. Who knows? Maybe I'm the Octavia, out here with my flak jacket on, baring my guts to the world and hoping they pay me for the privilege. Maybe someday I'll have a Dominic of my own, a brilliant, deep, take-no-shit beautiful son who looks at me and says "Mom, let's just be normal."

I can only hope I'll be so lucky.

Tini Howard, co-creator/writer

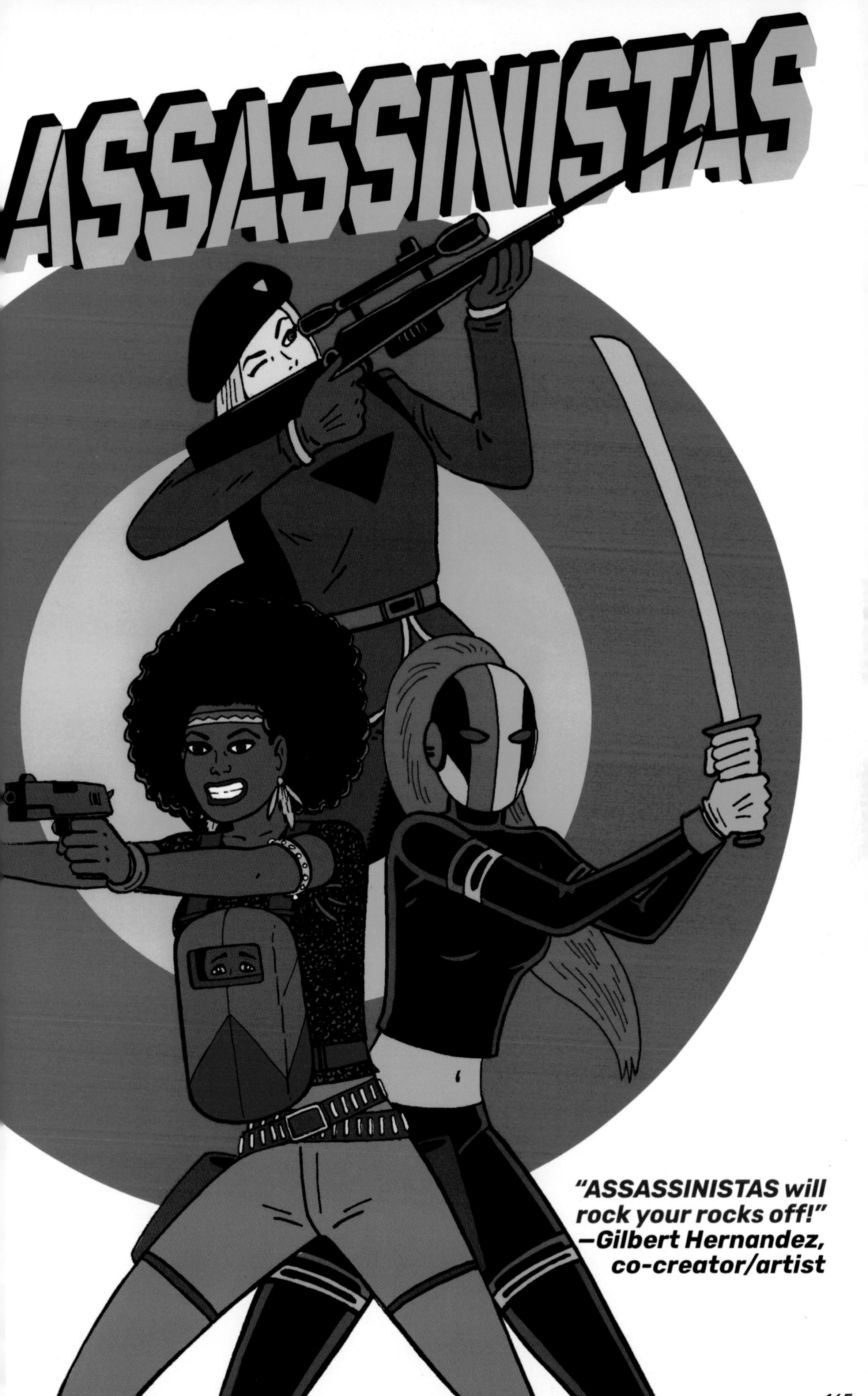
ASSASSINISTAS
"ASSASSINISTAS will rock your rocks off!"
—Gilbert Hernandez, co-creator/artist

Hey, AMATEUR!

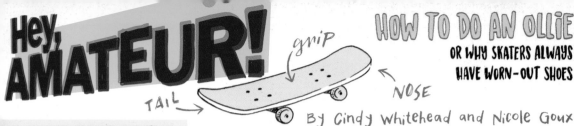

HOW TO DO AN OLLIE

OR WHY SKATERS ALWAYS HAVE WORN-OUT SHOES

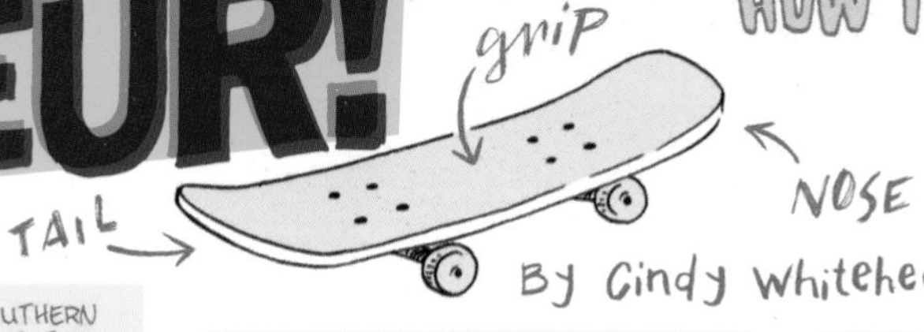
grip
NOSE
TAIL

By Cindy Whitehead and Nicole Goux

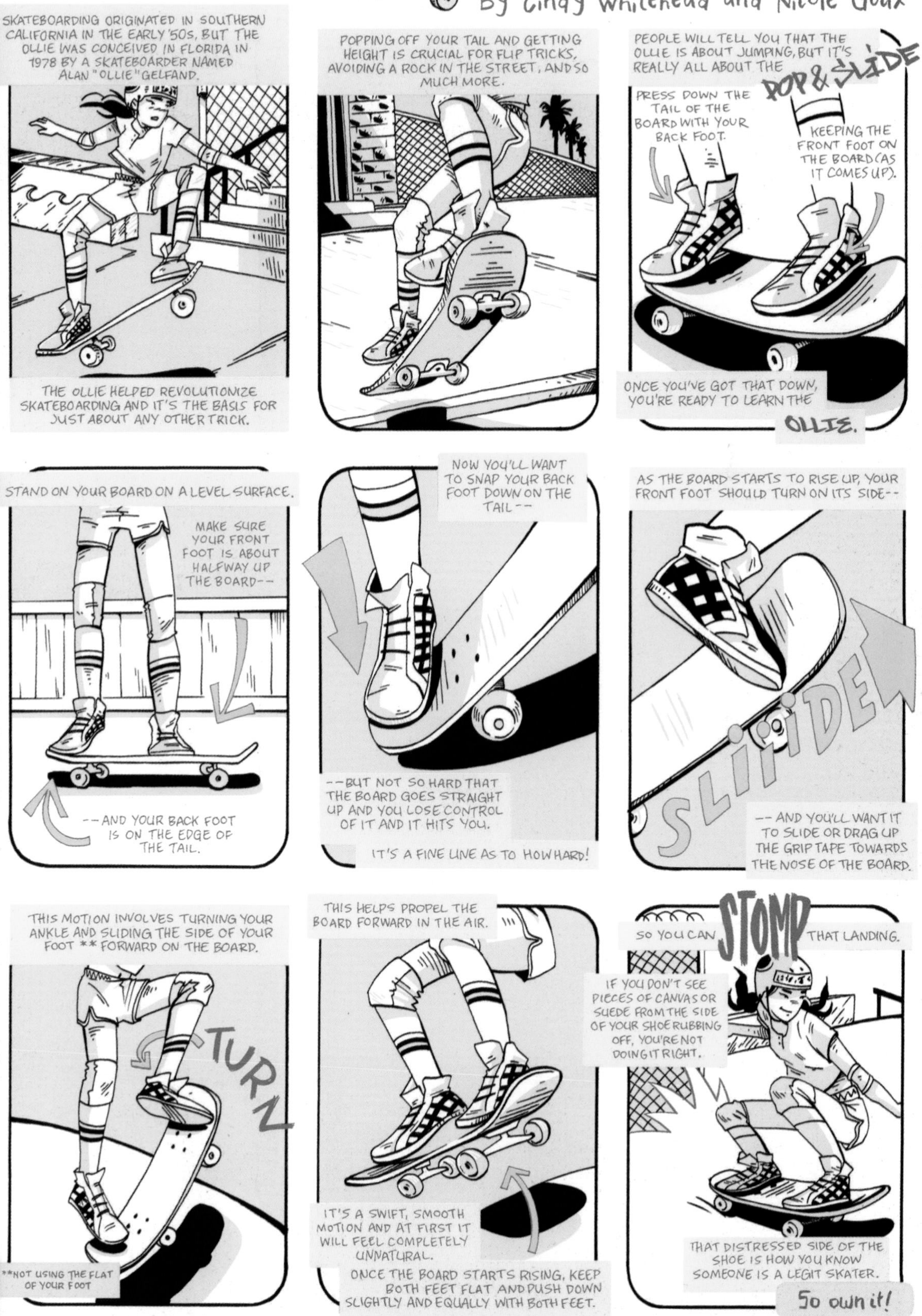
SKATEBOARDING ORIGINATED IN SOUTHERN CALIFORNIA IN THE EARLY '50S, BUT THE OLLIE WAS CONCEIVED IN FLORIDA IN 1978 BY A SKATEBOARDER NAMED ALAN "OLLIE" GELFAND.
THE OLLIE HELPED REVOLUTIONIZE SKATEBOARDING AND IT'S THE BASIS FOR JUST ABOUT ANY OTHER TRICK.
POPPING OFF YOUR TAIL AND GETTING HEIGHT IS CRUCIAL FOR FLIP TRICKS, AVOIDING A ROCK IN THE STREET, AND SO MUCH MORE.
PEOPLE WILL TELL YOU THAT THE OLLIE IS ABOUT JUMPING, BUT IT'S REALLY ALL ABOUT THE
POP & SLIDE.
PRESS DOWN THE TAIL OF THE BOARD WITH YOUR BACK FOOT.
KEEPING THE FRONT FOOT ON THE BOARD (AS IT COMES UP).
ONCE YOU'VE GOT THAT DOWN, YOU'RE READY TO LEARN THE
OLLIE.
STAND ON YOUR BOARD ON A LEVEL SURFACE.
MAKE SURE YOUR FRONT FOOT IS ABOUT HALFWAY UP THE BOARD--
--AND YOUR BACK FOOT IS ON THE EDGE OF THE TAIL.
NOW YOU'LL WANT TO SNAP YOUR BACK FOOT DOWN ON THE TAIL--
--BUT NOT SO HARD THAT THE BOARD GOES STRAIGHT UP AND YOU LOSE CONTROL OF IT AND IT HITS YOU.
IT'S A FINE LINE AS TO HOW HARD!
AS THE BOARD STARTS TO RISE UP, YOUR FRONT FOOT SHOULD TURN ON ITS SIDE--
SLIIIDE
--AND YOU'LL WANT IT TO SLIDE OR DRAG UP THE GRIP TAPE TOWARDS THE NOSE OF THE BOARD.
THIS MOTION INVOLVES TURNING YOUR ANKLE AND SLIDING THE SIDE OF YOUR FOOT ** FORWARD ON THE BOARD.
TURN
**NOT USING THE FLAT OF YOUR FOOT
THIS HELPS PROPEL THE BOARD FORWARD IN THE AIR.
IT'S A SWIFT, SMOOTH MOTION AND AT FIRST IT WILL FEEL COMPLETELY UNNATURAL.
ONCE THE BOARD STARTS RISING, KEEP BOTH FEET FLAT AND PUSH DOWN SLIGHTLY AND EQUALLY WITH BOTH FEET.
SO YOU CAN STOMP THAT LANDING.
IF YOU DON'T SEE PIECES OF CANVAS OR SUEDE FROM THE SIDE OF YOUR SHOE RUBBING OFF, YOU'RE NOT DOING IT RIGHT.
THAT DISTRESSED SIDE OF THE SHOE IS HOW YOU KNOW SOMEONE IS A LEGIT SKATER.
So own it!

Cindy Whitehead is a sports stylist and founder of girlisnotafourletterword.com. In 2016 she was inducted into the Skateboard Hall of Fame.

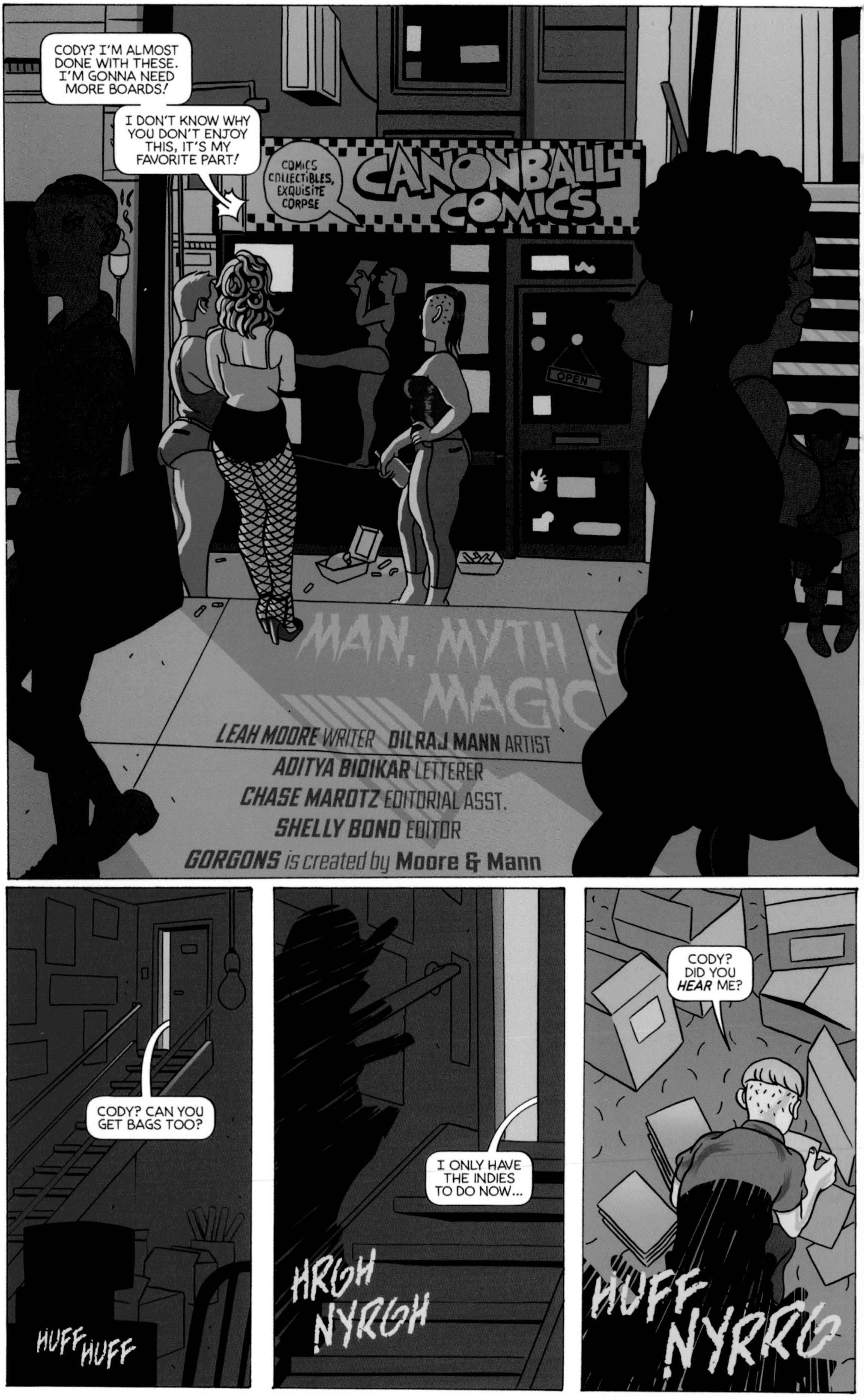

CODY? I'M ALMOST DONE WITH THESE. I'M GONNA NEED MORE BOARDS!
I DON'T KNOW WHY YOU DON'T ENJOY THIS, IT'S MY FAVORITE PART!
COMICS COLLECTIBLES, EXQUISITE CORPSE
CANONBALL COMICS
OPEN
MAN, MYTH & MAGIC
LEAH MOORE WRITER DILRAJ MANN ARTIST
ADITYA BIDIKAR LETTERER
CHASE MAROTZ EDITORIAL ASST.
SHELLY BOND EDITOR
GORGONS is created by Moore & Mann
CODY? CAN YOU GET BAGS TOO?
HUFF HUFF
I ONLY HAVE THE INDIES TO DO NOW...
HRGH NYRGH
CODY? DID YOU HEAR ME?
HUFF NYRRG

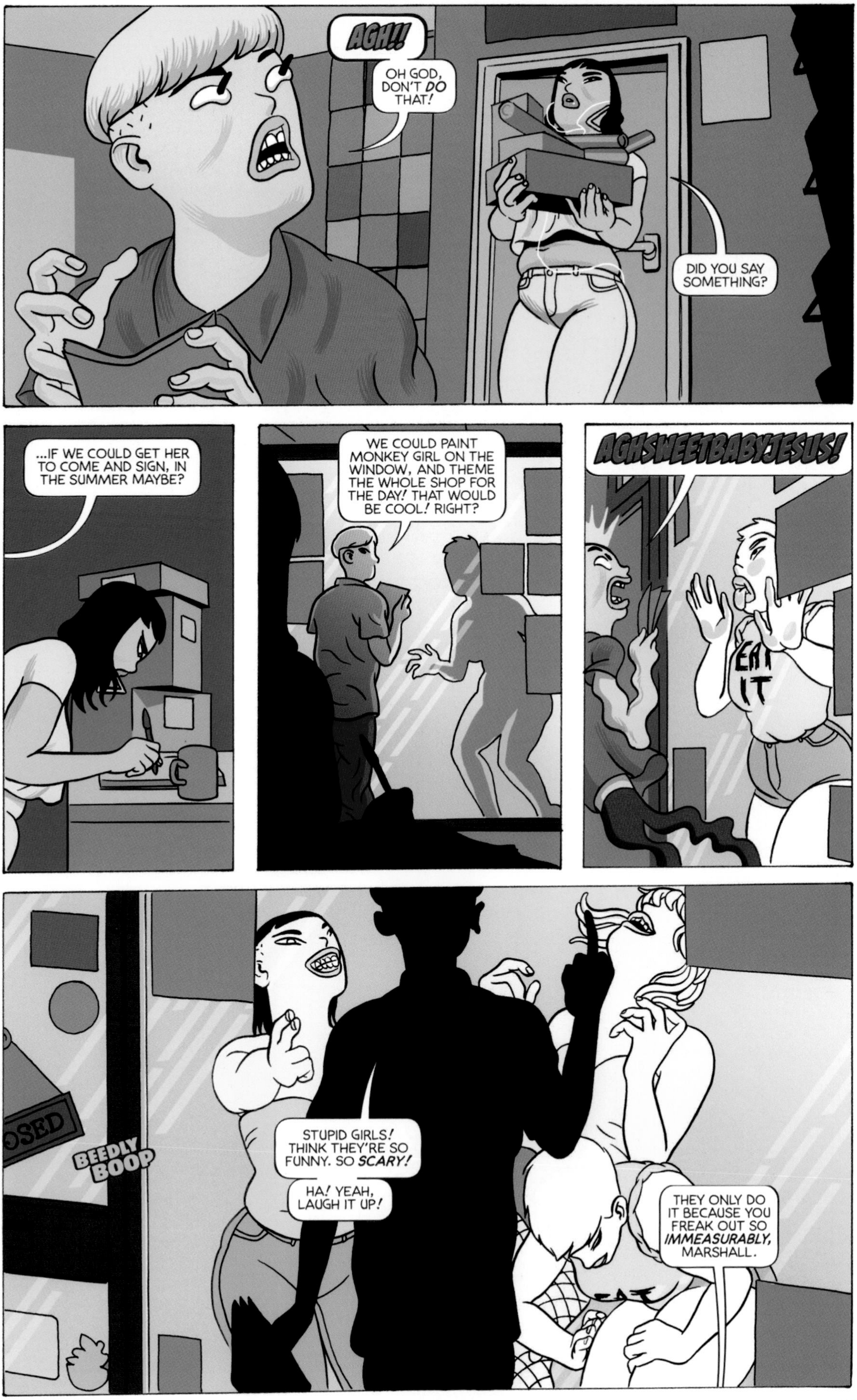
AGH!!
OH GOD, DON'T DO THAT!
DID YOU SAY SOMETHING?
...IF WE COULD GET HER TO COME AND SIGN, IN THE SUMMER MAYBE?
WE COULD PAINT MONKEY GIRL ON THE WINDOW, AND THEME THE WHOLE SHOP FOR THE DAY! THAT WOULD BE COOL! RIGHT?
AGHSWEETBABYJESUS!
EAT IT
OSED
BEEDLY BOOP
STUPID GIRLS! THINK THEY'RE SO FUNNY. SO SCARY!
HA! YEAH, LAUGH IT UP!
THEY ONLY DO IT BECAUSE YOU FREAK OUT SO IMMEASURABLY, MARSHALL.

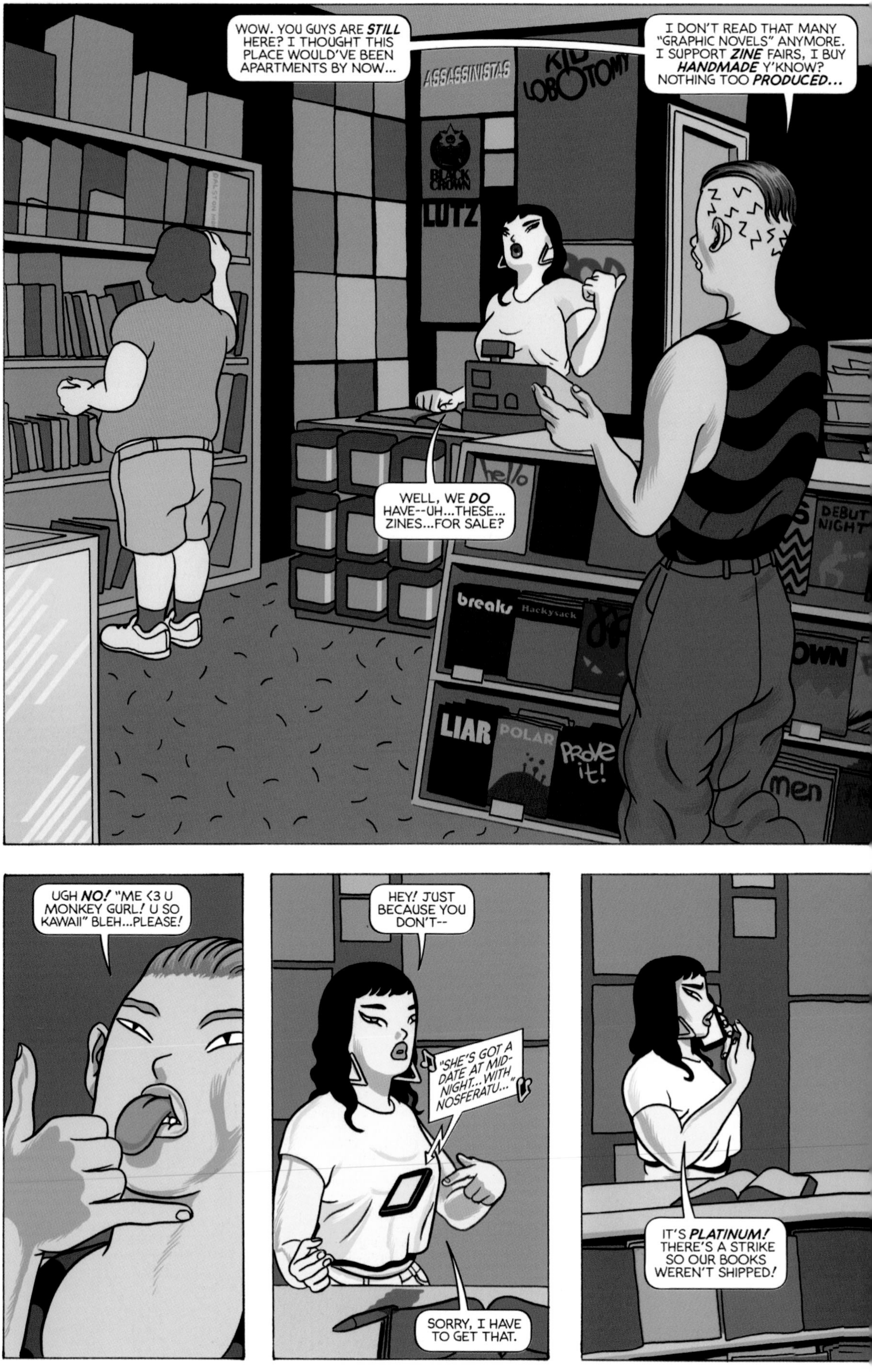
WOW. YOU GUYS ARE ***STILL*** HERE? I THOUGHT THIS PLACE WOULD'VE BEEN APARTMENTS BY NOW...
I DON'T READ THAT MANY "GRAPHIC NOVELS" ANYMORE. I SUPPORT ***ZINE*** FAIRS, I BUY ***HANDMADE*** Y'KNOW? NOTHING TOO ***PRODUCED...***
ASSASSINISTAS
KID LOBOTOMY
BLACK CROWN
LUTZ
WELL, WE ***DO*** HAVE--UH...THESE... ZINES...FOR SALE?
hello
DEBUT NIGHT
breaks
Hackysack
LIAR
POLAR
Prove it!
men
UGH ***NO!*** "ME <3 U MONKEY GURL*!* U SO KAWAII" BLEH...PLEASE*!*
HEY*!* JUST BECAUSE YOU DON'T--
"SHE'S GOT A DATE AT MID-NIGHT...WITH NOSFERATU..."
SORRY, I HAVE TO GET THAT.
IT'S ***PLATINUM!*** THERE'S A STRIKE SO OUR BOOKS WEREN'T SHIPPED*!*

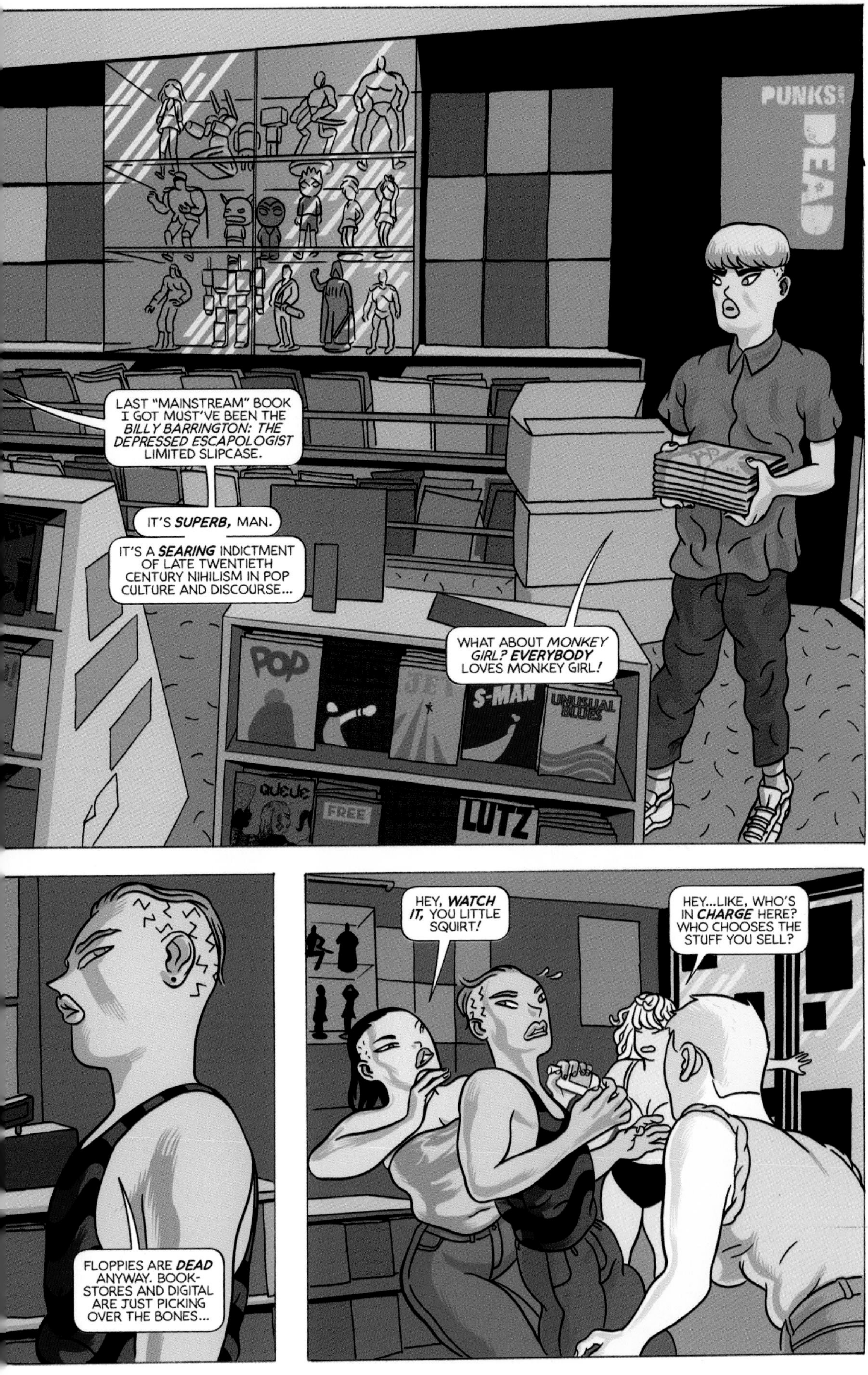
PUNKS
DEAD
LAST "MAINSTREAM" BOOK I GOT MUST'VE BEEN THE *BILLY BARRINGTON: THE DEPRESSED ESCAPOLOGIST* LIMITED SLIPCASE.
IT'S ***SUPERB,*** MAN.
IT'S A ***SEARING*** INDICTMENT OF LATE TWENTIETH CENTURY NIHILISM IN POP CULTURE AND DISCOURSE...
WHAT ABOUT *MONKEY GIRL?* ***EVERYBODY*** LOVES MONKEY GIRL*!*
POP
JET
S-MAN
UNUSUAL BLUES
QUEUE
FREE
LUTZ
FLOPPIES ARE ***DEAD*** ANYWAY. BOOK-STORES AND DIGITAL ARE JUST PICKING OVER THE BONES...
HEY, ***WATCH IT,*** YOU LITTLE SQUIRT*!*
HEY...LIKE, WHO'S IN ***CHARGE*** HERE? WHO CHOOSES THE STUFF YOU SELL?

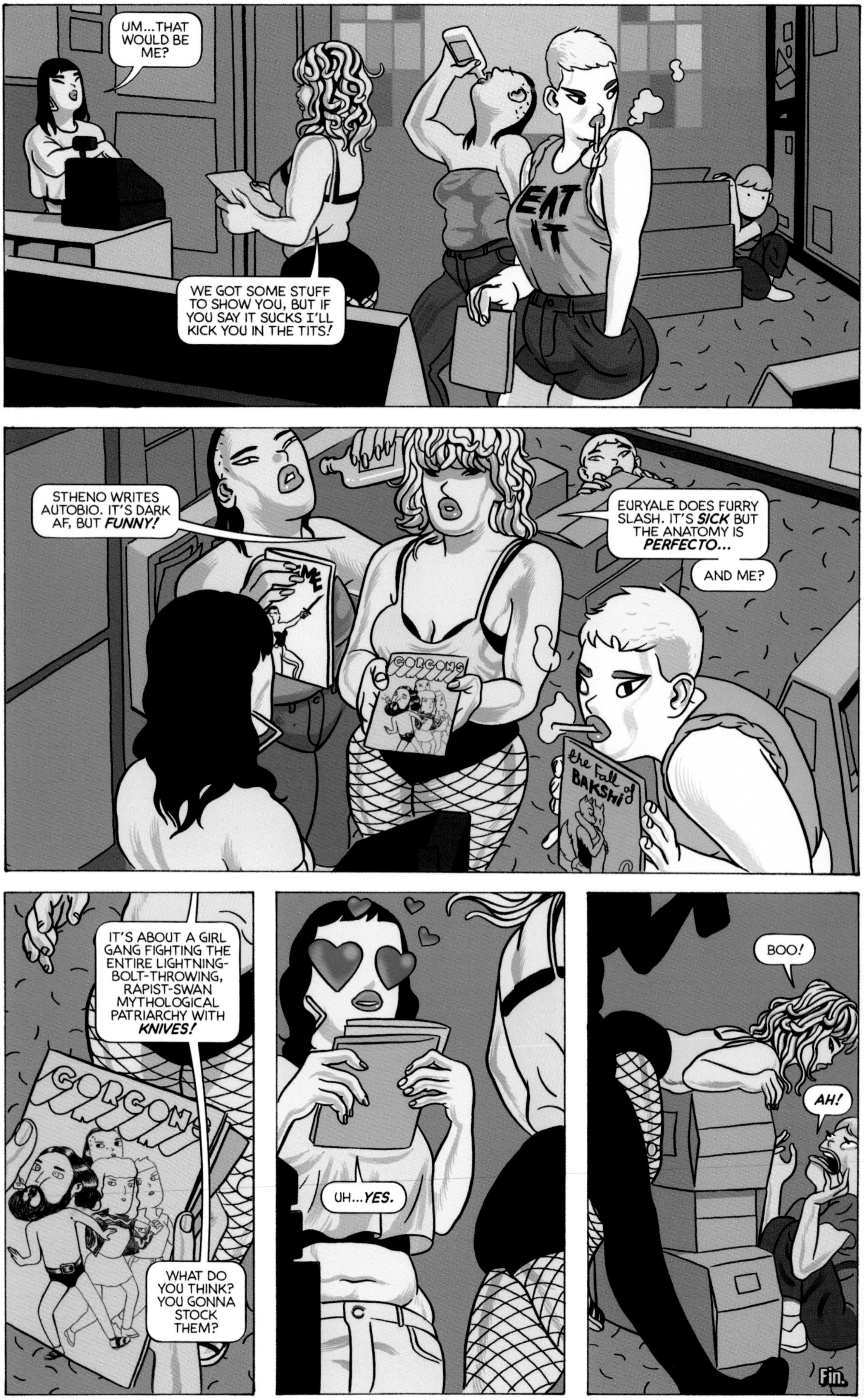
UM...THAT WOULD BE ME?
WE GOT SOME STUFF TO SHOW YOU, BUT IF YOU SAY IT SUCKS I'LL KICK YOU IN THE TITS!
EAT IT
STHENO WRITES AUTOBIO. IT'S DARK AF, BUT FUNNY!
EURYALE DOES FURRY SLASH. IT'S SICK BUT THE ANATOMY IS PERFECTO...
AND ME?
GORGONS
the Fall of BAKSHI
IT'S ABOUT A GIRL GANG FIGHTING THE ENTIRE LIGHTNING-BOLT-THROWING, RAPIST-SWAN MYTHOLOGICAL PATRIARCHY WITH KNIVES!
GORGONS
WHAT DO YOU THINK? YOU GONNA STOCK THEM?
UH...YES.
BOO!
AH!
Fin.

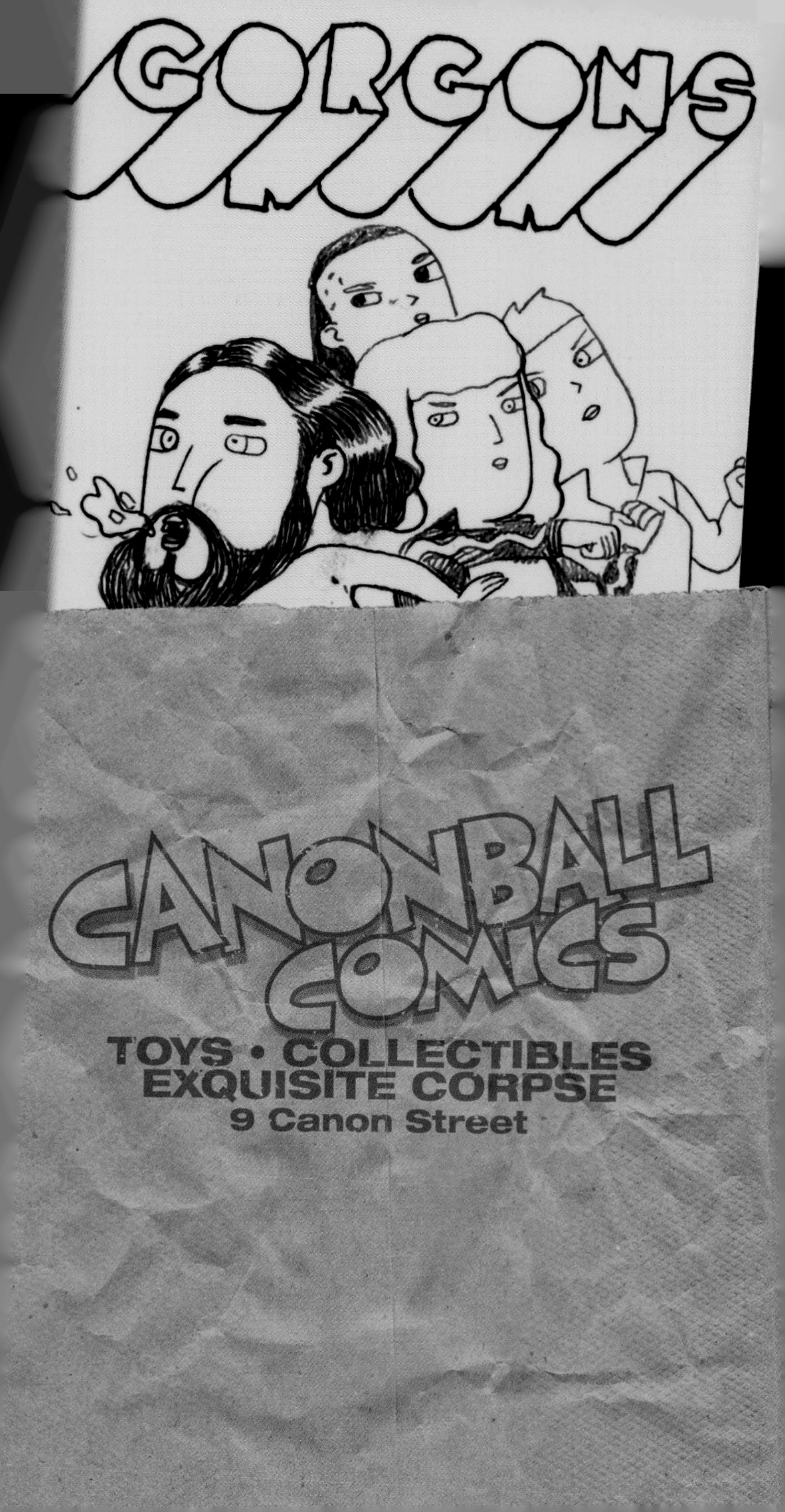
GORGONS
CANONBALL COMICS
TOYS • COLLECTIBLES
EXQUISITE CORPSE
9 Canon Street

JAIME HERNANDEZ
THE DEATH OF SPEEDY
TELEPHONE
A Love and Rockets Collection

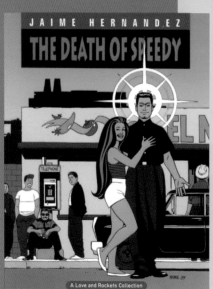

Love And Rockets: The Death of Speedy
Fantagraphics Books, 1989
by Jaime Hernandez

COMIC

I guess I first read *Love and Rockets* when I was ten or eleven; it was laying around the house and I picked it up. I loved Beto's *Palomar* like they were my family I could go and visit, but I loved Jaime's *Hoppers* with the pain and delicious heartache of a high school crush. Maggie and Hopey were too cool for me, but I could read their stories and sigh, and crush from afar.

As I grew up, *The Death of Speedy* stood out as my favourite. It wasn't just the best *Hoppers* story, it was the Best Story. Obviously, it's the classic *Romeo and Juliet* tragedy, with Dairytown and Hoppers set against each other, but it was the tiny incidental stuff that kicked me right on my arse. The way nice guy Ray never asks Maggie out, the way Hopey and Maggie argue, the real fear of getting decked by Blanca Rizzo. The older I grew, the more familiar these things were to me, and the more I cherished the story.

Speedy coming to Maggie, in the middle of the war with Dairytown, when Lito has just lost his eye, is the most moving and awful and doomed and wonderful thing ever made. His sudden declaration that she is the one he loves makes your heart leap, but her reaction to it is too true, and so brutal, and so honest, it tears it right out of your chest and stamps on it.

Jaime expertly dangles that pure crystalline romantic doomed hope right under your nose and then on the next page he crumbles it to dust. If you can find me a purer more profound moment, in comics, or film or books or whatever, then I'll buy you a drink.

BEAT SURRENDER

Wherein we wax nostalgic on the comic + record that made us drop to our knees.

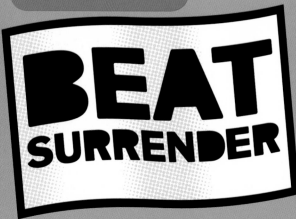

LEAH MOORE

writer –
CANONBALL COMICS: GORGONS

RECORD

Right up until grunge hit me in 1993 I raided my parents' records. I could listen to The Pixies, or Shriekback, or The Specials, or Roxy Music, or Lee Perry, or The Shirelles, or hundreds of others. When I was about five, I had a little one-speaker tape deck by my bed and one tape to play on it, which was *Legend*, by Bob Marley and the Wailers. I have no idea how this came to be my only tape, but I played it every night going to sleep.

Fast forward to me, aged ten, and I get a bigger room, and my mum lets me have her old stereo in it. It's a big old system with a space for albums so I go trawling through her records to fill it. The album that absolutely blew me away was *Are You Experienced* by the Jimi Hendrix Experience. It was like strapping myself to a train or a fighter jet and being pulled at 400mph through the most incredible soaring technicolour landscape that changed and shifted as soon as I thought I had a grip on it. Every song was different, but each felt like a bright, vivid piece of a huge, finely worked tapestry; part of the tapestry was possibly on fire, and part of it was probably dissolving into a colourful puddle, but then all of those things were fine, weren't they? Everything was fine, and everything was colourful and majestic, and astonishing.

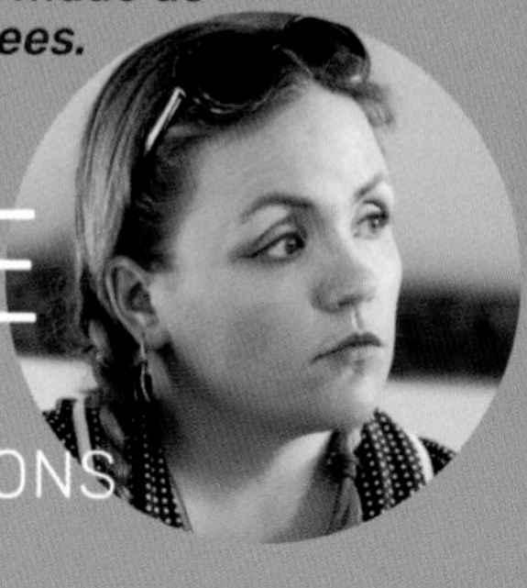

Are You Experienced by the Jimi Hendrix Experience
Track Records, 1967

MONO
ARE YOU EXPERIENCED
ARE YOU EXPERIENCED

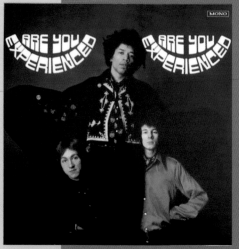

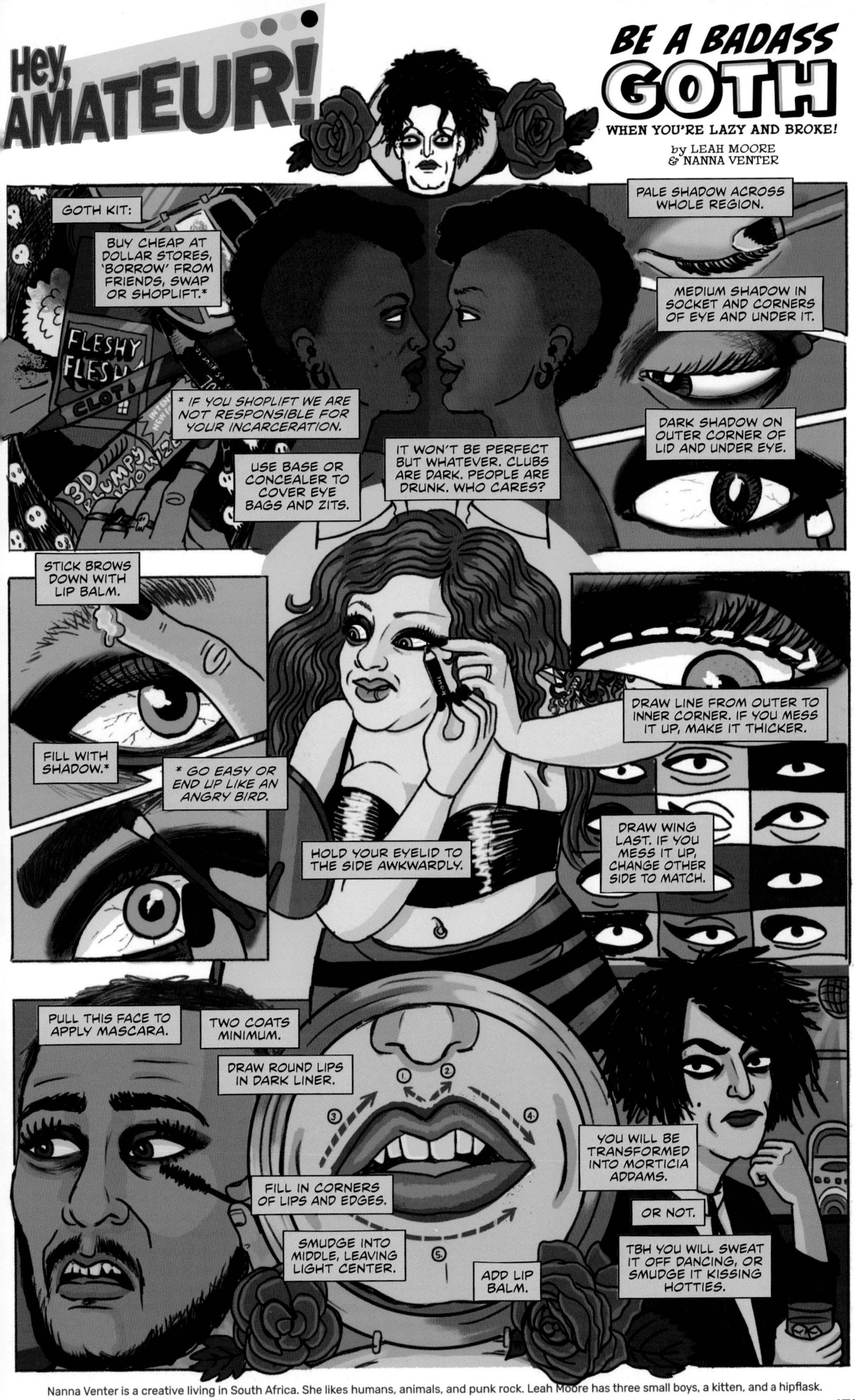
Hey, AMATEUR!
BE A BADASS GOTH
WHEN YOU'RE LAZY AND BROKE!
by LEAH MOORE & NANNA VENTER
GOTH KIT:
BUY CHEAP AT DOLLAR STORES, 'BORROW' FROM FRIENDS, SWAP OR SHOPLIFT.*
FLESHY FLESH
CLOT
* IF YOU SHOPLIFT WE ARE NOT RESPONSIBLE FOR YOUR INCARCERATION.
USE BASE OR CONCEALER TO COVER EYE BAGS AND ZITS.
IT WON'T BE PERFECT BUT WHATEVER. CLUBS ARE DARK. PEOPLE ARE DRUNK. WHO CARES?
PALE SHADOW ACROSS WHOLE REGION.
MEDIUM SHADOW IN SOCKET AND CORNERS OF EYE AND UNDER IT.
DARK SHADOW ON OUTER CORNER OF LID AND UNDER EYE.
STICK BROWS DOWN WITH LIP BALM.
FILL WITH SHADOW.*
* GO EASY OR END UP LIKE AN ANGRY BIRD.
HOLD YOUR EYELID TO THE SIDE AWKWARDLY.
DRAW LINE FROM OUTER TO INNER CORNER. IF YOU MESS IT UP, MAKE IT THICKER.
DRAW WING LAST. IF YOU MESS IT UP, CHANGE OTHER SIDE TO MATCH.
PULL THIS FACE TO APPLY MASCARA.
TWO COATS MINIMUM.
DRAW ROUND LIPS IN DARK LINER.
1.
2.
3.
4.
5.
FILL IN CORNERS OF LIPS AND EDGES.
SMUDGE INTO MIDDLE, LEAVING LIGHT CENTER.
ADD LIP BALM.
YOU WILL BE TRANSFORMED INTO MORTICIA ADDAMS.
OR NOT.
TBH YOU WILL SWEAT IT OFF DANCING, OR SMUDGE IT KISSING HOTTIES.

Nanna Venter is a creative living in South Africa. She likes humans, animals, and punk rock. Leah Moore has three small boys, a kitten, and a hipflask.

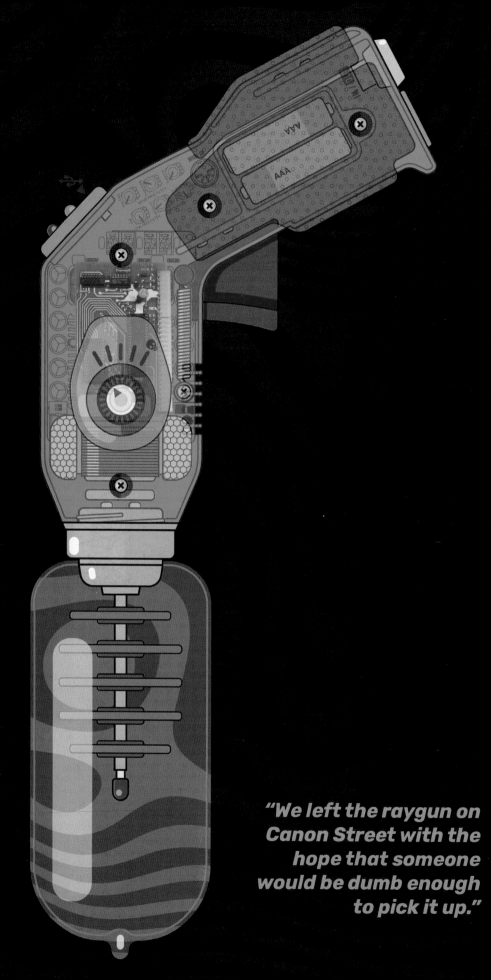

"We left the raygun on Canon Street with the hope that someone would be dumb enough to pick it up."

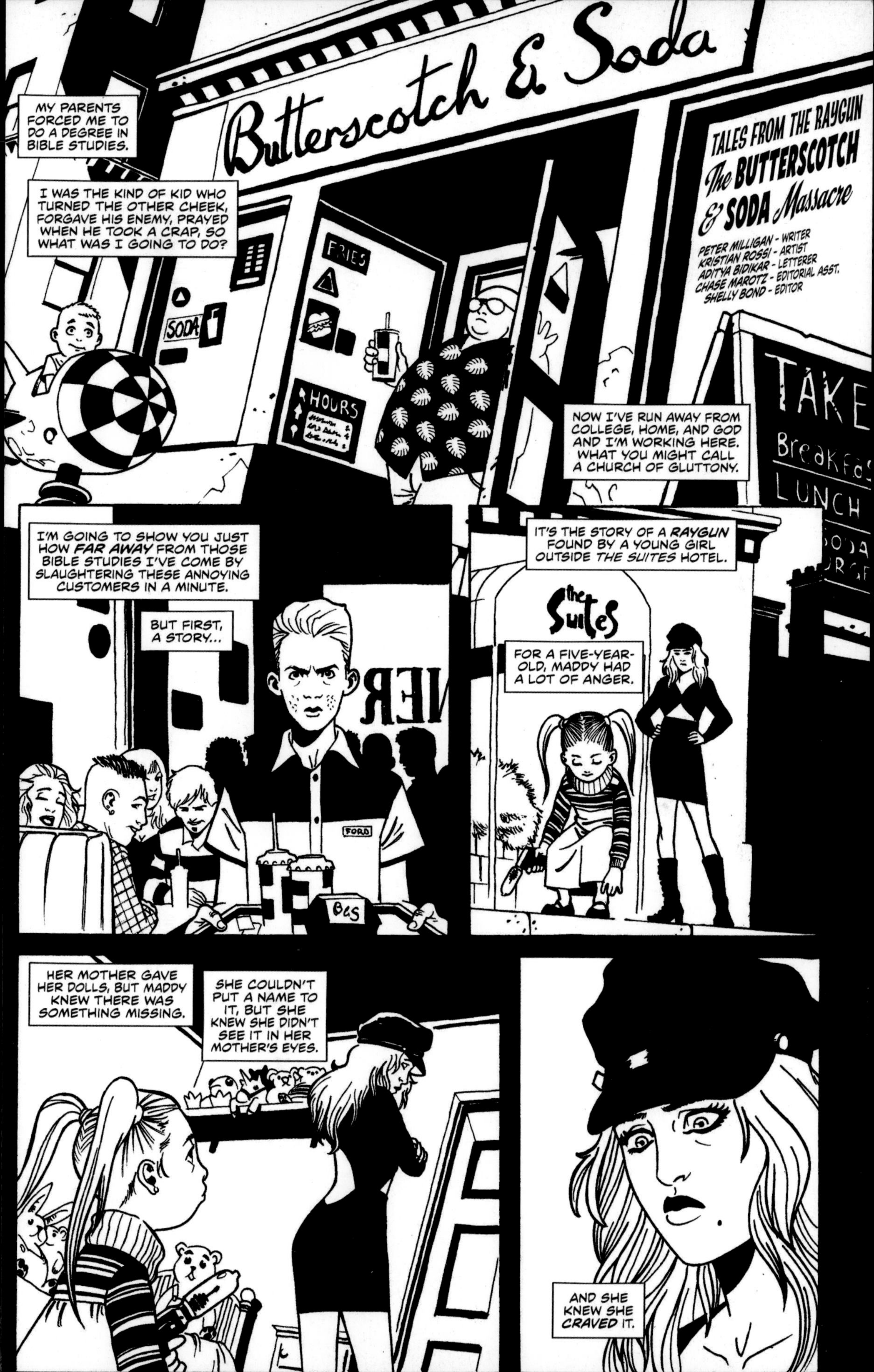
Butterscotch & Soda
MY PARENTS FORCED ME TO DO A DEGREE IN BIBLE STUDIES.
I WAS THE KIND OF KID WHO TURNED THE OTHER CHEEK, FORGAVE HIS ENEMY, PRAYED WHEN HE TOOK A CRAP, SO WHAT WAS I GOING TO DO?
TALES FROM THE RAYGUN
The BUTTERSCOTCH & SODA Massacre
PETER MILLIGAN - WRITER
KRISTIAN ROSSI - ARTIST
ADITYA BIDIKAR - LETTERER
CHASE MAROTZ - EDITORIAL ASST.
SHELLY BOND - EDITOR
FRIES
SODA
HOURS
NOW I'VE RUN AWAY FROM COLLEGE, HOME, AND GOD AND I'M WORKING HERE. WHAT YOU MIGHT CALL A CHURCH OF GLUTTONY.
TAKE
Breakfas
LUNCH
I'M GOING TO SHOW YOU JUST HOW FAR AWAY FROM THOSE BIBLE STUDIES I'VE COME BY SLAUGHTERING THESE ANNOYING CUSTOMERS IN A MINUTE.
BUT FIRST, A STORY...
FORD
B&S
IT'S THE STORY OF A RAYGUN FOUND BY A YOUNG GIRL OUTSIDE THE SUITES HOTEL.
the Suites
FOR A FIVE-YEAR-OLD, MADDY HAD A LOT OF ANGER.
HER MOTHER GAVE HER DOLLS, BUT MADDY KNEW THERE WAS SOMETHING MISSING.
SHE COULDN'T PUT A NAME TO IT, BUT SHE KNEW SHE DIDN'T SEE IT IN HER MOTHER'S EYES.
AND SHE KNEW SHE CRAVED IT.

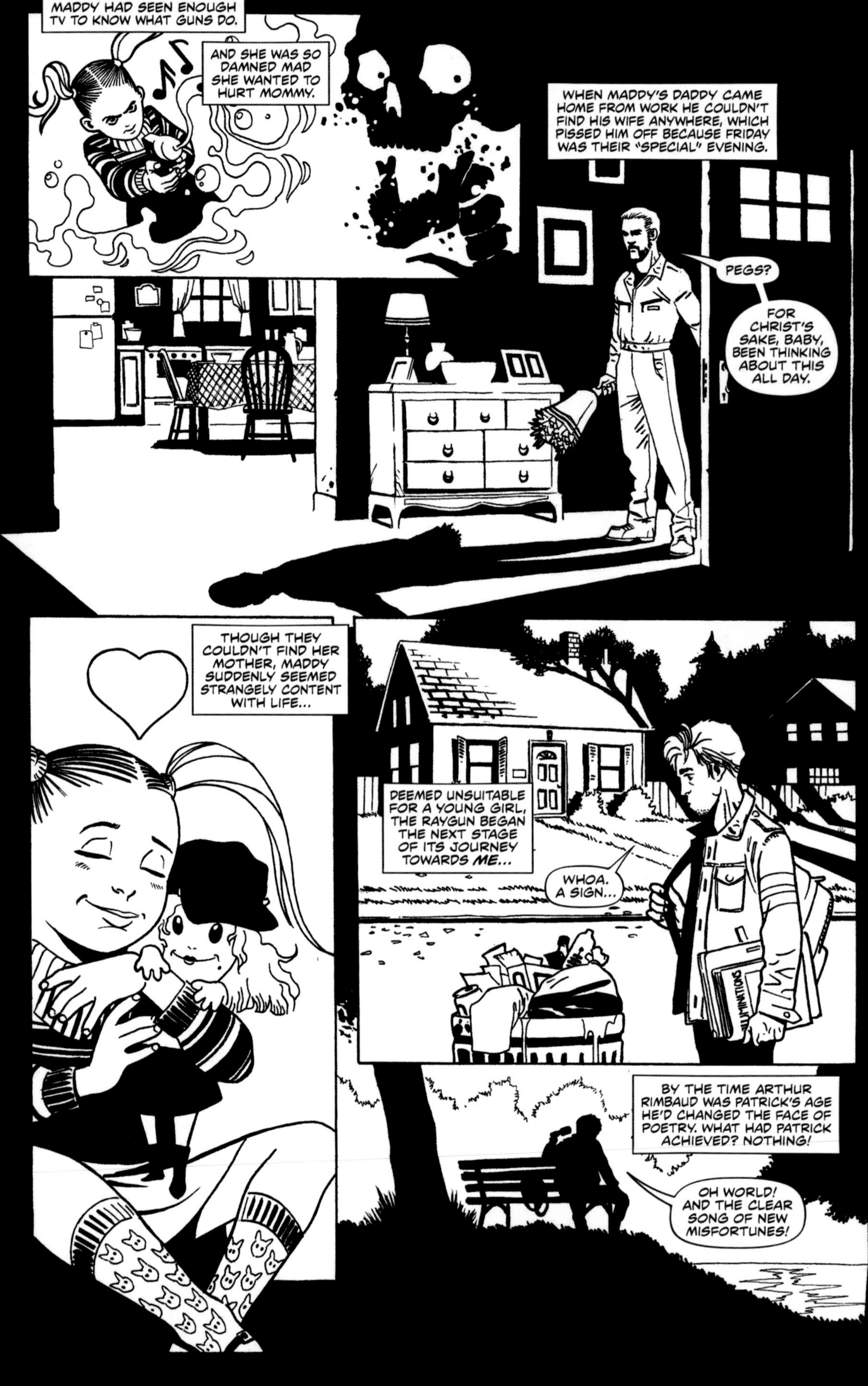
MADDY HAD SEEN ENOUGH TV TO KNOW WHAT GUNS DO.
AND SHE WAS SO DAMNED MAD SHE WANTED TO HURT MOMMY.
WHEN MADDY'S DADDY CAME HOME FROM WORK HE COULDN'T FIND HIS WIFE ANYWHERE, WHICH PISSED HIM OFF BECAUSE FRIDAY WAS THEIR "SPECIAL" EVENING.
PEGS?
FOR CHRIST'S SAKE, BABY, BEEN THINKING ABOUT THIS ALL DAY.
THOUGH THEY COULDN'T FIND HER MOTHER, MADDY SUDDENLY SEEMED STRANGELY CONTENT WITH LIFE...
DEEMED UNSUITABLE FOR A YOUNG GIRL, THE RAYGUN BEGAN THE NEXT STAGE OF ITS JOURNEY TOWARDS ME...
WHOA. A SIGN...
ILLUMINATIONS
BY THE TIME ARTHUR RIMBAUD WAS PATRICK'S AGE HE'D CHANGED THE FACE OF POETRY. WHAT HAD PATRICK ACHIEVED? NOTHING!
OH WORLD! AND THE CLEAR SONG OF NEW MISFORTUNES!

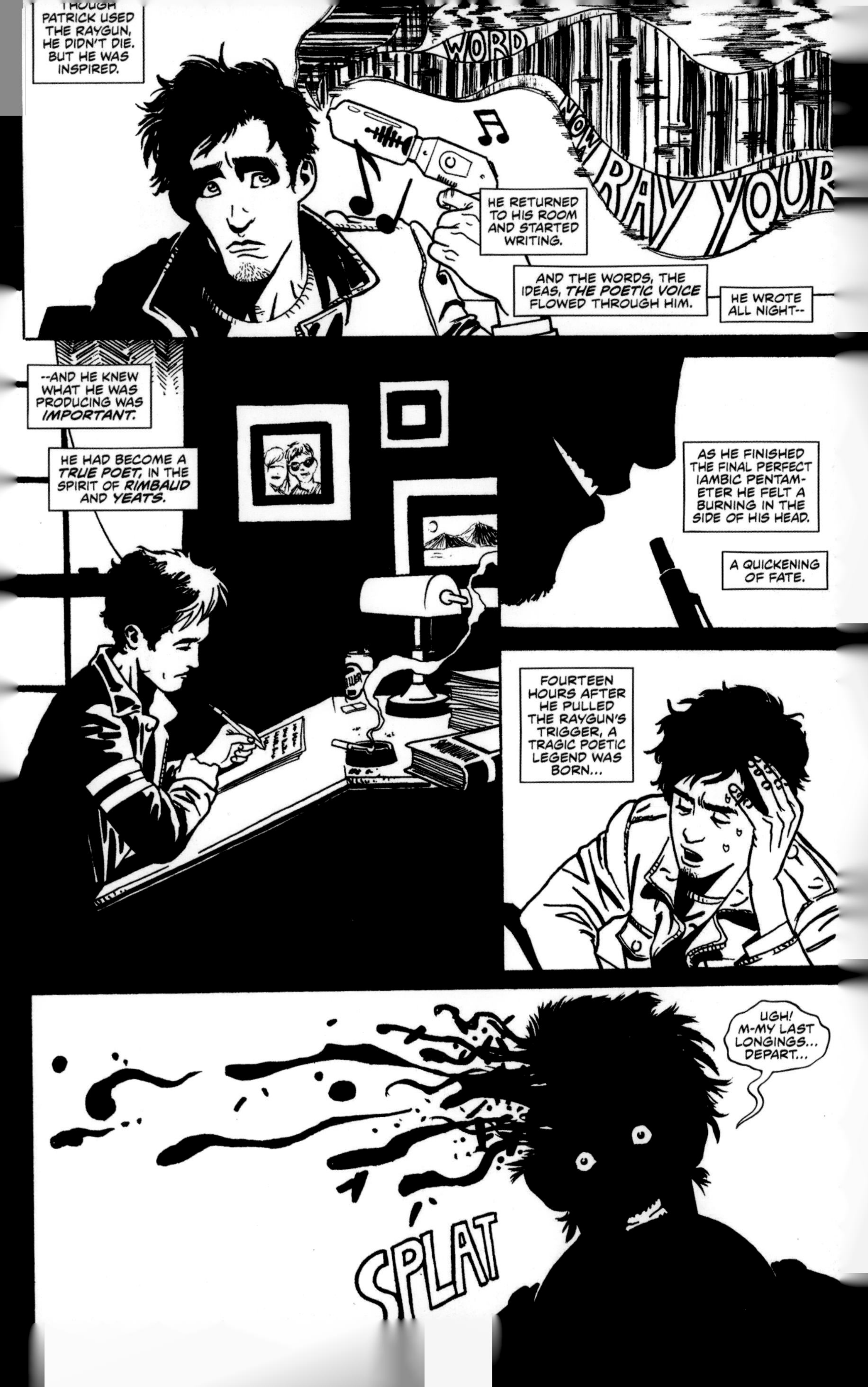
THOUGH PATRICK USED THE RAYGUN, HE DIDN'T DIE. BUT HE WAS INSPIRED.
WORD
NOW
RAY YOUR
HE RETURNED TO HIS ROOM AND STARTED WRITING.
AND THE WORDS, THE IDEAS, THE POETIC VOICE FLOWED THROUGH HIM.
HE WROTE ALL NIGHT--
--AND HE KNEW WHAT HE WAS PRODUCING WAS IMPORTANT.
HE HAD BECOME A TRUE POET, IN THE SPIRIT OF RIMBAUD AND YEATS.
AS HE FINISHED THE FINAL PERFECT IAMBIC PENTAMETER HE FELT A BURNING IN THE SIDE OF HIS HEAD.
A QUICKENING OF FATE.
FOURTEEN HOURS AFTER HE PULLED THE RAYGUN'S TRIGGER, A TRAGIC POETIC LEGEND WAS BORN...
UGH! M-MY LAST LONGINGS... DEPART...
SPLAT

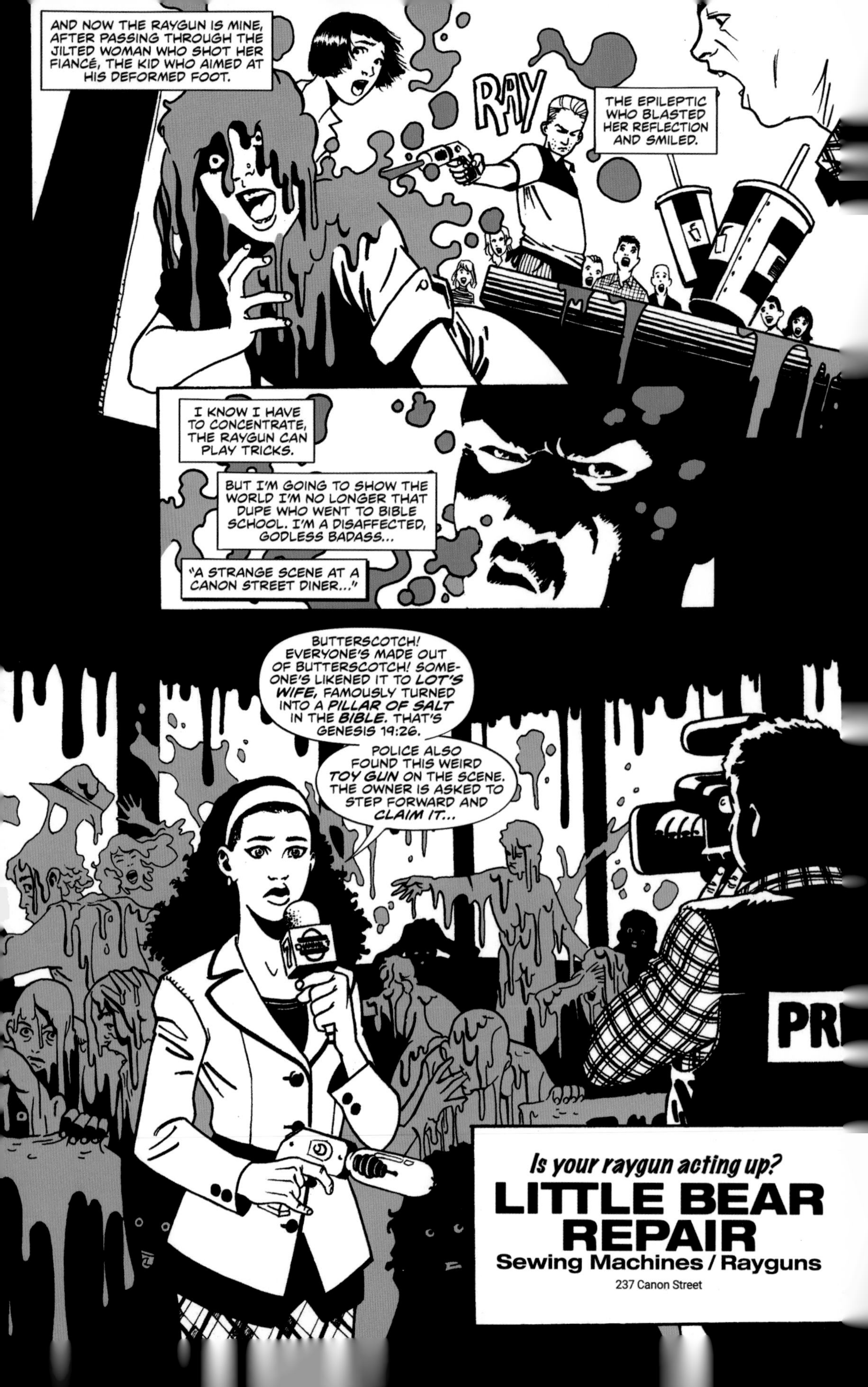
AND NOW THE RAYGUN IS MINE, AFTER PASSING THROUGH THE JILTED WOMAN WHO SHOT HER FIANCÉ, THE KID WHO AIMED AT HIS DEFORMED FOOT.
RAY
THE EPILEPTIC WHO BLASTED HER REFLECTION AND SMILED.
I KNOW I HAVE TO CONCENTRATE, THE RAYGUN CAN PLAY TRICKS.
BUT I'M GOING TO SHOW THE WORLD I'M NO LONGER THAT DUPE WHO WENT TO BIBLE SCHOOL. I'M A DISAFFECTED, GODLESS BADASS...
"A STRANGE SCENE AT A CANON STREET DINER..."
BUTTERSCOTCH! EVERYONE'S MADE OUT OF BUTTERSCOTCH! SOMEONE'S LIKENED IT TO LOT'S WIFE, FAMOUSLY TURNED INTO A PILLAR OF SALT IN THE BIBLE. THAT'S GENESIS 19:26.
POLICE ALSO FOUND THIS WEIRD TOY GUN ON THE SCENE. THE OWNER IS ASKED TO STEP FORWARD AND CLAIM IT...
PR
Is your raygun acting up?
LITTLE BEAR REPAIR
Sewing Machines / Rayguns
237 Canon Street

DC
VERTIGO
ENIGMA
The Head
The Lizard
The Enigma
MILLIGAN
FEGREDO
VAN VALKENBURGH

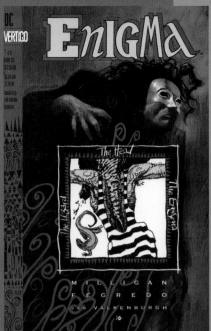

..........................COMIC

There's probably some sort of rule about not naming books by one's collaborators, but our Editor Supreme forgot to mention that to me, so let's keep this between us, shall we?

Unlike a lot of people working in comics, I was brought up on prose fiction and only came to comics as an adult, when I realized that there was some spectacularly weird stuff going on "in the gutters" which prose just wasn't up to doing for boring respectability reasons.

I discovered *Vertigo* soon after, and methodically made my way down the list of writers, and this Milligan fellow spoke to me in that space between panels, especially with *Enigma*, which was superheroes, but ... more, meta-fiction, but ... more. Just ... more of everything.

Simultaneously delicate and vulgar, sexy and gross, with Fegredo's scattershot lines coalescing to form fragile human figures, it was just what a young queer man needed to fall thoroughly in love with this fascinating, dangerous medium.

Seduction of the innocent—accomplished.

Enigma
(DC Comics/Vertigo, 1993)
by Peter Milligan & Duncan Fegredo

BEAT SURRENDER

Wherein we wax nostalgic on the comic + record that made us drop to our knees.

ADITYA BIDIKAR

BLACK CROWN
house letterer

Tom Waits
Rain Dogs
Island Records, 1985

TOM WAITS
RAIN DOGS

RECORD..........................

I remember the first album I bought for myself, with my own money. I was somewhere in my quickly lapsing teens, and till then, every album I'd bought had been shared with two of my best buddies, because none of us got enough pocket money to buy more than one album a month among the three of us. We'd read reviews of classic rock albums online and painstakingly settle on the one we felt worth the dosh.

Except one month, I wanted to buy something peculiar, that I'd seen reviewed in breathless but frustratingly vague terms, something the reviewers couldn't quite pinpoint, and understandably, my friends couldn't see why I wanted it. But I didn't really want to share it either.

And when I listened to it, sitting in my room watching the curtains swell and ebb on a Saturday afternoon, the first trills of "*Singapore*" came on, and I could instantly hear what couldn't be put down in words—the gruff, grizzly voice, the percussion as if played by ghost pirates, continuing through the next song—"*Clap Hands*"—and the next, something creepy, something alien calling to the human in me.

Not every track worked, but, going down the listing to the title track, the ones that worked unlocked a door into me, crouched inside my brain and have so far refused to move.

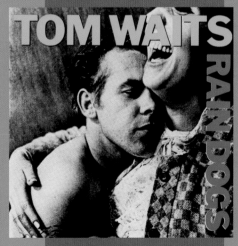

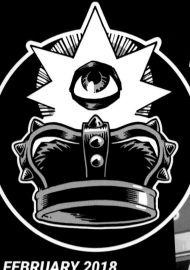

FROM THEORY TO REVOLUTION

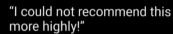

FEBRUARY 2018
PUNKS NOT DEAD by David Barnett & Martin Simmonds launches to cacophonous praise and incites all manner of bollocks on both sides of the Atlantic.

"Instant Club Hit!"
—*Bleeding Cool*

"A gorgeous comic that feels as fresh as the zits on Sid's sneering face."
—*DoomRocket*

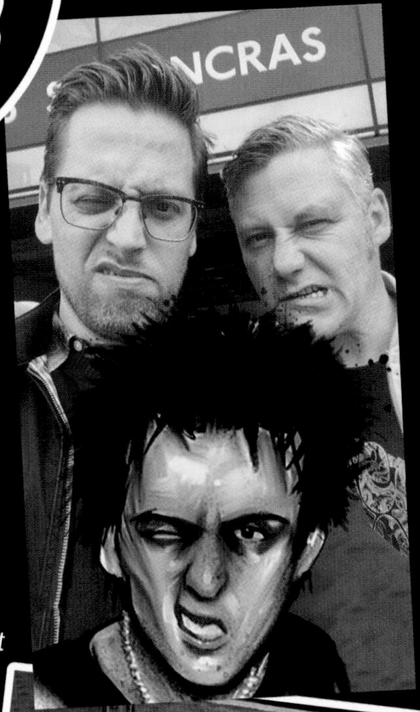

"I could not recommend this more highly!"
—*Mark Millar, Kick-Ass, Kingsman*

"Bang on target, no bollocks!"
—*Cathi Unsworth, author of Weirdo*

"It's punk as hell!"
—*Adventures in Poor Taste*

"A cheeky git of an issue, giving you that little fix that will leave you Jonesing for another."
—*Big Comic Page*

BLACK CROWN
PUNKS
NOT
DEAD
punksnotdead
#1 cover A
feb2018
BARNETT
SIMMONDS
BIDIKAR
IDW

BLACK CROWN
PUNKS NOT DEAD
THEME NIGHT
THE REVIEWS ARE IN
AND WE'RE OH SO PRETTY
Pull up yer bondage trousers and enjoy a COMPLEMENTARY MOLOTOV COCKTAIL
it's FRIDAY & WE'RE VACANT

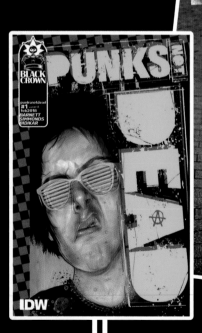

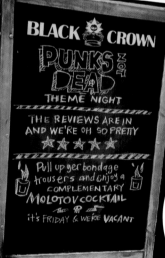

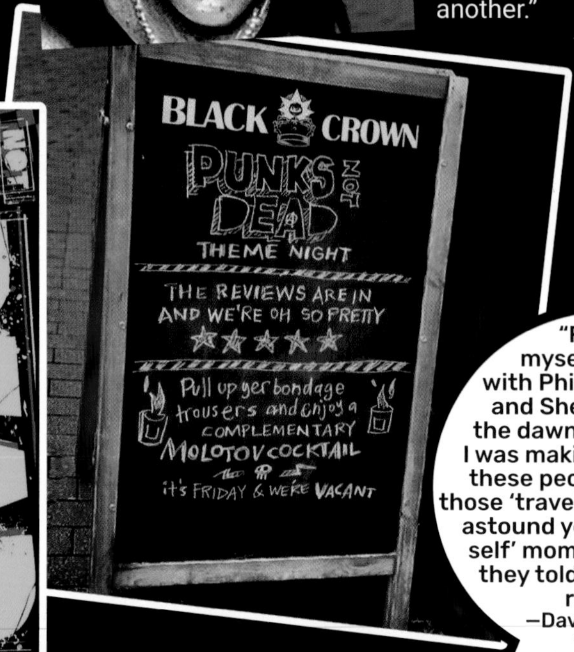

"Finding myself in a pub with Philip Bond, CUD and Shelly Bond and the dawning realisation I was making comics with these people was one of those 'travel back in time and astound your 19-year-old self' moments. And then they told me it was my round."
—David Barnett, writer

2018 FEBRUARY

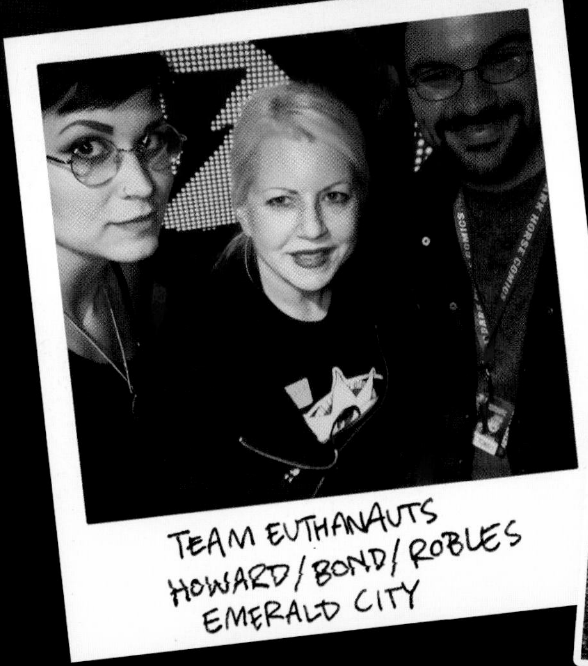
TEAM EUTHANAUTS
HOWARD/BOND/ROBLES
EMERALD CITY

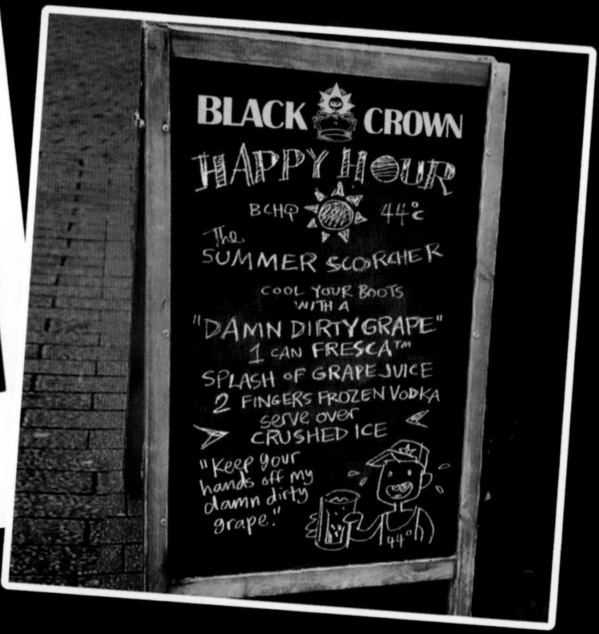
BLACK CROWN
HAPPY HOUR
BCHQ 44°c
The SUMMER SCORCHER
COOL YOUR BOOTS WITH A
"DAMN DIRTY GRAPE"
1 CAN FRESCA™
SPLASH OF GRAPE JUICE
2 FINGERS FROZEN VODKA
serve over
CRUSHED ICE
"Keep your hands off my damn dirty grape."
44°

MARCH
Two new titles are announced at Emerald City Comic Con marking BLACK CROWN's "phase II". EUTHANAUTS is a psychonautic deep-dive into the DeathSpace by Tini Howard and Nick Robles. HOUSE AMOK, by Christopher Sebela and Shawn McManus, follows a family on a violent cross-country summer vacation fueled by a shared psychosis.

APRIL
BLACK CROWN QUARTERLY #3 debuts.

JUNE
The BLACK CROWN SUMMER SCORCHER preview, featuring a wraparound artist jam cover, is ready for SDCC.

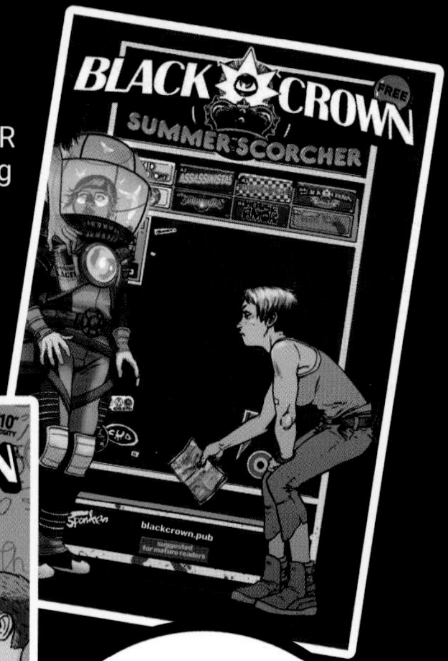
BLACK CROWN
FREE
SUMMER SCORCHER
blackcrown.pub
suggested for mature readers

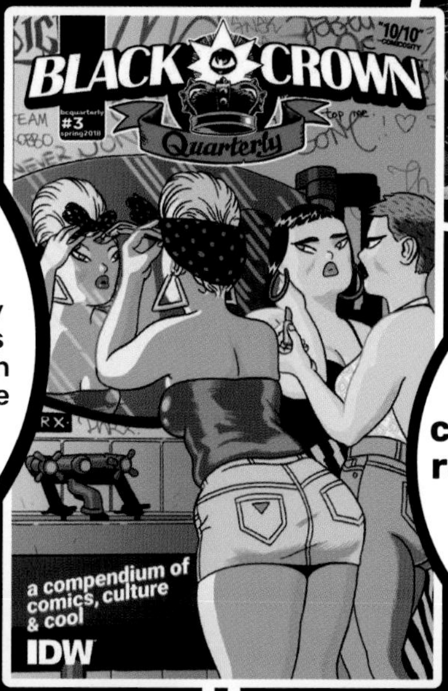
BLACK CROWN
"10/10"
bcquarterly
#3
spring2018
Quarterly
a compendium of comics, culture & cool
IDW

"My favourite moment would have to be losing my passport after an interview at ECCC in Seattle, finding it at a restaurant just minutes before the BLACK CROWN panel was due to start, and then relating the story to the audience. It's fair to say I was experiencing a huge adrenaline rush after the relief of knowing I'd be able to get home after the convention! I may have also mentioned Dot Cotton for reasons I can't remember."
—Martin Simmonds, artist

"Everything at BC is clearly a blast to make. You can see the creators really letting rip and loving it. That's priceless."
—Leah Moore, writer

MARCH ***APRIL*** ***JUNE***

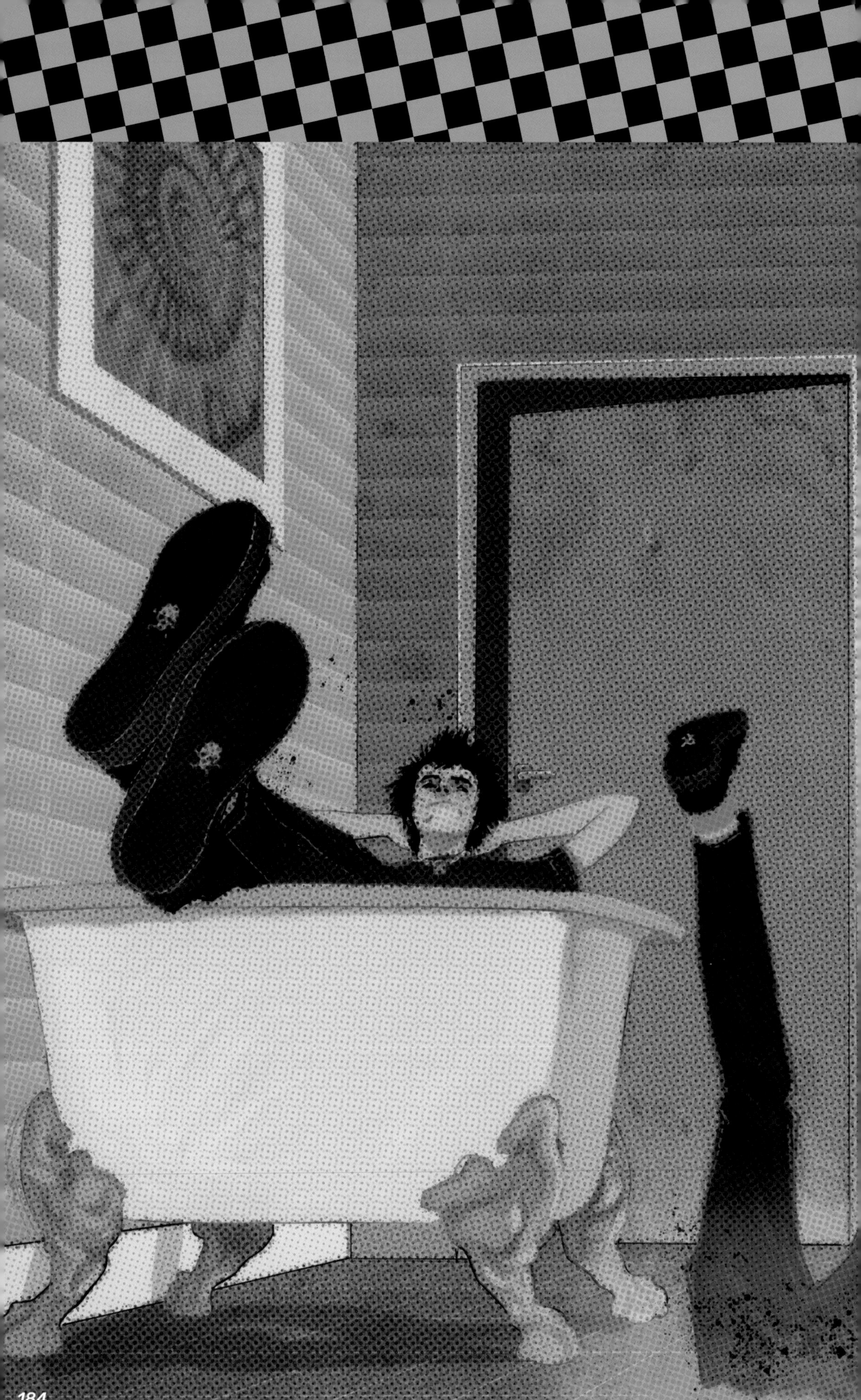

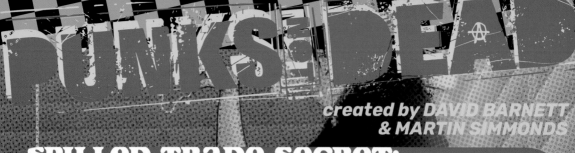

PUNKS NOT DEAD

created by DAVID BARNETT & MARTIN SIMMONDS

SPILLED TRADE SECRET:

LET THEM TAKE YOU ALIVE AT LEEDS

I met David Barnett in the fall of 2016 at the Thought Bubble convention in Leeds. I was a free agent that year, on vacation visiting my in-laws with my husband Philip and our son Spencer in tow. But secretly I was crafting the bones of BLACK CROWN. The family Bond was behind a table; Philip was selling sketchbooks, Spencer was pretending he wasn't related to us. A middle-aged Brit with a taller red-headed boy trying to hide behind him steps up to the table. He said he was a huge Vertigo fan. Then he looked me in the eye and told me two things we had in common:

1) He was a journalist and he, too, was made redundant from a company after devoting 20+ years of his life to the [fill in your own adjective] workplace.

2) He had an idea for a comic book. (Cue Gigantic Eyeroll. Doesn't *everyone*?)

We had a decent conversation and he seemed borderline legit. I quite liked the high concept: the ghost of Sid Vicious as father figure to an awkward teenaged boy being raised by a single mom. And then he blurted "It's called 'Don't Let Them Take You Alive.'"

Ladies and Gentlemen, the oxygen has left the building.

(Can it have another syllable — or ten?)

I told David that if he was lucky to hoodwink an editor willing to let him cut his teeth in comics, the title was a goddamn mouthful and if the series was collected it wouldn't fit on a spine! But the idea was intriguing. I gave him my contact info and we exchanged a few e-mails. I read his first script (impressive for a newbie) and we settled on the title PUNKS NOT DEAD. Absence of apostrophe entirely intentional.

NEVER MIND THE COLIC

I also met Martin Simmonds at Thought Bubble in Leeds, but a few years earlier circa 2014 and via portfolio review. I liked his work but it didn't blow me away. Two years later I was trolling Instagram for new artists when an incredible image caught my eye. It was a colorful, frenetic aerial shot of a girl in a convertible and my instant reaction was "Nice piece by Bill Sienkiewicz." Of course on closer inspection, it was illustrated by Martin Simmonds. This young punk had really levelled up. I told David I would sample him and a few others for PUNKS NOT DEAD, assuming I'd stick to my original strategy of uniting neophyte and veteran. But from first stab, Martin's Fergie and Sid had other ideas. This team was ready to pogo — including Martin's first-born son, Joe, who arrived just in time to be part of the original PND lineup.

BLACK CROWN
PUNKS NOT DEAD
punksnotdead
#1
feb2018
BARNETT
SIMMONDS
BIDIKAR
IDW

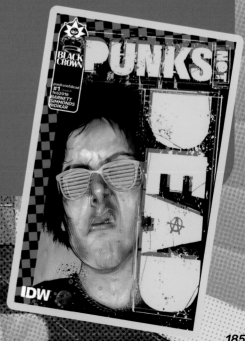

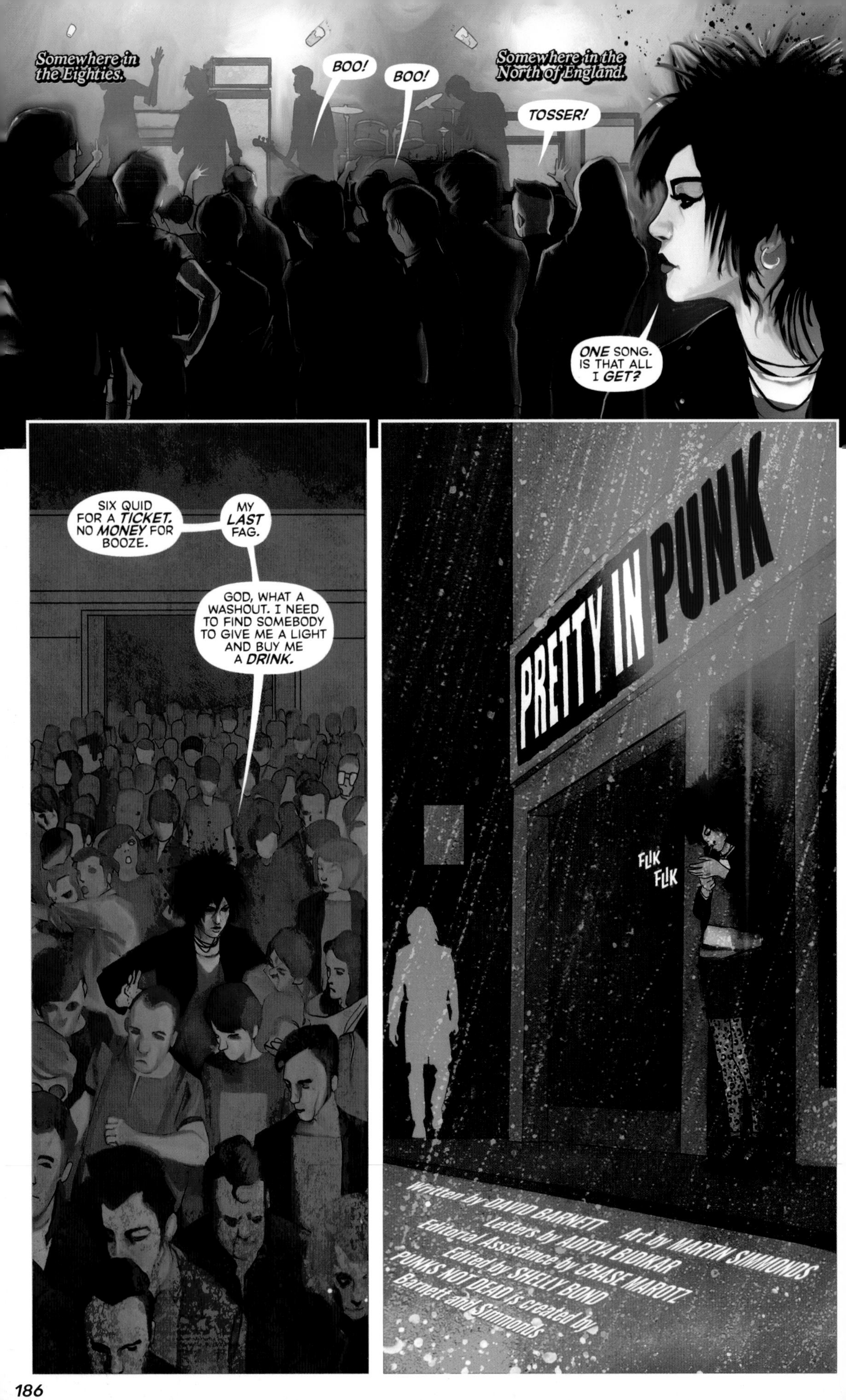
Somewhere in the Eighties.
BOO!
BOO!
Somewhere in the North of England.
TOSSER!
ONE SONG. IS THAT ALL I GET?
SIX QUID FOR A TICKET. NO MONEY FOR BOOZE.
MY LAST FAG.
GOD, WHAT A WASHOUT. I NEED TO FIND SOMEBODY TO GIVE ME A LIGHT AND BUY ME A DRINK.
PRETTY IN PUNK
FLIK FLIK
Written by DAVID BARNETT Art by MARTIN SIMMONDS
Letters by ADITYA BIDIKAR
Editorial Assistance by CHASE MAROTZ
Edited by SHELLY BOND
PUNKS NOT DEAD is created by
Barnett and Simmonds

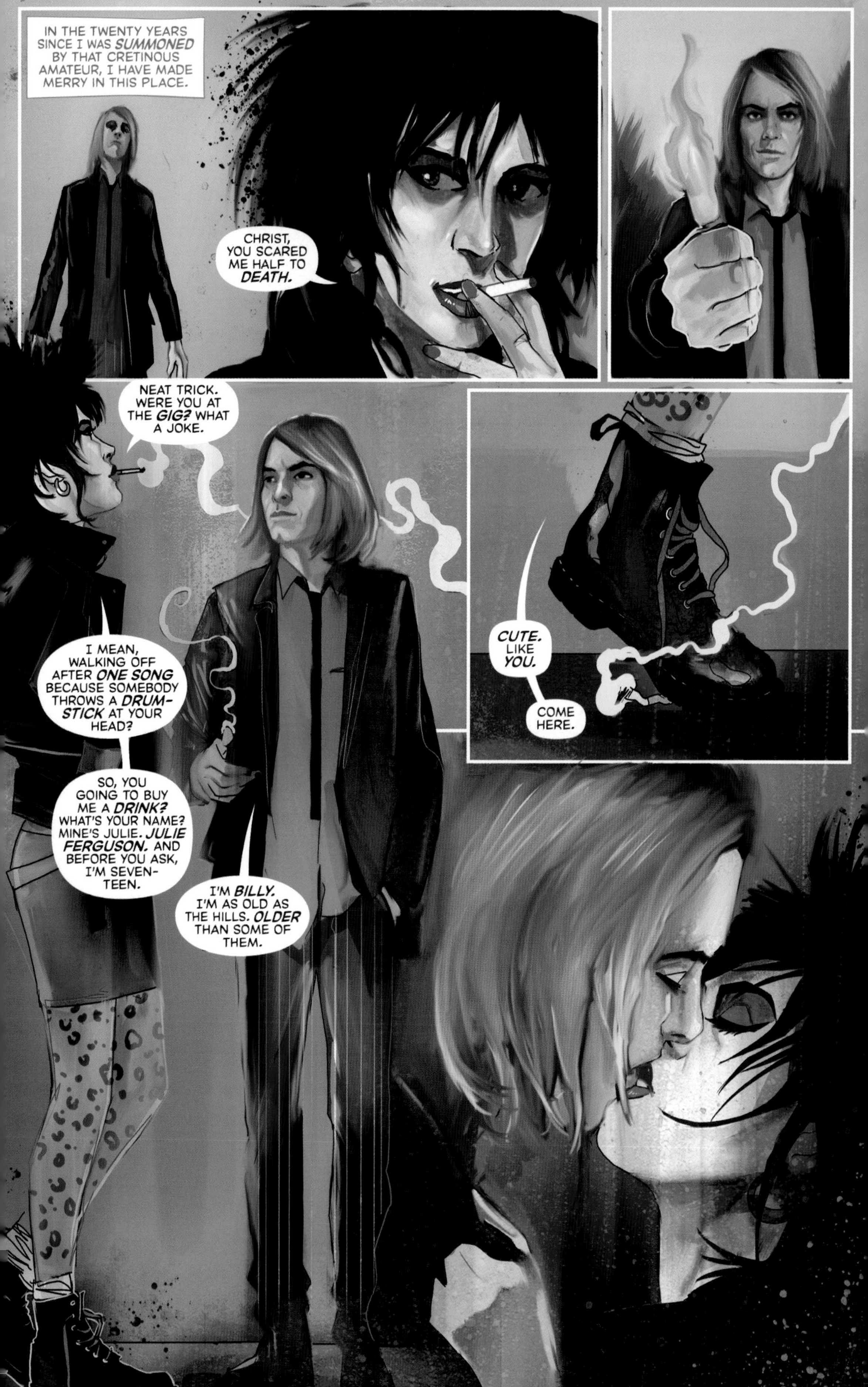

IN THE TWENTY YEARS SINCE I WAS SUMMONED BY THAT CRETINOUS AMATEUR, I HAVE MADE MERRY IN THIS PLACE.
CHRIST, YOU SCARED ME HALF TO DEATH.
NEAT TRICK. WERE YOU AT THE GIG? WHAT A JOKE.
I MEAN, WALKING OFF AFTER ONE SONG BECAUSE SOMEBODY THROWS A DRUM-STICK AT YOUR HEAD?
SO, YOU GOING TO BUY ME A DRINK? WHAT'S YOUR NAME? MINE'S JULIE. JULIE FERGUSON. AND BEFORE YOU ASK, I'M SEVEN-TEEN.
I'M BILLY. I'M AS OLD AS THE HILLS. OLDER THAN SOME OF THEM.
CUTE. LIKE YOU.
COME HERE.

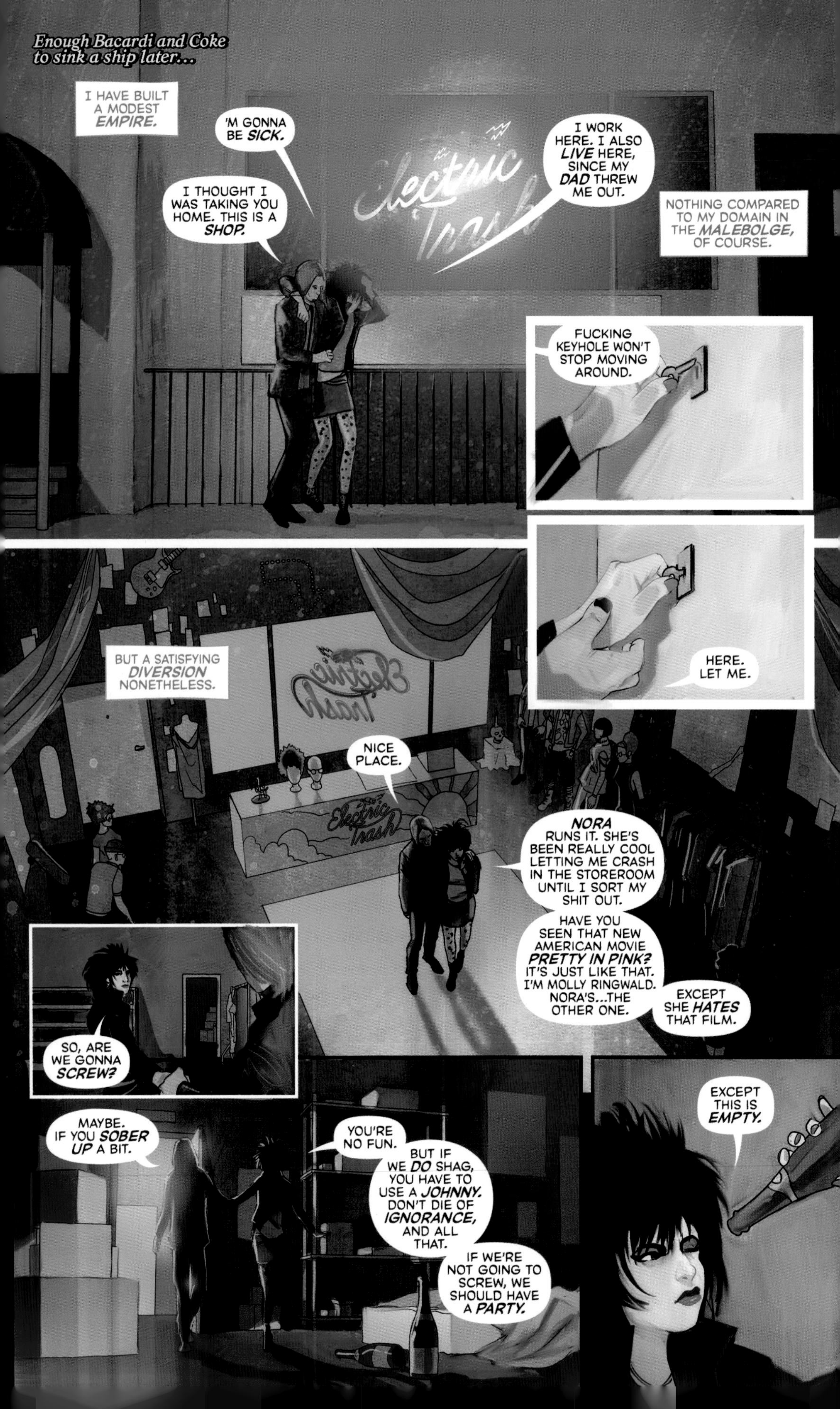

Enough Bacardi and Coke to sink a ship later...
I HAVE BUILT A MODEST EMPIRE.
'M GONNA BE SICK.
I THOUGHT I WAS TAKING YOU HOME. THIS IS A SHOP.
Electric Trash
I WORK HERE. I ALSO LIVE HERE, SINCE MY DAD THREW ME OUT.
NOTHING COMPARED TO MY DOMAIN IN THE MALEBOLGE, OF COURSE.
FUCKING KEYHOLE WON'T STOP MOVING AROUND.
HERE. LET ME.
BUT A SATISFYING DIVERSION NONETHELESS.
Electric Trash
NICE PLACE.
Electric Trash
NORA RUNS IT. SHE'S BEEN REALLY COOL LETTING ME CRASH IN THE STOREROOM UNTIL I SORT MY SHIT OUT.
HAVE YOU SEEN THAT NEW AMERICAN MOVIE PRETTY IN PINK? IT'S JUST LIKE THAT. I'M MOLLY RINGWALD. NORA'S...THE OTHER ONE.
EXCEPT SHE HATES THAT FILM.
SO, ARE WE GONNA SCREW?
MAYBE. IF YOU SOBER UP A BIT.
YOU'RE NO FUN.
BUT IF WE DO SHAG, YOU HAVE TO USE A JOHNNY. DON'T DIE OF IGNORANCE, AND ALL THAT.
IF WE'RE NOT GOING TO SCREW, WE SHOULD HAVE A PARTY.
EXCEPT THIS IS EMPTY.

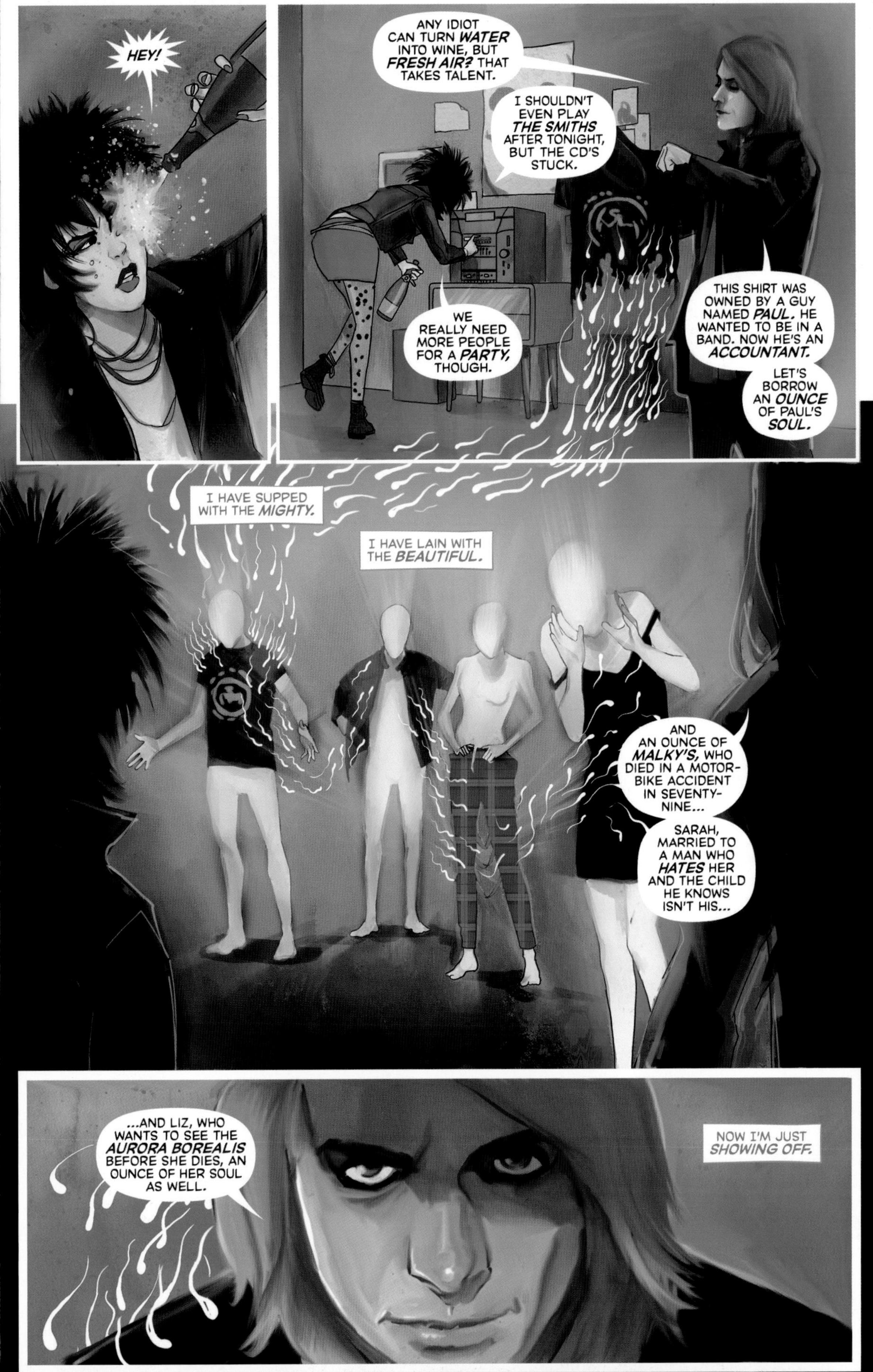
HEY!
ANY IDIOT CAN TURN WATER INTO WINE, BUT FRESH AIR? THAT TAKES TALENT.
I SHOULDN'T EVEN PLAY THE SMITHS AFTER TONIGHT, BUT THE CD'S STUCK.
WE REALLY NEED MORE PEOPLE FOR A PARTY, THOUGH.
THIS SHIRT WAS OWNED BY A GUY NAMED PAUL. HE WANTED TO BE IN A BAND. NOW HE'S AN ACCOUNTANT.
LET'S BORROW AN OUNCE OF PAUL'S SOUL.
I HAVE SUPPED WITH THE MIGHTY.
I HAVE LAIN WITH THE BEAUTIFUL.
AND AN OUNCE OF MALKY'S, WHO DIED IN A MOTOR-BIKE ACCIDENT IN SEVENTY-NINE...
SARAH, MARRIED TO A MAN WHO HATES HER AND THE CHILD HE KNOWS ISN'T HIS...
...AND LIZ, WHO WANTS TO SEE THE AURORA BOREALIS BEFORE SHE DIES, AN OUNCE OF HER SOUL AS WELL.
NOW I'M JUST SHOWING OFF.

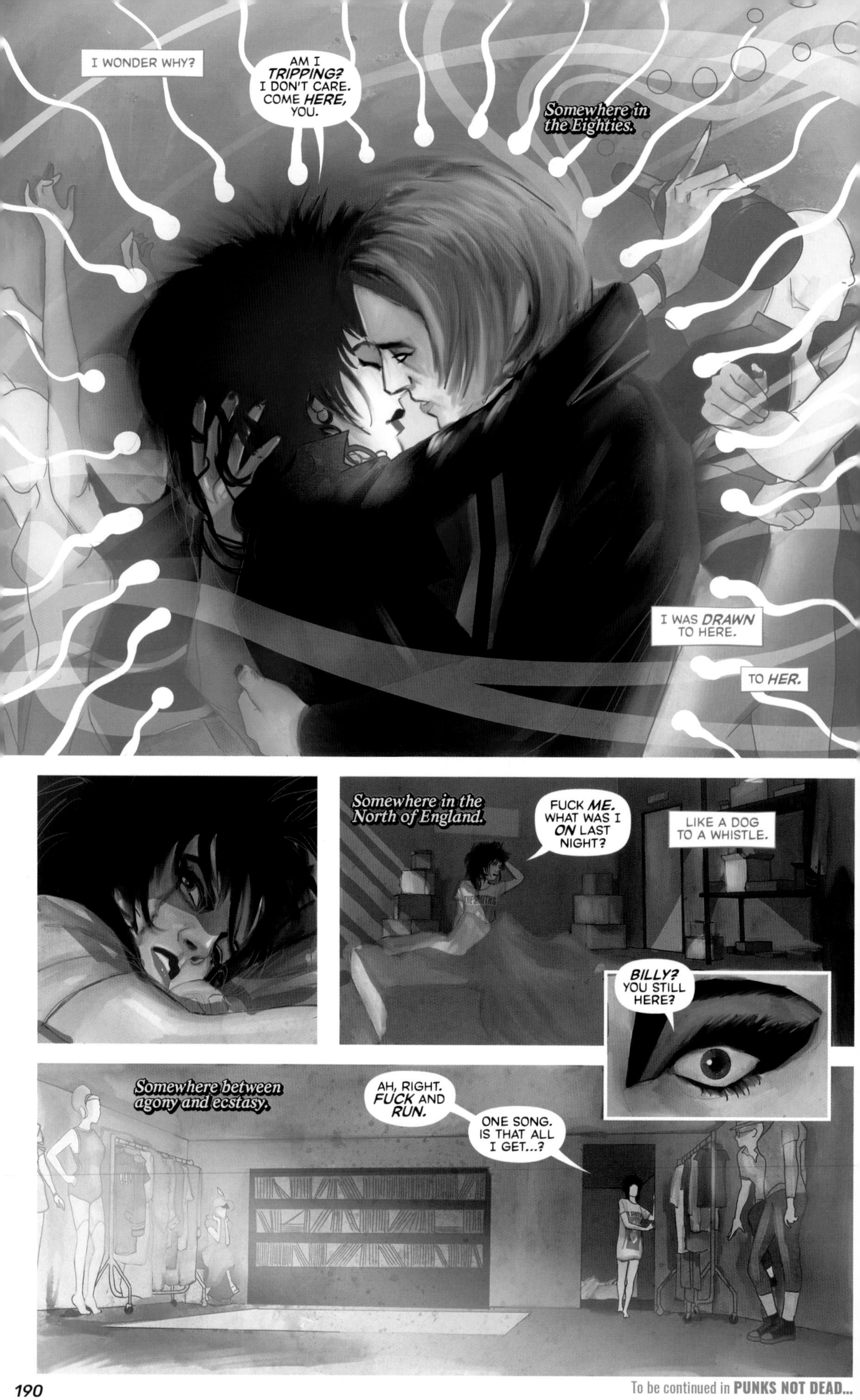
I WONDER WHY?
AM I *TRIPPING?* I DON'T CARE. COME *HERE,* YOU.
Somewhere in the Eighties.
I WAS *DRAWN* TO HERE.
TO *HER.*
Somewhere in the North of England.
FUCK *ME.* WHAT WAS I *ON* LAST NIGHT?
LIKE A DOG TO A WHISTLE.
BILLY? YOU STILL HERE?
Somewhere between agony and ecstasy.
AH, RIGHT. *FUCK* AND *RUN.*
ONE SONG. IS THAT ALL I GET...?

To be continued in **PUNKS NOT DEAD...**

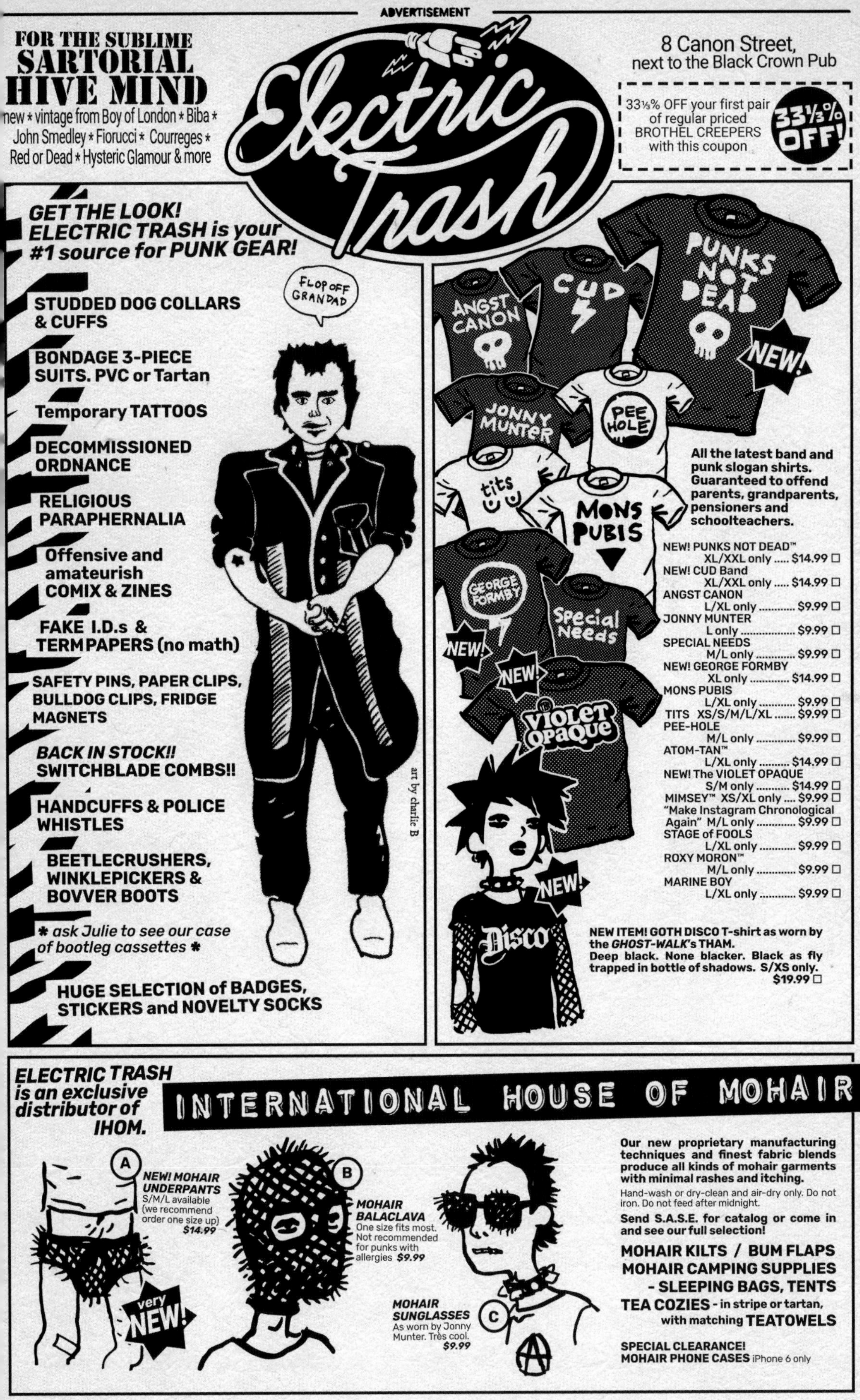
ADVERTISEMENT
FOR THE SUBLIME SARTORIAL HIVE MIND
new * vintage from Boy of London * Biba * John Smedley * Fiorucci * Courreges * Red or Dead * Hysteric Glamour & more
Electric Trash
8 Canon Street, next to the Black Crown Pub
33⅓% OFF your first pair of regular priced BROTHEL CREEPERS with this coupon
33⅓% OFF!
GET THE LOOK! ELECTRIC TRASH is your #1 source for PUNK GEAR!
FLOP OFF GRANDAD
STUDDED DOG COLLARS & CUFFS
BONDAGE 3-PIECE SUITS. PVC or Tartan
Temporary TATTOOS
DECOMMISSIONED ORDNANCE
RELIGIOUS PARAPHERNALIA
Offensive and amateurish COMIX & ZINES
FAKE I.D.s & TERM PAPERS (no math)
SAFETY PINS, PAPER CLIPS, BULLDOG CLIPS, FRIDGE MAGNETS
BACK IN STOCK!! SWITCHBLADE COMBS!!
HANDCUFFS & POLICE WHISTLES
BEETLECRUSHERS, WINKLEPICKERS & BOVVER BOOTS
* ask Julie to see our case of bootleg cassettes *
HUGE SELECTION of BADGES, STICKERS and NOVELTY SOCKS
art by charlie B
ANGST CANON
CUD
PUNKS NOT DEAD
NEW!
JONNY MUNTER
PEE HOLE
tits
MONS PUBIS
GEORGE FORMBY
Special Needs
NEW!
NEW!
VIOLET OPAQUE
All the latest band and punk slogan shirts. Guaranteed to offend parents, grandparents, pensioners and schoolteachers.
NEW! PUNKS NOT DEAD™ XL/XXL only ..... $14.99 ☐
NEW! CUD Band XL/XXL only ..... $14.99 ☐
ANGST CANON L/XL only .... $9.99 ☐
JONNY MUNTER L only .... $9.99 ☐
SPECIAL NEEDS M/L only .... $9.99 ☐
NEW! GEORGE FORMBY XL only .... $14.99 ☐
MONS PUBIS L/XL only .... $9.99 ☐
TITS XS/S/M/L/XL .... $9.99 ☐
PEE-HOLE M/L only .... $9.99 ☐
ATOM-TAN™ L/XL only .... $14.99 ☐
NEW! The VIOLET OPAQUE S/M only .... $14.99 ☐
MIMSEY™ XS/XL only .... $9.99 ☐
"Make Instagram Chronological Again" M/L only .... $9.99 ☐
STAGE of FOOLS L/XL only .... $9.99 ☐
ROXY MORON™ M/L only .... $9.99 ☐
MARINE BOY L/XL only .... $9.99 ☐
NEW!
Disco
NEW ITEM! GOTH DISCO T-shirt as worn by the GHOST-WALK's THAM. Deep black. None blacker. Black as fly trapped in bottle of shadows. S/XS only. $19.99 ☐
ELECTRIC TRASH is an exclusive distributor of IHOM.
INTERNATIONAL HOUSE OF MOHAIR
A
NEW! MOHAIR UNDERPANTS S/M/L available (we recommend order one size up) $14.99
very NEW!
B
MOHAIR BALACLAVA One size fits most. Not recommended for punks with allergies $9.99
C
MOHAIR SUNGLASSES As worn by Jonny Munter. Très cool. $9.99
Our new proprietary manufacturing techniques and finest fabric blends produce all kinds of mohair garments with minimal rashes and itching.
Hand-wash or dry-clean and air-dry only. Do not iron. Do not feed after midnight.
Send S.A.S.E. for catalog or come in and see our full selection!
MOHAIR KILTS / BUM FLAPS
MOHAIR CAMPING SUPPLIES - SLEEPING BAGS, TENTS
TEA COZIES - in stripe or tartan, with matching TEATOWELS
SPECIAL CLEARANCE! MOHAIR PHONE CASES iPhone 6 only

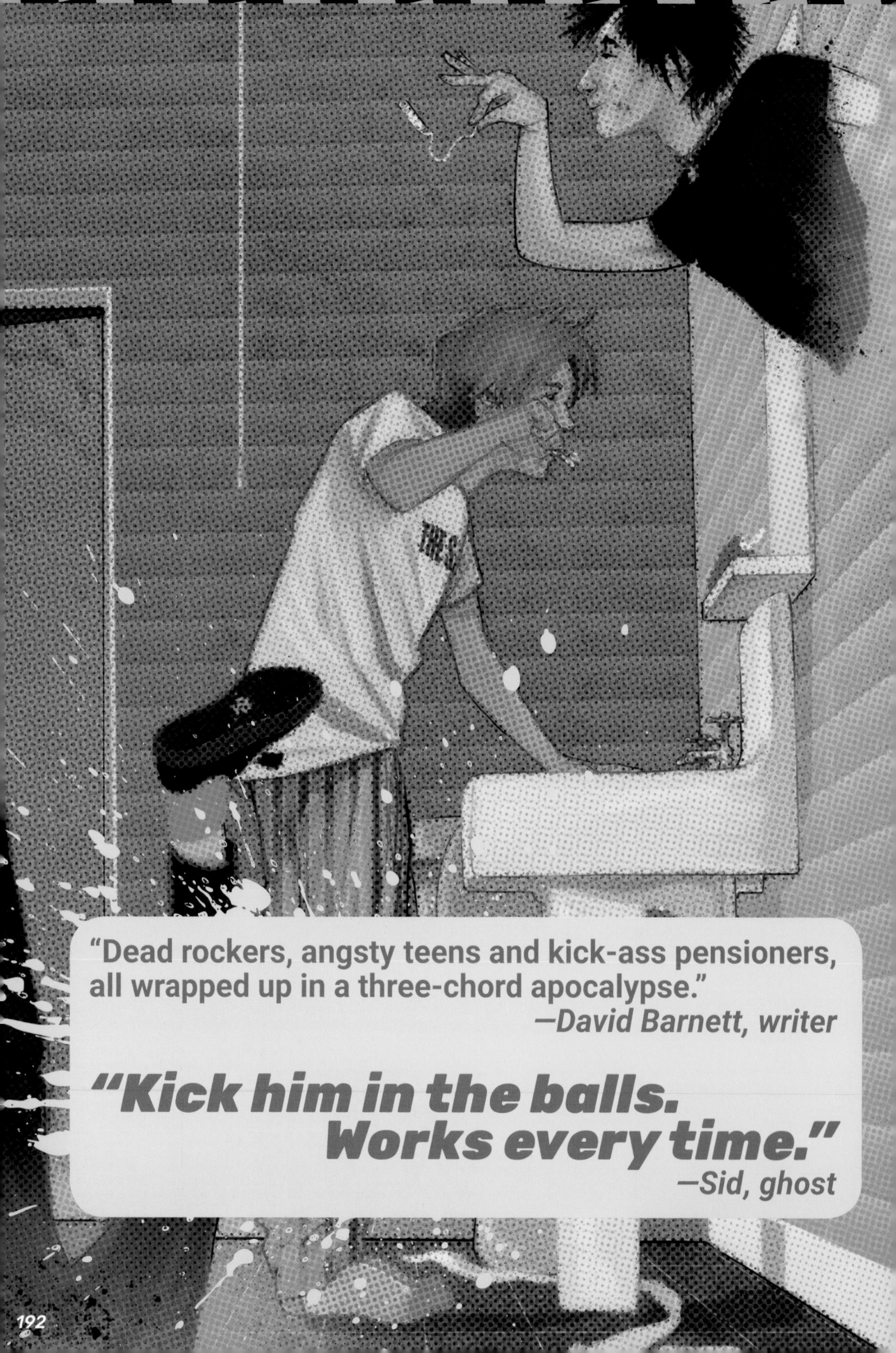

"Dead rockers, angsty teens and kick-ass pensioners, all wrapped up in a three-chord apocalypse."

—*David Barnett, writer*

"Kick him in the balls. Works every time."

—*Sid, ghost*

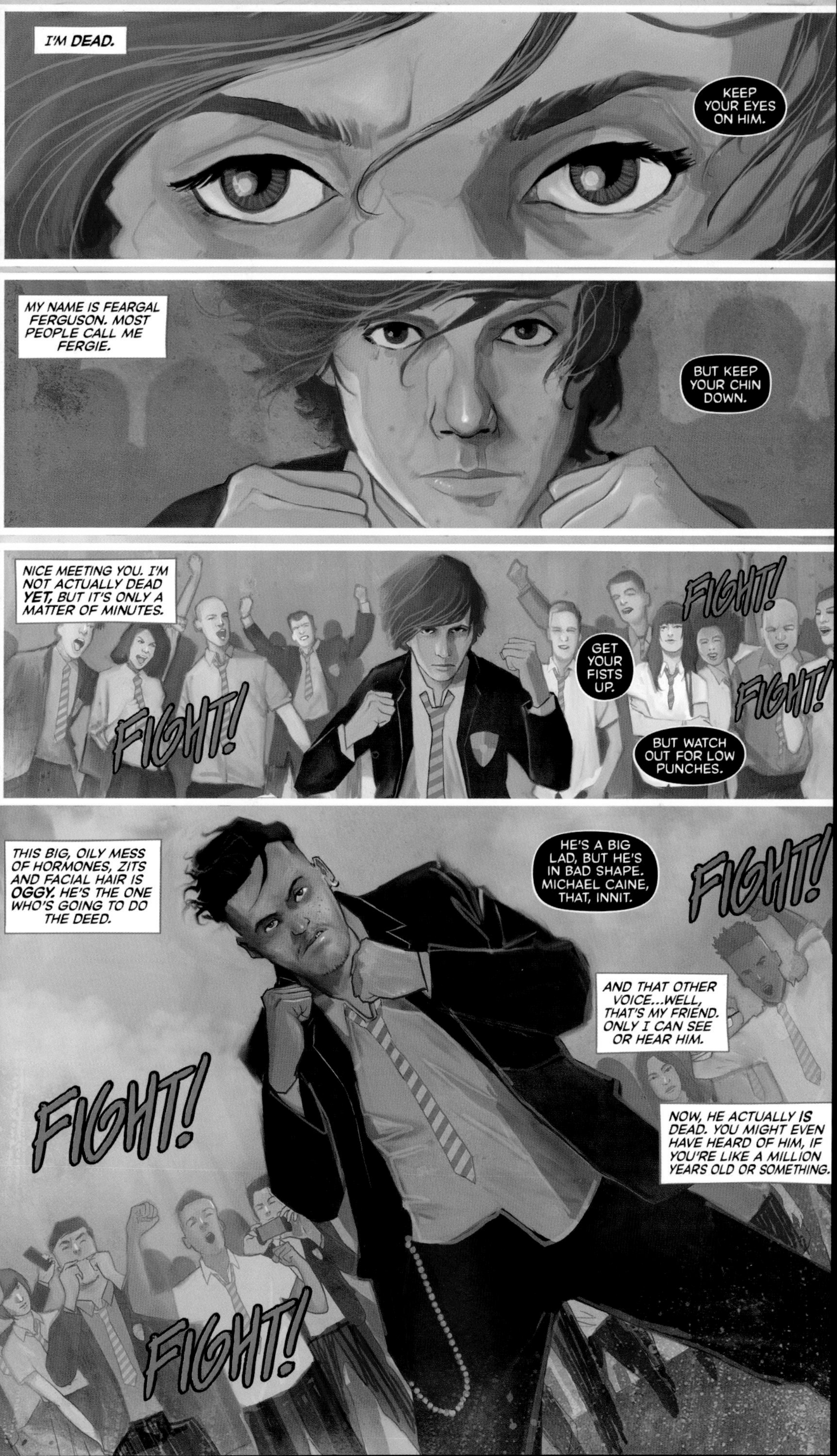
I'M DEAD.
KEEP YOUR EYES ON HIM.
MY NAME IS FEARGAL FERGUSON. MOST PEOPLE CALL ME FERGIE.
BUT KEEP YOUR CHIN DOWN.
NICE MEETING YOU. I'M NOT ACTUALLY DEAD YET, BUT IT'S ONLY A MATTER OF MINUTES.
FIGHT!
FIGHT!
GET YOUR FISTS UP.
FIGHT!
BUT WATCH OUT FOR LOW PUNCHES.
THIS BIG, OILY MESS OF HORMONES, ZITS AND FACIAL HAIR IS OGGY. HE'S THE ONE WHO'S GOING TO DO THE DEED.
HE'S A BIG LAD, BUT HE'S IN BAD SHAPE. MICHAEL CAINE, THAT, INNIT.
FIGHT!
AND THAT OTHER VOICE...WELL, THAT'S MY FRIEND. ONLY I CAN SEE OR HEAR HIM.
FIGHT!
NOW, HE ACTUALLY IS DEAD. YOU MIGHT EVEN HAVE HEARD OF HIM, IF YOU'RE LIKE A MILLION YEARS OLD OR SOMETHING.
FIGHT!

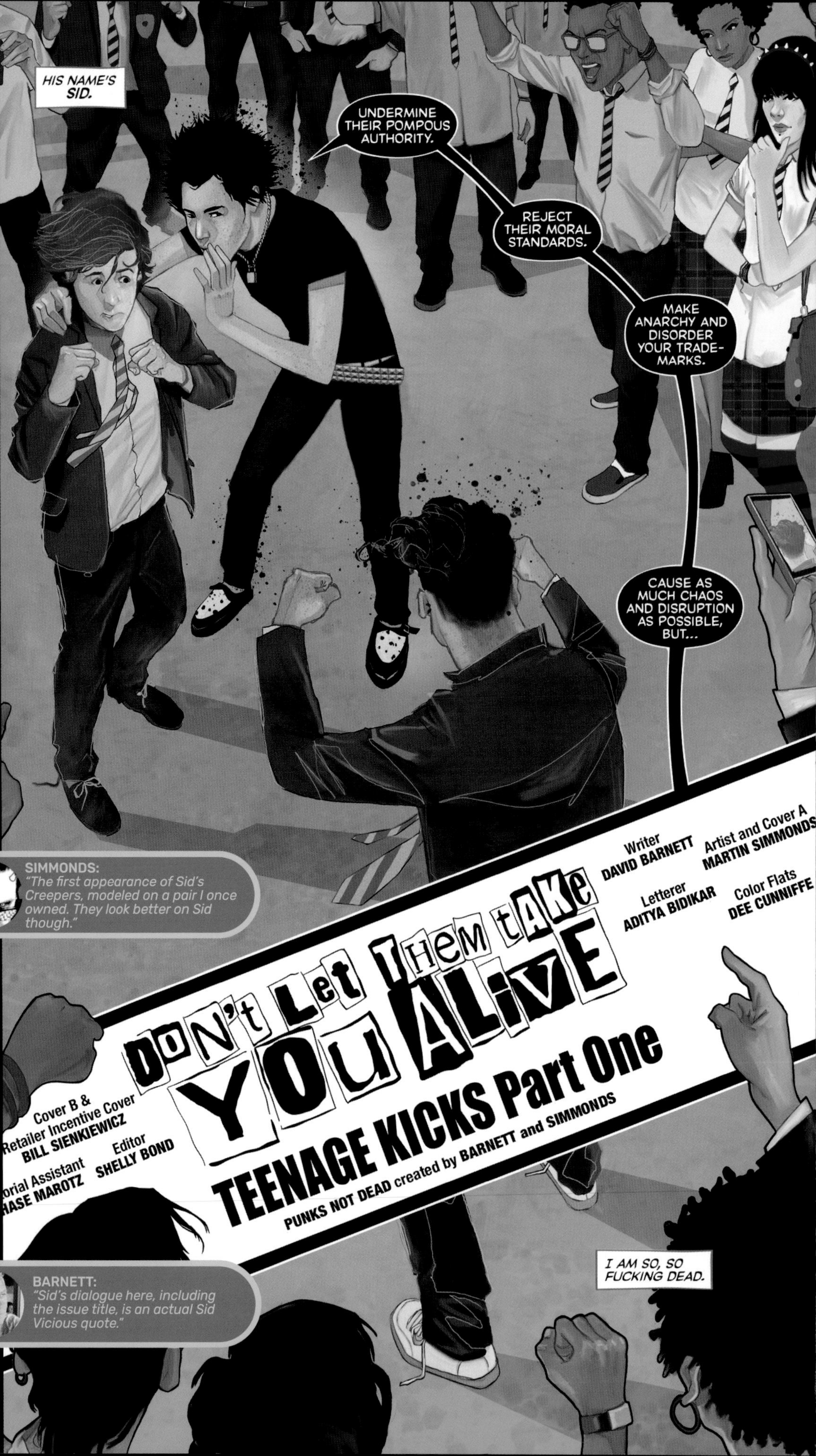
HIS NAME'S SID.
UNDERMINE THEIR POMPOUS AUTHORITY.
REJECT THEIR MORAL STANDARDS.
MAKE ANARCHY AND DISORDER YOUR TRADE-MARKS.
CAUSE AS MUCH CHAOS AND DISRUPTION AS POSSIBLE, BUT...
DON'T LET THEM TAKE YOU ALIVE
TEENAGE KICKS Part One
PUNKS NOT DEAD created by BARNETT and SIMMONDS
Writer DAVID BARNETT
Artist and Cover A MARTIN SIMMONDS
Letterer ADITYA BIDIKAR
Color Flats DEE CUNNIFFE
Cover B & Retailer Incentive Cover BILL SIENKIEWICZ
orial Assistant HASE MAROTZ
Editor SHELLY BOND
I AM SO, SO FUCKING DEAD.

SIMMONDS:
"The first appearance of Sid's Creepers, modeled on a pair I once owned. They look better on Sid though."

BARNETT:
"Sid's dialogue here, including the issue title, is an actual Sid Vicious quote."

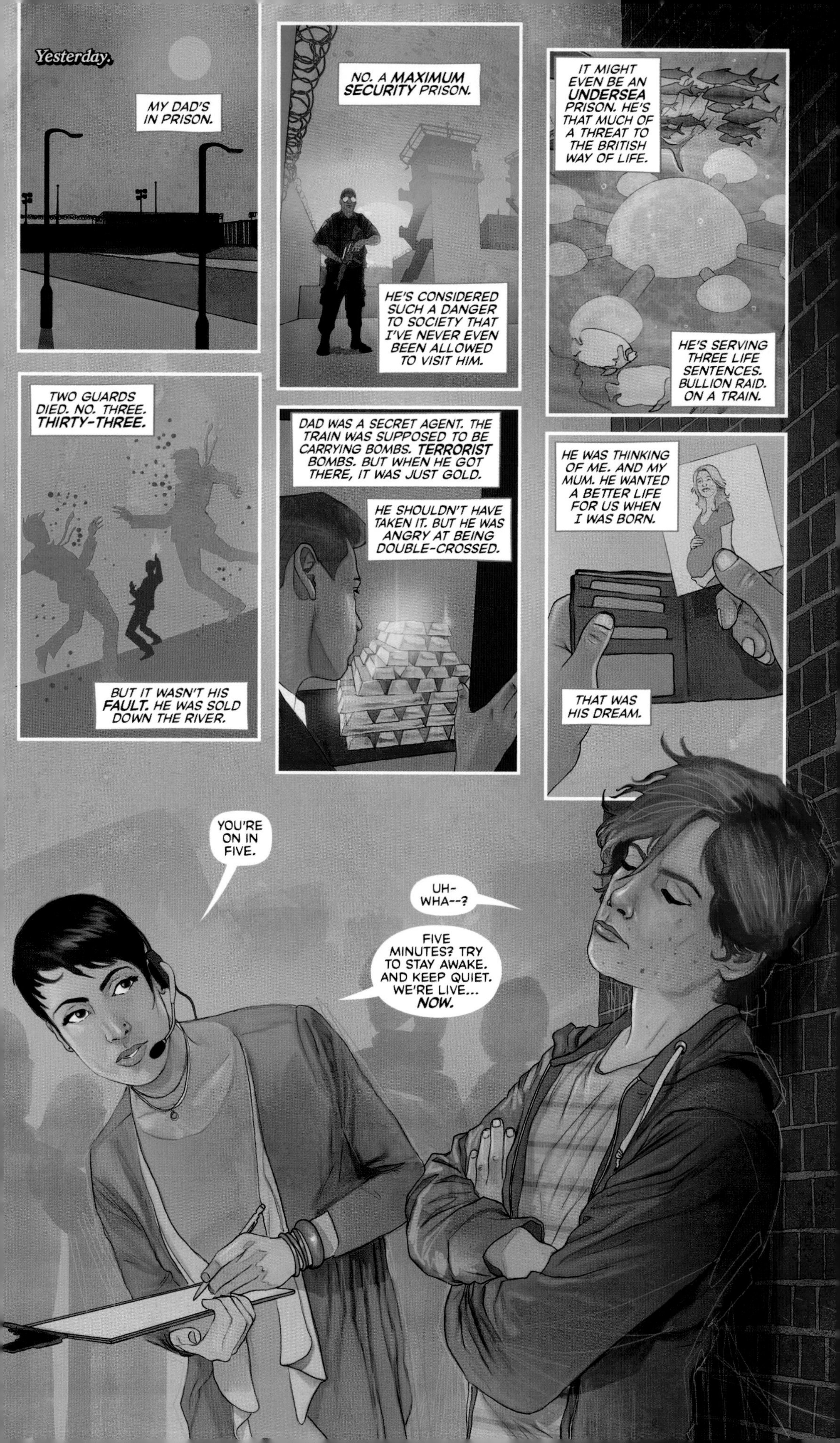
Yesterday.
MY DAD'S IN PRISON.
NO. A MAXIMUM SECURITY PRISON.
HE'S CONSIDERED SUCH A DANGER TO SOCIETY THAT I'VE NEVER EVEN BEEN ALLOWED TO VISIT HIM.
IT MIGHT EVEN BE AN UNDERSEA PRISON. HE'S THAT MUCH OF A THREAT TO THE BRITISH WAY OF LIFE.
HE'S SERVING THREE LIFE SENTENCES. BULLION RAID. ON A TRAIN.
TWO GUARDS DIED. NO. THREE. THIRTY-THREE.
BUT IT WASN'T HIS FAULT. HE WAS SOLD DOWN THE RIVER.
DAD WAS A SECRET AGENT. THE TRAIN WAS SUPPOSED TO BE CARRYING BOMBS. TERRORIST BOMBS. BUT WHEN HE GOT THERE, IT WAS JUST GOLD.
HE SHOULDN'T HAVE TAKEN IT. BUT HE WAS ANGRY AT BEING DOUBLE-CROSSED.
HE WAS THINKING OF ME. AND MY MUM. HE WANTED A BETTER LIFE FOR US WHEN I WAS BORN.
THAT WAS HIS DREAM.
YOU'RE ON IN FIVE.
UH-WHA--?
FIVE MINUTES? TRY TO STAY AWAKE. AND KEEP QUIET. WE'RE LIVE... NOW.

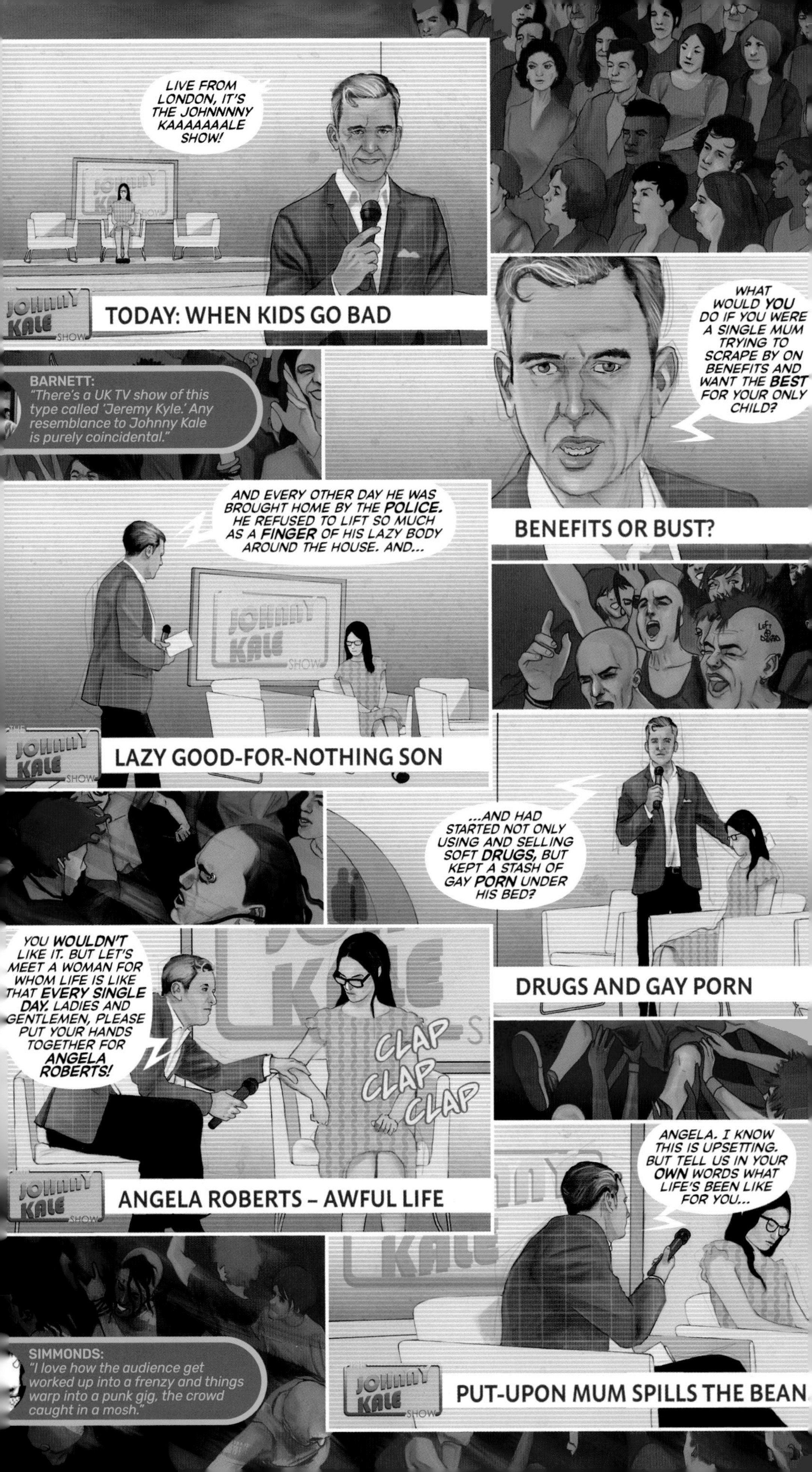

LIVE FROM LONDON, IT'S THE JOHNNNNY KAAAAAAALE SHOW!
TODAY: WHEN KIDS GO BAD
WHAT WOULD YOU DO IF YOU WERE A SINGLE MUM TRYING TO SCRAPE BY ON BENEFITS AND WANT THE BEST FOR YOUR ONLY CHILD?
BARNETT: "There's a UK TV show of this type called 'Jeremy Kyle.' Any resemblance to Johnny Kale is purely coincidental."
BENEFITS OR BUST?
AND EVERY OTHER DAY HE WAS BROUGHT HOME BY THE POLICE. HE REFUSED TO LIFT SO MUCH AS A FINGER OF HIS LAZY BODY AROUND THE HOUSE. AND...
LAZY GOOD-FOR-NOTHING SON
...AND HAD STARTED NOT ONLY USING AND SELLING SOFT DRUGS, BUT KEPT A STASH OF GAY PORN UNDER HIS BED?
DRUGS AND GAY PORN
YOU WOULDN'T LIKE IT. BUT LET'S MEET A WOMAN FOR WHOM LIFE IS LIKE THAT EVERY SINGLE DAY. LADIES AND GENTLEMEN, PLEASE PUT YOUR HANDS TOGETHER FOR ANGELA ROBERTS!
CLAP CLAP CLAP
ANGELA ROBERTS – AWFUL LIFE
ANGELA. I KNOW THIS IS UPSETTING. BUT TELL US IN YOUR OWN WORDS WHAT LIFE'S BEEN LIKE FOR YOU...
SIMMONDS: "I love how the audience get worked up into a frenzy and things warp into a punk gig, the crowd caught in a mosh."
PUT-UPON MUM SPILLS THE BEAN

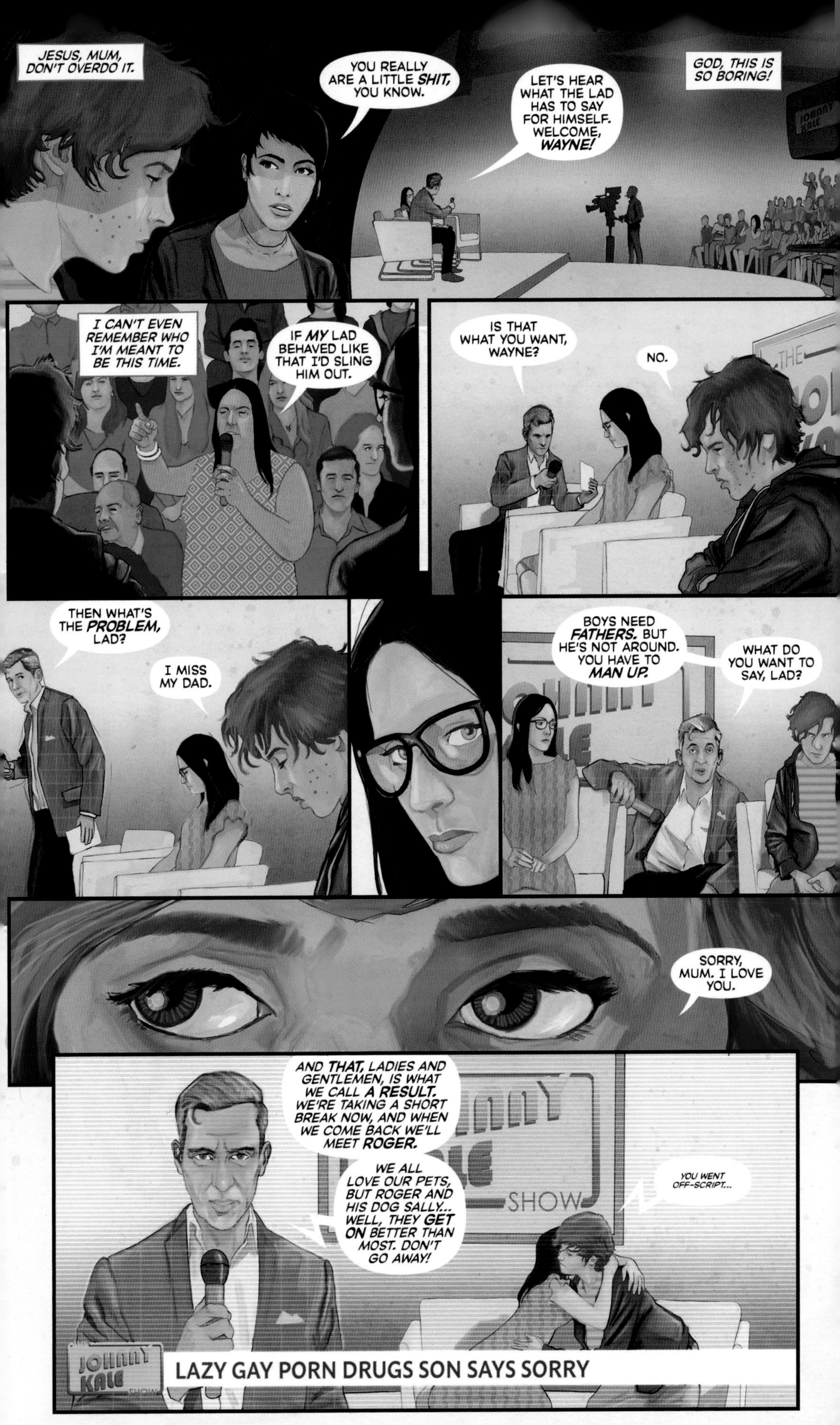

JESUS, MUM, DON'T OVERDO IT.
YOU REALLY ARE A LITTLE SHIT, YOU KNOW.
LET'S HEAR WHAT THE LAD HAS TO SAY FOR HIMSELF. WELCOME, WAYNE!
GOD, THIS IS SO BORING!
JOHNNY KALE
I CAN'T EVEN REMEMBER WHO I'M MEANT TO BE THIS TIME.
IF MY LAD BEHAVED LIKE THAT I'D SLING HIM OUT.
IS THAT WHAT YOU WANT, WAYNE?
NO.
THEN WHAT'S THE PROBLEM, LAD?
I MISS MY DAD.
BOYS NEED FATHERS. BUT HE'S NOT AROUND. YOU HAVE TO MAN UP.
WHAT DO YOU WANT TO SAY, LAD?
SORRY, MUM. I LOVE YOU.
AND THAT, LADIES AND GENTLEMEN, IS WHAT WE CALL A RESULT. WE'RE TAKING A SHORT BREAK NOW, AND WHEN WE COME BACK WE'LL MEET ROGER.
WE ALL LOVE OUR PETS, BUT ROGER AND HIS DOG SALLY... WELL, THEY GET ON BETTER THAN MOST. DON'T GO AWAY!
YOU WENT OFF-SCRIPT...
SHOW
JOHNNY KALE SHOW
LAZY GAY PORN DRUGS SON SAYS SORRY

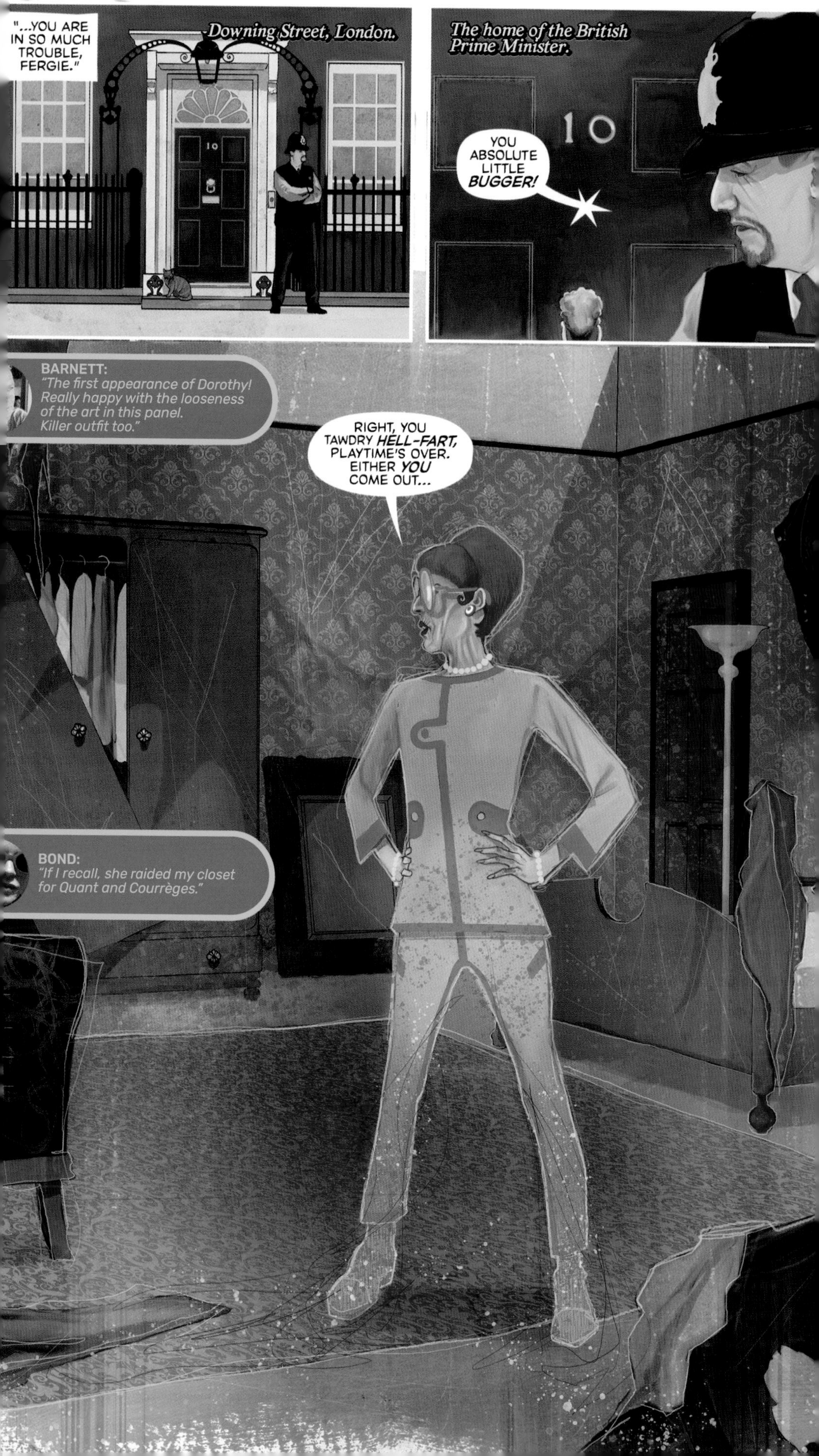

"...YOU ARE IN SO MUCH TROUBLE, FERGIE."
Downing Street, London.
The home of the British Prime Minister.
10
YOU ABSOLUTE LITTLE BUGGER!
BARNETT: "The first appearance of Dorothy! Really happy with the looseness of the art in this panel. Killer outfit too."
RIGHT, YOU TAWDRY HELL-FART, PLAYTIME'S OVER. EITHER YOU COME OUT...
BOND: "If I recall, she raided my closet for Quant and Courrèges."

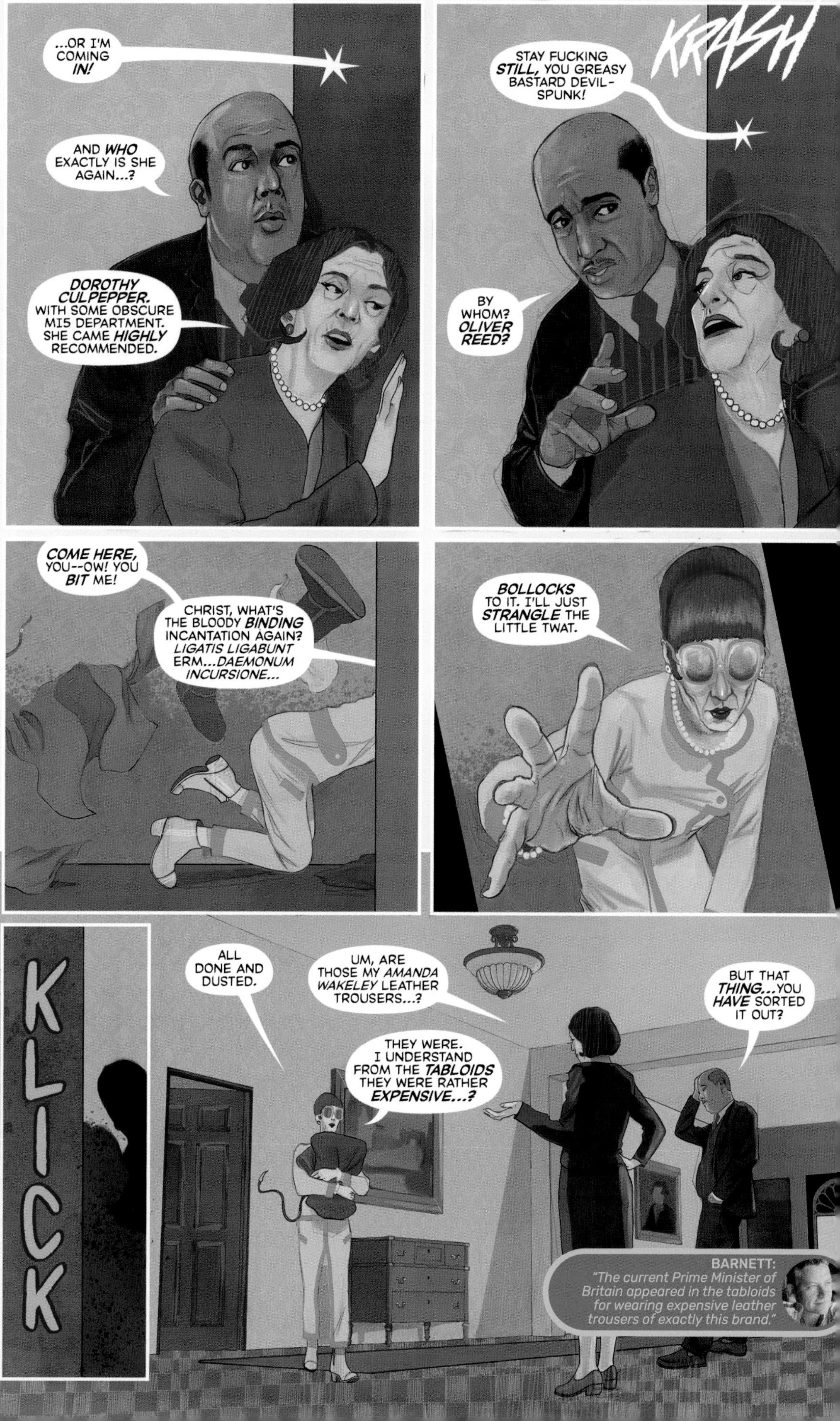
...OR I'M COMING IN!
AND WHO EXACTLY IS SHE AGAIN...?
DOROTHY CULPEPPER. WITH SOME OBSCURE MI5 DEPARTMENT. SHE CAME HIGHLY RECOMMENDED.
KRASH
STAY FUCKING STILL, YOU GREASY BASTARD DEVIL-SPUNK!
BY WHOM? OLIVER REED?
COME HERE, YOU--OW! YOU BIT ME!
CHRIST, WHAT'S THE BLOODY BINDING INCANTATION AGAIN? LIGATIS LIGABUNT ERM...DAEMONUM INCURSIONE...
BOLLOCKS TO IT. I'LL JUST STRANGLE THE LITTLE TWAT.
KLICK
ALL DONE AND DUSTED.
UM, ARE THOSE MY AMANDA WAKELEY LEATHER TROUSERS...?
THEY WERE. I UNDERSTAND FROM THE TABLOIDS THEY WERE RATHER EXPENSIVE...?
BUT THAT THING...YOU HAVE SORTED IT OUT?
BARNETT:
"The current Prime Minister of Britain appeared in the tabloids for wearing expensive leather trousers of exactly this brand."

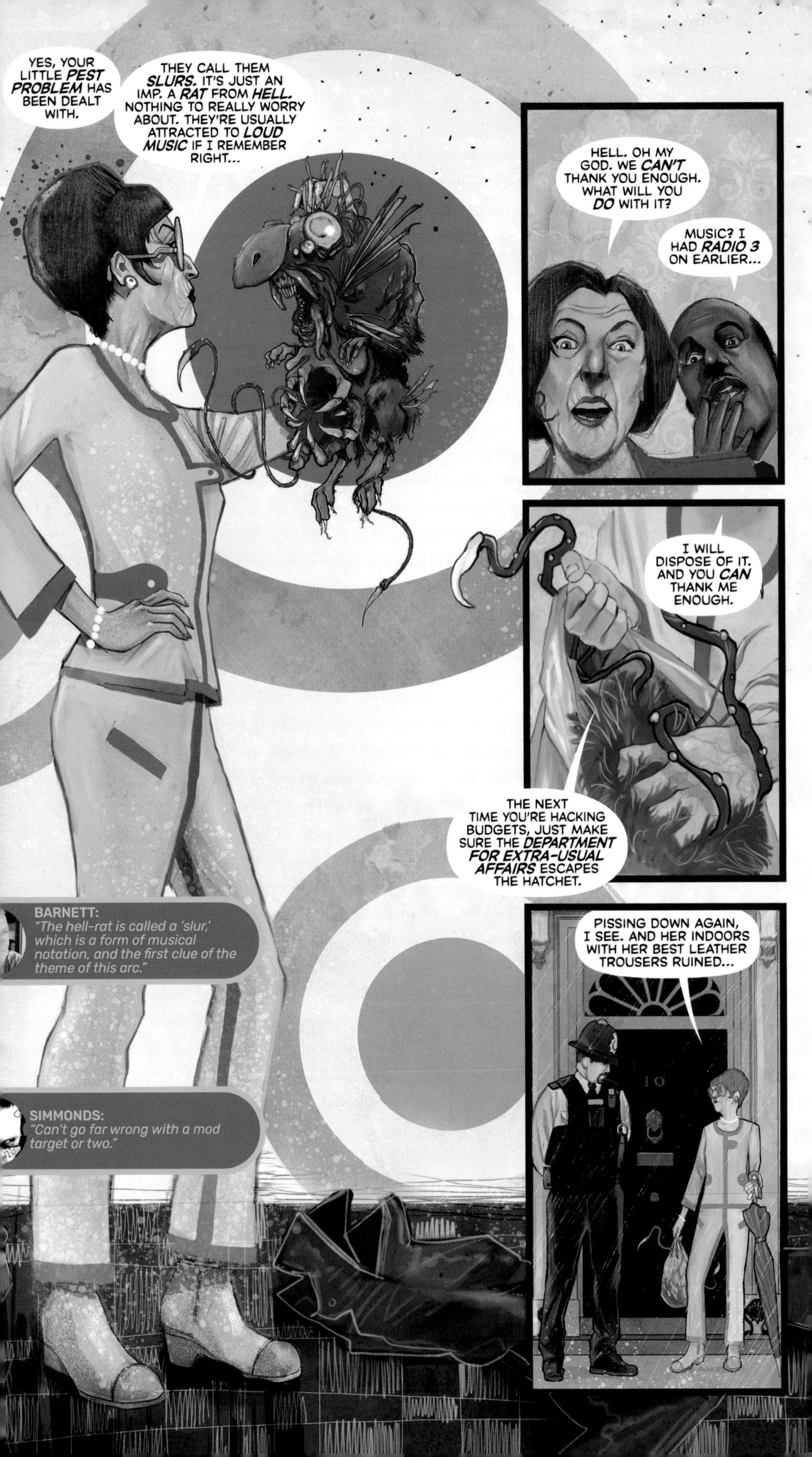
YES, YOUR LITTLE PEST PROBLEM HAS BEEN DEALT WITH.
THEY CALL THEM SLURS. IT'S JUST AN IMP. A RAT FROM HELL. NOTHING TO REALLY WORRY ABOUT. THEY'RE USUALLY ATTRACTED TO LOUD MUSIC IF I REMEMBER RIGHT...
HELL. OH MY GOD. WE CAN'T THANK YOU ENOUGH. WHAT WILL YOU DO WITH IT?
MUSIC? I HAD RADIO 3 ON EARLIER...
I WILL DISPOSE OF IT. AND YOU CAN THANK ME ENOUGH.
THE NEXT TIME YOU'RE HACKING BUDGETS, JUST MAKE SURE THE DEPARTMENT FOR EXTRA-USUAL AFFAIRS ESCAPES THE HATCHET.
PISSING DOWN AGAIN, I SEE. AND HER INDOORS WITH HER BEST LEATHER TROUSERS RUINED...

BARNETT:
"The hell-rat is called a 'slur,' which is a form of musical notation, and the first clue of the theme of this arc."

SIMMONDS:
"Can't go far wrong with a mod target or two."

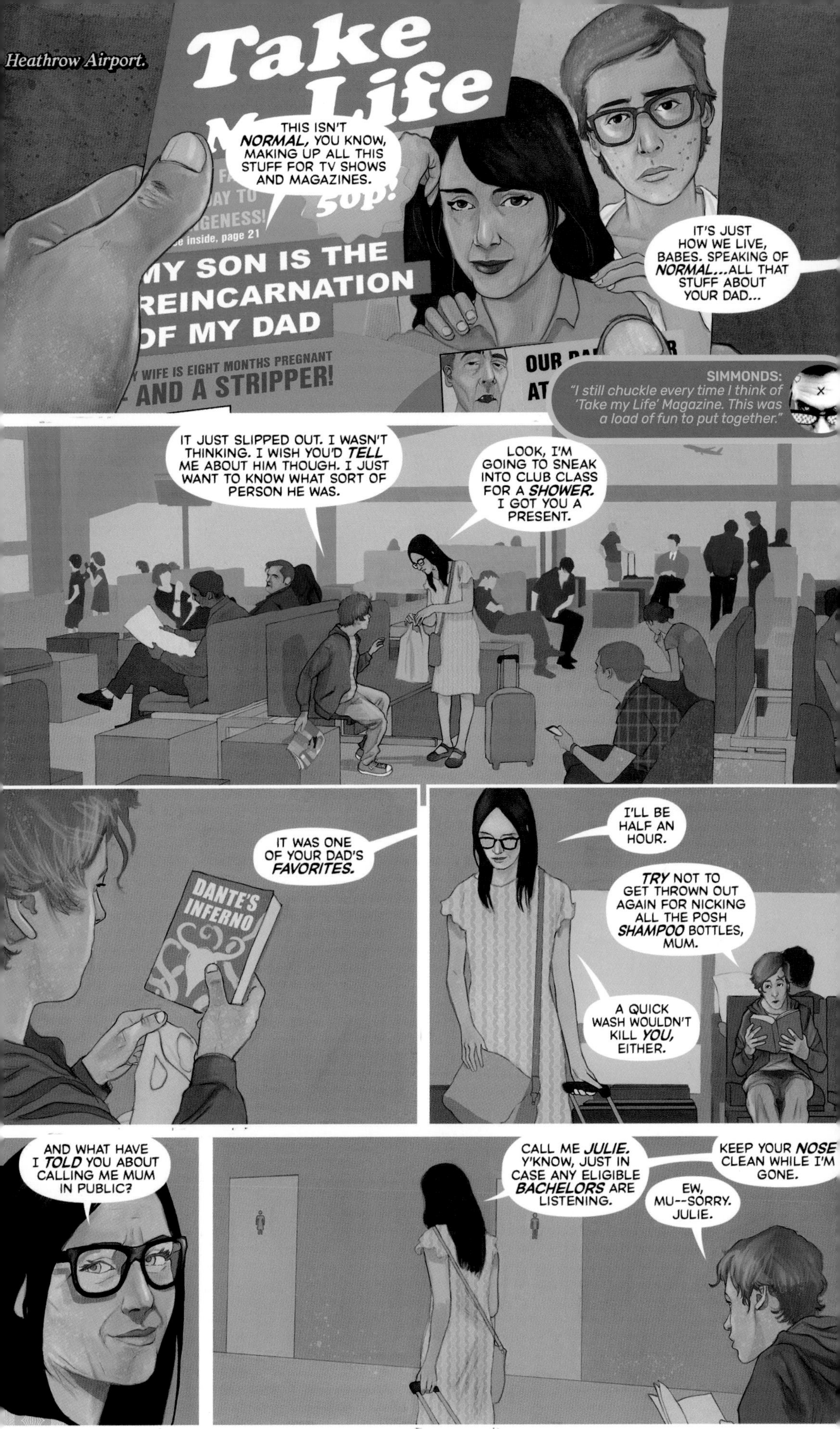

Heathrow Airport.
Take My Life
50p!
MY SON IS THE REINCARNATION OF MY DAD
MY WIFE IS EIGHT MONTHS PREGNANT - AND A STRIPPER!
THIS ISN'T NORMAL, YOU KNOW, MAKING UP ALL THIS STUFF FOR TV SHOWS AND MAGAZINES.
IT'S JUST HOW WE LIVE, BABES. SPEAKING OF NORMAL...ALL THAT STUFF ABOUT YOUR DAD...
SIMMONDS: "I still chuckle every time I think of 'Take my Life' Magazine. This was a load of fun to put together."
IT JUST SLIPPED OUT. I WASN'T THINKING. I WISH YOU'D TELL ME ABOUT HIM THOUGH. I JUST WANT TO KNOW WHAT SORT OF PERSON HE WAS.
LOOK, I'M GOING TO SNEAK INTO CLUB CLASS FOR A SHOWER. I GOT YOU A PRESENT.
IT WAS ONE OF YOUR DAD'S FAVORITES.
DANTE'S INFERNO
I'LL BE HALF AN HOUR.
TRY NOT TO GET THROWN OUT AGAIN FOR NICKING ALL THE POSH SHAMPOO BOTTLES, MUM.
A QUICK WASH WOULDN'T KILL YOU, EITHER.
AND WHAT HAVE I TOLD YOU ABOUT CALLING ME MUM IN PUBLIC?
CALL ME JULIE. Y'KNOW, JUST IN CASE ANY ELIGIBLE BACHELORS ARE LISTENING.
KEEP YOUR NOSE CLEAN WHILE I'M GONE.
EW, MU--SORRY. JULIE.

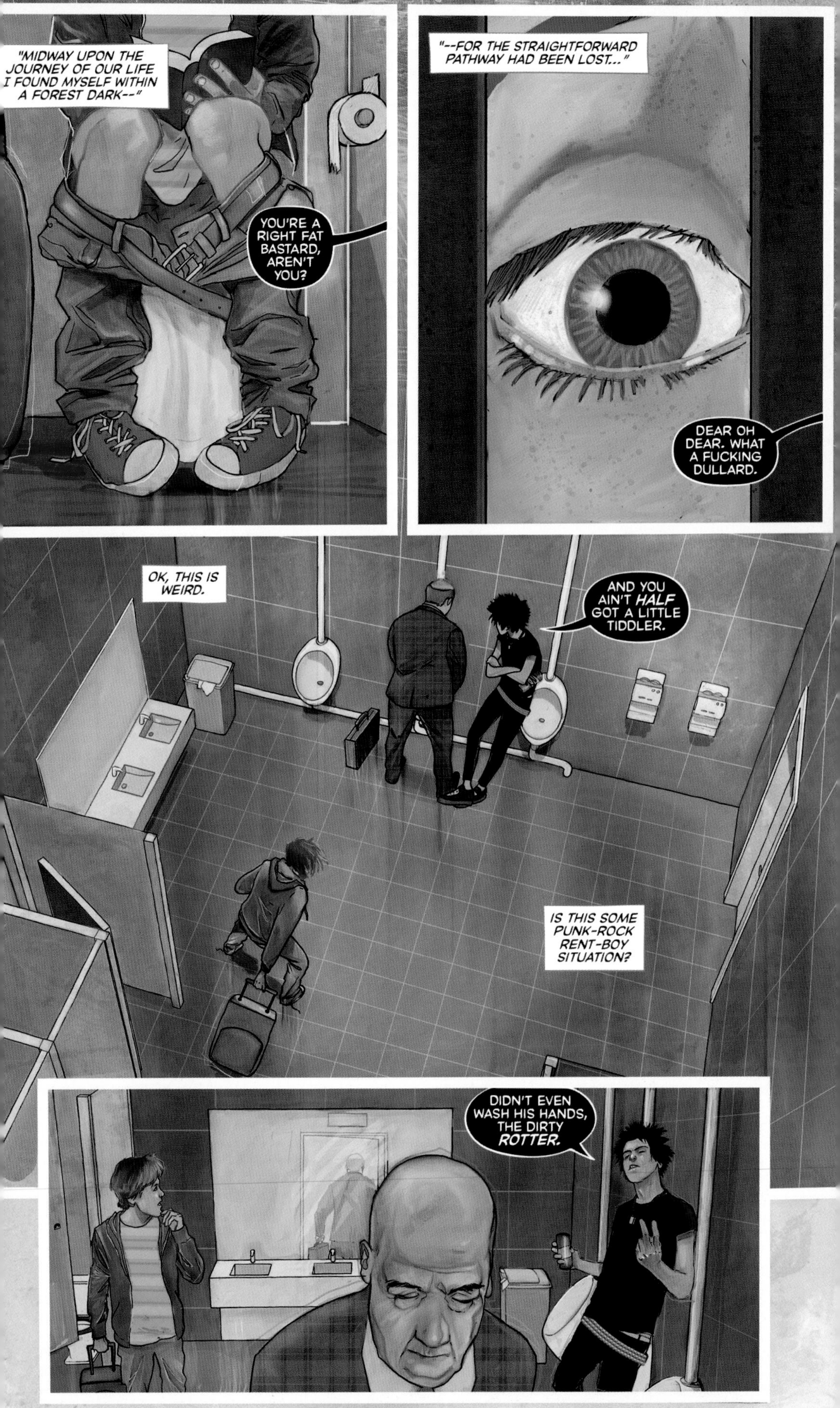
"MIDWAY UPON THE JOURNEY OF OUR LIFE I FOUND MYSELF WITHIN A FOREST DARK--"
YOU'RE A RIGHT FAT BASTARD, AREN'T YOU?
"--FOR THE STRAIGHTFORWARD PATHWAY HAD BEEN LOST..."
DEAR OH DEAR. WHAT A FUCKING DULLARD.
OK, THIS IS WEIRD.
AND YOU AIN'T HALF GOT A LITTLE TIDDLER.
IS THIS SOME PUNK-ROCK RENT-BOY SITUATION?
DIDN'T EVEN WASH HIS HANDS, THE DIRTY ROTTER.

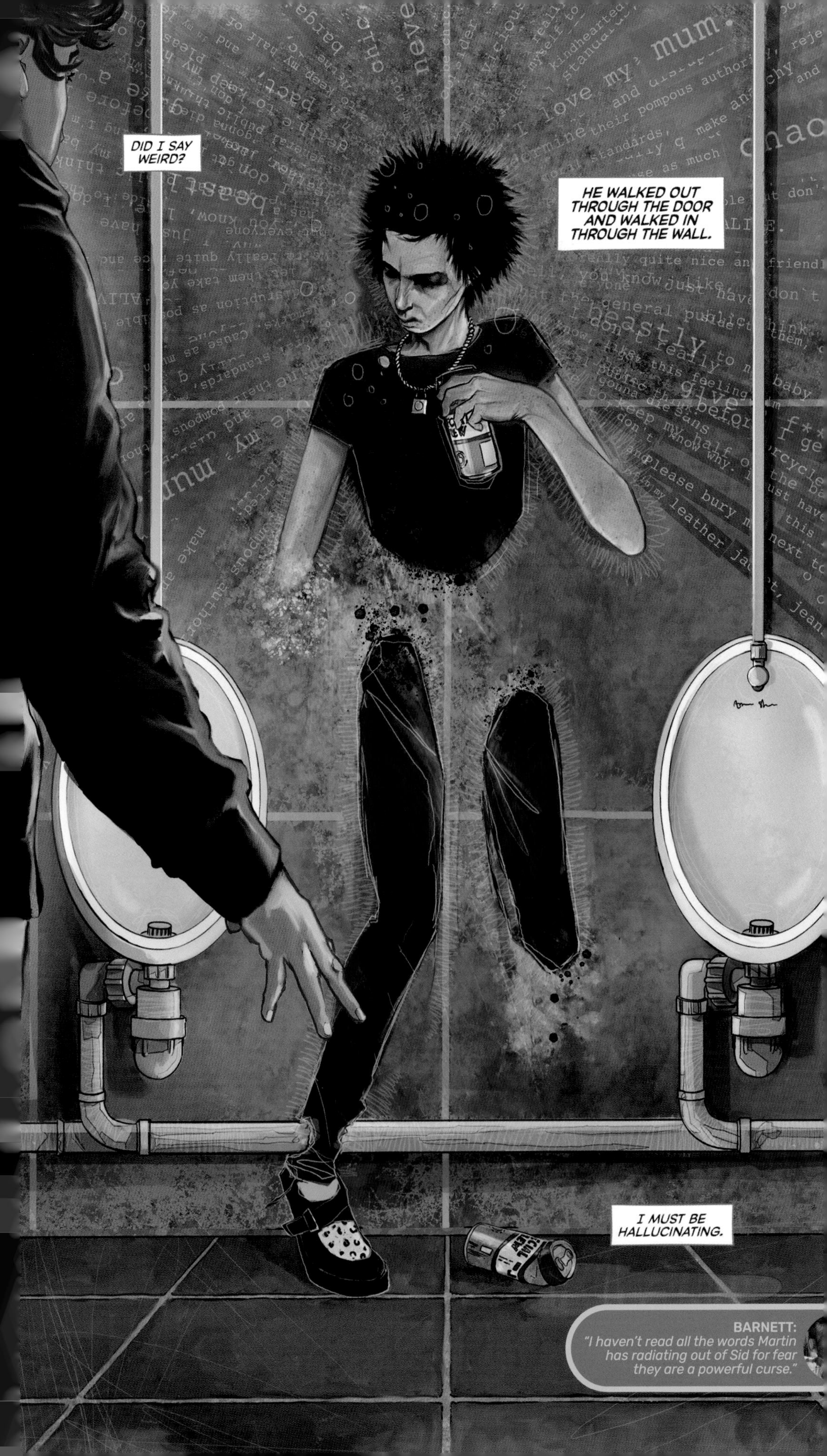
DID I SAY WEIRD?
HE WALKED OUT THROUGH THE DOOR AND WALKED IN THROUGH THE WALL.
I MUST BE HALLUCINATING.
BARNETT:
"I haven't read all the words Martin has radiating out of Sid for fear they are a powerful curse."

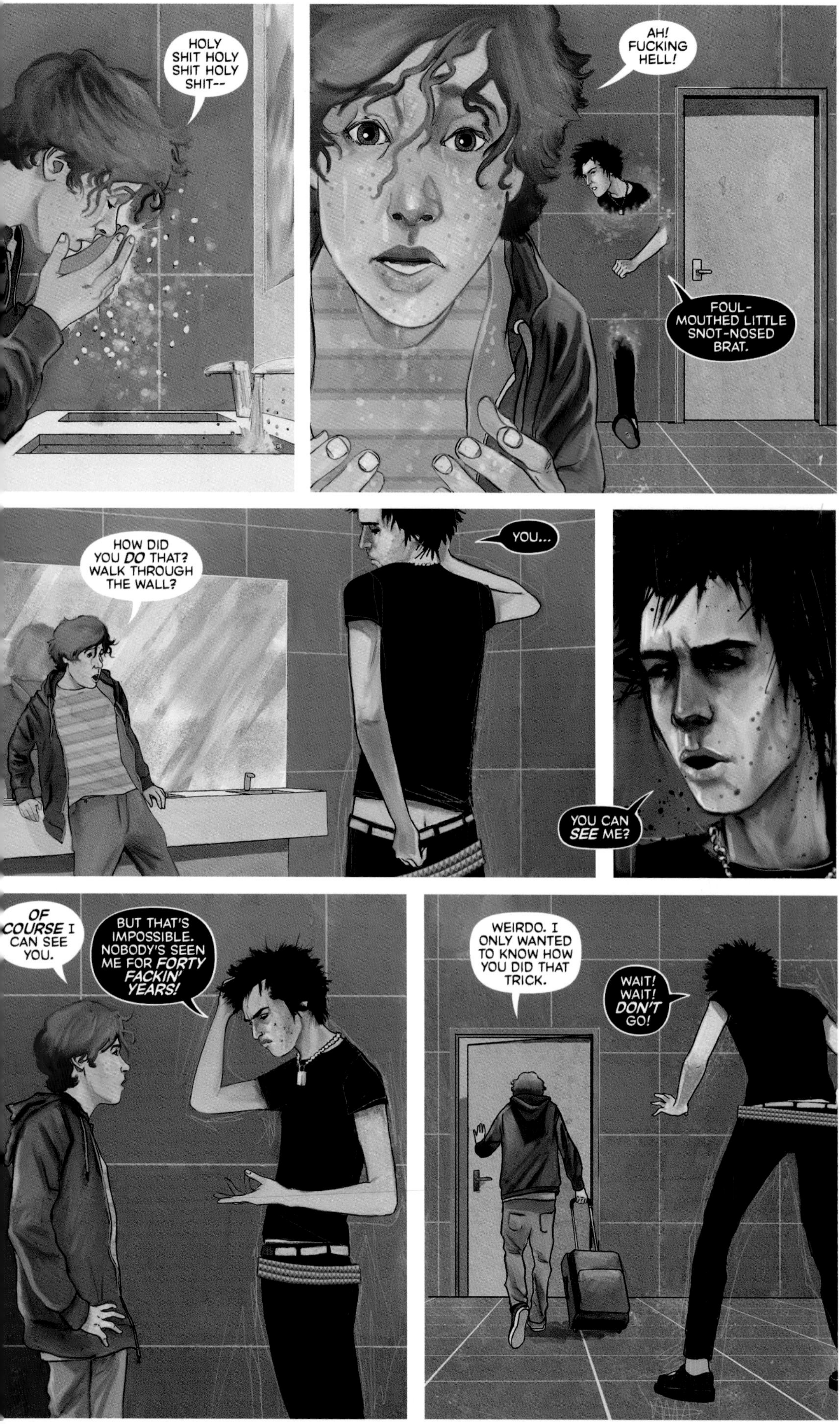

HOLY SHIT HOLY SHIT HOLY SHIT--
AH! FUCKING HELL!
FOUL-MOUTHED LITTLE SNOT-NOSED BRAT.
HOW DID YOU DO THAT? WALK THROUGH THE WALL?
YOU...
YOU CAN SEE ME?
OF COURSE I CAN SEE YOU.
BUT THAT'S IMPOSSIBLE. NOBODY'S SEEN ME FOR FORTY FACKIN' YEARS!
WEIRDO. I ONLY WANTED TO KNOW HOW YOU DID THAT TRICK.
WAIT! WAIT! DON'T GO!

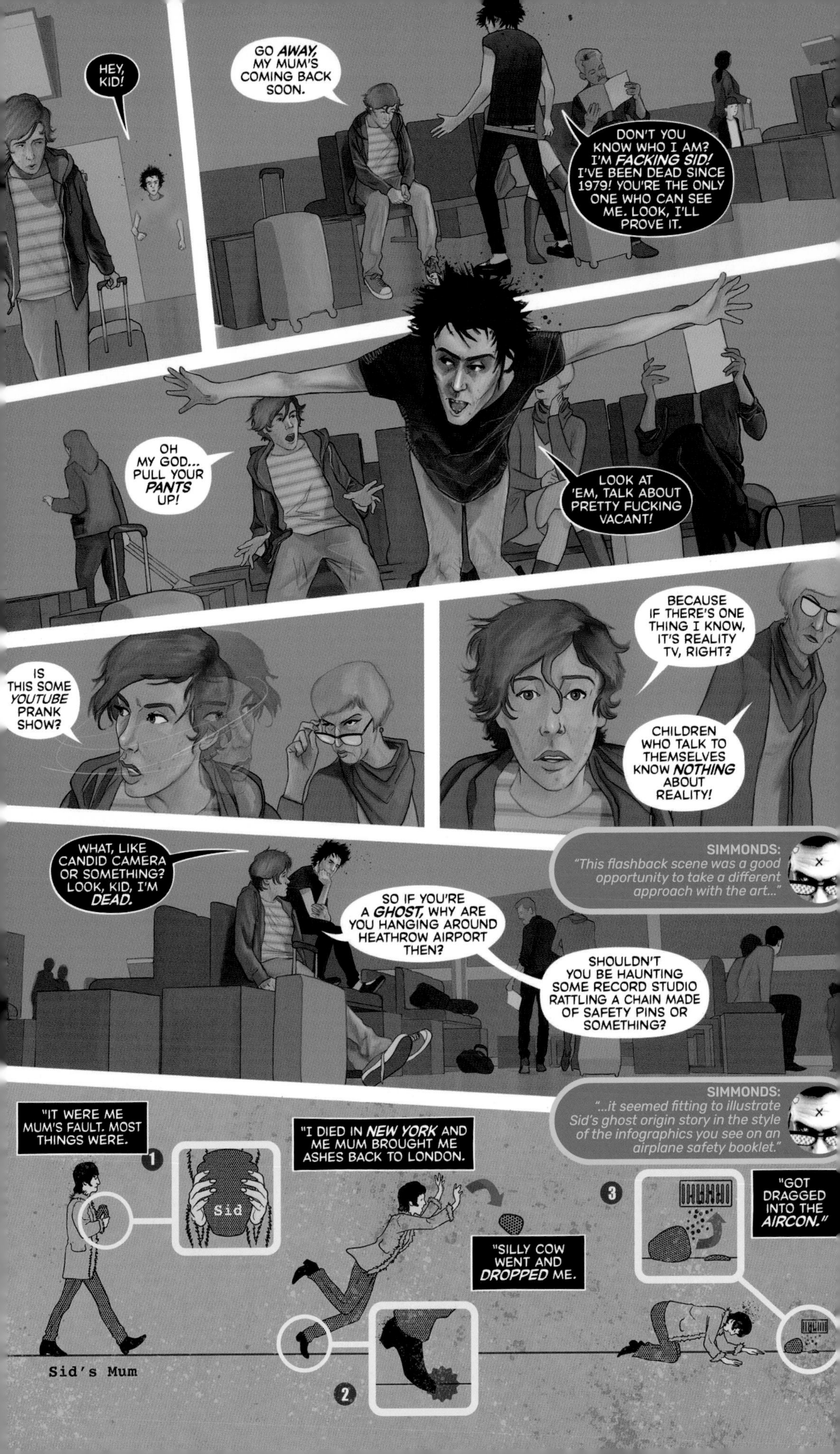
HEY, KID!
GO AWAY, MY MUM'S COMING BACK SOON.
DON'T YOU KNOW WHO I AM? I'M FACKING SID! I'VE BEEN DEAD SINCE 1979! YOU'RE THE ONLY ONE WHO CAN SEE ME. LOOK, I'LL PROVE IT.
OH MY GOD... PULL YOUR PANTS UP!
LOOK AT 'EM, TALK ABOUT PRETTY FUCKING VACANT!
IS THIS SOME YOUTUBE PRANK SHOW?
BECAUSE IF THERE'S ONE THING I KNOW, IT'S REALITY TV, RIGHT?
CHILDREN WHO TALK TO THEMSELVES KNOW NOTHING ABOUT REALITY!
WHAT, LIKE CANDID CAMERA OR SOMETHING? LOOK, KID, I'M DEAD.
SIMMONDS: "This flashback scene was a good opportunity to take a different approach with the art..."
SO IF YOU'RE A GHOST, WHY ARE YOU HANGING AROUND HEATHROW AIRPORT THEN?
SHOULDN'T YOU BE HAUNTING SOME RECORD STUDIO RATTLING A CHAIN MADE OF SAFETY PINS OR SOMETHING?
SIMMONDS: "...it seemed fitting to illustrate Sid's ghost origin story in the style of the infographics you see on an airplane safety booklet."
"IT WERE ME MUM'S FAULT. MOST THINGS WERE.
1
Sid
Sid's Mum
"I DIED IN NEW YORK AND ME MUM BROUGHT ME ASHES BACK TO LONDON.
"SILLY COW WENT AND DROPPED ME.
2
3
"GOT DRAGGED INTO THE AIRCON."

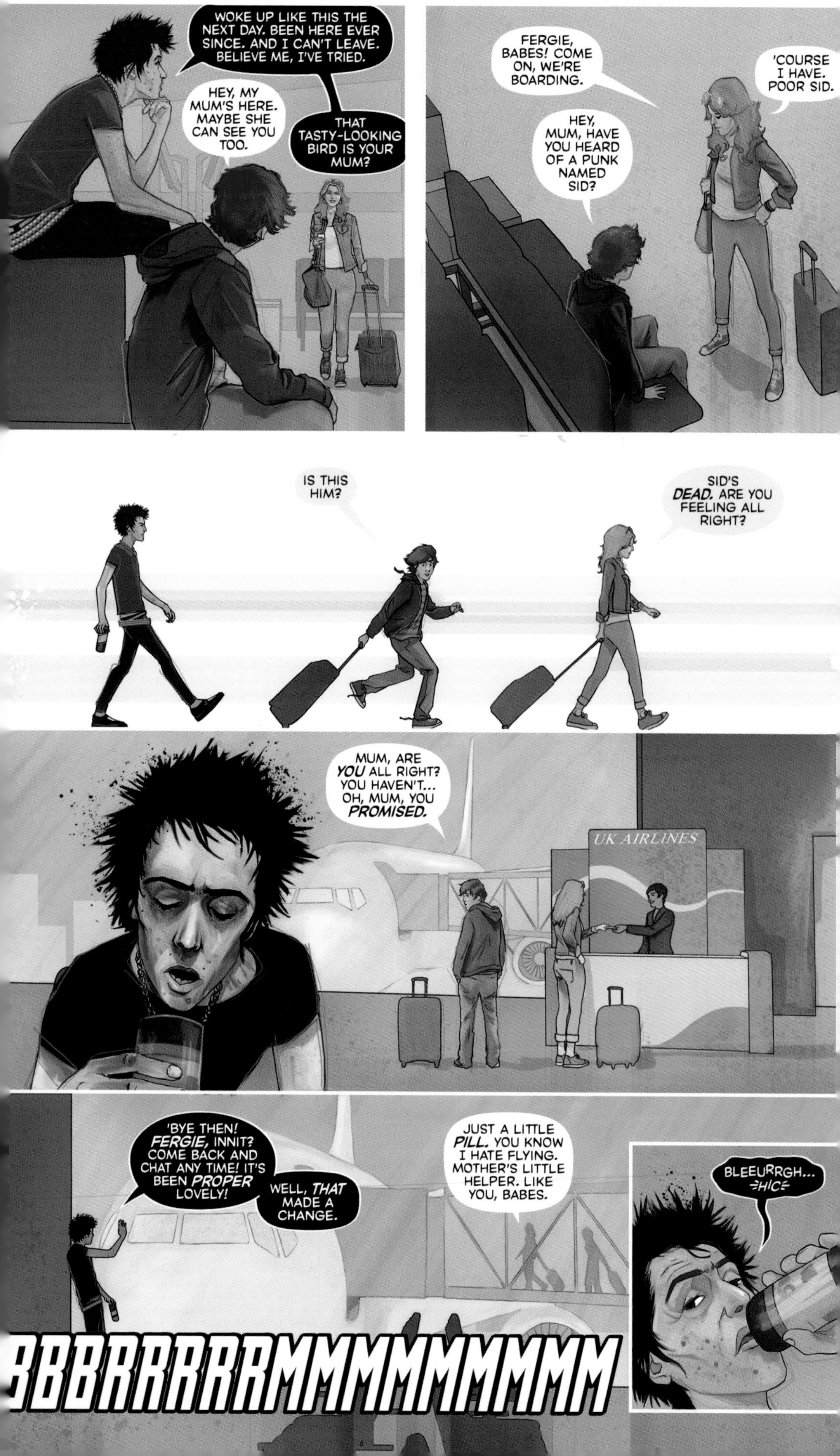
WOKE UP LIKE THIS THE NEXT DAY. BEEN HERE EVER SINCE. AND I CAN'T LEAVE. BELIEVE ME, I'VE TRIED.
HEY, MY MUM'S HERE. MAYBE SHE CAN SEE YOU TOO.
THAT TASTY-LOOKING BIRD IS YOUR MUM?
FERGIE, BABES! COME ON, WE'RE BOARDING.
HEY, MUM, HAVE YOU HEARD OF A PUNK NAMED SID?
'COURSE I HAVE. POOR SID.
IS THIS HIM?
SID'S DEAD. ARE YOU FEELING ALL RIGHT?
MUM, ARE YOU ALL RIGHT? YOU HAVEN'T... OH, MUM, YOU PROMISED.
UK AIRLINES
'BYE THEN! FERGIE, INNIT? COME BACK AND CHAT ANY TIME! IT'S BEEN PROPER LOVELY!
WELL, THAT MADE A CHANGE.
JUST A LITTLE PILL. YOU KNOW I HATE FLYING. MOTHER'S LITTLE HELPER. LIKE YOU, BABES.
BBBRRRRRRMMMMMMMMMM
BLEEURRGH... HIC

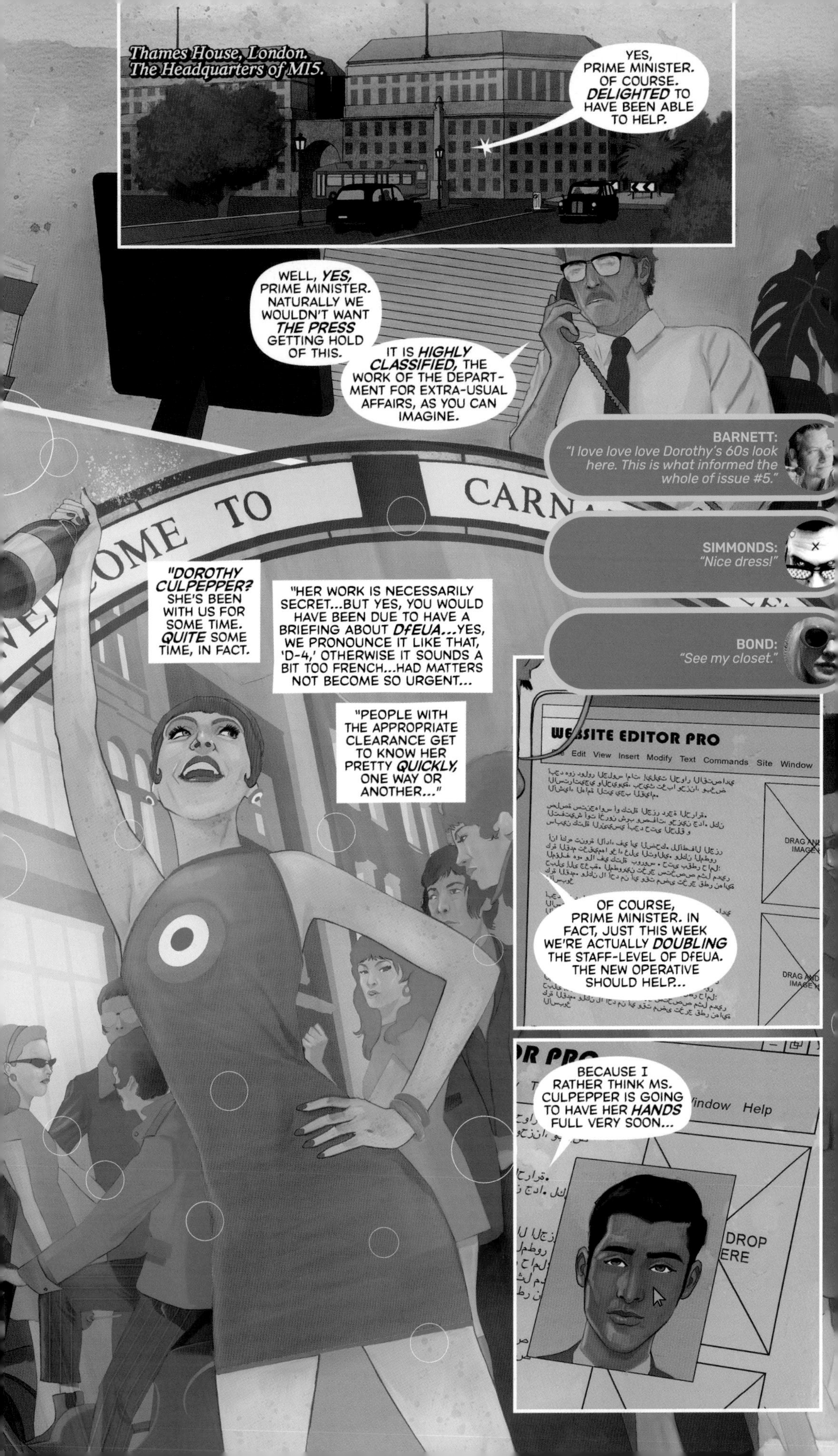
Thames House, London. The Headquarters of MI5.
YES, PRIME MINISTER. OF COURSE. DELIGHTED TO HAVE BEEN ABLE TO HELP.
WELL, YES, PRIME MINISTER. NATURALLY WE WOULDN'T WANT THE PRESS GETTING HOLD OF THIS.
IT IS HIGHLY CLASSIFIED, THE WORK OF THE DEPARTMENT FOR EXTRA-USUAL AFFAIRS, AS YOU CAN IMAGINE.
BARNETT: "I love love love Dorothy's 60s look here. This is what informed the whole of issue #5."
SIMMONDS: "Nice dress!"
BOND: "See my closet."
WELCOME TO CARNA
"DOROTHY CULPEPPER? SHE'S BEEN WITH US FOR SOME TIME. QUITE SOME TIME, IN FACT.
"HER WORK IS NECESSARILY SECRET...BUT YES, YOU WOULD HAVE BEEN DUE TO HAVE A BRIEFING ABOUT DfEUA...YES, WE PRONOUNCE IT LIKE THAT, 'D-4,' OTHERWISE IT SOUNDS A BIT TOO FRENCH...HAD MATTERS NOT BECOME SO URGENT...
"PEOPLE WITH THE APPROPRIATE CLEARANCE GET TO KNOW HER PRETTY QUICKLY, ONE WAY OR ANOTHER..."
WEBSITE EDITOR PRO
Edit View Insert Modify Text Commands Site Window
DRAG AND DROP IMAGE HERE
OF COURSE, PRIME MINISTER. IN FACT, JUST THIS WEEK WE'RE ACTUALLY DOUBLING THE STAFF-LEVEL OF DfEUA. THE NEW OPERATIVE SHOULD HELP...
BECAUSE I RATHER THINK MS. CULPEPPER IS GOING TO HAVE HER HANDS FULL VERY SOON...
Window Help
DROP HERE

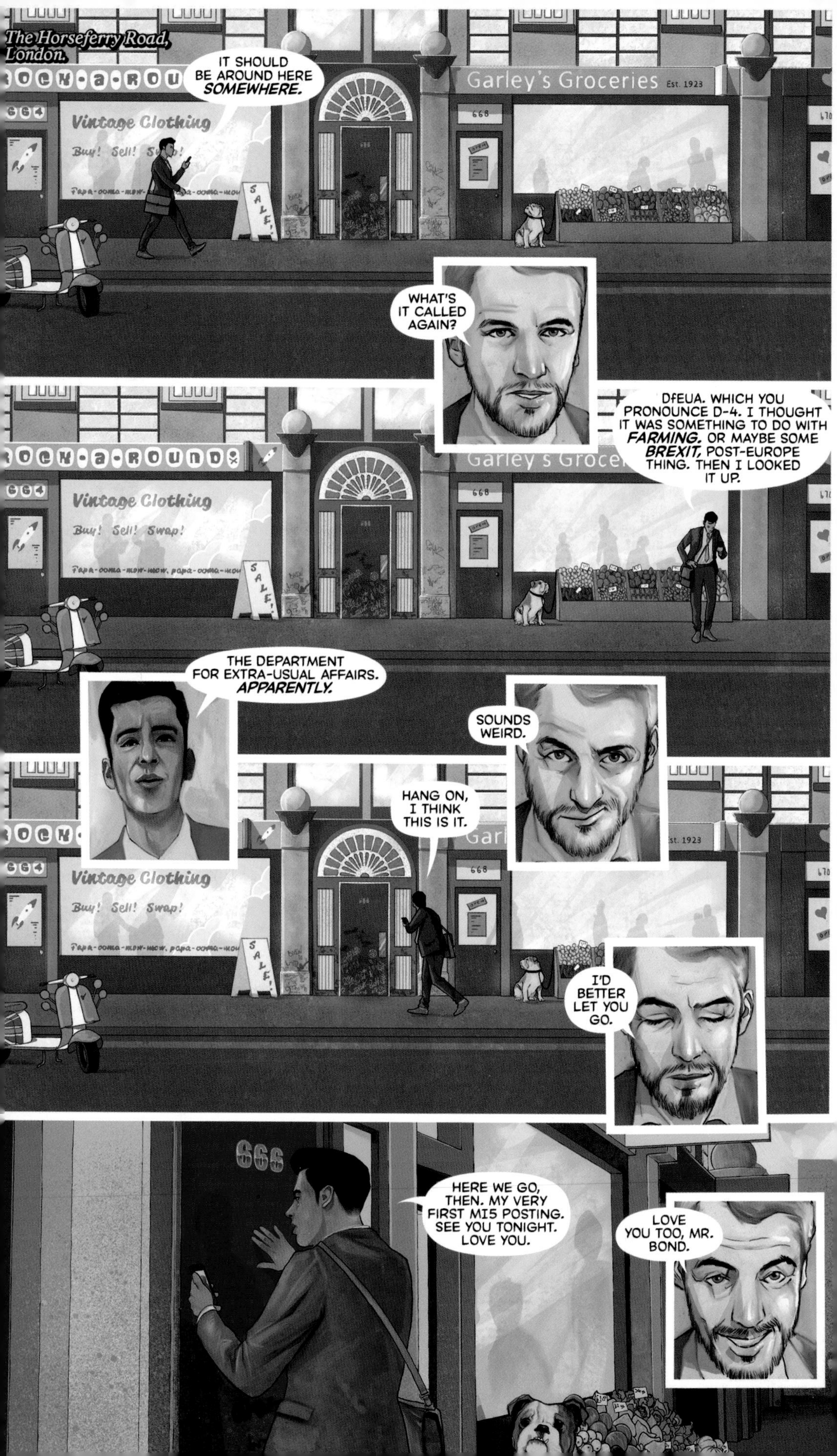
The Horseferry Road, London.
IT SHOULD BE AROUND HERE SOMEWHERE.
ROCK-A-ROUND
Vintage Clothing
Buy! Sell! Swap!
Garley's Groceries Est. 1923
668
SALE
WHAT'S IT CALLED AGAIN?
DfEUA. WHICH YOU PRONOUNCE D-4. I THOUGHT IT WAS SOMETHING TO DO WITH FARMING. OR MAYBE SOME BREXIT, POST-EUROPE THING. THEN I LOOKED IT UP.
THE DEPARTMENT FOR EXTRA-USUAL AFFAIRS. APPARENTLY.
SOUNDS WEIRD.
HANG ON, I THINK THIS IS IT.
I'D BETTER LET YOU GO.
666
HERE WE GO, THEN. MY VERY FIRST MI5 POSTING. SEE YOU TONIGHT. LOVE YOU.
LOVE YOU TOO, MR. BOND.

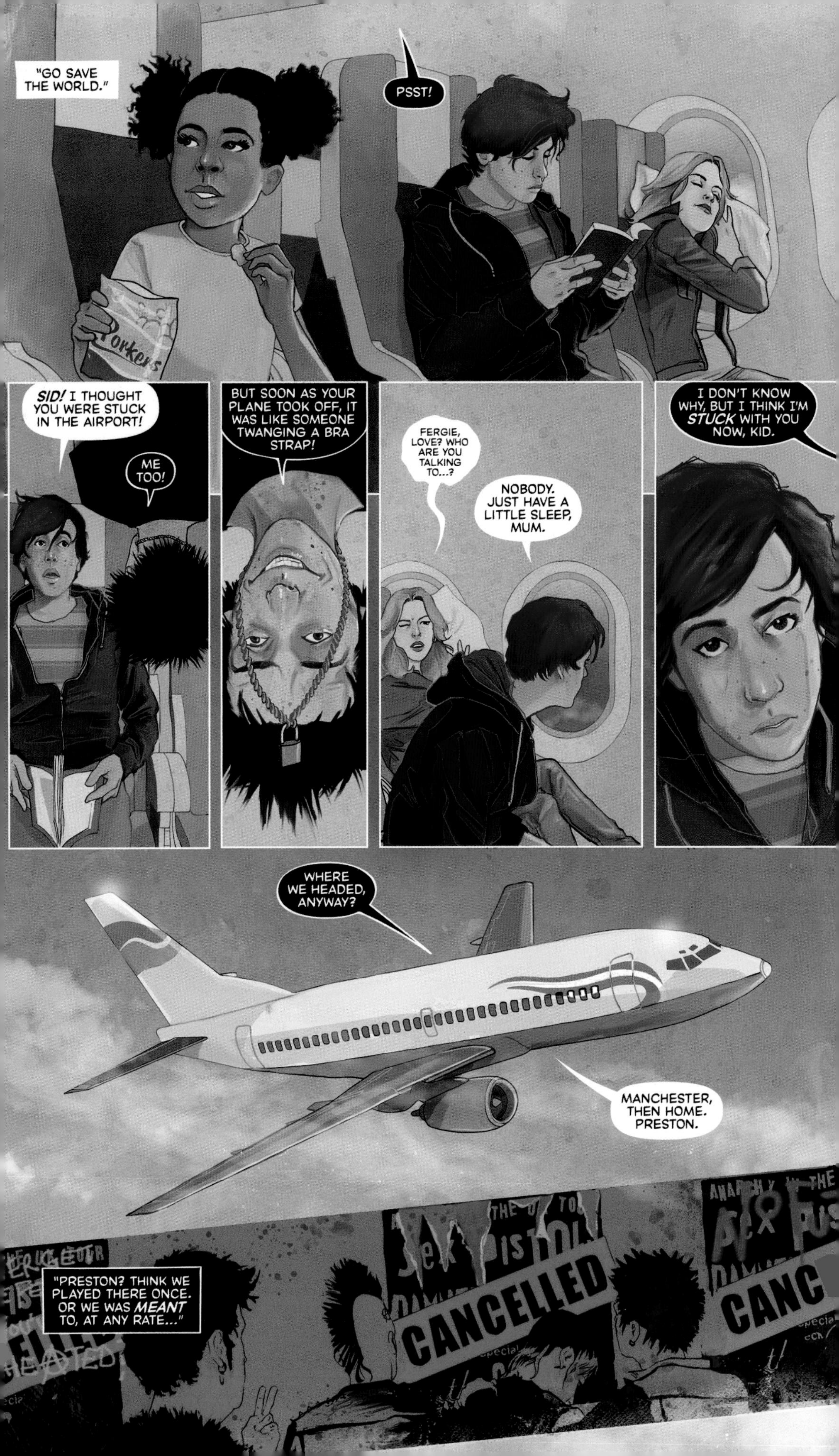
"GO SAVE THE WORLD."
PSST!
SID! I THOUGHT YOU WERE STUCK IN THE AIRPORT!
ME TOO!
BUT SOON AS YOUR PLANE TOOK OFF, IT WAS LIKE SOMEONE TWANGING A BRA STRAP!
FERGIE, LOVE? WHO ARE YOU TALKING TO...?
NOBODY. JUST HAVE A LITTLE SLEEP, MUM.
I DON'T KNOW WHY, BUT I THINK I'M STUCK WITH YOU NOW, KID.
WHERE WE HEADED, ANYWAY?
MANCHESTER, THEN HOME. PRESTON.
"PRESTON? THINK WE PLAYED THERE ONCE. OR WE WAS MEANT TO, AT ANY RATE..."
CANCELLED

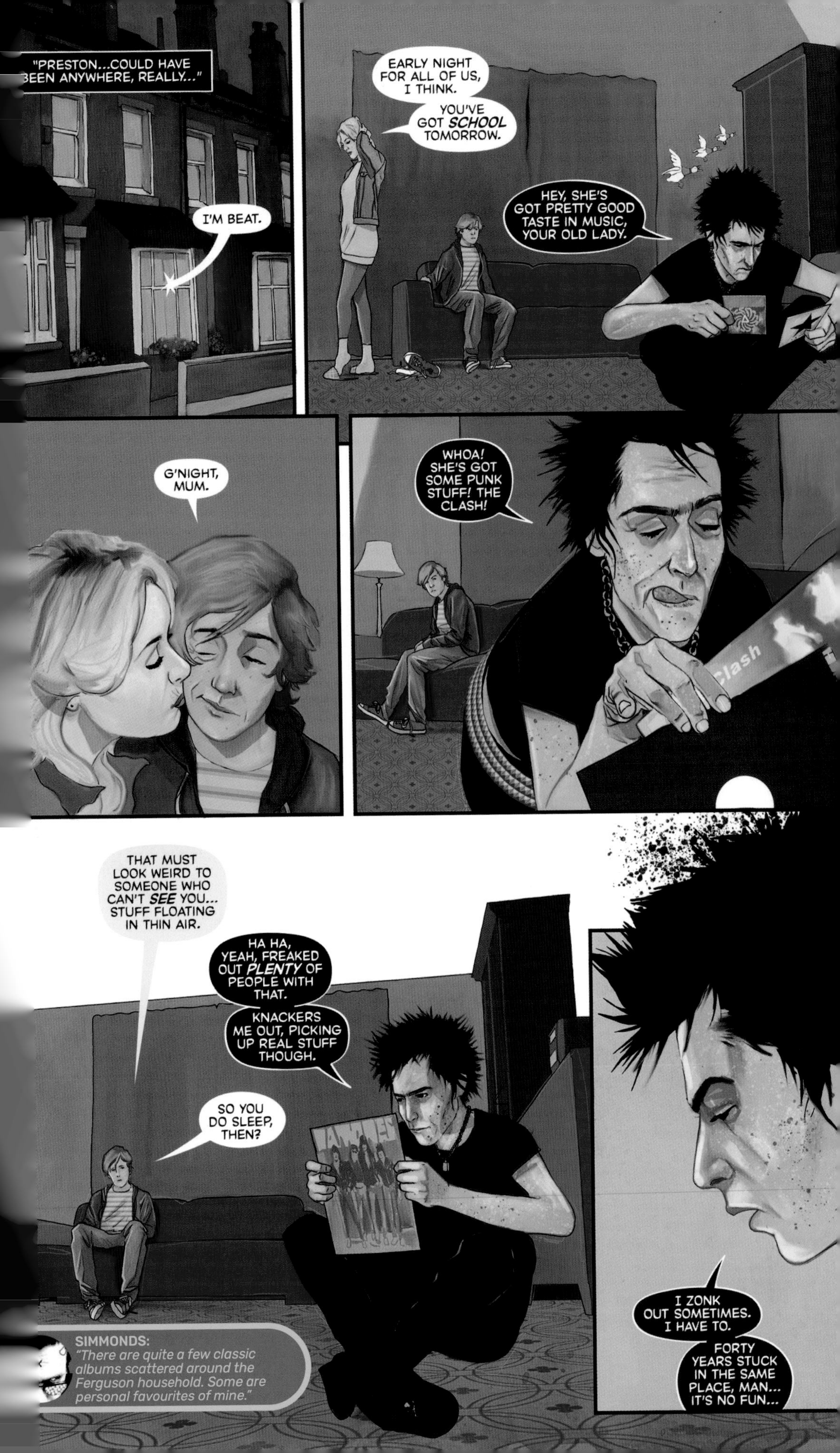
"PRESTON...COULD HAVE BEEN ANYWHERE, REALLY..."
I'M BEAT.
EARLY NIGHT FOR ALL OF US, I THINK.
YOU'VE GOT SCHOOL TOMORROW.
HEY, SHE'S GOT PRETTY GOOD TASTE IN MUSIC, YOUR OLD LADY.
G'NIGHT, MUM.
WHOA! SHE'S GOT SOME PUNK STUFF! THE CLASH!
Clash
THAT MUST LOOK WEIRD TO SOMEONE WHO CAN'T SEE YOU... STUFF FLOATING IN THIN AIR.
HA HA, YEAH, FREAKED OUT PLENTY OF PEOPLE WITH THAT.
KNACKERS ME OUT, PICKING UP REAL STUFF THOUGH.
SO YOU DO SLEEP, THEN?
I ZONK OUT SOMETIMES. I HAVE TO.
FORTY YEARS STUCK IN THE SAME PLACE, MAN... IT'S NO FUN...
SIMMONDS:
"There are quite a few classic albums scattered around the Ferguson household. Some are personal favourites of mine."

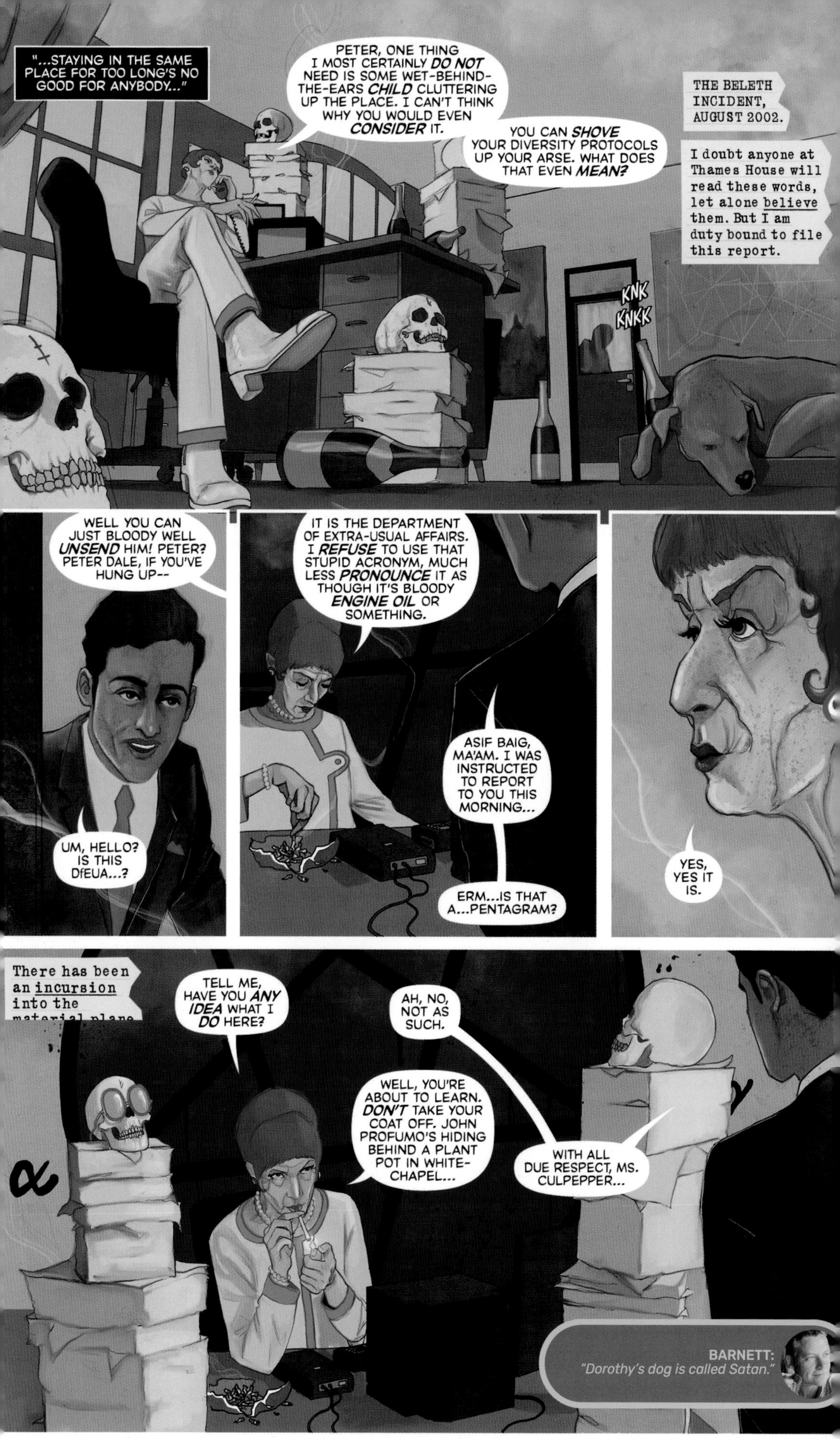

"...STAYING IN THE SAME PLACE FOR TOO LONG'S NO GOOD FOR ANYBODY..."
PETER, ONE THING I MOST CERTAINLY *DO NOT* NEED IS SOME WET-BEHIND-THE-EARS *CHILD* CLUTTERING UP THE PLACE. I CAN'T THINK WHY YOU WOULD EVEN *CONSIDER* IT.
YOU CAN *SHOVE* YOUR DIVERSITY PROTOCOLS UP YOUR ARSE. WHAT DOES THAT EVEN *MEAN?*
THE BELETH INCIDENT, AUGUST 2002.
I doubt anyone at Thames House will read these words, let alone believe them. But I am duty bound to file this report.
KNK KNKK
WELL YOU CAN JUST BLOODY WELL *UNSEND* HIM! PETER? PETER DALE, IF YOU'VE HUNG UP--
UM, HELLO? IS THIS DfEUA...?
IT IS THE DEPARTMENT OF EXTRA-USUAL AFFAIRS. I *REFUSE* TO USE THAT STUPID ACRONYM, MUCH LESS *PRONOUNCE* IT AS THOUGH IT'S BLOODY *ENGINE OIL* OR SOMETHING.
ASIF BAIG, MA'AM. I WAS INSTRUCTED TO REPORT TO YOU THIS MORNING...
ERM...IS THAT A...PENTAGRAM?
YES, YES IT IS.
There has been an incursion into the material plane
TELL ME, HAVE YOU *ANY IDEA* WHAT I *DO* HERE?
AH, NO, NOT AS SUCH.
WELL, YOU'RE ABOUT TO LEARN. *DON'T* TAKE YOUR COAT OFF. JOHN PROFUMO'S HIDING BEHIND A PLANT POT IN WHITE-CHAPEL...
WITH ALL DUE RESPECT, MS. CULPEPPER...
BARNETT: "Dorothy's dog is called Satan."

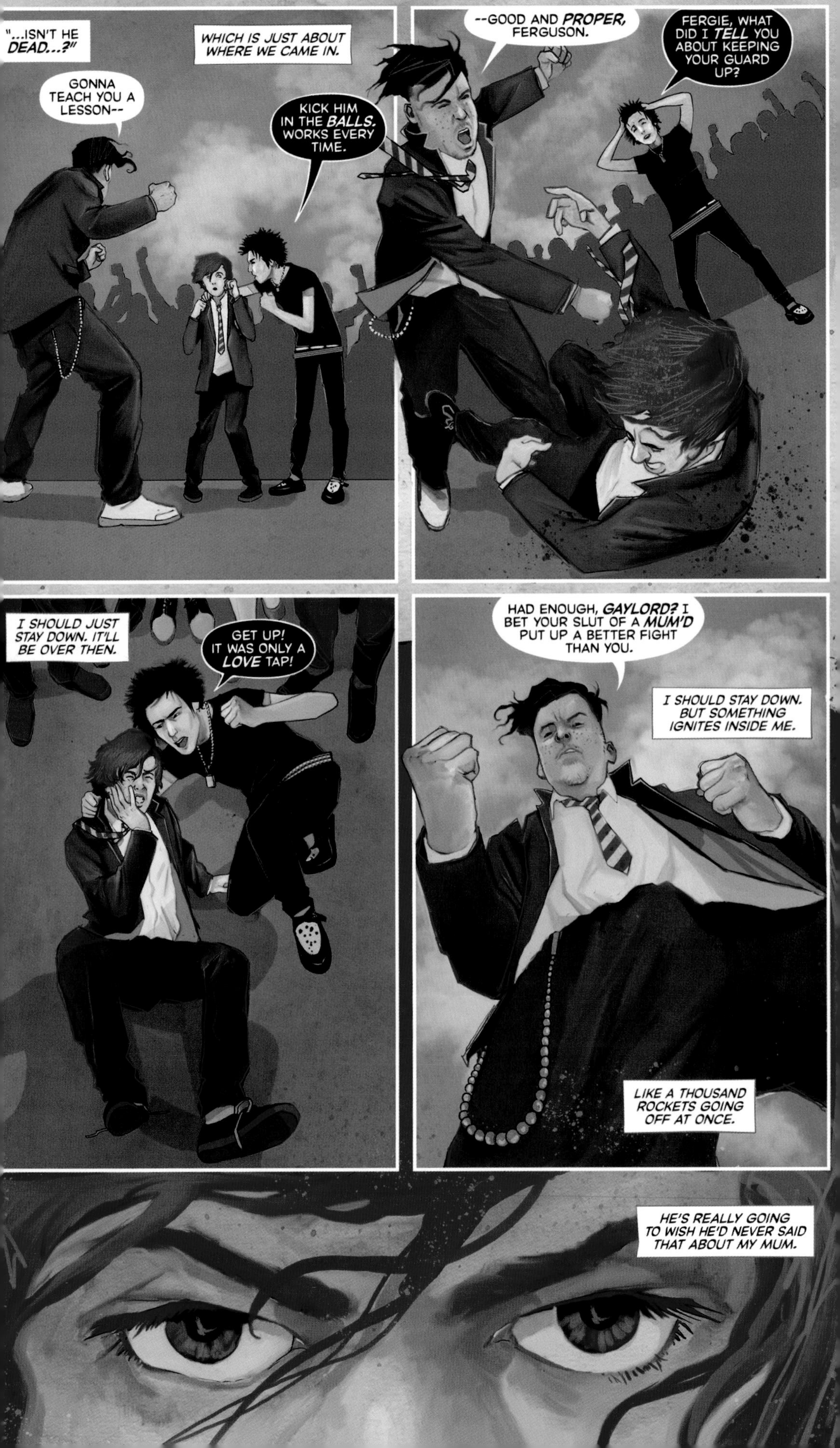
"...ISN'T HE DEAD...?"
WHICH IS JUST ABOUT WHERE WE CAME IN.
GONNA TEACH YOU A LESSON--
KICK HIM IN THE BALLS. WORKS EVERY TIME.
--GOOD AND PROPER, FERGUSON.
FERGIE, WHAT DID I TELL YOU ABOUT KEEPING YOUR GUARD UP?
I SHOULD JUST STAY DOWN. IT'LL BE OVER THEN.
GET UP! IT WAS ONLY A LOVE TAP!
HAD ENOUGH, GAYLORD? I BET YOUR SLUT OF A MUM'D PUT UP A BETTER FIGHT THAN YOU.
I SHOULD STAY DOWN. BUT SOMETHING IGNITES INSIDE ME.
LIKE A THOUSAND ROCKETS GOING OFF AT ONCE.
HE'S REALLY GOING TO WISH HE'D NEVER SAID THAT ABOUT MY MUM.

SIMMONDS:
"This page was a last-minute addition to the issue, and it's one of my favourite pages. It really pulls this scene together."

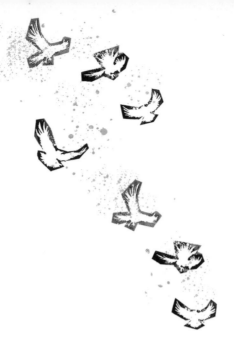

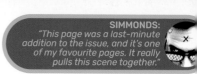

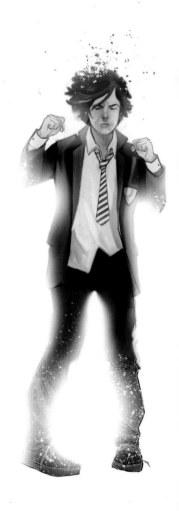

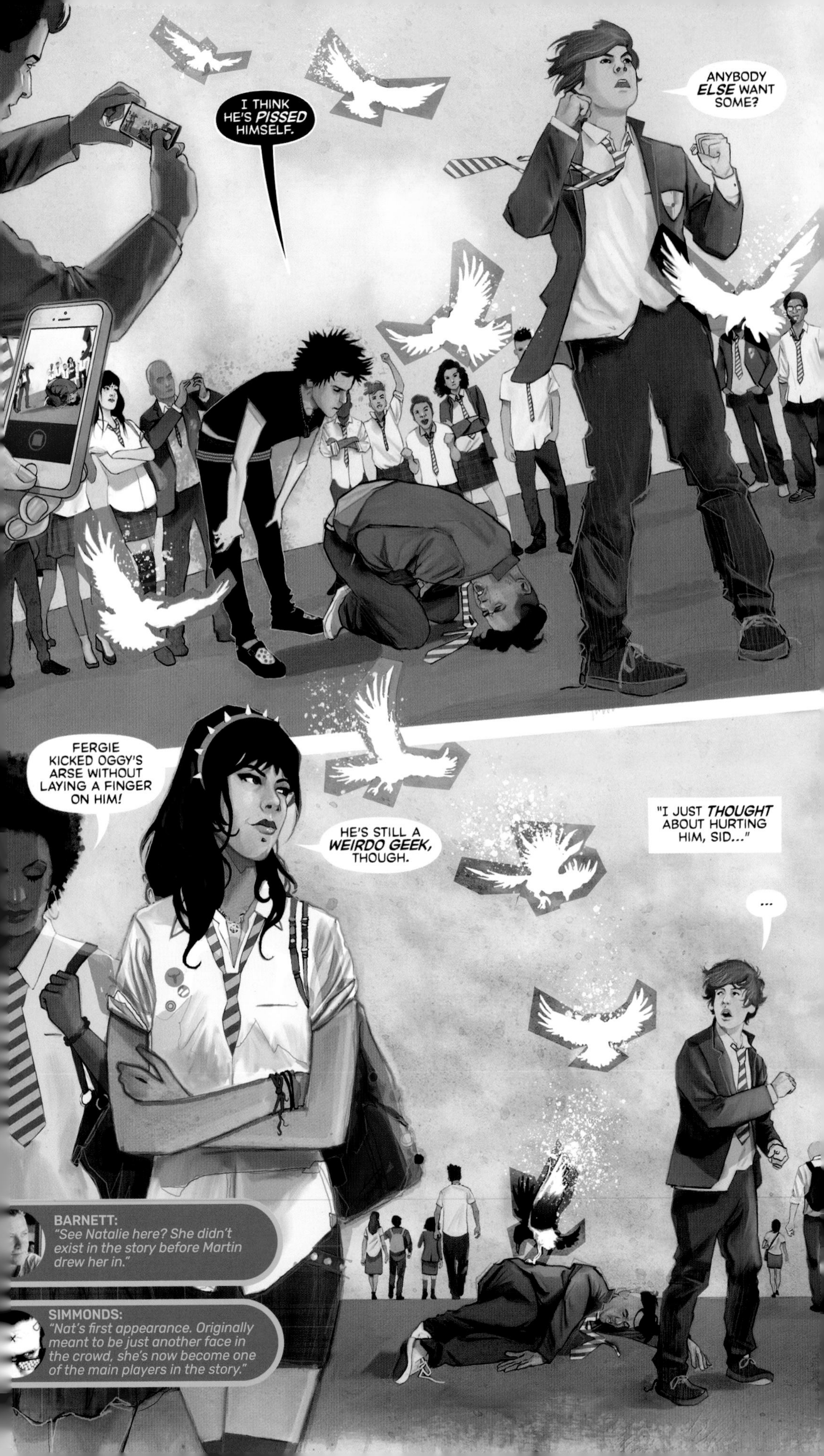

I THINK HE'S *PISSED* HIMSELF.
ANYBODY *ELSE* WANT SOME?
FERGIE KICKED OGGY'S ARSE WITHOUT LAYING A FINGER ON HIM!
HE'S STILL A *WEIRDO GEEK,* THOUGH.
"I JUST *THOUGHT* ABOUT HURTING HIM, SID..."
...
BARNETT:
"See Natalie here? She didn't exist in the story before Martin drew her in."
SIMMONDS:
"Nat's first appearance. Originally meant to be just another face in the crowd, she's now become one of the main players in the story."

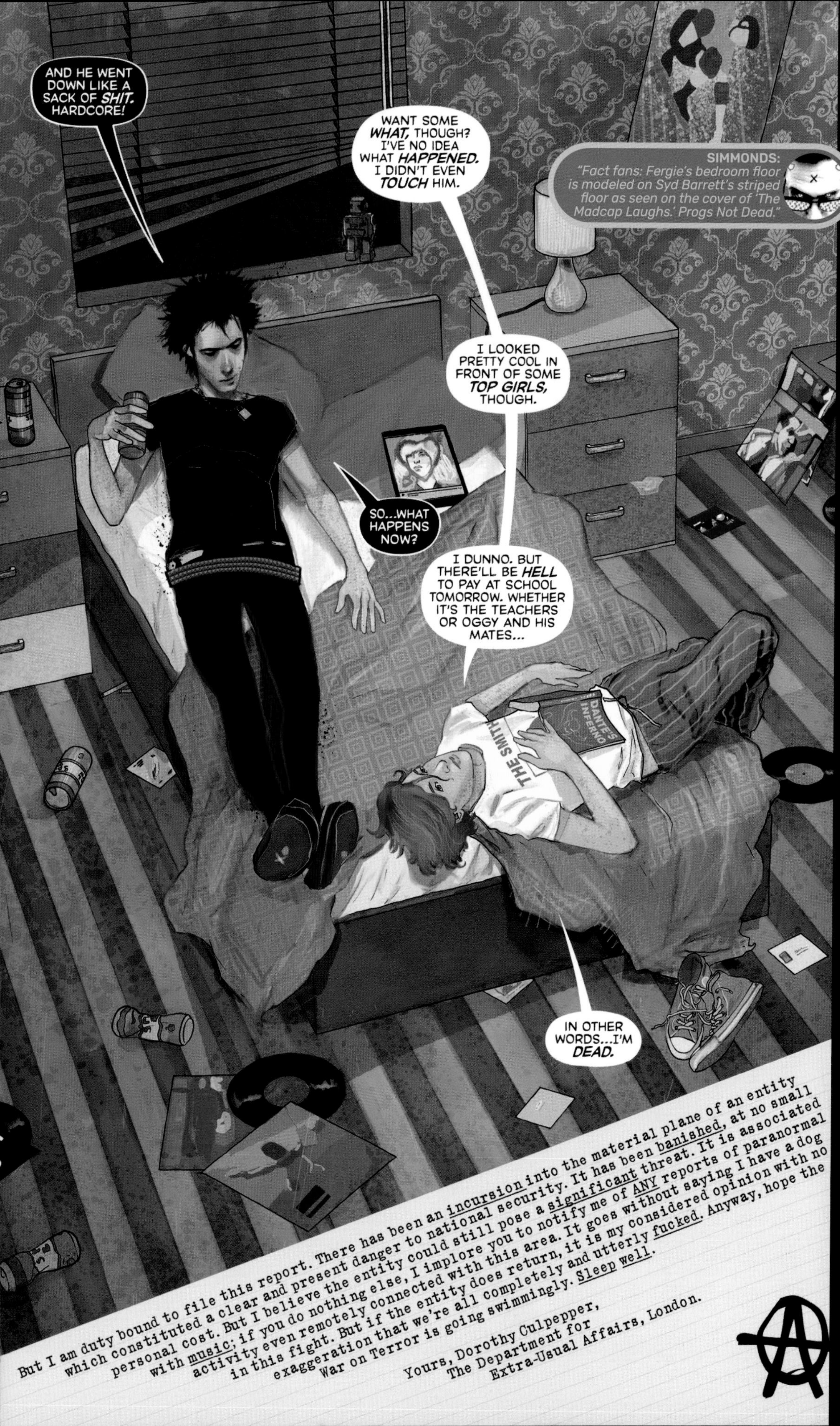

AND HE WENT DOWN LIKE A SACK OF *SHIT.* HARDCORE!
WANT SOME *WHAT,* THOUGH? I'VE NO IDEA WHAT *HAPPENED.* I DIDN'T EVEN *TOUCH* HIM.
SIMMONDS: *"Fact fans: Fergie's bedroom floor is modeled on Syd Barrett's striped floor as seen on the cover of 'The Madcap Laughs.' Progs Not Dead."*
I LOOKED PRETTY COOL IN FRONT OF SOME *TOP GIRLS,* THOUGH.
SO...WHAT HAPPENS NOW?
I DUNNO. BUT THERE'LL BE *HELL* TO PAY AT SCHOOL TOMORROW. WHETHER IT'S THE TEACHERS OR OGGY AND HIS MATES...
THE SMITHS
DANTE'S INFERNO
IN OTHER WORDS...I'M *DEAD.*
But I am duty bound to file this report. There has been an incursion into the material plane of an entity which constituted a clear and present danger to national security. It has been banished, at no small personal cost. But I believe the entity could still pose a significant threat. It is associated with music; if you do nothing else, I implore you to notify me of ANY reports of paranormal activity even remotely connected with this area. It goes without saying I have a dog in this fight. But if the entity does return, it is my considered opinion with no exaggeration that we're all completely and utterly fucked. Anyway, hope the War on Terror is going swimmingly. Sleep well.
Yours, Dorothy Culpepper,
The Department for
Extra-Usual Affairs, London.

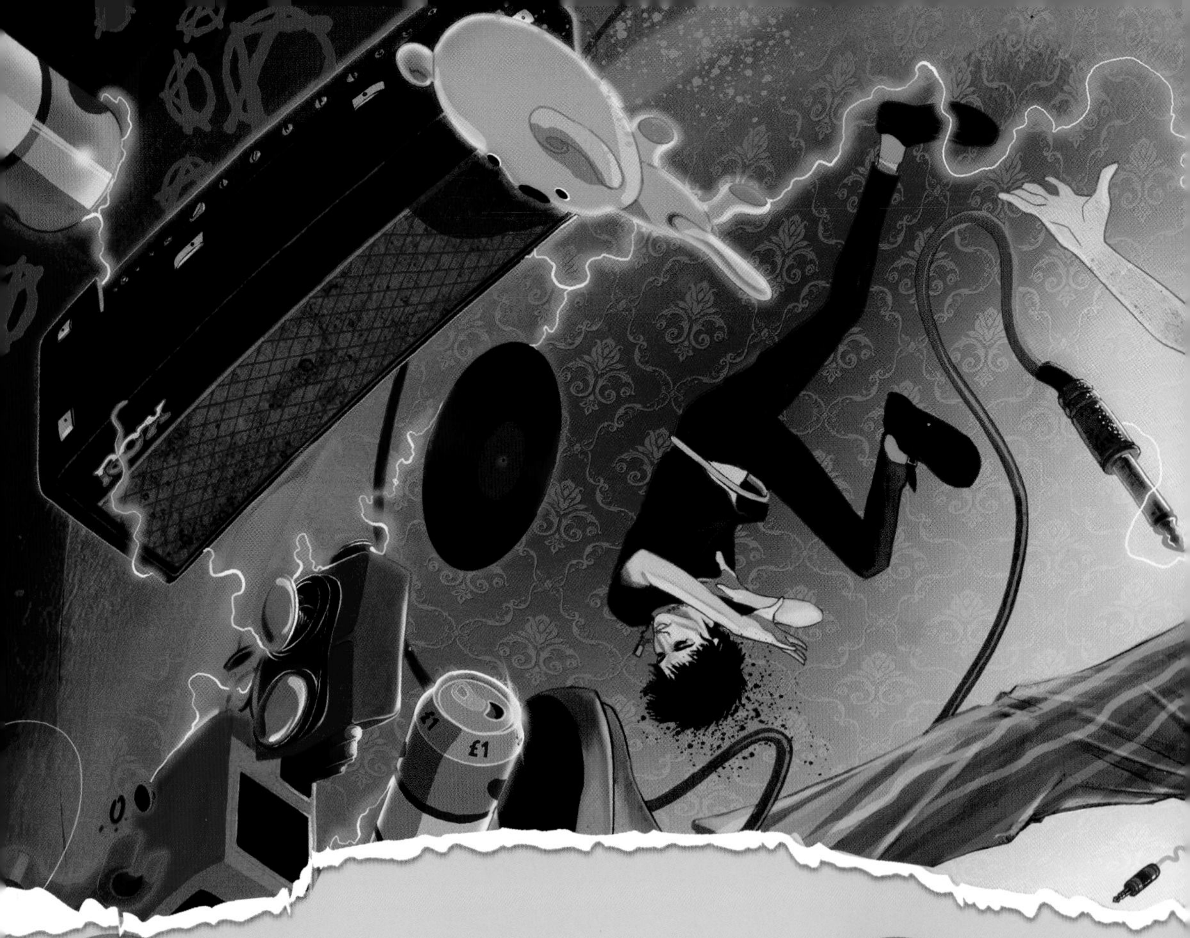

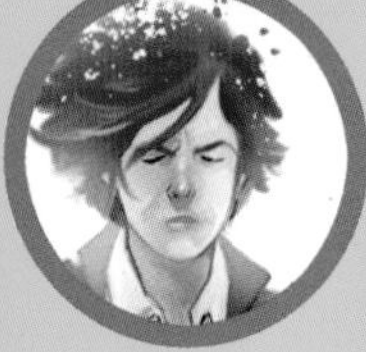

Feargal Ferguson is 15, and a loser. Literally nobody likes him. Except his mum Julie. Oh, and the ghost of a dead punk called Sid who Fergie gets stuck to in an airport. Like he didn't have enough to worry about.

What's on your bucket list that would shock even your close friends?

I suppose my closest friend is Sid, and I don't think there's much that shocks him. Probably if I said I was going to stay in and do my homework or something, that'd have him spluttering into his beer. He keeps finding these beer cans, by the way. No idea where he gets them from. I suspect he's nicking them. Or they're ghost beer cans. I suppose there is one thing on my bucket list: I'd like to know who my dad is.

Where were you when you heard the first two chords of "How Soon Is Now?"

I was probably like a day old or something. I love The Smiths. My mum got me into them. She went to see them when she was about my age, maybe a bit older. It was in Preston. They played one song and then stormed off stage because somebody threw a drumstick at Morrissey. He can say some things sometimes that make him sound like a bit of a dick. But maybe that's what happens when you get old. My mum says you have to be able to separate the art from the artist. I mean, for God's sake, I saw a picture of Sid wearing a T-shirt with a swastika on it. I need to have a word with him about that, actually. Not cool.

What's a misconception about you?

That I'm a total dweeb with no friends. Actually, that might be true. But I've just got these amazing powers and even this girl, Natalie, who is like the totally hottest girl in school, well I reckon even *she* thinks I'm pretty cool now. No, I can't fly or punch through walls or anything. In fact, I don't really know what I can do. Actually, it's a bit scary. Is there a right answer to this? This is like doing a test at school. I hate tests. I hate school.

What do you find beautiful?

That's, like, a dead embarrassing question. I don't want to say. OK, well, all right, then. This girl at school I mentioned before. Natalie. She's the most beautiful person I've ever seen. I've gone red, haven't I? My ears are burning. That always happens when I get embarrassed.

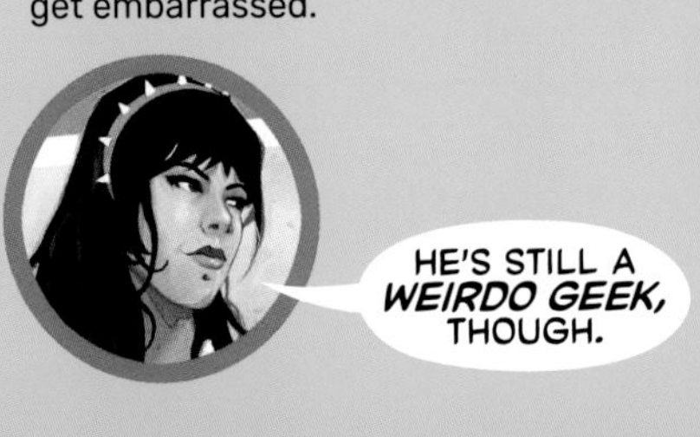
HE'S STILL A *WEIRDO GEEK,* THOUGH.

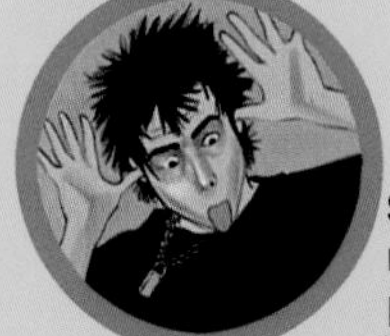

Sid is a punk rocker. A dead punk rocker. He's been stuck at Heathrow Airport for nearly 40 fackin' years and now he's stuck to some 15-year-old kid with the social skills of a brick. Can walk through walls. Can't fly. Might not necessarily be who you think he is. Or who *he* thinks he is, come to that.

What year in your life would you like to do over?

1979, innit. Year I died. Year... other people died. Might spend the year not so fucking strung out, maybe get a handle on what was really going on. Maybe not get myself in jail, get myself dead. From what I hear, though, the Eighties was well shit, so p'raps I was well out of it.

Famous quote that explains your raisons d'être?

"Don't do anything I wouldn't do". Me mum used to say that. Thing is, though, there's not much I wouldn't do, so that gives you a lot of scope, right? Pretty much to do anything. Wish that Fergie kid'd take a bit of advice. Lighten up. You kids today, not exactly a barrel of laughs, are you?

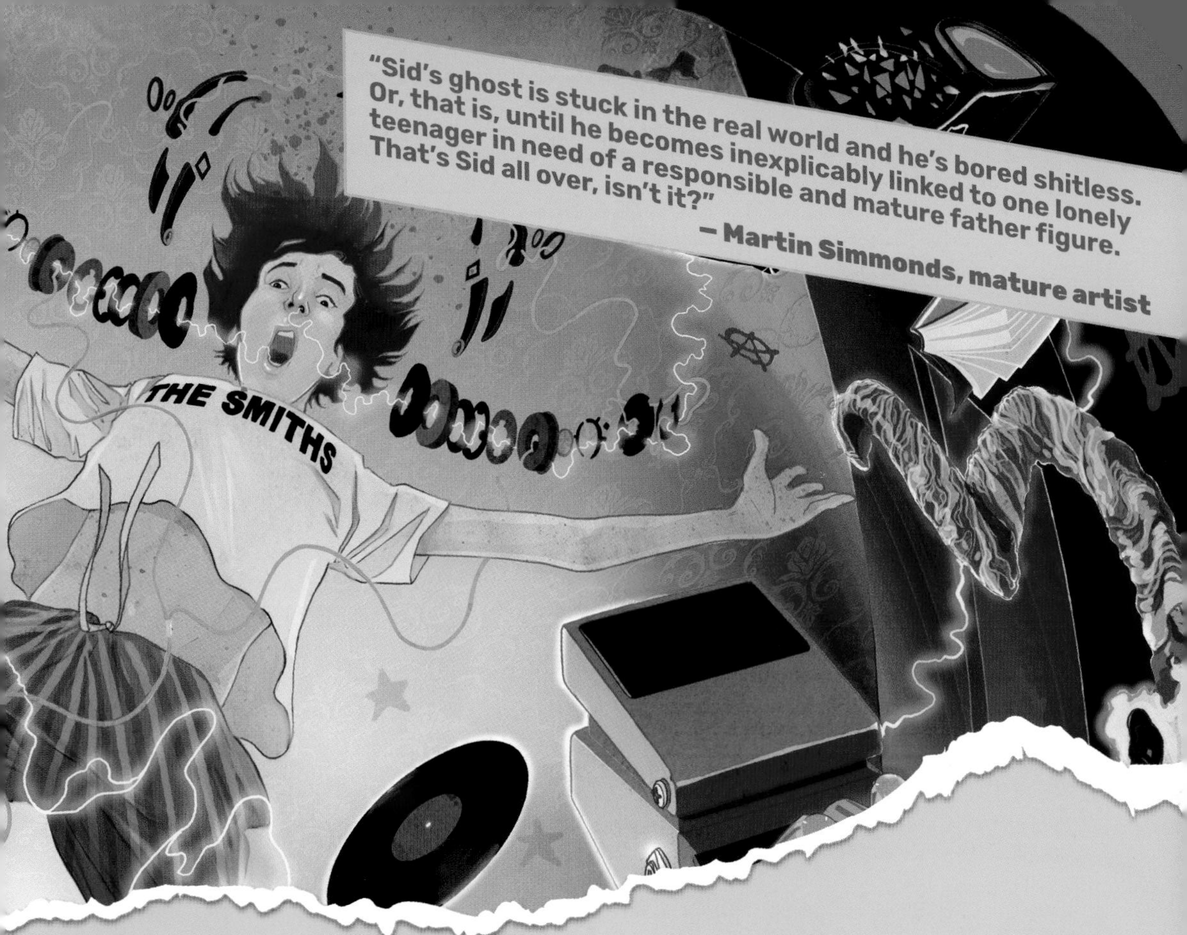
THE SMITHS

"Sid's ghost is stuck in the real world and he's bored shitless. Or, that is, until he becomes inexplicably linked to one lonely teenager in need of a responsible and mature father figure. That's Sid all over, isn't it?"

– Martin Simmonds, mature artist

Trouble and desire…

Is that a song title? Can I nick it? Be an ace song that. Trouble & Desire. With one of them little things in the middle. Anteater. No, not a fucking anteater. What am I like? Ampersand. Yeah, thing with trouble and desire is they go hand in hand, right? They do with me, anyway. I see something, I want it, and I get in a shitload of trouble. Even when I'm dead. Actually, that's not a bad lyric, is it? Have you got a pencil?

Worst career advice you were given?

Basically, variations on "You'll never amount to nothing." Ha ha, up yours, you old careers teacher fart. Who was on the telly then, me or you? Who made a record, me or you? Who's dead? Both of us! Who's still 21 and the sexiest fucking corpse in the world? You're looking at him.

What's on your bucket list that would shock even your close friends?

Bit late for that, innit? I've already kicked the sodding thing.

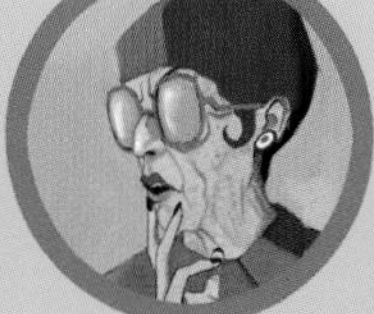

Dorothy Culpepper is the head of the Department of Extra-Usual Affairs, a department of the British intelligence service MI5. It is a post she has held since [redacted] and in the previous [redacted] years she has represented the Crown's interests vis-a-vis threats of a [redacted], [redacted], and [redacted] nature.

What's on your bucket list that would shock even your close friends?

Darling, my friends are unshockable, and those who aren't are dead. There's not a great deal I haven't done in my life, but fortunately the world keeps presenting me with new ideas. I suppose… skydiving naked with a bottle of Bollinger in one hand and a naked man (not over the age of 25) in the other. Oh, hang on. Bugger. I did that in '73. Anyway, a bucket list is things to do before you die, isn't it? I'm not planning on dying any time soon.

Famous quote that explains your raisons d'être?

I used to spend some time with Dorothy Parker. Between you and me, I gave her most of her best lines, to be honest. But two of my favourites she came up with herself are "If you want to know what God thinks of money, just look at the people he gave it to," and "The cure for boredom is curiosity. There is no cure for curiosity."

Finish the following sentences:

I wanted to be… drunk from quite an early age.

I suck at… following orders. Especially from men.

Trouble and desire… are my two middle names.

I collect… notches on my bedpost.

At the end of it all… I'll be there, drinking Champagne and smoking the last cigarette on the planet.

What do you find beautiful?

The smell of magic in the morning.

Best career advice you were given?

A toss-up between "Don't step out of the circle" and "If in doubt, fry the bastard."

Worst career advice you were given?

"If you know what's good for you you'll do what you're told."

DC
VERTIGO
THE INVISIBLES
No. 1
SEP 94
$2.95 US
$4.25 CAN
£2.00 UK
SUGGESTED FOR MATURE READERS
GRANT MORRISON
STEVE YEOWELL
DIRECT SALES

The Invisibles. Vertigo, 1994-2000, Grant Morrison and various artists

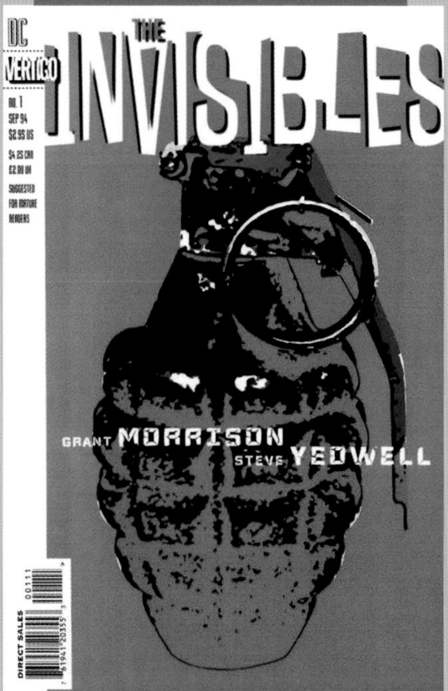

COMIC

From the moment Dane McGowan screamed FUUUUUUUUUCK! with a Molotov cocktail in his hand on the title page of the first issue of *The Invisibles*, I was hooked. It was 1994 and we were desperate for change. Two years earlier, the Tories had won their fourth consecutive General Election in the U.K., despite predictions that Labour would finally dislodge Thatcher's heir, John Major. Britpop was coming up and people were feeling scrappy. The time was right for *The Invisibles*, for this working-class kid from Liverpool who gets drawn into — what? A reality-spanning conspiracy where the worshippers of the authoritarian Outer Church are held at bay by the sexy, saucy, cool-as-fuck magician-terrorist-rockstars who make up the various cells of the Invisibles, the resistance in a battle that was life and death. Except it wasn't; as legendary Liverpool FC manager Bill Shankly might have said, it was more important than that. *The Invisibles* was written by Grant Morrison and art was by a wealth of creators, including Steve Yeowell, Phil Jiminez, Jill Thompson, Chris Weston, and a certain Philip Bond. It knocked my socks off. Every single issue got my head fizzing like a strong dose of ecstasy. None of it made any sense, except it all made sense. I thought Grant Morrison was a combination of god and my new best mate and had somehow got a direct line to my brain. None of this tells you what *The Invisibles* is about. It's about nothing and everything and by the end of it you weren't sure what was real and what was a lie and the only thing you wanted to do was throw a Molotov cocktail and scream "Fuck!," with exactly nine 'U's.

BEAT SURRENDER

Wherein we wax nostalgic on the comic + record that made us drop to our knees.

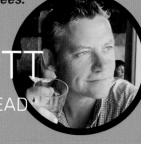

DAVID BARNETT

writer — PUNKS NOT DEAD

RECORD

By complete accident I've chosen an album from the same year as *The Invisibles*, music best experienced live in a darkened field performed by two men with bald heads, twin King Mobs effecting their own societal change from behind masses of electronic equipment. I'm not sure that *Snivilisation* is the best Orbital album, but is there such a thing anyway? The brothers Hartnoll commit their music to vinyl, to CD, to MP3, but it steadfastly refuses to stay solid. Go and watch them today and anything from this epic collection will have evolved to almost beyond recognition since this record was made. It was a funny old time for music, 1994. Guitars and electronic beats came together like never before. Bands claimed they'd always had a dance element to their music, indiekids and ravers got loved up together. I saw Orbital at Glastonbury in June of 1994, a couple months before *Snivilisation* was released. It was an epic gathering of the tribes, differences put aside. The music was grand and sweeping and progressive. Sid from PUNKS NOT DEAD would hate it, save for the punkish growl of Quality Seconds. He'd be wrong. This is a joyful experience, the soundtrack of a world on the cusp of change. It might be almost a quarter century old, but that's because Orbital were so far ahead of the game. Listen to it now and you'll realize we're finally catching up.

Snivilisation by Orbital, FFRR, 1994

SNIVILISATION
Orbital

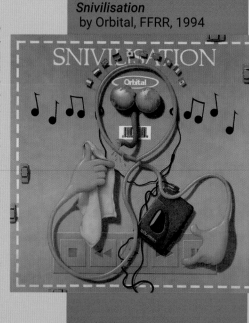

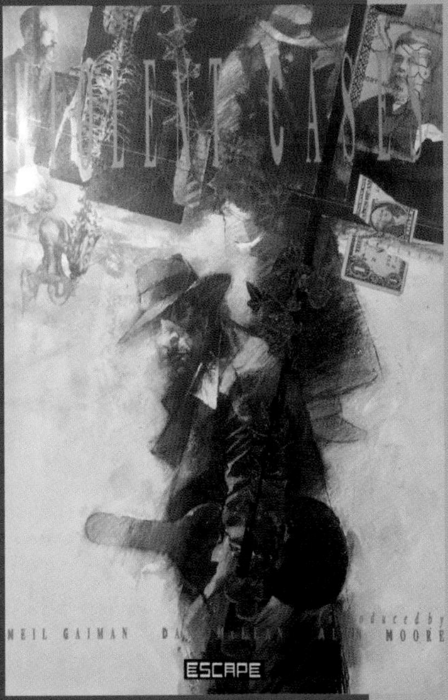
NEIL GAIMAN
MOORE
ESCAPE

Violent Cases
(Escape Books, 1987. Titan Books, 1991. Dark Horse 2002)
by Neil Gaiman & Dave McKean

..........................COMIC

I'm not ashamed to admit it: when I was a teenager, the Dave McKean covers were the principal reason I picked up *Hellblazer*. Of course, this changed once I started reading the issues, and I ended up loving it (what's not to love about a punk magician anti-hero?) for its intelligent writing and great sequential art. I couldn't get enough of McKean's work though, so I ended up tracking down any work that had his name attached to it. Before I got hold of *Arkham Asylum* and *Black Orchid*, I discovered *Violent Cases*, which was McKean's first published work, and it opened up a whole new world for me to discover.

Written by Neil Gaiman with art by McKean, *Violent Cases* was a genuine light bulb moment for me. It's a memoir that deals with childhood perception, misremembered experiences, and how reality and fiction can blend into one. As the story gets increasingly darker, the reader is left trying to separate the truth from the fiction. Obviously, being a Neil Gaiman story it's superbly written, and I loved the ambiguity that left me pondering the story long after I finished reading it. As for the artwork, up until that point I hadn't seen comic art like it. Yes, I'd seen the McKean covers, but not sequential art with a similar aesthetic (a breadcrumb trail from McKean's work would lead me to discover the work of amazing artists/painters Bill Sienkiewicz, Kent Williams and Jon J Muth). I love McKean's use of skewed perspectives to amplify the distortion in the narrator's memories, and how the artwork shifts in style throughout, adapting to suit the scene, mixing drawings, paintings, photography and collage.

McKean's art was truly something to behold, and I'd never seen comic art with so much life ingrained in it. His work was realistic, nightmarish and abstract, but above all else, completely immersive. *Violent Cases* is a great example of words and pictures working in perfect harmony.

BEAT SURRENDER

Wherein we wax nostalgic on the comic + record that made us drop to our knees.

MARTIN SIMMONDS
artist –
PUNKS NOT DEAD

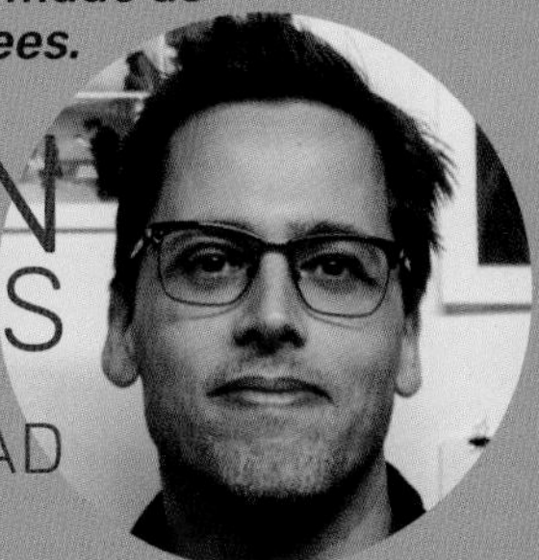

RECORD..........................

Fugazi
Repeater
Dischord Records, 1990

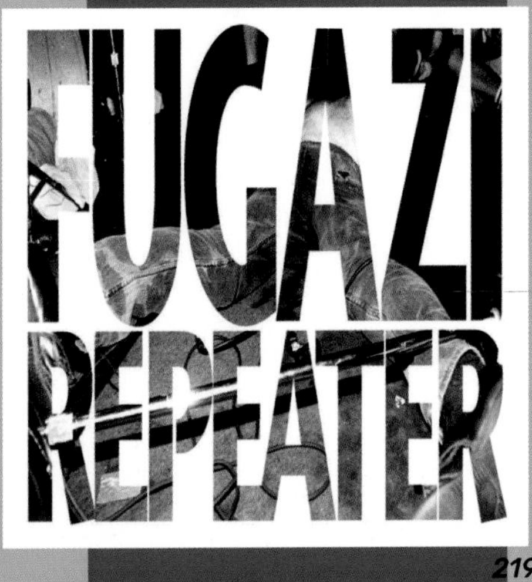
FUGAZI
REPEATER

Deep breath...
Fugazi's Repeater is the perfect punk album. There, I've said it.

Don't get me wrong; I love Sex Pistols, The Clash, Ramones, etc., but I discovered Repeater in my mid-teens; I'd never heard anything like it, and I've been hooked ever since.

Fugazi are pretty distinct sounding: Guy Picciotto's spikey, angular guitar sound is in perfect contrast to Ian MacKaye's more straightforward, heavier guitar playing. That same approach is evident in their vocal styles: MacKaye shouty and anthemic, Picciotto snarly and fragile. Brendan Canty's use of subtle hi-hat work and that distinctive snare rim-shot sound, both influenced by reggae and dub, is mixed with a good dose of punk aggression, and locks in beautifully with Joe Lally's distinctive bass playing.

Lally's dub reggae and funk-influenced bass playing adds a great melodic undercurrent to the whole album and perfectly underpins the guitars and vocals. Repeater is dynamic, aggressive, subtle and experimental, but that's not to say there aren't any pop sensibilities in there. That may sound unlikely for a punk/hardcore band, but there are plenty of hooks to keep you dancing/singing/shouting, if that's your thing.

Perfect punk album, right there.

swell maps

Welcome to GLASGOW, with your musical tour guide Cathi Unsworth
Illustrations by Cara McGee

GLASGOW is synonymous with heavy industry and sublime art. On its Coat of Arms, the miracles of **Patron Saint Mungo** symbolize the foundation of the city's prosperity in the form of leaping salmon. Over a quarter of the world's ships were once built on the banks of the River Clyde, including many that helped save the nation during World War II, when artist **Sir Stanley Spencer** portrayed the welders and riveters of Lithgows, who wore no safety equipment other than their tweed suits and caps. From such hard graft and high style were the city's distinctive sounds forged.

While Glasgow's industry flourished, so too did its artists. The Glasgow School was founded in the 1870s by architect **Charles Rennie Mackintosh**, his painter wife **Margaret MacDonald**, her sister **Frances**, and **Herbert MacNair**. Known as The Spook School, they defined an otherwordly Art Nouveau style derived from ancient Celtic. Mackintosh's School of Art building has alumni including "Fighting" **Robert Colquhoun**, YBA **Jenny Saville** and laconic scribbler **Dave Shrigley**. Punk fashion designer **Pam Hogg**, Time Lord **Peter Capaldi**, comedy bruiser **Robbie Coltrane** and acerbic *The Tube* host **Muriel Gray** also passed through its ranks.

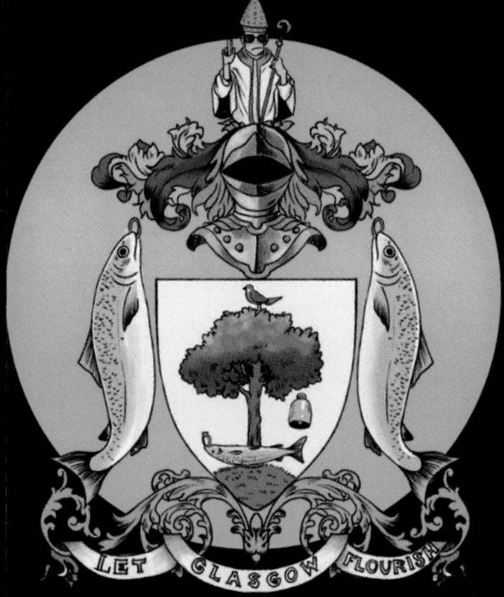
LET GLASGOW FLOURISH

Glasgow has produced as many influential musicians as artists and none more so than black-eyed **Alex Harvey**, who began his career carving tombstones and turned his graveyard blues into the potent hard rock of the **Sensational Alex Harvey Band**. Looking like a gypsy king, Harvey fully evinced the rock'n'roll lifestyle – he was dead at 46. His leather-clad heirs **The Jesus and Mary Chain** emerged in 1983 in a cloud of feedback and hair; brothers **Jim and William Reid** initially joined by **Primal Scream**-er **Bobby Gillespie** and managed by **Alan McGee**. Their incendiary 20-minute sets turned the fey world of Eighties Indie Upside Down, and their *Psychocandy* LP dominated the rest of the decade. Further descendants of this musical Spook School include fellow McGee protégés **Glasvegas**; **Mogwa**i ("evil spirit" in Cantonese); and polka-dotted *femmes fatales* **Strawberry Switchblade**. Other mad axemen who began their lives in Glasgow are **AC/DC** brothers **Angus and Malcolm Young**.

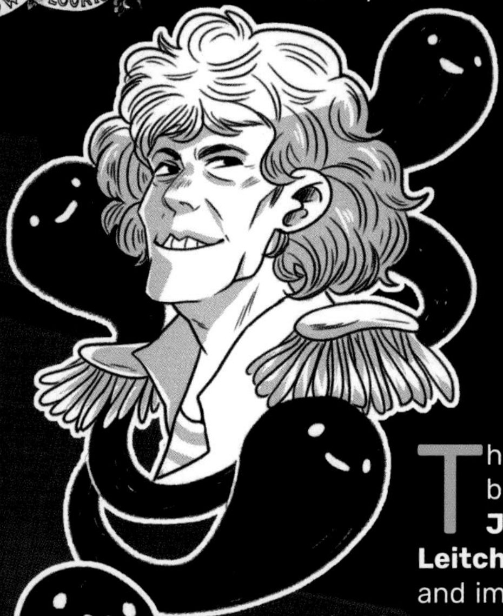

The city has a more whimsical side, beginning with **Pentangle** founder **Bert Jansch**, *"Hurdy Gurdy Man"* **Donovan Leitch** and **John Martyn**, who all explored and imbued traditional music with their own idiosyncratic airs. The magic they left lingering was inhaled again by a new crop of bands in the early Eighties. **Orange Juice**, who dressed like the Lithgows shipbuilders, had their own label, *Postcard*, which also accommodated fellow aesthetes **Aztec Camera** and **Josef K**. Then there were **Altered Images**, led by pixie singer **Clare Grogan**; **The Bluebells**; **Lloyd Cole and the Commotions**; **The Pastels** and **The Vaselines**. Later bands to rekindle these embers, **Bis**, **Belle & Sebastian**, and **Franz Ferdinand**, would all look equally at home in a Stanley Spencer painting.

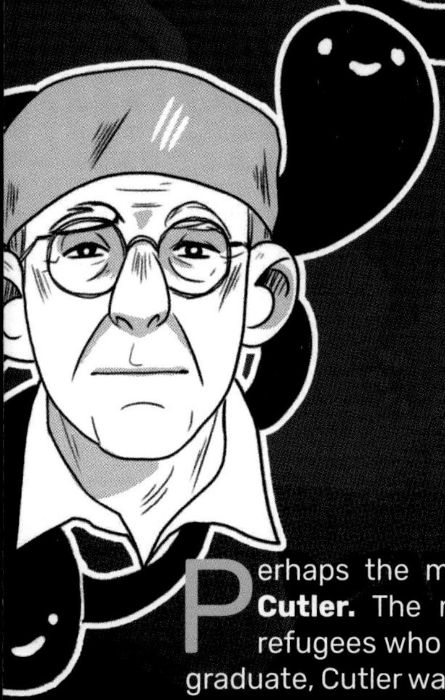

Perhaps the most surreal Glasgow voice of all belonged to **Ivor Cutler.** The mordantly humorous poet was the son of Jewish refugees who never got as far as America. Another Glasgow School graduate, Cutler was championed by **Ned Sherrin**, who helped him land a role in The Beatles' *Magical Mystery Tour* and the admiration of **Bertrand Russell**, **John Peel** and fellow Glaswegian joker **Billy Connolly**. The sound of applause was, however, anathema to Cutler – a member of the Noise Abatement Society, he forbade his audience to ever whistle their appreciation of his work.

Raised in a field in Outer Norfolk, CATHI UNSWORTH was a teenage goth whose spells actually worked when she made her way to London and became a journalist on *Sounds* at the age of 19. Before the weekly music press became extinct, she also worked for *Melody Maker*, then went on to co-create *Purr* and write reams more about music, film, fashion, noir fiction and general weirdness for everyone from the *Fortean Times* to the *Financial Times*. Over the past decade she has written five noir novels into which she pours all her obsessions with secret histories and pop culture. You can find out more at www.cathiunsworth.co.uk

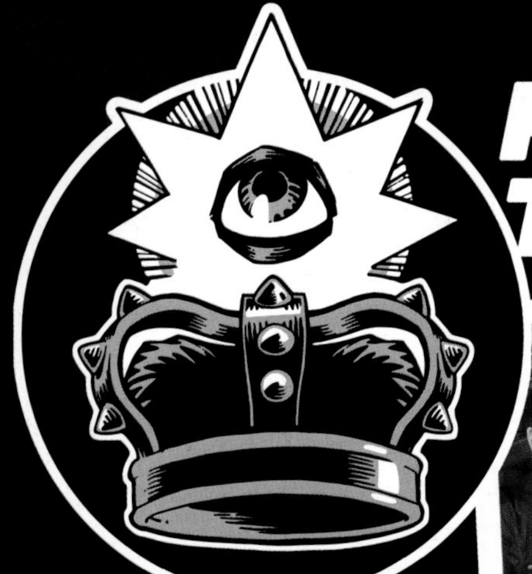

FROM THEORY TO REVOLUTION

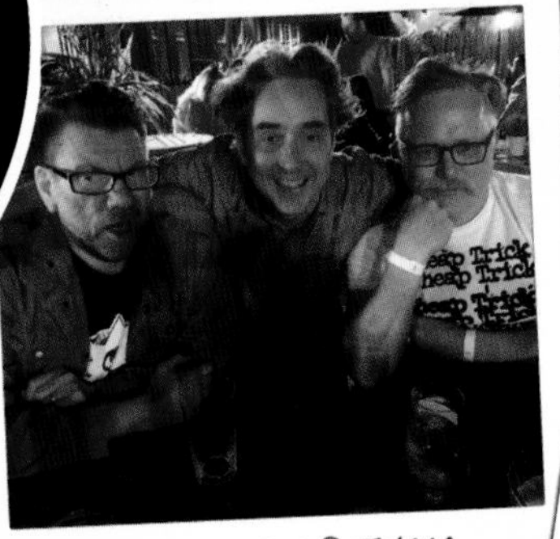

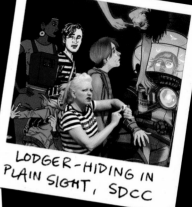

BOND, POTTER & PUTTNAM DISCUSS THE MERITS OF CIDER

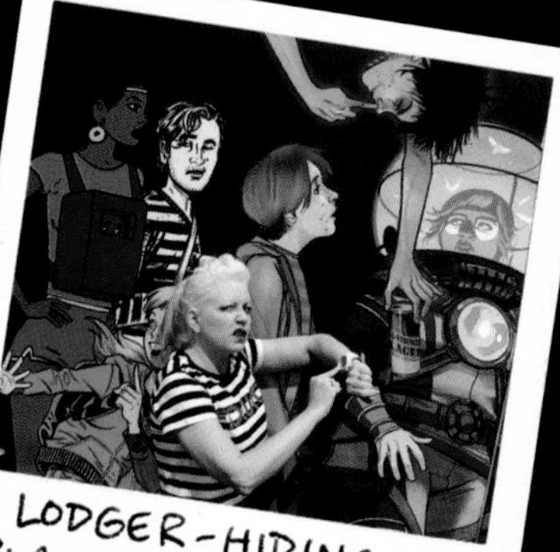

LODGER–HIDING IN PLAIN SIGHT, SDCC

MAY 2018

KID LOBOTOMY: A LAD INSANE, the first BLACK CROWN trade paperback, hits stores.

Philip and Shelly Bond are guests at the first Portsmouth Comicon in the U.K. BLACK CROWN talents David Barnett, Martin Simmonds, Will Potter and Carl Puttnam were in attendance.

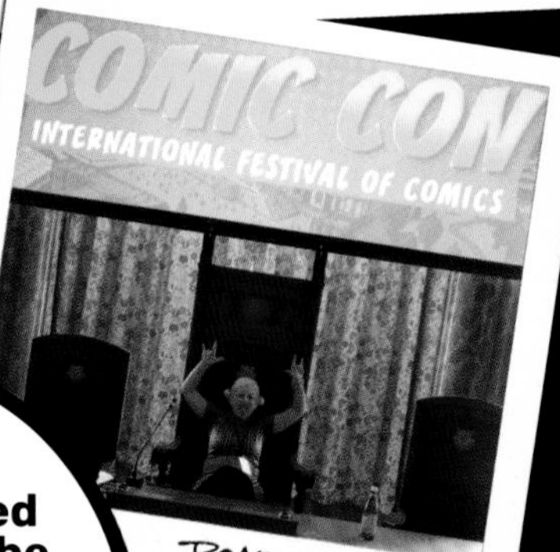
COMIC CON
INTERNATIONAL FESTIVAL OF COMICS

BOND TAKES HER THRONE – PORTSMOUTH

JULY

San Diego Comicon heralds the launch of EUTHANAUTS, and we bring writer Tini Howard to the convention to celebrate. The neo-noir thriller LODGER by industry vets David and Maria Lapham is announced to major fanfare.

"Forever changed and forever haunted by my time at The Suites. Kid lives under my skin. Ottla lives in my beating heart. And the hotel holds ghosts I'll never forget."
– Tess Fowler

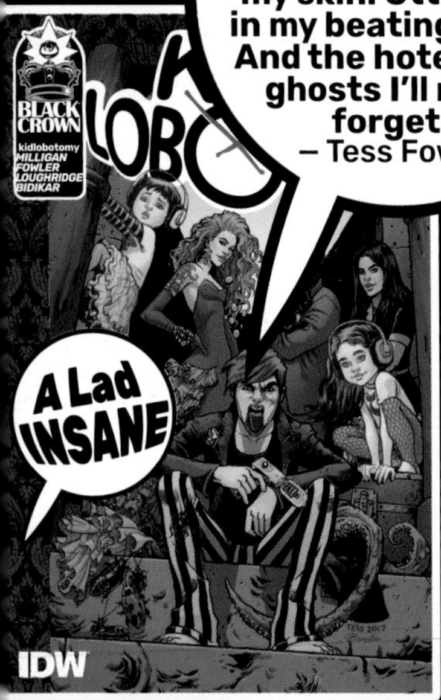
BLACK CROWN
kidlobotomy
MILLIGAN
FOWLER
LOUGHRIDGE
BIDIKAR
A Lad INSANE
IDW

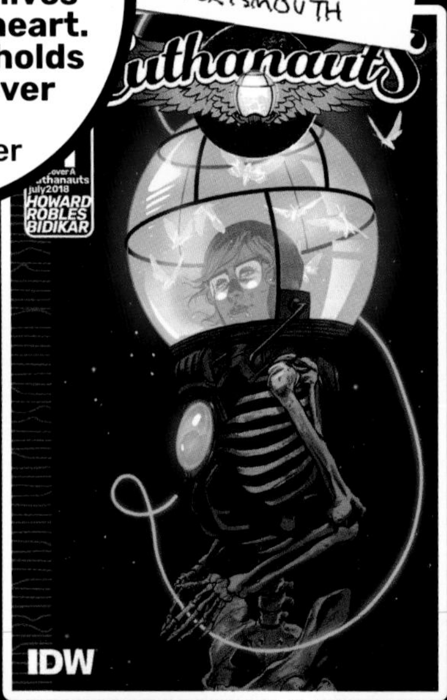
Euthanauts
cover A
euthanauts
july2018
HOWARD
ROBLES
BIDIKAR
IDW

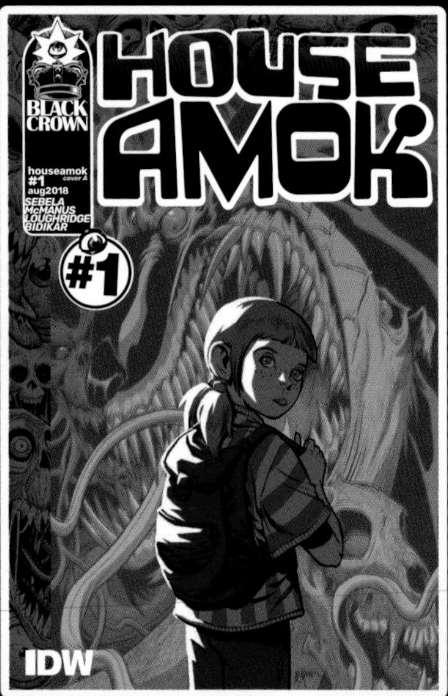
HOUSE AMOK
BLACK CROWN
houseamok
#1
cover A
aug2018
SEBELA
McMANUS
LOUGHRIDGE
BIDIKAR
#1
IDW

2018 MAY

JULY

AUGUST

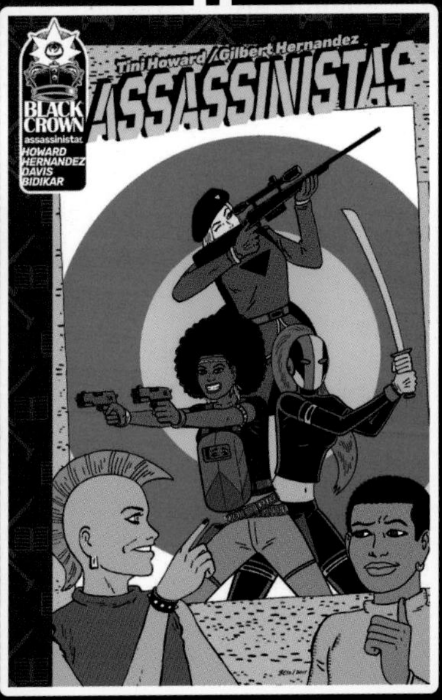
BLACK CROWN
Tini Howard / Gilbert Hernandez
ASSASSINISTAS
assassinistas
HOWARD
HERNANDEZ
DAVIS
BIDIKAR

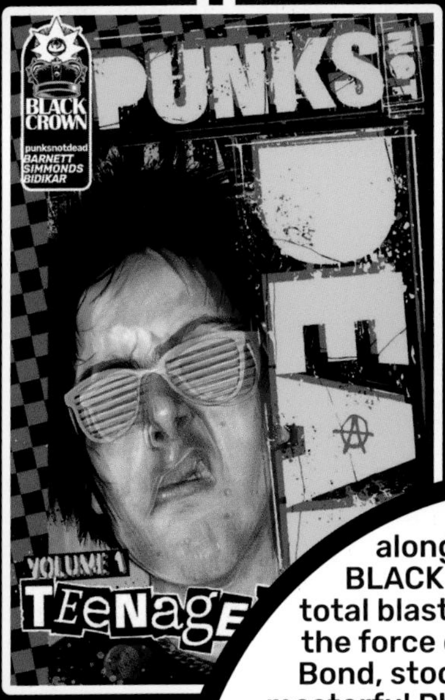
BLACK CROWN
PUNKS NOT
punksnotdead
BARNETT
SIMMONDS
BIDIKAR
VOLUME 1
TEenagE

SEPTEMBER

FEMME MAGNIFIQUE: 50 Magnificent Women Who Changed The World debuts.

OCTOBER

BCQ #4 debuts.

BLACK CROWN celebrates its one-year anniversary at St. Mark's Comics and announces PUNKS NOT DEAD: LONDON CALLING, a second arc for the hit series.

"Working alongside the team at BLACK CROWN has been a total blast. A gas! I've witnessed the force of nature that's Shelly Bond, stood in its lee next to the masterful Philip Bond, seen my older self rendered pen and ink by such titans as Rob Davis, Dilraj Mann and the selfsame Monsieur Bond, watched my words writ large by the terrific Aditya Bidikar, banged heads with David Barnett and Martin Simmonds and too many pints AND sat next to Pete Milligan while he signed books.
Of all these, if I had to pick one, it would be Dilraj's cover drawing. How many of us see an artist's imagining our older selves squatting unceremoniously, trousers round our ankles?!"

—Carl Puttnam, writer & lead singer of the CUD band

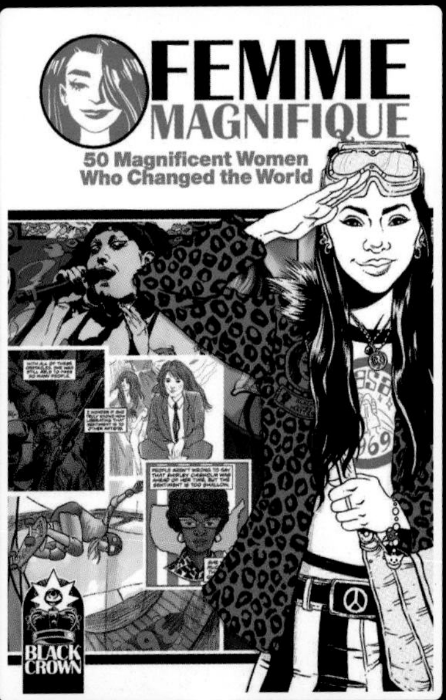
FEMME MAGNIFIQUE
50 Magnificent Women Who Changed the World
BLACK CROWN

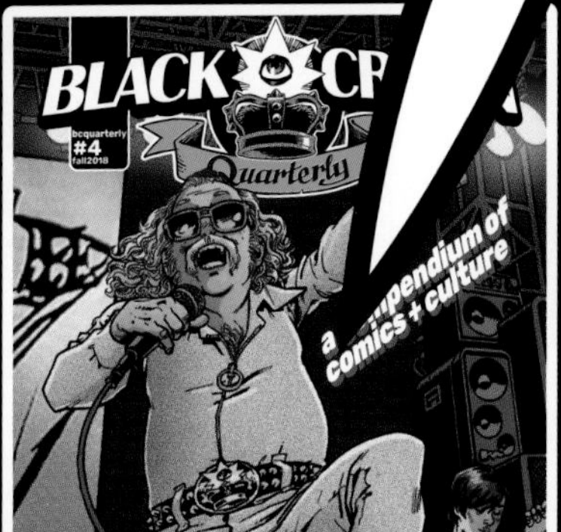
BLACK CR
bcquarterly
#4
fall2018
Quarterly
a compendium of comics + culture
IDW

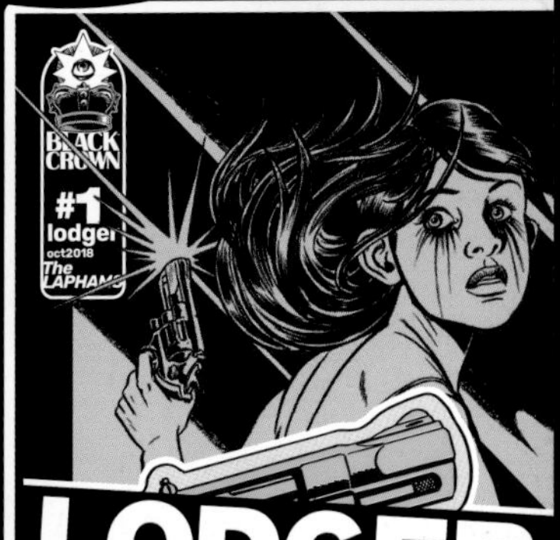
BLACK CROWN
#1
lodger
oct2018
LODGER
IDW

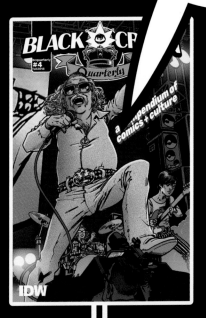

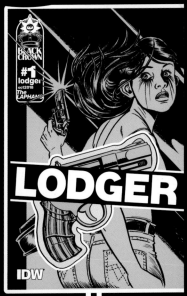

SEPTEMBER *OCTOBER*

LOOT

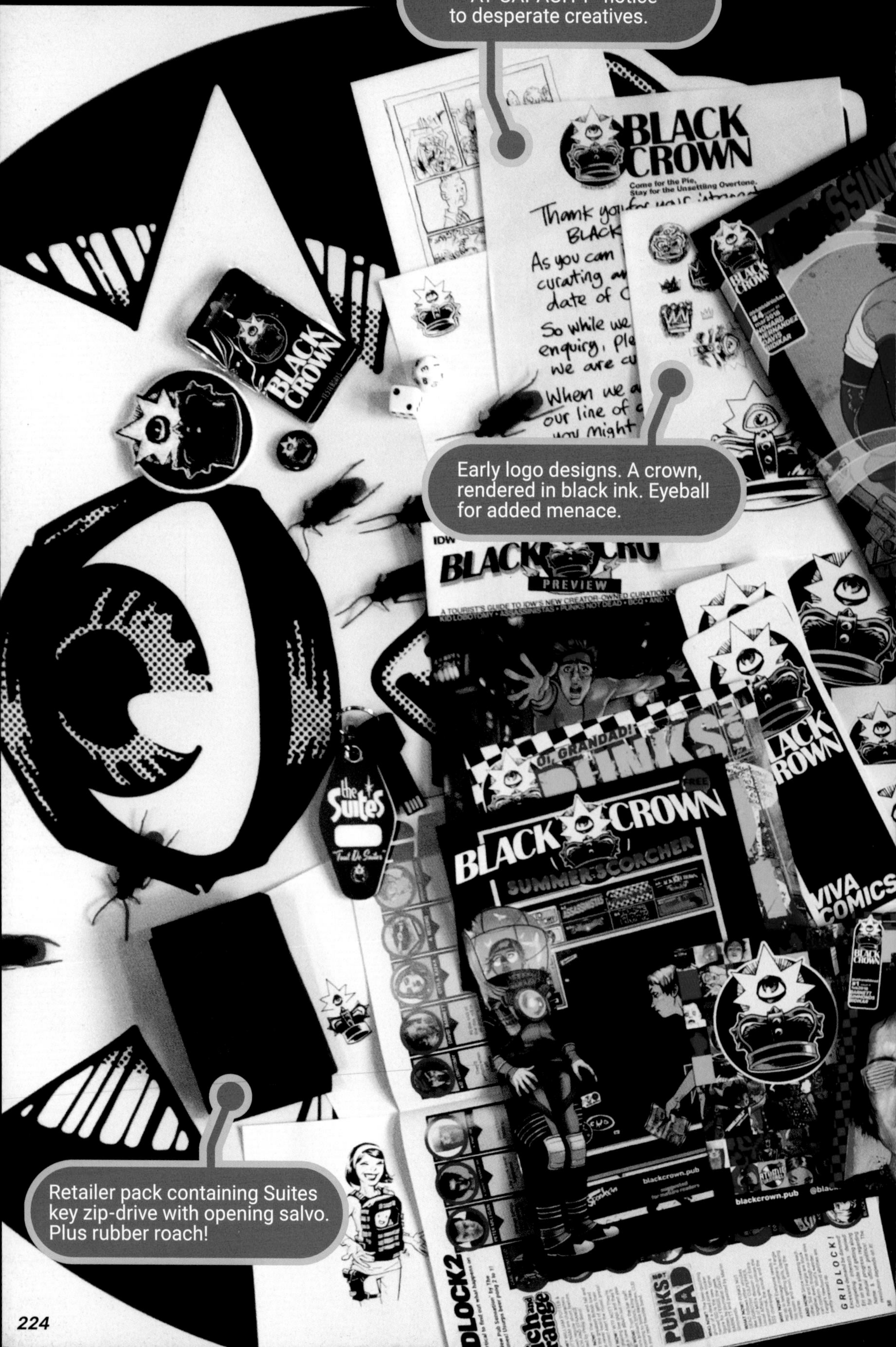
BLACK CROWN
Come for the Pie, Stay for the Unsettling Overtone.
BLACK CROWN PREVIEW
the Suites
BLACK CROWN SUMMER SCORCHER
OI GRANDAD!
VIVA COMICS
blackcrown.pub
GRIDLOCK2
PUNKS NOT DEAD

From the message board — "AT CAPACITY" notice to desperate creatives.

Early logo designs. A crown, rendered in black ink. Eyeball for added menace.

Retailer pack containing Suites key zip-drive with opening salvo. Plus rubber roach!

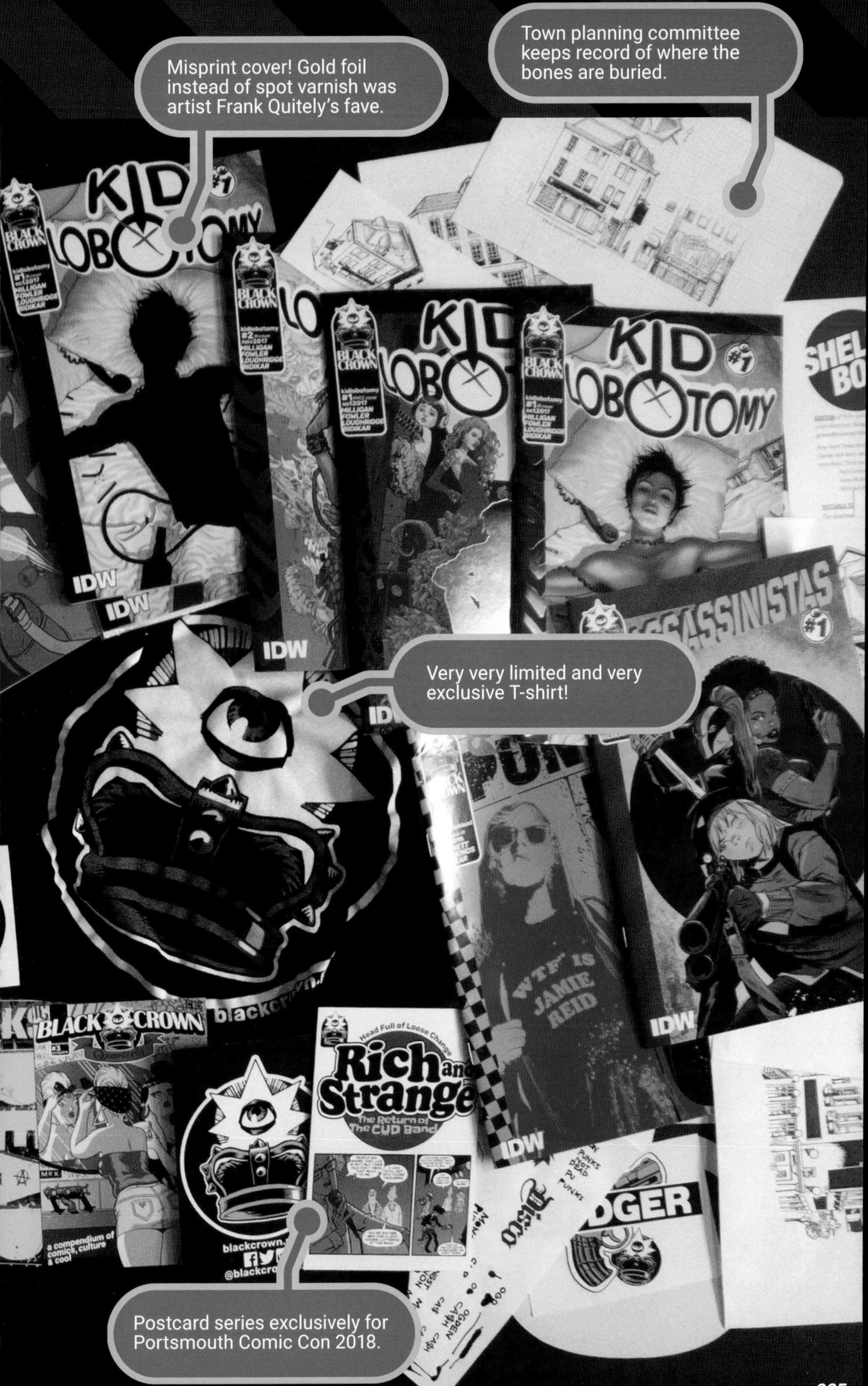
Misprint cover! Gold foil instead of spot varnish was artist Frank Quitely's fave.
Town planning committee keeps record of where the bones are buried.
KID LOBOTOMY #1
Very very limited and very exclusive T-shirt!
ASSASSINISTAS #1
Head Full of Loose Change
Rich and Strange
The Return of The CUD Band
a compendium of comics, culture & cool
Postcard series exclusively for Portsmouth Comic Con 2018.

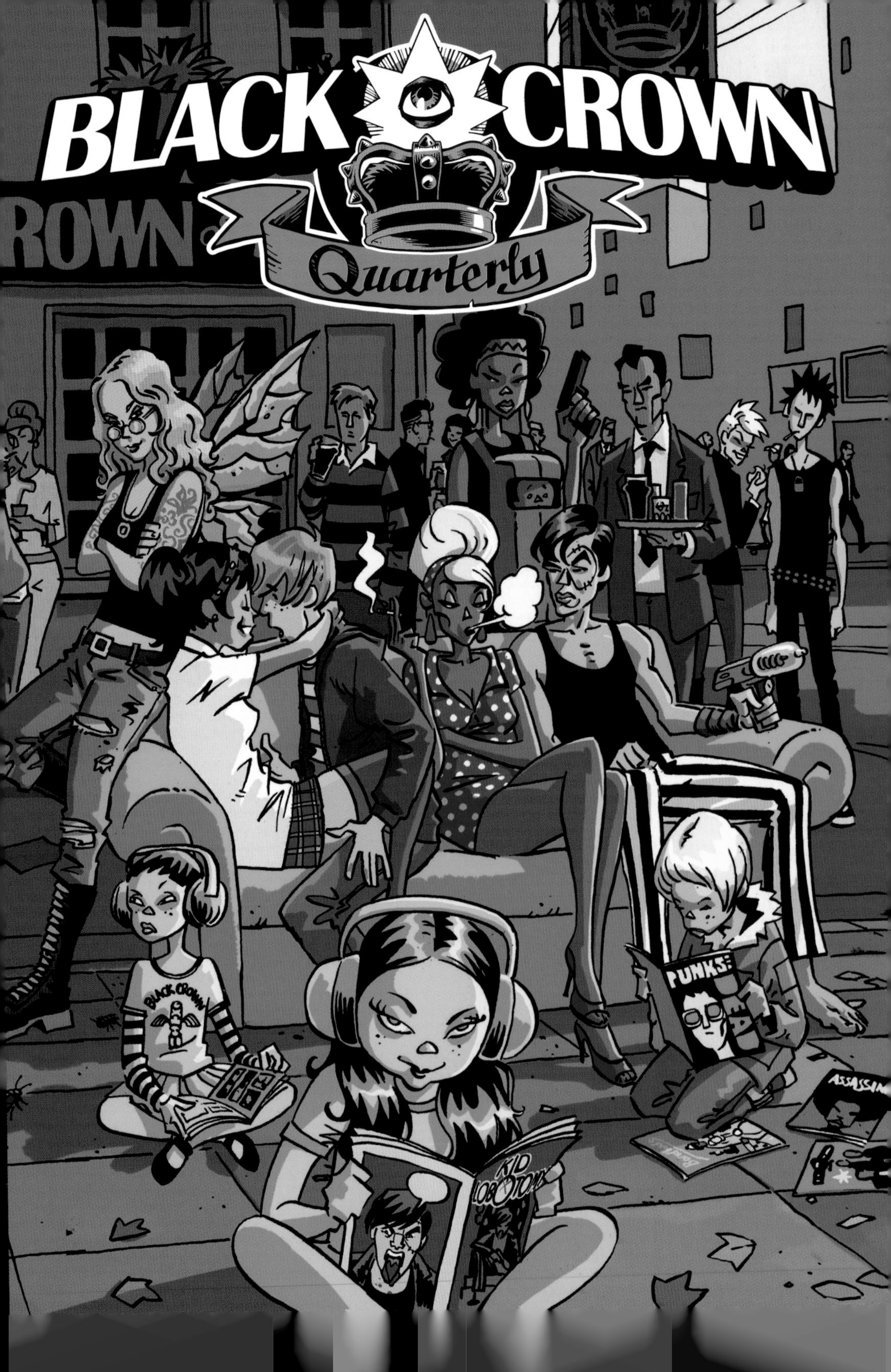
BLACK CROWN
Quarterly
ROWN
BLACK CROWN
PUNKS
KID LOBOTOMY
ASSASSIN

BLACK CROWN WRAPAROUND COVER KEY
*wherein we're in with the "in" crowd and
we find out who's who and what's what*

1 - ROSEBUD AKA Sis
First born • Nice tatts • Queen Bitch
KID LOBOTOMY

2 - DOROTHY CULPEPPER
Extra-Usual Champagne swigger
PUNKS NOT DEAD

3 - OCTAVIA PRICE
Former bounty hunter • roller disco
champion • should TM the Kevlar baby
carrier
ASSASSINISTAS

4 - DOMINIC PRICE
Former baby • likes video games and
making out with his boyfriend
ASSASSINISTAS

5 - THE NIGHT MANAGER
Apple tosser • spirit sater
KID LOBOTOMY

6 - SID
Spirit • tosser
PUNKS NOT DEAD

7 - JULIE FERGUSON
Something horrible this way comes
PUNKS NOT DEAD

8 - KID LOBOTOMY
Eponymous mad doctor • or mad
hotel manager
KID LOBOTOMY

9 - STACEY
Black Crown Barmaid • watch your
back
TALES FROM THE BLACK CROWN

10 - ERROL
Stacey's charge • talking clock
TALES FROM THE BLACK CROWN

11- FEARGAL FERGUSON AKA Fergie
British school boy • stuck to Sid
PUNKS NOT DEAD

12 - GHOST GIRL MOLLY
Protects Kid • likes red vines
KID LOBOTOMY

13 - GHOST GIRL BESS
Enables Kid • likes sushi
KID LOBOTOMY

14 - NATALIE
Too fast for Ridgemont High
PUNKS NOT DEAD

15 - RAM
Black Crown proprietor • mixes a
mean Lobotomy
TALES FROM THE BLACK CROWN

16 - CHRIS RYALL
On his third Guinness
Former Chief Creative Officer, IDW

17 - ROB DAVIS
Draws a crowd
TALES FROM THE BLACK CROWN

18 - ROBIN HENLEY
Laughs at his jokes
TALES FROM THE BLACK CROWN

19 - SHELLY BOND
Not shown
Thx, Rob

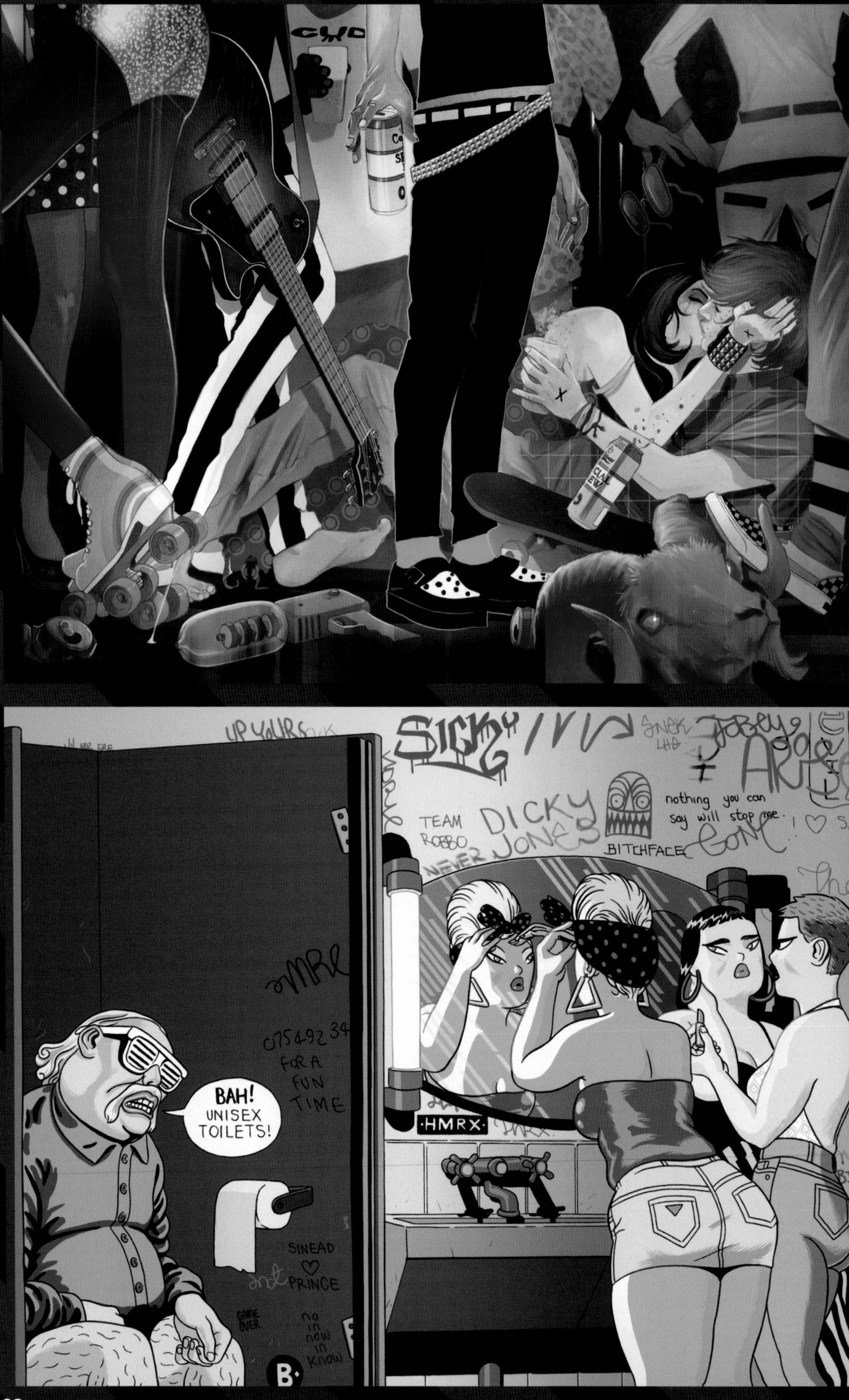
BAH! UNISEX TOILETS!
UP YOURS
SICK
DICKY JONES
TEAM ROBBO
NEVER
nothing you can say will stop me.
BITCHFACE
HMRX
075492 34 FOR A FUN TIME
SINEAD ♡ PRINCE
GAME OVER
no in now in know

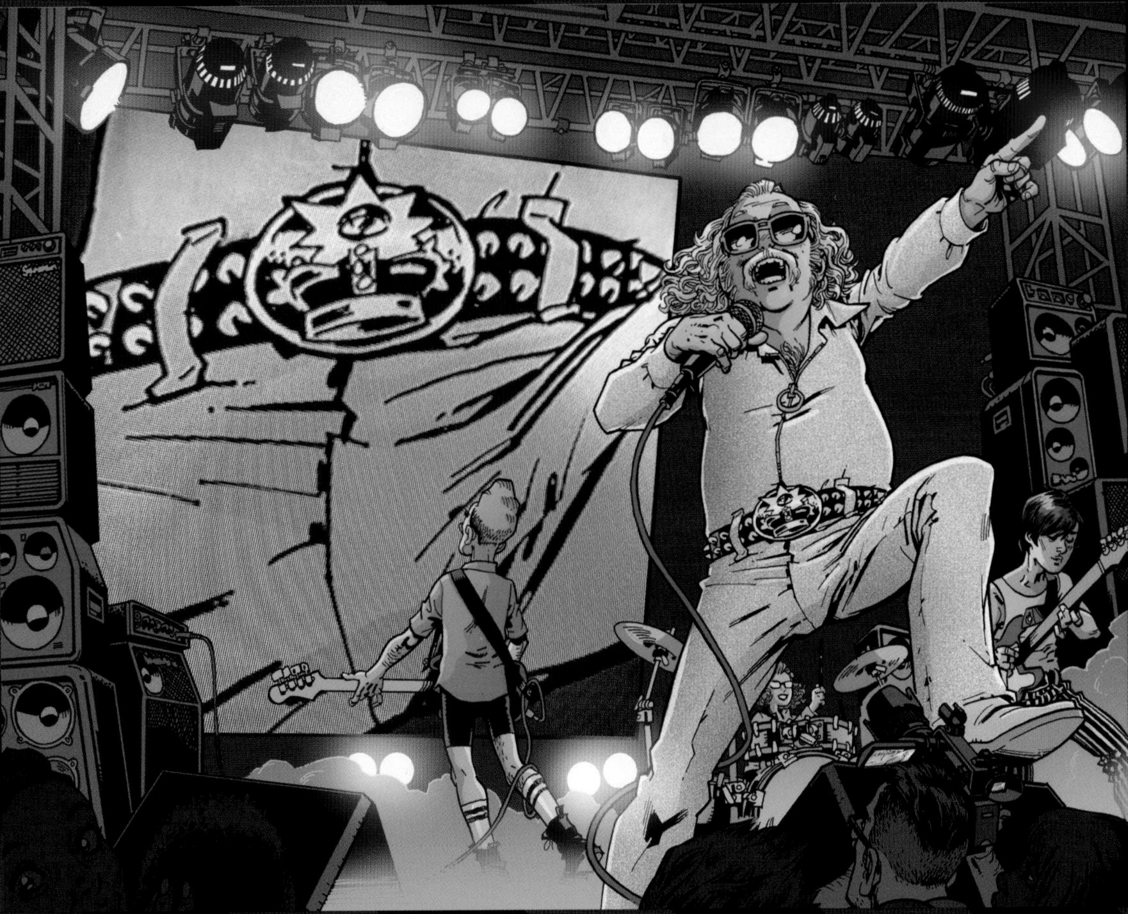

←BLACK CROWN QUARTERLY #2
cover by MARTIN SIMMONDS
←BLACK CROWN QUARTERLY #3
cover by DILRAJ MANN
↑BLACK CROWN QUARTERLY #4
cover by PHILIP BOND / LEE LOUGHRIDGE

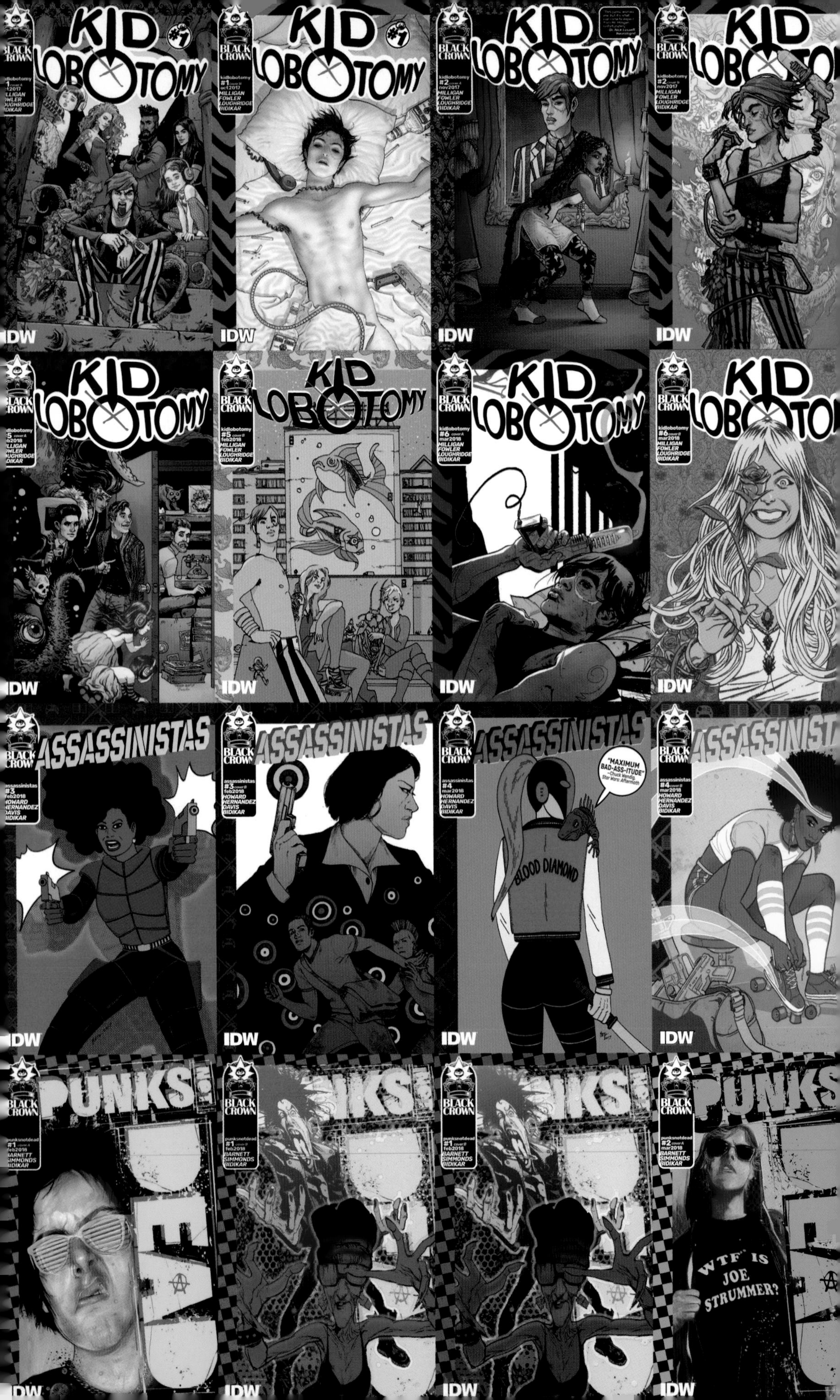

KID LOBOTOMY
#1
BLACK CROWN
kidlobotomy
MILLIGAN
FOWLER
LOUGHRIDGE
BIDIKAR
IDW
KID LOBOTOMY
#1
BLACK CROWN
kidlobotomy
#1 cover B
oct2017
MILLIGAN
FOWLER
LOUGHRIDGE
BIDIKAR
IDW
KID LOBOTOMY
BLACK CROWN
kidlobotomy
#2 cover A
nov2017
MILLIGAN
FOWLER
LOUGHRIDGE
BIDIKAR
IDW
KID LOBOTOMY
BLACK CROWN
kidlobotomy
#2 cover B
nov2017
MILLIGAN
FOWLER
LOUGHRIDGE
BIDIKAR
IDW
KID LOBOTOMY
BLACK CROWN
kidlobotomy
feb2018
MILLIGAN
FOWLER
LOUGHRIDGE
BIDIKAR
IDW
KID LOBOTOMY
BLACK CROWN
kidlobotomy
#5 cover B
feb2018
MILLIGAN
FOWLER
LOUGHRIDGE
BIDIKAR
IDW
KID LOBOTOMY
BLACK CROWN
kidlobotomy
#6 cover A
mar2018
MILLIGAN
FOWLER
LOUGHRIDGE
BIDIKAR
IDW
KID LOBOTOMY
BLACK CROWN
kidlobotomy
#6 cover B
mar2018
MILLIGAN
FOWLER
LOUGHRIDGE
BIDIKAR
IDW
ASSASSINISTAS
BLACK CROWN
assassinistas
#3
feb2018
HOWARD
HERNANDEZ
DAVIS
BIDIKAR
IDW
ASSASSINISTAS
BLACK CROWN
assassinistas
#3 cover B
feb2018
HOWARD
HERNANDEZ
DAVIS
BIDIKAR
IDW
ASSASSINISTAS
BLACK CROWN
assassinistas
#4
mar2018
HOWARD
HERNANDEZ
DAVIS
BIDIKAR
"MAXIMUM BAD-ASS-ITUDE"
—Chuck Wendig, Star Wars: Aftermath
BLOOD DIAMOND
IDW
ASSASSINISTAS
BLACK CROWN
assassinistas
#4 cover B
mar2018
HOWARD
HERNANDEZ
DAVIS
BIDIKAR
IDW
PUNKS
BLACK CROWN
punksnotdead
#1
feb2018
BARNETT
SIMMONDS
BIDIKAR
IDW
BLACK CROWN
punksnotdead
#1 cover B
feb2018
BARNETT
SIMMONDS
BIDIKAR
IDW
BLACK CROWN
punksnotdead
#1 cover B
feb2018
BARNETT
SIMMONDS
BIDIKAR
IDW
PUNKS
BLACK CROWN
punksnotdead
#2 cover A
mar2018
BARNETT
SIMMONDS
BIDIKAR
WTF IS JOE STRUMMER?
IDW

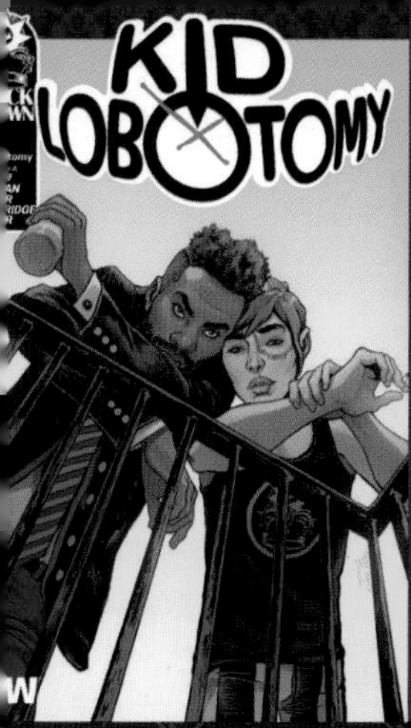
KID LOBOTOMY
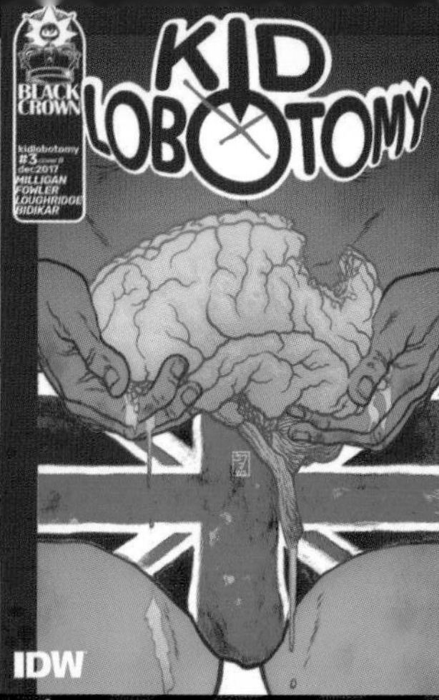
KID LOBOTOMY
BLACK CROWN
kidlobotomy
#3 cover B
dec2017
MILLIGAN
FOWLER
LOUGHRIDGE
BIDIKAR
IDW
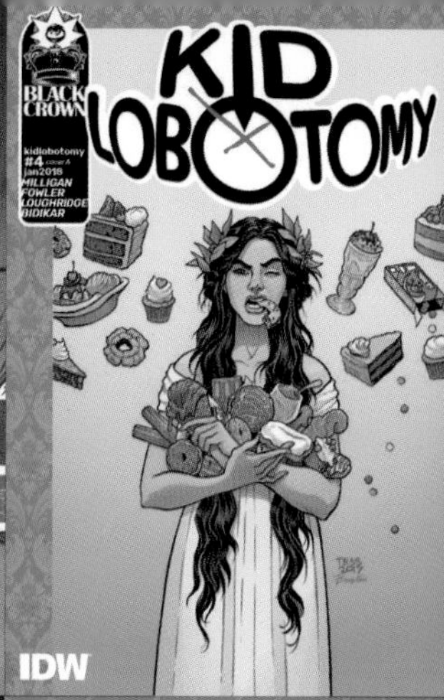
KID LOBOTOMY
BLACK CROWN
kidlobotomy
#4 cover A
jan2018
MILLIGAN
FOWLER
LOUGHRIDGE
BIDIKAR
IDW
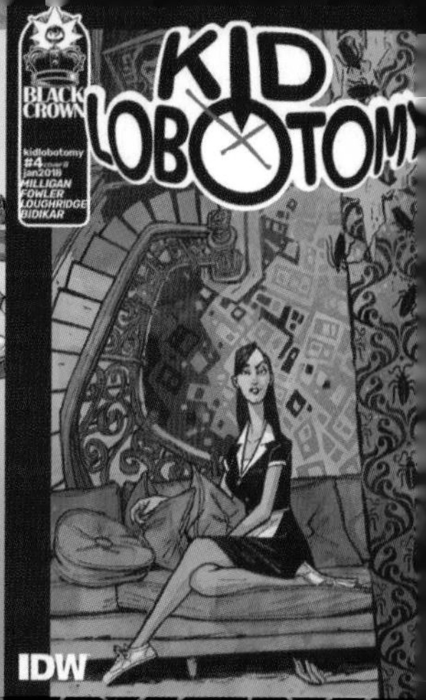
KID LOBOTOMY
BLACK CROWN
kidlobotomy
#4 cover B
jan2018
MILLIGAN
FOWLER
LOUGHRIDGE
BIDIKAR
IDW
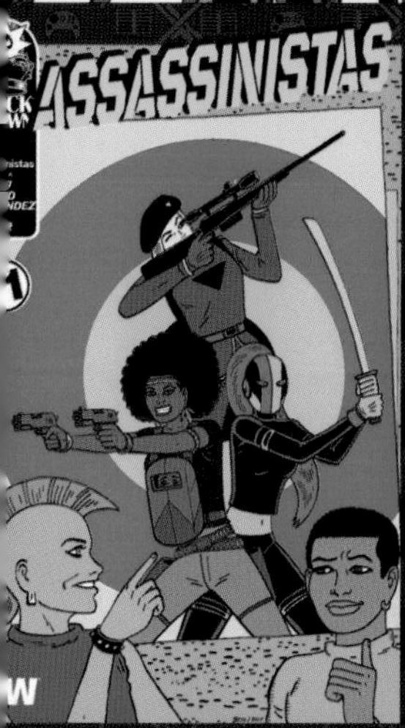
ASSASSINISTAS
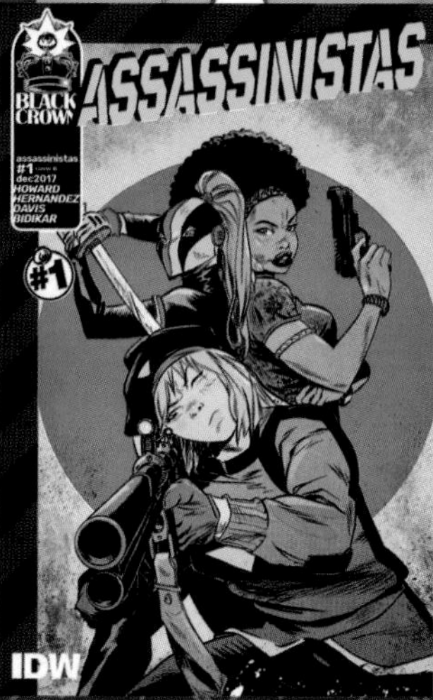
ASSASSINISTAS
BLACK CROWN
assassinistas
#1 cover B
dec2017
HOWARD
HERNANDEZ
DAVIS
BIDIKAR
#1
IDW
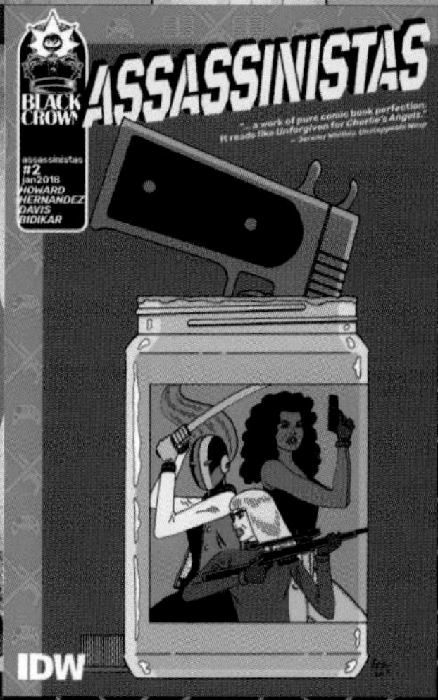
ASSASSINISTAS
"...a work of pure comic book perfection. It reads like Unforgiven for Charlie's Angels." - Jeremy Whitley, Unstoppable Wasp
BLACK CROWN
assassinistas
#2
jan2018
HOWARD
HERNANDEZ
DAVIS
BIDIKAR
IDW
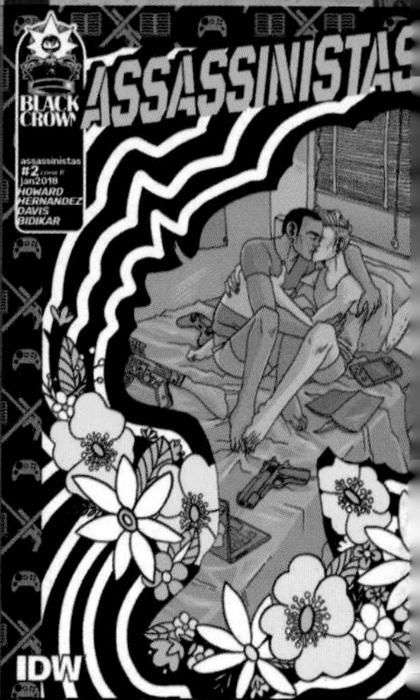
ASSASSINISTAS
BLACK CROWN
assassinistas
#2 cover B
jan2018
HOWARD
HERNANDEZ
DAVIS
BIDIKAR
IDW
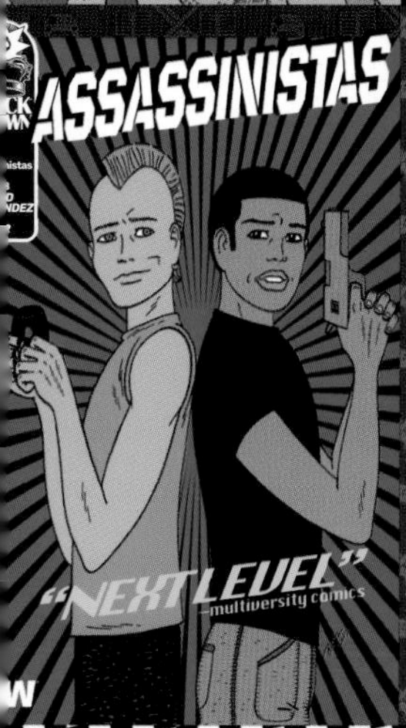
ASSASSINISTAS
"NEXT LEVEL"
—multiversity comics
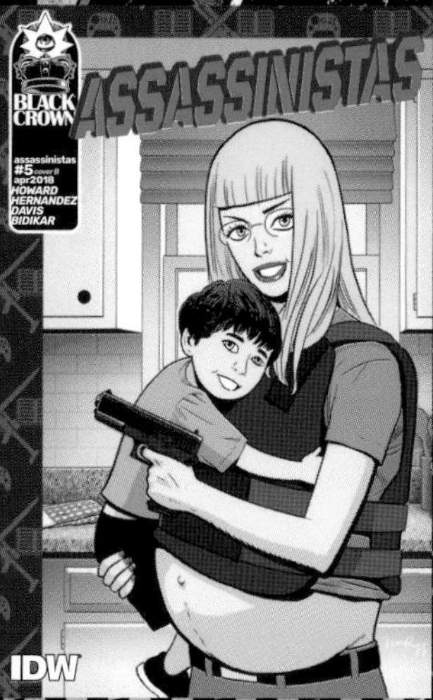
ASSASSINISTAS
BLACK CROWN
assassinistas
#5 cover B
apr2018
HOWARD
HERNANDEZ
DAVIS
BIDIKAR
IDW
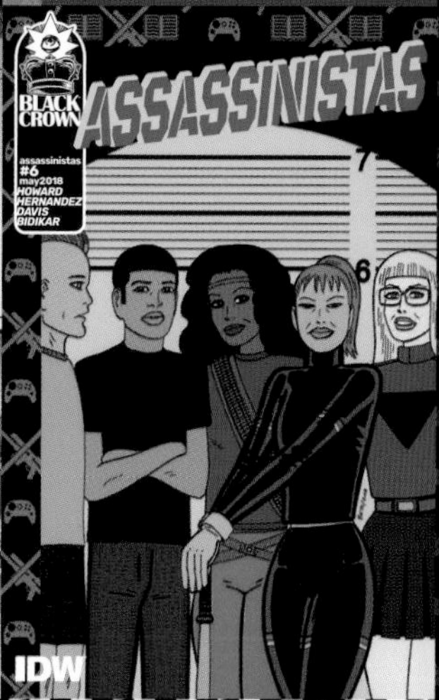
ASSASSINISTAS
BLACK CROWN
assassinistas
#6
may2018
HOWARD
HERNANDEZ
DAVIS
BIDIKAR
IDW
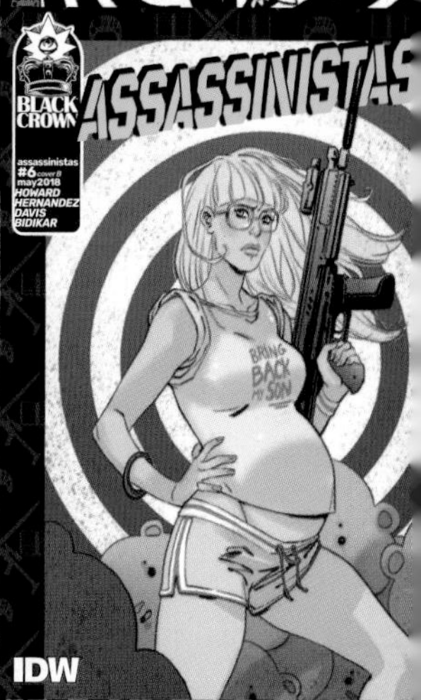
ASSASSINISTAS
BLACK CROWN
assassinistas
#6 cover B
may2018
HOWARD
HERNANDEZ
DAVIS
BIDIKAR
BRING BACK MY SON
IDW
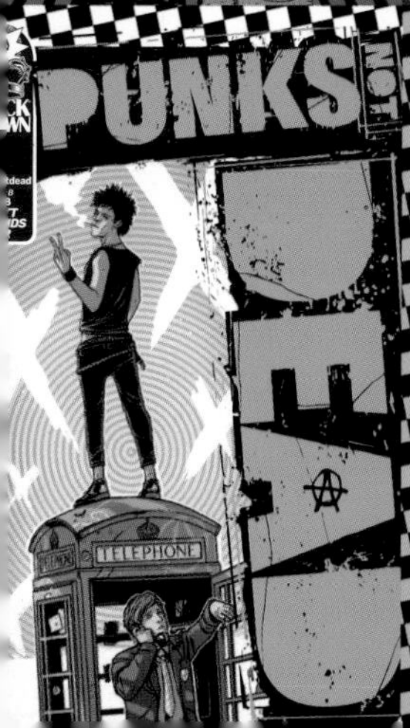
PUNKS
TELEPHONE
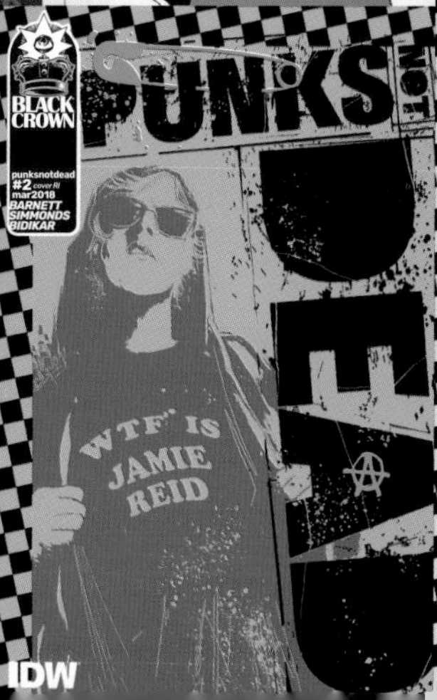
PUNKS
BLACK CROWN
punksnotdead
#2 cover B
mar2018
BARNETT
SIMMONDS
BIDIKAR
WTF IS JAMIE REID
IDW
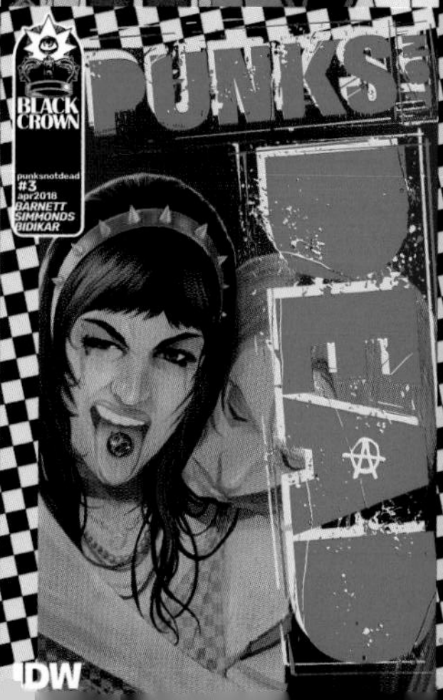
PUNKS
BLACK CROWN
punksnotdead
#3
apr2018
BARNETT
SIMMONDS
BIDIKAR
IDW
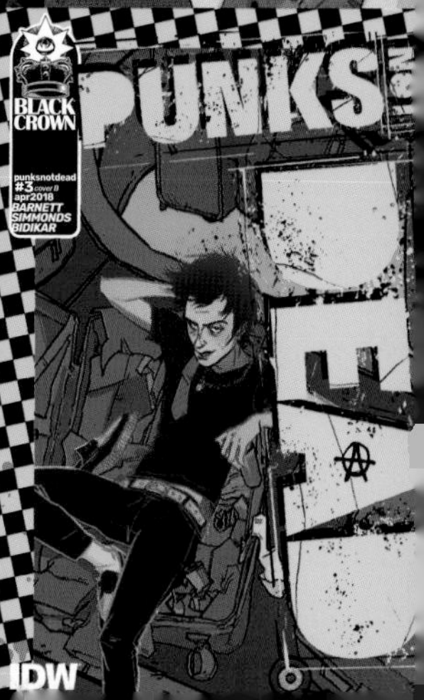
PUNKS
BLACK CROWN
punksnotdead
#3 cover B
apr2018
BARNETT
SIMMONDS
BIDIKAR
IDW

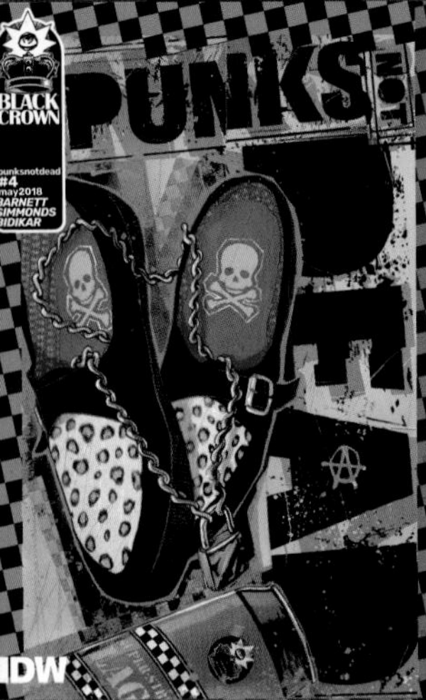
BLACK CROWN
PUNKS
punksnotdead
#4
may2018
BARNETT
SIMMONDS
BIDIKAR
IDW
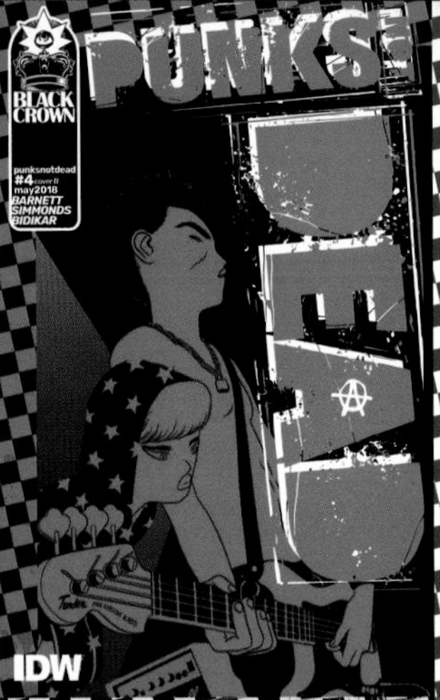
BLACK CROWN
PUNKS
punksnotdead
#4 cover B
may2018
BARNETT
SIMMONDS
BIDIKAR
DEAD
IDW
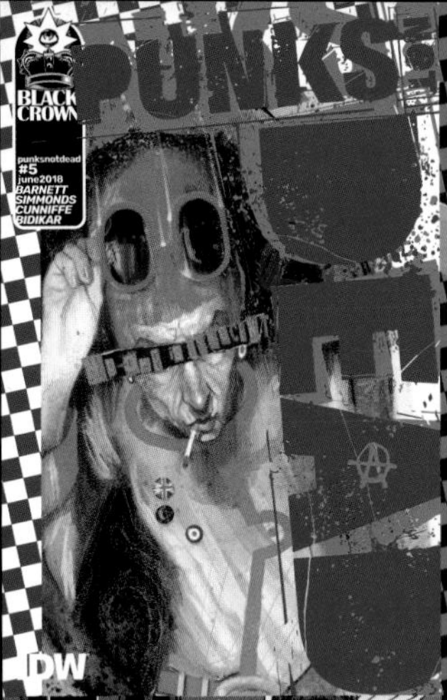
BLACK CROWN
PUNKS
punksnotdead
#5
june2018
BARNETT
SIMMONDS
CUNNIFFE
BIDIKAR
IDW
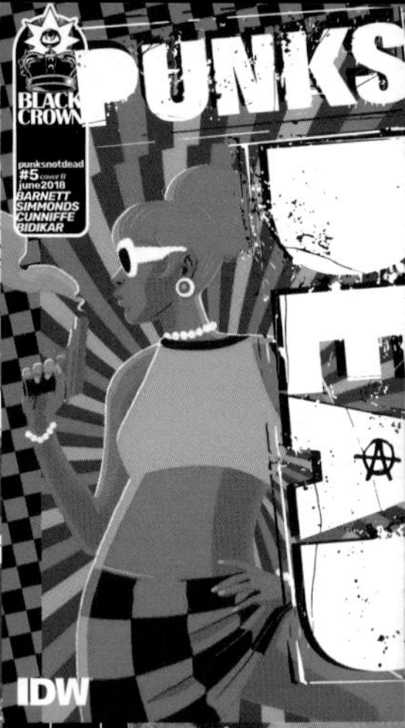
BLACK CROWN
PUNKS
punksnotdead
#5 cover B
june2018
BARNETT
SIMMONDS
CUNNIFFE
BIDIKAR
IDW
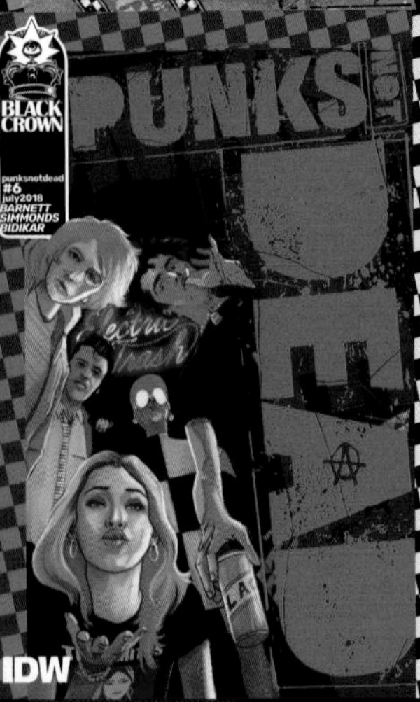
BLACK CROWN
PUNKS
punksnotdead
#6
july2018
BARNETT
SIMMONDS
BIDIKAR
IDW
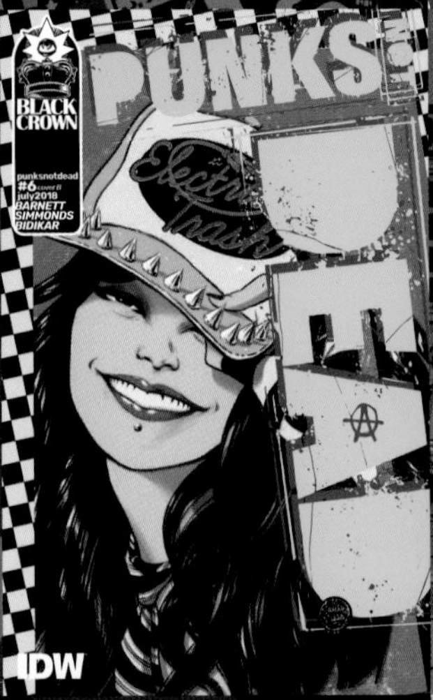
BLACK CROWN
PUNKS
punksnotdead
#6 cover B
july2018
BARNETT
SIMMONDS
BIDIKAR
IDW
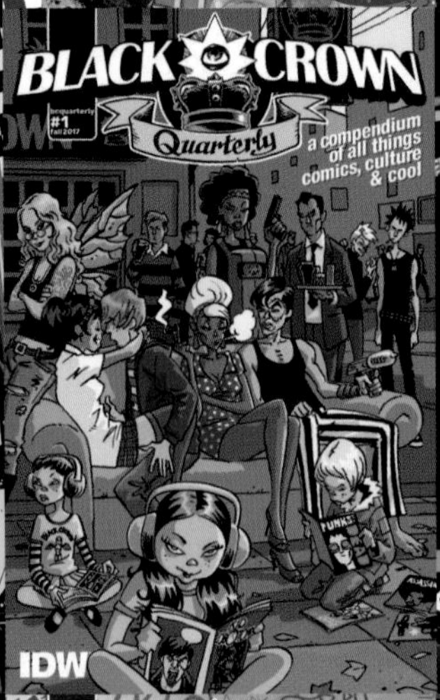
BLACK CROWN
Quarterly
bcquarterly
#1
fall 2017
a compendium of all things comics, culture & cool
IDW
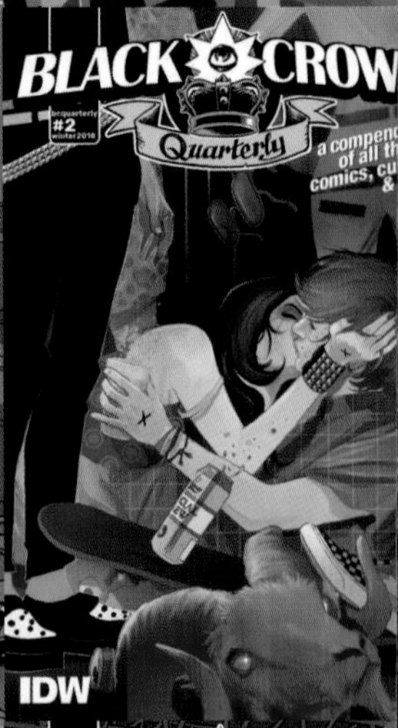
BLACK CROWN
Quarterly
bcquarterly
#2
winter2018
IDW
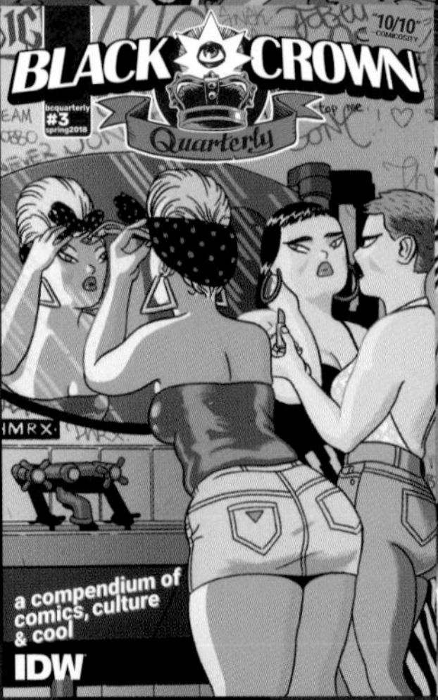
BLACK CROWN
Quarterly
bcquarterly
#3
spring2018
a compendium of comics, culture & cool
IDW
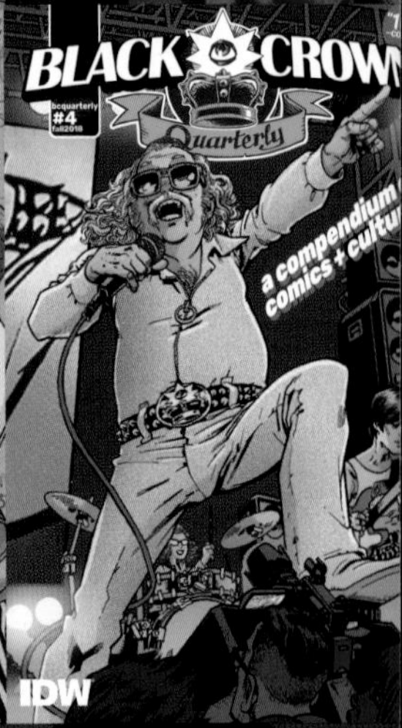
BLACK CROWN
Quarterly
bcquarterly
#4
fall2018
IDW

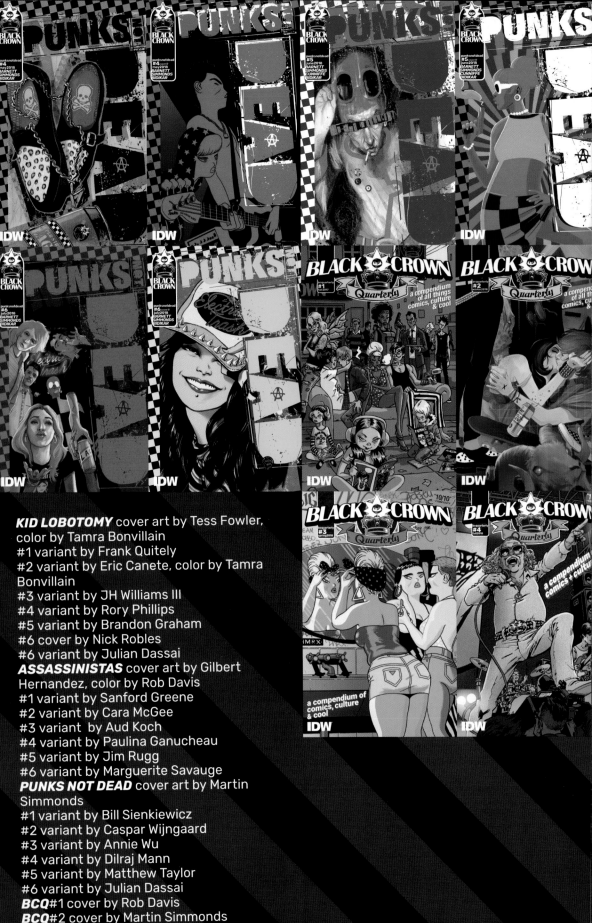

KID LOBOTOMY cover art by Tess Fowler, color by Tamra Bonvillain
#1 variant by Frank Quitely
#2 variant by Eric Canete, color by Tamra Bonvillain
#3 variant by JH Williams III
#4 variant by Rory Phillips
#5 variant by Brandon Graham
#6 cover by Nick Robles
#6 variant by Julian Dassai
ASSASSINISTAS cover art by Gilbert Hernandez, color by Rob Davis
#1 variant by Sanford Greene
#2 variant by Cara McGee
#3 variant by Aud Koch
#4 variant by Paulina Ganucheau
#5 variant by Jim Rugg
#6 variant by Marguerite Savauge
PUNKS NOT DEAD cover art by Martin Simmonds
#1 variant by Bill Sienkiewicz
#2 variant by Caspar Wijngaard
#3 variant by Annie Wu
#4 variant by Dilraj Mann
#5 variant by Matthew Taylor
#6 variant by Julian Dassai
BCQ#1 cover by Rob Davis
BCQ#2 cover by Martin Simmonds
BCQ#3 cover by Dilraj Mann
BCQ#4 cover by Philip Bond

BLACK CROWN
A1
KID LOBOTOMY
A2
ASSASSINISTAS
A3
A4
BLACK CROWN
Quarterly
B1
B3
Euthanauts
B4
HOUSE AMOK
B5
BCQ03
1 2 3
4 5 6
7 8 9
A 0 B
K-Y-M-C
109.9fm

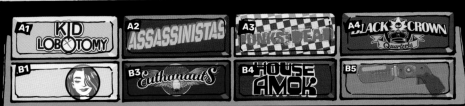

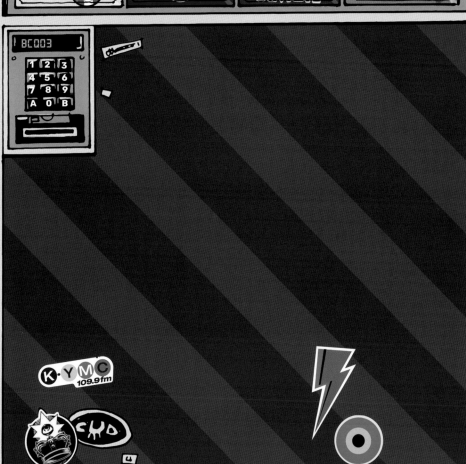

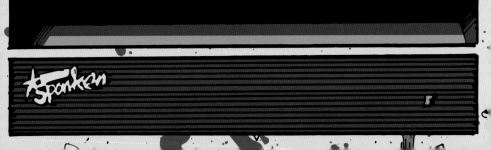

BLACK CROWN staff/regulars

ROB DAVIS is the writer/artist of TALES FROM THE BLACK CROWN PUB. He has been nominated for four Eisner Awards for *The Motherless Oven*, *Don Quixote* and the anthology *Nelson*. He won two British Comic Awards and the Lycean prize for *The Motherless Oven*. @Robgog

TINI HOWARD is the writer of ASSASSINISTAS and GHOST-WALK WITH ME. She is a writer and witch who lives in the Carolina wetlands with her partner and their two sons, who are cats. In addition to her work at the BLACK CROWN HQ which includes EUTHANAUTS, she writes *Rick and Morty* and *Captain America* among others. @TiniHoward

PETER MILLIGAN is the writer of KID LOBOTOMY. He is a comic book writer known for such controversial titles as *Skin* and *Enigma* as well as groundbreaking fan-favorites *X-Statix* and *Shade, the Changing Man*. Rumors that he despises cheese and being edited are at least 50% true. @1PeterMilligan

TESS FOWLER is the artist of KID LOBOTOMY. She is a self-taught comic book artist from Los Angeles where she lives with her husband Chris and fiendish hellcat Sam. She is a contributing artist on *Wonder Woman '77*. Fowler's other credits include cover work and interiors for Vault Comics, Image, IDW, Oni Press, Marvel and Black Mask. @TessFowler tessfowler.com

WILL POTTER is the co-writer and fictional character in CUD: RICH AND STRANGE, and the bassist in half-remembered Brit indie combo CUD. Will also corrupts the youth of today by writing numerous children's books and is the official mascot of the Rutland Trepanning Society.

CARL PUTTNAM is the co-writer and fictional character in CUD: RICH AND STRANGE, and the singer in half-remembered Brit indie combo CUD. His moustache is now less Dave Crosby and more Sundance Kid. He adds that "CUD's new album is less than a year away, at last."

ADITYA BIDIKAR is BLACK CROWN's esteemed house letterer and the recipient of Broken Frontier's 2017 Best Letterer Award. Based in India, Adi also letters *Motor Crush* and *Grafity's Wall*. @adityab adityab.net.

GILBERT HERNANDEZ is the artist of ASSASSINISTAS. He is the creator, with his brother Jaime, of *Love And Rockets*, a modern classic that debuted in 1981. In 2017, Gilbert and Jaime were inducted into the Will Eisner Hall of Fame. Gilbert has worked for DC Comics, Dark Horse, Drawn & Quarterly and others. He lives in Las Vegas with his wife and daughter. @BetomessGIlbert

DAVID BARNETT is the writer of PUNKS NOT DEAD. His novels include *Calling Major Tom* and *The Growing Pains of Jennifer Ebert*. He is a journalist for *The Guardian* and *The Independent,* among other publications. @davidmbarnett davidmbarnett.co.uk

MARTIN SIMMONDS is the artist of PUNKS NOT DEAD. He is also the artist of *Friendo* from Vault Comics and the series cover artist for Marvel's *Quicksilver: No Surrender*, and contributing cover artist for *Jessica Jones*. @Martin_Simmonds simmonds-illustration.com

DILRAJ MANN is the artist of CANONBALL COMICS and cover artist on the BCQ #3 and the PND#4 variant cover. Based in Lewes, U.K., he is the creator of *Dalston Monsterzz* published by Nobrow. @dilrajmanninstagram

LEAH MOORE is the writer of CANONBALL COMICS and HEY, AMATEUR! How To Be A Badass Goth. She is also the writer of *Sherlock Holmes: The Vanishing* and *Conspiracy of Ravens*. @leahmoore

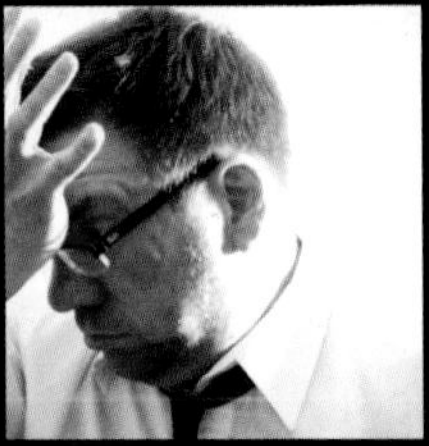

PHILIP BOND is the artist on GHOST-WALK WITH ME and CUD: RICH AND STRANGE, a regular feature in the BLACK CROWN QUARTERLY. He is also the logo and publication designer for many fine Black Crown titles. He's been held at the BLACK CROWN HQ so long he's gone Stockholmed and become complicit in the operation. @pjbond

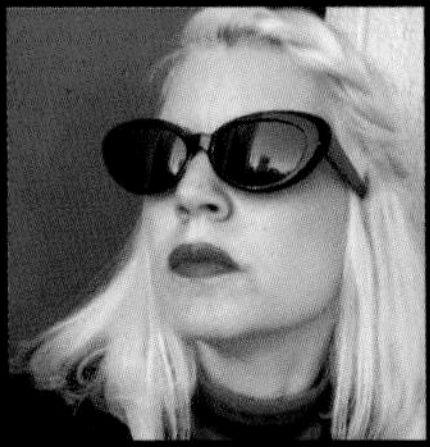

SHELLY BOND is the editor and curator of BLACK CROWN. She has been driven to edit + curate comic books, crush deadlines and innovate for over a quarter-century. She lives in Los Angeles with her husband Philip, their son Spencer, four guitars and a drum kit. You can follow her editorial + sartorial exploits on @sxbond @blackcrownhq and blackcrown.pub

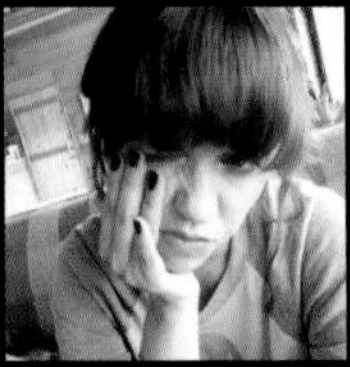

CARA MCGEE is the artist on SWELL MAPS. She has worked on a number of personal mini comics as well as comics, covers, and illustrations for BOOM!, DC Comics, IDW, and Cards Against Humanity. A BFA graduate of SCAD's Sequential Art program, she lives in the woods in the middle of nowhere.

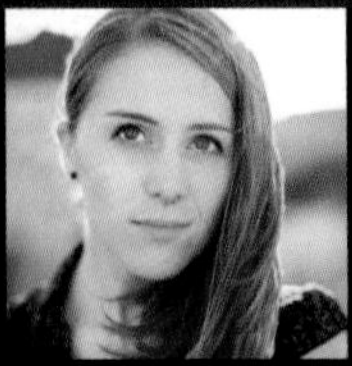

NICOLE GOUX is the artist on HEY, AMATEUR! How To Do An Ollie. When she isn't watching Buffy the Vampire Slayer for the 47th time, she draws comics for DC Comics, IDW, and Lion Forge as well as self-publishing works such as *F*ck Off Squad*.

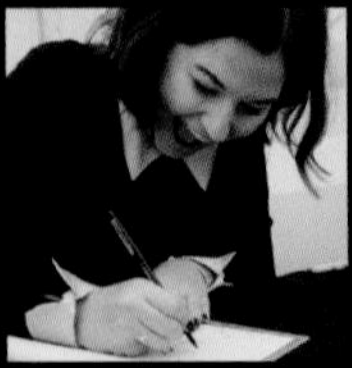

KATIE SKELLY is the artist on HEY, AMATEUR! How To Rock Barre Chords. She's an award-winning cartoonist who lives in Brooklyn, NY. Her comics work includes *Nurse Nurse, Operation Margarine, My Pretty Vampire* and *The Agency*. Photo: Frank Garland.

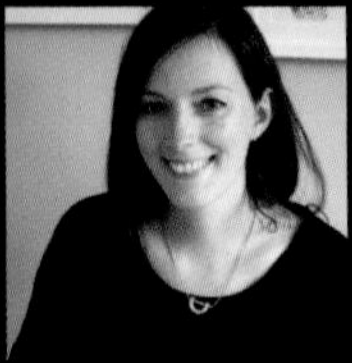

EMMELINE PIDGEN is the writer/artist on HEY, AMATEUR! How To Spot A Galaxy. A comics creator and commercial illustrator from North West England, Emmeline enjoys creating stories about imperfect humans, quiet moments, magic and discovery.

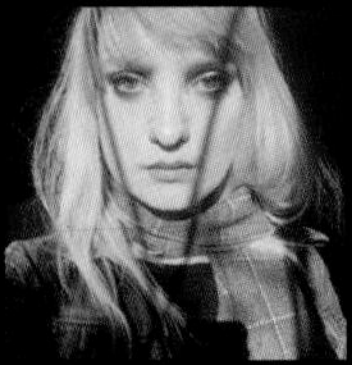

NANNA VENTER is the artist on HEY, AMATEUR! How To Be A Badass Goth. Her other credits include *Intrepid Astronaut*. 1/2 of Bad Form Podcast @nannaventer nannaventer.co.za

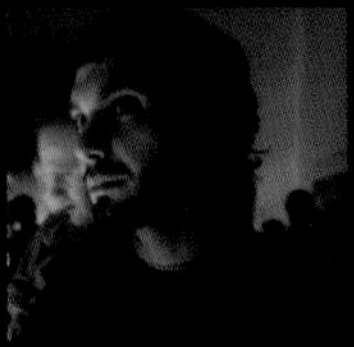

KRISTIAN ROSSI is the artist on BUTTERSCOTCH & SODA. He has worked under the guidance of Argentinian comics masters Marcelo Frusin and Eduardo Risso. Kristian worked on *Moonshine* and *Trespasser* among other comic books.

LEE LOUGHRIDGE is the colorist on KID LOBOTOMY and CUD: RICH AND STRANGE and he's colored over 100 issues of *Fables* for Vertigo. He surfs and colors comics 24/7. @leeloughridge

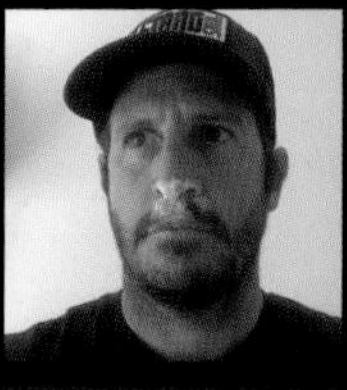

EVA DE LA CRUZ is the colorist of GHOST-WALK WITH ME. She has been collaborating with 2000AD and Vertigo/DC Comics for more than a decade and is currently coloring EUTHANAUTS for BLACK CROWN.

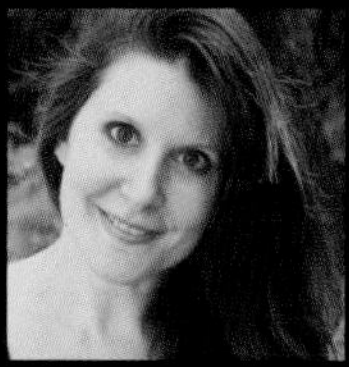

CATHI UNSWORTH is the writer of SWELL MAPS. Cathi was a journalist on *Sounds* and *Melody Maker* when they were still around, and writes for publications from the *Fortean Times* to the *Financial Times*. Cathi has written five obsessive noir novels.

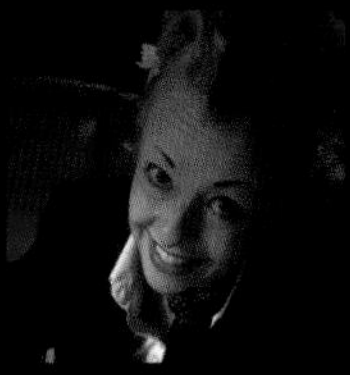

CINDY WHITEHEAD is the writer of HEY, AMATEUR! How To Do An Ollie. She is an OG Pro Vert Skateboarder who was inducted into the Skateboard Hall of Fame in 2016, a Sports Stylist and Founder of Girl is NOT a 4 letterword. @GirlisNOTa4LW

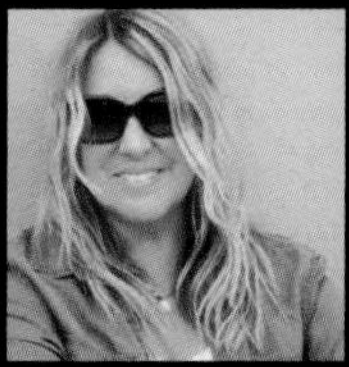

DEE CUNNIFFE provided color flats for PUNKS NOT DEAD and KID LOBOTOMY. He is an award-winning designer who gave it all up to pursue his love of comics. His colouring credits include *The Dregs, Eternal,* and *Redneck*. @deezoid

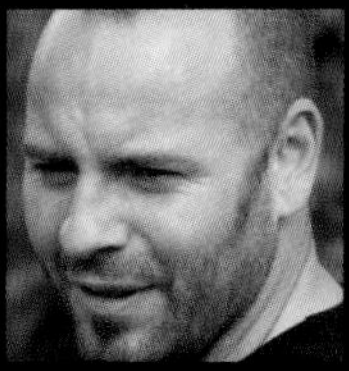

ROBIN HENLEY provided color flats for TALES FROM THE BLACK CROWN PUB and ASSASSINISTAS. She is a freelance illustrator and designer. @RobinHenley

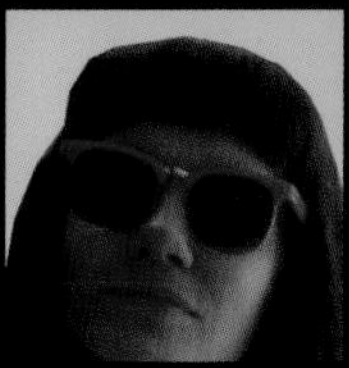

ARLENE LO is the BLACK CROWN house proofreader. After nearly 27 years proofreading for DC Comics, she will never stop having dreams about correcting mistakes. She photographs very badly, so here is a not-too-old picture of her with her handsome friend Cat, taken by her terrific husband, Allan Asherman.

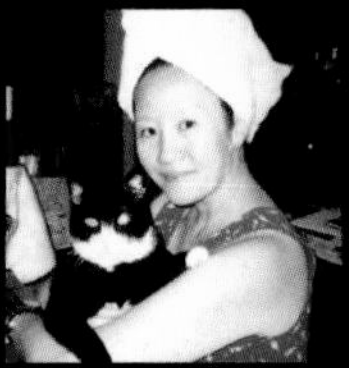

CHASE MAROTZ is the Associate Editor of BLACK CROWN. A self-proclaimed "Johnny-on-the-spot," he provides much-needed eyes, ears, hands and feet between the Los Angeles-based BCHQ and the IDW mothership in San Diego. @thrillothechase

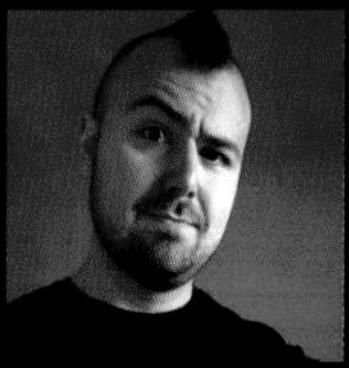

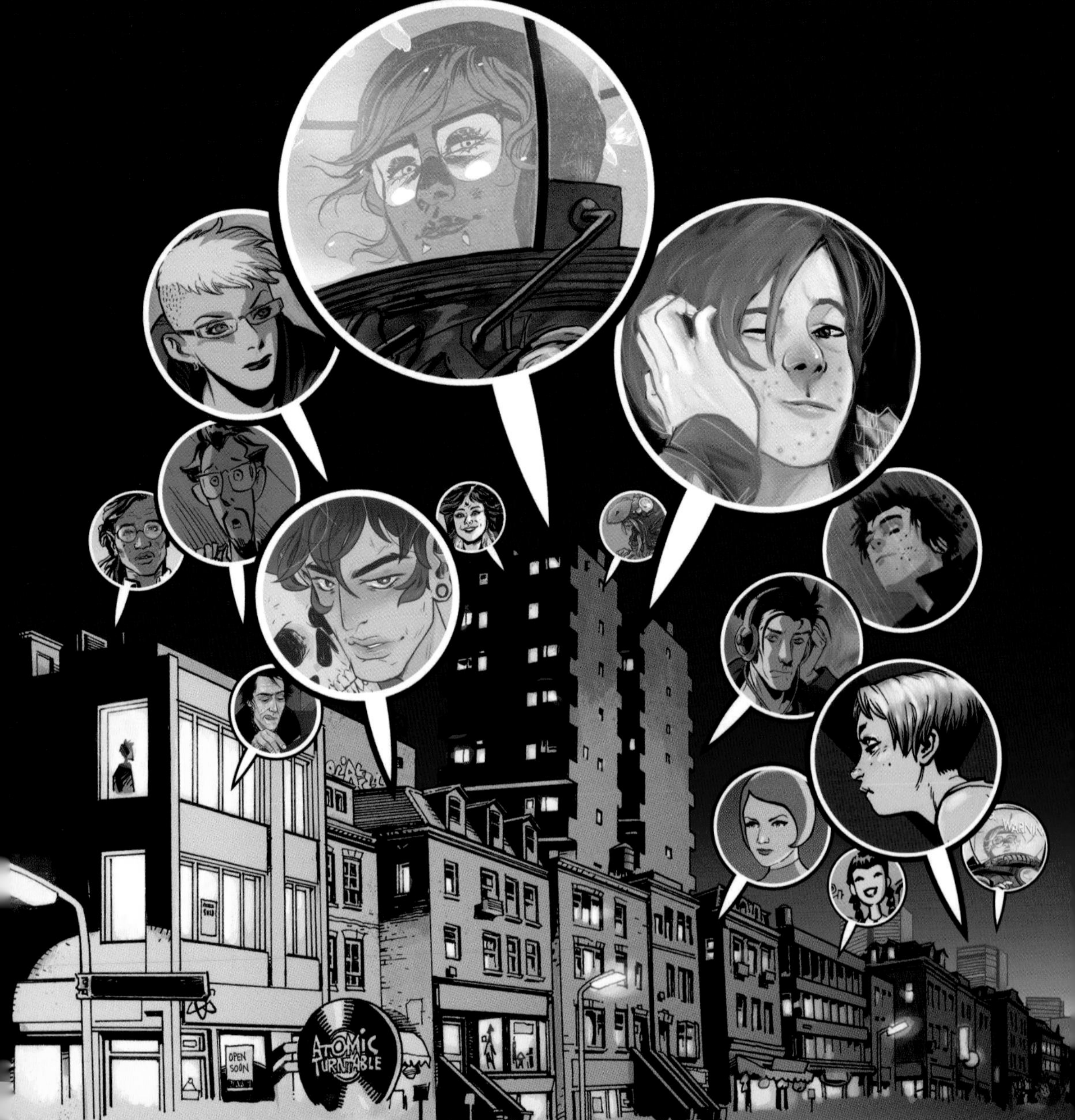
ATOMIC TURNTABLE
OPEN SOON

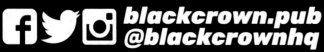

#therulingclass

blackcrown.pub